Tear
THE
WORLD
Apart

Praise for FALLEN GODS:

Beneath the fantasy and horror, a simmering love story brews. One that left me uneasy and completely unsure how to feel. Not because Ms. Simper failed, but because she succeeded so very, very well.
-Evie Drae, author of Beauregard and the Beast

Simper has created a brilliant combination of gruesomely dark fantasy and scorching romance. The protagonists are both so flawed, you are at once drawn to and repelled by them. Simper takes the idea of grey morality and writes it to perfection.
-The Lesbian Review

Simper has created a complex, immersive world for the series and that's not even touching on the well-developed characters or the complicated, fucked up relationship you can't help but ship anyway.
-Manic Femme Reviews

Praise for SEA AND STARS:

"If you like your fantasy with an extra dark twist, exceptional world building and deeply complex characters then reel this book in fast. You'll be hooked."
-The Lesbian Review

"The Fate of Stars, the first book in the Sea and Stars trilogy, is delightfully dark and sexy, full of lush imagery, vibrant characterization, and enough adrenaline to keep me up way past my bedtime."
-Anna Burke, award winning author of THORN and COMPASS ROSE

Praise for Camilla and Laura:

A beautiful retelling . . . perfect for anyone who likes darker-themed romance, horror stories, or plain ol' lesbian vampires.
-The Lesbian 52

S D SIMPER

© 2020 Endless Night Publications

Includes an exclusive excerpt from
The Moon, the Stars and the Desert Below

Tear the World Apart

Copyright © 2020 Endless Night Publications

Cover art by Jade Merien

Cover design and interior by Jerah Moss

Map by Mariah Simper

ISBN (Paperback): 978-1-952349-13-3

Visit the author at www.sdsimper.com

Facebook: sdsimper
Twitter: @sdsimper
Instagram: sdsimper

For Jaylee

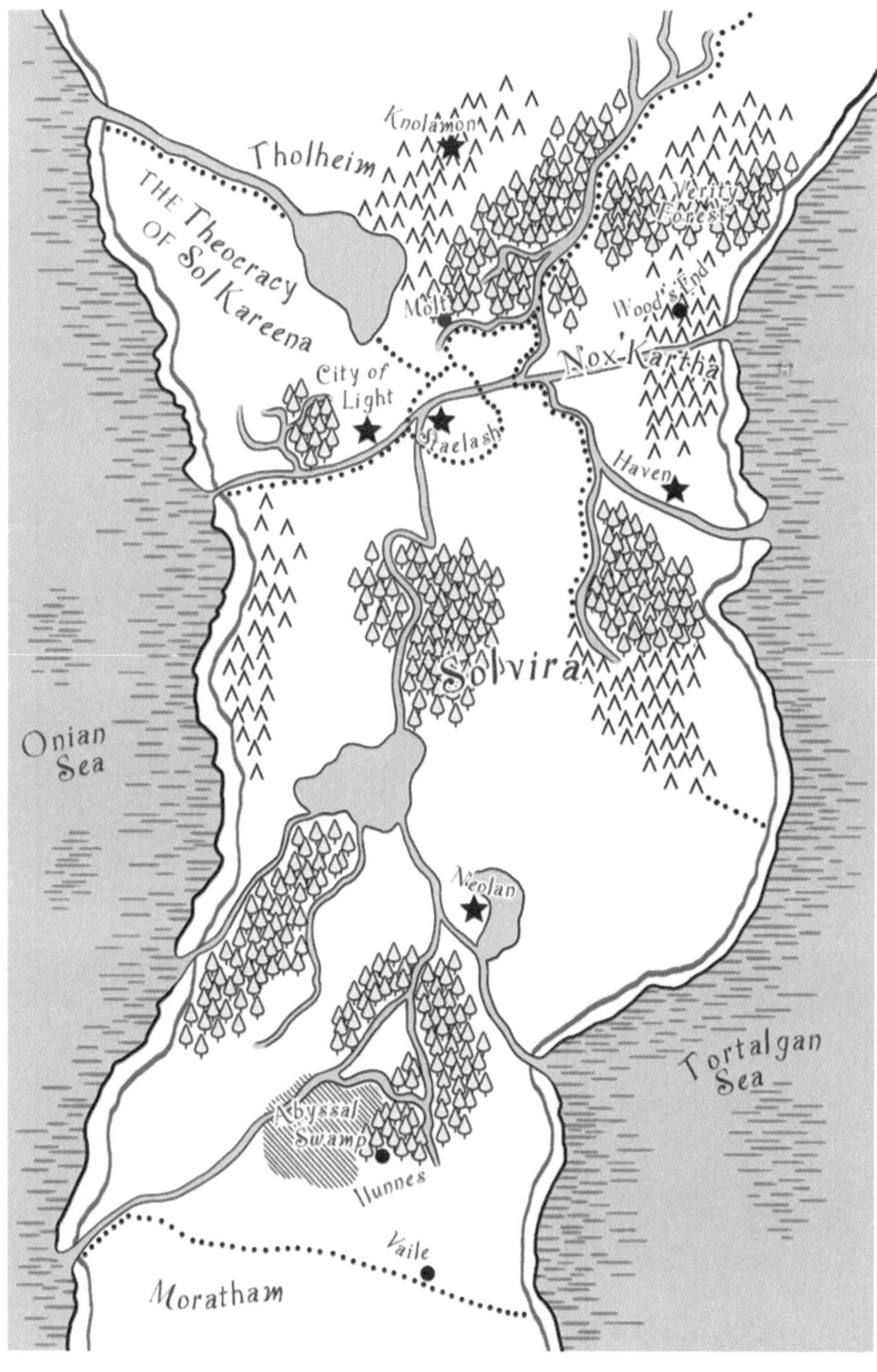

Tholheim
Knolamon
THE Theocracy OF Sol Kareena
Verity Forest
Molt
Wood's End
City of Light
Nox-Kartha
Faelash
Haven
Onian Sea
Solvira
Neolan
Tortalgan Sea
Abyssal Swamp
Ilunnes
Vaile
Moratham

Names

THE ROYAL COUNCIL OF STAELASH

Marielle Vors – Mair-ee-el Vohrs

Etolié – Eh-toh-lee-ey

Thalmus – Thah-muhs

Flowridia – Floh-rid-ee-uh

Sora Fireborn – Sohr-ruh Fire-bohrn

Zorlaeus – Zor-ley-uhs

THE ROYAL COUNCIL OF SOLVIRA

Flowridia – Floh-rid-ee-uh

Alauriel Solviraes – Ah-law-ree-ehl Sohl-veer-es

Reginal – **Reh**-gin-uhl

Jules – Jools

Irons – **Eye**-uhrns

FOREIGN DIGNITARIES

Casvir – Kas-veer

Murishani – Mer-eh-shah-nee

Xoran – Zoh-ran

Lunestra – Loon-es-truh

OTHER PLAYERS

Demitri – Dih-mee-tree

Ayla Darkleaf – Ai-luh Dahrk-leef

Khastra – Kas-truh

Odessa – Oh-des-uh

Soliel – Suh-lil

Mereen Fireborn – Mer-een Fire-bohrn

Zoldar—Zohl-dar

Tazel Fireborn – Taa-zuhl Fire-bohrn

Kah'Sheen – Kuh-sheen

VARIOUS GODS, ANGELIC AND DEMONIC

Sol Kareena – Sohl Kuh-ree-nuh

Eionei – Eye-uhn-eye

Alystra – Ah-lees-truh

Staella – Stey-luh

Neoma – Ney-oh-muh

Ilune – Eye-loon

Izthuni – Iz-thoo-nee

Ku'Shya – Koo-shy-uh

Onias – Uhn-eye-uhs

"Tell me a story, Etolié!"

Princess Alauriel Solviraes sat in her bed, five years old and infectiously smiley with her braided pigtails and soft nightgown. Etolié could deny her nothing.

"Let's see . . ." Etolié sat on Lara's bed, making a show of mulling over the child's request—she pursed her lips like a court jester, and Lara giggled. "Any requests?"

"Oo!" Lara's eyes sparkled, delight in her young face. "I like the one where you cut off the slaver's head."

"Which time?"

"With the axe," Lara said, her enthusiasm both innocent and radiant. "That's the best time."

And so, with shadowed illusion and copious amounts of glitter blood, Etolié illustrated a story from years' past, back when she'd taken off her clothes in the name of justice—though she generally glossed over those parts. ". . . and so I, having just dropped my invisible dagger like an idiot, had to resort to my best trick—*kissing.*"

"Ew!" Lara giggled as she squirmed away from Etolié's lips but was unable to quite escape the volley of kisses scattering across her precious skin.

"And that's when I decided to illusion an axe!" Etolié said, laying beside the laughing princess. Above them, a glittery axe swiped, a blast of bright red confetti bursting as it struck the air. "Needless to say, he died."

Well, it had taken a few swings, but Etolié wasn't here to explain how thick and meaty throat muscles could be—not to mention, bones. Lara didn't need to know the grittier details of life.

"And then you freed the camp?" the little princess asked.

"I freed the camp! I gave all the De'Sindai axes too. They're very useful in a pinch."

Lara smiled as she snuggled closer to Etolié. "I love it when you visit."

"Me too, Moonbeam." Etolié, typically touch averse, tolerated little kid cuddles because they really were too damn precious.

"What if you just lived here? You could be my mom!"

Though prepared to object, Etolié swallowed that bit of heartbreak. "I can't live here! Who would babysit my kingdom? You'll just have to settle on me being your aunt ninety times removed. Besides, you have a mom—and I don't doubt she's watching over you every second she isn't actively haunting your father."

Not true. Not true at all, and Etolié's heart ached to think of Ralaena. However, Lara giggled, and thankfully her five-year-old brain had already jumped to less guilt-inducing things. "Will you stay all night?"

"I'll at least stay until you fall asleep. That's a promise."

Etolié sat up enough to blow out the candle beside them, content to hold Lara and her little squirming self. The girl really was too cute, and while Etolié wouldn't say it was the definition of a wild time, her heart also couldn't deny the kid some maternal love, lackluster or not.

She kinda missed it too, some days.

"I told your momma about the axe," Lara's little voice said. "She said that story was scary."

"The *fu*—ther-mucker are you talking about?" Etolié snapped her fingers, and the candle flickered back to life. Not actually, but Etolié believed in her illusions pretty strongly.

"At night, when she talks to me. Sometimes she asks about you."

Etolié quickly illusioned a happy face, just in case her actual face wasn't convincing. "Are you sure you're not just imagining?"

"No, it's when I dream! You said the Goddess of Stars talks in dreams, and your momma is the Goddess of Stars!"

Etolié felt punched in the stomach by a tiny fist, even though Lara had done nothing more than smile with those silver eyes of hers.

"Sometimes she talks to me when I'm sleeping. She asks about you. I tell her stories!"

Etolié's hands had begun sweating, and she subtly wiped them onto the sheets, lest Lara notice and comment. "Of course you tell her *those* stories. I'm sure my sweet momma just loved that."

"She was worried. So then I told her nice things—like how you always take care of me and bring presents."

"What did she say to that?"

"She asked if anyone took care of you. I told her that Khastra makes you eat."

A scoffing, pained laugh left Etolié's throat at that. "All right. True."

"Your momma is very nice. She gives the best hugs." In Etolié's arms, Lara snuggled closer; Etolié clung tighter. "I love your hugs the most, though."

Etolié's words withered and dried like her empty wine glass. Instead, she simply held Lara tight, swallowing whatever painful feeling threatened to claw up her throat and leak out her eye sockets.

"But I love it when she visits. She's the nicest."

"She's, uh, she's something—" Etolié coughed, her throat suddenly threatening to clamp shut. "Tell her whatever you think she wants to hear. I don't want her to worry."

Lara's sweet smiling face held joy, and for a crippling, damning moment, Etolié realized this wretched feeling was envy. Lara rested back against her pillow, her little arms still wrapped tight around Etolié. "Will you sing?"

Once upon a time, Etolié had been serenaded to sleep by a voice as pristine and pure as gold. *"Sleep, little Starshine . . ."*

Etolié found her voice and sang her own for the child she loved:

Sleep, little moonchild
The night is not gone.
So be soothed by the stars
And the sound of my song.
Morning will come;
The night turned to day.
But, sleep, little moonchild
For my love never fades.

Gentle breathing filled the room. Etolié snuffed out the light.

Chapter 1

Flowridia had long ago stopped questioning whether life existed between the subtle, shifting movements within shadow. The realm of Sha'Demoni was real and tangible, coexisting with her own, though few knew how to step inside, much less navigate it. The cold of it was pervasive, cutting to the bone, but she felt no fear—not when her fingers were intertwined with the woman who knew it as a second home.

So surreal, to feel Ayla's cool touch in her hand.

They emerged from a shadow, the early morning sun illuminating Flowridia's realm in light. A bonfire cast deep shadows across the brutalized slave camp. Men moved about frantically, clearing the area of dead, desecrated bodies. Fearful faces—slaves of every race awaiting auction—stared from behind bars, unaware of the lurking presence.

Although Flowridia's heart ached for them all, her focus remained on only one. Magical lightning shot between stakes surrounding an enormous wolf chained beside them. Demitri perked up, and Flowridia resisted the urge to run to him.

Ayla stared upon the camp, a hunter upon prey, calculation in the sharp glint of her eye. "It appears someone wreaked havoc on this camp already."

"I may be to blame for that," Flowridia said, and the slight squeeze against her hand spread a blush across her cheeks.

"You, my sweet summer blossom?"

Something in Ayla's tone swept her smile away. Disbelief showed on the vampire's sharp features, her raised eyebrow not quite patronizing but certainly incredulous. With her cutting cheekbones and vibrant, icy blue eyes, all her expressions were eccentric.

Flowridia frowned. "I used necromancy to control the plants."

Ayla's disbelief faded into intrigue. "Necromancy?"

"So much has changed, Ayla."

So much, yes, but not the tender expression on Ayla's countenance, nor the glowing affection in her touch when she cupped Flowridia's chin and kissed her full lips. Flowridia savored the intimacy, the reminder of her victory. Ayla, once dead, had returned to her.

Ayla pulled away too soon. Always too soon. "I look forward to hearing it all. For now, I fulfill a promise to you." Ayla's lips brushed Flowridia's knuckle. "Rescue Demitri. Let me care for the rest."

The smile on Ayla's face twisted, something wicked in the gesture. Whether it was from the scent of blood or the prospect of battle, the meaning hardly mattered; fangs elongated in her mouth, her pupils expanding to hide any hints of color. White and black, the very vision of a predator before it pounced.

Ayla stepped from beyond the line of trees and into the clearing, sauntering casually, making no effort to hide her presence. Some men cried out to alert the rest of this interloper, who held malevolent glee in her smile. An arrow flew to her head. Inches away, Ayla's pale hand grabbed it, then shoved it through her temple, grinning at her attacker as she maimed herself.

When Ayla vanished into the shadow of a man swinging a sword, Flowridia willed herself to vanish. Not true invisibility, but enough to detour anyone not looking for her.

Screams met her ears. One by one, men fell at the outskirts of the encampment. "Pull together!" came the cry. Flowridia turned, recognizing the voice. "She's picking you off one by one," Shem yelled across the camp.

Perhaps Flowridia's spell hadn't even been necessary— Ayla became the center of gravity, all eyes upon her violent dance. Cries sang through the air. Men fell in severed heaps. Euphoria filled Flowridia as she stopped to watch, her breath stolen by the reminder of her love's brutality. Blood sprayed as Ayla eviscerated men with her claws, stealing knives from their corpses and casually flinging them through the air with perfect precision; others fell when metal lacerated their throats. Ayla tore heads from bodies, spines from their backs, gleefully stabbing approaching foes with her victim's severed ribs.

Though mesmerized, Flowridia tore her attention away. Demitri awaited, as enthralled as she by the display of violence, practically choreographed in its perfection. His golden gaze was reserved only for Ayla, but relief filled her when his beloved voice filled her head. *You've been busy.*

Elsewhere, pained cries met her ears. She ignored them, her focus only for her familiar. "Are you all right? Are you hurt?"

Just uncomfortable. They want me looking pretty for the auction.

Flowridia studied the four stakes surrounding the cart. Potent magic radiated; the lightning shooting between the stakes was not natural. "I have an idea." She looked at the battlefield, then cried, "Ayla! I need you!"

Within seconds, Ayla appeared from a shadow, fresh blood splattering her body. Entrails streaked her dress, her face a marvelous mess of gore. But her grin shone through, her fangs long and ominous, too large for her mouth as they peeked past her lips.

Gods, she was a vision, but now was not the time for admiration. "Can you use the Silver Fire to absorb the magic here?"

"Absorb the magic?"

"What's holding him is—"

It seemed she need not explain. Ayla reached a hand into the lightning, gasping when her body began glowing. Pain twisted her countenance, but soon she focused, bracing herself as power flowed through her. Pleasure softened her smile, a slight groan escaping her as the lightning flickered and faded.

Blinding light shone from her figure. Ayla shuddered, holding her head as she stumbled away.

Flowridia stepped forward cautiously, acutely aware of both the remaining slavers and the volatile magic imbued within her love. "Ayla—"

"Sweet Flowra," Ayla cooed, finally steadying herself, "what a gift you've given me." She looked to her hands, grinning darkly as she held them forward, toward the remaining slavers.

A blast of silver flame escaped, searing through the mob. It bore no finesse, merely pure power. Ayla ran towards them, another blaze of light bursting from her body. Men screamed. The forest burned. Overarching through the scene, Ayla's maniacal laughter seemed inescapable. Over and over, walls of flame burst, and with each surge of power, her glow steadily faded.

She vanished. Within the fray, she reappeared, and though their weapons turned upon her, nothing could touch the nimble woman.

Flowridia kissed her familiar's nose before inspecting the chains holding him thrall. "Damn it. I need a key."

Shem has it.

Flowridia had no intention of joining the battle and risking certain death. Instead, she gathered herself and expanded her senses to the grass at her feet. Smoke swirled from the pores of her skin, her mouth as she breathed, in unmistakable shades of purple. The grass around her wilted, desiccating at her will—

Then became flush with false life, imbued with necrotic energy. She bid the grass to rise, to grow at her will. The unnatural blades wrapped around Demitri's bonds, countless strands of greenery conjoining into a thick rope, and tugged—

The chain snapped.

Demitri shook off the rest, then leapt from the cart and stretched his long limbs.

"Demitri, are you—"

She was stopped when her gigantic companion bombarded her with his body. *I know it's silly to say, but thank you for coming back.*

Flowridia hugged him tight, engulfed on every side by warm fur. "I could never leave you forever, dearest Demitri."

In the fray, Ayla's sounds of glee cut off, replaced with pain. Flowridia looked to her but saw no attackers, no one to have caused this—only Ayla alone in a sea of carnage, her light blinding as she suddenly stared in shock at her hands, her arms, tore at her own skin—

Ayla's brilliant light expanded. Demitri grabbed Flowridia by the collar of her dress and ran into the woods. Flowridia struggled not to choke, scraped against the ground as a tremendous silver blast ravaged the camp. Heat met their back; trees rushed by in a blur as the ground tore at Flowridia's dress and flesh.

He stopped, immediately tossing her against his stomach and curling around her. From her pocket, Flowridia withdrew the green crystal, the arrowhead still stained in Lara's blood. The wall of fire hit them. The aura expanded.

Dazzling white light became their world. She focused the crystal's power, feeling nothing though all the world disappeared, engulfed by depthless power.

It faded.

All around, the forest lay ravaged and burned. Life ceased to exist; the skeletal carcasses of trees met their view. Only a small patch of grass and leaves, directly at their feet, remained.

What was that?

"As you probably noticed, Ayla is back." Demitri slowly uncurled, and Flowridia let the crystal's power fade. "It's a long story. Ask me when there's time." She glanced around, surveying the destruction. The eerie silence reigned ominous above all, more than the blackened ground and smoking, broken trees. "But the important part is that Ayla has the Silver Fire."

This will definitely end well.

From beyond came a shattered cry: *Flowra!*

Flowridia ignored his remark, instead staring in the direction of the camp. "May I ride you?"

No offense, but you smell like dead things. I don't want to smell like dead things.

As they ran, fewer and fewer trees stood. The ground became level, and then it stooped downward. A crater smoked where the camp had been. Fine black sand, as soft as powder, remained where there had once been earth.

The tents, the cages—all were decimated. Sorrow clenched at Flowridia's stomach. All the slaves . . . all the innocents . . .

Yet two figures remained—Ayla Darkleaf, frantic as she stared upon the perimeter of the camp, and a man lying near the center of the explosion, desperately clasping the very maldectine imbued collar that had once crippled Flowridia.

When she spotted Flowridia above the crater's side, Ayla gasped and ran to her. It might have been comical to see her feet slip against the slopping sand—but the terror on her face broke Flowridia's heart. "Flowra, I thought . . . Oh, my love."

Flowridia held her, though Ayla clutched her nearly hard enough to break her ribs. "Demitri dragged me away. I'm fine."

"I did not mean to . . ." Ayla pulled away. Her eyes remained wide, colorless, visible shock on her monstrous countenance. "I don't know what happened—"

Shuffling from below stole Ayla's focus. Her face became vicious as she peered into the crater, where Shem—the man with the collar, who owned the destroyed slave camp—attempted to make his escape.

With grace, Ayla slid down the crater's side. Flowridia followed, Demitri close by, though far less smoothly.

Shem froze at Ayla's approach. He bled from a plethora of wounds—whether they were from blades or claws, Flowridia did not know. His hands rose in defense, but Ayla grabbed him by the shirt collar. "You're familiar," she cooed, hunger in her gaze.

Shem, however, looked at Flowridia, recognition in his nervous smile. "Fancy seeing you—"

"Are you really so stupid," Flowridia said, fury rising with each word, "to think I'd speak in your defense?"

The color drained from Shem's tanned face. "I'm very rich, you know. Perhaps we can negotiate."

"Flowra, how do I know this man?" Ayla asked, languid as she studied his face and stance.

Flowridia's blood boiled to look at him, despising the residual fear his presence evoked. "Ayla, this is Shem. He's the one who sent his men to . . . how did he say it . . . 'break my spirit.' Not that they succeeded, but I believe intentions matter."

The words were apparently enough; realization flashed in Ayla's vibrant gaze. Her lip curled, revealing fangs.

"Shem, this is Ayla Darkleaf, affectionately known as the Scourge of the Sun Elves." From the corner of her eye, she saw Ayla stiffen at the title. The hunger in her eyes remained, but wariness matched it.

Months ago, at her death, Ayla had kept this all a secret. Now, Flowridia knew all.

"It's a ghastly legend," she continued, strolling forward. "For a thousand years, Ayla's people lived in her shadow. She would steal them, torture them, use them for all kinds of gristly experiments. A sort of mad scientist, known for being charming and deadly. She also served as a vessel for the demon god, Izthuni, creating a legacy as The Endless Night the whole world came to fear—perhaps you might know that title better."

Ayla remained frozen, her visage holding false severity. Flowridia placed a hand on her back, praying it reassured her. "I tell you this," she continued, though it was Ayla she truly addressed, "because I want you to just as well fear the woman who's claimed her." She smiled, praying it conveyed her sincerity. "Who loves her."

Ayla's fear settled. Her lip twisted into a faint smile. Flowridia turned her attention back to Shem. "Shem, I'm not going to give you to her. She's going to hold you while I take you for me."

"And what will you do to him, my love?" Ayla asked, curiosity flashing across her silver-tinted eyes.

"Consume him." Flowridia's hand shot out to grip his throat, her entire body crackling with purple lightning. Shem screamed as his skin withered, his essence and life absorbing into her, slow and steady, meticulously controlled. Desperation did not drive her—only the intent to hurt.

His fright, after what he'd nearly done to her, felt . . . delicious.

His face thinned. His body desiccated. From behind, Ayla watched with fascinated interest, dropping him as soon as he stood dead in her grasp.

Flowridia breathed deep, letting energy flow through her. From deep within, that faint purple glow emanated, and any weakness, any injuries she had smoothed over.

Then, she blushed as her attention returned to the moment. "I wanted to show off."

"You've changed," came Ayla's voice, unquestionable lust bleeding into the words.

"So have you," Flowridia replied, her breathing finally settling. All around, the destroyed scenery stood testament to that statement; Ayla was back. Ayla had changed. Ayla held more power than ever before.

A hand gripped Flowridia's collar and yanked her forward. Ayla crushed their mouths together, pure lust radiating from her touch as she held their bodies together. A hand tangled into her hair, gentle at first, but when it twisted, Flowridia became *raw.*

Sunlight burst from over the horizon. Infused with power, adrenaline pounding, Flowridia wanted nothing more than to feel Ayla's body against her, but all that faded when something slimy touched her lip. She pulled back in horror, realizing that whatever gore stained Ayla's face had slipped down to her mouth. She spat on the ground, resisting the urge to retch as she frantically wiped her lips of blood. "Bath. Now."

Ayla's frown was nothing less than pitiful. "You did not mind earlier."

"I was caught up in passion and adrenaline earlier. I'm more worried about diseases now." Ayla's apparent offense surprised her, and Flowridia composed herself. "Of course I want you, darling. But find us a river or something to bathe in."

Ayla's pout might have been endearing had Flowridia not sensed actual hurt—and were she not splattered in buckets of blood. Ayla released her. "Give me a moment."

She slipped into Demitri's shadow.

Flowridia stroked her hand along her familiar's fur. "Do you need a bath too?"

Not with you and Lady Ayla.

"I accept that."

Ayla soon reemerged, her good mood having apparently returned. Without a word, merely a leering grin, she lifted Flowridia into her arms and whisked her into a shadow.

The world shifted into black and greys, yet it held more substance than the few times she had traversed the foreign realm near Staelash, the scenery formed and nearly solid as Ayla carried her through the odd terrain. Bright, blinking eyes watched from the distance, true demons looking curiously upon the rare interlopers. Or perhaps Ayla was a common sight, having danced freely between the realms for nearly two millennia.

Izthuni, the Demon God of Shadow ruled here, and with her quest complete, Flowridia held his favor.

"Why does this look different than the Shadow Realm in Staelash?" Flowridia asked.

"Some parts of Sha'Demoni are more and less broken. The area around Staelash might be the most ravaged. Across the sea, in Ku'Shya's Realm, there's even color."

"Remarkable."

The mortal world reappeared. A forest surrounded them, but the trees had grown sparse due to the bank of a river. Ayla held her as she stepped into the water, nonchalant to the chill even as it rose to her hips; Flowridia clung to her as she dipped her blood-soaked form into the water. She shuddered, the cold discomforting. "Don't release me. I'll be swept away."

"I have you," Ayla whispered, and the words held weight. Oh, she was so new and wonderful—Flowridia helped to clean her face as the water cleansed them both of gore and grime. When she saw her beloved again, her sharp cheek bones and pallid skin, they kissed, her heart soaring when Ayla touched her beneath her dress. "Take this off. Otherwise I will rip it away."

Ayla carried her to shallower waters, where the river only rose to Flowridia's knees, supporting her as she slipped it over her head. "It's one of yours," Flowridia said. "One of your gifts to me. Did you make it?"

"I did." Ayla's eyes darted back to the cream-colored gown. "A thousand years of cutting people up and stitching them back together in odd ways has given me embroidery skills I pride myself in. I know the work spent on it; that's why I didn't want to rip it needlessly."

For Ayla to speak so freely of her sordid past sent a shiver down Flowridia's spine. They washed, though Flowridia remained demure in the open woods—a sentiment Ayla did not share, given how casually she tossed her own dress aside and basked her nude form in the open air.

She was perfect, in her different, fearsome way. Flowridia loved to watch her, each lithe muscle shifting beneath the thin skin of her back. Small in every dimension, but such was the nature of elves, though Ayla might have looked sickly had she lacked that subtle aura of death. There existed not a single bit of hair on her body beneath her neck, but Flowridia knew that to be normal for elves, though the current style of the rich, dark hair on her head did give her pause—cut just past her chin, instead of the luxurious locks Flowridia had known. In the murky swamp, she hadn't noticed the change, but in the light she had to admit it was terribly cute—and 'cute' had never been a word she would have previously granted The Endless Night.

She didn't know of any elves as short as Ayla, but it did not matter—when she turned, the tiny peaks of her breasts chilled from the water and breeze, Flowridia shamelessly admired her, blushing when Ayla caught her. "Enjoying yourself?"

"Endlessly," Flowridia replied, her own posture such to hide her slim curves. "You're beautiful."

"I know," came Ayla's curt reply, and she chuckled, embracing Flowridia in the stream. With her head pressed to Flowridia's neck, Ayla held her there, becoming as still as the ice she radiated.

Flowridia kissed her hair. "Why is your hair different?"

To her relief, Ayla grinned, her hand making tender strokes against Flowridia's bare back. "I have been restored to my most perfect form—which, in this instance, is the form I had upon my original death. My hair was short. Not my personal preference, but there are spells for that. You will also note I have two ears."

Flowridia laughed, gleefully touching the precious, pointed appendages. "And thank every god for that." She kissed the one once severed, delighted to feel Ayla's grin. "Let's go back to my mother's house."

"Is that where we were?" Ayla pulled away, taking care to lead her to the shore, then handed her the wet dress. "You never cease to amaze me."

Flowridia blushed as she dressed.

They held hands through the shadow realm, soon coming upon Demitri, alone in the ruined forest. *That was fast.*

"We really did only bathe, Demitri."

Whatever you say.

Flowridia frowned, her motherly heart struggling to internalize her baby boy's words—much less his understanding of adult relationships.

But Ayla, who did not know Demitri's words, released Flowridia and tentatively approached the gigantic wolf, hesitating before offering her hand. When Demitri touched her with his nose, Ayla caressed the fur of his snout. "Astounding, how much you've grown," Ayla said. "You are as handsome a creature as I have ever met."

How did we ever let her die?

Flowridia smiled but said nothing as Ayla pulled her hand back. "Stay by my side in Sha'Demoni," she said to Demitri, then she touched them both as she stepped into the shadow of a tree.

They vanished from sight.

Etolié held a weight as precious as gold, but at least a thousand times as heavy, given she couldn't have lifted Khastra if their lives depended on it.

But Khastra wept into her chest, bearing her own unfathomable burdens.

Etolié gazed upon the forsaken city, the rising scent of blood and carnage sickening. Entire streets had been leveled—likely by the giant fucking dragon surveying the scene, its skeletal body fascinating under any other circumstances.

A second dragon sat docile beside it, covered in gruesome burns and bearing stitches around its neck. Etolié recalled Flowers' story about a gentle dragon named Valeuron, a being of peace and life, only to be burned to death and beheaded by Soliel.

Speaking of whom . . . Etolié cast her gaze down toward the small pile of ash before the base of the statue of Sol Kareena, still protected by a glass dome. Too many omens this night—what of Lara and Flowers? The silver light and now this damning piece?

The most condemning remained the pulsing pile of gore beneath Khastra's legendary, gemstone hammer—the remains of Imperator Casvir, First and Last of His Name, Tyrant of Nox'Kartha and Marshal of the Deathless Army.

Though Etolié suspected she would be a fool to think he would be gone forever.

She cradled Khastra's face to her breast, content to clutch the tentative peace of the moment as she ran her fingers through the half-demon's hair. The strands soothed her anxious mind as she gently separated them, piece by piece, and the occasional brush against Khastra's horns brought the reminder of their different heritages.

Khastra was the daughter of a wicked demon goddess, and Etolié's own angelic heritage held equal merit, for the Goddess of Stars, her mother, had once nearly held the world in her soft embrace, but it mattered not. Etolié recalled the blessed words passed between she and the half-demon: *"I love you."*

And even in the midst of a city of death, surrounded by corpses and the memory of splattering gore, Etolié's heart could warm for that.

A few children slept. Some sat at the feet of the statue of Sol Kareena. One—her darling Ceile, barely three years old—softly cried from hunger, and Etolié's heart ached. Lunestra consoled a few others, her grandmotherly aura much more effective for that than Etolié's . . . everything. As it was, larger hands clung to her. Khastra no longer wept, but Etolié resolved to protect her all the same.

Murishani, a yappy little dog without a master, approached, his robes covered with streaks of gore and black, gruesome blood. "Khastra," she whispered, ignoring when Sora, too, responded to the name—the half-elf had been carving the same stick for at least an hour now, and it bore an impressive point. Her tawny skin was covered in the same ash and ichor as the rest of them, and her misery showed upon her resolute countenance. Upon her shoulder was Leelan, her familiar, who seemed content to hide in her impressively long ropes of blonde hair.

But Khastra gazed up, her eyes swollen and red, revealing the truth of her unprecedented biology—undead, yet half alive, capable of tapping into the crazed blood powers of her progenitor.

And capable of sobbing in Etolié's arms, causing her face to puff and swell. Etolié had never witnessed anything so vulnerable, not from the most powerful woman in the world. Khastra said nothing, merely watched from her seat beside the statue.

"Murishani's coming."

Etolié had learned long ago not to offer Khastra help to stand, well aware she served as a poor counterweight to her dearest friend's mass. Khastra shook as she stood, towering above Etolié, who barely reached her sternum in height.

Magnificence returned to her stance, and Etolié stared in awe at the half-demon, her daunting presence enhanced by her musculature and sheer size. Khastra was beautiful, from her deep blue skin and silver tattoos—covered in blood and ash today—to her hooves and tail, every piece of her something perfect.

"General Khastra," the viceroy said, his hands spread wide in welcome, "I'm glad to see you're feeling better.

Tensions have been high, and I'd certainly benefit from a good cry myself."

Etolié stepped forward, more than happy to make this fuckface cry, but Khastra's hand on her shoulder stopped her. "Viceroy," her demon said, all semblance of weakness gone from her rough tone, "I feel more alive than I have in months."

"There remains the matter of what to do with these darling wards of yours. I'd be happy to conjure transportation to Nox'Kartha—"

"Do not be cute with me," Khastra spat, and Etolié shivered at her vicious tone. "As you said, they are my wards; I will get them home." She looked back, the legacy of her years as a famed military leader returning to her stance as she surveyed her ragtag team of children and priestesses. "We should go. The canals await." Lunestra immediately responded, gently waking the few who slept. "Etolié, you should help. There is work to do."

There was nothing of exhaustion in Khastra's countenance anymore—only spite. "Yes, General," Etolié said, giving a brief salute, though with the wrong hand. She passed Sora by, the half-elf still more focused on her stick than their current task, and gently roused Ceile.

"Be that as it may, General Khastra," Murishani continued, more pathetic than Etolié had ever heard—did he genuinely fear Khastra? He'd be a dumbass not to. "There remains the fact that half the imperator is still, um, squished beneath your hammer. If you wouldn't mind moving it—"

His words cut off when Khastra's hand closed around his throat. "Do you think I am stupid?" Etolié's stomach clenched as Murishani's hands clung to Khastra's, his breaths suddenly heaving. "My soul is all but forfeit, and the only thing standing between my life and a torturous hell is that hammer."

His voice seeped out in painful wheezes. "I-I could reason with him—"

"Your promises mean nothing." She released him; Murishani collapsed, coughing his dainty little lungs out. "How I long to kill you. But I would not be foolish enough to try. You masquerade well, but do you think I do not recognize your smell?" She spat at his feet, then returned her gaze to Etolié—who admittedly had frozen and not accomplished her task of rousing Ceile. "Etolié—"

A great *roar* tore across the sky.

The rotting dragon, Valeuron, remained docile, mindless in death, but the skeletal dragon suddenly writhed. It roared, shooting noxious purple flame into the sky. It turned on its counterpart, ripping off its massive claw in one horrific tear—Valeuron did not even react.

Realization struck Etolié. "Khastra! The orb!"

The dragon clutched the black orb, its body immediately sparking with power, flashes of unnatural lightning dancing across its boney body. Khastra stepped forward; Etolié ran to join her, and when the dragon turned its gaze upon them, purple flame filled its eye sockets. By Eionei's Asshole—it could eat them both in one snap of its jaws.

It spread its wings, puffing up like a frightened cat as Khastra took another step forward. It roared; Khastra roared right back.

Etolié might've swooned, except the dragon seemed to take this as a personal affront—purple flame welled in its throat.

Khastra held out her hand, and from the splattered gore heap that was Casvir, her magnificent hammer rejoined her. Taller than even she, the gargantuan weapon held a glowing, gemstone head, and when the dragon breathed its horrible flame, Khastra swung it like a fucking windmill, scattering the unnatural fire.

The flame relented. Khastra held her battle stance, tense and prepared to charge—but the dragon no longer looked at her.

It looked at the gruesome remains of Casvir.

Keeping its defensive stance, the dragon crept forward and flinched when Khastra feinted a strike. It clasped the orb to its ribcage like a baby, and Etolié suddenly . . . understood.

"Wait," she said, careful to avoid being within range of Khastra's weapon as she stepped to the side, keeping an eye on the dragon as she approached Casvir's remains. For all Etolié's pitfalls with empathy, animal empathy was something she begrudgingly had to admit she held some talent for—and this oversized, winged feline was scared. "Dragon! Look at me—not her."

She didn't miss Khastra's look of horror, nor the dragon's fiery gaze as it watched. Etolié pointed at the pile of squished Casvir. "He's gone," she said, loud enough for the dragon to hear. "Imperator First and Last is feeling a little under the weather, and I bet his influence on you is waning. You still have your mind, don't you?"

Holding its defensive pose, the dragon's boney tail flicked against the ground, visibly agitated, and Etolié couldn't shake the image of a cornered cat.

"Listen, kitty, if you need to go, now's the time." She looked to the orb held protectively in the dragon's claws and sighed. "And if you need to take that thing with you, just swear you'll keep it away from the God of Order. It's likely safest with you, anyway."

The dragon studied the ruined city, daring to tear its gaze away from Etolié, then lingered on the children and Lunestra. With visible trepidation, the dragon took a step toward Etolié, then flinched when Khastra suddenly rushed to stand behind her.

"Etolié, what are you—"

"Khastra, it's scared of you. Just . . . let me try this." Etolié approached the dragon, who looked fully prepared to spread its wings and bolt away at the first sign of danger. But Flowers had befriended Valeuron—so why would his counterpart be any different? "You have a metaphorical brain in that skull of yours, don't you. Maybe even a heart too. Why aren't you running away, kitty?"

Kitty—that was the dragon's name, she decided—looked again to the children, then back to Etolié.

"All right, you're worried about the kiddos. Listen, the resident beefcake and I got this, though if you're offering to help, I won't say no."

Kitty offered a claw forward, and it was easily large enough to carry a Celestial or two, but not enough to carry eight children, as well as three adults—much less a massive half-demon. "I think I see where you're going with that, but you'll have to explain the rest."

The dragon's claw stretched farther. Kitty didn't move forward, however, and her continuing glances toward Khastra likely explained why. And so Etolié met her in the middle, ignoring whatever maternal-esque glare Khastra was undoubtedly giving her, and touched Kitty's outstretched claw.

A feminine voice, as soft as a night breeze, played like music in her head. *Where can I take you?*

"Um..." Etolié sounded like an idiot, which was a mortifying thing to be in front of an unfathomably old and intelligent dragon. "Staelash."

"Is it very far?"

"A week, by carriage."

Kitty took her claw away, and from the ravaged piles of buildings began... digging? Etolié wasn't going to try and explain the mind of a dragon-cat. Instead, she ran back to Khastra, whose glowing eyes held severity. "Kitty is going to help. She wants to get the children somewhere safe."

Khastra said nothing, her stare relentless, her grip on her hammer constant.

"What's going on in that horned head of yours?"

"I am very glad I insisted the dragon be kept intact instead of turned into a throne," she said, soft enough that the dragon might not hear. "Did not realize it still had a mind."

Etolié glanced back to her new dragon friend, realizing its brother stood not fifty feet away, mindless and monstrous. "She's like you, then."

"She may have had awareness all along."

Etolié couldn't stand to dwell on that, instead watching as Kitty pulled a ruined, bloodstained carriage from a collapsed building. Etolié called toward her companions. "Kitty's gonna bring us to Staelash. Let's get moving."

It was Lunestra and Sora who lingered—the children were fearless as they approached the massive dragon, their dirty faces in various states of awe. Murishani watched from a distance, all the practiced charm gone from his visage. Contempt sneered his lip, and Etolié found the rare glimpse of his real face woefully uninspiring. When he caught her eye, he smiled; she was happy to smile right back, with no kindness at all.

Sora and Lunestra finally approached, the former still holding her makeshift spear. "We trust the dragon now?" the half-elf said and Etolié nodded, surprised at her own confidence. "I suppose it would've eaten us already if it wanted to."

"She would've. For now, her name is Kitty." Etolié ran to join the children, amused to see Kitty watching them almost fondly. They dared to touch her offered claw, and perhaps the dragon needed the gentle touch—how long had it been since she'd been shown an ounce of kindness? Here she was, bothering to rescue a group of refugees, and Etolié found that . . . inspiring. "I'm assuming you want the kiddos to pile into the carriage?"

Kitty gave a rather obvious nod, not unlike a certain wolf Etolié adored. She relayed the message, amused to watch the children scramble to obey and Lunestra call them to order.

On the steps of the cathedral, Khastra remained, the hammer still grasped in her hands. Etolié ran to her, heart suddenly sinking. "There's room for you too, Beefcake."

Khastra spared a glance for gory Casvir, and Etolié's stomach squirmed to realize he was . . . pulsing. "He will not be gone forever, Etolié. Perhaps not even for long."

"It would've been too good to be true. But do you still feel him whispering in your brain?"

"It was never a whisper, merely a presence. Like a shadow that followed wherever I went. It feels lighter. But it does remain." Khastra watched Kitty, quiet acrimony on her ashen features. "The dragon was not transformed by his power, and so she may truly be free. I am not. And I do not want you to be in the way when he comes for me."

Etolié frantically shook her head, daring to grab Khastra's wrists—her hands were still occupied with the hammer. "There's a time to be noble, and there's a time for me to beg for you to forget that and come with me. Please."

With care to avoid Etolié's toes, Khastra set the hammer down. She stroked Etolié's gore-soaked hair, her face surely a mess from Casvir's ichor. Etolié floated up to meet her, wings aloft, and spared a moment to gaze upon Khastra's pained countenance, finding her beautiful despite the gore and ash coating her face. It was so surreal, so strange, to think she loved this woman, that she was in turned loved, and without any true thought behind it, she pressed their lips together, as impassioned as she dared given she was covered in blood.

Khastra's hands came to rest on her body, evoking memories of their unexpected, impossibly beautiful encounter. "Come with me," Etolié pled, and though Khastra's glowing eyes held sorrow, Etolié nearly sobbed when she nodded. "You can always leave the hammer, if you're worried about Imperator First and Last."

Khastra shook her head as Etolié gently floated down. "I would have to keep an endless vigil. Though I may fear Imperator Casvir's return, the world would fear if my mother stole back what I took."

Right. Khastra had her self-imposed duty. "Fair enough."

Khastra hefted the hammer up and followed Etolié toward the dragon—who metaphorically fluffed up her fur at Khastra's approach. "No, no—Kitty, she's a friend. Or something like that. But she won't hurt you. She's a slave to the imperator, just like you were."

Though Kitty's defensive position remained, she made no move to stop Khastra from strapping her hammer to the roof of the carriage. "It will be a tight fit," Khastra said, studying the children and priestesses already in the carriage.

"Good thing we're already covered in gore," Sora said, and to Etolié's relief, Khastra smiled.

They managed to squeeze in, even locked the door. Etolié curled into Khastra's lap, not complaining about the seating arrangement in the slightest when those strong arms held her close.

The children squealed—half in fear and half delight—when the carriage lurched. Kitty placed one claw beneath it and the other to steady it.

The dragon launched into the air, leaving the forsaken city far behind.

Chapter 2

They traveled in silence, and Demitri sniffed at every new thing, growling at the eerie shadows and the eyes far beyond. But the world soon shifted back, the nauseating stench of decaying bodies and swamp filth penetrating her senses. The familiar, waterlogged cottage awaited them.

Surrounding it were countless corpses, some years old and others mere hours. Evidence of fire ravaged the roots of a large tree, where Flowridia had nearly been burned alive, and before it lay a pile of bodies, disemboweled and torn apart.

Demitri absorbed it all with his young eyes, and Flowridia's heart ached.

The door creaked as Ayla pushed open the thick, damp wood. Fungal growths grew unattended in the walls and the sides of the cottage, but what had been purposefully cultivated had long ago died. Bloodied footsteps led from the cauldron room to the front door—Ayla's, Flowridia realized, surreal at the thought. Beside the ajar door was a closed one—a bedroom—and behind a small wall in front of them was the kitchen.

Ayla stopped in the center of the main room, her keen eyes studying every inch of the macabre building, missing nothing, Flowridia was sure. "This is where you spent your childhood?"

"A few years of it."

Demitri sniffed about, nearly too tall to comfortably fit. Ayla's lips pursed as her gaze shifted from the walls to Flowridia's face. "I imagined it larger."

A smooth voice said, "I never felt the need to expand it."

Ayla whipped around, nails digging into Flowridia's skin as she clutched her hand tight. Behind, ethereal and glowing a faint blue, Odessa the Swamp Witch serenely floated, the carving knife in her neck the only mar to her loveliness, even in death. Flowridia's own spitting image—surely Ayla would also think so, and her stomach churned to think her love might equate her to this wicked woman. "I am Odessa, Flowridia's devoted mother." She offered a hand, but Ayla stood utterly frozen. "You must be Ayla Darkleaf. She's spoken of nothing else since bringing your body here."

"Flowra," Ayla said, her cool tone a mask to what Flowridia feared was brewing hatred, "seems you have a story to tell."

"It's all right, Ayla," Flowridia said, but Ayla's nails threatened to draw blood. She bit back her words at the lifting of Ayla's lips, her revealed fangs elongating as she glared.

"Now, now," Odessa said, taking back the offered hand, "you wouldn't be standing here if it weren't for me and my accommodations."

Demitri appeared beside them, frantically sniffing the air. *Mom, something is different.*

But Ayla smiled, though her fangs still engulfed her mouth. "Of course," she said, her voice charming though muffled slightly by her teeth. "Perhaps gratitude is in order."

"Oh, but there's something a bit more pressing," Odessa said, floating in front of them; Ayla walked right through her, dragging Flowridia along. She gasped at the bone-chilling cold. "Fine. Perhaps it was a mistake to apprehend the vampire in my work room."

Ayla froze, glaring as she turned. But Flowridia's mind worked faster, realizing it could be only one. "Mereen?"

"Well, she didn't give a name, but—" Odessa's words cut off when Ayla walked straight through her again, marching to the cauldron room.

Light radiated from the enchanted meat-hooks above the cauldron, currently wrapped around a familiar figure, clad in leather. She was beautiful, her pale skin reflecting the light, her white-blonde braid disheveled. She dangled above the blood-stained cauldron, her smile bright as she set her eyes on Flowridia. "Oh, wonderful!" Mereen said. "I came to find you. Glad to see you found your wolf."

"Hello, Mereen," Ayla cooed, delight on her tongue; Flowridia shivered at her murderous tone.

"Ayla Darkleaf," Mereen said, her resignation apparent. "The one constant in my life."

Odessa appeared behind them, her radiating light matching the chains around Mereen's captured form. "I saw her skulking around the cottage, peeking through the windows and such. Once she came inside, well, you know I don't trust anyone."

Flowridia clung to Ayla, feeling her tension. Yet something lay missing—something that caused Flowridia's heart to race. "Mother, where is—"

"The *condemning* thing you don't want our interloper to see?" Odessa smiled, but her eyes were crazed. "I hid it."

Thank the gods for Mother—and those were words Flowridia never thought she would think. "Mereen," she said instead, "what are you doing here?"

"I wasn't going to save your life only to leave you to die elsewhere," Mereen said, her smile too broad to be sincere. Her eyes had not left Ayla, whose grip on Flowridia threatened to break bone. "Had to make certain you were safe, sweetie."

Ayla looked to Flowridia. "What is she talking about?"

"She saved me from the slavers. I don't know if you remember that, given I was wearing maldectine—"

"No, no—I do recall her voice," Ayla whispered, wonder on her tongue. "So strange, to remember a life I didn't live. But . . . it was not the first time you had met, however."

"She saved me from the God of Order."

Ayla returned her leering eyes to Mereen, all good humor fading. "Why?"

"She was a lost little girl in the woods. It's what decent people do."

"And then you conveniently came across her in a slave camp?"

Mereen's smile turned vicious. "I saved her from rape and possible death. I think that deserves some credit. Perhaps even a show of mercy—"

"Mereen, shut up," Ayla spat, and to Flowridia's surprise, Mereen obeyed, sneering as her lips clamped shut.

Ayla finally released her; blood flowed painfully through Flowridia's arm and hand. "Flowra, my love, I can already feel your soft heart prepared to bequeath mercy upon this woman, but she is wicked, and she is ruthless."

"She knew who I was to you, yet she still saved me," Flowridia said, recalling her own slip.

Ayla gave a curt smile, visible annoyance twitching her lip, but Flowridia did not bend. She met her beloved's eye, standing as tall as her stature would allow. "We will let her speak for herself." Ayla stood up, stance poised to fight as she said, "You may speak, Mereen, but only speak the truth. Why were you following my Flowra?"

Mereen struggled to muffle her words, but they came out nonetheless. Was this magic? Flowridia did not understand it at all.

"I heard there was a girl you loved," Mereen finally said. "Had to meet her for myself."

So it had not been pure luck that led Mereen to the dark woods where she and Soliel had been. Flowridia frowned, yet Mereen's actions remained baffling, even if she held ill-will.

"How did you know to follow her south?"

"I was following the slavers."

Ayla frowned; Flowridia did too. "Elaborate," Ayla said. "Speak no lies."

Mereen spat at Ayla's feet. "You will only kill me after—"

"Speak, or you will be clawing your own eyes out when I'm done with you."

Mereen fought, pain scrunching her beautiful face before the words, "I sent the slavers to her," burst from her mouth.

Appall dropped Flowridia's jaw, but Ayla said, "Why?"

"It was the only way I could think of to separate her and the empress from the rest."

So it had not been a coincidence.

Victorious, Ayla's smile twisted into something cruel and wicked. "And how did you know to do that?"

"People talk."

"Who talks?"

Mereen struggled, mouth clamped shut. Ayla suddenly slapped her across the mouth, leaving two large gashes across her lip. "Izthuni wasn't quiet. Other vampires overheard the ritual. I heard it from them."

"But why?" Flowridia said, the cold pulse of betrayal numbing her limbs. "Why would you assist in bringing Ayla to life?"

"You're pretty for a human," Mereen said, her smile almost sweet as her mouth slowly healed. "Clever, too. Much more than my sister, bless her heart—"

Again, Ayla's claws swiped across her face, this time leaving five deep gashes. No blood pooled, but raw red showed within the split flesh. "Do *not* speak of—!"

"Who, Sarai?"

Ayla lifted her hand to strike, but Flowridia grabbed her shoulder, releasing her quiet plea. "Kill her or let her go. I won't watch you torture her."

"Then in deference to her saving your life, I will kill her quickly," Ayla spat, but Flowridia held up a hand.

"Wait," she said gently, then she returned her attention to Mereen and repeated her question. "Why did you help me?"

Mereen, wrapped in chains, lost all her good humor and plainly said, "Because I cannot kill what's only sleeping."

Ayla looked to Odessa, watching serenely from the door. "Release her. I'm going to rip her head off."

With surprising care for enchanted, chained hooks, they unraveled, slowly releasing Mereen. "You'll allow this, Flowridia?" Mereen said, her body twisting like a dancer in ribbons. "Whatever my selfish ends, I did save your life. Twice."

Flowridia stayed silent, fighting the guilt rising in her heart.

"I will not hear her name from your damned tongue," Ayla said, watching like a lion presented fresh meat. Her fangs elongated as Mereen was placed upon the ground. "Instead, I shall hear you beg for mercy."

"Oh, Ayla, *please,*" Mereen said, mockery at her tongue. She slowly lifted her arms defensively, kept well away from the weapons at her back and hip. "Do I sound enough like Sarai?"

In the split moment of Ayla's rage, she lifted a hand against Mereen, leaving Flowridia to stand on her own feet. "No more words from you!"

Mereen plunged her fingers into her ears and screamed. Ayla swiped; Mereen dodged, rolling backwards, the soul-curdling cry still radiating from her lips. *"Mereen, freeze!"*

But she did not hear it, Flowridia realized, and the truth of Ayla's power over Mereen washed over her like a cold bath—

And then Mereen's foot struck Flowridia's chest.

Bone cracked. Flowridia smacked into the wall and collapsed. Escalating pain pulsed with each heartbeat. Mereen ran, but when Ayla followed, Flowridia's mild whimper gave her pause.

Ayla fell beside her, panic hastening her voice. "Flowra, Flowra, *no!*"

Each wheezing breath felt like drowning. Flowridia grabbed at Ayla's hands, willing her sight to steady. "I can—I can heal it—"

Ayla frantically shook her head, then tore Flowridia's beloved dress and all beneath it down the center, revealing her bare chest. With acute precision, she ran her fingers along the sides of Flowridia's ribs, when a sharp pain shot through her chest. Flowridia cried out, short and airy, and Ayla gently cupped her face, the ice in her eyes brimming with tears. "You have a fractured rib, possibly multiple. Judging by how blue your lips are turning, one has punctured your lung, which means the air is leaking out and will compress all your organs until one of them fails and you die. Take as deep a breath as you can."

Flowridia did, or tried—she gasped, yet felt so little.

"I'm going to save you, Flowra," Ayla said, calm despite her frantic words. "All you must do is stay awake. If I fail . . ." She suddenly tensed; she clutched Flowridia's arms, hard enough to bruise. ". . . let me turn you. Please."

Flowridia's desperate breath drew nothing. Darkness encroached on her vision. With a final burst of strength, she nodded.

Ayla stood and whirled toward Odessa. "I need a knife," she cried, all semblance of composure quickly fading. "I need honey. And I need a large needle, preferably hollow."

Odessa gestured to the wall of shelves beside her cauldron, pointing at her quarry as she spoke. "Knife. Honey. Can't promise the needle—"

"Then a reed, witch—a hollow reed!"

Flowridia focused on breathing, though she felt so little air. Pressure rose in her chest, along with ineffable, impending doom.

Something cold touched her hand—Demitri's nose nuzzled her palm. *Mom, it'll be all right. Lady Ayla will save you.*

She couldn't summon the air to speak. Threads of black threatened to cloud her vision. Instead, she focused on the fine hairs of his snout, her mind grasping them and their sensation as she fought to stay conscious.

Ayla returned, her focus upon a blood encrusted knife. Frantically, she spat on it, then scrubbed it with her dress, flakes of gore falling to the floor. "Let us pray you do not contract sepsis," she muttered, the vibrant blue of her eyes nearly engulfed in black. Her gaze narrowed; her hand suddenly glowed with silver light, which steadily grew into a flame—which she held to the knife's blade. When the knife shone, residual heat casting a faint glow, she coated it in honey. A sticky hand brushed lightly against her ribs . . . counting? "Try not to move," Ayla said, her calm merely a mask. "This will hurt, but it will save your life."

Flowridia managed a faint, "Ayla . . ." before Ayla stabbed the knife between her ribs. It seared and *burned*, but when she flailed, an impossibly strong arm forced her back down. The thin knife twisted, shooting pain across her side. It withdrew; Flowridia gasped yet felt so little air.

Fresh pain filled her when Ayla thrust something into the wound. She dared to look and saw that the reed had been inserted into her side. Ayla placed her lips to the end of it and apparently sucked, and with each breath, Flowridia felt the pressure in her chest . . . ebb.

In time, Ayla removed her lips, her mouth stained in blood, then carefully placed her hand onto Flowridia's chest. She slowly removed the reed; Flowridia winced but did not scream. With care, Ayla spread fresh honey onto the wound. "Heal yourself now," she whispered, words as tense as the air around them.

Flowridia shut her eyes, focusing on her body through the pain, felt the cracked bones and punctured organ, and willed life to flow through them.

Demitri touched her; she grasped onto his presence, his innate connection to her fueling her magic. With each breath, the pain faded. Flowridia opened her eyes, trembling as she met Ayla's gaze. "Ayla," she whispered, and the tension shattered.

Ayla pulled her into her arms, and Flowridia clung to her, desperate for comfort after so much pain. Ayla's lips ghosted her hair; her hand, sticky from honey, settled against her hip and the torn fabric.

"I'm sorry about the dress," Flowridia said, fearing reprimand, but Ayla only clung tighter, silent in the still morning. She sat as a statue, for she had no need to breathe, becoming cold stone around Flowridia's body.

A ghostly apparition crossed her vision. Odessa watched them, her gaze withering, then said, "Well, is she going to live?"

For as cruel as Odessa's gaze was, Ayla's disposition could have clouded the sun. "Yes."

"Good," Odessa said, her impatience only thinly veiled. "With that all in order, perhaps my daughter didn't tell you, but I was promised a little something in exchange for my aid, and I grow impatient—"

"Your daughter very nearly died, so perhaps show a modicum of empathy." Ayla's gaze softened when she looked to Flowridia instead. "You need rest, my sweet summer blossom, and perhaps another bath, lest the honey get into your hair."

Flowridia shook her head, managing to sit up with help. "You have to find Mereen. She couldn't have gone far in the daytime."

"Fuck Mereen," Ayla spat, the pure vitriol shocking, even on her. "She cannot speak, so let me stay with you."

"Is she . . . She's helpless to your will?"

"Precisely. Hence her cowardly retreat. If she cannot hear it, she cannot obey it. This is the nature of vampirism— the slave is helpless to the will of their creator."

"Ayla, she wasn't here to seek me out, I'm certain. There's still enough she can do to condemn us." Flowridia looked to Odessa, a question in her gaze. "Where is it?"

Odessa gestured to a trunk in the corner.

"Ayla, please," she whispered, leveling their faces. She placed a lingering kiss on her love's lips, cherishing the feeling after so much pain. "I'm shaken, but I'll live. Please, go. I want nothing more than to be held, but I won't relax until you try to find her."

Ayla released her, still mindful of the hand smeared in honey. "If that is your will . . . I do see the merit."

"Soon we'll have all the time in the world, my love, but there are a few ends left to tend to." Ayla helped her to rise. Standing, they shared a final kiss. "Go," she whispered, and Ayla whisked herself away into a shadow.

With utmost trepidation, Flowridia crept toward the truck, trembling as she lifted its lid.

There she was, a cold bastion of horror—Empress Alauriel Solviraes, dead. Streaked in blood; nearly decapitated from Soliel's knife. Her eyelids opened as mere slits, and

Flowridia dared to reach down and touch her clammy skin, gently shutting those silver eyes forever. Emotion struck; for all her joy, the pain still cut like a dagger to her heart. Amidst her glowing victory, there had been an unbearable cost.

A cost . . . she had not chosen to pay.

There was a time to mourn, but when Mother's radiating light shifted the shadows of the room, Flowridia knew it was not yet. Instead, she shut the lid, biting back any prayers of peace, and instead found a dried cloth and spat upon it, rubbing her own sticky chest. Though it was only her mother, she shied at her own immodesty, instead focusing on removing the honey so she could hold the ruined her dress together.

"Flower Child, your beloved is much less amiable than she was promised to be." The door shut on its own volition; beyond, she heard Demitri growl. Mother floated beside her, and Flowridia dropped the cloth and held her dress together. "I grow impatient."

"Once this is dealt with, I promise she'll—"

"She'll what? Bring me something as decrepit and ruined as the body in the trunk? I can't say I'm impressed—she's disrespectful to your mother, which is hardly a good sign for your future."

Stepping back, Flowridia had only the wall to greet her. "It's a stressful time. She was only just revived and now—"

"No time for me, I know. She does have time to fuck you in the filthy swamp water and rescue your familiar, and now she has time to chase this . . . vampire? If I'd known 'Mereen' would have been such a nuisance, I would have let her go," Mother seethed, her blue outline glowing brighter. "Here I am, punished for my own good deed."

Flowridia straightened her stance, wary of her mother's fury. "I have sworn this to you. You need only be patient—"

A spectral hand lashed across Flowridia's face, corporeal enough to topple her to the ground. Outside, Demitri howled and scratched at the door. Held up by her hands, Flowridia looked up from the dirty floor and gingerly touched her face, feeling something cold and burning.

"She's 'rather weak to begging,' yes?" Mother's face twisted into an ugly sneer, cold cruelty in her gaze. "Then start *begging,* Flower Child, lest you beg me for mercy instead."

Flowridia stumbled to her feet, too shocked to be angry, but behind Odessa came a shadowed figure, silent until it burst into silver flame. "I wondered when you'd show your true character," Ayla said, her luxurious words cruel yet calm. Odessa gasped as silver-lit fingers wrapped around her ethereal neck. Ayla stood behind, fangs elongating as Odessa struggled. "Pure magic sustains your being. The least I can do is touch it."

The ghostly witch wailed, twisting her body to try and escape Ayla's grasp.

"She needn't beg for this," Ayla said, striking and furious. "Command me, my sweet. This monster will never touch you again."

Flowridia stared at Odessa, at the woman struggling in a monster's grasp and dug for empathy, for any residual shards of love she could assemble to defend her. "I-I don't—"

"Flower Child," Odessa managed to say, her smile becoming kind and maternal, though marred in desperation, "all I have ever done is love you."

The words plunged like a dagger in her stomach.

"I know I can be strict, but it is because I know you have the capacity to be better."

In her lowest moments, Flowridia still thought of the lives she had taken beneath Odessa's roof, the familiarity of splitting skin, the inescapable smell of blood, the repulsive sensation of flesh between her teeth—

Mother struggled, but Ayla's body merely flared with flame, subduing her immediately. "My darling Flower Child, you know I loved and cherished our time together."

Flowridia recalled three years of a twisted hell, the memories entangled with moments of sweetness, scraps of love for her starving self, but so many more of hate.

"Flower Child—"

"You aren't capable of love," Flowridia said, voice breaking at that final word. It cut like a knife, this severance of her desperate craving for maternal affection. "Long ago, you might have been. But the world broke you. Suffering changed you into something wicked."

Cruelty twisted Mother's visage. "You aren't better than me, you know—"

"Just do it," Flowridia whimpered.

Odessa's fearful anger bore into her. "Flower Child, please—" She shrieked, her form glowing bright, but not so bright as Ayla. Wisps of light and energy tore as Ayla ripped in her two, protected by the Silver Fire covering her undead skin. Odessa screamed, flailing in vain against the claws splitting her apart.

Flowridia expected grandeur, a spectacle. Lara had died in a flash of light radiating across the sky.

Instead, Odessa was shredded to bits and faded away, her wailing disappearing in tandem.

Flowridia wrapped her arms around herself, tears falling fast.

Ayla's skin held a silver glow. She went first to the door, opening it to allow Demitri to peer in and stop his howling. "It is over now, Demitri," Ayla said, the faint light of her skin enough to illuminate the room. "Odessa is gone."

Demitri immediately perked up. Were he able to fit through the small door frame, Flowridia held no doubt he would pounce on her. *We don't have to worry about the bitch in the swamp?*

Despite her heartbreak, Flowridia managed a scoffing, painful laugh. She wiped her falling tears. "And how long have you been sitting on that joke?"

Since we entered Neolan.

Ayla stood on her toes and placed a lingering kiss on Flowridia's cheek. Her touch was tender, body cleaned of sticky residue as she wrapped her arms around her. "What are you feeling?"

"I hurt," Flowridia said, exhaustion bombarding her fragile form. She clung to Ayla's body, weeping in her embrace.

In silence, Ayla held her, her fingers writing soothing lines across her back.

The ruined dress hung in shambles off Flowridia's body, but there was no one here to care or judge. Her heart ached. She had killed Mother once before, but it had been an accident. That foolish hope had remained, that perhaps there might still be something between them. Flowridia wept, mourning the hole in her heart.

"Come with me," came the soft whisper in her ear. "You need cleaned up. You need sleep."

Flowridia let her lead, let Ayla's cold hands caress her nearly naked form as she wiped blood and honey from her skin. The touch was kind, almost healing, yet she ached from something far deeper. "I feel so stupid," she whispered, when she finally calmed. Her tears fell lightly now, as quiet as her words. "I thought I'd finally found the courage to hate her, but look at me. I suppose . . . I suppose no matter what, she's still my mother, and I—"

She was stopped by a finger on her lip. "Look at me," Ayla said darkly, and Flowridia obeyed. "You can mourn what she was not, but you cannot mourn what she was. All she ever tried to do was break you, and in many respects, she succeeded. You share her blood—who cares? She birthed you, but it does not mean she is your mother. You can cry, Flowra, but don't you dare blame her failings on yourself."

There was truth in the harsh words, but it did not change how badly she ached. "I suppose you're right. But then that leaves me with no mother, and I don't know if that's better."

Ayla resumed wiping grime from Flowridia's form, the affection kind and innocent. "Being alone is not the same as being lonely. But it does not help, being here—I do not know much of magic yet, but I swear her essence permeates this place. I think you shall feel better once we have left it behind."

Flowridia didn't disagree but kept her silence as Ayla washed her. Beneath her sorrow, her pain and tears, there remained the underlying surrealness of Ayla's presence. Ayla was here, she was real, and nothing could take that away.

When Ayla had finished, she helped Flowridia rise. "Your body has been through more than most mortals can take in just the past few hours; I really do insist you sleep."

"You need to find Mereen. There's not much else for you to do, while I'm sleeping."

Ayla caressed her thick hair as she led her to bed. "Plenty I could do, but I suppose you are right. Demitri can watch over you while I'm gone." When Ayla cupped her cheek, she placed her hand to cover it. "But indulge me. Let me stay until you fall asleep." Gentle, thin fingers removed themselves from her cheek. "I love you, Flowridia."

"I love you," she whispered back. "Be careful."

Ayla hummed a gentle tune, the familiarity of it like radiant light breaking through the dark of Flowridia's mind. Especially now, to know something of its origin—written by a woman Ayla had once loved, whose name upon Mereen's tongue had incited Ayla to rage.

So many questions swirled in Flowridia's mind. But despite her misgivings and sorrow, sleep stole her quickly.

Their party flew for hours. Etolié slept for nearly all of it.

She vaguely recalled the children and their incessant comments about how small the world appeared from so high in the air. Sora remained quiet, and Etolié wondered if she were hurting more than she led on.

Lunestra said little as well, but more because of the side-glances she kept giving to she and Khastra's less-than-platonic cuddling. Then again, when had she and Khastra ever been strictly platonic? The more Etolié considered it, the more humorous it became, to think how desperately she'd craved Khastra's touch and affirmation all these years.

She thought idly of Khastra's weighted words: *"I have loved you for so long . . ."*

Despite the pain and heartbreak of the past day and night, the world became quiet in Khastra's arms.

Light shone over the horizon. All was serene, until a giant claw of bone suddenly poked through the window. The children startled, but Etolié's sleepy mind got the point. Without leaving her cozy place on Khastra's gore-covered, armored chest, she touched it.

"I see a city far ahead. Is that where you want to go?"

Etolié looked out the window—rather, as well as she could given there was a dragon claw blocking the view—and recognized the rolling green hills, even spotted the expansive river. She sat up, grateful when Khastra steadied her—her head spun, the world was loud, and her first order of business upon landing would be to grab her favorite flask. Though sobriety was impending, she leaned her head out the window and screamed, "YES, THAT'S RIGHT, KITTY. TO THE MANOR."

When she sat back down, her chest warmed at Khastra's chuckle. "I adore you, Etolié."

Her smile came unbidden. Was this what it felt like to be smitten?

Upon Lunestra's lap was Ceile, who watched all the while. When Etolié shared her smile, the girl returned it, despite her drying tears.

So strange, to feel such fragile joy after heartbreak. The looming threat of Casvir remained, but for now, they had a dragon flying them home.

A much more literal fluttering in her stomach caused her to sit up. They slowly descended, and rather than cause panic among the populace, Etolié stood up as well as she could in the packed carriage. "Help me outside, Beefcake."

Khastra didn't argue, instead helping steady Etolié as her slim figure slipped out the small window—thank Alystra's Fine Ass for self-imposed starvation, right?

Her wings spread, and though she didn't fly nearly so fast as the dragon, she managed to catch Kitty's rib as she floated behind. Kitty, feeling the touch, glanced back, then slowed and gently grabbed her. The massive dragon held Etolié to her face as she flew. *"Yes, little one?"*

"I'm going to make you invisible!" Etolié shouted amidst the whipping winds. "Land in the manor courtyard!"

"A wise plan."

With one claw clutching the carriage to her ribcage and the other keeping Etolié close, Kitty descended toward the city. Etolié focused, intent on turning the dragon into a particularly opaque patch of clouds. Although she had wings, Etolié had never flown so high, and while the wind threatened to deafen her, the sights were magnificent. Staelash approached, and she laughed, invigorated by the sudden sensation of victory.

For fuck's sake—they had actually lived.

However, while Etolié could make Kitty invisible, she couldn't mask the earth-shaking *thud* of her landing. Etolié immediately freed herself, becoming visible as a volley of guards tentatively approached. "Hello! It's me! You know me. Don't come closer, please!"

Etolié landed and held out her arms—thankfully, they listened. "Magister Etolié," one said, inspecting the gore and ash and nastiness on her hair and body—perhaps they wouldn't notice the dragon-shaped indent in the grass, "what's going on?"

"I brought a friend. She helped save our lives. Don't panic." Etolié held up a defensive hand toward the guards. "Don't panic."

She released her spell. The dragon appeared. One man gasped and drew his sword; the others looked faint.

"She's not going to hurt us," Etolié said, watching as Kitty carefully placed the carriage onto the ground. The door swung open, and a pile of children literally fell out—bloodstained, tear-stained, and sleepless. Then came Lunestra, visibly relieved to be touching solid ground again, her once pristine robes soiled from dirt and blood.

When Sora emerged, she fell upon the ground and gripped the luscious, green grass. The little bird familiar she kept chirped merrily as it hopped around beside her, and Etolié thought Sora might burst into tears—her eyes certainly watered.

Khastra was the last to appear, busying herself by removing the hammer from the carriage, but Etolié's attention was stolen by the sudden cry of, *"Etolié?!"*

That was the only warning before Etolié was bombarded by twice her girth in ginger.

Queen Marielle, apparently returned from her honeymoon, sobbed into her shoulder, and Etolié patted her back, content to pretend the queen wasn't on thin fucking ice. "Hi, Marielle."

Zorlaeus, who Etolié had recently decided had a personality and was actually quite pleasant, stayed farther back, visibly wary of the dragon. "She's been despondent," he said softly, "ever since she heard about the Theocracy."

"You were at the funeral!" Marielle cried, and when she pulled back, tears had streaked down her painted face. Blood stained her hair and dress, but to her credit, she didn't seem to care. "You could have died!"

"Yes, well, long story short—we didn't."

"Explain the dragon!" Marielle screamed, but then she returned to weeping.

Etolié resigned herself to her itchy touch, her arms awkwardly hovering around but only barely touching her crying companion. "Well, she used to be Casvir's dragon, but now she belongs to no one but herself."

Marielle pulled away from Etolié, falling into Khastra's embrace next. Khastra, who had significantly less patience for Marielle, kept her arms at her side. "We are fine, Marielle."

"You must tell us everything!" Marielle cried, stepping back to face all three of them. To her credit, she didn't seem to mind the blood and ash now staining her own dress.

"It's a very long and fascinating story," Etolié said, "and I'm sure Sora would love to tell it."

The half-elf blinked. "What?"

"After we get these children situated, of course," Etolié said, gesturing to their small party. "And Lunestra."

Thalmus emerged from the manor, apparently not giving a shit about the dragon, which Etolié admired. Instead, he stared at her like she was a ghost, then at Lunestra and Sora and to the smiling, albeit traumatized children . . . but then it darkened.

He stared warily at a certain Nox'Karthan General, whose glowing eyes unabashedly met his. Etolié stepped between them. "Hello, Thalmus. No, I'm not dead. I think we should celebrate by giving these kiddos some food and a bath, yes?"

"Etolié," Thalmus said, his words rare and thus not to be discounted, "she can't be here."

"Who? Sora? Didn't know you hated half-elves . . ." She let her lame joke trail off, because Thalmus had no sparkle in his eye. "Listen, it's complicated, but she's here because I asked her to come. She . . ."

Khastra had pled for anonymity: *"I beg of you—say nothing."*

". . . it's for the best. Please. You've known her for years. You know she's good. You know she's not . . ." Etolié swallowed, floundering when Thalmus merely stared. "You know she didn't have a choice."

"Tensions are high," Thalmus said, his dark features flickering briefly to the undead general, "and you know what statement this will make to the world."

Etolié snapped her fingers—Khastra flickered out of sight. "Poof! She's gone. No harm done. She was never here."

Etolié had spent years of her life bending over backwards to avoid speaking to Thalmus. This might've been the longest conversation they'd ever had. "You know the risks," he said.

"I do." She looked at the four guards and frowned. "Keep your mouths shut."

"Magister," one said, "we all served General Khastra for years. We'll say nothing."

The others nodded in agreement. Etolié recalled that Khastra had a reputation here, largely beloved by all. "Thank you."

"But *why* is there a dragon?" Marielle said, her own composure not quite so strong as Thalmus'.

That really did warrant more explanation. Etolié realized Kitty watched, as though waiting—likely to say goodbye. "We'll need to have a meeting about the fate of Imperator First and Last, but like I said, this was the dragon he enslaved. He's not in a state currently to keep her enslaved. She's actually a very nice and polite lady and was kind enough to fly us here." Etolié stepped toward Kitty, a smile on her lip. "I suppose you're going to take that orb with you."

Kitty spoke, this time without touch. *"It is my duty upon this world; I fear I am the only one left."*

"I mean, your brother was willing to give it to my friend, Flowers, but then dragon daddy showed up."

"I know nothing of Valeuron's intentions for your friend. Is it true though—the Great Father killed my brother?"

Etolié nodded, unprepared for the wash of grief that rolled over her—yet it wasn't her own.

"This bespeaks an ill fate for the world."

"He's trying to gather all six orbs to undo the Convergence."

Kitty remained quiet a moment, her boney countenance surprisingly expressive—Etolié all but saw her anguish. *"Then I must not allow it."*

"Would you help us?" Etolié said, grasping any hope she could. "We're fighting a losing battle, but with your help, we could stop him for good."

"Whatever atrocities he has committed . . ." Kitty's words ceased, and Etolié again felt that sorrow. The dragon could not speak aloud, but damn, she could emote. *". . . I cannot kill my own father. I do not have the heart."*

"Fair enough," Etolié said, not relating to that sentiment at all.

"Besides, there is a greater part I must play. If my Father is here, then my Mother will surely follow."

The words settled about as comfortably as a sucker punch to the gut. "Y-You mean—?"

"Somewhere on this realm, my Mother's spirit waits. I must find her."

Etolié smiled, well aware her eyes were full of crazy. "Is that . . . good news?"

"None can predict the will of the Great Mother, but I cannot fathom her joining Father after what he's done to Valeuron. I must

go." Kitty's purple, gaseous eyes flashed. Etolié knew what scrutiny felt like, and this dragon wasn't looking at her quite the same as before. *"Thank you. What is your name?"*

"Etolié," she replied, and she swore the dragon's gaze grew more intent.

"You are . . . the Goddess of Stars."

Etolié forced a smile. "That's my mom, but close enough."

"My mistake."

"Anything we mere mortals can do to help?" Etolié asked, increasingly unnerved with every passing minute. "Not to be pessimistic, but I'd prefer your Godly Mother be sweetened to our lowly cause of keeping the worlds right where they are."

"Fear not. When the time comes, you will know what to do. You did in the time before. Farewell."

And with that cryptic bullshit, Kitty launched into the air. Etolié watched those boney wings somehow keep her aloft—science said *no*, but dragons were magical creatures—until she was a tiny speck in the distance.

Exhaustion threatened to cripple her. Her mind reeled from Kitty's words, but she stuffed those feelings into a box. Etolié was a gore-encrusted mess, and so were the rest. "Thalmus, we need baths for everyone, as well as somewhere for the children to sleep before we decide what to do with them. We need to have a meeting, but I think Archbishop Lunestra deserves better than bloodstained robes."

"I will help the children," Thalmus said, and then he looked to Marielle. "Will you—"

"Archbishop, I'd be more than happy to assist," the queen said, her smile genuine.

Etolié shared a look with Sora, the half-elf looking near collapse, but the quiet joy of victory remained.

On the ground remained the faintest imprint of goat hooves, and Etolié kept her spell of disbelief, even as she touched blood-streaked armor, trailing down the gem-studded masterpiece until she grasped a filthy, callused hand. "Let's go," she mouthed, and the invisible presence followed.

The manor was home in ways Celestière never had been. And no matter how often Etolié felt itchy and confined in her city, it held comfort. With Khastra's hand in hers, she wound familiar halls and stairs, not going to her library, no, but somewhere far more somber.

After Khastra's death, there had been speculation on how to disassemble her bedroom and distribute her grand swath of trinkets and boundless wealth. Khastra was fucking loaded, which seemed appropriate given she was older than money. But Etolié's gut still clenched to remember the meeting wherein they had read her will.

In Khastra's beautiful script, it had given only three instructions:

Her hammer would be returned to her mother—though the eternal, final jest had been that no one could lift it and fulfill those terms.

A set of journals would be given to someone named Kah'Sheen—her sister, Etolié now knew.

All the rest, all her earthly possessions, her mountains of wealth and priceless collections of treasures, were for Etolié to do with as she saw fit.

And Etolié, distraught and adrift for the anchor she had lost, had decided to do absolutely nothing with any of it. The room had remained stagnant until Marielle's wedding, wherein it was cleaned in anticipation of Khastra's return.

When Etolié twisted the locked doorknob of Khastra's suite, it clicked open. Locks were a nebulous annoyance at best to the Savior of Slaves. Warmth lay in every object, every dresser, every blanket on the large, demon-sized bed. Khastra's room in Staelash was a sorcerer's hoard of beautiful things, rare gems, its own small museum of elegance, and when Khastra's body flickered back into view, Etolié saw the barest ghost of a smile on her face, splattered with blood and ash.

"Let's get you out of that armor," Etolié said, releasing her hand. She locked the door, then led her demon to the adjacent washroom. The crystal sconces glowed in gentle shades of amber at their entrance. It bore more finery and style than the other washrooms in the manor, windowless and decorated by the general herself. Khastra had loudly refused to share a bathing space during the manor's initial construction, and thus had been given her own space, though Etolié had been dunked into it more than once over the years.

An enormous, pond-like tub had been built into the floor, more than large enough for Solvira's former general to relax in and filled with water purified by magic. It bore stones around the perimeter, decorative and damp, beautifully reflecting the ambient lights.

Khastra's armor was coated in gore, her skin streaked with blood, hair matted, and Etolié painstakingly helped her remove every piece of the gem-laden shell. They could be cleaned later; for now, Khastra needed to be freed from the prison of horror branded onto her body.

When she removed Khastra's breastplate, Etolié saw the letter tuck inside, dirtied from crusted blood but far from ruined. Its seal had been broken.

Khastra knew. But they'd kissed upon the battlefield, so perhaps she had not made a fool of herself by revealing her heart.

Etolié laid the pieces in a neat arrangement, then beckoned for Khastra to sit. The half-demon wore only the thin garments separating her skin from the crafted armor and gambeson. Etolié had seen it a thousand times, deeming it more of a second skin than clothing, and spared a moment to study the sharp lines of her oblique, her pectoral and breast and small bud of her nipple and wondered what it would be like to touch it all, to luxuriate in her body without the fear of time.

Making love to Khastra the first time had been a one-sided affair, and Etolié wanted so badly to touch her in return, to connect them the way Khastra had and see the half-demon undone.

Her heart craved that bonding, but now was not the time, both of them coated in gore and blood, emotionally wrecked by unspeakable horrors. Instead, as Khastra sat on the floor before her, Etolié summoned her flask and took a few long sips, then offered the rest to her favorite demon, who accepted with a joyless smile. She took a quick drink as Etolié carefully pulled out the putrid filth caught in her lengthy, lavender hair. She unbraided Khastra's matted locks, taking great pains not to tug, though she surely failed. The blood had been dry for hours, resulting in a crusty, macabre mess.

They were silent for all of it, both clinging to peace, though Etolié realized she couldn't speak for whatever passed through Khastra's mind. When she peered over, Khastra's face was streaked with tears.

She asked, "What's on your mind, Beefcake?"

"It was a mistake for me to come here," Khastra said, and Etolié had never heard her sound so exhausted. She set the open flask on the ground beside the tub. "I am endangering Staelash, and I am endangering you."

Etolié stepped around her, cupping Khastra's face as she directed it to look at her. "Nox'Kartha and Staelash are friends by marriage, remember? Zorlaeus and Marielle were good for something. Casvir wouldn't fucking dare."

Khastra's expression said otherwise, but she smiled through her quiet tears.

"The water's warm, ya big lug," Etolié said, gesturing to the bath. "You can go first. I'll track down some towels—"

She was stopped by a gentle grasp on her hand. "I do not know how long I have with you," Khastra said. "Stay with me, please. Let me savor your presence."

Etolié blushed, because *damn*—Khastra knew how to say poetic bullshit. "Yes, general," she replied, and oh fuck, did she sound breathless? She certainly felt it.

Khastra stood and began removing her remaining clothing; Etolié looked away, suddenly shy to see her. They'd made love in the dark, illuminated by Khastra's tattoos, Etolié's wings, and filtered moonlight through the skylight— romantic, certainly, but Etolié only recalled flashes of Khastra's beautiful body.

As she picked her flask up off the ground, covered by Khastra's shadow, she wondered if Khastra ever thought about Etolié's body, surprised at how self-conscious she was to consider it. She took a long drink, though the world was quiet enough here.

A voice spoke softly amidst the faint trickling of water. "Etolié?"

Etolié glanced over her shoulder, enough to see that Khastra had stepped into the water.

"You do not have to join me, but you are invited to."

Etolié dared to hold a mirror to herself and peek into the cesspool that apparently housed her emotions—just for a moment.

Khastra had seen her naked. Khastra had quietly teased her on countless occasions about her aversion toward itchy, confining clothing, had judged her outfits at Etolié's insistence, had once given a very close inspection to her side- boob when a crossbow bolt had nearly torn it away. They'd already had sex but . . .

Khastra had said she was beautiful.

She swallowed her fear. Her wings illuminated the scene as she disillusioned her clothing, then she shyly turned around, demure as she covered her breasts with her hands.

Khastra said nothing as Etolié approached, merely gazed at her as she had their entire friendship—as though she were the most precious person in all the worlds. She was seated, as far as Etolié could see, the hint of her breasts peeking in and out of the water, fully visible when she offered a hand to help Etolié step in. Starkly taboo, allowing herself to look, but more daunting than that was the vicious scarring between them.

Yet with the sight came the confirmation that Khastra's tattoos really did cover all of her, including her nipples, and all sex-thoughts aside, Etolié found the idea of tiny, illuminate nipples hilarious and snickered.

Khastra withdrew her hand. "What is funny?"

"Did it hurt to tattoo your nips?"

Khastra laughed, and it was the most wonderful sound in all the world. "Very much. But that was three thousand years ago."

When offered again, she accepted Khastra's hand. Warm water enveloped Etolié like a cherished hug. She moved instinctively to help Khastra wash the grime from her body, grateful when the half-demon did the same for her. Where the blood touched the enchanted water, it swirled away and vanished—for which Etolié was thankful, given the alternative was for her to be bathing in entrail soup.

It was as sensual as Etolié had ever experienced, helping another woman bathe, the innocent intimacy a glowing, precious thing.

As she scrubbed further blood from the long, tangled locks, generous with the soap, Etolié whispered, "You read my letter?"

"I did."

"I asked you a question. I need to know—what are we now?" Etolié's nerves threatened to overtake her tongue, but she pushed onward, nevertheless, always a glutton for punishment. "My better judgement says we aren't only friends anymore, given we keep touching lips, but you know what they say about assumptions."

Khastra cupped Etolié's cheek, pulling her from her task of untangling the matted locks. "I mean what I said—I love you, Etolié."

"You didn't quite phrase it like that," Etolié teased, daring to wink. "'I have loved you for so long,' I think was the real bit."

Khastra's smile became gentle, something dark coloring her cheeks. "Etolié . . ." She said her name like it was as fragile as a dove. "I loved you the moment I first saw you, all those years go. You were dynamic. And funny. And so very beautiful. I resolved to tell you, but you confided in me your proclivities toward attraction, as well as your discomfort at being seen that way." She brushed her thumb across Etolié's jaw, the callused touch a comfort. "You were a person who needed to be loved, but not in the way I had initially thought. I devoted myself to you as a friend and was blessed every day for it.

"As for what it means," she continued, and Etolié's heart glowed, "I would hope it means we do what we have always done, but with more honesty in our actions."

"So, exactly the same, but with sex."

Khastra nodded. It sounded unbearably perfect.

"I fear," Khastra said, letting her hand fall from Etolié's face, "that my own words are prophetic—we can only be as close as our kingdoms allow, at least publicly. With the Theocracy's destruction, I do not know how close that will be. You say Nox'Kartha and Staelash are united by marriage, but Staelash belongs to Solvira, who will not dismiss this lightly." Khastra kissed her forehead, unbearable warmth in the gesture. "May I hold you? Not with intention. But you are naked, and I do not want to make you uncomfortable."

"Please hold me," Etolié said, surprised at her own pleading, and Khastra, seated upon the bench within the tub, pulled Etolié into her lap and held her to her bare chest. Where their skin touched, those silver tattoos glowed, and Etolié habitually traced the ones on her shoulders, too shy to touch her breasts or scars. Instead, she looked up and kissed her jaw, overjoyed when Khastra met her in the middle. Their lips touched.

So strange and wonderful, to bask in the feeling of Khastra against her, their naked forms chaste as they exchanged soft, slow kisses. Fluttering warmth filled her stomach with each tender gesture, the disbelief of it still jarring—Khastra loved her. And that was all right because Khastra was . . . *Khastra,* and she needed no other reason than that.

"Wait," she said, a rather loud and invasive thought interrupting her quiet moment. "Exactly the same, but with sex?"

A slight frown deepened the faint lines on Khastra's face, her confusion apparent in her nod.

"No wonder everyone thought we were fucking."

Khastra laughed; Etolié's favorite sound in all the worlds. She grabbed her flask and drank, then moved to offer more to the half-demon—

When the liquid suddenly funneled on its own from the small opening. Etolié immediately pushed away from Khastra, scrambling to the opposite side of the tub as a tiny figure formed from the swirling booze. Leaning back, she relaxed casually against her fist, sinking into the water enough to cover her naughty bits and forcing a smile. "A little busy here, Grandpa—"

"Oh, Etolié—thank the Triple Suns!" Tiny Eionei stood no taller than her middle finger, but his tears were as loud as a normal man's. He made no effort to hide his sobs. "We were so worried! You disappeared, I couldn't feel you at all, the Theocracy was destroyed, Sol Kareena is devastated, and—"

"Grandpa, I'm fine," Etolié said, the emotional outburst unexpected though admittedly touching. She had never seen Eionei cry. Still, she shied away from strong displays of distress; anxiety spiked within her. "I'm all right. Just cleaning up at the moment, so it's not the best time."

Tiny grandpa's liquid form—amber and slightly foamy, as any good beer should be—wiped his tears away, his wings mere speckles of foam as they gently floated behind him. "I understand. But will you tell us what happened soon? Not even Sol Kareena could hear her followers' prayers."

"The short version is that Imperator Casvir used a Convergence Orb to cut off contact to Celestière. I don't know how."

As Eionei nodded, Etolié kept a silent spell readied, prepared at a moment's notice to illusion the naked half-demon away if he looked backwards. He sniffed, composing himself as he wiped his liquid eyes. "I don't know the last time I told you I love you, but . . . I do." He shuffled uncomfortably, clearly remiss to leave despite the awkward meeting location. "Sol Kareena is unwell, but knowing you're safe will hopefully help."

"Tell everyone I'm well," Etolié said, not saying a particular maternal name, as much as she wondered if her momma even knew. "I promise to reach out to you again soon."

"Your, uh, neck is looking better."

Etolié's smile was suddenly painted. Right. That had been an uncomfortable previous conversation. "Well, running into bookshelves is a hazard in my chosen profession, but fortunately bruises heal quickly. Grandpa, I really should go."

"Of course. Stay safe, Starshine."

His liquid self fell back into the flask. Etolié took a sip, then shut it and tossed it back into its extra-dimensional space. "He never does that at convenient times," she said, returning to Khastra's lap.

"What happened to your neck?"

"Like you don't know." She pointed at the now unblemished, pale skin. "You got a little carried away. Left a mark. Sora noticed too."

It was rare to see horror in Khastra's glowing eyes, but there it was, and Etolié resisted the urge to chuckle. "I sincerely apologize. It was not my intention."

Etolié smile as softly as the memories of the night evoked. "Fuck, I don't even have a joke for that. Just kiss me."

When she pressed their lips together once more, Etolié melted, wonderful warmth flooding her body. If this were love, she wanted to keep it, bottle it, let it intoxicate her, yet she feared studying would scare it away. Like a small bird—to cage it would kill it.

Etolié chose to let it soar.

Chapter 3

The sky was dark when Flowridia finally blinked into wakefulness.

On the small table beside her was a dress, likely placed there by her love, as well as a bowl filled with raw nuts. Flowridia took a handful, ravenous from a day of no food. She stripped the ruined gown from her body and slipped this new one onto her body—amused to realize it was her own, stolen from Staelash. Through the open door, she saw Demitri's sleeping form, but someone else was missing. "Ayla?"

Rustling from outside pulled her focus. "Ayla, love?" Flowridia peeked her head around the doorframe, her eyes keen in the dim lighting. Her expression softened when she saw the woman kneeling beside a trunk of Flowridia's things, engrossed in a document.

But at the mention of her name, Ayla turned, eyes wide and severe. "*The time spent with you has been enjoyable,*" she recited, mouth twisting into a grin. But her eyes still spoke murder. "What is this?"

Flowridia stepped through the doorway, leaning demurely against the post. She knew the words the letter held. Her eyebrows furrowed as she whispered, "It's exactly what it says—a letter from Casvir. T-The imperator."

Ayla's gaze returned to the document. "*Watching you grow and change over these last few months has been a great pleasure to me and a memory I will treasure,*" she read, her mocking tone pulling a frown to Flowridia's lips. "*You have been a rare joy to have in my life—*" Ayla let the paper flutter to the floor and stood focused on Flowridia. She stepped forward, menace in each motion. "When did you meet Casvir?"

"He and I worked together for a time," Flowridia said, standing tall despite Ayla's approach. The elf placed a hand on Flowridia's chest, letting her finger drag down her skin, pulling the collar of her dress down with it. "Ayla—"

Ayla drew her finger back. "My Sweet Summer Blossom," she said, each word tumbling luxuriously off her skilled tongue, "it seems he was awfully close to you."

"He cares for me, yes."

Those words caused something to shift in Ayla's demeanor—her cool sensuality cracked, and rage suddenly marred her sharp face. She ripped her hand away as though struck.

Flowridia ran to grab the document and scanned it, wondering what sort of damning information lay hidden between the lines. "You must've known, though," she said, still struggling to understand. "Whatever awareness you had . . ." Except for the months she had left the ear behind, Flowridia recalled, but what difference would that have made?

Before she could comment, Ayla snatched it back, the edges tearing where Flowridia had grasped it. *"You are counted among my friends, and if you are ever in need of aid, call upon me and I shall answer,"* Ayla read, the barest hints of ire marring her smooth tone. *"Your presence will be sorely missed."* Her hand fell, her harsh gaze cruelly juxtaposed to her cool tone. "Adorable, his affection for you. Tell me—did he speak just as prettily in your bed?"

"I beg your pardon—" But Flowridia's words were stolen when Ayla crumpled the letter in her fist. She dropped it to the floor—Flowridia fell to her knees to steal it back, frantically smoothing the edges, hands trembling when she realized Ayla' nails had punctured it.

"I had wondered what changed about you." Ayla paced, her feet silent upon the floor. "My sweet, timid Flowridia, grown up and murdering monarchs for love. How quaint. I never thought Casvir could dig his fingers in quite so deep—in your head, and all sorts of secret places."

Flowridia smoothed the document as well as she could, carefully folding it back along the worn lines. Her breathing shallowed with every cruel word.

Ayla paused, taking in the sight as her gaze rested solely upon Flowridia. Her voice took on a sardonic edge, even more patronizing than before. "How did you do it, I wonder. Did you draw him in with your innocence? Kiss his cheek? Wait in his bed and touch yourself? The tactic did not work for me, but you're awfully cute. He never looked twice at me, but you . . ." Her eyes narrowed into a glare, a storm of icy blue and silver. "Did you cry his name? Or was it mine and mine alone?"

With a gentleness betraying the brewing typhoon, Flowridia set the folded letter back into its envelope, then set it aside, safe from the storm. "Ayla Darkleaf, I can't even fathom what leaps you're making in that letter, so let me make this crystal clear—I never slept with Casvir."

Ayla tilted her head, eyeing Flowridia like a snake about to strike as she stood up. "Did you want to sleep with him? It would have been a luxurious throne—you, the Imperatrix of Nox'Kartha—"

"Ayla, he's my friend!" She stepped forward, the very air growing faint and dead around her. When she breathed, she saw the barest hints of purple. "He was my mentor, my guardian—and I endeared myself to him as a student. Not once was he ever untoward. Not once did he ever wish to be. And I swear to you, Ayla, there wasn't a moment when I ever stopped wanting you!"

Ayla's gaze fell briefly to the floor.

Frustration tore a cry from Flowridia's throat. "You say that I've changed, and I have! I have, Ayla, but not because I fucked my way to a throne. Instead, I've lied and murdered, destroyed myself, turned away from what I held dear, and all for you." Her voice shook as fresh tears fell from her eyes. "I'm not the girl you died for. I killed her to bring you back."

A frown pulled at Ayla's mouth, and Flowridia could just see the hints of fangs, thorns piercing the red rose of her lips. Several tense seconds passed. Ayla's expression reminded her of an abused kitten, claws at the ready but with eyes as wide as saucers.

Perhaps, deep down, that's all she was. A pitiful kitten who masqueraded in a pompous mane.

"Forgive me then," Ayla spat, "perhaps I was just misled. You did fuck the Empress of Solvira, after all."

Cold pulsed through Flowridia's veins. The swirling mist of purple dissipated as she released a controlled breath. "It was the means to an end—"

"The promise to abandon your quest was the means to an end? Forgive my double standard—I care far less that you fucked her than I would have about Casvir." Those wide eyes twitched, revealing the turmoil beneath her anger. "But you loved her, didn't you."

The lingering question of what precisely Ayla remembered during her time of death remained—but it seemed she recalled one damning, wrenching piece. "It's not—it's not that simple—"

"Then look me in the eye and tell me I'm wrong."

Ayla stared—waiting, watching. Flowridia swallowed a painful lump, the weight as heavy as the guilt she carried. "Ayla..." She blinked; her vision misted. "I was tired. The road had been long. I . . . I did falter, but I . . ."

Ayla's lip sneered, but she remained silent. The house creaked, and near them, Demitri watched, doing an admirable job at pretending he did not exist.

Flowridia grasped at any and all thoughts, seeking the answer to her own jaded, broken heart. "Lara and I . . . She saved my life, Ayla. I couldn't just kill her."

When Ayla finally spoke, the silence finally shattering, it held all the wickedness of her deeds. "You could kiss her on the battlefield, though. You could spare a moment for that."

"I don't want to fight with you," Flowridia said, breath catching at the final word. "And I don't know what you want me to say. What's done is done."

"Were you not going to mention it? Sex is sex, sure; have your fun—but do not lie to my face and say you never stopped wanting me."

"Ayla, when have I even had a moment to breathe, much less—"

"Will you say a single damn thing that isn't a deflection?!"

Ayla's outburst lingered in the air like a fog. Flowridia swallowed guilt, her tears welling anew. "I need to be alone."

In a blink, Ayla appeared in front of the entry door, blocking it with her small body. "Where are you going?" she asked, voice rough. Her eyes still held that wide expression, thinly veiled panic underneath palpable anger.

"I need to be alone," Flowridia repeated, her words pathetic, choked by tears. She took another step forward, and when Ayla made no move to leave, she continued, "Ayla, please. I need to think."

The battle raged behind Ayla's eyes, and Flowridia knew without question that her love could hold her prisoner from now until eternity if she so chose. "Go then," Ayla finally spat, and she stepped aside. "You clearly have no need for me."

The words were bait. Flowridia pressed her lips shut and stepped out the door, feeling that gaze on her back even after the door clicked shut.

The moist, noxious scent of the swamp met her senses, but Flowridia stepped forward without fear, knowing the dead would only rise at her word. The scattered corpses were a small army, a bloodied pile by a tree half burned. Ayla had returned, and what a magnificent moment it had been. All her work and sacrifice had reached its zenith, yet reality now seemed bent on toppling all her pride.

The first inklings of insecurity seeped into her soul. By every god—had it been a mistake? Ayla's death had martyred her, but with each sloshing step through the boggy terrain, Flowridia recalled her cruelty. Once, Flowridia's own blood had been used to summon The Endless Night. Once, Ayla had masqueraded in a burnt mask, hellbent on destroying every ounce of confidence Flowridia's abused self had desperately clung to. Once, she had plotted her death, yet the acts were never so wicked as her words.

Yet . . .

Flowridia swallowed threatened tears to think of Ayla's tear-stained apology, her anguish and shame at her own cruelty. Flowridia had told her the awful and terrible truths of her past, and Ayla had told her she was strong to have survived it, instead of ruined. Ayla had so starkly begun to change . . .

And now, so had Flowridia. Perhaps that was the problem.

Behind her, the cottage flickered nearly imperceptibly from the light within. She had wandered far in her musing. Shadows surrounded her, and perhaps Ayla watched her from one of them.

If she kept walking, would Ayla follow?

Flowridia stopped, hugging herself as her lip trembled. She blinked; her sight became hazy from tears. Here, the ground was muddy, but no water lapped at her ankles. And so she sank to her knees, not caring for her skirt.

She wept.

The anguish, the guilt—all of it escaped in her tears as she sobbed. Tears seeped through her fingers, her hands covering her face, and though the swamp had never been welcoming, it was at least familiar. There was comfort in that.

Lara was dead, and Flowridia did not know what to make of that, of her.

An agonized cry tore from her throat. She ached to remember the corpse in the cottage, the final words between them, their kiss before Lara's death at Soliel's hands . . .

Forever discontent. Perhaps it was merely the fate of her world.

Something shuffled before her, and Flowridia knew Ayla would never let herself be heard unless she wanted to be. When she looked up, there Ayla was, her skin pale enough to nearly reflect what minimal light broke through the trees, her eyes unquestionably glowing, like a cat in the dark. Bright and blue, there remained quiet acrimony within them.

Ayla sat, apparently uncaring of the mud. Idly, she picked up a stick and drew shapes in the ground. Flowridia struggled to see her, so thick were her tears, so dark was the atmosphere, but Ayla's voice, when she finally spoke, was quiet.

"I never met Empress Alauriel," Ayla whispered, her tone melding seamlessly with the darkness. "She was only a princess during most of my time in Nox'Kartha, and Murishani always took the lead in negotiations with Solvira, per Casvir's request. They did not trust me enough for that. But her reputation preceded her—her wisdom and her kindness both, the whispers that she would be a grand ruler, when the time came. She was the very last of the legitimate Solviran line, and the world watched, wondering who she would choose to marry."

Flowridia wiped tears from her eyes, her sleeves dirtied from dirt and sorrow. Ayla's form gained some clarity, still shadowed by night, but something glistened against her cheeks.

"Were there justice in the world," Ayla continued, her words smooth despite her tears, "you would have walked away from this place with her. Perhaps you would have been the one she chose, and it would have been everything you deserved."

Anxiety brewed at the words. Flowridia struggled to breathe. "Ayla, no—"

"Flowra, you can deny a great many things, but you cannot deny that you would have been the ruler of the greatest empire in the world. And more importantly, Empress Alauriel wouldn't have left you a sobbing mess in a swamp."

Flowridia didn't have to see to feel the shift in Ayla's demeanor, the slight gasp in her words—and Ayla wasn't one who needed to breathe.

"Let me ask one terrible thing," Ayla said, anguish twisting her words now. She dropped her stick, her arms wrapping around herself instead. "And swear you will not lie, because I cannot . . ." A sob stole her words, and it took all Flowridia's will to not leap up and embrace her. "If she were to walk out of these woods right now, alive and wanting you, who would you follow?"

Flowridia looked to the dirt, trying to make sense of her scribbling, but the darkness obscured it. "I . . ." She hesitated, but not because she didn't know—but because she so painfully knew, and she nearly sobbed to feel its weight. "I would follow you until the end," she whispered, and she meant it with all her soul.

"I have nowhere to take you," Ayla said, heartbreak in the words. "I have nothing to give you. My greatness was stolen over four hundred years ago, when they locked me in that damn box. I am not even Lady Ayla Darkleaf, Grand Diplomat of Nox'Kartha anymore. I am merely a monster in a swamp with a particular talent for making you cry."

With utmost care, Flowridia took her hand, stroking gentle, purposeful lines across her love's palm. "I don't want greatness. I don't need anything, except for you and Demitri. I think there's something romantic in having nothing—we're a blank slate. Our future is whatever we make it. We can go anywhere. We can be anything. Just you and me, remember? And Demitri."

Ayla's hand closed lightly around Flowridia's fingers, the other coming to clasp them fully. "I am so sorry," she whispered. Her pose deflated, defeated, her words sounding the same. "My spirit recalls very little of these past six months. The farther back I look, there are no memories at all. Feelings, yes. But it's all as scattered as sand. Mostly I remember you. I remember your presence. I remember trying to scream your name but only reaching you in your sleep. But in the moments leading to my rebirth, I hold not memories nor images, but ineffable knowledge, like understanding how to walk—as though it has always been there. And so yes—I know what you said to Lara. I know what you did."

Blood pulsed hot through Flowridia's veins, her icy limbs uncomfortable at any reminder of Lara and her death.

In the ensuing quiet, Flowridia softly gathered her damning words. "You were gone. I was lonely. And she was someone kind and lovely." Fresh tears welled in her eyes, but there was more she had to say. "If Soliel, the God of Order, hadn't come, you wouldn't be here. She died to save my life because she loved me, even though she knew what I had intended for her. And that's the damning truth of it, Ayla. Please know that I love you so much, but I . . ." She shuddered, a sob nearly stealing her words. "Having sex with her truly was the means to an end—opening up my heart was my betrayal. For all my joy at your return, I'm still mourning her death. She was a friend who could have been more. It broke my heart. But none of it had anything to do with you. None of it means I love you any less. Had I walked away, I still would have wanted you."

"Empress Alauriel is dead," Ayla said, yet it sounded far more like a plea. "She's gone. You are mine now, and if you wanted me to carve out my heart for you to hold, I would do it. If you wanted to do it yourself, I would let you. Your story hurts, but not so painfully as the thought of leaving you because of it. If you can find it in yourself to forgive me and accept a legacy of nothing—"

Her words cut off when Flowridia rose. With care to not trample on whatever she had drawn into the mud—idle shapes, she saw, hearts and perfect circles—Flowridia sat beside her, no reserve in holding Ayla in her arms. "We'll make our own legacy," she whispered, and Ayla clung to her, her head resting against Flowridia's shoulder. "To return Lara to Solvira would damn our future, but she deserves a final resting place. Will you help me bury her?"

Ayla softly kissed her fingers. "Yes."

In quiet contemplation, they retrieved a corpse of infinite worth.

At her own insistence, Ayla carried the body, volunteering to dump it in the ocean where it would never be found, but Flowridia's heart hurt too much to contemplate the notion.

Instead, with Demitri in tow, they left the swamp. Though Sha'Demoni beckoned, the longer path seemed most appropriate—time to clear their heads and let the last vestiges of their argument fade. Flowridia carried a shovel from her mother's home, but her other hand clutched Lara's destroyed dress, soaked with blood and swampy water, cut in twain by her own knife before she had hung the precious corpse up to drain. It bore the barest hints of embroidery at the edges, the patterns of stars and moons, and though dirtied and torn, there was precious beauty to be found.

When they reached the edge of the swamp, Flowridia beckoned them forward, the damp, murky grass steadily drying. Soon, it tickled her dirt-caked legs, and in the distance appeared a wrenching sight.

She ran. A tree, taller than those of the swamp, became her destination. Illuminated by blissful sunlight, it marked the beginning of a beautiful meadow, and at the base, a smoothed mound covered in grass created a pit in her stomach. A stone marked the top, weather worn, utterly unreadable. But Flowridia could still touch and imagine the etched words: *Here lies Aura—a friend.*

She slowed and stopped, dropping carefully to her knees beside the grave. "My friend," she whispered, the breeze carrying those words into the meadow. Insects chirped here; owls cooed. Life held on. And Aura, her dearest Aura . . .

Ayla appeared at her side, and Flowridia wondered how disappointed Aura would be, to think she walked a dark path. Aura was not her mother, but she had practically raised her—raised her to be good.

It stung. Tears welled but did not fall. Instead, Flowridia stood and stared at the empty spot beside the fading grave. "My familiar lies here," Flowridia said simply.

"Aura?" Ayla said, eyebrow quirking up.

A smile tugged at Flowridia's lip. "You remembered."

Ayla set the body down with care and stepped over the mound. "I remember everything you've ever said."

With unnatural speed, Ayla plucked the shovel from her hands and began digging, cutting through the soft earth with the ease of paper. Meanwhile, Flowridia placed a hand on the mound, contemplating whether pursuing an answer to a dangerous question was worth the cost.

To drag back Aura's spirit... The wolf had died so quickly. Flowridia had never been able to apologize. She had never said goodbye.

This is who I replaced?

Flowridia gave Demitri a quiet smile. "Replaced isn't the word. You are neither better nor worse, but different. She was more of a parent—whereas you are a child."

She gave a teasing smile, but with it came a bittersweet thought—if Aura had not died, Flowridia wouldn't have her darling boy, and there was no way to find peace with that. Purple smoke rose from her palm but just as quickly vanished.

Let Aura rest. It was the last gift she could offer.

Is Ana dead forever?

The question jarred her from her tentative peace, the sound of those crunching bones beneath Shem's heavy boot flashing like lightning through her memory. "You saw?"

They had me chained up, but I watched everything.

From her pocket, Flowridia procured that tiny sliver of bone, the anguish of loss flooding her. "She's gone, yes."

Demitri bumped her with his nose. *I'm sorry. But, since you have a bone, could you bring her back?*

She hadn't considered it, the idea both hopeful and ... daunting. "I don't know if I should."

Why?

"I don't know how intelligent she really was. She was a happy little thing, filled with life, but ..." Flowridia's hand closed around the bone as she swallowed tears. "... perhaps it is best to simply let her move on."

Demitri nuzzled her hair with his nose, giving a small lick to her cheek.

Still, the idea haunted her, and as she stared at her closed hand, she shut her eyes, seeking to grasp anything connected to the shard of bone, any presence, any lingering spirit.

With focus, her mind grasped onto something far away.

There was no kindness in necromancy. No invitation. Merely exacting control over whatever fell within your domain.

Yet Flowridia merely beckoned, the command so soft, she prayed it could be a suggestion and nothing more. *Will you come say goodbye?* she asked into the void.

Something called, and when Flowridia opened her palm, from the shard of bone sprung a sparkle of light.

Not a darling skeleton, no—but a translucent, blue-tinged fox, bearing fur and a fluffy tail. Doe eyes studied her as the ghost floated at eye level, but just as soon it twirled around her with the fluidity of a sea creature, and Flowridia laughed through her seeping tears. "Oh, Ana," she said, and when she tried to touch the little thing, her hand fell right through.

Ana licked her fingers, the sensation cold and discomforting, like tiny needles of ice. When she gave a raspy *yip*, Flowridia gasped, overwhelmed by bittersweet joy.

When she fell upon Demitri, he stiffened but remained stoically still, despite her chilling touch. *She seems happy.*

"Perhaps there was something to her after all," Flowridia replied, beckoning to the little spirit. Ana floated back—zipped about like a hummingbird, really—eventually peeking out from the recesses of her hair and rubbing against her cheek.

Ayla was watching, Flowridia noticed, a charming sort of confusion on her features. "What in the world is that?"

"This is Ana," Flowridia said, and she began the tale, of the little fox's death and rebirth. Ana seemed to sense a friend, and immediately floated around Ayla, sniffing her, or giving the appearance of it.

And Ayla, as Flowridia spoke, illuminated in the faintest tone of silver. Flowridia silenced as her glowing hand touched the little ghost, afraid until—

Ana nuzzled against it, as though it were solid; which it was, to her. Flowridia resumed her story, her motherly heart warm as Ayla cautiously, but dotingly, caressed the little ghost, eventually holding Ana in her arms when she settled. "This requires massive concentration, I'll have you know," Ayla said, her words stiff and short. "But I am committed to not destroying this . . . Ana."

"I appreciate that," Flowridia replied, feeling bittersweet to watch Ayla cradle her—for Flowridia could no longer. "It's silly to think of her as mine."

"She never had the chance to have a life," Ayla replied, stroking her fingers through Ana's translucent fur; the fox yawned contentedly. "Instead you've given her a loving death. Ghosts are as intelligent as they were in life, which means if Ana were not happy to see you, she would have left."

It settled an unspoken question lingering in her heart. Flowridia gestured for Ana to come closer, and she obeyed, trotting along the ground as though she had substance. "I can't care for you the way I did before," Flowridia said, still clutching the bone in her hand, "and you deserve to move on and rest, perhaps even find friends. Knowing you, you already did."

Ana did not understand, those large eyes watching as she fell against Flowridia's leg. When she offered a hand, Ana nipped it affectionately, though the sensation was uncomfortable, even without corporeal teeth.

She doesn't have to go forever. Surprised at the words, Flowridia met Demitri's golden eyes. *You can't care for her like before, but she could visit if you ever need her.*

She could, and Flowridia cried as she bid the little creature goodbye, knowing she didn't understand and simply couldn't. Flowridia could bring her back, but she wouldn't, for it would be cruel to disrupt Ana's final departure into the world of the Beyond.

And so she kissed Ana farewell, lips tingling from cold, told her a precious truth—*"I love you, sweet thing."*—and lingered in her uplifting presence a final moment, absorbing the memory of those beautiful, empty eyes.

Ana dissipated peacefully into the void, as she deserved. Flowridia clutched the bone shard to her heart, breathing through her tears.

"Flowra."

Ayla's voice returned her to the present.

"I do not wish to interrupt your mourning, but the grave is dug."

The tranquility of Ana's final reunion vanished, leaving her cold.

Flowridia slipped the shard into her pocket, then knelt beside Lara's corpse, trembling as her fingers glossed over her blood-stained hair. Ana's end had been violent, yet peace had finally come; such would not be Lara's end, instead torn from life by a knife wielded by a mad god.

She slid her hands beneath the nude body but struggled to rise—she had no adrenaline fueling her now, only her small arms and determination.

She rose, cradling Lara close, but stumbled, gasping as she and the corpse tilted toward the ground. But a pale figure stepped from Flowridia's shadow, smoothly righting her and supporting Lara's body.

Together, they carried Lara to her final resting place. At the edge of the hole, Ayla brought Lara to her chest, relieving Flowridia of her great burden. A quiet sort of resignation flickered in Ayla's countenance, but with all the fluidity of the dancer she was, she dropped down into the grave. The vampire laid Lara down at the bottom and crossed her arms comfortably across her chest. "Anything she should hold?"

Flowridia shook her head but offered the ruined dress. Ayla folded it neatly and arranged it to cushion her head.

"I have nothing she would want," Flowridia whispered. "But if you wouldn't mind, some flowers would be nice." She glanced at Aura's grave and smiled faintly.

Ayla lifted herself with ease from the deep hole. "Any particular kind?"

Sorrow marred Flowridia's smile. "Bring me a tulip. A white one."

"Only one?"

Flowridia's powers over death had exponentially increased, resulting in macabre miracles, her capacity to slay and control all life around her. And she wondered what it meant for the light side of that coin, an impossible thought welling in her mind. The field spread far and wide, lit by the sun and nourished by earth and rain. "Only one. It's all I'll need."

Ayla vanished into the shadows. Flowridia gazed down upon the body, trying to find any semblance of Lara in this mutilated corpse. "I'm sorry," she whispered, for there was only Demitri to hear it. "You were the best person I've ever known. You loved me—" Her voice cracked, words catching in her throat as a quiet cry escaped. "I'm sorry it became your downfall. I'm so sorry."

Lara was gone, her death a violent offense to a legacy of grace and justice. She had chosen her path, but the guilt of that sacrifice tore at Flowridia's heart, knowing Lara's love of someone undeserving of that devotion had been her end. She had chosen her death, but Flowridia had desecrated her body and used her blood for an abominable task. She prayed Lara's soul did not look back upon the living, that her allegiance to Staella would be enough to grant her rest.

And she wondered, darkly, whether there was a lifetime wherein Flowridia had chosen Lara from the start, what kind of happiness that might've brought.

Yet with that thought came a brutal reality, that if Lara hadn't gone, there would be no Ayla—there was also no peace in that.

Soon, a soft arm wrapped around her waist. Ayla knelt beside her. She held a single, perfect tulip in her hand, the purest white. It shone in the sunlight, and Flowridia plucked it gently from Ayla's grasp.

When Ayla stood, she stole a handful of dirt and sprinkled it inside.

Demitri, not to be outdone, shoved a respectable mound of dirt inside with his enormous paw. *You said I was sweet once.*

Flowridia waited for more, then laughed when Demitri merely pushed more dirt into the grave. "Demitri, say something nice."

I did.

Flowridia rolled her tear-filled eyes, clutching the single flower as Ayla's arms wrapped around her from behind. Oh, how surreal it was—beneath her heartbreak and anguish and all the pain of these past few days, there remained the perfect truth. Ayla was here. And Ayla was loved—Flowridia's conflicted heart had never questioned that.

When Demitri finished burying the fallen empress, Flowridia dug a small hole in the loose dirt and placed the flower in the center, supporting it as she covered the base. A bit of healing magic, and words flowed through her mind: *Take root, sweet one.*

The roots spread. Flowridia felt that faint and perfect life stabilize. She smiled, but an instinct within her bid her for *more.* A deep breath fueled her before she spoke her spell. *"Now, grow."*

The earth rumbled. The energy flowed from her core and into the dirt in twisted lines, not unlike the roots of the tulip. She felt the natural world welcome the intrusion, caress her with open arms.

Nature. Life. Her dearest and oldest friend. It welcomed her back with nothing but love and acceptance.

Throughout the meadow, thousands of tulips burst free from the earth, growing tall and strong within seconds.

Each one shone the purest white. Fragrance bombarded Flowridia's senses.

When she stopped, she fell to her knees, head light from the sudden burst of power. Though her vision spun, it came with a glimmer of pride. All around, covering the mounds and spreading beyond the horizon, flowers decorated the field. They spread to the base of the trees, even dotted them in places.

For a moment, Flowridia forgot her anguish, shaken at what she had done. She had expected results, but not of this magnitude.

A gentle hand, as white as the tulips, wiped a tear from her cheek. "Impressive," Ayla said, a certain wonder in her eye. "I can honestly say, in all my years, that I've never seen anything like that."

Flowridia's breath hitched as Ayla knelt at her side. "Tulips ask forgiveness," Ayla whispered, and Flowridia shut her eyes, tears streaming down her dirt-stained face.

She dug a grave far smaller than the others and tucked the little bone inside, burying it softly. Here lay three precious figures, and Flowridia held boundless guilt for each one.

She said nothing, finding no peace among the dead.

Chapter 4

A blast of cold wafted through the doorframe as Etolié and Khastra stepped outside. Snow gently fell, the air smelling fresh and moist. Etolié didn't mind the cold, was actually entirely unaffected by it, but illusioned a winter coat, nevertheless. Thankfully, not enough had fallen to leave footprints yet, lest Etolié have to illusion away goat hooves.

They had remained chaste in the tub. A foreign anticipation expanded in Etolié's stomach, some tumultuous mix of fear and excitement and self-conscious madness, but she had subdued that for now. There would be time to rest. There would even be time to do a bit more than that, though Etolié was shy to consider it.

But there was work to do.

In her lovely main city, comprised of the majority of Staelash's population, Etolié waved at those who acknowledged her—children and adults alike. No one bowed, because she didn't like it. Many of these people had been slaves all their lives, and for them to give up one master just to bow to another made her feel . . . gross.

The Nox'Kartha Embassy loomed behind the other buildings, its great tower a beacon of dread now. With so uncertain a future, Etolié wondered what this apparent alliance would mean. Would they be tied into a war? Staelash couldn't handle that.

But not too far away was the post office, which years and years ago had set up an extremely efficient letter carrying service between Staelash and Solvira's capital city, Neolan. Etolié stepped into the warm building and offered a wave to the De'Sindai man at the desk. "I need paper, please. And a quill. Also ink. I didn't plan ahead."

The man quickly gave her what she needed.

Etolié sat at a desk, her hand never far from her half-demon as she sat beside her on the ground. After a deep, steadying breath, she wrote to one of the few remaining friends she had.

To Magister Reginal of the Solviran Council,

I write first and foremost to inform you that Sora and I are alive. We survived the destruction of the City of Light, which I am confident you have heard of. If not, this might be awkward. We are safely back in Staelash by means of a dragon, which I will happily explain when we next meet.

The most important order of business, however, is the matter of Archbishop Lunestra. She is alive and safe with us, though I do not know for how long. Nox'Kartha will be stalled in its onslaught for the time being, assuming it plans to move forward at all. We must find a place for her.

There is also the matter of Imperator Casvir. He's currently not a threat, for reasons purposefully unspecified.

All of this leaves more questions unanswered than answered, but you know the important pieces now. I will happily answer those follow-up questions upon your reply, even be willing to meet in person, however I must ask of a potentially more pressing matter:
Where is Empress Alauriel? Is she safe?

Your friend and colleague,
Magister Etolié of Staelash

She sealed it in wax and handed it to the postmaster. "Expedite this, please."

The postmaster, well used to Etolié asking to expedite everything from state secrets to birthday cards, opened the latch to a permanent portal and slipped the scroll inside.

Now it sat upon a hopefully small pile of letters in Magister Reginal's office and would be read soon.

Etolié left with a polite goodbye, then paused on the doorstep, squeezing Khastra's hand. "The whole world has turned upside down," Etolié whispered. "I've done all I can for now. Tell me it's all right to rest."

"There is no shame in rest, Etolié. You are right; the work is not done. But your duty now is to wait."

When Khastra gently tugged her along, back onto the familiar path to the manor, Etolié clung tight to her large hand. "You all right? Your hand is freezing."

"I will not die, but my hair is wet, and I am half-frozen—"

"We could have *waited,*" Etolié said, stopping in her tracks, but Khastra laughed, apparently finding amusement in her distress.

"Duty could not wait," the half-demon replied. "Come with me again to my room. I have the largest fireplace in the manor." Something different and new bled into her tone, full of implication and delight and reservation unbound, something Etolié had never heard before from the half-demon, nor could have fathomed. "You can always help me to warm."

Etolié could say nothing, managing only to nod, and wondered if Khastra felt the same anticipation in her stomach as she.

When they returned to the manor, no one passed them on the path to Khastra's old bedroom. The half-demon wasted no time in stoking the fireplace, and Etolié was left in silence to watch her and study every motion of her incredible body. They'd made love before, but Etolié felt shy, so shy—perhaps even afraid.

Not of Khastra. Not of her dearest and most treasured person. The root of her fear lay in something else, and Etolié hated that she couldn't seem to shut it off.

"Etolié—"

Etolié's gaze immediately darted to Khastra's face.

"Would you be bothered if I removed my clothes?"

"Thought that was the plan," she said, feigning bravado, yet was breathless to watch her, the reveal of her endless assortment of back tattoos, the fire casting every muscle in flickering shadow. Etolié admired Khastra's girthy arms and shoulders, her abdominals—all the parts of her she loved, though now in an ineffably different way. She was entirely hairless, like all elves and half-elves, save for her eyebrows and the gorgeous mane of purple hair spilling from her head, clinging to water and tiny shards of ice.

Etolié averted her eyes when Khastra turned toward her, suddenly shy, but a gentle voice said, "Do not be demure. I love it when you look at me."

"I realize we were naked cuddling a few minutes ago," Etolié replied, finally meeting her gaze, "but it still feels unreal."

"You used to harass me with comments about my thighs quite often," Khastra said, her wink conveying her teasing. "I hope you will do it again."

"I mean, I was thinking . . ." Etolié's words trailed off; she remained safe behind illusionary clothes, still too nervous to show herself. "I'm as oblivious as a pile of bricks, so I'm assuming this is an invitation to do the fuck thing."

Khastra's laugh surely resonated through the manor, and Etolié's heart soared to hear it. "Yes, Etolié. It is an invitation to do the fuck thing."

Except, it didn't quite sound like 'fuck,' because the odd, crushing sound of 'ck' was something Khastra couldn't quite pronounce, resulting in a strange gagging sound that sounded half caught in her throat and definitely not conducive to someone overjoyed to do the aforementioned word.

Etolié didn't verbalize that; she simply laughed. "Beefcake, you might be the most endearing motherfucker in the realms."

Khastra came down to her, their lips touching, lingering, then separating for the half-demon's tongue. Etolié loved it so, this strange new world of kissing someone she adored. Although she was still deciding what to name this anticipation inside her, Khastra's kiss spoke of thinly masked urgency, desperation, and while it scared her—by the gods, it scared her so—it also brought excitement.

When she pulled away, Khastra's glowing eyes held infinite softness, depthless and wonderful. "I would take great comfort in your touch, Etolié. But only if you want it too."

Etolié did, she realized, the mere idea of being so close to her beloved demon enough to make her heart palpitate. Her clothing flickered away, though she tried to cover her breasts and boney hips. "I-I'm still processing the idea of wanting to be wanted," she admitted, though she couldn't meet Khastra's eye. "I'm used to people wanting me, to seeing me like an object—you know I had to play to that to get Staelash any goddamn favors. But I love it when it's you. I love the way you look at me." Though she trembled, she let her arms fall away, catching a glimpse of herself in the full-length mirror—boney and half-starved, at least in her eye. But she dared not illusion it away. Khastra would know. She always did.

And Khastra thought she was beautiful.

"I'm sorry I'm not . . . more." She couldn't find another word to use, but her hand skimmed across the protrusion of bone that was her hips as she shut her eyes, breath hitching when Khastra's hands gripped her waist.

"I know you struggle," came that beloved voice. "More than anything, I want you healthy and secure. I know it is a complicated thing, and I will ask you to eat, but do not think it is because I want you to be different. You are beautiful because you are you, and what you need more than anything else is to know you are loved. Everything else will follow." Khastra's hands skimmed up past her hips and waist to her back, and when Etolié opened her eyes, she realized the half-demon knelt before her, her horns reaching the top of Etolié's chin. "And you are so loved. I adore you, Etolié. Amorously and innocently, both."

Etolié couldn't help her smile, heat filling her cheeks when Khastra placed her lips to her collarbone. A gasp, but then laughter as Khastra trailed those sweet kisses up to her neck. The half-demon grinned against her skin. "Will you come to bed with me?"

"Yes, General," she teased, but then she squealed when Khastra scooped her up, silenced by her mouth as they kissed.

Khastra pulled back the comforter, then laid Etolié down on the sheets below. Etolié often forgot their stark size difference—you got used to staring at a lady's sternum all day—but when Khastra's forearm flexed, it was easily larger than Etolié's thigh. She grinned, finding that exceptionally neat, but then heat filled her cheeks when Khastra's gaze roamed her nude body.

Muscles taut, Khastra joined her, one knee on either side of her supine form. Etolié's eyes widened as she took in every curve of her musculature, her abdominal muscles jutting from her core, the tattooed lines across her torso. And, of course, her breasts, small but proportionate to her figure, the wards discoloring even the centered, peaked buds.

Khastra leaned forward, but Etolié held out a hand, her fingers stopping when they touched a literal wall of muscle. "Hold on. I'm basking."

Khastra raised an eyebrow, smirking in tandem. "Admire all you like," she said, gesturing down her stomach.

"There's my favorite asshole." Etolié's hand stroked down Khastra's abdominal wall, the tattoos glowing at the contact, and she found she adored the feeling, the half-demon's skin both a comfort and a new world to explore. She pushed ever so slightly, taken aback when Khastra obeyed the unspoken command. She pursed her lips, glancing from Khastra's body to her face. "You look good."

"Thank you," Khastra replied as her hands returned to Etolié's body, those callused fingers gentle as they stroked across her skin, skimming the sides of her breasts, a question in the gesture.

But as Etolié lay beneath her, body alight with every touch, she realized this wasn't quite what she wanted. Not yet. Instead, she spoke words she only hoped she could follow through with. "Lay down," she said, though it was far more a command, and the barest hint of a smile twisted Khastra's parted lips.

When Etolié pushed on her abdomen, Khastra followed, matching her pace before setting her back onto the bed, something demure and foreign in her glowing eyes. Etolié straddled her hips but realized that was much too far from her face and scooted up.

Hesitant, she placed her hands down, slowly touching the smooth musculature beneath her as she slid up. Etolié felt power in the ink of the tattoos, but stopped when she reached Khastra's breasts, hesitant when her fingers brushed beneath.

Khastra grabbed her wrists. "Please, do not be shy, Etolié."

She placed Etolié's hands on her breasts, and when Etolié squeezed the soft flesh—the only bit of softness on Khastra's body—she felt Khastra tense, a slight moan escaping her throat.

The sensation sent a thrill down Etolié's spine. Khastra had always been untouchable, powerful, yet here she lay beneath Etolié, willingly subduing herself to her touch.

Etolié liked that. By Eionei's Asshole, she liked that *a lot.*

Feeling bold, she took one of Khastra's tattooed nipples into her mouth, grinning when the half-demon gasped beneath her, more so when Khastra's hand settled into her hair.

She briefly pulled back; the small nipple had, indeed, begun glowing. With a slight tap, its opposite illuminated, and

Etolié giggled like a madwoman, more so when Khastra scoffed and joined her.

What a joy it was, to hear her laugh. Etolié forever chased that wonderful sound.

There Etolié stayed, content to kiss Khastra's breasts, finding unbridled joy in the intimate touch and in the half-demon moaning beneath her.

Etolié's hand wandered down, realizing that while she could reach between Khastra's legs, she could not quite do it comfortably. With chagrin, she removed her mouth from the sensitive bud and sat back, realizing that a faint, purple blush covered Khastra's cheeks, but also blossomed across her neck and chest. Etolié smiled. "That's adorable."

"What is?" Khastra asked, breathless but smiling, the softness returning to her features.

"Your blush. It's cute."

Khastra shut her eyes, pulling away as though shy, yet her smile grew wide, beaming. "I am not often called 'cute.'"

A powerful half-demon, yes, a near demi-goddess and general to the most feared armies in the world, but here in her bedroom, Khastra blushed in soft purple, and Etolié silently swore to never tell the secret. Instead, she kissed along her chiseled abdomen, her hands stroking Khastra's obliques, and down to the hip bones threatening to tear from her skin.

A faint purple hue covered the glistening folds of Khastra's vulva, and Etolié blushed at the erotic display. The tattoos ended there, though lines curled around Khastra's powerful thighs. Still, Etolié's inexperience was at the forefront of her mind now. Perhaps she should have drunken more for nerves, but then Khastra interrupted. "Etolié?"

"I have no idea what to do here," Etolié said, glancing up to Khastra's face.

"Whatever you would do for yourself," Khastra said, mischief in her smirk, "do to me."

That precluded Etolié often spent time touching herself, but she was willing to play along for Khastra's sake. Etolié placed a kiss upon her demon's thigh, then let her fingers lightly touch the inner lip, loving how Khastra twitched at the touch.

Etolié explored, a new world presented. Khastra seemed content to let her, and Etolié appreciated the soft sighs her companion gave.

But never did Khastra appear breathless or excited, and Etolié saw no sense in trying to do the fuck thing until she was. Etolié finally asked, "Am I doing it right?"

"You are doing well," Khastra said, and she propped herself up onto her elbows to better face Etolié. "Take your time. You are new."

"Yes, but I want to make sure my practice is worthwhile," Etolié said, realizing it sounded much more like a whine than a remark. Was she embarrassed? Gods, she *was* embarrassed.

But instead of commenting on that, Etolié lowered her head, daring to kiss Khastra's most intimate parts, loving every soft hum her companion made. The taste was bitter yet wonderful, and Etolié longed to bottle it and know precisely what it was about undead demonic discharge that excited her so.

Still, whatever Etolié did was not quite right, even as she kissed the half-demon's swollen lower lips, and finally a hand caressed her hair. "Etolié, humor me. Come up here."

Contrite and fearing reproach, Etolié obeyed, but Khastra's strong hands grabbed her arms and pulled her up to her mouth. Their lips pressed together, and Etolié was intimately aware that bitterness stained Khastra's tongue as well.

"Kiss me here," Khastra whispered. "I will touch myself."

"Was I that bad?"

"No, no! Etolié, you are inexperienced and will learn." Khastra kissed Etolié's cheek, and her arms prevented Etolié from hiding her embarrassed blush. "Help me to help myself."

Etolié accepted that. Khastra released her, her own hands sliding down her body, and Etolié kissed her lips and neck and squeezed her breasts, loving the half-demon tensing and moaning beneath her.

Something gratifying came from the sensation of sucking on the sensitive skin of her neck, leaving those lovely marks. The most powerful woman in all the world, laid out for her to explore and claim? The stirring between Etolié's legs was foreign and new, heat welling at the mere thought of Khastra belonging to her and her alone. She had always been possessive of the half-demon—she'd known this and didn't care. But this put it into more than mere feeling, those blossoming purple marks Etolié's personal signature.

Soon, tremors shook the half-demon's body, and Etolié clung to her, kissing Khastra through the peak of her pleasure. Her cries were held in Etolié's mouth, little whispers of, "Oh, Etolié . . . I love you."

And when Khastra finally stilled, Etolié smiled against her lips. Strong arms wrapped around Etolié's slight form; the half-demon curled around her. "I am overjoyed to have you," Khastra said, her body reverberating against Etolié's.

Etolié smiled, her hand stroking idle lines along the tattoos of Khastra's chest. "It feels . . ." She glanced up at Khastra's face, blushing at the sincerity in her demon's smile. ". . . unreal."

Her demon.

Fresh tears brimmed in her eyes, yet she felt no shame because she had cried to Khastra a thousand times, the spawn of the War Goddess a shockingly good listener, the first true confidant Etolié had, and when she posed it that way, as simply an extension of the friendship Etolié already cherished above all others, falling in love didn't seem quite so terrifying.

Her demon. And when Etolié thought about it, it was everything she'd wanted all along—Khastra by her side.

Khastra's voice reverberated against Etolié's ear. "I do not disagree."

"You've wanted me for a long time, though. Like, twenty-four years, long time."

Khastra's purple blush returned. Etolié grinned, conveying her tease. "Passively, yes. I did not entertain the notion often. I presumed it would never happen. Besides, I was acutely aware of how young you were. But there were occasions when I would be struck by your beauty."

"Oh?" Etolié said, wiping away the brimming tears from her eyes. "Tell me more about that."

"You are very attractive, Etolié."

"I'm three-quarters angel—tell me something I don't know."

Somehow, Khastra looked more like a blueberry than a half-demon, with how starkly purple her cheeks and chest had become. "You went through a phase where all your dresses were translucent, and you would ask if the color clashed with your nipples. How am I supposed to react?"

Khastra looked terribly embarrassed, that oh-so-endearing blush returning to her cheeks. Etolié grinned as she sat up. "And my little pink nips always matched my color palette, so thank you. Besides, you could have told me to stop." She sat up and pinched said nipples with her fingers, erupting into laughter when Khastra bit her lip, looking suddenly pained.

"I should have, for propriety's sake." Khastra's lips became a line, and Etolié got the sense she was bracing herself to be slapped. "But they are lovely nipples, and I am a weak woman."

And Etolié, who acknowledged she was traumatized and generally remiss to ever be looked at like an object to fuck by absolutely anyone, realized nothing felt more invigorating than the most powerful woman in all the world telling her she had nice nipples. A broad smile overtook her face, and with it, a blush. She felt safe and cherished, and that was enough. "Tell me everything you've held back."

Khastra did so, something about her silver hair being as lustrous as starlight and her ass being rounder than Alystra's—which Khastra claimed to have personally seen— her laughter as melodious as elven windpipes—which Etolié assumed was a compliment—and her lips as tempting as fabled forbidden fruit of legend, at which point Etolié finally shut her up by sitting on her face.

They returned to the cottage, Flowridia, Ayla, and Demitri. It was as good a home as any, for now, though it bore the taint of sorrow. Flowridia gazed upon the rotting dead, their decay hastened by the moist atmosphere. Where the water was deeper, they might stagnate, but Odessa had built her home on a drier patch of swamp.

On the porch, she paused a moment, looking upon a body half-submerged, its glassy eyes staring back. Though gruesome, it wasn't what drew her in—but the spear protruding from his stomach. Flowridia gripped the finely carved handle, but the body wouldn't release it; as she tugged, it threatened to emerge.

In silence, Ayla offered a half-formed smile and coaxed her away, then with her foot on the body and her hand on the weapon, she slid it out of its gory resting place.

Flowridia accepted it, clinging to this tiny spot of joy amidst all the sorrow—her beloved spear, a gift from Thalmus, safe from watery rot. Its glass head reflected the minimal light, casting a tiny rainbow upon the cottage's porch, and the carvings of flowers and other plants were familiar and beloved.

When they entered the vacant building, she leaned it against a wall and instead busied herself with sweeping.

But Ayla lingered, nothing prideful in her stance. Her hand clasped her forearms, nails digging into the skin. "Flowra, I'm sorry."

Flowridia set the broom aside, then approached her beloved, remiss to touch her yet. "I know you are."

"I have been a brute, and I am so sorry. I do not want to fight with you. I do not wish to hurt you. I want . . ." She shut her eyes, as silent and still as a stone. There she remained, stagnant, and Flowridia waited, her own breaths the loudest sound of all. When Ayla finally spoke, it held pain. "I do not know what I want."

"It's been six months, Ayla," Flowridia whispered. "Six months, and you were revived only, what—six hours ago? The whole world is different, and while I missed you for every second of it, it doesn't mean I'm the same person as before."

Ayla's hold on her arm released, revealing ghastly punctures, slowly healing before Flowridia's horrified gaze. "You have changed. You're *whole.* You are not a shattered little waif, afraid of reprimand. You're a necromancer, for Chaos' sake, and there is no necromancer upon this realm who is weak of will. You're vibrant. You're perfect. You're . . . healing." Ayla cast a joyless smile, still unable to meet Flowridia's gaze. "I pray I still fit into your narrative."

A horrible pit expanded in Flowridia's stomach. Dread stilled her tongue. "I am different. Do you still want me?"

"I did not love you because you were a shattered soul. I loved you because you were gentle and kind, because you cared for me and worried even though you were foolish to do so. You were a safe place, and you don't know what . . ." Ayla silenced, visibly forcing her composure to steady. "You don't know what that meant to me," she finally whispered, "to feel peace."

Flowridia pulled Ayla into her arms, relieved when the elven woman all but melted into the embrace. "I'll bring you peace and joy for all your days, if you'll let me," Flowridia said, fingers entangling in rich locks of black hair. "We would be fools to not expect some friction, but so long as we value one another above ourselves and work for our love, we will make it."

"I will." Ayla pulled back, still clutching Flowridia's arms, the strength of her grip revealing her tension. Her jaw trembled. "But I am so sorry. I accused you of an outlandish crime because of my own stupid insecurities."

"Oh, Ayla—"

"Do not try to make it right; I made an ass of myself and nearly destroyed something you love." She glanced at the crumpled, torn letter.

"May I ask what in the letter made you think . . ?"

"If I reread it, likely nothing," Ayla said, releasing her. She stepped back, looking unsure of where to stand, where to place her hands—so strange to see Ayla so apprehensive. "But when you are wielding a hammer, everything begins looking like a nail—and I may be sensitive on the subject of *Lara* for some time." Ayla said the name with notable disdain, and Flowridia bit back a retort. "When I died, you did not know Casvir. Now he is saying you're a treasure? I am not trying to justify what I did, but you have to understand . . ." She slumped, unquestionable melancholy in her pose. ". . . that *I* do not understand."

Flowridia stayed in her own small square, wondering when she had jaded herself into thinking all would simply resume as it was. Six months had passed, like they'd finally acknowledged. So much had changed. "To summarize a long story—a story I'll happily tell you—Casvir is my friend. He granted me my magic all those years ago. We travelled together after your death to find an orb, and all I did was mourn you. I don't know quite what awareness you had, but truthfully the idea of you haunting me kept me moving. He grew to care for me in our time alone and I for him, but it was never more than that. He was actually incredibly discomforted by the idea, when rumors started spreading."

To her surprise, Ayla scoffed . . . then laughed. "Forgive me," she said, though she did very little to stifle it, "but if it had been anyone but you, I would have *reveled* in spreading that rumor myself."

"Did you mean to imply earlier that you had tried to seduce him?"

"Yes. Many times." Ayla smiled, curt and wicked. "It is a sore spot that I failed."

Flowridia fought to hide her appall. "You were very insistent before that you hadn't. I thought you hated him."

"Hate and sex are well intertwined, Flowra, though I understand that it may not be something you can fathom. In politics, there is no greater weapon, so you can imagine my ire when I was rejected. I hate what I cannot control. I spent years trying to coerce him into my bed before I finally snapped and settled on assassination—whatever it took to gain any semblance of power over that horrible man. To this day, I do not entirely know how to feel about it, given he seemed practically gleeful over my attempts to take his life. Bit of a blow to my self-esteem—" Her words stopped abruptly, something stark and worrisome stealing her countenance. "Am I saying too much?"

"Well," Flowridia began, careful in her choice of words, "you're right that I don't fathom it, at all. But I also don't fully understand why you hate him."

She let the statement linger, hoping Ayla would hear the unspoken question. It was an invitation, and ire twisted Ayla's glower. "If Casvir were on fire, I wouldn't even spit on him. The feeling is mutual. No matter how you spin it, I was a slave, and he was my keeper. To know you are pledged to him as a god is better than thinking he slept with you, but it is still something I will have to adjust to."

Flowridia shook her head. "I'm not."

Was she?

"He granted you your powers, Flowra," Ayla said, voicing her own thoughts. "It is unheard of, for a child to become a witch, yet here you are. You received Aura as a little girl."

"My mother pledged for me," Flowridia said, the connection suddenly clear, "before I was even born."

Ayla shook her head. "Look at you—your soul sold before you were even conceived. I can hate him all I like, but it does not change the truth. Irony dictates he must own the one thing I love."

Oh, Flowridia hated that, her heart sinking to contemplate the truth in those uncomfortable words. Was she truly owned?

She was silent a moment too long, it seemed. "You were cleaning," Ayla continued, her hands twitching as they clutched the other. "How can I help you?"

Flowridia looked past her, to the macabre, horror-stained room. "Would you take care of the blood?"

Ayla nodded, the smile on her thin lips softer than the lingering silence. She disappeared behind the door and shut it.

Demitri, that lazy boy, laid against a wall, the damp wood groaning against his weight. *You fight a lot.*

Flowridia picked the broom up from beside the wall. "We had one fight. And we worked through it. It's what happens when two adults try to coexist."

You and I never fight.

"You and I fight constantly," she said, sticking out her tongue. "And you're not an adult, anyway."

She didn't have to see his grumble to feel it. *We're not going to stay here, right?*

"For a little while, but not forever."

Good. It's too small. I need a mansion, at minimum.

Flowridia swatted him with the bushy end of the broom. "And when did you become so entitled?"

I have needs.

Flowridia rolled her eyes.

Why are we even cleaning if we're just going to leave?

"The way I see it," Flowridia muttered, "leaving any evidence that I performed a blood ritual will end badly."

Good point.

When she had finished sweeping the living space, she segued into the cauldron room. Ayla was on her hands and knees scrubbing the floors, the tiny footprints all but gone, leaving only a coagulated puddle around the cauldron itself. The black iron shone as much as iron could, the inside cleaned of gore. A wooden bucket held macabre matter.

Ayla smiled but said nothing at her entrance, her fangs long and sharp from the presence of blood. Flowridia set her broom against the wall. "May I empty that for you?"

"Yes, thank you," Ayla said, her pupils all but consuming her pale gaze. Alarming, yes, but juxtaposed with her soft countenance, it was nearly endearing.

Flowridia clutched the bucket's wooden handle, though just as quickly flinched when what was certainly a splinter stuck its way into her finger. Sighing, she released it, choosing to remove it now rather than risk the sliver of wood burrowing deeper into her skin.

"What's wrong?" Ayla said, and Flowridia waved off her words.

"Only a splinter. I'll have it out in a—"

Flowridia's heart skipped when she swore, within the span of her blink, Ayla had gone from kneeling on the floor to uncomfortably close to her ear. "Let me see," she said, and when Flowridia offered her hand, Ayla's visage hardened. "Damn it, Flowra—this could have gone septic within hours."

"That's highly unlikely," Flowridia replied, trying to laugh off Ayla's panic, but her love grabbed a knife—the same used earlier to stab her between her ribs.

With finesse unmatched, the tip of the blade flicked against the diminutive sliver of wood, driving it painlessly out. "Who knows what touched that thing." Ayla squeezed the tip of Flowridia's finger until a small droplet of blood welled, which she let drip to the floor. "Now you may heal it."

"Of course, Lady Darkleaf," Flowridia replied, perturb in her tone, though she did let the spell flow to staunch the blood and heal the laceration. "I appreciate the doting, but I'm not a fragile bird."

Flowridia swore one of Ayla's eyes twitched. "No, I suppose not. Instead, you're a human—a living human—which is the far more delicate thing."

"I don't know if that's true—"

"I appreciate your offer of help," Ayla said, lifting the bucket herself, "but I will take care of this."

Flowridia frowned as Ayla carried the bucket from the room, uncomfortable for reasons she could not quite name. After a stabilizing breath—*Ayla was new; Ayla was paranoid; Flowridia had legitimately almost died earlier; it was fine; all was well*—she followed her to the front room, ignoring Demitri who feigned sleep against the wall.

When Ayla opened the front door, a noxious smell swept into the home, lingering as she dumped the bucket's contents into the boggy mud beyond the porch. "Ayla, I fear this paranoia of yours will only grow." It took all her will to keep her voice gentle, but she succeeded, even if Ayla's ensuing frown threatened to topple it. "Accidents happen. You have to let me live."

Ayla slammed the door shut behind her, then dropped the bucket onto the floor. Her sanguine smile held thinly veiled panic. "What happens when you die, my dearest heart? I live. Forever."

The words held a terrible truth, and Flowridia's heart sunk to consider it. "That isn't something I want you to worry about yet."

A predator faced her, from the void of her eyes to the fangs threatening to pierce her lips, but Flowridia felt her anguish. "My love," Flowridia whispered, "I don't know what you want me to say."

Ayla's stare remained inscrutable, yet her fangs grew ever longer, sneering her lip. With feet lighter than air, she came forward, and though her face remained monstrous, her eyes pled; they watered. "There is one solution."

The silence held implication. Flowridia's pulse thumped in her ear. Despite six months of grief, of yearning, of *fighting*, the idea of what the future would hold had somehow never unraveled, aside from the longing for her name.

Because Ayla was right. Someday she would die. It was the way of mortality—but Ayla was something different.

"I-I will consider it," Flowridia said, but then Ayla suddenly stole her arms, faster than a whip.

"There is joy in becoming a creature of the night, my love," Ayla cooed, her voice bearing both temptation and panic. "You were more than willing when faced with imminent death. What is the difference?"

Flowridia leaned away, feigning a smile. "As I said, I will consider it."

"You don't want it," Ayla whispered, and something dangerous laced that statement. Black pupils, barely rimmed with blue, stared daggers.

"I never said that. But never seeing the sun again would pain me."

"You would have the moon, my sweet. The moon and all the creatures of the night."

Flowridia frowned. "My garden?"

"Some plants thrive under moonlight."

"Ayla—"

Pain shot through her. Ayla's nails had drawn blood. "What would you propose instead?!" Her outburst echoed through the small cottage.

Black eyes glowered at her. Flowridia steadied herself. "Let me go," she whispered, shaking at the exertion to remain in control. "You're hurting me."

Immediately, Ayla shrunk back, horror twisting her countenance. Blood seeped from Flowridia's upper arms, ten perfect cuts where nails had broken skin. Ayla covered her mouth and cowered.

In careful movements, Flowridia crept toward her. "Why are you afraid?" she whispered, and when she reached forward, Ayla shook in her grasp.

"You're so fragile," Ayla managed, staring at the blood dripping down her skin.

"As any mortal." She moved closer, letting their forms brush against the other. "I have a long life ahead of me, my love."

Ayla shut her eyes, flinching when Flowridia touched her. "I don't have a life ahead of me. I have eternity alone."

Ayla had been alone for a millennium. She would never die a natural death, and Flowridia wondered if anything could break the apparent curse that had twisted her form and granted immortality.

"Anything you want. Anything. I will give it," Ayla pled, desperation driving every word. "But let me, please. In the few hours I have returned, you have already nearly died twice—one of those times by my own hand. I cannot bear to lose you."

Flowridia grew cold at the thought. To become a vampire meant to be helpless to Ayla's will. Given an order, she would be compelled to follow. She recalled how Mereen had frozen when told to stay still, had knelt when told to kneel . . .

Would Ayla be able to resist the temptation?

She would own her.

Flowridia reached up to stroke Ayla's cheek. The black eyes staring back held fear. Ayla asked a high price for her trust.

"I need time to consider it," Flowridia whispered, heart aching to feel Ayla's fear. "Not because I don't love you, and not because you're wrong. But I need to wrap my mind around it."

Blood dripped down to her elbow, leaving violent streaks across her russet skin. Before any could fall to the floor, she touched the droplet, catching the blood, then coated her finger as she ran it up the tender flesh.

When she offered it forward, Ayla stiffened, transfixed upon the dripping liquid. "Might as well not waste it," Flowridia said, praying she sounded more tender than terrified.

Fangs touched Flowridia's fingers as Ayla succumbed, breathless though she had no breath. As Ayla sucked the blessed life fluid from her finger, no color at all in her eyes, Flowridia saw a woman desperate for deliverance, and when a spot of blood stained her lip, Flowridia kissed it away, lingering and savoring Ayla's presence as well as the metallic sting. When she pulled away, she wiped the blood from her opposite arm onto her finger as well, but when Ayla reached for it, Flowridia shook her head. "I can think of a better place for you to lick this from."

The statement lingered. Ayla cocked an eyebrow, then offered a hand to lead her into the bedroom, and Flowridia practically saw her salivating.

Such a silly thing, to distract the thousand-year-old monster with sex, but as Flowridia kissed her, taking care to keep her bloodied hand away from her hair and dress, she felt Ayla's crippled power return. Thinly veiled strength rested behind her groping hands, and her elongated teeth scraped her skin but never drew blood—merely forced gasps from Flowridia's throat.

Oh, she longed to succumb and let Ayla tear the dress from her body and consume her, meld them as one. But she could prolong the moment. There was no hurry. Ayla was hers, and they had all the time in the world.

With the same gentleness she knew Ayla adored, Flowridia pushed her away with her unsullied hand, her own eyes large and batting, Ayla's a monstrous sea of black. She stepped back to her childhood bed, adoring Ayla's gaze as she removed her underclothes—a somewhat ungraceful task with one hand, but Ayla simply lounged against the wall, licking her lips when Flowridia sat and lifted her skirts. She spread her legs, invigorated by the hunger in Ayla's gaze.

There was no place for shyness here, though her breath failed at the first touch of her bloodied finger to her lower lips, flush with want. She rubbed the tender skin, the motion smoothed by blood and the want between her legs, invigorated beneath the judgement of her lover's gaze—who finally sauntered over, hips swaying as she pulled down her sleeves, letting the dress fall and pool at her waist. Oh, her subtle curves were a delight, a sight Flowridia could study for hours, the alabaster white of her skin as smooth as polished marble.

Ayla knelt before her spread legs, nothing humanoid in her visage or gaze. Blood dripped from Flowridia's aching cunt, the pleasure of her own touch merely the calm before her lover's storm. When she removed her hand, she beckoned Ayla to come with bloodied fingers, gasping when she stole them into her mouth, this unholy blend of life and desire.

Ayla kissed her soft thighs, leaving the bloody imprint of lips trailing toward her feast. At the touch of lips, they moaned—Ayla, of hunger; Flowridia, of pleasure. Flowridia held her there, fingers twisting in the dark shadows of her hair, bidding her to drink.

The threat of her fangs remained, but Flowridia felt no fear. Ayla's tongue was the grandest delight. Amidst their unholy union cried the purity of true love, for Flowridia adored her, savored the intimate truth that Ayla was hers and hers alone.

The hunger in her gaze pulled tenderness from Flowridia's very soul, and when she cried out and finished, body pulsing from pleasure, she bid Ayla to rise. The monster did, her mouth and jaw a bloody mess, but Flowridia craved more. She crushed their lips together, metallic bitterness assaulting her tongue, then pressed Ayla's mouth to her neck. "Please," she said, desperate for bonding, for lust.

"You're certain?" came the alluring voice, rough with want.

"Enough to satisfy; not enough to kill," she managed, gasping when a sharp prick stung the sensitive skin. Below, Ayla's fingers caressed her pulsing clit, soaked from want and blood, then pushed inside.

Flowridia danced upon a tightrope between pleasure and death. But lost in the mess of a blood-stained bed, gasping from pleasure unparalleled, she felt truly immortal.

She trusted Ayla to guide her fall.

"You know what's nice?" Etolié said, Khastra's hand clutched in her own. Her body hummed in their afterglow, and she couldn't seem to keep her free hand from stroking up and down Khastra's invisible bicep as they walked down the hallway.

"What is nice?" the incorporeal voice said, and Etolié forcibly believed nothing was there, lest the magic fail.

Etolié squeezed her hand, leaning against the bicep that definitely wasn't real as they walked. She kissed the obviously false wall of muscle, certain it would glow were it visible. "Not being abandoned minutes after having sex."

She didn't have to see Khastra's expression to feel it; the half-demon faltered slightly in her steps, though she quickly resumed when Etolié didn't stop. "You are unhappy."

"Yes? I don't know." Etolié gave a brief nod to passing servants, then resumed talking to herself. "It was a shitty thing to do, but I don't know if staying would have made it better."

"I had been anticipating that being our last moment because you would hate me for what I had done," Khastra replied. "I had to go. Nox'Kartha was leaving. But when you kissed me, I lost myself. What happened between us that night was sacred, and I could not shatter the silence, even with a goodbye. When I left, I wondered if it had been a dream, but I could not deny your scent on my skin."

"Listen to you, getting poetic on me." As they climbed the stairs in the manor, Etolié smiled, her hand still touching Khastra's bicep, her thumb stroking her hand. She couldn't stop, even if it made it ridiculously difficult to illusion Khastra away. "If you're trying to distract me, it's working."

Khastra squeezed her hand, and for a moment she flickered into view. "You deserve better than that, and I am sorry. Never again. I swear it."

Etolié let her vision linger for a moment, like taking a breath, before holding it anew and letting her disappear.

A reply to her letter had finally come. It had delivered no news, but Reginal wanted to meet. On the third floor of the manor waited the council chamber. Etolié took a few long sips of her flask as she approached, then tossed it back into her extra-dimensional pocket realm, never drunk enough for a meeting with world leaders.

As the first to arrive, Etolié technically had her choice in chairs, but propriety dictated she take her same seat next to Marielle's, opposite what was once Khastra's but was now Sora's place, and so on. Too anxiety ridden to sit, she leaned against the chair, gripping the dark wood.

They were alone, so Etolié let her focus wane. Khastra's form appeared, and Etolié smiled at her, enamored after a few hours spent napping in her arms. Nothing they hadn't done before, but it was different to sleep naked—or visibly naked, on her own part—next to someone you loved, to wake up pressed against their bare skin. She loved it. Adored it.

Khastra rubbed her hands across Etolié's shoulders, gently touching her thin frame. Shivers burst across her skin; the touch certainly welcome but on the verge of over-stimulating when Khastra's thumbs dug into her muscles. "Breathe, Etolié. You need to relax."

Despite her mythical strength, Khastra had never hurt her, not once—a fact Etolié found inspirational. But the half-demon had lived among mere mortals nearly all her life, so perhaps their fragility was simply ingrained into her memory.

As it was, Etolié was about three seconds away from literally purring when the door swung open. She immediately straightened her stance, her face hopefully suggesting that she had not just been intimately, though innocently, touched by her favorite demon, but then it was only Sora, followed by Lunestra. She let Khastra flicker back into view. "You two are looking much cleaner."

Sora wore her typical, non-priestess attire—breeches and boots and a comfortable tunic, void of finery. Lunestra, however, must have worn borrowed clothing, but not Sora's— the half-elf was at least half a foot taller than the elderly woman. Given the cut and size, Etolié guessed it was an old dress of Flowers'—one of the fancy ones she'd never worn.

"I can honestly say I've never been happier to be home," Sora replied, and she beckoned Lunestra into her own seat—predictable, but polite.

The Archbishop of the Theocracy had a pleasant, innocuous smile, one Etolié had seen a few too many times during their years political-ing at each other. Lunestra sat and said, "I should say you make a lovely couple, you and your friend, Khastra."

Funny, how her expression could be both so neutral and shit-eating all at once. "It's a recent thing," Etolié mumbled, her back pressed against her demon.

"She is being truthful, Archbishop," Khastra said, her arm coming to cross over Etolié's torso—a gesture both protective and possessive, enough to bring a blush to her face. "Our relationship changed after Marielle's wedding."

"I see," Lunestra said, most likely honest, but it was difficult to tell, given how well she masked. But she had a great many things to mask, Etolié recalled—her country was in crisis, and her brother had died hardly a week ago, in the aforementioned aftermath of Marielle's wedding.

Life was fragile and fleeting. Etolié held Khastra's hand and refused to dwell a second more on that.

Thalmus entered, and Khastra exited view fast enough that he hopefully didn't notice. If he had, he didn't show it. He gave a polite nod to Archbishop Lunestra and sat silently in his seat.

Peace was fleeting—Marielle burst in, and Etolié cringed when the door banged against the wall. "Oh, wonderful. We're all here."

Zorlaeus followed behind her, as skittish as an unearthed crab. He all but hid in his seat, across from Marielle's, and while Etolié still fought against his nomination as a council member, on a personal level he was all right.

Marielle stopped before Lunestra's seat. "All the world is in mourning," she said, genuine and kind. "I know politically there's little Staelash can do. But, on a personal note, if there is anything any of us might do to offer comfort, please don't be shy. You're a guest, but you're also a friend."

"I appreciate that," Lunestra replied.

Marielle smiled sincerely and took her seat—whatever the drawbacks of wearing her heart on her sleeve, Etolié did have to admire her capacity to give condolences.

Lunestra said, "Forgive me, but you seem to be missing someone."

Aw. That someone. Etolié, who had survived an undead siege and could probably do with a few more years of napping, offered a rather caustic smile and said, "Off the record, Archbishop, but I have no fucking idea where Flowridia is."

Lunestra's eyes widened, though not with any anger, and Etolié thought this might've been the first authentic reaction she'd seen since arriving in Staelash.

"Lady Flowridia, Grand Diplomat of Staelash, disappeared shortly after the wedding," Etolié continued, three degrees away from laughing from sheer nerves. "I don't believe she's in or currently affiliated with Nox'Kartha, but I suppose we just don't know now do we. This might be concerning, but somehow I think she's fine."

Given she had an orb? That she'd stolen? Flowridia had all the protection she needed, even if Etolié's eye couldn't stop twitching whenever that came up.

"Once we get this all squared away, I'll call a search party. But we should contact Solvira now." Habitually, Etolié withdrew the silver mirror she kept in her pocket dimension and tapped it.

Nothing. Therein lay the concerning part. Lara wouldn't answer.

She slipped it away, then withdrew a small scroll, one she knew bore no words. Instead, a wax seal imbued with power bore the sigil of the Solviraes Royal Family.

She ripped it. When she dropped it, it unfurled on its own and landed with a gentle touch upon the wooden floor, then unleashed a blast of light.

The magical rays gained form and substance, creating humanoid figments. Etolié recognized the two Celestials depicted in the light, their forms more like the angels of Celestière than mortals.

Magister Reginal of Solvira was a man Etolié rather liked, bemused by his eccentric clothing and waist-length beard—pure white, juxtaposing nicely with his dark, umber skin. He stood beside High Priestess Jules, who Etolié knew to be a total stick-up-her-ass type but nice enough.

Instead of a greeting, she asked the obvious: "Where's Lara?"

"Oh, you don't know," Reginal replied, and he began stroking his beard in a manner Etolié had come to recognize over the years meant he was about to say something he'd much rather not. Etolié forced a smile, nervous at that. "She left with Lady Flowridia and a small party to find one of the Convergence Orbs. She claimed to know the location of one far south, in the Abyssal Swamp."

Her eye twitched. "Listen, if I saw that nasty lunar explosion all the way from fucking apocalypse town, you saw it too."

"I think the whole world did."

Eye twitch. Eye twitch. Keep calm. "So where the fuck is she?"

Reginal would likely start pulling out beard hairs if he didn't stop stroking quite so frantically. "We lost track of them. After the explosion, we sent a search party—"

"*YOU NEGLIGENT DICKHOLES LOST THE EMPRESS OF SOLVIRA?!*" Etolié released Khastra's invisible hand and stormed toward the figures. The world was red; oh, her blood fucking *boiled.*

"She went with General Irons—it was supposed to be a short mission—"

"And now she's missing after an extremely suspicious explosion, and you haven't even alerted the fucking kingdom! The literal last of Neoma's line might be dead and we're just sitting here having a pleasant fucking meeting?! We should be *burning down the countryside looking for her—*" She stopped, because it suddenly occurred to her that something was wrong. Through gritted teeth, she said, "Convergence Orb?"

The question lingered, and Etolié forced a smile as Reginal coughed. "Yes, Magister Etolié," he said. If he had the audacity to be angry, Etolié would have a few more fucking things to say. "Like I said, Lady Flowridia came. Lara wished for discretion and took only a small party."

"Reginal, your math is broken," Etolié said, liable to grind her teeth into powder at this rate. "Soliel has four orbs— he stole Emperor Malakh's, he stole Marielle's, he stole the green one from the dragon, and then there was a certain incident a week ago involving a dead former archbishop that conveniently ended with him having four." Who was she to not throw in a good lie now and then for sanity? Yes, she quietly had the orb tucked away in a box in the library, but they didn't need to know that.

"Correct," Reginal replied, "and then Lady Flowridia found the fifth with Imperator Casvir—the one from the ocean. She presented it to you at the wedding, or so I was told. There was one more unaccounted for, and—"

"Funny, because Casvir had it. It was used in his attack on the City of Light. His dragon stole it back, but it's definitely accounted for." The first snicker of laughter left Etolié's throat, because damn it—she laughed when particularly stressed. "There's not an orb in that swamp, so why the fuck was Flowers taking her there?"

Thank Morathma's Whore Mother—Reginal had the good sense to frown at that, even furrow his ancient brow a bit. "Oh my."

"Maybe double that search party, hmm?" Etolié failed to quite subsume her laughter, but she at least managed to bring it down to an annoyed giggle. "Put me in charge; I won't fail."

"Magister Etolié," Priestess Jules said, and Etolié prepared herself for another furious tirade, "I don't disagree that this has taken a suspicious turn. But spare a few minutes for the issue at hand—the Theocracy of Sol Kareena is in crisis, and the archbishop is a refugee."

Etolié blew out what would hopefully be her final attempt at a stabilizing breath. "A fair rebuttal."

She cast her spell, and a doppelganger from her imagination stepped gracefully to the seat waiting for her— real Etolié turned into Khastra's side, invisible as she clung to her half-demon. Khastra led her to the corner of the room and coaxed her to sit—and she did, embraced by those massive arms as she sat on her lap.

"Tell us what happened," Jules said. "All of you—we should hear it from reputable mouths."

"Well, it all started when I saw a giant invisible army coming over the horizon," doppelganger Etolié said, because throwing her voice was the easiest trick up her metaphorical sleeve.

Eionei had taught her that when she was just a tiny girl living in her momma's house, told her it would be a hilarious prank to pull on the Goddess of Stars. And it probably would have been, had tiny Etolié thrown her voice to sound like giggling or a song. Instead, she had screamed bloody murder and cried for help—and her frantic momma had searched the house in hysterics, bursting into sobs when Etolié had finally revealed herself.

Not funny at all. She hadn't done that again.

Sora had resumed the story, she realized. Everything sounded purely clinical, though Marielle's eyes would burst from her skull if they grew any wider. Lunestra merely listened, quiet anguish twisting her elderly features. For a moment, Etolié felt a modicum of pain for her, this woman she'd previously dismissed as just another political asshole. Lunestra had risked her life to save the orphans in her care, and Etolié respected that.

Sora told it all, though faltered when she mentioned the tunnels. Etolié spoke up then. "The tunnels were massacred," she said, the day and night of screams still haunting her memory.

"What of the protections?" Jules said, because she'd studied history, Etolié guessed.

"If you know about the protections, you know that Goddess Ku'Shya set them. Nox'Kartha's General could speak her momma's tongue and deactivate the runes."

In the corner, Khastra's grip tightened on Etolié, and she feared what she would see were the half-demon visible. She'd witnessed Khastra's regret, felt it vibrate against her entire body when her demon had sobbed.

The two Solviran Council Members had turned ashen. "By Sol Kareena's Light..." Reginal muttered, and Jules looked somewhere between tears and screaming.

"She didn't have a choice," Etolié said. "She's a slave to the imperator just like any of the undead. But that's what happened."

She remembered staring opposite a false wall, the Bringer of War leering above them, gazing directly into Etolié's eyes.

The Bringer of War had spared them. But Etolié could say nothing. Instead, Etolié said they had hidden in the tunnels, and when all was clear, they left.

They were caught, she said, aching to say Khastra's role in it all and clear her name. But Khastra had begged her to stay silent, lest she face eternal pain. "The story ends in an unconventional way," Etolié continued, "because you'll notice we're not dead or captured. In fact, a dragon brought us.

Um . . ." She thought of how to say it, realizing there was little tact to have. "But Imperator Casvir was . . . squished."

Reginal merely blinked. "Yes, you mentioned that."

Jules had turned stark white. "He's dead?"

"No. He's squished. Khastra said he'll be back. But that's how we escaped—with Imperator Casvir out of commission temporarily, one of his dragons managed to escape."

"One of his dragons?"

Right. "Just ask me whatever you want. There're a lot of details that—"

Reginal suddenly turned around, and though his gaze technically looked toward Zorlaeus, Etolié knew he looked at something far away. "The empress?"

Something spoke from beyond, though Etolié couldn't hear it. She managed a breath, anxiously waiting.

When Reginal turned back, Etolié couldn't see color on his light-filled form, but she suspected he had lost it. "It seems we need to cut off this meeting early. A portion of Lara's party has returned. Without her."

Panic pulsed through Etolié's blood. "What?!"

"Our scouts came across General Irons carrying one of their party members, both of them injured."

"What?!"

"They ran into a team of slavers. Half a day from a southern village called Ilunnes. I am going to speak to them."

Etolié's tongue froze. Marielle ended the meeting. The light faded, but Etolié had been punched, or something like it, standing from Khastra's lap but stumbling against the wall.

Slavers? The word pulsed hatred through her blood.

Doppelganger Etolié remained by the chair until real Etolié stepped into the illusion, blending them seamlessly.

Sora approached. "We don't know what's happened," the half-elf said, and she offered a hand. Etolié held it, letting their quiet pseudo-hug at least convey comradery. "Just because the general was taken doesn't mean the empress or Flowridia were. Perhaps they escaped."

Emptiness expanded in Etolié's stomach. She released Sora's hand and withdrew her flask instead, drinking as Marielle stood and said, "No use panicking yet," though she clearly didn't believe it, for how ashen she had become.

Etolié's jaw trembled as the room slowly cleared out, a somber mood stealing their words.

Lunestra remained with them, the little bird on her shoulder quiet as she stood up. Sora came to Etolié's side. She supposed they were friends now, since that was what tended to happen when you shared a pipe and your daddy trauma. "Is Khastra still here?" the half-elf asked, once they were alone.

"She's right there," Etolié said, her voice trembling, and Khastra appeared, still seated on the floor in the corner. "If anything's happened, I'll kill every last slaver on this fucking realm."

"I thought that was the plan anyway," Sora replied, but Etolié couldn't smile.

The first of her tears fell when Lunestra came up beside her. "Magister Etolié, I don't know if this is rude to offer to an acolyte of Eionei, but I would happily give you a blessing of comfort, if you think it might help."

Etolié forcibly bit back her instinctive sass, because Lunestra was a foreign monarch and not a pillow to punch out her frustrations on. Instead, she shook her head. "I appreciate it though. I really do."

Lunestra offered an unoffended nod. "If I may ask, do you know anything of the happenings of Celestière? Despite my prayers, I've heard nothing from Sol Kareena—neither her presence nor her voice."

"Eionei made a mention of her being unwell, but I don't know anything else."

Lunestra looked as though she waited for more, but Etolié had nothing more to say. Soon, she and Sora left.

Etolié leaned against her chair until a great weight pulled her away, then cradled her against her warm, strong chest. She set her head against Khastra's sternum, quietly crying.

She felt . . . empty.

"I don't know what any of this means," Etolié whispered. "I have all these puzzle pieces and nowhere to begin."

"The tiny one has made herself a suspicious character."

"She has a lot to answer for. I'm just praying it's stupidity."

Khastra's arms tightened around her, and when she spoke, she sounded almost nervous? "I need to tell you something."

Etolié sat up, mist obscuring her vision. "Are you about to ruin my day even more?"

"I do not know why the tiny one stole the orb, but I witnessed the theft."

So rare, for Etolié to fail to conjure a single emotion—she replied with an utterly vacant stare.

"The morning after Marielle's wedding, you were asleep. I did not want to wake you. The tiny one came into your library to take back the orb."

"And you didn't wake me up?"

"You needed sleep."

"And you didn't bother to tell me after?"

"It was not my business."

Resignation bled into Etolié's ensuing groan. "Oh, fuck you and your weird Demoni morality."

And then she collapsed again upon Khastra's chest, worried beyond measure, relieved when strong arms held her anew.

When their orchestral union of souls concluded, Flowridia held Ayla's head against her heartbeat.

The pleasure was bliss, yes, Ayla's touch a dark paradise, but the true bonding of hearts happened in the quiet afterglow. Flowridia breathed, savoring the moment of peace.

So rare, for them to bask and simply be in the time before Ayla's death, when her soul was held in a vice. But Ayla held no bonds now, save the ones she tied herself. No bargains or contracts to pull her away—simply the freedom to remain in Flowridia's embrace. That she would choose to stay still brought fluttering to Flowridia's stomach.

"I promised Demitri we wouldn't stay in the swamp for long," Flowridia whispered, the words softly breaking the blissful silence. "Is there anywhere in particular you would like to be?"

"The idea of running away with you was once impossible, and so I had given it only idle thought," Ayla said, clutching Flowridia's naked form, buried in the bed. "You had remarked that you would be content to live in the woods—just you and me. And Demitri, of course. Although . . ." She stroked her fingers through Flowridia's hair, the cool touch soothing. "...if that dream became real, you would never see your loved ones again. Would you be content with that?"

Flowridia's heart sank. "I had accepted that would be the price of your return—that no one could know. Casvir shall, but he knew my quest to resurrect you already. I cannot return to Neolan with no news of Lara, so I fear this is the end."

Flowridia's visage must have shown her anguish—Ayla placed a leisurely kiss upon her lips. "Let me give it some thought." Flowridia watched that calculating glint return to her eye, even as her smile faltered.

Ayla remained silent, and Flowridia leaned up to kiss her. "You worry me," Flowridia said, but her love shook her head.

"Trust that there is madness to my methods, sweet Flowra—"

A knock ruined her perfect world.

Fully nude, she half sat up, supported by her hands, though Ayla remained a sleepy heap upon her—despite having no need for sleep. Flowridia listened, swearing she must have imagined it.

There again came the knock. And then a pathetic whine of, *"Ayla Darkleaf, please don't kill me."*

This time, Ayla perked up, stance not unlike a cat listening to the soft squeaking of her prey. Her icy visage glared as Flowridia slowly stood up, transfixed at the impossible convergence of worlds. She slipped on her dress, but Ayla remained mostly nude, breasts exposed from her disheveled dress and making no effort to change that. "Is that—"

The knock came again. *"I need to talk to Lady Flowridia. It's very important."*

Flowridia returned to the main room, where Demitri sat tense and quietly growling. *Smells pretentious. You should let Ayla eat him.*

"I'm not saying no, but I do want to know why he's here," Flowridia replied, smoothing her modest attire. Ayla appeared beside her as she twisted the doorknob, still half nude, but that was her own prerogative. "Viceroy Murishani?"

Murishani looked as out of place as a pristine cupcake on a pile of cockroaches. He glowed, somehow, despite the dank atmosphere, his flowing blonde locks luxurious, his opulent robes impeccable. He smiled with his lips, but his eyes were stale, and Flowridia thought this odd, given his charming, charlatan nature. "What a delightful honeymoon home," he said pleasantly, glancing around the terrain. "I think it's the corpses that really add that personal touch. May I come in before I stain my robes in shit water?"

"Absolutely not," Flowridia replied, matching his polite tone.

"And Ayla Darkleaf!" Murishani placed a hand over his exposed chest—the slit of his robes nearly hit his navel. He did a marvelous job not acknowledging her exposed chest, maintaining perfect eye contact instead. "Oh, how you've been missed. Nox'Kartha hasn't been the same without your creative mind."

"Nox'Kartha can miss me all it likes," Ayla replied, her sultry tone bespeaking murder and little else.

Though his presence unnerved Flowridia to her core, there remained a more pressing matter. "How did you know we were here?"

"Context clues. Subtlety was never your strong point."

"Flowra, you know this man?"

When Ayla slipped her hand into Flowridia's, their fingers quickly intertwined. "Well enough. He's not supposed to talk to me, you see, or come within ten feet of me."

"Why—?"

"That threat would be absolutely respected," Murishani interrupted, his smile lacking any sincerity, "were there anyone to enforce it."

The words lingered; Flowridia frowned. "Excuse me?"

Ayla raised a hand. "I will happily enforce it."

"What happened to Casvir?" Flowridia's blood ran cold at the words, unable to stop the sudden trembling in her hands.

"That's why I'm here," Murishani replied, hands outstretched defensively. "Might I come in?"

"No, you may not," Flowridia spat. "What happened?"

Murishani's smile faded completely, leaving nothing but a grimace. "Khastra happened."

Those two words said nothing, yet the implications were clear. Flowridia's breath caught in her throat.

"I tried to warn him," Murishani said, drama in every word. "Now he currently holds more resemblance to a squashed mosquito than a man. He's no more dead than he was before—there are advantages to becoming a lich—but it's taking much longer than I'd hoped for him to repair himself—by which I mean, he's still mostly a pile of meat. And that's why I'm here—to humble myself and ask for you to come and assist because if we can agree on one little thing, it's that we both prefer Casvir's taut, barrel chest to be in one piece, yes?"

Flowridia looked to Ayla, hardly able to breath as her limbs became cold. Ayla looked merely disdainful. "I have many questions," Ayla said simply. "But I suppose they can wait."

"Why, though?" Flowridia asked, grateful for the doorframe, lest she sway. "What aren't you telling me?"

Murishani's sneer seemed genuine, and not only for the stench. "You're really going to make me tell it here?"

She didn't grace him with a response, and he told it. In muted tones, he spoke of death, of the imperator's onslaught against the Theocracy.

Flowridia, standing in her mother's home, surrounded by dead things and the stifling, choking atmosphere, could not even fathom it. His words didn't settle, simply swirled in her mind, unable to be processed. Yet she trembled, breathless to think of the beautiful city burned and destroyed, its citizens fodder for the Deathless Army, all the slaughtered children—

"Lady Flowridia?"

"You have an orb," she said, shock muting her words. "I'm certain you can fix it yourself."

"Well, the dragon took it back, but . . ."

His words faded as she shut the door.

"I'll accept that as a 'maybe,'" came his pervasive voice, but Flowridia struggled to walk. Her legs failed her; she leaned against the wall housing the fireplace, then slid down, her imagination straining to visualize his awful words.

Ayla sat before her, her dress finally put properly together, and took one of her arms, gently coaxing blood to flow through the numb limb as she rubbed her tawny skin. "Flowra?"

Not two weeks ago, Casvir had asked for her final answer—to know if she would accept her throne. Flowridia managed a shallow breath, too stunned to feel anything at all. "I can't believe him," she whispered, the pulsing reality of betrayal surging through her body. "How . . . How could he? All those people—those *children.*"

"Flowra, I say this with all the kindness I can muster—this is entirely in his character."

"I could have stopped this," she whispered, but then Ayla furiously shook her head.

"This was not your fault—"

"It wasn't, but I could have stopped it. If I'd known. If he'd told me."

Demitri said nothing, though his nose rubbed against her hair. Ayla, meanwhile, kept with her soothing gestures, switching to Flowridia's other arm. "You clearly know something I do not then."

"I was pledged to Casvir before I was even conceived," Flowridia said, an echo of their previous words, "which meant he meddled and orchestrated my parents' union. My mother was Odessa, but my father ..." She shut her eyes, trying hard to picture a man she'd never known, whose blood she shared but whose face would be a mystery forevermore. "My father's name was Zanoram, the son of Archbishop Xoran. The Theocracy's throne was my right, my inheritance. I didn't want it, but now ..."

Ayla's cold touch glossed across her face at her failed words, lightly touching her hair. "I have so many questions," Ayla said, intrigue in her words, "but I shall ask the most important first. What do you need?"

Flowridia focused on Ayla's touch, letting it guide her spirit back into her body. Eyes shut, she considered those weighted words, and the answer surprised her. "I need to see it for myself."

"Easy." Ayla's touched disappeared as she stood up; Flowridia was offered a small hand. "Come. I will take you there."

"I don't know what perils we might come across," Ayla said, her voice as cold as the atmosphere of the demonic realm, "so forgive me when I drag you and Demitri into Sha'Demoni at the first sign of danger."

"I accept this," Flowridia replied, and then the world filled with color and a sickening stench.

The sun rose, but it could not combat winter's chill. Clouds covered the world, and a flurry of snow fell to cover the graveyard before them. It took Flowridia a moment to realize this was the entrance to the City of Light—for though pieces of the wall remained, the great statue of Sol Kareena, once bidding visitors welcome, was nothing but a pile of stone.

In silence, she entered.

Magnificent, truly, the absolute magnitude of the destruction. So little stood in one piece—every building had collapsed or nearly so; all the beautiful fountains were rubble. The stench rose as she tracked through puddles of blood and ichor, her breath a blending of fog and swirling ash. Pieces of bodies lay strewn about, but never as a whole—anyone whole was standing, some wandering.

All she passed stared upon her with vacant, hungry eyes, but it was child's play to detour them, to simply cast her spell and watch them walk away. Casvir's influence had waned with his temporary demise.

The Deathless Army had grown, she knew, and as she entered what she thought might have once been the city square, there stood a mass of undead, idle without their master.

Valeuron sat among them, his vacant gaze and burned figure an eerie addition. Blood stained his claws, one was missing, and Flowridia felt the first rising of fury at his fate, his spirit gone but his body—this peaceful, beautiful creature—used for monstrous deeds. She stared upon the army, but it could barely be called that. There were newer recruits, stolen from among the Theocracy citizens. No weapons. No shields. Merely well-dressed nobles missing limbs, merchants in blood-stained, tattered clothes—and children.

So many children, some half torn apart.

Flowridia forced herself to stare and memorize their vacant gazes.

The disquieting peace was stolen by a sudden snickering, quickly cut off. Flowridia turned—to Ayla, who stood before a collection of stairs leading to what was once the grand cathedral. Demitri was with her, and as Flowridia approached, Ayla covered her mouth, eyes wide, visibly fighting an impulse Flowridia saw right through.

An enormous, black, *pulsing* stain lay strewn upon the stairs, the stone beneath it shattered by a force she could only envision one source for. Bits of shattered armor remained around it, but most of it had been cleaned away. No body or large pieces—that had been taken away, it seemed—but what had been left behind painted a gruesome image.

Murishani hadn't exaggerated the damage. "Go ahead," Flowridia said, glowering when Ayla burst into a fit of laughter.

Demitri nuzzled her, who didn't need to speak or even have the biological capacity to laugh to also convey his amusement. Ayla wiped tears from her eyes, absolute delight escaping her throat as uncontrollable wheezing. "I-I'm sorry. I am so sorry." She resumed her laughing fit.

Somehow, the vision of Ayla joyous and cackling, uncaring of the carnage around her, completed the vision of all Flowridia had learned and sought to reconcile. It fell into a single picture, of a woman unhinged, so calloused and cruel that she would laugh hysterically for one fallen enemy amidst a sea of slaughtered innocents.

Though to be fair, Demitri laughed too.

And so Flowridia merely waited, studying the gruesome stain of gore where Casvir had fallen. When Ayla finally calmed enough to speak again, she said, "This is the best day of my life."

"This may be the worst day of mine," Flowridia replied, forcibly pleasant as Ayla visibly fought to control herself.

Ayla wiped tears from her eyes. "Darling, are you angry?"

"I can't fathom what grudge you have with the Theocracy," Flowridia replied, her sniffling loud amidst the quiet scene, "but I can't imagine you would ever celebrate the deaths of thousands of innocents."

"I am indifferent, but that is a little better, right? Honestly, I am gleeful at Casvir's, uh, *predicament.*"

Rather than respond, Flowridia stared upon the stain of Casvir, who Murishani claimed was not dead—or any more dead than before—yet she struggled to imagine how or what good she could do. She studied the jagged lines of shattered stone forming the perfect outline of a hammer's head.

There was only one thing that could have caused Khastra to crack. She wondered of Etolié's fate—if she lived or if her death had been the trigger.

She should be heartbroken. But she didn't feel much of anything at all.

Beyond, the faint moaning of death slowly grew louder as patrolling undead approached, drawn toward their living essence. The great mass of fresh recruits remained stagnant, but the others peered hungrily at them, some approaching faster than others.

Flowridia did not fear them, and instead she walked the rest of the way up the stairs, passing shards of stained glass and coagulated, drying blood. Where the doorway once stood, she paused and stared ahead, upon what little remained.

A statue. Sol Kareena and her son.

Flowridia could come no closer, the rising waves of guilt threatening to drown her. She swallowed tears, but then came a soft touch upon her arm. "Your lips are purple," Ayla whispered. "Your skin is ice. Are you certain you wish to stay longer?"

"We can leave," Flowridia whispered, her stare still upon the goddess' visage, evidence of blood on its base.

Ayla wrapped her arms around her, something alluring in her dark words. "I think a proper bath would warm you up. We can leave your bloodied dress behind."

Flowridia spared a glance for her skirts, only then noticing the gore and other fluids.

"And with Casvir gone, there's no one to stop us from luxuriating in my personal favorite."

"Your private bath?"

Ayla's grin finally stole her gaze. "You're half-frozen to death. Let me spoil you."

Flowridia spared a final glance for the ravaged city, for the watching undead, and finally for the statue beyond, shame filling her to face it.

She could have stopped this.

They left through a shadow—she, Ayla, and Demitri.

Flowridia walked in a daze through the shadow realm, ignorant of whatever eyes and creatures followed them.

All those people . . . thousands of them . . .

Though many minutes passed, she felt nothing at all—not until they stepped into a room of stone and ambient sconces, enveloped by a soothing warmth. A stone bath bearing carvings of roses and thorns was the main attraction, but a closet filled with robes could not be dismissed as their own, unique comfort. The walls held no door, save for the enticing entrance to the underground hell beneath their feet—

which somehow, after witnessing absolute carnage, seemed like such a small thing.

Demitri sniffed about, even as Ayla leaned in and whispered, "Are you comfortable with me bathing in front of your familiar?"

"He won't care."

Ayla's ensuing grin precluded her stripping from her soiled dress, the ends of it stained in what Flowridia was certain were Casvir's entrails. "I have to ask. I don't actually know what his mental age is."

"He's still a little boy."

Demitri perked up at her words. *I'm a grown up.*

"You're really not though," Flowridia teased, her smile appearing unbidden, despite her exhausted state. "You were barely born a year ago. Even if you were a normal wolf, you would be young."

But I'm not a normal wolf. I'm big.

"Fine. Do you care if Ayla bathes in front of you?"

I'm always naked. I see you naked all the time. I don't care if she is.

Flowridia only then noticed Ayla, her raised eyebrow and subdued smirk. "Demitri doesn't mind if you're naked," Flowridia said, hoping it explained the one-sided conversation, "citing his own nakedness as proof."

"Fair enough," Ayla said, and as Flowridia stripped away her own ruined dress, the vampire offered Demitri her hand, uncharacteristically cautious when he bumped his large ahead against it. "You are a gorgeous creature, Demitri. Once I've helped your . . ." A slight frown marred her visage when she looked to Flowridia. "What would I call you, to him? 'Mistress' comes to mind, but it does not seem like you."

In her precious year with Demitri, no one had ever asked. As she arranged her filthy clothing in a pile, she realized she didn't know. "He's always called me 'mom,'" she finally replied, though a question lingered at the final word.

Ayla seemed content to accept that. "Once I've finished helping your mother, we'll figure out how to wash the dirt from your paws."

If you get married, do I have to call Lady Ayla 'mom,' also?

"That's between her and you."

"Pardon?" Ayla asked, and Flowridia resisted the urge to laugh.

"Demitri asked if he has to call you mom, if you and I ever . . ." Flowridia shrugged, shy to admit the rest.

However, Ayla's grimace caused her heart to sink. "I will respectfully decline the title of 'mother'."

Flowridia fought to hide her relief as she looked to the tub. Ayla was not opposed to marriage, it seemed. Sconces cast light in gentle jewel tones across the walls, and when she twisted the knobs to fill the basin, she recalled her idle thoughts of joining Ayla here someday.

She hadn't anticipated Demitri being here too, but he was an accessory to her perfect world. Still, soon Ayla embraced her from behind, chaste for Demitri's sake only, Flowridia was sure, as she dragged her into the warm water.

Yet washing the dirt and grime and nightmares from her skin only brought reminders of what had brought them.

When the filth was but a memory, Flowridia basked a moment in the serene dream of Ayla's bath—all the more perfect with Ayla herself. Soon Flowridia settled into her arms and wept, hardly aware when Ayla placed a kiss upon her brow. Gods, this should have been perfect, but any time she blinked she saw those undead children staring back.

"Do you need to talk about it?"

Flowridia frantically shook her head, unable to articulate any of it into words. Not yet.

"May I ask something else, then?"

Flowridia looked up from her spot between Ayla's breasts and nodded.

"Last I recall," Ayla said smoothly, "I had killed Khastra. Broke her spine in two. Won't you explain?"

"That story spans about six months."

Ayla gestured to their shared washroom, revealing a timeless spectacle and a snoozing wolf in the corner. "We have all the time in the world, darling. I want to hear everything."

Flowridia managed to smile and began at the beginning.

A letter came. Etolié feared it.

She had come to recognize Reginal's writing over the years. Nude in bed, pressed close to her favorite, equally nude demon, her trembling hands could hardly hold it—in the end, Khastra read it aloud.

With Etolié pressed against her chest, Khastra read the contents, confirming that General Irons had, indeed, returned. He had carried back a priest named Coal, who was nearly dead but would now live. The Solviraes weren't the only ones with the power to transport people across impossible distances, though the royal family did it the best and the easiest.

The people of Ilunnes had called for help when they had appeared. And then there was something about some ancient evil returning to the nearby swamp. Etolié didn't listen to that.

"Just get to the part about Lara."

Lara had escaped. General Irons could see her cage from his. Apparently Flowridia was taunted by their captor. When he sent men to molest her, she had somehow freed herself of her confines and slew them with her dark powers.

Etolié was neutral on the subject of necromancy. To hear that Flowers had used it to detour probable rapists leaned her opinion toward positive.

Etolié perked up at the mention of Flowers apparently destroying half the camp. "How?"

"It does not say. But that was when Irons escaped. It does say she left her wolf behind."

Etolié's stomach clenched. Oh, Demitri . . .

"But she did escape with Lara. They know nothing more."

"Does it say anything about the silver light?"

Khastra shook her head.

"Fucking hell." Etolié snatched the letter and let it float to the ground. She settled fully atop her demon's chest, idly distracting herself by tracing the tattooed lines on her breasts.

"You are stressed," Khastra said, pointing out the obvious.

Etolié didn't even grant that phrase a reply. She simply spared Khastra a withering look and resumed tracing the ancient words along her skin.

Khastra's sigh held the weight of all her years of friendship with Etolié—which, even now, Etolié was astounded Khastra agreed to carry. "Speak your mind," the half-demon said.

"I feel so useless. Moonbeam is missing or dead, Flowers too, I have a house full of orphans and a displaced archbishop, a dragon spouting cryptic nonsense, your own impending doom that I'm forcibly not thinking about—"

"Cryptic nonsense?"

Etolié scooted closer to Khastra's face, entertaining herself with the tattoos on her neck instead. "Kitty said . . ." The words replayed in her head, and Etolié felt cold at the memory. ". . . She said that the Goddess of Chaos would be coming soon."

Khastra's hand stroked a soft line along Etolié's brow. "And this is burdening you."

"I mean, she did follow it up with a very helpful, 'Oh, you'll know what to do when the time comes,' or some shit. I'd say that's worth being burdened by."

"Very strange," Khastra replied, but she seemed far less bothered than Etolié. "Would you like me to help you in researching Chaos? Perhaps we might learn something more."

Etolié plopped her head upon Khastra's chest. "Later, but yes. I'm too jittery to do anything useful."

"If you are seeking suggestions, I would happily engage in useless activities with you."

Taken aback, Etolié sat up and faced her demon. "That's the worst seduction I've ever heard."

Khastra's laughter soothed her agitated heart. "Are you saying no?"

"I'm saying that you're normally full of poetic nonsense so that was pathetic." Etolié kissed her. "Try again."

Khastra pressed their lips together, this time choosing a silent route—her large hands gripped Etolié's ass, pulling a moan from her throat. "Much better," Etolié said, and then she squeaked when Khastra rolled them over, leaving Etolié pressed between the bed and her half-demon love.

As much as Etolié adored dominating her indomitable companion, gods there was something primal in withdrawing all control and letting Khastra lead, and when the half-demon buried her face between her thighs, Etolié grabbed her horns and knew she had chosen right.

Flowridia told her the tale of six months of grief—the true and honest story, of being kidnapped by Ku'Shya's youngest daughter, of fighting the skeleton dragon for the orb, of Khastra's return, of meeting Tazel Fireborn and their ensuing friendship, though she glossed over the pain of discovering all the horrid truths of The Scourge of the Sun Elves—

"It did hurt, finding out everything," Flowridia said, her fingers having long shriveled, soaked in soapy water.

In Ayla's beautiful, dangerous gaze, was quiet abashment. "I did say you wouldn't like who I was in Nox'Kartha."

"Whatever my feelings," Flowridia whispered, "I accept it as truth. You aren't your deeds, but your deeds are yours. It was Casvir who helped me reconcile it all. He validated the nightmare I witnessed in your dungeon underground but spoke earnestly of the love you had for me. He said . . ." She smiled, and it surprised her, for the memory ached as much as it brought joy. ". . . that I evoked something new and beautiful inside of you. And I can't imagine a more romantic sentiment than that."

Ayla looked shyly away—how strange, to see her love so reserved. "I would be blushing, were I capable."

"He's the one who encouraged me to do whatever it took to bring you back. But that's jumping ahead."

She resumed, the grief of those months alone healing with each story, with each smile and laugh she evoked from Ayla. She spoke of embracing her talents as a necromancer, of learning to heal, of finding joy in her journey with Casvir.

She spared only one detail—Murishani and his gut-twisting plot to have her carry his child. Not to protect him, no. She would tell Ayla in time. But not when they were so sweetly entangled in his own house. Not when she knew it would disrupt this perfect, quiet moment.

The dragon caused Ayla to place a finger on her lip. "You met two dragons? That's more dragons than I think anyone in the world has met."

"He was wonderful," Flowridia said, sorrow filling her at the memory. She spoke of their brief time together, the vision she witnessed. "I don't know what he saw in my past and future that made him willing to give me the orb. And it haunts me, Ayla. I can't let it go."

"Could you not ask him?"

Flowridia told the rest—that Soliel had come and slain him. "He called me by your name," she admitted, breathless at the thought. Her fingers brushed across Ayla's skin, her focus far away. "He called me 'Flowridia Darkleaf' and said he knew my death."

When she finally met Ayla's gaze, she saw contemplation, but little more. Her guarded countenance remained serene as she said, "Strange."

"I questioned Soliel on it, months later. He wouldn't say anything."

"I don't know that I like the idea of you running into him over and over," Ayla said.

"I have every intention of holding a dagger to his throat if that's what it takes for him to answer my questions," Flowridia said, and she resumed her tale, speaking of Valeuron's gruesome death, of Casvir's inexplicable survival, and of her own accidental victory, when she'd wielded the black orb for a single, blissful act.

Demitri yawned then, coaxing them back to the present. When he stretched, flecks of dirt fell onto the ground.

Ayla kissed Flowridia's cheek. "I look forward to hearing the rest, but in the meantime, I'll take him somewhere to bathe."

Ayla stole a bathrobe from the closet, then left with Demitri. Flowridia dressed, mind spinning from the day. It was so easy, in this windowless room, to pretend the world was well, to let time simply stop. She ought to wait. Ayla would return soon.

Like a sickening siren's song, she looked instead to the false wall opposite the entrance. The beauty of this space led to so much horror beyond, and she could not say why she listened—only that the path beckoned.

The steps were as cold as she remembered. But unlike time past, as she traversed the endless maze, she felt neither fear nor sorrow—simply nothing at all.

Her thoughts merely floated, never settling as she found her quarry. First the chemical stench of death, and then the ominous sign above the magnificent arch—*"The light shall burn away all your fears."*

With the cathedral destroyed along with the city, this construct of horror remained the only living memory of its grandeur. Flowridia stepped into a hall of death, revealing the vile machination of her mad lover's mind. The leather patches upon the wall bore gruesome scenes of demonic gods, and in the pews waited eternal supplicants before the massive construct of horror—Sol Kareena herself, fashioned from the skins of her followers.

Although she had not pledged to the Sun Goddess, Flowridia mourned, the thought of those thousands of lives lost lacerating her heart. Though not in spirit, they were her people in blood. Her father had once been a great name among them, though she had never known him. Casvir had offered her this kingdom, and she had said no.

If she had accepted, would it have spared it this horrific fate? Tears welled in her eyes as she gazed upon the eternally weeping goddess, the construct's tears embroidered with jewels.

Upon the altar was scrawled the elven word for *burn.* Flowridia ran her finger across the script, surely drawn in blood long dried, her heart aching for the self-fulfilling prophecy.

The whole city. Every citizen. Gone. The first of her tears fell as she knelt before the altar, facing the macabre mockery of the goddess. "I'm sorry," she whispered, jaw trembling as she mouthed the words. "If I had known . . ."

But did her words mean anything at all? She sat within a cathedral of death, having resurrected Sol Kareena's great antithesis hardly a day ago. She shut her mouth. Her words would only be an insult.

"Flowra?"

Flowridia knew the voice, not bothering to wipe her eyes before she looked back to Ayla Darkleaf, the architect of this horror, shadowed by an enormous wolf.

Ayla looked right at home among the garlands of entrails and bloodstained floors. In shades of monochrome, save for those brilliant eyes, Ayla was a piece not yet finished, pristine as she aided Flowridia in standing.

Flowridia gazed upon the brutal architecture. "I don't know how to describe in words what I felt when I first discovered this place. Terror, yes. Shock. I was disgusted and horrified, but that still doesn't encapsulate my sorrow."

To her surprise, Ayla crossed her arms, ambivalence in her stance and words. "I like it."

"It's magnificent. There's no denying that. This is who you were—it's who you *are,* and I accept that. I don't understand, but I accept it." Flowridia released a stabilizing breath, praying her words were true. "Even if it's hard."

"I do not have to feel what I do is wrong to acknowledge that others might feel differently," Ayla whispered, utterly unreadable—a closed book in every respect. "Of course you would disapprove—you are pure light, my sweet summer blossom."

Flowridia took Ayla's hand, her tears slowly stilling. "Not to the world, but perhaps still to you." She gazed back up at the statue and released a stabilizing breath, the weight of those deaths heavy upon her tired soul. "Had I known what Casvir intended, I would have gone. I would have presented myself and gained a kingdom. Not a fate I have ever desired, but my life is not worth more than thousands."

"I respectfully disagree," Ayla said, her voice a serpent among a vineyard as she cooed into Flowridia's ear. "And need I remind you that, had you gone, you would not have me?"

The truth of it settled like a thousand shards of glass upon stone. "Casvir is upstairs," Flowridia whispered. "Murishani said so. He said I could help. I *should* help. He's my friend. He's done so much for . . ."

Her words faded away for the stark severity on Ayla's features. "After all you've seen?" Ayla's touch left her hand, instead settling upon her waist, a certain possession in her grip. "My darling, may I say something cruel?"

Dread pulsed through her blood as she nodded.

"You are woefully shortsighted."

Frowning, Flowridia looked to Ayla, seeing merely callused indifference upon her sharp features.

"You claim to care for these people," Ayla continued, the low tonality of her voice melding with the dark atmosphere, "say you might have given up your aspirations to save them, yet you would go and condemn them, all the same. Do you think the war is over, with the capital's destruction? Have you given no thought to the people beyond the walls? There are vast amounts who live in smaller cities and in the country now fearful for their lives, and rightfully so. Nox'Kartha will not cease its march. Its relentless might will fall upon them, and they will be given the choice: surrender or die."

Ayla's gaze left hers for a mere, flickering moment, cast thoughtfully upon the walls. Severity filled her icy gaze. "How many of them do you truly think would forsake their goddess and pledge to the imperator? Some, yes. Those who value their lives and their families. But most will die in Sol Kareena's name. An afterlife of perceived paradise does not change that they are dead. If you aid in healing their fallen oppressor, it will be a matter of days, if not hours, before the army marches again. Not that there is anywhere for them to go, but they have a few weeks to come up with a plan for retaliation—or escape."

"Will he really return without my help?"

"Of course he will. If Murishani is to be believed, he's a lich—and those are damn near unkillable."

The word *lich* was foreign and sparked questions, but for now, Flowridia looked upon the macabre goddess. Fists clenching, she swallowed her tears.

"They're condemned all the same," she whispered. "Funny, how I have the power to ruin the world yet hold no way whatsoever to save it. I hold no influence. Even if I could return, Staelash is a small kingdom. It could not save the Theocracy. It could not stand against Nox'Kartha."

It brought a frightening query. In the fulfillment of her dream, in burying herself to be reborn anew, who was she now?

"What if I could give you that power?"

The statement jarred her from her oppressive spiral of thoughts. Flowridia tore her gaze away from Sol Kareena's visage, only to see cruel calculation upon Ayla's. "Explain yourself."

"Flowra, my darling," Ayla cooed, the darkness of her tone sending shivers down Flowridia's spine, "I have been contemplating a little . . . something." From her hand came the first spark of silver flame. It slowly spread across her arm and body. When it reached her face, she grinned in ecstasy. "The Solviraes were known for all sorts of magic—not just fire. I have been experimenting in my quiet moments with a few more obscure aspects of their powers, to see what I can do. And the results have been gratifying."

She turned, facing away. Unease welled in Flowridia's stomach. "You're making me nervous, but I know you have a plan. You always do."

With meticulous posture, Ayla took several slow steps away, monologuing all the while. "You may recall that your friend, Etolié, shares half the bloodline of Ilune. Her illusion talents are legendary, a birthright from her mother. The Ilune half of her blood doesn't hold those same abilities to nearly the same regard, but many of the Solviraes could conjure at least minor illusions—and I do believe Empress Alauriel was among them."

Ayla's body shifted. Flowridia watched, dumbstruck as the woman turned around—and it was Ayla's wicked grin, her piercing stare, her stance, her poise . . .

But the face and body and hair was Alauriel Solviraes, perfectly recreated, save for that unremitting stare. "What do you think?" she said, and Flowridia felt faint to hear that familiar, sultry croon from Lara's lips. "The magic is easy—it's like drawing, but with only my mind."

Flowridia could manage one breathless word. "Why?"

"At first, because you were fond of her. I have not let that go. I was processing, trying to understand that errant grain of sand in my perfect world. If you needed one last fuck to get her out of your straying mind, I would give you that. I would even playact the part." Lara—Ayla—approached as she spoke her vitriol, her touch confusing when she traced a line across Flowridia's collar bone. "But then it occurred to me, that with Alauriel's body and powers, who was I but Alauriel Solviraes herself? You were worried about what to do with her body, knowing you could never see your friends again without an explanation, but what if that were not necessary at all?"

Lara paused, and Flowridia contemplated her words, deeming them extremely foolish, if not outright stupid. "I hate this."

Glaring, Lara took her hands, those silver eyes all Ayla. "Staelash can do nothing. But Solvira is the greatest kingdom in all the world. Take it. You will have more power than Casvir. You will have the influence to save a nation. I do not propose war, but I do propose . . . *subterfuge.*"

"Need I remind you that Empress Alauriel holds the power?" Every fiber of Flowridia's being reeled at her words, but nothing Ayla said as wrong. "Not me."

"My sweet summer blossom, from what you told me, you had the capacity to whisper a great many things in your Lara's ear. And do not forget I owe you a grand debt." The woman stood on her toes, her lips ghosting Flowridia's as Lara's visage disappeared, becoming the predator she loved. "I do believe they said I was your monster on a leash, yes? Command me, my sweet."

Though they were a siren's call, Flowridia managed to lean away from those thin, perfect lips, step away from that enticing gaze. "I . . ." Her breath caught; Ayla put on the mask of the supplicant, but it was merely that, and Flowridia knew it. "You have everything to gain from this as well."

"Obviously." Bemusement colored Ayla's sultry stare. "If you've read my history, you know I once played the political game for my own gain. I have always wanted to rule the world, so let me have a piece of it. We both win. I see no reason to hesitate."

Yet Flowridia did, for what would this be but a cruel subterfuge? Lara's legacy would not be to have fallen valiantly to the God of Order, no, but something vast and unknown.

But it could save thousands of lives.

"I would be placing my life and Solvira's in your hands," she whispered, and when Ayla frowned, she continued. "Refugees from the Theocracy would live and die at your word—yes, yours. Not mine. You would hold the power to destroy everything, and I wouldn't be able to stop you." She shut her eyes, familiar fear seeping through her limbs. "And what of your plea for me to become like you? What of my so-called fragility? How would you explain to the world the death and rebirth of Lara's beloved?"

"Are you saying you accept?"

The words lingered, thick and weighty.

Rather than answer, she took Ayla's hand. "Come with me?"

Ayla nodded and let herself be led. Demitri followed, silent but always listening. At the back of the blasphemous cathedral waited a door leading to what Flowridia knew once housed horror unbound. Truthfully it still did, but at least nothing here lived anymore.

Ayla's laboratory was a frightening ensemble of brilliance, her sketches of anatomy matchless in their attention to detail, the dissections pinned to the wall perfectly preserved. Upon the slab, the once-victim had become merely a stain. Dress forms of preserved torsos dotted the walls, each with their own gowns in varying states of completion—one stood out, white and embroidered with plants and flowers.

Upon the floor was a ream of discarded cloth, slightly dirtied from harboring Ayla's corpse and touching the floor. Flowridia knelt before it, gently gathering the embroidered, translucent fabric into her arms. She knew its meaning. She knew it matched the incomplete dress. As she stood back up, she hugged it to her body, this spot of beauty in a hellscape of horror.

"What is this?" Flowridia said, though she already knew.

Perhaps Ayla sensed it too, her body slightly hunched as she brushed aside her hair, blacker than ash. "Do you hate it?"

Flowridia gazed upon the embroidered piece, the individual pastel colors perfectly matched, the stitches smaller than a needle's prick. Every flower bore life and personality; this was a treasure, pure art. "No. It's the most beautiful thing I've ever seen."

So rare, to see her proud lover demure. Ayla's eyelashes fluttered as she straightened her stance, her doll lips pulling into a slight smile. To the world, she was a monster; here alone, she was a smitten maiden, shy to accept praise. "I think you know what it is."

"I fear what I may become, Ayla. In throwing away my past life, I have yet to know who I am. If I commit my life to good, am I a good person despite what I've done? If I live a selfish life, does that mean I am wicked? You have begged for me to accept immortality, but I'm scared. There are so many things I don't know." She held the veil to her heart, eyes shut as a single ray of hope shone through her clouded mind. "There is one thing I know. There is a name I desperately crave. If I am to live forever with you, I need a promise of your love."

She cupped Ayla's cheek, stroked that cutting bone with her thumb and said, "Marry me, Ayla Darkleaf. You may turn me on our wedding night."

Ayla stared. Her eyes were as wide as the moon her blood now hailed from, but before Flowridia could worry and recant, she grinned as wicked as her soul. "Done."

Flowridia laughed, unexpected relief flooding her limbs. Before she could speak, Ayla clasped her hands together and stepped away, staring at nothing—a vision in her own mind. "So much work to do. It will be a spectacle, my Flowra. An absolute beacon of a day. Your last day as a mortal should be celebrated—not mourned."

This . . . was not what she'd expected. "I don't know that I want it to be a spectacle."

"It is my wedding too, so at least hear me out." She spread her arms wide, eyes shut in bliss. "A wedding for ages, and you'll be the star. We shall set all your affairs in order first. I acknowledge the sacrifice this is for you, and I will not have you regretting the most important day of our lives. But can you imagine? Oh, you'll be dressed in white, your hair in curls—Flowra, it shall be the greatest celebration this realm has ever known." Pointed fangs grew from her lip, her excitement made manifest. "A wedding day for you . . . and a night for me."

"Are you proposing I wed Lara?"

"No, I'm proposing you wed me, but let me have some fun. Let Solvira pay for it. Let me give you the crown you deserve."

Flowridia stole a deep breath. "Will this make you happy?"

"Exquisitely so. And the moment it goes wrong, we run. Who can stop us?"

Flowridia's objection died in her throat. "Explain."

"We live a while as rulers of the greatest empire in the world. We rescue the people you feel responsible for, providing a haven for any refugees who cross our borders. We wed, and it is the most beautiful day of our lives. I turn you, and it's the greatest tragedy the world has ever known." She placed a dramatic hand upon her forehead. "The empress and her new bride—attacked on their wedding night by a monster—perhaps even The Endless Night, given my presence upon the world will surely be known soon. But Lara loves you all the same, you remain the vampiric Empress Consort, and when it finally all falls apart, whether it be days or years from now, you and I disappear into the sunset as wife and wife. Someday it will surely fall to ruin, but let us revel in the meantime," Ayla cooed, trailing her finger down Flowridia's sternum. "Love your friends. Say goodbye. Leave no regrets in your mortal life. The adventure of a lifetime awaits us, and we shall live our perfect life with all the pieces put neatly in place."

Swallowing her better judgement, Flowridia said, "Fine. We'll do it. You'll need to work on your voice, though—you sound nothing like Lara."

"Spectacular!" Ayla planted a kiss on her cheek, then carefully took the wedding veil from her hands. She threw it over Flowridia's head, giggling cutely all the while. "All shall be well, Flowra."

Flowridia didn't quite believe her, but as she gazed at her love from beneath the veil, she felt the first spark of genuine joy.

She would do this for Ayla, for the refugees of the Theocracy of Sol Kareena—for the people she could not save otherwise.

And she would be lying if she said it was not a little bit for herself.

Chapter 7

"Oh, Lara—we have been so worried!"

The gleaming, shining towers of the Glass Palace cast a wide shadow, but not nearly as wide as the grin spreading across Lara's face. She made a show of placing a hand over her heart, of summoning tears to fall down her cheeks.

Flowridia knew she loved every moment of it.

When the older woman embraced her, her own tears falling fast, Lara returned the gesture with one arm, keeping Flowridia's hand held in her own. "There is much to tell you," the false empress said.

Flowridia didn't know the older woman greeting them, but her robes suggested both finery and Sol Kareena worship. "When Coal and General Irons returned without you," the woman said, "we feared the worst."

Lara made of show of gasping. "They have returned?"

"Are they all right?" Flowridia asked, stepping beside them. She had prepared Ayla for everything she could think of . . . The fate of their party hadn't been among it. "Where are they?"

"In the infirmary. Neither are in good form," the woman admitted, and she shook her head. "But they will live."

The lift descended then, and a man Flowridia recalled as Magister Reginal appeared, relief apparent on his elderly features. He had the darkest skin she had ever seen on a man, juxtaposing delightfully with his long, snow white beard. "Lara, you've given us all a scare. General Irons told us a harrowing tale."

When he offered a hug, Lara accepted, her smile feigning worry. "There is nothing to worry about anymore.

But we do have a story for you. I think a council meeting is in order."

"Etolié asked to be informed of your return. With your assistance, we would happily bring her here."

"I am afraid I'm not in the health to do that," Lara said, feigning despondence, though only Flowridia could sense her subtle dramatics. "I shall explain why in the meeting."

Reginal nodded, though warily. "I can try something else, then. I shall meet with you in a few minutes."

Hand in hand, Flowridia, Lara, and Demitri followed the old woman to a circular room, and Flowridia was stunned at the beautiful décor. Brilliant tapestries colored the windowless space, and above the crescent moon shaped table, fluttering, glowing lights lit the enclosed ceiling. Demitri managed to fit behind them and sat himself on the floor.

"My name is Jules," the old woman said, offering a hand to Flowridia. "High Priestess of Sol Kareena to this kingdom. Etolié has spoken highly of you and your talents."

When Flowridia accepted, she smiled, flattered to know Etolié spoke of her at all. "Thank you. I can only hope I live up to the image."

"General Irons says you are a powerful necromancer," Jules said, and Flowridia genuinely couldn't say if she was being tested, but she did know Jules was condensing what had likely been an expletive-filled rant.

"I do hold some talent, yes," Flowridia replied. "But I take more pride in healing arts."

"There is something you must be told," Jules said, and she launched into a harrowing tale, one Flowridia pretended not to know—of the City of Light's destruction, though she shed further light on Etolié and Sora's fate.

"Oh, Etolié," Lara said, her hand covering her mouth. "I had forgotten about the funeral in all this madness. Of course she would have been there."

"She and High Priestess Sora both, yes. We have yet to know the full scope of the damage," Jules said.

Flowridia swore Lara's perfect control slipped for just a moment, revealing confusion. But the beginning of a plan stirred in Flowridia's head. "You said Lunestra is in Staelash?"

"Yes. We have yet to decide where to take her."

Reginal entered, carrying what appeared to be a small scroll. "Etolié is prepared to join us."

Behind him followed General Irons, who looked unharmed but likely only because of the castle healers. His sneer immediately fell upon Flowridia, but he said nothing, merely took his seat.

"General Irons," Lara said, smiling with charm at the glowering man, "I'm glad you could be here. I was distraught to hear of your injuries."

"Whatever I'm feeling, I had no intention of missing a debriefing," he said, curt and formal. "I am grateful to know of your survival." His condemning gaze returned to Flowridia, though he said nothing else.

Reginal dropped the small scroll, and as it unraveled, it cast a beam of light. Flowridia had seen nothing like it before, gasping slightly when Etolié's form appeared within, glowing like the illusion it was.

But more alarming than that—Etolié immediately burst into tears. "Oh, thank fucking Eionei's Asshole, you really are alive!"

Flowridia swallowed her discomfort at the words—for they were unquestionably a lie, and only a taste of Etolié's anguish when their ruse inevitably came to light.

Lara stepped forward, gently caressing the figment's hand. Not true touch, but the gesture remained. "All is well, Etolié."

"And *you!*" Etolié turned a withering gaze onto Flowridia, though tears still streamed down her face. "I'm fucking furious, but I love you."

Flowridia recoiled at the words. "Why?"

"All right—pausing the heartfelt reunion now." Etolié took a deep breath, and Flowridia had the sinking understanding that she was about to be interrogated. "You stole an orb."

"I did," she muttered. There was no use in denying it.

"Where is it?"

Flowridia's hands gripped the other, and she silently cursed Ayla for her insistence on returning. "Soliel stole it."

"Oh, did he now," Etolié said, audibly pained.

"You might've known he was involved, if you hadn't screamed at me on the mirror—which he destroyed."

"It's replaceable." Etolié crossed her arms. "You two went to find an orb. Which orb?"

Flowridia braced herself. "I felt an orb in a swamp. I stole the blue orb so I could find it—"

"Why didn't you ask for help?"

"You had enough to worry about, with the Archbishop's death—"

"You stole it before that."

She had. Flowridia pursed her lips, desperately trying to summon a lie, when Lara coughed. "Etolié, she came to me because she knew I was the only one who could help. There were layers and layers of protections within the swamp, and only the Silver Fire had the capacity to absorb them."

"That doesn't explain why there were suddenly *seven* orbs. Math doesn't lie, Flowers."

"It was a trap," Lara continued, and now Etolié closed her mouth, "set by the God of Order, seeking to lure another orb to him. We found this out when he attacked us."

Etolié's frown was permanently etched, it seemed. "I did see a spectacularly large flash of silver light. Anything to do with that?"

"It was an awful battle," Lara said, and she waxed poetic on a fight she hadn't fought, spinning an elaborate tale for Etolié and the Solviran Council. She spoke with her hands as well as her voice, and Flowridia realized she'd need to have a conversation about Lara's typical body language—given she wasn't a dancer, nor one for dramatics, and thus would move with significantly less grace and flourish.

But as she spoke, Flowridia remembered it all. A star gone supernova; Lara had blown herself to pieces. That light, bright as she had ever seen, and then gone so suddenly—like Lara herself.

Emotion struck her, but she wrestled it aside. To feel Ayla's cold hand on her shoulder gave the cruelest of reminders, but she could not regret, not now, not when her vampiric love had kissed her lips and held her only an hour before.

And so, she remained frozen all the while, though the rest seemed enraptured. "If it were not for Flowra," Lara continued, "I would have succumbed to my injuries. However, she pulled me from the brink of death. It took time for me to recover, but we returned as soon as I was capable of travel."

"You still seem a little roughed up," Etolié said, genuine worry on her features. "Your voice is different. I'm worried you're getting sick."

"Oh, very likely," Lara replied, adding a purposeful gravel to her voice.

"There was a casualty in all of this," Flowridia said, recalling their script. "Lara..." She braced herself, willing herself to relay the agreed upon lie. "...is suffering from memory loss."

"The powers I drew from," Lara affirmed, nodding gravely, "have affected me in ways we couldn't have foreseen. Flowridia is correct; much of my memory is damaged. I have done my best to compensate, but forgive me if I am lost in my own home for a time." She offered a humorless chuckle. Flowridia was astounded at the sincerity of the performance. A thousand years, and Ayla's best skill might still be her capacity for lies and acting.

"Lara, won't you let me look you over?" High Priestess Jules implored. She leaned forward, withered hands clasping each other. "Perhaps I can help you."

"You really ought to." General Irons made no effort to hide his disdain. "Make sure there's nothing *lingering* that shouldn't be there."

Lara waved away the words. "What's done is done. With each day, little bits return. It will simply take time. But if there is anything drastic, I certainly won't be a stranger."

"In any case," Magister Reginal said, staring off at space, "we should gather our defenses and start an investigation. The God of Order has five orbs, and we should be prepared for him to retaliate."

"Honestly," Etolié said, and all turned to look at her, "the dragon is likely the best defense we could have for any of the orbs. Now it's just a matter of getting the rest back."

"What dragon?" Flowridia asked.

"Casvir's dragon. Her name is now Kitty. You could have told us he had an orb."

Condemnation rightfully colored Etolié's tone. For once, Flowridia settled on the truth. "I was a coward. It was the artifact he used me to find."

"At least you're honest sometimes."

"The God of Order is not our most pressing concern," Lara said, more muted than before. Flowridia squeezed her cold hand. "Despite what he did to me, there is the matter of the war. What happened to the Theocracy is distressing." She turned aside, dramatic as ever, but this had been all but recited before they'd arrived. "Priestess Jules said that Archbishop Lunestra is in Staelash. Send her here. Solvira is much better equipped to protect her."

Whatever Flowridia's reservation toward the archbishop, the woman was a part of the people she had vowed to save. However, the rest of the council looked less certain. "It's a good deed, assuredly," Reginal said, "but I fear what we would be tying our country into."

"Send the orphans as well," Lara continued, ignoring his remark. "Unless you're willing to accept the task of rehoming them. I have no doubt Imperator Casvir would destroy them from spite if he found them."

"Lara," Reginal said, exasperation coloring his tone, "as I said, Nox'Kartha would not take this lightly."

"We do not tell them." Lara held out her hands, silently asking for a rebuttal. "Imperator Casvir is busy repairing himself as we speak—when he finally awakens, he may ask Staelash where she's gone, but if they say she's elsewhere, he will not attack them. They have a treaty." She turned to Etolié. "We will take her, at least for a short while. Let me sort out the details."

"That's kind of you, Moonbeam," Etolié said, though she sounded uncertain as well. "I'm trusting your wisdom."

"I have the beginnings of a plan."

Reginal sighed and said, "Let me see if I can help you conjure a portal. It would be far safer for the archbishop to come here through magic than by carriage—"

Etolié's scattered brain suddenly blurted out a change of subject. "The slave camp! Where's the slave camp?"

Lara's chuckle brought to memory fangs and coy grins. Nothing of the late empress in the gesture. Flowridia would have to reprimand her later. "Be assured, Etolié, there is nothing left of the encampment. Send an envoy if you wish, to study the remains. What matters is my—*Flowra's* familiar is safe."

Flowridia felt certain that everyone noticed the slip. Judging by the smile spreading across Lara's face, she suspected it was no accident.

"My friends," Lara began, letting her fingers slide from Flowridia's shoulder. She moved behind her chair, grabbing the sides with her small hands. "There is another matter I should draw some attention to; a matter that I feel will surprise none of you." A regal laugh escaped her throat this time, purposeful and perfect in its mimicry. "Flowra and I fostered the beginnings of a relationship back during Marielle's wedding, but what feelings had been kindled have only continued to grow." She stepped to the side, taking Flowridia's hand. "I make no assumptions for the future, but she makes me happy." The sweet sincerity in the statement was no act. Those silver eyes glistened.

The others at the table watched with interest—Etolié in particular, one eyebrow quirked. Reginal looked nearly as radiant as Lara, but General Irons' glare turned more severe. Even Jules' smile had suddenly fallen, clearly painted.

"So, to settle any gossip, we are courting," Lara continued, pride lacing her tone. "And all I can hope for is your support."

"I have seen you smile more in the days spent with her than in all the months following your father's death," Magister Reginal said, his smile endlessly happy.

A cough interrupted his statement. "This is a council matter," Irons said sharply. "May we speak as strictly a council?"

Lara twisted her grin to a dangerous degree. "I don't believe it's presumptuous to say that Flowra may soon be joining our council."

"My point stands. I request we speak in private."

"General Irons—"

"Lara," Flowridia said softly, capturing Lara's gaze. "He's right. I'll leave; I don't mind."

When Flowridia stood, Lara pulled her close, planting an innocent kiss on her cheek. It brought a blush, along with a vicious glower from across the table. "Wait outside," Lara cooed.

"Of course." With Demitri close behind, Flowridia stepped into the expansive hallway. Once it shut, she placed an ear to the door, unsurprised to hear absolutely nothing.

Demitri's voice interrupted her plotting. *So Etolié gets to stay, but not us?*

"I think Etolié is on the council."

General Irons isn't doing much in regards to self-preservation.

"That's what I'm afraid of," Flowridia whispered, stroking the fur on his neck. "I don't need to hear; she'll rant all about it."

Before or after she strings him up by his bowels?

"Creative, aren't you." She bit her lip, staring at the door. "Hopefully before." Grimacing, she took Demitri's face in her hands and kissed his nose. "You've grown."

Golden eyes studied her. *So have you. I think that might be the secret.*

"I'm the same size, dearest Demitri."

No, but your power has grown. With a sly slip of his tongue, he returned the gesture, kissing her on the nose. *Just a thought.*

"Perhaps I'll ask Ayla to help us figure out the correlation between your growth and mine."

You should ask her. It'll give Lady Ayla something to distract herself from all the people she could be sewing.

A pained groan escaped her throat. "You know, Demitri, the fact that you're always right hurts me."

The doors opened a few minutes later with Lara the first to emerge. She held a smile, but Flowridia saw ice freezing it in place. To her surprise, Lara shut the door behind her. "They wish to discuss the matter further, in private."

"Ay-Lara," Flowridia said, cursing her slip. Slips like that burned kingdoms to the ground. "Lara, let's talk."

"What's there to discuss, my sweet summer blossom?" Lara stepped forward and took Flowridia's hands in her own, kissing them before planting a third on her lips. "Our wedding will commence. That is what matters."

Flowridia moved to interlace their fingers. She squeezed affectionately, holding her attention. "There was bound to be opposition. General Irons—"

"Irons may object all he'd like," Lara cooed, a vicious grin spreading across her face. Murder glinted in her silver eyes, and Flowridia saw the cracks in the façade. Perhaps it was Lara's face, but it was all Ayla, all fury.

Flowridia leaned in close and whispered, "If you kill him, they'll think it was me. And I suspect he would happily die for that cause."

The truth of the statement settled between them both, and the tension in Lara's stance ebbed. "What do you propose instead?"

"First, we go somewhere private," Flowridia replied, glancing quickly at the closed door. "Then, we kill it with kindness. Now that I'm staying, I'll be forced to interact with him, but I don't think he'll pose any physical danger."

"The moment he does," Lara said, voice seething, "I will bake his organs into treats for Demitri."

She's so thoughtful.

"No one is going to be baked," Flowridia said, her glare set on Demitri.

The double doors creaked open. The Magister was the first to appear, and from within she saw General Irons standing with obvious pain. "I apologize for that," Magister Reginal said quietly. "Etolié and I agree that Lady Flowridia is a bright spot in your life."

"Time will sway the rest, I am certain," Lara replied, and she graced the magister with as sweet a smile as Flowridia had ever seen. "I need to take care of something. Would you escort Flowra to my bedroom? I shall join her shortly."

Reginal gave a slow nod, clearly confused by the request. "Of course, Lara," he said, and he gestured for Flowridia to follow.

Flowridia did not quite understand what her ruse was but followed along. At the lift, Reginal spared a frown for Demitri. "He's a bit large for the lift, but I shall happily summon him once we've arrived." He stared a moment longer, curiosity in his words as he said, "Will your familiar need his own room?"

Flowridia looked to Demitri, who stared right back. *Well I do need somewhere to go while you and Lady Ayla have your naked time.*

"Demitri would love his own room," Flowridia replied, resisting the urge to roll her eyes at his turn of phrase.

She and Reginal stepped into the lift, which quickly rose, her stomach unsettled at the motion. Up they went, and Flowridia counted floors. The Magister remained quiet, purposefully avoiding eye contact.

"We will have to expand the lifts," he muttered, staring out the window. Below, the city expanded in every direction, bustling with life. "For your wolf, I mean. I don't believe it's presumptuous to think you will be staying with us for some time."

Heat filled Flowridia's cheeks. When she glanced at the Magister, a slight smile rested upon his face.

"I mean it when I say she's happier than I've seen in years," he continued, the lift stopping at the appropriate floor. Flowridia matched his footsteps as he escorted her out. "When her father died, Lara all but shut herself away. But with you, I think she might finally heal."

Flowridia forced a smile at that, the panging guilt of her ruse striking her stomach. To think of Lara, vibrant and happy, only brought memories of her bloody and cold in the dank swamp.

He escorted her to a set of elegant, carved wooden doors. Within, the darkened room lit at their entrance. Glowing crystals dotted the walls, casting shadows on the tapestry bed. A desk and several bookshelves covered an entire wall, and an ajar door led to what she could see was a washroom. Rich, comfortable, and appropriately royal, Lara's bedroom promised luxury.

There, on the desk, sat a familiar bouquet of flowers, gifted long ago as a warning. Flowridia's blood chilled in her veins.

"I presume Lara will join you shortly," Magister Reginal said as he gestured forward. "But if you need anything all, don't be shy. I will have the room next door made up for your familiar and bring him there."

She gave her thanks as he exited. Her steps tread silently upon the dark wood floor, wary of the ghosts she might awaken—metaphorical or not. The bookshelf alone held boundless treasures; so many spellbooks and scrolls, books on history and science. Flowridia marveled at each one, knowing Lara must have read and cherished them all.

The damned bouquet stared like an omen, but what could she do? Throw it away, perhaps. It seemed so cruel to be rid of it.

She emptied her pocket of its one valuable possession—her small piece of maldectine, once piercing Lara's back. The barest hints of blood had dried upon the tip, and Flowridia quickly shoved it into a drawer, hating the reminders it brought, wishing her bracelet had not been taken by the slavers.

Alone, she sat upon a worn chair by the bookshelf and drew her legs to her chest. Lara had sat here. Lara lived a lifetime here.

She shut her eyes, the vivid image of a red-streaked, mutilated body dangling just behind her eyelids.

Her hands stiffened, clutching the armrests of the chair. How many more would die for this? Worn leather creaked under her nails, the dead flesh against her skin drawing an eerie reminder of the cold body resting beneath a meadow of tulips.

At least half an hour passed before Lara appeared from the shadow of the bookshelf, and for a moment Flowridia forgot the illusion, saw the empress herself and felt dread. But when her eyes rested on Flowridia, they were silver but not soft. No, this was the gaze of her love. "I didn't know where her bedroom was," she said simply. "So, thank you for indulging me." Lara's form swirled away in a cloud of glistening smoke.

Ayla's visage could topple kingdoms from mere terror, that predatory grin matched only by the intensity in her pale blue eyes—flecked with the barest hints of silver around the pupils. For Flowridia, however, it soothed her troubled heart, and when Ayla neared, she pulled the undead woman into her lap. She rested her head against Ayla's slight chest, no heartbeat to distract her from the comfort she drew from the cold embrace.

"Where were you?" Flowridia asked.

"Reginal and I were caught up in something. Nothing concerning."

"You need to reconsider your cadence of speech," Flowridia said. "You don't sound at all like Lara."

"Lara was a royal," Ayla cooed, her fingers stroking through the thick locks of hair. "Royals speak with flair."

"Lara was a royal, yes, but not nearly so illustrious." Flowridia sat up enough to see her lover's face and chuckled at her obvious aggrieve. "You sound like you. I adore your words. But you sound like a well-educated elf speaking a second language—not a Solviran noble speaking her first."

"Fine, fine." Ayla rolled her eyes, and Flowridia fought a grin. "I will mask better, because you are right."

She laid her head back down against Ayla's hollow, cold chest. Ayla's fingers resumed their tender motions, and Flowridia hummed contentedly into her skin. "Forgive me if I misheard," Ayla muttered, "but did they mean to imply that Sora Fireborn is alive?"

Flowridia's good mood immediately evaporated, replaced by stark realization. "Sol Kareena resurrected her, after slaying you."

Unquestionable perturb settled on Ayla's countenance. "Insulting. Do you want me to try again?"

"I would prefer to let it go. I've forgiven her and moved on."

"Whatever you say," Ayla continued, and then she softened by small degrees. "We have a beautiful home here."

"The magister believes I'll be staying. I think he approves."

Dark laughter met her ears. "I am determined to make them love you. With some, it will not be so difficult. Etolié even spoke in our favor." Her tone took a turn, menace caressing each smooth word. "Others may take some convincing. The High Priestess smiles but I know a viper when I see one. And we need not speak more of General Irons. They do not trust you. They expressed dissatisfaction with you knowing the location of the Theocracy's Archbishop given your ties to Nox'Kartha—personally, I think it would be easier to wipe the slate clean. We are a new monarchy, and we deserve a new council."

Flowridia attempted to sit up, but that cold hand held her enthralled. "Ayla," she whispered, shutting her eyes, "I don't want anyone else to die."

Pursed, mocking lips drew into a smile. "And what will you do when you join me in death? Death is inevitable, my sweet summer blossom, and you'll have to cause a few, if you want to live forever."

Teeth grit, Flowridia's gaze sharpened. "If that's fate, I reject it. You said yourself once that you didn't have to kill them, that your victims didn't even feel it if you tried. Perhaps I won't be as strong as Mereen and never touch mortal blood, but I have no intention of—" She bit back her next words, for they had been harsh.

Ayla watched warily, defensive as her mouth twisted into a frown, promising castigation. "Of what? Becoming like me?"

"That's not what—"

"It's what you meant," Ayla purred, yet it held cold cruelty.

The tension between them stretched long, slowly boiling. "I—" Flowridia shut her mouth; anything she might say would only escalate this. "I don't want to fight with you."

Tension settled between them. Flowridia drew herself away, meeting no resistance as she left Ayla's embrace. Standing now, she mulled over her words, resigned to the trap she had dug for herself.

Becoming like Ayla . . . Wasn't it inevitable?

Would her humanity slowly trickle away?

Behind her, Ayla shifted, and Flowridia remained still as sharp nails coaxed along her gown—not tearing, but the threat remained, intentional or not. "I don't typically waste time articulating my feelings," Ayla said, menace in her gaze when she came to face her. "Usually I just kill whoever's frustrating me."

Flowridia frowned, hands clenched behind her back. "Is that a threat?"

"No. It's an observation. Do you think you're better than me, Flowra?"

"I—"

"Do you think you're stronger?"

The question was a trick, Flowridia knew, just like the last. She said nothing, merely waited for Ayla to finish.

"First you give your pretty speech about love and acceptance—but faced with the prospect of immortality, you suddenly have the audacity to judge me?"

Flowridia hoped her glare was scathing enough, but the prickling, uncomfortable sensation of *truth* coexisted with her rising anger. "I'm not judging you," she said evenly, forcing her voice to remain steady, "and I'm sorry you felt like I was. I see how that happened, and it wasn't my intention."

"Then what is it? If it is not judgement, then what am I seeing?"

Flowridia looked her in the eye, the temptation to yell still virulently strong. Instead, she breathed it out. "You're seeing fear. My fear. Fear of the unknown."

Ayla remained in her proud stance, but her anger had gone. "Why?"

"I'm scared, Ayla," Flowridia said, hating how vulnerable she sounded, hating the emotions rising in her throat. "I'm going to do this because I agreed to do this. This is the inevitable conclusion; I know. You're completely right that someday I'll die and you'll be alone, and I don't want that. I don't want to leave you alone. But it doesn't mean there are not a thousand unknowns I've been keeping at arm's length. The fact remains that I don't know how I'll be as a vampire. You're right—I don't know what the bloodlust feels like, so I can't stand here and judge. I'm afraid of so many things, but I think the greatest one is knowing you'll have full and complete power over me, and no matter how much I trust you—that terrifies me."

Flowridia blinked, tears misting her vision of Ayla— who looked entirely cut off at the knees. She shuffled forward, awkward as she pulled Flowridia against her. So terribly out of character, and Flowridia nearly laughed despite herself. "Flowra, I . . . I did not realize."

"I didn't tell you," Flowridia whispered. "I don't think I really understood it myself."

Ayla rested her head against the crux of Flowridia's neck, managing to be the one holding her, despite her smaller frame. "You raise an interesting point. Let me think on this."

They lingered in silence, and Flowridia felt more weighed down than before, having admitted to them both that she was afraid.

"Flowra, my darling . . ." When Ayla faced her again, her countenance familiar yet gloriously new after so many months apart, she resumed her proud stance, her radiant confidence blinding and bright. "In the meantime, we have this beautiful palace housing gardens of grand beauty, a luxurious bed, access to every sort of rich cuisine . . ." Her smile twisted, bearing conspiracy. "The question remains of which you'll choose to indulge in first."

Flowridia smiled, nearly laughing, because Ayla was inexplicable and charming in strange and endearing ways. She leaned in to kiss her love, content to let the world fade away.

But she kept it chaste, lest it escalate—rather, lest it escalate on terms she hadn't yet set. Their lips parted, and she sorted her conflicted feelings. "I'm afraid of so many things, Ayla," she admitted, yet her dread faded away to say it, lost in that drawing gaze. "I'd like to forget them." Her voice lowered, though she felt suddenly shy to say what she wanted . . . if she could even articulate it. "Tonight, I want to be afraid of only you."

Confusion marred her love's visage. Flowridia grabbed Ayla's hands and placed them on her breasts.

"I see," Ayla said, and for a moment she chuckled, and Flowridia feared a moment she was being mocked, only for Ayla to suddenly steal her lips, content to consume her whole. Ayla touched her, seizing control, her hand twisting in Flowridia's hair to hold her thrall. They kissed, and it was not loving no—but *raw.*

Oh, her desire brewed quickly. Ayla's roaming hands caused her to moan, to sigh, and when she met Ayla's eyes, a rush of need coursed through her blood at those blown pupils. Only a faint ring of ice surrounded the expanding black holes, and Flowridia was helpless in their orbit.

Arms wrapped around her form and lifted her with ease. Ayla carried Flowridia to the neatly made bed, dropping her and crawling on top of her. Her slight form carried almost no weight, yet her unholy strength kept Flowridia dominated utterly. Bruises would surely appear at her wrists, but she did not care—in fact, she would love them, cherish the proof of their lovemaking. She sighed, gasping at the teeth marking her neck. With pain came pleasure, and desperate words escaped her lips. "Ayla, Ayla, I'm—" Her own cry broke her stumbled attempt at speech. "I'm ready. Take me, Ayla."

Ayla's face appeared in her vision. "Already?"

Heat colored Flowridia's cheeks. "It's the hair thing," she admitted, biting her lip. She blinked prettily, shy as Ayla quirked an eyebrow. "You pulled my hair."

Ayla laughed, her claws withdrawing from Flowridia's wrists. "Oh, Flowra," she managed, shaking from her own laughter, "how you amuse me."

Flowridia frowned, her pulse suddenly loud in her ears. "Do I?" Ayla continued her hysterical giggling, wiping a tear from her eye. Self-conscious, Flowridia attempted to pull herself away.

A hand suddenly wrapped around her neck. Flowridia could mostly breathe, but nails scraped the soft skin. Ayla's joyous outburst quickly twisted into menace, her smile growing much too wide. Fangs elongated from her lips; her eyes turning black. "Darling, if a little fight is all it takes for you to spread your legs, I will gladly comply."

The nightmarish stare left her limbs feeling cold and what lay between her legs burning hot. "Yes, please," Flowridia said, and her ensuing cry cut off when Ayla pressed her into the pillow.

Ayla leered with pointed fangs as her fingers slid up to grab Flowridia's hair. Her grip tightened, twisting sharply. Their gaze met, the force between them thick enough to slice with one of Ayla's knives.

A pathetic whine passed through her lips. Flowridia's hands grabbed the sheets, her breathing labored. Ayla's mouth crushed her own; teeth scraped her lip. Flowridia's numb hands reached up to encircle Ayla's back, embracing her captor in a shaking embrace.

Ayla suddenly released; Flowridia's vision spun as blood rushed to her head. Her shirts rustled as Ayla dove underneath. Hands brushed her thighs. Teeth bit at her hip.

Ayla tugged her underclothes away, and the first caress of her tongue against Flowridia's vulva was bliss.

Rough, cold fingers slid inside her. Lips encircled her aching bud, and Ayla's tongue made skilled work of the tender nerves. With each thrust, Flowridia's moans grew more desperate. It wasn't enough. It was never enough. *"Harder, please,"* she begged, and Ayla complied. Perhaps she would tear apart, but the deeper she felt Ayla move, the closer she felt to absolute ecstasy. Close, so close, and the whispered words, *"Ayla, I love you,"* fluttered from her lips.

Her pleasure peaked, stars passing her vision as her body arched at the force of her orgasm. Still, Ayla moved; her tongue made easy work of her desperate form.

It wasn't until Flowridia slowed that Ayla matched her, lingering a moment before her head appeared from under her skirt. Her grin remained, but her eyes practically glistened. Reverence carried each weighted word. "Flowridia, my love, my heart, how I long to face eternity with you."

Ayla's fingers twisted gently as she removed them from Flowridia's body. Though her head still swam, Flowridia smiled sweetly, and when Ayla's weight rested beside her, she placed a kiss on those flush lips. "Can I ask . . . Is *this* something you want? Something rougher?"

Ayla made no effort to cover her wince. "If that's what you want, I will do it, but pain is not gratifying for me."

A blush filled Flowridia's cheeks. "Sorry if that bothered you . . ." Her words trailed away at Ayla's slight shake of her head. "I can only count on two hands the amount of times I've had sex. I'm still learning what's normal."

"I am confident there's nothing I haven't tried at least once," Ayla replied, her grin positively lurid. She sat up, making of show of removing her dress, revealing her sensuous figure. "We have nothing standing in our way tonight, and while I cannot speak for you, I greatly look forward to knowing your beautiful body as well as I know my own."

Something in her turn of phrase made Flowridia's stomach flutter. Her blush surely darkened. "I desperately want to know yours too," she shyly said, and with no preamble Ayla placed Flowridia's hand between her legs, the wetness brewing from her cunt already dripping.

"Just in case you questioned how much I adore making love to you," Ayla said with a wink.

Flowridia hadn't, but she relished the invitation, content to savor her well into the night.

Chapter 8

Etolié shut the door behind her after an awkward meeting. Lunestra had agreed to go to Solvira. Now it was a matter of packing up the children's minimal belongings—gifted by Staelash—and getting them ready to go.

With a heavy sigh, Etolié all but fell against her invisible Beefcake waiting in the hallway. Lacking the emotional fortitude to keep her hidden, Etolié's magic faltered. Khastra flickered into sight.

"What is wrong? Did it go badly?"

Etolié shook her head. "It's all fine."

She couldn't actually say the plan. Khastra had insisted she not. The less she knew, the less Casvir could torture out of her later—as she had so reassuringly put it.

"But Lunestra's heartbroken," Etolié continued, "and she's bottling it up. It doesn't take an empath to feel that." She forced a smile. "Time to deliver the verdict."

Thalmus, that mother of a man, had moved beds from the various guest suites into one large one so the orphaned children could stay together. When Etolié came near, she already heard the screaming giggles children often emitted, and when she opened the door, a few of the older ones had taken to smacking each other with pillows. "Calm down, kiddos," Etolié said, casting glitter from her hands to draw their focus. "Chosen of Eionei, here—gotta make an announcement."

They mostly obeyed—except for Ceile, Etolié's secret favorite, who ran toward her and grabbed her leg. But she was only three, and Etolié forgave three-year-olds for not having perfect attention spans. She shut the door, leaving Khastra out, then lifted Ceile up, supporting the little girl with her hip and arms. "We have a new home for you lovelies—Solvira is going to take you in. You'll get to stay in a castle—"

Some of the older children gasped at that. Ceile stopped sucking her thumb long enough to ask, "Do we get to meet a princess?"

"No princesses, but there is a very nice empress who I'm certain would love to meet you." As well as Flowers, who Etolié had no doubt would charm them through sheer princess aura. "She's going to find you all somewhere safe to stay."

The mood among the children was of radiance, but not of joy. "But what about Priestess Lunestra?" one asked.

The pang in Etolié's gut came in tandem with the door creaking open. "Oh, I don't—I don't actually know—"

"It's all right, Magister Etolié," came a familiar voice, and Lunestra herself came up beside her. "I'll explain. It would be better coming from me."

Etolié nodded, the weighted mood suddenly more than her limited emotional capacity wished to try and handle. She squeezed Ceile tight, smiling when the girl returned the hug, and handed her to the Archbishop, who stepped forward into the circle of children. "I love each and every one of you dearly," she began, and Etolié took that as her cue to leave.

As Lunestra gathered them together, bidding them to sit in a circle around her, Etolié quietly shut the door behind her.

In the hallway, Khastra pulled Etolié into her side. "She is the only mother many of them ever knew," the half-demon said softly, perhaps sensing Etolié's discomfort. "While they could have been adopted out, some might have chosen to stay and become priests and priestesses to Sol Kareena."

"That's one way to indoctrinate the next generation," Etolié said, trying very hard to be blasé and failing. "It's . . . It's not fair. They've lost their home, their people, and now they have to lose the only family they've ever known. It's for the greater good; I get that. It's the only way they can be safe from Tyrant Deathless. If they're separated, there's no way for him to find them, but . . ." She shut her eyes, gritting her jaw. She would not cry for this.

She would get angry.

"Orphans have always been the price of war," Khastra said, her hand gently grazing Etolié's shoulder. "Children are innocent, no matter what side of the battle lines they were born on or the sins of the parents, yet they pay the greatest cost."

Etolié swallowed, fists clenched. "There's nothing I can do."

"You are the reason they get to live at all. That is enough."

"It's not, though!" She bit back her words, too loud for the late hour. "I haven't saved them at all. I've saved them from death for now, but now I'm tossing them into the unknown."

"It is enough, Etolié," Khastra said, both her hands on Etolié's shoulders. "It is enough. You are enough. There are more battles coming, and you will not be able to fight them if you stay and hold their hands until the end. No one ever saved the world alone—and it is all right to release them into someone else's care."

Etolié shut her eyes, a small smile tugging at her lips when Khastra's lips brushed her hair. "I'm tucking these feelings into a box now."

"Very good. We can open it when you are ready."

With a final thought for the children, Etolié released a small sigh and slumped. "Back to business. We have a Goddess to research."

Holding hands, Khastra pulled her along, then suddenly scooped her up. Etolié's shriek turned quickly into a giggle, and then into a soft sigh when Khastra kissed her lips, still walking. "Couldn't wait, Beefcake?"

"I have waited long enough," Khastra replied, her smile unbearably tender. "I will waste no time now."

They kissed; Khastra walked. It turned out that kissing and walking meant that neither of them were paying attention because the next thing Etolié knew, she was squished between Beefcake and an even larger half-giant rounding the corner.

Thalmus flinched. Etolié would have fallen had Khastra's grip not been so inspirationally tight. They stared at each other a moment, all parties fully aware of what had just transpired, judging by the shock on Thalmus' face. "Hi," Etolié said, and the half-giant merely glanced between them.

Thalmus was taller than Khastra, though not by much, but any height larger than Khastra was impressive. He lacked her definition, years of indoor work and a quiet life spent glassblowing having softened what was once probably an impressive physique. "I didn't realize you two had become so close," he said simply, and all he gave to Khastra was a nod.

"It's a new thing."

"Clearly."

Thalmus stepped past them, and Etolié nearly let him go, content to give him a wide berth, but there was news. "Flowers is in Solvira," Etolié said, knowing he would care very much to hear it.

He did stop at that, his dark eyes watchful as he waited for more.

"She's officially courting Empress Alauriel."

His expression softened, and were they even remotely friendly, she might have told him it was cute. "Good," he said, that fatherly reminiscence filling his countenance.

This time, when he turned to leave, Etolié let him. "Anyway. Library?"

Khastra wasted no time, though she did refrain from kissing her until the door had successfully closed behind them. Etolié loved the smell of books and booze, but not as much as she adored the taste of Khastra's mouth. When she was pressed against a bookshelf, Khastra's passion not relenting, she whined and pushed her away. "I gotta warn Zoldar. My bug got an eyeful last time."

Khastra placed a final kiss on her forehead, then carefully set her on her feet. Etolié immediately ran through the arrangement of hexagonal shelves, until she reached the skylight in the center. A plethora of stars shone down, as well as a crescent moon, and Etolié forcibly didn't think about the jeweled box among her shelf of trinkets. "Zoldar! Come on down, ya little night bug."

Skittering echoed from above. Etolié grinned at the approaching Skalmite, waving as it crawled down from the shelf. "Khastra, I don't think I properly introduced you to my bug. This is Zoldar. He's my new bookkeeper, since Flowers is as good as stolen."

The green, mantis-like creature stood nearly as tall as Etolié, the only clothing on his exoskeletal body a pendant with a large shard of maldectine. He clicked at Khastra, his spindly hands working in tandem to articulate his meaning. "He, uh . . ." Etolié frowned, then remembered their previous and awkward interaction. "He does not say hi and says he doesn't like you because you made me cry."

The little bastard spat his goop before Khastra's hooves and tried to walk away. "Listen," Etolié said, strutting after him. "She and I have talked. It turns out we're madly in love. You don't have to like her, but at least be polite."

When he looked back to Khastra, Etolié realized the half-demon remained forcibly stoic, but her twitching lip revealed her intense amusement. "You be nice too," Etolié continued. "He comforted me after you fucked me and left, so I do get it."

Khastra chuckled. "Zoldar, I would be happy to make peace—"

Zoldar, not sharing the sentiment, crawled straight up the nearest bookshelf and disappeared among the dark rafters. "We're gonna fuck so plug your earholes," Etolié called. "We do have housekeeping to do first though."

A fact Etolié usually didn't admit to was that she couldn't actually read every book and scroll in her extensive collection. Many had been smuggled from the Solviran Library—most without the knowledge of the late emperor— but Khastra had always been around to fill in the gaps in her understanding of languages.

And so, they studied.

Between books, Etolié held Khastra's hand. This was not a new thing at all; she had done it countless times when they were platonic. Yet her heart fluttered, as every little thing made it do lately. If this were the apparent 'big deal' about relationships, Etolié was starting to understand the appeal.

People met and fucked and fell in love—it was the way of the world. She'd never thought it might be the way of hers, but Khastra was real and wanted *her* and that knowledge would never be anything less than pure joy.

But her good feelings dissipated when she opened a book on Solviran history.

Solvira once worshipped the Triage—the grand trio of Neoma, Staella, and Ilune. All were gone now—Neoma, slain by Ilune; Ilune, imprisoned underground for eternity; Staella . . . merely gone.

The book showed paintings of them at their finest, and Etolié could admire most of them—Ilune surrounded by an army of death, the sort that would give even Casvir a scare; Neoma and her vast Silver Fire, waging war against Morathma . . .

But one gave her pause. She stared at the perfect likeness of Staella, Goddess of Stars, her estranged momma. Once, her constellations had illuminated the sky. Once, she had been the hero to sailors lost in horrific storms. Her gentle heart had given humanity to Solvira's brutality, or so Eionei had said. Here, she held a weeping supplicant in her arms, for once momma had taken on the pain of others, had healed empathically—physical and emotional wounds; curses and spells. A double-edged sword—a great power at a great cost, to take on the burdens of the world and burn them through her godly blood.

Etolié recalled an idle memory, of a time she had fallen as a little girl, testing her wings, and scraped an impressive hole in her knee and shattered the kneecap. Staella had held her, softly wept into her hair as Etolié screamed, and she remembered with perfect clarity when the pain vanished—

Only for momma to grit her teeth and swallow tears, bidding Etolié to run along. She had, but she remembered the vicious, fleeting image of the horrible gash on momma's own ethereal form, despite her efforts to hide it.

A weight on her shoulders brought Etolié back. Khastra pulled her against her chest, the top of Etolié's head reaching the half-demon's sternum.

Khastra said nothing. She didn't need to. She knew every secret Etolié stubbornly clung to—even if some were well known. One did not simply murder her own father and be banished from Celestière without the entire angelic populace finding out.

They didn't know the years of trauma and tears leading to that gods-awful moment, though.

Etolié shut the book and set it aside.

They moved forward, Khastra guiding them until every book bore a foreign tongue. The half-demon's callused hands released Etolié, instead skimming the array of spines, her elegant face serene.

"It's so weird that the God of Order is technically my cousin," Etolié mused, as she dug through a collection of scrolls tucked into their shelves in the wall. "I mean, by marriage. Auntie Kareena and I are only related on the technicality of her dead sister loving my momma, but she sees me as a niece. Which means baby Soliel is my cousin."

Baby Soliel, who somehow grew up to be a time travelling God hellbent on separating the three coexisting planes. Etolié didn't pretend to understand how it worked; she simply accepted that it was true.

"He is eight months, yes?"

"Something like that," Etolié replied, but then her frown came unbidden. "Well, no. Time moves a helluva lot slower in Celestière. Eight months have passed here, but he would still be a tiny thing."

A horrible thought struck her. "If we killed the baby, would it stop the God of Order?"

"I truly cannot say, Etolié," Khastra replied, thankfully not sounding horrified at the thought of infanticide. "But it would not sit well with me to slit a baby's throat on a hunch. If we knew for certain, it would be a conversation worth having, however."

Khastra's amorality was startling at times, but not so much as the realization that Etolié agreed. She was already banished from Celestière. What worse could they do?

"This one is written in elven," Khastra finally said, holding up a particularly yellowed book. "The title translates into *Mother of Worlds*. Might be what you are looking for."

Etolié accepted when Khastra offered it. "Well, unless it has pictures, I'm gonna need your help."

Khastra sat against the wall and beckoned for Etolié to sit next to her, but Etolié shook her head—Khastra's lap was much more comfortable.

When Khastra's arm crossed over her, protective and properly weighted for comfort, Etolié felt a semblance of peace, despite the stressful day. "Was *Mother of Worlds* one of Chaos' titles?"

"It still is. They pray to her, across the sea. They believe she will return someday."

"What I'm hearing is that Kitty's statement about her momma returning soon isn't so outlandish?"

Khastra's large hand opened the yellowed pages with infinite care—she dealt with delicate objects daily, like her gemstones, and Etolié's fragile heart. "It is not, though there is no way to know when it will be. If the dragon says it, however, there is no one who would know better."

Khastra idly turned pages, her glowing eyes scrutinizing the foreign words, and Etolié wished she also spoke seventy-six dialects of elven—then she might be slightly less useless. "I don't know what I'm looking for," Etolié admitted. "But I can't forget what she said. I'm turning into Flowers—letting dragons get inside my head."

"You care for the world. There is no shame in that."

When a picture appeared on the next page, she stopped turning, and Etolié stared at a humanoid figure, shrouded in shadow and with six colored orbs floating between her hands. "What does it say?"

"Nothing of grand interest," Khastra replied. "Across the sea, Chaos is often depicted as wielding all six orbs."

"What do *you* know?" Etolié asked, shutting the book before Khastra could turn the page. "The history books will all say the same thing—but you were literally alive for all of that."

Khastra softly rested her head against Etolié's, who hummed a sigh of innocent pleasure. Sex was new and exciting and resulted in an intense rush of bonding hormones, but Etolié was slowly learning she didn't care how they were intimate—to cuddle with her in the library was wonderful. To kiss her was bliss. Etolié simply wanted her and wanted to be everything to her.

"My first wife was a Priestess to Chaos," Khastra said, and Etolié remembered that much, the little anecdotes about Khastra's previous spouses surreal to hear about. "And I recall her vehemently insisting Chaos would return in her lifetime. She could feel it in her bones, that the time neared. She said she dreamt of it and felt her Goddess' presence grow stronger each night." Khastra shook her head. "Every generation believes they are a chosen one, Etolié. I held her as she passed away in her sleep as an old woman, still certain of Chaos' return.

"I know facts," Khastra continued, and Etolié stroked her clothed bicep, adoring the strength she felt. She always had. "I know she is a Goddess of Death and Creation. Conception and pregnancy are considered the culmination of chaos, to turn something unstable into something beautiful. During her reign, mothers who died in childbirth were said to be taken directly up to her side and promised that their baby would be protected all its life."

"That's a sweet sentiment." Etolié's hand slid from her bicep to her shoulder, admiring the strong curve. When she touched skin at the collar of Khastra's shirt, magic sparked in the tattoos peeking from above the fabric. "But what I'm hearing is you don't think she's coming back anytime soon."

"I am saying you should not stress."

"But the dragon said . . ."

Khastra's free hand settled on her back, the weight of it soothing, drawing an immediate smile to Etolié's face.

"Perhaps you serve some grand purpose. There is no way to know. Keep your eyes open—if you are meant to know, it will happen. Otherwise, do not spend your life looking for something that is not there."

"I know you're right, but . . ."

"You want to know?"

"I wanna *know.*" Etolié set her forehead against Khastra's shoulder and moaned. "I have to know things."

"The scientist in you will live on. There are better things to prepare for."

Another frown left Etolié's lips. "In all honesty, Beefcake, I'm scared. Soliel is winning. Despite all our efforts, he has four orbs. What's the use in his counterpart returning if he's already won? And he *will* win, at the rate he's going. He would have last felt the white orb in Staelash, and eventually he'll burn it down to retrieve it—and with that many orbs, he might succeed."

"I would not allow that," Khastra replied, and Etolié was surprised to hear the faintest beginnings of a grin.

"You'll be in Nox'Kartha."

"Perhaps. Perhaps not. Depends on when he comes."

"Last time, you ended up with a severed spine."

"That was Izthuni. He is a god. It was two against one. Ayla Darkleaf is dead, so there is no threat of The Endless Night."

Etolié sat up, confirming her suspicions that Khastra had started smiling again. "He was a god that Soliel feared, even with two orbs. Do you think you could have taken The Endless Night in a fair fight?"

"I could not fight Izthuni in Sha'Demoni, when he has his full power. But channeled through a host? I might."

"We were kicking Soliel's ass in the cathedral." Etolié stroked Khastra's elegant face, adoring the subtle laughter lines around her eyes. "Do you think we could try again?"

The glint of excitement in Khastra's countenance held the hint of something Etolié had not seen in well over six months—they harkened to a simpler time, when Khastra was a bombastic asshole and not the subdued woman enslaved to Nox'Kartha. Little flashes of light shone in her happy moments, but Khastra was different now.

"I think," Khastra replied, a calculating glint in her eyes, "it would be a brutal fight, given his power has doubled and more. He nearly slew Lara with three, if the tiny one is to be believed, and she is a Solviraes." Her grin broadened, showing her white teeth. "But I am the Daughter of Ku'Shya, and there is no stronger blood than that."

When Etolié looked up at Khastra, excitement brewed within her at the half-demon's confident smile, that wicked shine in her eyes. Etolié leaned up and kissed her. "I love you; you know that?"

"I love you too, Etolié," Khastra replied, immediately a puddle of softness with the return of that delightful purple blush. So endearing—from Bringer of War to this cuddly puppy with just a simple *I love you.*

They kissed, and though Etolié's fears didn't go away, at least she felt a semblance of calm, until—

Inspiration struck. "But what if we just did it?"

Khastra's mild, purple blush slowly spread across her cheeks and neck. "Did what?"

"Why don't we go kill Soliel? Literally what is stopping us?"

Khastra suddenly burst into laughter, pompous and loud, everything Etolié loved though she didn't understand it. "This is what I have been saying all along, and now you think of it?"

"Look, Lara's near death has put a few things into perspective. I have an orb. He already likely knows it's here. So why not use it to find him? Then, we kill him."

"Do it," Khastra replied, and Etolié adored every piece of her. "We need not tell Lara."

"We need not, indeed." Etolié extracted herself from Khastra's lap and ran to the center of the library, beneath the skylight. The night sky cast minimal light, but her wings spread wide, illuminating the dark atmosphere.

She went to her favorite shelf of trinkets and withdrew a jeweled box.

To touch it brought back memories, of she and Khastra's fight and subsequent make up, and then their make-out—a confusing assortment of emotions, but Etolié shoved that all aside.

When she opened the box, there it lay—a pure white orb, radiating light and power. Khastra peered around the bookshelf, watching Etolié study. "Would this hurt you?" Etolié asked curiously.

Khastra shook her head. "I am both dead and alive. Consequentially, neither dark nor light magic can heal me. Or hurt me."

"That's not very reassuring." She plucked it from the box, power pulsing through her veins as she melded with the artifact. Her headache spiked, but she'd anticipated that and managed to avoid grimacing. The light from her wings radiated brighter, the illumination spreading across her skin.

Strange, wielding it. Etolié sensed no malevolence—simply the compulsion for good, for healing. This orb was not for combat, but for aid.

Time was scarce—the longer she held it, the more likely Soliel would sense its precise location. She shut her eyes, letting the power fill every recess of her body and mind as she asked, *"But where are the rest?"*

The most powerful, panging compulsion sang that its counterpart was far away, across oceans and mountains. But then came dissonance and with it, ineffable knowledge.

A conglomerate: three of its counterparts were south—far south, yet moving rapidly north.

And another . . . near it.

But not near enough for them to be together.

Etolié opened her eyes and set the orb back inside the box, the awareness cutting off suddenly. She shut the lid, hiding it. "Khastra, someone else has an orb. Soliel has company." Etolié scowled at the jeweled lid. "Here's hoping he didn't make a friend."

"We should start walking if we wish to find out."

Scoffing, Etolié pulled a wine glass out of her pocket dimension, along with a bottle. "I'll do you one better. Go sit behind a shelf. I have a plan."

Khastra raised an eyebrow but placed a quick kiss upon her cheek and obeyed.

Etolié popped the cork with merely a flick of her thumb—it counted as a lock, she'd learned—and poured the liquid into the glass. She summoned her voice and lightly sang:

"Oh, Eionei, who gives us joy
Bless my cup and—

She didn't even get to finish the rhyme before her liquid swirled like a tiny whirlpool. A figure appeared as it rose above the rim of the glass, and Etolié knew the man well. "Etolié! Always delightful to hear from you." Tiny grandpa, a rich shade of maroon, showed a shocking amount of emotion for being sentient wine. "Are you all right? We still haven't been able to discuss the Theocracy, and Sol Kareena would benefit from your account."

"I'd tell her myself if I could," Etolié said, and she winked to soften that sore point. Being banished from Celestière had its drawbacks. "No time, yet. I actually need a favor—horses."

Eionei brought a hand up to his chin, thoughtfully stroking it. "Horses, you say?"

"Yes. But I need two this time. One for me and one large, beefy one for, uh . . . supplies. Like, six hundred pounds worth, probably."

"You want a flying horse capable of carrying a six-hundred-pound object?"

"No, six hundred pounds *worth* of objects. That's an important distinction."

Eionei's lips became a thin line. Whatever he suspected, and Etolié knew he did, he couldn't simply accuse her—all the world was in disarray, and it'd be a pretty damning thing for Etolié to be in cohorts with the woman tangentially responsible for the fall of the Theocracy. "Uh-huh. Well, I do have something that might work. Give me an hour—I need to take them to someone who can transport them to your realm."

Etolié smiled, because she knew perfectly well who 'someone' was—you know, a certain Star Goddess capable of inner-planar travel and the reason the Solviraes could do the same—but decided playing dumb would save everyone heartache. "Someday I'll figure out how to do that. Just for you."

"I'll hold you to it. We'll talk soon?"

"We will," she said, though she hoped it was a lie. When Eionei's image disappeared, she drank the entire glass and groaned. "All clear."

Khastra emerged from her place behind the bookshelves. "We should decide what to tell him."

"Realistically we should tell nobody anything, for now. Eionei won't ask. Lunestra won't tell. And Sora is pretending she heard nothing." She sighed when Khastra wrapped her arms around her from behind, leaning back into the touch.

"I despise secrecy," Khastra said, her hands making a blessed mess of Etolié's hair, "but I do understand."

"I hate it."

Once upon a time, the world had been simple. The world had assumed Khastra and Etolié were in bed together. But now that they actually were, it had to remain merely a rumor once more.

Though, that was assuming they lasted long enough for the world to risk finding out. Imperator Casvir would return. The thought filled her with dread.

Etolié took the jeweled box and stuffed it into a small bag, along with her maldectine knuckles—Khastra's gift deserved to be used.

As she considered what else to pack, Khastra's lips touched her hair, the half-demon all but hunched over to reach, and Etolié twisted around to meet her. She smiled at the fluttering in her stomach and heart, every ounce of affection from Khastra not new but exciting and joyful. "If I am hearing correctly, we have an hour?"

Etolié grinned and disillusioned her clothing.

So strange, to be back where they'd first made love. So easy, to fall back into the nest of blankets and scarves and soft things, to giggle as Khastra's fingers grazed lightly across her wings—as sensitive as anything down below, and just as taboo to touch—and gasp when those callused hands brushed across her breasts.

And Etolié loved it, yes, but not nearly so much as she enjoyed pushing the half-demon down and straddling her hips, watching Khastra's eyes widen in want as she pled for Etolié's touch.

Although she remained self-conscious, Etolié kissed Khastra's thighs and vulva, breathing through her fear of being judged, knowing Khastra never would. Khastra knew everything about her, every dark secret and subsequent flaw, every painful step of her healing journey.

If this were Etolié's reward for taking those steps, to rub her face in Khastra's cunt and love it, it had been a journey worth taking.

She dared to push inside her—her entire hand fit . . . very easily—careful as she moved, terrified to hurt her, which had never been a thought she'd considered before; Khastra was indomitable. But it delighted her to watch her demon be vulnerable, hear her soft cries and match her gaze and feel . . . something. Love, yes, but more. Connection, yes, but deeper.

Etolié didn't think too much of it, simply savored the tender moment.

When Khastra touched herself, Etolié used all her minimal strength to thrust harder, breathless to watch her finish. When she trembled, Etolié moved with her, helped to push her over the edge, gratified to watch her finish.

And when Khastra finally stilled, Etolié carefully withdrew. Realizing her hand was coated in demonic pleasure, she plucked a single scarf to wipe it off on, then tossed it aside when Khastra teared up. "You all right, big lug?"

The half-demon responded by grabbing her and pulling her into her chest. Etolié settled into the embrace, smiling when Khastra curled around her. "It is very surreal, still, making love to you," her demon whispered, "and wonderful to be vulnerable and hand my fate to you, for a few moments."

"Fucking hell, Khastra—everything you say is poetic bullshit," Etolié teased, squirming up to reach her face. She kissed Khastra's full lips, adoring the sensation. "Can't believe you'd been hiding it for twenty-four years."

Khastra chuckled, and her inability to ever be offended was likely the only reason they had stayed friends for so many years. "It seems you have evoked something new inside of me."

"Oh, shut up," Etolié said, unable to help her laughter.

Khastra's grin only widened. "You do not want to hear about the melodious perfection of your laugh? Or how endearing it is that you tremble when I touch your wings?"

"No, I do not," she teased, like a dirty liar. She laughed when Khastra kissed her forehead, then gasped when she touched the aforementioned wings. "You're ridiculous."

They kissed and touched, but not for long enough. Time escaped when they made love, until suddenly Etolié's grandpa sixth sense starting ringing like a bell. "Wait," she said, pausing her grinding against Khastra's mouth—her horns made very convenient handholds. "We need to go outside—"

She laughed when Khastra flung her into the blankets, apparently content to finish what she'd started.

So, a few minutes later, the sex-delirious duo quietly emerged in the late-night hour. In theory, everyone would be asleep—everyone except a former stablemaster who nearly collided with them in the doorframe. "Etolié—!"

"Sora!" Etolié peered past her into the starry, winter night. "What are you doing?"

Sora held up her smoking pipe. Etolié didn't have to ask further. "Perhaps you know why there are a pair of winged horses by the stables?"

She perked up. "Yes, I do. Deliver the message for us, would you? Khastra and I are gonna go kill Soliel."

Sora nodded, as though this were a perfectly acceptable and leisurely excursion. "Have fun."

"You can join us if you'd like," Etolié continued. "You're good with a sword."

Sora shook her head. "Unlike you two, I'm not a demi-god. I'd rather keep my organs unfried, thank you."

Etolié accepted that. "Fine, fine. Miss all the fun."

"Also, and forgive me for being presumptuous, but after our conversation in the carriage—our many, *many* egregiously exhausting conversations in the carriage—you two need alone time."

"All right. I see how it is."

Khastra's glowing eyes were always far more scrutinizing when she raised a dreaded eyebrow. "What conversations?"

"I'll explain in private, lest Sora be forced to relive massive trauma." She smiled at the half-elf. "Don't tell Solvira we're doing this. Lara got her ass kicked, and I don't want her to worry. If they ask, tell them not to worry and to wait it out. Unless we die, in which case let them know they aren't required to give in to Soliel's demands for ransom in exchange for our carcasses."

In response, Sora brought the pipe to her lips and puffed. "Don't die, please."

"I promise nothing."

Etolié and Khastra skipped out into the night.

As promised, two winged monstrosities waited obediently outside the stables. Etolié grimaced as she approached. "Gods, they're ugly."

The horses glowed, as was appropriate for something hailing from Celestière. The white one sparkled, a subtle rainbow hue in its long mane and tail. A larger, grey beast seemed fully capable of dragging a stagecoach all on its own, with ease. Both bore wings of light, and Etolié had chosen to not question what in Celestière a mortal horse had bred with to result in these.

"I think they are beautiful, Etolié," Khastra said, offering a hand to the larger beast. "You simply despise animals."

"I love Demitri. He knows how to bathe and not bite my face off." Already uneasy, Etolié patted the glittery monster's nose, shivering when it sniffed. "I'm indifferent to animals. It's horses specifically that need to fall off a cliff and die."

"These ones would not die because they have—"

"Oh, shut it."

Khastra laughed, easily mounting the saddled monstrosity—which, yes, was meant for a humanoid because Eionei wasn't a dumbass.

"Not taking your hammer?" Etolié asked.

"The horse cannot carry it, even if I were to hold it. I will summon it whenever we camp."

Etolié kept her distance as she crept to the horse's side, flinching when she touched it—the beast didn't even react, which meant it was either indifferent or conniving.

When she did finally manage to climb aboard its back, she pulled out her flask and drank. "Oh, just kill me now."

Khastra laughed. "Lead the way, Etolié."

Etolié kicked the creature in the haunches, stomach lurching when it shot into the sky. "Fly smoothly, ya glittery shit."

Thus began a nauseating journey.

A night of pleasure, and then Flowridia collapsed into Ayla's cool embrace and slept until the morning burst over the mountaintops, framing the outline of the pulled curtains.

To awaken in the pool of her lap, with Ayla reading serenely above her, was as blissful a scene as she could have imagined. A taste of perfection, once lost and now found; her shattered dream, the cracks repaired in gold.

A luxurious voice said, "Good morning, darling."

Ayla set the book aside and graced her with a smile, her cold fingers running leisurely through her hair. If this was Flowridia's fate, to awaken each day to a sweet, *"Good morning,"* and a gentle touch, eternity didn't seem so daunting.

But soon she would no longer awaken. Soon she wouldn't need sleep. An odd thought, one that clenched at her heart. They hadn't spoken more of her fears, and Flowridia personally preferred that.

She smiled, despite the worry. With her head in Ayla's lap, she finally replied, "Good morning, my love. What were you reading?"

"Pre-Civil War Solviran History. If I am going to rule a country, I wish to study it at its greatest. Pity though—the book is old. I swear I find missing pages in every chapter."

"Strange," Flowridia muttered, content to melt into Ayla's lap.

"Have you slept enough?" Ayla asked, continuing with her tender gestures.

"Yes—"

Flowridia gasped when Ayla slipped her hands beneath her sleepy form and pulled her up. Cradled now, Flowridia sighed as Ayla resumed stroking her hair. "You're so wonderfully soft when you've just woken up," Ayla said. "A pity you'll have no need to sleep soon." She hummed gently, her face lingering at the crux of Flowridia's neck. "I have a present for you. Look at your nightstand."

Flowridia glanced over, charmed to see a bouquet of fresh flowers—small and white, delightfully lovely. "Where did you get those?"

"It is not winter everywhere. Southern Solvira has some delightful blooms, even this early in the season. And it has been days since I have seen you with your lovely hair accessory."

Flowridia blushed, utterly enamored, and kissed her love's cheek. "You went all that way for me? Thank you."

Ayla returned the gesture, lingering by her ear and whispering, "Are you feeling all right?"

"I am." The question sparked no curiosity, until Ayla began pawing at her waist and stomach, kneading her dress in cat-like motions. "Are you?"

Ayla nodded, an odd pout on her lip. "I have a question, and I hope you don't find it rude. And please do not be embarrassed; personally, I am enamored." Her wide eyes batted prettily. "You started your monthly some time during the night, and I cannot stand such a waste of blood."

Flowridia had grown up in an orphanage of girls and had no reservation about feminine things—this was, however, the oddest request she had ever been given in her entire life. Her stare surely reflected that. "You want my menstrual blood?"

"Blood is blood, Flowra," Ayla said, and all cuteness in her gaze disappeared behind the expanding black in her eyes. The first peek of fangs appeared at her lips. "Indulge me. Assuming you don't feel ill."

Flowridia laughed, the request too strange for words, but offended was nowhere near how she felt. Oddly flattered, actually. "All right, you insatiable woman. Do whatever you like. My body is yours."

They kissed, then Ayla's teeth scraped gently across her lip. Faster than Flowridia could react, she crawled beneath the blankets, content to find her feast beneath. Flowridia giggled at first contact, her tired body joyfully responding, and quickly fell into pleasured moans—

A knock interrupted their play. Ayla's eyes spelled murder as she rose from the depths of the bed, the barest hint of blood on her lips and chin.

Another knock, and with it came an apologetic voice. "Lara," came Reginal's voice, "forgive the interruption, but a meeting has been called."

Ayla's face and form shifted into that of the belated empress, glowering as she pulled a robe over her exposed form, though it hardly covered her. Were she seeking to make a point, she would succeed. Flowridia sunk back into bed, covering her nude body with the plush blankets.

Ayla—as Lara—cracked open the door. "Yes?"

"I apologize for interrupting," he said, quickly averting his eyes to the ground, away from Lara, barely clothed. Lara had been demure and modest in life; Ayla had no such insecurities. "But there remains the matter of Archbishop Lunestra and the orphans from the cathedral. A meeting has been called, and your presence will be needed to bring them here."

Lara's voice held ice. "You mean to steal me from my lady's side?"

"Others might object, but I would take no issue with her joining us."

Tension showed in Lara's form, illusionary or not. "Fine. Give me a moment."

She shut the door, fists clenched, and from the bed, Flowridia said, "Please tell me you illusioned away the blood—"

"What is the use of ruling by your side if we never get a moment alone?"

Flowridia stood from the bed, her body alight but still able to settle back down. At Ayla's side, she gently said, "This is what you agreed to, when you stole Lara's place." She cupped Ayla's face, admiring its sharp contours and light blue and silver gaze. "This is ruling. Lara was beloved by her people and her council, and you've agreed to uphold that legacy." Her hand fell to Ayla's. She squeezed tight, both a comfort and a warning. "Don't give them a reason to suspect anything amiss."

Ayla glowered as she dressed in her finery. Flowridia asked, "What *do* you think about the Lunestra situation?"

"It must be handled carefully," Ayla replied, having no difficulty with the jeweled clasps. "I have no doubt Casvir intended to slaughter every man, woman, and child in the

Theocracy, and while he would be willing to overlook eight mangy orphans, for the Archbishop of the Theocracy to have escaped his grasp will be a massive blow to his pride. For Solvira to harbor her would be an insult, assuming he finds out."

"Would we be risking a war with Nox'Kartha?" Flowridia asked, relieved when Ayla immediately shook her head.

"I would say no, if only because Casvir is intelligent enough to know that it would be a complete stalemate. I sat in on many of his tactical meetings, wherein he discussed Solvira's defenses and concluded on his own that he did not have the means. Now, the Bringer of War does beg the question of whether or not he would try again, and his capacity for shock-and-awe on the battlefield is enough to bring most countries to their knees—hence the Theocracy's fate.

"But even if the battlefield would be lost to the Deathless Army, a siege is another matter entirely—even without the Bringer of War, Neolan has the capacity to defend its capital indefinitely. Bear in mind that the Solviraes can literally pluck items and people through the planes—a talent I'm slowly unlocking—so it does not matter if we are surrounded, though the true risk will be to the countryside and all the mountain villages beyond direct influence of the city. Solvira has enough of them that Casvir could still stir terror into the masses. But bear in mind, Casvir has sworn to his citizens that they will never be sent to war. Any retaliation upon his own capital would be devastating to his reputation, even though he, too, could sustain himself indefinitely. There would be no victor. It would be a stalemate for years to come. Too expensive of an endeavor for him to bother to take, even if he knows we harbored the orphans."

Flowridia stared, taken aback by the sheer amount detail. "Those were incredibly thorough insights."

Ayla secured a necklace around her neck, eyebrow raised as she said, "Flowra, you do know I used to be a politician, right?"

"Yes, you were a diplomat for Casvir—"

"No, before that. In Zauleen. Did the history books really not write of it? I am offended."

Flowridia thought back to those dreadful texts, recalling countless brutal details. "Yes, they did. Though not so much as they wrote of your . . . everything else."

Ayla's annoyance bled out into her chuckle. "A pity, for I personally find that to be the most interesting part of my story. You think I was born charming? Hardly. I had to learn."

"I can't imagine you as anything but . . ." Flowridia said, but Ayla laughed uproariously, stealing her words.

"Darling, while I was a literal legend, I was more the sort of monster who lurked in the woods on dark nights waiting for lost souls to pass—no charisma necessary. Honestly, I cringe to dwell on how absolutely *inept* I was in social circles. So many mishaps. The Endless Night may have been born in a night, but Ayla Darkleaf? Becoming a vampire made me alluring—but not *charming.*"

Flowridia grinned at her dramatics, unabashed as she stole her lips for a quick kiss. "I would love to hear every detail."

"Perhaps after the meeting." Ayla's returning smile showed fangs. "There is business to finish first."

Ayla pushed her onto the bed, and Flowridia had no wish to fight her.

Not too much later, they left the bedroom hand in hand, able to piece together the path from memory.

They were the last to arrive in the council chamber. General Irons poured over a series of documents, a quill in his hand as he wrote notes in the margins. Reginal smiled at their entrance, as did Jules.

"I recall you were having difficulties summoning portals and channeling your magic," Reginal said. "Would you allow me to help you? I'm not so precise as Etolié, but I've done well enough before."

Lara agreed, and the duo fell into a conversation about the principles of portals. Flowridia, meanwhile, sat as far from General Irons as possible, contemplating her next words. Ayla had set the stage for her proposal, to house the refugees—the time to act was near.

Her stomach lurched when a portal appeared in the center of the room. Lara stumbled back, her grin broad and painfully reminiscent of Ayla. But Reginal clapped his approval and stepped through.

"I suppose I'll have to practice," Lara said, a feigned apology in her stance.

The only sound became the occasional rustling of paper from Irons. Flowridia glanced up, unfortunate enough to coincide with him doing the same, their awkward shared glance apparently appalling to them both as he glared and looked back down.

When she looked to Lara, the imposter empress had noticed as well, her icy gaze trying to freeze him where he sat.

The portal flared, and from it emerged a small child, and then another and another. Eight children appeared, the eldest no more than perhaps nine, each carrying a folded nightgown in their arms. Flowridia's heart immediately bled for their nervous eyes as they looked around the council chamber, especially for the tiniest one—a little girl, perhaps three.

Reginal stepped through, followed by Lunestra, who gave a pasted smile.

Guilt filled Flowridia to face her, this woman who had lost her entire kingdom—a loss Flowridia might have prevented, had she only known. However, a spot of amusement filled her, to realize Lunestra was wearing one of her old dresses.

"Archbishop Lunestra," Reginal said, pointing to a vacant chair, "feel free to have a seat. Uh, children, you may sit wherever you are comfortable."

Most happily plopped on the ground, admiring the reflective floor, but when the littlest looked lost, Flowridia beckoned to her. "Would you like to sit with me?" she said softly, and when the girl nodded, she beamed and lifted her into her lap. The girl sucked her thumb, but just as quickly wrapped her chubby hands into Flowridia's long hair, apparently finding comfort in clinging to the thick locks.

"Magister Etolié of Staelash has apparently disappeared," Reginal said, his frown deeply etched, "but we have been told, and I quote this directly, 'not to worry and to wait it out.'"

Flowridia's frown matched his, but knowing Etolié, she had simply given up and run away for good, or perhaps set herself on fire to escape, as she had often threatened.

"It has been proposed that we house Archbishop Lunestra for the time being, until a more secure location can be found," Reginal continued, the eccentricities of his motions not unlike a more wholesome Murishani. "All in secret, of course. However, there remains the matter of the orphans."

Ever the fidgety hostess, Lara stood from her chair to pace, though grimaced when one of the children on the floor brushed against her dress. "Surely we have temples equipped to house a few. We also have many perfectly respectable orphanages, though I was told this would not be ideal."

Flowridia swallowed her fear, taking courage from the innocent child in her arms. "I simply fear," she said, grateful for the small weight in her lap, "that given the opportunity, Casvir wouldn't hesitate to finish his slaughter of the entire capital. We must make it as difficult as possible for him to know their identities, and to separate them would be the simplest way. Ideally, we would find them homes. He wouldn't think to look for children with parents."

"I entirely agree," Priestess Jules said, "but to simply adopt out eight children overnight is impossible."

"We start with trusted referrals then," Flowridia said. "If you know anyone considering adoption, please speak up. But otherwise, we split them up among the temples and orphanages, perhaps even send some out of Neolan."

"My husband might know someone," Reginal said thoughtfully, "but let me speak with him first."

Flowridia smiled. "Wonderful. I might even propose we send a few back to Staelash. Thalmus is as good a man as I have ever met, and he personally oversaw the maintenance of the orphanage in the city, ensuring it was safe.

"That said," she continued, fully aware of Lunestra's indecipherable gaze upon her, "there may be future homes open to housing a few children, given the inevitable influx of refugees Solvira will undoubtedly see in the coming weeks. They won't flee to Tholheim, and Solvira is the only other option unless they wish to cross the ocean."

"Are you suggesting that we accept the refugees?" Reginal said, his stark discomposure visible on all the other council member's faces as well—save for Lara, who gave her most reassuring smile.

"I'm saying we should prepare for the inevitable and have a plan in place."

"You have quite a few opinions," General Irons said, making no effort to hide his disdain, "on council matters, for someone who isn't a part of the council."

"We actually discussed this at length," Lara interjected, her own smile wearing thin. "All her opinions echo my own, though she should receive the credit for brilliance."

Jules' expression softened. "There is precedence for this. You were praised for accepting the Skalmites into our catacombs. Risks aside, the world is watching us."

Flowridia had nearly forgotten the news that the Skalmites were living their lives in the Solviran Library. Lara blinked at the initial mention of 'Skalmites' but just as quickly smiled and said, "An excellent point."

On Flowridia's lap, the girl fell against her chest, still sucking her thumb. Flowridia cradled her, offering the sweet girl a smile before returning her attention to the council. "Assuming we don't cross the border or provoke Nox'Kartha, they would have no reason to retaliate. We aren't in any way engaging in an act of war by accepting Theocracy refugees from the outlying cities."

"Be that as it may, we simply do not have the resources to suddenly care for so many people," Reginal said, anxious as he stroked his long beard. "There are likely to be thousands by the end. Where will we house them? How will we feed them?"

Excellent questions, and Flowridia's optimism withered. But before she could retort, Irons said, "You also seem rather keen to predict Nox'Kartha's military procedures. What if this does antagonize them?"

Flowridia recalled Ayla's previous sentiments, content to echo them herself and add her own personal knowledge. "Casvir has shown the world his purpose, to establish himself as a formidable force and dominate the country that had been antagonizing him—"

"Oh, were they?" Irons said, sparing a glance for Lunestra.

". . . for a reaction for years. He will finish the job, but he won't stand by and gloat when his actions speak for themselves. But while he was apparently confident in his victory against the Theocracy, he can't recreate the same tactic with Solvira—we'd be watching for it—"

"We?" Irons said.

". . . as well as have measures in place to counteract any magic attack he could bring," Flowridia continued, rather fired up now, in the face of Irons' rudeness. "He has no desire to fight Solvira because it's not a fight he's confident he can win."

"As a foreign diplomat," Irons spat, "you certainly know a lot of Nox'Karthan military tactics."

"You know I spent months with Casvir—"

"Somehow that makes me suspicion of your motives, *my lady—!*"

"General Irons," Lara said, unquestionable venom in her eerily calm words, "take care how you speak. My lady has valuable input." The sweetness in her smile returned as she looked to Flowridia. "Kindly continue."

Irons looked properly victorious, and Flowridia bit back her annoyance. "I . . . I don't have much more to say," she replied. The girl in her lap stared warily at Lara, and Flowridia gently stroked her hair, conveying what comfort she could. "Reginal has offered a rebuttal I don't know how to . . ."

Except she did. Only days ago, she had grown a field of tulips. What if . . .

"What if," she whispered, breathless at her own insane idea, "I could solve the issue of food? Would that be incentive enough for someone to helm the housing dilemma?"

"I would say so," Reginal said, wariness coloring his words. "What did you have in mind?"

"I wish to experiment before I make any sort of commitment. Where does Solvira grow its food?"

"We have farms stationed outside the city. But there's not much happening now, given the winter season."

"That won't matter for my purposes. Contact someone whose field I might borrow."

Reginal's intrigue bordered on amusement. "Happily so, my lady."

"As for the orphans," she continued, "Jules, can I ask you to compile a list of all the orphanages and temples accepting orphans for me? I would like to discuss options with you, but I need to know what the options are first." She looked to Reginal. "And speak with your husband, yes. I would gladly find any one of them a proper home."

"I think that covers the important points, for now," Lara said, her smile infectious, though Flowridia knew it to be false. "The children need a better place to wait, in any case, so I propose we adjourn for now."

She was referring to the ones lying on the ground, and the others drawing shapes with their greasy hands on the polished floors. Flowridia bit back a laugh as servants were called to escort them to their prepared room. Lunestra left with them, though not without a lingering glance to Flowridia—utterly indecipherable, and it made her stomach churn.

But instead of thinking too much of it, she roused the girl in her arms, placing a soft kiss in her hair. "Breakfast is waiting for you," she said lightly, but the little girl simply curled in tight.

"Are you the princess?" she said, her voice muffled by her thumb.

Charmed, Flowridia shook her head. "I am not a princess, no."

"Lady Etolié said there wasn't a princess, but I didn't believe her."

Flowridia laughed, and then she stood and carried the girl to the other children. "Unfortunately, Etolié was telling the truth. But you can pretend that you're the princess while you stay in this castle."

She visibly perked up, apparently having never considered the idea. "I will be the princess."

Enamored, Flowridia pulled one of the long, woven stems from her hair. She quickly measured it around the little girl's head, then tied the end to near the bulb—then used magic to seal it together, bidding the stem to fuse.

She placed it onto the girl's head, much to the child's delight. The flower petals blossomed behind her ear, a green stem making a near perfect ring around it. "There. Every princess needs a proper crown."

The girl beamed, radiating light until the servants finally came to escort them away. She waved goodbye and Flowridia copied it, her cheeks sore from happiness.

"Flowra, darling," Lara said, a mischievous glint in her eye, "I believe you and I have unfinished business to attend to—"

"Lara," Reginal said, perhaps not realizing he had interrupted, "if your health permits it, there is still much to discuss, as well as an impressive piling of paperwork that needs your attention."

The subtle, murderous shift in Lara's countenance bore evidence of the predatory interloper—so much so that Flowridia stepped between her and Reginal, who looked terribly confused. "Of course," Lara finally said, the forced niceties of her tone alarming even to Flowridia. "Flowra, you'll sit with me, won't you?"

Flowridia moved to obey, but Irons spoke with his usual disdain. "Given we are discussing matters that no longer concern Lady Flowridia, we should reconvene as strictly the private council."

Lara clasped her hands together, her smile showing teeth. Her words were as sweet as honey. "Given your comparative worth to me, perhaps you should take your beloved sword and shove it up—"

"Lara, let's speak in private." Flowridia's panic manifested in a joyless smile. She grasped Lara's shoulders and all but shoved her out of the room—leaving the flabbergasted council behind.

Alone in the hallway, all signs of the kindly empress vanished from her visage—though she wore Lara's face, she was every part the wolf masquerading as a lamb. Flowridia crossed her arms, furious. "You can't just say things like that."

"And what is so wrong with wanting time with you?!" Lara snapped, boorish as she spread her arms wide.

Flowridia heaved a controlled sigh, her nails digging into the fabric of her sleeves. "Can you please lower your voice?"

To her credit, Lara obeyed. "I love you. Gods forbid I spend a little quality time between your legs."

"I don't want you there if you're going to act like this."

Taken aback, Lara's visage shifted by degrees, ice breaking through the sheen of silver coating her eyes. "Pardon?"

"Ay—Lara, you're the one who chose to run a damn kingdom, so do it."

For a moment, Lara's posture bristled, her lips became a thin line, and Flowridia braced herself to argue here and now in the hallway. But to her surprise, she slumped dramatically against the wall and crossed her arms, scowling instead. "I don't miss the days of pandering to vermin, but here we are."

"We could still leave,' Flowridia replied, her anger seeping away at Ayla's defused mood.

But Lara shook her head. "I have plans, my love. And so do you. I shall try to control my anger in the meantime."

"You were only trying to defend me. Under most circumstances, I appreciate it, but Lara never would have lost her temper like that. They'll only wave it away as stress and lingering trauma for so long."

"You must be careful, Flowra." Lara's sneer twisted her entire face. "General Irons had previously implied you were an ambitious social climber, hopping from Casvir's throne to mine, and unfortunately it does look suspicious. You cannot let him provoke you. And you must be careful how you speak of Casvir in official meetings. Speak the truth, yes. But bear in mind how you say it, lest it sound like an endorsement. And use his title, for gods' sake—or you really will sound like a hussy."

Flowridia sighed. "Politics are complicated."

"I could always kill him."

"Please don't," Flowridia replied, knowing full well this wouldn't be the last time she had to say it.

"You're a woman of kindness and gentleness," Lara continued, taking Flowridia's hand in hers, "and that does well for interpersonal relationships. I do not doubt you will win them over with your wit and smile in due time. You were wonderful, truly. Very well spoken. You simply have to bear in mind what your words will mean out of context."

Flowridia smiled at that, her blush burning bright. "Thank you. I'm trying."

"I suppose this is a reminder for me as well," Lara said, annoyance manifesting in her rolling eyes. "There are politer ways to tell someone to shove their opinions up their ass. My charm is a bit dull."

"You can always practice by saying pretty things to me," Flowridia teased, giggling when Lara grabbed and groped her over her skirt.

"Go on and garden," Lara said, "or whatever. You may not see me until this evening. Reginal and I have a few things to discuss in private, and I do not know how long it shall take."

Curiosity overshadowed her pride at her love's initiative. "What about?"

But Lara waved it off, her smile quiet and uncharacteristically shy. "I shall tell you once it's done."

They kissed in the hallways, and Flowridia set off on her own.

Flowridia spent her time outside with Demitri practicing the nuances of necromancy.

That was a neat trick, in the camp with the plants.

Flowridia smiled as she sat in the grass outside the garden. Neolan held far warmer weather than Staelash, which was likely still an icy wonderland. Here, though the chill remained, spring had come, shown in the buds of flowers and tiny sprigs of grass at her feet. Someday soon, she would explore the garden's grand recesses—even in the winter, it rivaled Nox'Kartha's, perhaps even surpassed it—but her skin yearned for sunlight after so long spent in a swamp.

"I did a neater trick," she admitted begrudgingly, "while defending Ayla's body." She practiced arbitrarily worthless tricks, coaxing the grass to rise, promoting new growth. "It's funny, the things you'll do when you're desperate. Sometimes they're things you said you would never do." She released a heavy sigh, a dandelion sprouting in tandem with her finger rising. "I raised the dead. I controlled a small army of death. And it was . . ." She shut her eyes, hesitant to admit it aloud. "*. . . invigorating.*"

You enjoyed it?

"I had never felt more powerful," she said softly, "but it scares me, how much I liked it. Power is never something I aspired for, but once you taste it, you want more."

Demitri's nose nuzzled her hair. *It's like you always say: it doesn't matter what your powers are. It matters what you do with them.*

She reached up and patted his nose. "I have no way to practice, short of sneaking around the Solviran graveyards at midnight."

You'd get caught. You're not very sneaky.

"I don't disagree."

She heard approaching feet and chattering children. When she looked to the castle, Lunestra and the orphans approached, no doubt coming to enjoy the beautiful day. She said nothing as they neared, content to let them be, then was reminded that Demitri was a spectacle.

"Is that your dog?" one asked.

"Can I touch him?"

"Can I ride him?!"

Lunestra quietly tut-tutted their antics—she held a small girl in her arms, the same Flowridia had previously cuddled in the council meeting. "Children, be polite. Lady Flowridia is a witch, and her wolf is not a pet; he is a familiar. Remember how we treat Yaril?" She gestured to the little bird at her shoulder, and the children seemed to understand. "It would be disrespectful to treat him that way."

Flowridia looked to Demitri, a question in her gaze.

The attention would be nice, actually.

"If you ask him politely," Flowridia said, still seated on the ground, "he won't mind. He understands everything you say."

Demitri sat, for which Flowridia was grateful, given his massive size, and when the children offered their hands, he nuzzled them sweetly, even licked the braver ones who dared come close. Lunestra set the youngest child on the ground, watching her run to Demitri—and less than politely ram into his leg. When he raised his head to howl, a few jumped back, giggling nervously, but the rest joined in. A small chorus of little howls joined with Demitri's beautiful, somber one, and Flowridia couldn't stop her laugher.

"I appreciate you humoring them," the archbishop said.

Flowridia shook her head. "It is no trouble."

"They have been through more horror in the past two days than any person should experience in their entire lives," Lunestra said, her guarded expression ever-present. "Any distraction is a kindness. Thank you."

"I only hope we can find them stability soon," Flowridia said, and behind her back, Lunestra's aged hands suddenly clutched the other. "The moment Jules brings me that list, I'll have the orphanages and temples contacted."

"With all possible respect, I would rather not discuss this now."

Flowridia looked between her and the children, her heart aching to realize the awful truth. "You've known them all their lives," she said softly.

"Yes, I have." Sharpness made up her tone, and Flowridia said no more of it.

She thought of Ana, the sweet, silly thing, and though she hurt, she knew it was nothing to the depth of losing an actual child. She thought of Demitri, her pulse spiking to even consider the notion.

Familiars were an extension of one's soul, she had heard. While she believed that to be true, Demitri had come to her as a baby. He had been helpless. He had been hers.

Soon enough, Lunestra bid the children to thank Flowridia and Demitri for their time, then escorted them to the garden.

Flowridia quietly resumed her work, melancholy for reasons she understood but could not voice. Demitri recognized it; he knew every feeling she had. *Are you really going to try and find all of them homes?*

"I'm going to try and do a great many things, Demitri," she replied, but even as she grasped a dandelion, her heart dwelled upon Lunestra and her quiet anguish.

They were not friendly, no. In their first meeting, Flowridia had toppled an entire discussion off the table for her own childish needs and thus set the tone for every meeting since. But in times of tragedy, needs changed.

At her bidding, Flowridia grasped the inherent power within the small flower and bid it to expand, and around her sprouted new growths, small yellow sprouts bursting from the ground. Remarkable, yes, but it would mean nothing if she could not do it again.

Lunestra would be here for the foreseeable future, and Flowridia decided it was time to make amends.

That evening Flowridia gathered her courage and took the first step.

Alone, she knocked upon the door to the guest room. At the soft, 'Enter,' she did so, her steps silent upon the carpeted floor.

There sat Lunestra upon the bed, grey hair free of its normal crown, falling in thickly braided loops. She wore nightclothes but showed no sign of reticence at Flowridia's fancier attire. "Good evening, Lady Flowridia."

She looked sincere, too exhausted to have any false airs. Flowridia smiled and said, "May I join you, Archbishop?"

Lunestra gestured to the bed beside her, and Flowridia sat, smoothing her dress, revealing the many embroidered patches.

"What brings you here?" Lunestra said.

"I know you and I have had friction in the past," Flowridia said, her eyes fixed to Lunestra's aged hands, the skin nearly translucent, revealing the outline of bones and veins behind its dark hue. "But my heart weeps for you and your people."

A polite smile spread across Lunestra's face, bearing all the lies of politics. "You are very kind—"

"I don't say that as the empress' beloved." Flowridia's hands clutched the other, Lunestra's pain a thinly veiled mask over her elderly countenance. "I say that as Flowridia, a girl raised as an orphan in a small village whose visit to the City of Light was her first ever vision of a great city. I thought the cathedral was the most beautiful sight in all the world. But that isn't the true tragedy—my heart weeps for the slain children, for the families, for the brave people who lost their lives. I . . ." She swallowed her feelings, praying her sincere humility showed. "I know you're hurting. I wanted you to know you aren't alone."

Lunestra's passive expression remained. "Thank you, Lady Flowridia. You have a kind heart. But given your ties to Nox'Kartha, you must understand why it stings."

It held no cruelty—merely finality, and Flowridia offered merely a nod, not wishing to offend her guest. She prayed the gesture had done more good than harm, despite coming with the pain of rejection. She stood and smoothed her skirts, withholding her tears, but when she touched the door, Lunestra said, "I must thank you, though."

Flowridia turned around, her hand lingering on the knob.

"I don't fear for myself, but I do fear for those children." Lunestra's gaze held no reserve as she met her eye. "I fear that Imperator Casvir will not stop until he hunts the final few of us down. My death is inevitable, whether it be by his hand or my own health, but they have their whole lives before them. Whatever my reservations about you, I trust you would never purposefully lead them toward harm. You agreeing to helm their safety means more to me than you can ever know."

"Archbishop, it's an honor to help," Flowridia said, approaching the bed once more. She stood beside the bottom post, her hand gently wrapping around the carved wood.

"I never bore children," Lunestra said, her face holding a spark of hope, "but over the years, the children who have come through the cathedral were and are as dear to me as though they were my own. Sol Kareena herself called me to that role, and they are my legacy upon this world. It will hurt to see them go, but I know they would be happier with a family, instead of merely a grandmother."

"They'll be safe here, wherever they end up," Flowridia said, conviction in her words. "Casvir is fearsome, but he's not omnipotent, and whatever comradery there is between us . . ." Her smile twitched, to think of the tragedy performed by his hand. ". . . I don't condone what he's done. It's broken my heart."

Lunestra's smile held light. "Thank you."

"You said you have no children," Flowridia continued, her gut twisting as she contemplated her next words. This woman likely hated her, but she had done right so far. "Did . . . Did your brother leave any behind? Or does your bloodline truly end?"

Lunestra shook her head, her joy fading. "He had one son, but he disappeared twenty years ago. My nephew was dear to me. When his mother passed away in childbirth, I aided my brother in raising him."

"Tell me about him." Flowridia's soul longed to know.

"He was the kindest person I ever knew," Lunestra replied, something wistful in her countenance. "As a boy, he had the unfortunate habit of bringing home wild animals and trying to convince Xoran to keep them. He loved all creatures and felt their happiness and pain in ways that were truly remarkable. When Sol Kareena granted him a familiar, I had never seen a more talented healer. He learned to wield a sword so he could better protect his loved ones. He was a paladin. He left a legacy of kindness. My hope, when I pass on, is that I might ask Sol Kareena of his fate."

To hear of her father brought bittersweet joy. Flowridia gripped the wood tight, swallowing back her threatened tears. "He sounds like a wonderful man."

"He would have led the country with grace," Lunestra said, affirming the words. "He had resisted taking the throne for many years, insisting he could better serve his goddess on the road than on a throne. Perhaps he was right. He had reached his fortieth year when he disappeared."

Bracing herself, Flowridia whispered, "What if I could tell you his fate?"

Lunestra frowned, her posturing stiffening. "With witchcraft?"

"His name was Zanoram, wasn't it?"

Her frown deepened. "Yes," Lunestra said, watching her warily.

"He was travelling to visit his family in the southernmost parts of Solvira," Flowridia began, maintaining careful eye contact with Lunestra, "when he was stopped by a De'Sindai man." Her mother's horrid words replayed in her head, the story of a paladin in the Abyssal Swamp. "He was told of a kidnapped maiden, stolen by an evil witch. As you said, his heart was kind and valiant; of course he went. He killed the monstrous witch, or so he thought. When he found the maiden, she enchanted him. Then she seduced him." She swallowed the lump in her throat, Lunestra's expression utterly indecipherable. "A-And then she killed him. It was what she did to all her victims. Her name was Odessa, and she was a monster."

Lunestra searched her face, her skepticism apparent. "That's a rather fantastic tale."

"It was what the witch told me," she whispered, "and she would have no reason to lie."

"Odessa is a Solviran legend."

"She was quite real," Flowridia replied, knowing there was more to say, yet feared it, feared rejection. But would it give this woman hope to know? "Odessa did as much many times, luring in men to seduce them, slay them, and birth their children. Sometimes eating them; sometimes allowing them to live. She let Zanoram's child live, deeming the girl worthy of her power, and dropped her off at the doorstep of an orphanage in a small village called Ilunnes."

Lunestra kept her studious gaze, then beckoned Flowridia forward. "Sit before me."

She obeyed. In slow measures, Lunestra reached out and stole a long strand of Flowridia's curled hair. "Zan took great pride in his hair," Lunestra said. "Is the auburn from your mother?"

Flowridia nodded.

"It's beautiful."

She smiled, shy and sincere.

"It's so strange, to say I've seen that smile before, but it is unmistakable," Lunestra said, wonder in her gaze as she studied Flowridia's face, her amber hue, and released the curl of hair. Instead, she took Flowridia's hand in her darker one, yet a connection remained in their palette, in the daintiness in their wrists and the texture of their hair—the ineffable connections of blood. Lunestra released her. "In the Theocracy, it is traditional that when someone takes the mantle of priest or priestess, they shed their family name— even royalty. When I became Priestess Lunestra, nearly sixty years ago, I shed my family name. My brother, Xoran, did the same when he became archbishop. It is to show allegiance to the goddess above all. But your father, as a paladin, kept his, and would have until he became the archbishop. He was Zanoram Makosa—my own name, at birth, and my brother's. It is yours too, by right of blood."

Lunestra's smile held kindness, even as Flowridia's own visage twisted from tears. By every god—she had a name. Not one she sought or had to earn, but granted by nature of being born, a birthright as valuable as sustenance and air.

Flowridia Makosa, Daughter of Zanoram—she wished she could have whispered the blessed name to the little orphan girl who wept in her bed from loneliness, dreaming of the family she would never find.

Genuine curiosity twisted Lunestra's aged features. "What do you mean when you say he was visiting his family?"

"I don't know. Apparently, he told that to the demon. Did you not know?"

Lunestra shook her head, then stopped and sat back, frowning as she stared at the wall. "He would often disappear to go 'crusading' as he jested of it—in truth he was spreading the teachings of the goddess, or so he said. He would be gone for weeks or months at a time, but I recall . . ." Her frown deepened. "There was a woman. It would have been many years before your birth—he was only a young man when he proclaimed his intention to marry her. I never met her, but I am told she came from a well-known family in her homeland and they wouldn't allow it. Xoran, too, forbade it—though I never knew why. I thought the matter was done with but . . ." Lunestra remained quiet a moment, even as Flowridia contemplated the implication. "Though he had many potential suitors at home, he never gave them a second thought. He claimed it was the season of his life to bring glory to Sol Kareena's name, but I wonder if, perhaps, he never let her go."

Flowridia's breath left her. "Then his family might still be out there. Did you know the woman's name?"

"It was a foreign name." Lunestra shut her eyes, lips pursed as silence settled. "Mariam. Her name was Mariam. I don't know any more than that."

Flowridia had never met anyone by the name but repeated it, resolving to remember. "For the sake of my father's legacy, I will find her." She smiled unbidden, nearly laughing. "Perhaps I have a sibling."

When Lunestra finally met her gaze again, tears welled in her eyes. "Even if it is only you, I'm overjoyed."

"I know you and I have had uncomfortable interactions in the past," Flowridia whispered, the truth of it pounding heat into her cheeks. "And I want you to know that I'm sorry. I've made many mistakes in my short political career, and I'm bound to make a few more."

"You did cast yourself in an untrustworthy light," Lunestra affirmed, but her countenance was kind. "In all sincerity, I saw you as a child. Had I not, I would not have gone to find you in the woods." She studied Flowridia the way she had minutes ago, when she had learned of their shared blood. "You're not a little girl anymore, though. You carry yourself differently. And I would be happy to cast aside the image of the child I knew and instead know the woman you are now."

"I would love to know you," Flowridia whispered, and when she looked to Lunestra she saw, for the first time in all her years, a piece of her heart she had been so dearly missing. Her mother had been wicked, but Lunestra was her blood, her grandmother in spirit, and the warmth in her heart spilled into her tears.

When Lunestra offered an embrace, she accepted, and it was the maternal love she had missed all her life.

She finally pulled back; both of them cried quiet tears. "Will you tell me more about my father?"

Lunestra told her treasured tales all through the evening.

It was late when she returned to the bedroom.

She hadn't any expectation, but she certainly hadn't presumed she'd see Ayla seated elegantly on the bed, her black dress provocative and tight, making even her small breasts look substantial in the dim lighting. "Good evening, darling. I've been waiting."

"Are you seducing me, Lady Darkleaf?" Flowridia asked, bemused at her shameless antics, but though Ayla perked up at the title, she shook her head.

"No, though I would never deny you. This is me taking advantage of the opportunity to wear something to my tastes, instead of the illustrious gowns of Solviran Royalty. I do see the merit of them, but I prefer Nox'Karthan styles."

Flowridia's unremitting smile only grew. "But you're not seducing me? Even after all your promises this morning?" A wink punctuated her teasing.

Ayla sat up, nearly cute as she batted her eyelids. "I have a present for you. A . . . pre-engagement gift."

"May I tell you of my day first? My heart is close to bursting."

Ayla leaned forward, curiosity twisting her smile. "Of course."

"The most wonderful thing happened," she whispered, and already she felt the return of her tears. She joined Ayla on the bed, the woman before her of unfathomable worth, yet Ayla had not completed her heart entirely—not even the truest love could. Now, however, she felt . . . *whole.* "I found something I have searched for my entire life."

She spoke of Lunestra's words, crying when she spoke of their embrace, and Ayla listened, sincerity in her gestures. "I have a family. I have a *name,*" she said, and she spoke it aloud for the first time—*Flowridia Makosa,* and Ayla's visage softened to hear it.

When Flowridia's story had ended, Ayla said, reservation in her words, "I have never understood the need for a family, but your happiness brings me joy."

"What do you mean?" she asked, though her eyelids drooped from want of sleep.

But Ayla shook her head. "Well, that is a lie, actually. I say I do not understand, but I would like to think I found a family all the same." She brought Flowridia's hand to her lips, lingering as she whispered, "That is what we are, is it not?"

Fresh tears welled in Flowridia's tired eyes. "Of course, it is. You and me, remember? And Demitri."

Ayla hugged her, sinking into Flowridia's arms like a tired child. "Are you sleepy?"

"A little," Flowridia admitted, "but I'd like to see your gift first."

Squeezing her hand, Ayla looked like a small kitten, nervous and shy, her eyes as large as the moon. "I may have eavesdropped in a shadow. You were talking to Demitri and bemoaned that you had no way to practice your necromancy."

Unsettled, Flowridia nodded.

"So, I prepared a gift, like I said."

Ayla smiled, but it so desperately sought approval. Flowridia laughed, though mostly from nerves. "All right."

"Come with me."

Flowridia agreed, prepared for the cold of Sha'Demoni as Ayla led her into a shadow.

She would be used to the Shadow Realm in time, she suspected, though navigating it indoors was another task entirely. Ayla led her through winding halls with perfect precision, while Flowridia feared she would end up stuck in a wall.

But soon the outside world greeted them. The eerie eyes of distant demons watched from afar, curious and bright. Flowridia held tight to Ayla's hand, knowing there was nothing to fear. "Have you gone to see your god, yet?"

"No," Ayla replied, her voice as dark as the atmosphere. "I have been far too enamored with you, my sweet Flowra. I suppose I should, however. He did endorse your quest."

"He called you his greatest creation," Flowridia replied. "That's a high compliment."

Ayla laughed, and it echoed across the shifting landscape, all color having faded except Flowridia's own self. "I suppose it is."

Darkness soon engulfed them as Ayla seemed to go underground, but Flowridia forced herself to simply breathe and move forward. Though she saw nothing, the world shifted back to her own—she felt it against her skin, the subtle change in cold. Pitch black surrounded them. A putrid smell assaulted her nostrils. Flowridia instinctively covered her nose, resisting the urge to vomit—so horrendous it was. "Don't forget I'm blind in the dark," Flowridia said, then shielded herself from the sudden light in Ayla's palm.

Silver flame illuminated Ayla's visage, casting it in frightening shadows. "Give me a moment," she said, her voice as dark as the atmosphere. She released Flowridia's hand, the light revealing stone walls and frightening figures—faces cast in eternal horror.

Flowridia balked, her stomach screaming of the wrongness of it all. Ayla touched a torch, the light it stole turning into a natural orange. Bright flame filled the dungeon. She touched another, and another, the light slowly increasing.

They stood in a simple room, large and made of stone. Piles of corpses lay before her. Flowridia waited for some trap, some trick, noting only their stages of rot and their dirt-covered clothing and fingernails—these bodies had been dead for some time.

Ayla approached, charm twisting her grin. "What do you think?"

Flowridia stared, knowing she was missing something. "I think I'm in the presence of quite a few dead people," she replied, slow and unsure.

"You are too sweet and innocent—my darling, they're for you!"

Her face conveyed the excitement of a woman presenting an anticipated birthday present, a nice cake, something pleasant, but this was Ayla, and Ayla was hardly typical. "Oh, to practice with," Flowridia said, her unease likely palpable.

"I plan to find a few living victims for some of your more, uh, detailed exploits, but what use is there in waiting . . ." Ayla's joy faded by a mere glimmer. "Do you not like it?"

"I simply wasn't expecting it." Flowridia dared to step forward, not wanting to offend her eccentric love. "They're very nice corpses."

"Mausoleums are easy to steal from." Ayla approached from behind, her large eyes conveying disappointment. "You do not like it."

Honesty was all Flowridia had. She sighed and said, "It's thoughtful. But . . ." She bit back the words, mulling them through her mind before she dared to speak them aloud. ". . . I don't know that I should move forward in this."

"Why not?"

"I once told myself I would never raise a humanoid corpse," she said, lightly stepping toward the bodies, most half-rotted, staring with mouths agape. They were human once, or Celestial, but she had the means to make them something more. She had nothing to fear from them—only herself. "I broke that promise to save you, and I don't regret it. But to do it for gain seems . . ."

She struggled to find a word. Ayla eventually touched her lower back, contemplation on her sharp features. ". . . selfish?"

"Something like that."

"Evil?"

Flowridia shook her head. "Casvir turned me away from that notion. These people are dead. Their spirits have gone on to the Beyond. Their bodies were merely vessels, and now they are food for the earth to consume. As long as I don't pull their spirits back, I take no issue with my powers." She breathed, coaxing power out with her breath. Purple mist seeped from her pores, swirling around her fingers. "The power is intoxicating," she admitted. "Invigorating. *Addictive.* I fear who I might become if I continue down this path."

"Describe her."

Confused at the remark, Flowridia frowned. "I beg your pardon?"

"You fear who you will become—describe her. Who is she, this apparent monster?"

Amusement shone in Ayla's raised eyebrow, the mild twist of her lip. Flowridia stared at the gaseous substance in her hand, watched it weave and flow around her fingers. "I . . ."

She truly didn't know. This shadowed future . . . Was it merely that? A shadow and nothing more?

"A necromancer once owned Solvira," Ayla cooed. "She founded it. The God of Death was wicked, but she was respected. However, you need not be like her—you are Flowridia, my gentle, beautiful Flowra, and I do not believe any amount of power could corrupt your tender heart." Ayla took her hand, the one caressing dark magic, immune to its necrotic touch. She kissed her knuckles. "If you must reject my gift, do not let it be because of fear."

Flowridia looked to the corpses, a whispering within her pleading for her to act. With trepidation, she stepped forward, still holding Ayla's hand.

She held her free hand out toward a corpse on top of the pile and bid it to come.

Purple mist rose within him, seeping from his mouth, his eyes, his pores. In shambling, erratic motions, the man lifted himself from the bodies, shuffling toward her with glazed eyes and a slack jaw. It only unearthed more of that horrendous, rotting stench. Stringy hair fell from his head, his open mouth revealing worms and maggots. Ruined clothing hung in tatters, the buttons plated from gold, evidence of silk at the ruined seams. This was once a nobleman. Now, he was a puppet.

He moved perfectly in time with the strings she pulled, though his rotted physical form was its own nuisance. A dangerous thought sparked within her as she touched his putrid flesh. Releasing Ayla, lest the magic be confused, she let her focus expand, studying his physique, the dead flesh stagnant, roused unwillingly by her probing.

Her energy pulsed as she poured it into him, commanding the flesh to seal, the muscles to stitch together once more. Before her very eyes, his bones repaired; his skin smoothed over. He still bore dirty hair and tattered clothing, but his face became handsome, though a bit grey. He could not pass for living, but he was hardly a frightening creature.

The man watched, perfectly obedient. Flowridia released her touch, feeling faint not from her depleted reserves, but for shock.

Beside her, a girlish laugh sounded. "You are incredible," Ayla said, and Flowridia smiled at her palpable delight.

"I suppose I have a future as a mortician," Flowridia replied, blushing when Ayla's lips brushed her cheek.

"Show me another miracle, darling," Ayla cooed, a hint of lust in the words. "I adore watching you work."

Enamored at the words, Flowridia obeyed, finding she rather liked showing off.

Chapter 10

Flowridia's heart pounded as she sat inside the large, ornate carriage.

At her own insistence, they rode with no sigils or finery—she wished to draw no attention to them in case her plot did not work. She sat across from Magister Reginal, and outside, two guards in street clothes drove the carriage. Beside her, Archbishop Lunestra, keen to be involved in any plans regarding her citizens, wore street clothes, unrecognizable as the refugee monarch. Were it only them as passengers, they might have chosen a smaller ride, but Demitri filled most of the space, insisting on accompanying them.

It's my right.

"You're a wolf; you don't have rights."

Ayla had stayed, to her own chagrin. *"My entire day is meetings, constant meetings! Everyone is always angry over something . . ."*

Ayla had ranted and raged all morning, as Flowridia had readied.

". . . hate that you will be going without me. You are much more important. I could cancel them all."

"Ayla, no."

So, with the eccentric magister and disguised archbishop, they rode out of the city walls, and to the fields beyond. Flowridia stared, enamored by the lake, its crystal surface glittering in the sunlight.

"Lady Flowridia, I should tell you," Reginal suddenly said, startling her, "that I have spoken to my husband on the matter of the orphaned children. He and I had actually been discussing expanding our small family. We have a son, but he's grown. Erlyn, my husband, has agreed that now is the best time."

Elation filled Flowridia. "You'll take one?"

"That littlest one deserves a family before she's accustomed to life without one."

Her heart soared at the thought. "I can't imagine a better life for her," she replied, and beside her, Lunestra held a sincere smile. They spoke of family life—of Reginal and his husband and child.

When the carriage stopped, outside was a small cottage, surrounded by fences and fields and a barn. A guard opened the door, and she gathered her skirts as she exited, overjoyed by the crisp breeze and warm sunlight.

Cities were wonderful, but her heart yearned for the outdoors, for the woods and the fields. Demitri shadowed her, and Flowridia offered a hand to the elderly woman emerging behind her, who graciously accepted. When Reginal appeared, he beckoned them forward. "The gentleman's name is Beckett, and in the spring and summer months, he employs a small army of farmhands to assist with the labor of his crops. He's the city's largest producer of agriculture."

"This is all very foreign to me," Flowridia admitted. "I understand farming and gardening but providing enough food for a city as large as Neolan boggles my mind."

"Given you're proposing providing enough food for Neolan and the refugees," Lunestra said, clearly bemused, "I assume you plan on studying."

"Something like that. But don't thank me yet."

They stared at her oddly, and Flowridia accepted that as a victory.

They were introduced to Beckett, the man who owned the sprawling fields. He offered a tour, and she accepted, but with the caveat that she see the fields first.

"I will say," the man said as he escorted them past the barn and a small selection of livestock—all of whom cowered at Demitri's passing, "I was surprised to hear you would be coming personally. That's not what I would have expected from a noblewoman from Nox'Kartha."

"I'm actually from Solvira," she said kindly, practiced charm in the words. "I grew up south of here, then spent time in Staelash, employed by Magister Etolié."

"I had heard that."

Did the whole world know her? She recalled a girl in the woods months ago proclaiming to Casvir that she gave no care to her reputation, and now she wondered if she had been wrong.

The field was little more than dirt, though plagued with spots of wild grass. "Once the last of winter clears away, we'll be planting again," he said.

She studied the vast field, contemplating the cost and prayed she could pay it. This was far larger than a meadow beyond a swamp. "Might I have a seed? Just one."

The man agreed and left to fetch one.

Reginal had kept his robes hiked all the while, apparently remiss to dirty them. Flowridia braced herself and asked, "Reginal, is it true that people think I'm using Lara for social gain?"

The aged man grimaced, and Flowridia internally withered at the honest response. "Many do, yes. There were, uh, *salacious* rumors regarding you and Imperator Casvir, so when you and Lara had your rather public moment at Queen Marielle's wedding, many people . . . made assumptions."

Someday she would wring Murishani's neck. She feared this rumor would plague her for life. "I understand. Let me at least reassure you that there was nothing untoward between Imperator Casvir and I."

"Etolié explained your relationship to me," Reginal replied, "so while I heard the rumors, I chose to take her word."

"What irks me," Lunestra said, her polite demeanor covering thinly veiled ire, "is the presumption that Flowridia, a child, was the one at fault. Even if they had been sleeping together, the imperator is centuries old."

"I wasn't a child." Flowridia looked to Demitri, taller than she, who had been just a pup when they had embarked on that journey all those months ago. "Not in age, at least. I suppose in spirit, I was still very young."

Lunestra chuckled, soon joined by Reginal. "You were a child enough. You're still one now, to people like us."

Flowridia smiled at the tease. Her elderly companions did have a point. "I'm nearly twenty—only a few years behind." Her wry grin revealed her jest, and behind them, Beckett quickly ran to join them.

He offered Flowridia a single seed. "I don't know what good this little thing will do."

Flowridia clutched it in her fist, feeling the dormant power within. In silence, she stepped forward, Demitri trailing as she went into the field.

The notion was impossible, unheard of, yet she had performed this miracle before. Flowridia knelt in the dirt, buried the small seed, and placed her hand over where it lay. "It's so strange, Demitri," she whispered, gathering her focus. "Ever since I raised those dead in the swamp, it's as though . . . as though some door has opened. I feel different. I feel changed."

Perhaps it was what you needed in order to grow.

Flowridia felt the seed and poured her power into it. At the first vibration of life, she coaxed it along until a single, beautiful sprout of wheat poked from the dirt. *"Hello,"* she said, the words laced with power. *"I need a few more of you."*

The earth trembled, not unlike when she'd summoned the dead to rise, yet this bore emblems of light. The entire field shook as thousands of stalks rose to match their sole progenitor, spreading from the center as they grew at impossible speeds.

Flowridia felt nothing at all, no drainage of power—not until the growth ceased and a beautiful field of wheat surrounded her.

Dizziness struck. She stumbled forward into Demitri, whose jaws gripped the collar of her dress, preventing her from falling. Though her vision blurred, she felt him tugging her along. Her attempt to say something amusing ended in only a pathetic groan.

Demitri dragged her to the edge of the field, a puppeteer with an unwilling prop. When they approached the archbishop and the two gentlemen, Flowridia still reeled at the outpouring of energy. But Beckett was struck dumb, jaw slack as he gazed upon the field, ready for harvest.

Reginal burst into joyful accolades, but Flowridia merely settled in the dirt when Demitri set her down.

She caught one important phrase, however—*"This is more than proof enough! I accept your proposal."*

She managed a smile. When she opened her eyes, she saw Lunestra's blurry countenance kneeling beside her. "That's beyond anything I've ever seen. How did you do it?"

"I dunno," she slurred, finding the dirt and the pillow of her hair sufficiently comfortable for a nap. "Just . . . somethin' inside me said I could."

Admittedly, she remembered very little else until they reentered the carriage.

Demitri's tongue lapped across her hands, never stopping. *I'm trying to help. Is this helping?*

"It's keeping me conscious," she replied, her limbs an impossible weight to lift.

"That was remarkable!" Reginal said, his enthusiasm having not staunched. "You could solve famine! The whole world could benefit from your talents."

Flowridia smiled behind her closed eyes. "After a nap."

When they rolled through the gates, guards stopped them, prepared to ask for their business in the city, but immediately recognized Reginal. "Magister," one said, "with due respect, we must ask that you go straight to the castle. There's been a murder."

Flowridia's stomach clenched.

Reginal said, "What has happened?"

"We don't have details yet, sir, but some are speculating it's supernatural in origin. We can't say with any confidence that the streets are safe."

"Of course," Reginal replied, and the carriage kept moving along. "How ghastly."

How ghastly indeed, Flowridia thought, and somewhere deep inside, she suspected something vile.

Reginal waxed poetic at length of Flowridia's miracle at the wheat fields in the ensuing council meeting. Flowridia wished to melt into her chair and hide, and her blush surely conveyed that.

"Don't be so shy to accept your dues," Lara said, her smile filled with unbearable pride; Flowridia could barely face her. "Though now we must pay up—housing."

"I will put some thought into it," Reginal replied.

"Some consideration should be given to where to send Archbishop Lunestra," Jules said, and Flowridia's gut clenched at the words.

"She's only just arrived," Flowridia said.

"Yes, but the sooner the better. The Glass Palace is not a long-term solution."

"What of Staelash?" Lara asked.

"Assuming we trust Queen Marielle's new husband," Reginal said, hesitant and perhaps even apologetic, "it could be a solution. She would be right under their noses, but there is merit to it."

Lara's smirk betrayed her poor mood. "Zorlaeus doesn't have the spine enough to betray anyone."

Reginal visibly fought to subdue a chuckle. "I don't disagree, but I wasn't going to say it."

"Alternatively, though it might be a stretch of our goodwill, but what of the Sun Elves in Falar'Sol?" Lara proposed. "It would send her much farther away, and even if Casvir were to discover her whereabouts, he wouldn't wish to antagonize them."

"We have no connection whatsoever with the Sun Elves," Jules said.

"Aside from their common goddess," Lara added, but Jules shook her head.

"Yes, but the Theocracy itself maintains no official ties. I fear it would be a waste of our time."

Lara looked to Reginal. "What do you say?"

Reginal shook his head. "I'm highly skeptical, but the worst they can say is no. It wouldn't be an insult to ask. I can pen a letter to the executor."

"Then the matter is settled for now," Lara announced, with a flourish far more dramatic than the true empress would have made. "Reginal shall write to the executor, but Lunestra shall be sent to Staelash as a final resort."

"I take no pride in reporting what my soldiers found last night," General Irons said, producing handwritten documents, the ink still drying on the topmost one. "An entire family torn apart. I will spare you the details, but they can be read in here."

Flowridia immediately slid over the documents from across the table, stomach sinking at his words. "Lara, this is . . ."

Madness, is what it was. A husband and wife and their three children, their blood used to fill a bathtub—presumably for their opulent murderer to bathe in. Flowridia's own blood boiled as she scanned the documents. "It says here one family member was left alive—a grandfather. Do you have his testimony?"

Irons shook his head. "Not yet," he said curtly. "He's currently in custody of the Temple of Sol Kareena. He was too shaken to say much of anything. He bore distinctive bite marks on his neck, however, as you may note further down. We fear there may be a vampire in our midst, or something else that works with blood."

Despite the condemnation in his words, Flowridia's gaze returned to the paper. "This is . . . *beyond*. Generally, vampires try to be discreet. They don't want their hunting grounds investigated."

"Kind of you to shed light on something we've already made note of," Irons said, his glare unrelenting. "If you have any other brilliant insights, I'm desperate enough to entertain them—"

"Take care how you speak to her," Lara said, but Flowridia shut her up with a glare.

She remained quiet as they spoke more of the crime, her anger quietly simmering any time Lara, ever the actress, said a single word. There could only be one culprit, and Flowridia internally raged over the audacity of it. For Ayla to do this to her own people? And to be so blatant? Ayla had to feed; this was a fact. But this was much more than a regrettable disappearance in the night.

"Flowra, are you all right?"

Startled from her musing, Flowridia forced a smile at Lara's question. "I feel ill from this morning. May I be excused?"

"Of course." Lara looked to the rest and said, "May we take a short recess? I would like to escort Flowra myself."

No one argued with the obviously enamored couple. They quickly swept into the hallway, but once alone, Lara lost her theatrical facade. "You are not sick. You don't smell sick. What is wrong?"

Flowridia braced herself, glancing briefly behind to be certain no one would hear them. "How could you?"

Lara's gaze held utmost sincerity, and it made Flowridia's blood boil. "I beg your pardon?"

"Those murders. That was you." When nothing at all changed in Lara's demeanor, Flowridia nearly screamed from frustration. "How could you?"

"Honestly, Flowra, I know nothing of it. Simply awful."

Despite the glamour of her disguise, Flowridia knew this face—this was not Lara, the empress, nor Ayla, her intended; this was Lady Ayla Darkleaf, master of deceit, her face a perfect decoy. A stranger would buy it, perhaps even a friend; Flowridia knew her better than that. "You would have the audacity to lie to me?"

"Flowra, I would never—"

Flowridia walked away. Magic pulsed through her system, and when she breathed, the cloud of purple would have choked someone passing by. But she wouldn't lose control; not here and now, and not over this.

But then came an infuriating phrase: "Flowra, your behavior is stupid."

She refused to turn around. "And you're a liar, so forgive me for not wanting to stand here and be disrespected."

"I have my reasons."

Flowridia whirled around. There Lara stood, directly at her heels. "You admit you lied? This thing you know absolutely nothing about?" Flowridia matched her glare, fury rising. "Did you truly think I didn't know? How *dare* you shut me out. You can tell me to shove off when something isn't my business, but you can't lie to my face and expect me not to know."

"Shove off, then," Lara cooed, but Flowridia shook her head.

"Did you hear General Irons? He thinks I'm responsible. I'm involved, whether either of us like it or not." Flowridia stood tall, taller than her lover, but Ayla was not one to back down. "If you would let me in, perhaps I can help with whatever harebrained scheme you have going on in the city."

"No. I refuse. You're too—" Lara's mouth flattened to a thin line, her words stopping abruptly.

"Too what, *darling?*" Flowridia dared, the word purely mocking.

Ayla's lip twitched, her face otherwise indecipherable. "Nothing."

"Too what? Fragile? Human? *Stupid,* as you so eloquently put it?"

"I didn't call you stupid. I said your behavior was—"

"Is that better?!" Flowridia shut her mouth; her cry echoed throughout the hall, and they were hardly alone. "There is a massive difference between privacy and keeping secrets," she continued, voice lowered, "and you don't know the difference at all. All I have ever done is be vulnerable to you, so how can I possibly pledge my heart to someone who won't return that?" Flowridia blinked, hating her tears, but not so much as the sudden panic in Ayla's eyes. "Gods, that's not what I . . ." She swallowed her words, knowing the truth in them. To lie would make her no better. "We'll talk later."

Flowridia turned on her heels, fury and sorrow driving her steps, but frantic footsteps followed. "You're too pure," Lara said, though it was all Ayla behind the façade. She grasped Flowridia's hand, as nervous as a child facing reproach. "I'm trying to protect you."

"After all I've done, you think I'm pure?" Flowridia laughed, though it was heartless and cruel. She tugged her hand away, continuing her exit.

"Flowra, please."

Something in those words broke Flowridia's heart. When she turned, it was Lara's image, yet there was no mistaking Ayla's remorseful visage. How strange, that she could be a monster in one moment and then so pitiful in merely a blink.

"I'm sorry," she said, lip trembling. "Yes, I lied. I didn't want you to know."

"Why?"

Lara's stance remained small, and Flowridia waited as she gathered her thoughts. "Because you hate it."

"I do," Flowridia affirmed, her own words muted, "but that doesn't mean I hate you. I don't understand why you do what you do, but I accepted that I simply never would. I had to decide if I loved you more than I hated what you did. Accepting that the answer is 'yes' was not a decision I came to lightly. I won't reject you for doing what you've always done. I'm not going to try to change you. But lying to me tells me you don't respect me. Instead, you're trying to manipulate me into feeling what you want me to feel. You've spent your entire life manipulating people and using them—and that *is* something that must change if I'm to be yours forever. There will be times that I'm disappointed and angry with you, but I will love you regardless."

Lara stared at the floor, looking pitiful. "I have to go back. We will talk later."

Flowridia nodded, too tired to be angry, and left her there.

"Unfortunately, I see the merit," Lunestra said as they walked through the garden paths. "It would be best if I didn't stay in Neolan."

In spots of shade, the lingering chill of winter quickly settled, but the sunlit patches brought the promise of spring. Flowridia's heart sank at the words. "If not here, is anywhere safe?"

"There are certainly spies in the capital city," Lunestra replied, kindness in her aged voice. "I trust Empress Alauriel to know where would be safest."

"I do too." And it was true—Ayla would know precisely where Casvir's assassins might search for the missing archbishop.

Thoughts of Ayla brought a frown to her face; Flowridia prayed Lunestra didn't notice. She hadn't seen Ayla in hours and still quietly fumed. "Lara mentioned something about the Sun Elves potentially taking you in."

"I would be surprised if they accepted," Lunestra admitted. "The elves across the sea are known for being isolationists, and I doubt even worshippers of Sol Kareena would want to risk being involved in the war. However, I see why she would at least ask—it would be a safe option." She smiled, then released a soft, scoffing laugh. "So morbid, to discuss my own death. I wonder if it's even worth the fuss. I shall drop dead of old age before the assassins even reach me." When Lunestra laughed, Flowridia joined her, amused at her progenitor's macabre humor.

Still, the reminder wounded her heart. "I hope it isn't strange for me to admit how dearly I'll miss you," Flowridia said, the words nearly lost in the gentle breeze. "I don't wish to speak of my mother, but suffice it to say she was not the family I'd always hoped for as a child." Emotion rose in her throat. She swallowed it, knowing that once she began crying, she wouldn't stop. "To know who I am, to be Flowridia Makosa..." She stopped her wandering, idling in a sunny patch. "I barely know you, yet it means so much to me."

Lunestra took her hands, their dissimilar hues still bearing emblems of shared blood. Her smile held sorrow for that same impending loss. "Family doesn't disappear because of distance. Blood is eternal. When I die, my legacy lives on in you—and *nothing* can change that. Even if Casvir succeeds in taking my life, I live on in you."

The words were a farewell. Flowridia could not find it in herself to feel guilty for her ruse with Ayla—for a moment, her legacy was pure. If she could offer nothing else, it would be for Lunestra to die with that hope. Tears welled in her eyes as she blinked; Lunestra's own dark eyes glistened. "And you're quick to assume we'll never see each other again," Lunestra said jovially. "I will die someday, but I'm filled with enough spite to keep moving for now."

Flowridia managed to chuckle through her tears, stealing her hands away to wipe her eyes.

"And beyond that," Lunestra continued, gentler now, "life must move on. I am in the winter of my life, but you have barely left spring. People like me must leave the world to people like you and hope you flourish. My legacy is set in stone, but your life has only just begun."

"You said your legacy was the children of the cathedral, that Sol Kareena herself called you to that role," Flowridia mused, finally resuming her steps through the garden. She wiped her final few tears upon her sleeve. "If it isn't too personal, I would love to hear that story."

Lunestra followed, admiring the few blossoms among the winter's chill. The frost had melted, leaving an arrangement of muted colors—in only a few more weeks, it would explode in a rainbow of hues. "I wish it were a happier tale. It began when I was a little girl. I was royalty, but I was still expected to attend school with other children. My brother and I walked every day, and on the path was a large monument. It depicted Sol Kareena embracing a little child, and I remember loving it. It became the face of my own vision of the goddess—she is justice and light, but she can also bring comfort and happiness. It was years later that I actually learned what the monument was for—*In Memory of Evandalin's Fire,* it said, followed by the names of the twenty-four children who died in the flames."

Flowridia's heart ached at the words. "That's awful."

"Did you ever hear of the cathedral fire?"

Flowridia nodded. "All that was left standing was the statue of Sol Kareena and the altar. That's what Etolié told me."

"History had not forgotten it, but there was so little information to be found," Lunestra said, a certain spark in her words. "I have a keen interest in history and have written many books on my country. I'm working on a piece now, lest the victorious write the story of the day the City of Light fell to Nox'Kartha. But I digress—I studied the fire and was heartbroken to recognize the panic those children must have felt, locked in their rooms for the night as the building burned. Some would have died of smoke inhalation before they burned, and those were the lucky ones. I studied the names on the monument and wept, because someone needed to weep for those poor children."

"That's good of you," Flowridia, understanding the sentiment. Perhaps tender hearts simply ran in her bloodline. "Do we know what started the fire?"

Lunestra paused in her wandering, shoulders sinking. "No. It's one of those great mysteries, but for the statue to have still been standing gives me hope that she saw it all. There was a body identified by its jewelry and vestments lying before the statue—the high priestess of the temple, Evandalin. The fire was named for her, to celebrate the legacy of peace she had left, despite her awful end."

Yet Lunestra remained tense, the silence holding no finality. Flowridia sought to gather words, but the high priestess finally did say more. "It is dangerous to speak of demons, lest we summon their presence. But there was evidence of activity. The fire was not the true evil; it was what was discovered in the ruins."

The words lingered, asking permission. "I highly doubt it will be the worst thing I've ever heard," Flowridia said.

"Unfortunately, I believe you," Lunestra replied, an apologetic smile on her lip. "The mystery remains of why no one could escape. The fire is thought to have originated in the chapel, perhaps a knocked over candle. But that would have been a slow burn, not nearly enough to destroy a temple made of stone. There were no survivors, and so no witnesses to what occurred behind the walls, but written in blood on the altar— which did not burn, despite the great blaze, were Demoni symbols. Eventually they were discovered to mean *burn.*"

Flowridia recalled the shadow of Ku'Shya that had loomed over Khastra's funeral. And once, she had stood before

Izthuni, whose emanating dread haunted her on sleepless nights. "You believe a demon was behind it?"

"It would have been a mortal acting in their stead, but the evidence cannot be denied."

"Forgive me for insinuating it," Flowridia said, pondering the story, "but you said the high priestess' body was found beside the altar—might she have been behind it?"

Lunestra's gaze lingered on a patch of frost, untouched in the shade. "I suppose we cannot know a person's true character, especially so many years later, but the treatises written on her legacy would say no. High Priestess Evandalin was famed for her work in reforming the cathedral as a home for the orphans. Before her time, there were countless scandals and endless stories of abuse. She sought to make it a home. For her to burn down the place of peace she had worked so hard to build doesn't make sense to me."

A sudden memory struck her, of a cathedral of horror, decorated with demons and gore. Too recently, she had gazed upon an altar bearing the bloody elven word for *burn*. Flowridia dug through her memories, hating that she had forgotten Ayla's age, tried to recall the history books she had devoured on The Endless Night. She simply asked, because though it could have been a grand and terrible coincidence, but her gut said something different. "Was this before or after The Endless Night first manifested?"

Lunestra looked contemplative, and Flowridia feared what she thought. "I do not know for certain, though I think before. There were no Sun Elven refugees mentioned in the texts I studied, and they were commonplace later."

"Just curious," Flowridia said, and she prayed Lunestra accepted it. "Tell me, if you can, of your own reforms of the orphanages. If I can continue your legacy, let me."

They spoke for hours—not of lighter things, but of hope. Flowridia's mind remained distant, memories of horror bleeding into the pleasant afternoon—Ayla's macabre cathedral recreation, her casual disdain of Sol Kareena . . . Yet it was impossible.

Surely impossible. So why couldn't she shake it?

All was well, here in the light, until distant thuds signified a familiar and beloved presence. Flowridia was surprised to see Demitri rapidly approaching. "Well, hello," she said, content to embrace him, but the wolf looked uncharacteristically frantic.

Lady Ayla is being crazy.

"What?"

I heard strange noises and went to your room. She let me in, but she wouldn't stop ranting about you and . . .

Flowridia couldn't say she had ever heard Demitri at a loss for words.

Just go please.

"Lunestra, forgive me, but Demitri says my intended needs me." Demitri pawed at the ground, visibly anxious. "It sounds urgent."

"Of course. Go on," Lunestra said, no offense in her smile.

"Demitri, can you escort Lunestra back to the castle?"

I can do that. But then I'm coming to find you.

"I would expect nothing less," she said, and she kissed his nose. Then, she grabbed her skirts and ran down the path, fear driving her steps.

What had Ayla done now?

Flowridia ran through the hallways, heart racing as she waited for the lift to rise. Something in her stance must have suggested panic—servants tried to stop her and ask what was wrong, but she waved them off, said it was nothing.

When her room came into sight, she did not stop or knock—she barged inside.

Ayla sat on the edge of the bed, hunched over as she slid her thumbnail *beneath the skin of her forearm*—skin that was already bunching up like a sleeve around her wrist, revealing pallid muscle beneath, even a hint of bone. They matched eyes, Ayla's wide with shock, and Flowridia collapsed against the shut door, aghast and sickened by the display. "Darling!" Ayla said, pausing in her apparent attempt to deglove herself. "I had wondered where you were—"

"What are you doing?!" Flowridia cried, too nauseated to step forward. On the floor before Ayla was what Flowridia realized was a small pile of flesh. When Ayla held out her mutilated arm, Flowridia shut her eyes and shook her head.

"Practicing. Passing time. Pain does not bother me."

Flowridia heaved a heavy breath yet drew no air. Lightheaded, she stumbled forward as Ayla smoothed the gathered skin across her forearm where it belonged—before Flowridia's very eyes, it began healing.

"I can only stop it for so long, remember? You've seen me do worse to myself—remember the burn?"

Flowridia did but violently shook her head. "No, this is worse," she managed to say, sickened even as the flesh sealed back into place, the damaged spots healing and regrowing. The pile of flesh remained, and Flowridia wondered how long she had been doing this before Demitri ran to find her.

"It's nothing, I promise." And Ayla, misguided, sweet Ayla, proceeded to grab the pointer finger of her left hand and *yank*.

The sickening crack of bone and squishing flesh churned Flowridia's stomach—yes, she had seen worse, but this was the woman she loved—and when Ayla offered her own severed finger forward, Flowridia recoiled and waved it away.

Kneeling, she clung to Ayla's dress, fingers grasping fabric and her small hips. Her breathing became labored, even as Ayla carelessly held the finger back to her mutilated hand; the skin sealed, but Flowridia didn't care. She took Ayla's hand and kissed the scarred finger, even as it became porcelain perfection. She stroked gentle lines across Ayla's forearm, knowing she would feel nothing amiss but unable to shake the memory of horror.

"I don't care if it's nothing," Flowridia said, cradling the arm to her neck like a child. She kissed Ayla's palm, her wrist, savored the chill touch of her skin before gently setting it back into Ayla's lap. On her knees, she remained a supplicant, bracing herself as she picked up the layer of flesh on top of the pile—nearly an entire hand, though just the skin, peeled off to make a glove. It had ripped at three of the fingers yet was unmistakably Ayla's pale coloring.

"It's a game I play," Ayla said, her words tight and tense, "when I am stressed. Degloving requires near perfect concentration, so..." Her words trailed off, perhaps in response to Flowridia's welling tears.

Flowridia dropped the ruined flesh and managed to rise to her feet. In silence, she went to Ayla's side, knelt on the bed beside her, and pulled her into an embrace, Ayla's head pressed against her chest. She clung tight, sickened down to her soul though she struggled to describe *why*—even to herself. "I love you," she said, and to her surprise, Ayla slumped over.

"I did not mean to worry you…" She trailed off at Flowridia's gentle *shh.* Flowridia simply held her, savored her presence, grateful to hold her for as long as they had.

"You scared Demitri. He sent me to find you."

Flowridia didn't know if this were a cry for help or simply another quirk to discover. When coaxed to lay down, Ayla obeyed. "I sometimes forget he talks."

"He's constantly chattering about something," Flowridia said, pulling Ayla into her arms. "I just don't repeat it unless he wants me to." She clutched her lover like a doll, hoping it conveyed some comfort. Knowing Ayla, it did, though she would never say it. "Is this because of our fight? Is that why you're stressed?"

Ayla stared at the wall, her hands flexing against the blankets. She said nothing, but her silence was answer enough.

"Ayla, I love you." Flowridia sat up, just able to see the first hints of Ayla's eyelashes, but she could decipher nothing else. "I don't have to know every thought in your head, but your secrets and hurts are safe with me. They're a burden I would gladly help you carry, if you'll let me. I plan to be your wife, and that's not a duty I intend to take lightly."

Ayla said nothing, merely stared at the wall. Flowridia's heart ached, fearing she had misspoken. In the ensuing silence, she dared to pull away, just enough to see her love's face. Though she feared reproach, it paled to her worry of being shut out of Ayla's inner world. She steeled her resolve and crawled on top of her, then fell on her opposite side, facing Ayla now.

Ayla barely reacted, though her searing gaze did settle onto Flowridia instead. "Everything is fine, Flowra," she repeated, sounding reserved, but Flowridia pressed their lips together instead, grateful when Ayla returned the gesture.

"May I offer you a gentle touch instead?" she whispered, and Ayla nodded, sighing into her mouth. Flowridia shoved aside memories of gore and pain, and instead held her love in an innocent embrace, gently stroking soft lines across her back.

In slow measures, Ayla melted into her touch, the tension in her form ebbing away. Ayla kissed her neck, settled with her head against Flowridia's breast. "I apologize for scaring you."

"It's in my nature to worry," Flowridia managed to say, drawing Ayla closer, holding her tight.

"I have always wondered if I could strip enough flesh off my body to recreate myself," Ayla said, contemplation in her gaze. "I have never quite had the fortitude to skin my own face, though."

Flowridia *tsk-tsk-ed* as she shook her head. "I don't know how you can stand to *face* yourself."

Ayla opened her mouth, then shut it abruptly. "First you sob at my feet over it, and now you are making jests?" Her incredulity faded into an amused chuckle. "Flowra, you are an enigma."

In response, Flowridia placed a chaste kiss in Ayla's hair, grateful to have seen a glimpse of her joy once more.

Ayla's words, when they finally came, were shy. "I am . . . embarrassed."

"You don't need to be," Flowridia said, but Ayla wouldn't meet her eye, her shame apparent.

"You are angry with me. You should not comfort me."

Flowridia kissed her yet again, praying it conveyed her sincerity. "I can set my anger aside and hold you when you need it."

In silence, she did so, pressing close to her love. To simply be near her was its own magic.

But to her surprise and worry, Ayla suddenly tensed in her arms. Wetness stained Flowridia's shoulder as her love shed quiet tears.

Flowridia said nothing, merely held her, this enigmatic and sensitive lover of hers.

They remained in silence for some time—time Flowridia lost track of in her own quiet distress. Ayla's words, when they came, were soft and contrite. "I am sorry."

"I know."

"No—Flowra, I am sorry. I am awful at loving people, and I have fucked this up in a horrible way." Ayla's grip tightened, and while her nails were not painful, Flowridia was acutely aware of them piercing her dress. "Please do not leave me."

"Ayla, no," Flowridia replied, breathing in the cool scent of her lover's hair. Faint but unmistakable, the scent of blood clung to her black locks. "I forgive you."

"I do not deserve that."

"Stop," Flowridia said gently. "We deserve nothing, my love. I offer kindness because I love you. I ask only for the same in return."

Ayla gently touched the thick, layered curls, sinking her entire hand and part of her arm within the mass. "I have to be in control, else the whole world falls apart—I am introspective enough for that. My life is a play, and it is up to me to manipulate the players into enacting my narrative." She withdrew her hand, content to caress the hair by Flowridia's face.

"That's a little narcissistic," Flowridia said gently, and Ayla gave a scoffing, pained laugh.

"Your capacity to understate my flaws is truly remarkable."

Flowridia kissed her, caressed her, and coaxed her love to face her. "You berate yourself much more than you deserve."

"Flowra, let us not contemplate my body count."

And despite the somber mood and truly gruesome statement, Flowridia laughed. "Whatever your flaws, you're self-aware."

Ayla did not join in her amusement, but she did manage a small smile. When she opened her mouth to speak, a knock interrupted her.

From beyond, a voice said, "Empress Alauriel?"

Ayla tried to rise, but Flowridia stopped her. "Let me talk to them," she whispered. "I shall tell them you're sick and can't be bothered."

Ayla shook her head. "No, no—I should run my damn kingdom, remember? But . . ." She sat up, though her posture remained small. So strange, to see her utterly unconfident. "But I have been contemplating how to make this up to you. You will let me, won't you?"

"Ayla, you don't—"

"I owe you an explanation, at the very least."

Flowridia took her hand, praying Ayla believed her sincere intentions. "I will accept an explanation."

"Tonight, then."

Ayla removed her touch, and Flowridia hated watching her go. Her love's figure became Empress Alauriel's, and when she might've opened the door, Flowridia suddenly said, "Wait."

Lara paused, waiting for an explanation, but Flowridia simply rolled out of bed, cringing when she picked up the discarded pile of her intended's flesh. "What should I do with this?"

Lara smiled and took it, then tossed it into a dark shadow—where it disappeared. "I will take care of it."

Lara left, joining the servant waiting at the door. Flowridia remained alone, contemplating every new development.

Flowridia eventually busied herself with Demitri, Lunestra, and the orphans, but quietly awaited any news of Ayla. She wasn't at dinner, and when Flowridia asked, Reginal said simply that she was busy with some pet project—but wouldn't say what.

Flowridia worried all the while.

After, she traversed the halls alone. Her bedroom was dark, but the door to the washroom was opened, revealing the first flickering of candlelight.

Flowridia tiptoed inside, gasping at the display. Countless candles dotted the counter and the sides of the tub, reflected by mirrors, and floating in the water were flower petals in pastel colors. Ayla herself sat on the side of the tub, her scandalous attire revealing the pale curves of her hips and translucent enough to show the barest hints of her breasts. "Hello, Flowra," she said, but it lacked the confidence Flowridia had come to know and love.

"Hello," Flowridia said, shutting the door behind her.

"Come. Relax." Ayla stood and beckoned her forward, sensuality in every fine motion. "I have made up my mind to care for you this evening, so indulge me, won't you?"

Tentatively, Flowridia accepted her outstretched hand, interlacing their fingers as she stepped forward. "This is beautiful," she whispered, even as Ayla leisurely busied herself with the buttons on Flowridia's dress.

"I know a thing or two about setting a mood." Ayla helped remove her dress, leaving her in her underclothes, and folded and tucked it aside. She quickly returned to Flowridia's side to ease her out of her underclothes, her touch upon her bare skin innocent but dripping with sensual delight. "Go make yourself comfortable," she cooed, and she whisked Flowridia's clothing away, disappearing a moment through the doorway.

Flowridia quickly tied her auburn hair up, remiss to wash the lengthy curls again so soon, then slid into the tub, the water's warmth embracing her like a lover's touch. Whatever Ayla was plotting, this was a wonderful start.

She settled against the side of the tub just as Ayla returned. In silence, she stepped into the tub, still wearing her barely-there gown, the fabric floating to the top of the water as she slid in and sat across from her. With a distant smile, she stole one of Flowridia's feet and kneaded her fingers into the flesh, evoking a hum from its owner.

"I owe you an apology," Ayla said, her focus entirely on the water and Flowridia's foot. "A far better one than this, but I hope you will accept this as the first step. I have been selfish. I see that now. I thought, by lying, that I was protecting you; instead, I was treating you like the delicate flower of the time before—who it also would have been wrong to lie to, but hopefully you can understand why it would have been my first instinct. But you have grown, and I was an ass. You deserve an explanation."

Flowridia offered a reassuring smile, finally comfortable after the stress of the day.

"Yes, I am behind the murders," Ayla continued, resignation in her tone. Her touch brought boundless relief to Flowridia's tired limb, even as a sneer marred Ayla's lip. "Yes, there are multiple, though they have not discovered it yet—aside from making a scene, I have turned at least one person, assuming they are buried soon enough. I have spent the better part of the day contemplating why, aside from the most pressing part—which is setting up the pieces for your journey into vampirism. If there is a threat plaguing the kingdom, what a beautiful tragedy it shall be, for the empress consort to fall into damnation—yet retain her character, of course. There is nothing in the charter that says the consort may not be an undead creature."

The reminder of Flowridia's imminent immortality caused her gut to twist, and she prayed Ayla didn't sense her sudden spike in distress.

"However, even I can see the holes in that statement," Ayla continued, gently lowering Flowridia's foot back into the bath. She lifted the other, repeating the same, tender motions. "Realistically, I am acting out. I am bored. Politics are stifling, golden shackles, and I am trying to stay sane. I feel like a feral cat suddenly caught and caged."

"We don't have to stay," Flowridia said, though her heart sank to say the words. "We could run away right now, and they'd never find us if we didn't want them to. I would be sad to leave some pieces of my life behind, but you're the most important part of it. If you're miserable, we can fix that."

"I do not wish to leave," Ayla said, and the words were surprising. Her undead lover visibly mulled over her thoughts. "But I am already tired of this masquerade. Empress Alauriel, bless her departed soul, was *boring*." At Flowridia's ensuing frown, Ayla held up a hand. "Yes, yes—she had a lovely cunt, but now she is dead, and I have to slog through her insufferable legacy."

Flowridia kept her mouth shut, furious at the words. But any mention of Lara, no matter how kind or crass, brought boundless amounts of shame—and it was a conversation she would simply rather avoid.

"I have fallen so far from where I once was," Ayla mused, her gaze a thousand miles away. The candlelight reflected against the pale shades of her eyes, casting them in hues of flame. "You have read my history; you know I was a legend. I had gained something of a following—not worshippers, but . . . *supporters*. People who appreciated my brutality and sought to place me on a throne. I had my eye on becoming an executor. Not for any true end; just because I could. It was a different sort of challenge because I could not simply murder my way to the top. I had to make friends and gain endorsements. I had to win people's trust, despite my history. Understand, the Sun Elves were mocked by their Chaos-worshipping neighbors in my day. Funny, don't you think, that no one ever tried to stop me from killing them?"

Ayla's ensuing grin bore malice. "It is because the other four elven kingdoms spit upon Sol Kareena. They worship the Old Gods, predominantly Chaos. Most of the world found my actions abhorrent—yet the other elves hardly cared. I was not a hero to them, but I was also not the villain the rest of the world painted me to be. Their only reservation was that I acted through Izthuni, another false god."

Flowridia kept her expression neutral, actively fighting to hide her appall. For the rest of the elves to be indifferent to genocide seemed unfeasible, yet Ayla had said it. "I did wonder how you had managed to gain power, given your reputation."

"Understand, Flowra, there were endless rumors circulating about my character. Some did not believe I conspired with demons at all. Some did not even think I vivisected people and sewed them to other people, even when it came from my own tongue!" Ayla chuckled as she placed Flowridia's foot back into the water. "Amazing, how people will lie to themselves. So many politicians have scandals that people sweep under the rug. If Mereen and her ilk hadn't stuffed me in that damned coffin, I would be ruling the Iron Elves right now, perhaps even all of Zauleen—I could have united the elven kingdoms."

Ayla sunk back into the tub, melodramatics in every motion. "Instead, I rule Solvira, which was once the greatest country in the world, ruled by incestuous tyrants who went mad more often than not. But the issue, Flowra, is that *I* do not rule Solvira. *My* plans for Solvira would involve a more totalitarian hand—not out of cruelty, no, but for simplicity. There would be far fewer crimes if we simply killed all the criminals. Then I would not be cursed to deal with them." Ayla *huffed*, staring fitfully at the ceiling. "This was what the Solviran Civil War was fought over, you know—Goddess Ilune began restricting free will and called it safety. I see the merit, to be honest."

"How so?" Flowridia asked, fully prepared to regret the words.

"How what?"

"How did she restrict free will? Was her mistake to act too quickly and scare her people off? I know nothing of history—how do we not repeat it?"

Ayla sat up, gaze guarded. "The God of Death had the ability to essentially bestow a 'living death' of sorts—fully alive but given the mindlessness of the dead. She would curse it upon anyone who defied the crown. It was said there were simpler variations of it, such as removing memories or simply forcing you to speak the words she implanted into your head, but the heart of it meant using necromancy to control the living masses."

"The utopian world you're describing sounds very similar to Nox'Kartha," Flowridia said, "assuming you're planning to offer the same benefits to its citizens."

"Oh, Casvir said many times that he modeled a decent amount of his decisions after Solviran rule beneath the Triage—meaning, before Neoma's death, Ilune's imprisonment, and Staella's subsequence disappearance." Ayla leaned forward, her hands held prettily beneath her chin. "Keep talking."

"I hate seeing you miserable," Flowridia said, nervous at her own words, for they could not remain idle statements once spoken aloud. "Your ideas for ruling Solvira aren't bad at all. It's like you said—you *do* understand politics, your temperament aside. I'm hesitant to enact full totalitarianism, but I can support a strict regime, so long as it's fair and just. If I can help you shape Solvira into something greater and new, let me."

In a gesture hilariously unlike her prideful lover, Ayla batted her eyelashes and pouted her bottom lip. "May I kiss you?"

"Of course," Flowridia said, laughing even when Ayla surged forward, the water sloshing out of the tub and snuffing out some of the candles.

Ayla placed a single, passionate kiss upon her lips, enough to make her breathless in mere moments. "Say more words, darling. I want to hear all your plans."

Giggling, Flowridia held Ayla against her, adoring her enthusiasm. "They're your plans. Tell me *your* plans."

"A question for you, then," Ayla cooed. "Can you bestow a living death?"

"I don't know. I've never tried."

Ayla's grin spread eerily wide, a snake ready to devour her prey. "I shall find you some worthy victims to experiment on."

Flowridia's good mood fell at that. "Forgive me— *worthy victims?*"

"Flowra, for all your benevolent ideals, there are still people you consider lesser, or at least worthy of death. I was *shaken* when you destroyed that slaver." Flowridia swore Ayla growled, a sensuous, guttural echo radiating lust. "It was so far from the vision I held of you, as glorious as seeing you naked anew. I love my pure and innocent Flowra—the one who's shy and sweet and so *deliciously* submissive in my bed." That grin remained, hungry and wild, practically salivating as she straddled her in the tub. Warmth welled between Flowridia's legs. "But there is a different side of you now, a brewing storm as dangerous as you are beautiful. And I cannot wait to rule beside her."

The barest hint of Ayla's fangs poked from her mouth, her eyes a rich black—all that excitement made manifest. Palpable tension brewed between the two of them, and Flowridia's body pulsed with want. "All right. We'll do it."

"Splendid," Ayla replied, her visage utterly inhuman.

"There's a lot to discuss, and I want you to promise only that we make no decisions alone. You have to trust me, and I . . ." She trailed off a moment, basking in Ayla's glorious form before her, barely clothed, the barest hint of her breasts peeking in and out of the water. ". . . I'll trust you too." Ayla chuckled, but stopped abruptly when Flowridia placed a finger to her lips. "If you're going to get yourself all worked up in front of me, you'll all least allow me to watch, right?"

She raised a teasing eyebrow, and Ayla's colorless eyes glinted with unparalleled glee. She parted the plunging neckline of her dress, revealing her breasts, peaked in the cool air. "Darling, you know I always love putting on a show." Beneath the water, cool fingers stroked across Flowridia's thigh. "Do you mind if I borrow this?"

Flowridia shook her head, not entirely certain what she was agreeing too, when Ayla shifted slightly, straddling the one thigh, and groaned as she rubbed herself along the soft skin. Her taut abdomen shifted with every motion, her hands free to touch and tease her breasts. The candlelight served to cast her in alluring, flickering light, the sounds evoked from her throat the sort to keep Flowridia up for nights to come. Oh, Flowridia adored her, and Ayla so obviously reveled in the attention, drawing out her pleasure until her face conveyed nothing but pain.

Flowridia dared to touch her then, to gently stroke between Ayla's legs, and nearly laughed at her lover's shock— and subsequent finish. Flowridia held her as she shook, kissed her as she rode the last waves of her pleasure, then basked in the silence as Ayla pressed their foreheads together. "Want anything?"

Flowridia bit her lip. "Perhaps a little something."

Ayla chuckled and dove beneath the water.

It felt like old times, but without the shackles of politics.

They flew for days, Etolié and her glittering shit, but Khastra by her side made riding the sparkling death trap almost tolerable.

When they needed a break, they descended into the fields or forest—whatever lay scattered beneath them—and sat among the trees or grass or snow, usually talking, occasionally kissing, and sometimes with Khastra stuffing food down her throat. Etolié wondered if she'd ever been so happy in all her days.

Staelash had been golden shackles for many years, though the work was still rewarding. But there had been moments of joy amidst her perpetual annoyance, precious moments with the best friends she'd ever had in her life.

Marielle's father had been a dear friend, and she mourned him. Khastra had been her dearest, and now she was something more. To sit in her lap and stroke her hair and kiss her lips in the woods was perfect.

Endless.

All was well.

Late one evening, they descended for a break.

The ground could not come soon enough. The moment the white steed's hooves touched the forest floor, Etolié slid down, fell to her knees, and vomited.

Trees surrounded them, and according to their map, they had plopped into Hillshire Forest, deep within Solviran territory. Creatures cried out in the distance, grating on Etolié's tired mind. Mist rose to cover the ground, adding to the admittedly eerie ambience.

A shadow fell upon her, followed by a large hand on her back. When she was offered a water satchel, she drank enough to fill her mouth, then spat it out, hoping the last bits of vomit left with it. "Why me?"

Khastra chuckled as she gently scratched her back. "I find this funny. You have wings, yet you are sickened by creatures with wings."

Etolié laughed at her awkward phrasing. "Your language barrier is showing, Beefcake."

In response, Khastra pulled her back, away from the evicted contents of her stomach, and held her in her lap. "Be certain you eat when your stomach has settled."

"Technically speaking," Etolié managed to say, "I live on starlight, so food is—"

"Still necessary for nutrition."

"Fine, fine," Etolié said, and from one of her pockets she withdrew a flask of alcohol. She wouldn't say she drank— more that she let the noxious liquid pool into her mouth and trickle down her throat. Yes, it was disgusting, the sharp taste absolutely vile combined with the lingering hints of vomit, but life was about priorities.

"Do you need sleep?"

"You know I never admit the answer to that nasty question," Etolié said, tossing the flask away. "Likely, but I would like to keep going for a while longer."

Khastra kissed her hair, an action that brought a fierce blush to Etolié's cheeks. "I will accept that answer for now, but next time you are sleeping."

When the half-demon stood up, far laxer with Etolié's poor decisions than normal, she resumed her typical camp-setting habits.

First, she held out her hand for an indeterminable amount of time. The fact remained that her flying horse, despite being fully capable of carrying six hundred pounds or so of half-demon, could not lift a hammer that for all intents and purposes weighed as much as the sun. But magic tied it to Ku'Shya's bloodline—after a few awkward, silent minutes of Khastra standing like a pleading statue of old, her massive weapon whirled through the air and into her waiting grip.

Etolié, expecting the sudden rush of air, shut her eyes, only cringing slightly at the impact of hammer against beef.

Second, Khastra picked the perfect tree by a method of selection Etolié did not pretend to understand. There was no pattern in type of tree or size or even location—Khastra would swing the blasted weapon against a trunk and essentially decimate that chunk, leading it to collapse.

And third, the fallen tree became a sturdy place of rest for the duo. Khastra began clearing out underbrush to start a fire.

Etolié watched the predictable series of events with amusement, finding the habit superfluous given she had offered to bring her cozy tent, but Khastra walked an unpredictable path between luxury and 'roughing it.' Etolié had long ago given up trying to understand her.

Soon, a fire burned before them, casting fiery hues upon Etolié's silver hair. She savored the smokey scent, for it reminded her of years on the run, years of finding her place in the world, of becoming the 'Savior of Slaves.' Not that she was happy then, but she was fulfilled.

But Khastra was better than any memory of her years before she'd been wrangled into the title of 'magister.' Their meeting coincided with the founding of Staelash, so in a very real way, it was the day her life began.

Habitually, Etolié reached into her pocket dimension to touch her half of the silver mirror she shared with whatever ward needed it—before recalling that the other half no longer existed due to an unfortunate but still suspicious God of Order incident. "Not gonna lie, Khastra, I'm worried about Lara."

"Explain," Khastra replied, pulling jerky from her pouch. When offered, Etolié shook her head, leading Khastra to somewhat forcibly take her hand and set the jerky onto it.

Now stuck holding dried meat, Etolié gave her answer. "The idea that this battle was awful enough for her to lose touch with her magic? That's not a little thing."

"She very nearly died, Etolié. Some consequences are to be expected."

"I try hard not to think about that first bit." Etolié did take a small bite, finding it palatable. The dried gristle forced her to slow her words, her thoughts rampant as she chewed and swallowed. "And look . . . I love Flowers. I do. But that explanation was absolute bullshit. She would have *known* the orb in the swamp was false, because she definitely knew Imperator Asshat had one." Etolié exhaled, illusioning smoke for emphasis. "She also never actually explained why she stole back the same one she found."

"The tiny one's actions are erratic," Khastra replied, the fire casting lovely shadows across her face. She was ageless and immortal, yet those subtle signs of living remained, the laughter lines at her eyes as beautiful as anything Etolié had ever seen. "When we see her in person, we should question that."

"Damn straight we should." Etolié took another bite, the flavor unpleasant this time, the seasoning stronger than her picky palate preferred. "Sometimes I wonder if Nox'Kartha got more into her head than we realize."

Khastra's glowing eyes looked to the stars high above, far away from the flame. "I observed nothing untoward during our months in Nox'Kartha, but she and I were never particularly close. She has left far more confident; I will say that."

"Confidence doesn't equal ill-intention." Etolié leaned against Khastra's arm before wrapping one arm around it. How she adored that strength, thinly veiled behind cotton and skin. "All I wanted was for her and Lara to get married, but now they're together and for some reason my skin is crawling."

"The tiny one has changed," Khastra replied, and Etolié would never find it less than hilarious that Flowridia had a forced pet name due to the limitations of Khastra's unwavering accent. "And it is all right for your opinion to change. However, you must let them make their own mistakes."

Etolié sneered to think she was right. "I can't put my finger on it anyway. I was thrilled when they locked lips at the wedding. But seeing them at the castle . . . I wasn't even physically there, but something was off."

"I was not there, so I cannot cast judgement yet."

"Am I just overly protective?"

In response, Etolié felt Khastra's lips against her hair, refreshing the blush on her cheeks—perhaps the sensation would never fade, and Etolié wouldn't mind that at all. "Perhaps, but it is to be expected. You have loved her since her birth."

"True," Etolié said, having never forgotten that visceral connection upon holding the three-day-old infant, how her heart had softened despite ten years as the vigilante "Savior of Slaves" turning it to stone. Alauriel Solviraes was her family, her niece ninety times removed or so, and she had felt that instinctively, this baby with whom she shared her momma's blood. There were things to joke about—her love for Lara wasn't one of them. "She was a lovely little thing."

"And your role in her life should not be discounted," Khastra replied, though her gaze became melancholic. "You have loved her when her own mother could not."

Ralaena Solviraes—who did not wield the Silver Fire, and who had died because of the fetus' radiant power. Her soul had been destroyed, absorbed by the baby she had died to bring into the world.

"I'm a piss poor substitute," Etolié said, but something old and bitter rose within her, and as much as she hated introspection, it smacked her like a punch to her stomach.

A noble death from every conceivable perspective, a mother dying to save her unborn child—except Etolié's. She had watched the late empress Ralaena choose every day to move forward despite the risks, the cost, despite her body failing and weakening with each passing hour. She had been so frail; skeletal, even.

She should have never been asked to conceive it. She and Emperor Malakh had married thinking they would never need to. But when Malakh's older brother had passed, leaving the throne empty, an heir had to come, lest the bloodline end.

At eight months, Ralaena had succumbed, collapsing in the hallway—dead. The baby had been cut from her womb, premature but crying and healthy, still glowing from the soul she had absorbed.

Etolié hadn't been there. She was in Staelash when the news had come, had comforted Clarence through his tears— Ralaena's brother, someone left behind in her sacrifice. She attended the funeral and saw the late Emperor Malakh's own anguish. She watched a beautiful life extinguish for a cause she couldn't fathom and saw the broken pieces left in the aftermath of the tragedy.

She had met baby Lara after the funeral, fully expecting to hate the helpless little thing.

Instead, she had fallen instantly in love, and as she had held the tiny girl in her arms, Etolié wondered if, perhaps, she did not lack empathy, but instead held too much.

Seducing evil men to slay them during her ten years as a vigilante came with risks, the type of risks that had led a too-young Etolié to make the decision the empress had not, though under far different circumstances.

Little else to do when you were small and alone.

"Etolié, are you all right?"

Etolié, seated next to Khastra, blinked away tears. "I'm fine," she whispered, praying Khastra couldn't guess her thoughts. Of course, she knew—she knew every dark and bitter secret Etolié held, but there were stories she didn't want to repeat. "Just, um, thinking about tiny Lara. Precious little squish."

Khastra didn't believe her, as told by the half-demon pulling Etolié into her lap and holding her tight—which was justified, given Etolié didn't generally go misty-eyed over babies.

"Is this normal?" Etolié asked. "To worry every second of your life?"

"If you have a child? Absolutely." Khastra kissed Etolié's hair, because Khastra had raised nineteen children in her thousands of years of living and somehow lived with the heartbreak of their extinguished lives.

Etolié would outlive Alauriel, who wasn't even her child, yet the knowledge haunted her on sleepless nights.

"It is equally normal to worry about who your child chooses to love," Khastra continued, extracting her arm to instead wrap it around Etolié's body. "And if I have learned nothing else in being a mother, it is that except in cases of certain death, it is best to let them live and make mistakes. I do not know if the tiny one and Lara will be happy together—but if they are, you do not want to villainize yourself by speaking out against them. Not without very good reason."

Etolié, who considered herself a flagrant narcissist, had to brace herself before she nodded. "It might be fine," she said, committed to lying to herself—it was what she was best at.

"It truly might," Khastra said, the laughter in her words enough to bring a genuine smile to Etolié's face. "Lara is a good and wise woman. And the tiny one's most questionable decision was loving The Endless Night—who is dead."

"That, and stealing the orb," Etolié said, unwilling to let that tidbit die.

"She should explain that decision, I agree."

When Etolié finally finished her jerky, she waved away the offer of a second strip. "I don't want to lose any more lunch than necessary."

But Khastra didn't relent, eventually taking Etolié's hand and placing the meat in it. "Then sit a while longer and let it digest."

Etolié begrudgingly obeyed, secretly overjoyed to spend more time in her presence.

Representatives from the Temple of Staella came the next afternoon, along with a matron from one of the outlying orphanages.

Flowridia clutched a letter from Thalmus, any correspondence from him as precious as gold. Beside her, Demitri thumped his furry tail upon the floor, expressing his boredom, and Lunestra held the children's hands, loving them for as long she could.

It was a bittersweet meeting, for the children to face their new futures. Lara had done restoration work on the Temple of Staella, Flowridia recalled, and it showed in the High Priestess of the Goddess of Stars' gratitude and radiant kindness. "Is Empress Alauriel here?" she asked. "I would love to speak to her. She hasn't visited in a while."

Truthfully, Flowridia didn't know where the empress had gone and responded accordingly, saying she would deliver the message for her to visit. Instead, she supervised the priestess' meeting with a few of the older children, watched her charm their young hearts and steal a few away to their new homes, acolytes to a new goddess.

It was the same with the orphan matron, who seemed much kinder than the one Flowridia had grown up with. She took a small group as well.

A few were to be taken to Staelash, per Thalmus' agreement. Jules escorted them away, saying Lara was busy but could be bothered for this.

The final one, the littlest girl Flowridia now knew to be named 'Ceile,' was to be taken home with Reginal and his husband, Erlyn, a fact which still made Flowridia's heart soar. Erlyn, when he came, seemed reserved, juxtaposed with

Reginal's eccentric self, as well as noticeably younger, but it was difficult to guess ages in Celestials, which she assumed they both were.

There was immediate love in his eyes when he held Ceile, and Flowridia knew it was where she was meant to be.

Lunestra bid each child farewell, lingering to give every one of them a proper send-off. It wasn't until Ceile left with one of her new fathers that the mask of motherly kindness was lifted.

Lunestra stared wistfully at the door as she sat upon a chair. She wore the garb of her goddess, the golden and white robes settling around her as she sat, her thick ropes of hair plaited into her impressive crown—once black, now greyed with age.

"Are you all right?" Flowridia asked, for this had to ache.

"I am well," Lunestra replied, a resigned smile finally settling upon her wrinkled face. "Better than I thought I would be."

Flowridia pulled up a small chair to better sit beside her. A fireplace roared, keeping them warm in the chill afternoon. Demitri curled behind their chairs, always listening. "What do you mean?"

"I mean that I thought I would be devastated. Instead, I feel calm. It's strange, to feel the mantle lifted from your shoulders, but my responsibility is over. I shall love them all their lives, but . . ." She shut her eyes, serenity settling upon her aged features. ". . . the cathedral and the orphans were my life's work. My watch has ended, and I am at peace."

"You should be commended," Flowridia said, but Lunestra already shook her head.

"I do not need a reward or commendation. It was my duty. I devoted my whole heart to making the best and safest place possible for the children in my charge, and I would like to think I succeeded as well as I could."

"They obviously adored you."

Lunestra hesitated before she spoke, mist filling her gaze. "Thank you."

"There's more good news," Flowridia said, recalling that morning's meeting. "I have been told that a group of Theocracy refugees crossed Solvira's borders yesterday. They're being directed here, where they can receive the support they need."

"That is wonderful," Lunestra replied, her aged countenance alight from her smile.

"Is there anything more we can do? If I have the power to help, let me wield it. These are my people, in spirit."

"They're yours by right," Lunestra said, the weight of the words more than Flowridia expected. "With the capital destroyed and their archbishop presumed dead, it is safe to assume that hope is not high. But I fear, if you were to simply come out and reveal your identity, you would be rejected, assuming they believed you at all. Your reputation precedes you; unfortunately, your name has become synonymous with Nox'Kartha's."

Flowridia's stomach sank, a chill spreading across her skin. "I accept that."

"In time, it may fade, especially if you continue courting Empress Alauriel. You would be surprised what a change in surname can do for a political career." In a gesture both charming and terribly suspicious, Lunestra winked in a grandmotherly sort of way.

She likely knew something, given the magnitude of gossipers in the palace. Whatever innate joy filled her at the tease, Flowridia resisted the urge to convey it quite so brightly. "If you were to speak on my behalf, might it help?"

Lunestra nodded gravely, her countenance falling into something subdued. "Yes, but I fear my continued life must remain a secret for the foreseeable future."

"I know you're right," Flowridia said, "but I fear no one would believe me. The only proof I have is my mother's story and . . ." Her voice trailed off, but Lunestra's questioning gaze lingered. ". . . the demon's own word, though he would speak on my behalf if I asked."

"The demon from your story?" Lunestra asked. "Do you mean to imply . . ?"

Flowridia braced herself for regret. "It was Casvir."

Lunestra sat back in her chair, face ashen as she stared into the fireplace.

"He orchestrated it all," Flowridia admitted, the first welling of guilt rising in her stomach. Was this a betrayal, to speak the truth? She doubted Casvir would be angry, yet it felt like a step away from the man she still considered a friend. "Casvir sent my father to Odessa, knowing Odessa would do as she always did. He wanted a child he could groom from birth and grant power—he's the patron of my witchcraft. He gave Demitri to me."

"That explains it," Lunestra whispered, her gaze still fixed to the fire.

"He also said it was his intention to hold power over the heir to the Theocracy. But then he took a liking to me." She couldn't bring herself to smile, despite the treasured memory. "He said I was destined for greatness beyond what he could have anticipated."

Bitterness twisted Lunestra's tight lips. "And he burned my kingdom to the ground instead."

"Yes. I'm sorry."

Lunestra looked directly to her, filled with vehemence and ire. "Sorry? You have done nothing. He is the chorister orchestrating this madness. You were a chosen instrument, but you are not to blame."

Flowridia forced herself to nod but could not summon any words. Lunestra was right; Flowridia was not at fault. Yet the haunting truth remained that she could have stopped it, had she known. "I suppose I needed to hear that. From you."

Lunestra came to the edge of her seat, then beckoned Flowridia forward. Flowridia obeyed, gently sitting in her progenitor's lap, nearly crying to be held in her arms. It felt so juvenile, to sit on her lap like a child, yet it held a comfort she realized she had always craved. "Casvir was right about one thing—you are destined for greatness. And that greatness is whatever you choose. You do not have to play into his hands. You do not have to choose the path he laid for you."

Instead, she had chosen something worse—to resurrect the very monster Lunestra had long feared. But for the moment, Flowridia curled into the embrace, content to hide behind the lie and wonder . . .

Would it mean anything at all now, to salvage the goodness in her life?

They spoke for hours. It was night when she emerged.

As she traversed the halls with Demitri, she heard a voice shout, "Lady Flowridia!" Reginal approached, looking pleased. "You weren't at dinner."

"My apologies. I was speaking with Archbishop Lunestra."

"No harm done, but I am supposed to tell you—Lara has requested your presence in the ballroom."

He was hiding something, as told by his shifting smile and nervous eyes. Had Flowridia thought he were capable of malice, she might have been worried. "Thank you," she said, "though I don't know where that is."

Once given directions, she and Demitri left him alone. Instead of expanding the lift as initially promised, they had added a second one, citing that for the sake of the servants, it had been planned for some time. Still, this new one could easily accommodate a horse, and Demitri only needed to tuck in his tail.

The lift ascended. Demitri nudged her ear. *I think she wants you alone.*

Flowridia raised an eyebrow. "You think?"

I do. I'll wait in the hall."

Outside the glass walls, streetlamps lit the bustling city. The moon rose, full tonight. Flowridia's expression, however, didn't change. "I think you know something."

The lift stopped, and Demitri nuzzled her hair as she left. *She's nervous.*

Elation filled Flowridia at the words, butterflies fluttering about her stomach. She instinctively smiled, unable to meet his eye as she blushed. "She's going to propose?"

Go be surprised.

Flowridia kissed his nose.

Alone, her steps echoed across the stone hallway like a whip, but massive double doors soon stood before her, carved from wood, gilded from gold, and bearing elaborate designs.

Staelash's ballroom was the grandest room in the manor, impressively large and suited for lush parties and gatherings. But Solvira's castle was ancient, and its ballroom stretched to the stars. Massive walls held spiraling pillars, decorated in silver and gold, bearing depictions of angels. A balcony surrounded it, as well as an elevated stage, perhaps for instruments, but the room alone was larger than the manor in every dimension. Her eyes fell first upon a small portal near her by the door, the rounded edges lined in what looked like sparks. It nauseated her to be near, but she hardly paid it any mind.

For all her confusion and wonder, it paled to the graceful figure twirling in the center. The windows let in the light of the full moon, but the only other illumination was the delicate display of silver flame at Ayla's hands and feet—and it was truly Ayla, in her undead form. She stilled at Flowridia's entrance, the fire in her hands snuffing out, but Flowridia shook her head as she shut the door. "Please, continue. I love watching you dance."

She could not see Ayla's face, but she imagined it well enough—her serenity and joy, how freely her body obeyed every precise command. The flame rose anew, though not hot enough to scorch the stone floor, and in delicate motions, Ayla twirled it around like a ribbon. It flowed with her as smoothly as water, and though the motions were limited, oh, the display was beautiful.

When Ayla danced, Ayla was free, the fire showing the quiet joy on her face as she stepped in time. For all her brutal endeavors, nothing compared to the grace of her movements. She was a creature of violence, yes, her body a weapon, yet she held the fire with all the finesse of her knife, letting it become one with her, a partner as much as a weapon.

She came near, the fire snuffing out as she twirled around Flowridia. With care, she stole Flowridia's hands, wasting no time in placing one upon her shoulder before leading her in a silent dance. Flowridia stumbled, but she laughed at the attention, overjoyed as Ayla led her across the floor. "Do you imagine music?"

"Sometimes," Ayla replied, not winded at all—she need not breathe. "More often, I simply hear a beat in my head and follow in time. I prefer real music, but that is a luxury."

She slowed her pace, then parted, bowing with depthless grace and poise.

Flowridia curtsied in response. "You're so lively when you dance. It's beautiful to see."

Ayla took Flowridia's hands in her smaller, colder ones. "Thank you. I find it calming during times of stress. Healthier than degloving, I would say. Or at least less distressing to you."

"Are you stressed?"

Ayla's smile didn't falter in the slightest, despite her words. "Very much so."

In her heart, Flowridia knew why, and it was increasingly difficult to keep that to herself. Excitement radiated from her skin like small sparks of lightning. "Your fire is magnificent."

"Thank you. I do not dare try anything too elaborate yet, but I am enjoying the challenge."

"Where did you learn to dance?"

"That is a much longer story," Ayla replied, gazing up with vibrant eyes. "Will you come with me?" She gestured to the portal, then intertwined their fingers when Flowridia nodded.

Slipping through the portal caused her stomach to turn, even more than her anticipation. Stars dotted the sky when they emerged, brilliant and sparkling. Directly above, the moon beamed down, illuminating what appeared to be a valley.

Mountains grew up around every side of this expansive, hidden meadow. Tall grass caressed her legs when she took a step, chilling her feet with wet dew. Yet the air was warm and when Flowridia saw flowers—moon lilies, she realized—she wondered what haven she had entered.

Ahead, a small cottage stood centered below the moon. Flowridia took a step toward it, but Ayla shook her head. "That's for our wedding night," she said, smiling as bright as the moon.

Behind, the portal remained. Ayla took her hands and kissed them. "Ayla, what is this place?" Flowridia asked, feeling the radiant energy of this valley. Magic fluctuated against her senses.

"The Valley of Neoma. The barriers between the planes are weak here," Ayla said. "They say one can walk right into Celestière if they know how. The Solviraes have protected this place for thousands of years, or so Reginal said. It is a place of eternal night, where they say Neoma and Staella first made love here, and it's traditional that a Solviraes comes here twice in his or her life, once on their wedding night and . . ." Ayla trailed off, her eyes reflecting the silver light. Hesitant, she dropped to one knee, and from her neckline she withdrew a small ring bearing a diamond. ". . . a-and once when they proclaim their true love, in honor of their late goddess' love."

Flowridia had known a proposal would come, and had expected some bombastic display, something akin to Marielle's wedding parade, or perhaps even Ayla's labyrinth, something baptized in blood and artistry. She had prepared herself for embarrassment, to blush at Ayla's audacity.

Not this. Not a simple ring in the middle of a meadow beneath the full moon. The peace of the moment touched her, bringing tears to her eyes. Trembling, she took the ring, immediately sensing a spell set into the simple swirls of thin metal.

"I worked with Reginal to enchant it," Ayla said, swaying as she stood, words rambling as she stared at the ground. "It protects your mind from any sort of magical compulsion. I recognize the sacrifice of being with me for eternity, for allowing me to turn you, and I would never wish for you to think that I would hurt you, or exploit you, or try to control you because, Flowra—" When Flowridia looked up, Ayla's eyes glistened. "Flowra, I love you." For Ayla to be so visibly nervous tugged at Flowridia's heart. "Please, say something."

Flowridia smiled, still holding the ring in her hand. "You didn't ask," she teased. "All your words, and you never asked the important part."

Ayla shut her mouth, shyly taking Flowridia's free hand as her jaw trembled. "Flowra," she whispered, reverence in her voice, "will you marry me?"

"Yes."

At the word, Ayla burst into tears, tackling Flowridia to the ground as sobs wracked her body. With the ring safely enclosed in her fist, Flowridia held Ayla tight as wet, tearful kisses sprinkled across her cheeks.

Flowridia slipped the ring onto her finger, finding it a perfect fit. "I love you, Ayla."

Ayla lingered at her jaw, clutching tight at Flowridia's hair, but not for lust. She continued sobbing, curling into an embrace.

"I-I am sorry," Ayla stammered. "I do not mean to cry." Flowridia stroked her sharp cheekbones, adoring the smooth skin. "With you, I feel joy. It's a rare and beautiful thing."

Flowridia set Ayla's head against her breasts and held her tenderly, allowing them to bask in the moonlit night. The chill of the grass and the night sunk into her bones, but Ayla's presence, cold or not, warmed her heart and limbs. "I promise to bring you joy for every day of my life and—"

And after, her mind finished, but her tongue turned to stone at the words. She held Ayla tight, praying she did not push for words Flowridia couldn't bear to say.

The days of her life were numbered.

But for now, Flowridia pushed aside her dread and fear. Instead, she held the woman she loved, savoring the sensations of living.

Stepping back through the portal, they were met with applause.

Magister Reginal stood at the front, alongside Demitri, but it seemed he had gathered the entire household. Servants clapped, guards cheered, and High Priestess Jules stood to the side summoning what appeared to be small fireworks erupting across the ceiling. Even Lunestra clapped with the rest. Drinks and dessert had been brought—a small party awaited.

Hand in hand, Lara, her disguise impeccable, led Flowridia forward, beaming and making a show of laughing and bowing at the gathered crowd. She held up their united hands, Flowridia's wedding ring reflecting the display of light. "I present to you, your future empress consort," Lara announced, her voice easily belting above the crowd. "Lady Flowridia, Grand Diplomat of Staelash, has agreed to be my wife."

The crowd cheered. Flowridia blushed, unable to hide when Lara kept a hand on her waist and lightly pushed her forward. Her smile remained, but she shied at the attention, trying to avoid eye contact with anyone among the applause.

When the applause dwindled, well-wishers came forward, the first of whom was Demitri. He pressed his face against hers, and when she pulled him into a hug, she heard his voice. *It's difficult to feel you when you're so far away.*

"I'm sorry if it scared you."

I'm an independent wolf. I'm also happy you're happy.

Reginal went straight to Lara. "I'm glad to see that all went well."

"Thank you for your assistance," Lara said, and she accepted his hug when he offered it. "It seems my grasp on summoning portals is still shaky. I will have to practice."

"Come to my office anytime." With a glance to the crowd, he whispered, "It wounds me to know you still suffer from memory problems. Perhaps, with Jules' help, we could try and help."

But Lara shook her head. "No need to waste time on my account. Everything is slowly coming back."

Reginal shook Flowridia's hand and offered his congratulations, and Priestess Jules had already engulfed Lara in a hug. When Lunestra came, Flowridia accepted her warm embrace. "Your father would be overjoyed," she whispered, and Flowridia's gut twisted, guilt marring the beauty of the moment. "Just as I am."

"When will the wedding be?" Reginal asked.

Lara glanced to the window, illuminated by the full moon. Her smile turned eerie, conspiring. "At the next full moon."

Jules' eyes grew wide. "That's awfully soon."

"Twenty-eight days," Lara said. "But should we not magnify my ancestral mothers' glory? Twenty-eight days, and then we shall be wed."

Jules shared a glance with Reginal, who stood at her side, visibly dazed. "Then, we shall begin planning," he said, articulating each syllable.

"We shall meet tomorrow morning," Lara said, purposefully ignoring their obvious hesitation. "Where is General Irons this evening?"

"He has his own opinions on the matter," Reginal said, resignation in his words.

Flowridia merely nodded, not missing the painted smile on Lara's features. "Well, as my father told me once, you are on the right path once you've made a few enemies."

Flowridia couldn't say with any confidence that the late emperor would have said anything like that, but Lara stole her hand and led her toward the drinks before Reginal could reply.

Ayla was an indulgent drinker, a *connoisseur,* as Zorlaeus had long ago described her, but Flowridia recalled that the late empress had been as well. The difference was Ayla's difficulty in getting drunk, given her undead biology—fortunately, she could act the part of the tipsy empress perfectly well.

And she did, charming servants and nobility alike, graciously accepting their congratulations. Flowridia picked at the dessert table, finding joy in the decorated tarts but dearly missing baking her own pastries.

As the future empress consort, the least she could ask for was time alone in the kitchens, right?

She didn't drink—it wasn't her preference—but joined in the small revelry, attached to her intended's side. Idly, she spun her ring around her finger all through the evening, delighted every time she recalled its presence.

Yet a strange dread lingered, the knowledge that her days were now definitively numbered. Twenty-eight sunsets until the next full moon.

She would never see the sun again.

When she grew tired, she whispered to Lara, who immediately proclaimed that the party must end.

They held hands as they walked through the hallway to return to their room. "I'm amazed you managed to put that together so quickly," Flowridia said, "much less get anyone to agree to help."

"Reginal agrees to anything I say, I'm noticing," Lara replied, though merely in looks; she gave no care to acting like the late empress when they were alone. "He simply wants me happy. He was curious when I told him how I wanted the ring to be enchanted, so I may have alluded to you being an extremely paranoid person, for which I am sorry."

Flowridia laughed at that, then grinned at the beautiful ring—simple, elegant, perfect. "I forgive you."

"Is it too soon? Twenty-eight days? I may be letting my excitement get ahead of me." Lara's visage flickered a moment, revealing Ayla herself, her oft-severe gaze as doe-eyed as Flowridia had ever seen. "I cannot wait to be your wife."

With tenderness, Flowridia pressed their lips together, savoring her kiss, then whispered, "Watch your illusion, my love."

Ayla blinked, then chuckled, Lara's image returning.

Twenty-eight days left to cherish the sun . . .

"I simply wonder," Flowridia teased, casting the anxious thoughts from her head, "just how against propriety it is for me to be spending my nights in your bedroom."

Behind them, Demitri followed, and she was surprised when he answered her strange inquiry. *They think you sleep with me.*

"I beg your pardon," Flowridia said, before Lara could give her own reply.

That's what the servants assume. There's a human bed in my room; they think you sleep in there.

"What is Demitri saying?" Lara asked, and Flowridia laughed as she told her.

In their shared bedroom, Demitri left them alone. Though hand in hand with Ayla, Flowridia's gaze landed briefly upon the bouquet on the table. Guilt filled her. Were there justice in the world, this would have been the real Lara's moment.

Yet she did not regret; she could not regret—not when Ayla stood beside her, pure love in her eyes.

Instead, Flowridia willed her good mood to return and embraced her, kissed her lips, enslaved by that captivating touch.

"There is the matter of the guest list," Reginal said in their morning council meeting. "Lara, no need to stress—I will invite your relatives and all the appropriate nobles, though let me know if there's anyone I might not take into consideration. But, Lady Flowridia, while the council in Staelash will be invited, do let me know if you have any friends among the populace you wish to include."

"I'm sad to say I wasn't there long enough to make any outside the council ," Flowridia said, abashed to admit it.

"There is also the matter of Nox'Kartha."

The unspoken implications soured the light mood. Flowridia's hands clutched each other, suddenly sweating. Withering gazes stared from across the table—from Jules and General Irons both.

"Aside from the matter of Flowridia's friendship with the imperator," Reginal continued, "we should not forget the treaty between Nox'Kartha and Staelash—and by proxy, to

Solvira. It could be perceived as an insult if they are not sent an invitation."

"But there is the matter of the refugees as well," Lara said, apparently finishing his thought. "To invite Imperator Casvir and his envoy when we are sheltering those he's actively oppressing will cast us in a suspicious light."

Casvir's memory brought only conflict. Flowridia knew she loved him, but could she face him? After what he had done to the City of Light? "Would it be possible," Flowridia said, though hesitation slowed her tongue, "to invite him but keep it quiet? I could make it a personal request that he come accompanied by only a few guards and attendants, assuming he even needs them. No entourage. Then it really is as a friend instead of a political maneuver, but we still save face."

Irons still glowered, but Reginal seemed appeased. "The viceroy is known for giving extravagant gifts," the magister said, perhaps hinting, but Flowridia shook her head.

"I'd rather he not be there." Flowridia offered her best false smile, the sort she'd seen on Lunestra and Etolié's faces more than once—that polite sort of smile that said she was utterly insincere but needed to be tactful.

Lara frowned, and it was assuredly Ayla's frown—the murderous one Flowridia hated to see. "Why?"

"I don't know if the story is appropriate for an official council meeting."

"It's a council meeting with strictly Solvira," Reginal offered, thinly veiled intrigue glinting in his eye. "We're always keen for gossip."

Irons' eyes might roll right out of his head before the end of the meeting, but Jules did a terrible job pretending she didn't care.

Flowridia's stomach churned at the memory, however, subtle dread filling her to remember what he had nearly done. "We don't get along." They visibly awaited more, but Flowridia kept her mouth closed.

Lara wore a calculating glare. "You've never mentioned that."

"It hasn't come up."

Lara's countenance suggested they would certainly be addressing this later.

Reginal sighed with more than a little melodrama and said, "Well, I will issue that invitation straightaway. In unrelated news, we received reports of an earthquake in the Forest of Hillshire."

Even Lara stared incredulously at that. "An earthquake?"

"I agree it is strange. I would propose sending a small investigative party. I fear there may be something magical afoot, and with the God of Order still out there, we can discount nothing."

"Yes, send someone," Lara said, waving it off. "Moving on—I have something of a pet project I wanted to push forward," she continued, offering her own assortment of paperwork to the council. "I have been perusing prisoner files. Do you realize just how much money is spent on their upkeep? These are people who will rot in their cells, yet we spend precious taxpayer money keeping them alive—but for what? And then there are pettier criminals serving outlandish sentences for minor offenses." She pushed one smaller file forward. "If you can justify this man spending twenty years in prison for stealing cornmeal for his family, please do. But otherwise, I think this speaks of a deeper, more insidious problem in Solviran society."

"I'm inclined to agree," Jules said warily, "but what are you suggesting?"

"Flowra and I have been discussing this at length, actually," Lara said, her smile steadily more vicious, radiating excitement through her twitching legs and fingers. "All this food my Flowra is creating for the refugees—we expand that to all our citizens. No one shall go hungry in our borders. If Nox'Kartha can do it, so can we.

"Second," she continued, before she could be interrupted, "we abolish the prisons."

They were met with stark silence at that.

"The money used to fund them pays the farmers harvesting the food we are freely distributing—seems fair. And we execute the life-long prisoners."

Flowridia's gut twisted at that. Lara could have said it better.

"That seems excessive," Reginal said, tugging on his beard.

"My compromise is we send them to toil the fields instead—but we have untapped potential sitting in our prisons, idly wasting away. We kill it, or we put it to work.

Reform who we can, I suppose. But I see no purpose in wasting money."

The ensuing argument was expected, Flowridia supposed—mostly Jules and Lara issuing polite, albeit combative words about ethics and what Sol Kareena would want—and she remained silent, instead making eye contact with Irons, who oddly had said nothing on the matter.

"It's barbaric," Jules said. "Were we to do that, we would be no different than Nox'Kartha."

"Yet, Nox'Kartha modeled their justice system after the one Solvira held in time past—back when we were the uncontested greatest country in the world." Lara's smile bore the falseness of political lies, but at least it was polite. "We can be so again, with a little reformation."

"I vote," Reginal offered, interrupting the arguing council members, "we table this discussion for today and negotiate tomorrow. Let it settle. It *is* a significant change that you're proposing, Lara."

"Fine." Her curt response signified the end. When she sat in her chair, Flowridia reached over and squeezed her knee. "What other news is there?"

General Irons spoke next, sliding over his own pile of paperwork. "Multiple deaths last night, though less dramatic— a woman drained of blood and left in an alleyway. There's evidence her body was violated *after* she passed on."

Flowridia frowned, but Lara accepted the paperwork without further reaction. Instinct said this was her doing, yet the details were immensely out of character.

Well, presumably. If Ayla had a love of necrophilia, they would need to have a talk. She glanced to her intended, hoping her alarm was clear as she caught her eye.

Lara passed the paperwork along, then furrowed her brow at Flowridia's questioning gaze. Discretely, she directed her finger at herself, eyebrow raised in inquiry.

Flowridia nodded.

To Flowridia's relief, a grimace passed Lara's features, the subtle shake of her head conveying her innocence.

Thank goodness.

"There was also a young couple attacked last night in the upper district—apparently the man's throat was torn out by the attacker's teeth. His wife survived, though I know nothing else of her condition. The pattern here is very clear. I request permission to enact martial law before this becomes an epidemic," Irons said, though not without his characteristic glower to Flowridia. "Vampires, assuming that's what this is, quickly lead to more vampires. We cannot let this continue."

"Two nights of violence, while tragic, doesn't mean this is an epidemic," Jules said. "We'll only risk causing panic, for there to be a battalion of paladins storming the streets. And what if there is no supernatural cause?"

"Then there is a serial killer in our midst, and I stand by my request. A curfew should be set until this matter is done with."

To Flowridia's surprise, amusement twisted Lara's smile. "I agree."

"Lara, I oppose this," Jules said. "It will do more harm than good. I do not give my consent."

"Our citizens should be informed that there's a threat," Lara replied, innocence in her gaze; Flowridia admired her commitment to the part. "General Irons, rest assured that an edict shall be sent out before the day is through. At sunset, all citizens must return to their homes."

"Thank you," Irons said. "This will, of course, need to be extended to residents of the palace. The timing is such that I am concerned and suspicious."

He didn't say it to her, but Flowridia felt an accusation, nevertheless. "Timing?"

Irons gave no reply. Her blood boiled.

When the meeting concluded, Flowridia glared as he went, contemplating how to best administer a poison that wouldn't be traced back to her. Would she do it? Likely not. But even her patience had its limits—and the image of him choking on his own vomit was truly gratifying.

Once the room cleared of council members, Lara revealed her true, vampiric self. "What did Murishani do and how painful do I need to make his death?"

"I worry that killing him would bring trouble," Flowridia replied, though she quietly reveled in the idea. "If he knows you're back, Casvir knows you're back, and while I doubt he'll do anything without provocation—killing Murishani would definitely be provocation.

"But," she continued, because there was no use in lying to hide it—not when she'd yelled at Ayla for the exact crime, "to sum up the story, he was jealous of my friendship with Casvir and wanted to. . . use me to become more important to him . . ." She steeled herself for Ayla's inevitable fury at her next words. ". . . by coercing me to have his baby, by which I mean he put a metaphorical knife to your throat and insisted I fuck him."

To watch the subdued worry in Ayla's features melt into rage was truly a sight to behold, her countenance becoming the monster of legend. "He *what?!*"

"Ayla, it's in the past. Nothing happened. Casvir swatted him on the wrist and—"

"It's not fine! Don't say it's fine!" Ayla stepped away from the table, and Flowridia gasped when flame appeared at her feet. As did Ayla—she lurched and tried to stamp it out.

"Ayla, you need to . . . well, not *breathe,* but—"

"I will kill him!" From Ayla's mouth came fire, silver and bright. Flowridia sunk deeper into her chair. "I will strip his skin off in pieces and leave him to hang by his wrists and die of exposure!"

"I'll happily discuss that idea at length once you've calmed yourself—"

Instead, Ayla vanished into a shadow. In the ensuing quiet, Flowridia swore she heard a feminine scream, as though from underwater, a thousand miles away.

Soon, Ayla emerged, looking placated. No sign of flame at all. "Forgive me," she said curtly. "I had to go blow up a little."

"That is completely fine and honestly healthy." Flowridia reached for her, still in her chair, and Ayla accepted her hand. "Your temper is something to work with, not against."

Ayla's countenance returned to a pout. "You don't want me to kill him?"

"I would sleep better at night if you did, but as I said, I'm worried what it would bring. If we kill Murishani, Casvir would retaliate."

Ayla collapsed dramatically against the side of Flowridia's chair. "I shall think on it. Kindly don't hate me if I snap his neck anyway."

"I would never. That said . . ." Flowridia shut her eyes, still plagued by images of horror, the Theocracy's downfall an atrocity. ". . . like I said, if Murishani knows, Casvir knows. You've said before that Casvir wouldn't dare attack Solvira, but would he ever try to dismantle us? Would he use the knowledge of who you truly are against us?"

"He would need proof, Flowra. And he would need someone trusted to advocate for him." Ayla's face fell into contemplation, and Flowridia was grateful to not be simply disregarded. "We operate under the knowledge that he knows. He will come to the wedding, and all will be well, because we still hold the upper hand from every possible angle. My presence may even be a protection, given any insidious corruption he might try to seep into my kingdom would never be tolerated beneath my reign. Perhaps when we leave, he will grasp Solvira in the ensuing power struggle, but that will be many years from now. Nothing to trouble yourself with."

Though the words held logic, Flowridia still feared. "I think I may worry until the end," she admitted, but Ayla's ensuing smile was kind.

"It is in your nature to worry, Flowra. But it is something that endeared me to you back when I resolved to hate you. There is wisdom in caution, and it is something I need to be reminded of."

Flowridia smiled, blushing when Ayla kissed her cheek.

"Regarding the meeting," Ayla continued, "I suppose we shall be letting our citizens live in fear for a time. Honestly, this is splendid. Better than I could have hoped. What better way to ease our citizens into our trust and good graces than a threat to bind us together? Flowra, I think General Irons may be an unwitting ally."

Flowridia glowered at that final statement. "He thinks I'm behind it."

"Yes, but he can prove nothing."

She stared at the door, skin prickling at his accusations, his bigotry. "I'd like permission to do something very stupid."

"Granted. What precisely?"

Flowridia told her. Ayla thought it was fantastic.

Ayla stepped into the shadows. Flowridia and Demitri tracked down General Irons.

Sconces passed, and the dark wood of the interior walls were cast in deep shadow. With her familiar beside her, she picked up her pace until she came upon him, his armored steps not nearly so bold as Casvir's. "General Irons!" she called, and the man stopped, standing alert as she approached.

"Lady Flowridia," he said, not even offering a nod of deference.

"I won't mince words. You so clearly despise me," she said, when she finally stood before him. She remained a full head shorter, but she had learned from watching Ayla that size meant absolutely nothing; she kept her head high. "Tell me. Throw my sins at my feet. I'm tired of this game between us."

Irons studied her, his demeanor not shifting in the slightest. The tension between them could have forged diamonds. "Everyone else may have fallen for that innocent demeanor," he finally spat. "but I know you've done something to her."

"And pray tell what it is I've done," Flowridia said, acutely aware of both the sword at his hilt and the gigantic wolf beside her—as well as the monster watching in the shadows.

"Whatever enchantment you've cast upon the empress, it's clear she's fallen completely under your spell, and most of the council and kingdom have followed suit." He bowed, arms spread wide with mockery. "You've won. Congratulations, Empress Consort Flowridia Solviraes. You'll be the ruler of the greatest empire this world has known, and you hold ties to both Staelash and Nox'Kartha. Perhaps they'll fall next under your watchful eye, eh?"

Flowridia refused to fall to his taunt. "You have clearly made up your mind on this."

"I sleep with holy sigils beside my bed because I know there is an evil in this kingdom that relies on blood to survive. Blood magic is dark necromancy. Could the victims speak, I'm sure they'd have a damning story to tell."

"Accusing your future empress consort of a false crime is treason," Flowridia said. "Defamation. Be careful who you say this to."

"I will say nothing, out of a hope that my warning might be heeded. Marry the empress. Rule this kingdom, and take your victory. But know that I am waiting for you to slip and show your true nature."

Flowridia steeled her jaw. "General Irons," she said, pushing down the brewing fury within her, "you need not believe my sincerity in marrying your beloved empress. I love her, and I have done nothing to compel her mind to love me."

Her nails dug into her palms. "But I will affirm one thing. There is an evil in this kingdom."

"So, you have brought the demons you serve here?"

"I serve no demon. Merely myself." Flowridia softened her stance, sincere pleading in her voice as she continued. "There is a plague upon this kingdom, one that feeds on innocent blood, and you and I waste time seething at the other when we might be the only ones who could stop it."

Irons frowned, but not from anger. "Explain yourself."

"Each day, there are circling rumors of vampiric activity in the slums of the city. Perhaps I could help. If there is an undead monster, who better to stop it than a Paladin of Sol Kareena and a necromancer?"

The scrutiny in Iron's stare might've been intimidating, were she telling the full truth. As it was, she felt oddly more confident by lying. "You would offer to assist me after I've threatened you?" Irons said.

"I would set aside our feud for the greater good."

Irons' glare only magnified. Looking down, for he towered over her petite form, he said, "None of this changes what I've said. I do not trust you." He released a tense breath, fury in the gesture. "But I will allow you to help. If this is a trick, I will run my sword through you where you stand, whatever your status."

"I would expect nothing less." She offered a hand; he did not accept. "Let me shadow you on your next investigation. I shall offer whatever insights I can."

"I intend to personally go to the Neolan Graveyard this afternoon. You are welcome to accompany me."

She would not say he looked pleased, but he did appear surprised, and that was victory enough.

Once he disappeared around the corner, Ayla appeared from Flowridia's shadow. "Gain his trust," Ayla whispered, every word from her lips a temptation she loved to entertain. "Then the real fun begins."

"I don't know that I would call this 'fun,'" Flowridia replied. "But it is for the greater good."

Ayla kissed her with cold, dead lips.

The path to the graveyard wound through the slums of Neolan, and Flowridia's steps remained slow as she soaked up the dank atmosphere. Children giggled as they played in piles of refuse, and for all the delicious smells drifting from windows, the unmistakable stench of urine and shit permeated the alleyways, overpowering any pleasantness. Even in daylight, she saw women on street corners, their attire bespeaking their wares, and when wandering eyes followed her and her rich clothing, she kept close to General Irons and Demitri, glad she had brought the wolf along.

At Ayla's insistence, she had worn shoes today, and was grateful now, given the prevalence of glass shards and splinters of wood.

As a child in Ilunnes, she had grown up with no understanding of wealth—everyone was poor, but everyone was happy for the most part. The orphans were fed and clothed and sometimes scavenged enough coins to buy a sweet at the shop. Staelash was an anomaly, given most of its citizens were former slaves, and she had so often heard Etolié rant and rage about the unofficial caste system in Solvira, how racism kept the people she had worked so hard to free in perpetual poverty—hence why Staelash had been formed. In Nox'Kartha, all were equal by law, the menial tasks performed by undead.

Here, in the ancient empire, Flowridia saw half-elves and descendants of giants, humans, even a few De'Sindai, all living in poverty in the dilapidated outskirts of the massive city. When she reached into her pocket to give a wandering beggar a coin, General Irons placed his armored glove on her hand, the slight shake of his head a warning. "Don't flaunt what you have. You'll attract the entire district," he whispered. He hovered beside her like a moth to flame; whatever his hatred of her, it seemed she was only allowed to die by his hand. "And you'll find a knife in your back as soon as you can't pay the lot of them."

Flowridia nodded, her resolve as fragile as glass as the homes grew sparser. They stepped along the stone-paved path, their destination straight ahead and marked with an iron gate. Ivy hung over the walls; patches of lichen grew across the stones. "I'm told there was a disturbance in the graveyard last night," Irons said, and he pushed open the gate, the creaking of metal singing in response. "Normally this wouldn't fall under my jurisdiction, but I'm taking no chances."

Within, Flowridia saw some semblance of order among the graves by the entrance, the stones aligned in eclectic but organized lines. But when she peered farther back, disarray punctuated the plant-strewn collections of mausoleums and stone markers. "What happened?"

"Witnesses heard screaming sometime after midnight. When my guards investigated, they found evidence of blood in one of the newer mausoleums."

Graveyards were peaceful places, the somber atmosphere melding with the outpouring of love from mourners. Flowridia had often visited the designated plot in Staelash, small but beloved, seeking to mend her brutal view of death after three years of hell in the swamp. She would wander it like a ghost, a quiet observer of funerals and mourners, but while she sometimes stumbled upon tragic deaths, more often it was a farewell to an elderly loved one, a celebration of life. Absorbing its energy had been healing.

But here, that peace had been shattered. Something vile lingered in the air.

Two guards stood beside a mausoleum, nodding at their approach. "We were told to postpone cleanup until you arrived," one said to the general.

"You were told correctly." he said, but one of the guards blocked their path.

"With due respect, my lady," the guard said to Flowridia, "it is not for the faint of heart."

"You are welcome to wait outside," she said, expression fully earnest as she smiled; from the corner of her eye, she saw General Irons fight a smirk. "I entirely understand."

The guard appeared shocked. General Irons clasped him on the shoulder. "Son, she knows what she's in for." He plucked the lit torch from the guard's hand and stepped inside without another word; Flowridia followed, unhindered.

Demitri, however, paused at the stone entrance. *This is too small.*

Flowridia frowned within the dark hallway. "I'll be quick. Keep these nice young men safe from whatever crawls out."

You're just full of spite today.

Perhaps she was.

Flowridia followed Irons through the dark hall, intrigued by the smell of ancient dirt and fresh blood. Irons waited, the torchlight illuminating an endless array of cobwebs, as well as skeletons laid to rest within inlets in the walls—all marked with their own individual plaques. The hallway led into a larger antechamber. Flowridia heard *scratching.*

She stopped, managing to grab Iron's arm. She held a finger to her lip and tapped her ear; he frowned as he listened. They were hardly discrete, with his half plate armor, but perhaps whatever moved hadn't heard them yet. In silence, she held out a hand, bidding him to wait, then shut her eyes, expanded her senses, asking whether something dead were hiding here . . .

Her eyes shot open.

Like a boiling pot, sensation radiated from one of the fresher coffins. Flowridia slowly stepped into the antechamber, reeling at the coagulated blood on the floor. It brushed against her skirts, staining the edges, but she held her breath and pointed at the offending coffin.

Irons offered her the torch, then drew his sword, his own steps far louder as he came forward. He held up three fingers, then two, one—

And tore open the wooden coffin's lid, revealing a twitching occupant.

The man—the vampire, for fangs pierced his lips; blood caked his face—turned in his grave, far more shock than hatred on his features. When he tried to sit up, Irons brandished his sword; Flowridia's hands glowed with holy light. "Don't move," Irons said, and the vampiric man held up his hands in defense. "Tell me your name."

The man hissed, revealing his fangs.

"Who did you kill?" Irons said, louder this time. From beyond, rapid, metallic footsteps approached. "Whose blood stains this tomb?"

Flowridia brought her hand close to his face, a rising sense of euphoria filling her as he recoiled into his tomb. With his gaze caught between them, his hand darted out to grab Flowridia's hair—

She grabbed his face, his sizzling flesh malleable beneath her touch. The vampire screamed—but it suddenly cut off, Irons' glowing sword sticking out of his throat. Flowridia pulled her hair from the vampire's grip, trembling with adrenaline as Irons grabbed the dead man and dragged him from the coffin.

The two guards appeared, both paling at the macabre sight. "What happened?"

"Nothing I want leaving this mausoleum," Irons replied, positioning the vampire so its body lay strewn across the coffin, leaving his neck and head to dangle off. He lifted his sword high, then brought it down in a violent swoop.

The head fell to the ground with a sickening bounce, before rolling to the side. Flowridia grabbed it, careful to keep it away from her hair, lest the dripping blood stain it. "It would be best to keep this away from the body. Vampires have a habit of refusing to stay dead."

"Agreed." As he positioned the body back into the coffin, Irons told the guards, "Bring me a box," before looking back to Flowridia. "Good work.

The guards left. Taken aback, Flowridia smiled. "Thank you. I've witnessed more than one vampire death in my life. I know a few things."

He offered a hand. Flowridia nearly took it, though confused, before recalling the head. Irons accepted the severed head by the hair. "What do you make of this, necromancer?"

With her torch low to the ground, Flowridia inspected the plaque on the coffin. *"Louri Belgrau,"* she read. "Is the victim's name familiar?"

"No, but I will do a search for suspicious deaths in the past week."

"Last night was likely his first night rising," Flowridia replied, frowning as she inspected the blood on the floor. "He's sloppy. Whoever he killed won't rise as a vampire. Have you discovered any others? Vampires, I mean?"

Irons shook his head. "This is the first, but I will have my guards do a sweep of all the graveyards in town."

"Most won't be in graveyards," Flowridia said. "That's a myth, I think. We were lucky to find this one."

"Be that as it may, it is worth a try," Irons replied, and in the distance, footsteps approached. When the guards approached, Irons placed the head in the wooden box they brought and latched it shut. He placed it in the coffin beside the corpse. "Good enough?"

"I would say so. Do we tell the family?"

"No. No need to desecrate their loved one's memory. This crime was not his. He became a monster." He looked to the guards. "Now you can clean up."

Flowridia withheld a grin for their groans.

"There is more to do," Irons said as they left. "There remains the matter of the other victims of last night. I would like you to accompany me to inspect the man's body. You can tell me if it looks like a vampire attack. I suspect we may have just killed the perpetrator, but I worry there will be more. Something had to create this one."

Demitri bombarded her at the entrance. *First, I smell blood, and now you're covered in blood.*

"I'm not covered in blood, Demitri," Flowridia replied, though she cringed at the stains on her dress. "Just splattered a little."

Irons watched with his usual sneer. "As I was saying," he continued, "I will also try to set up an interview with the wife, but that will take more time. Tomorrow, likely."

"We'll come with you," she said, and she followed him into the unknown.

In the evening, Flowridia curled up in a chair with *Gods of Life and Death: A History of the Triage yet* was met with a strange dilemma.

Missing pages.

Flowridia skimmed through centuries of history, amused at any mention of General Khastra of Solvira, who it seemed held greater influence than she had thought. Dissertations on Ilune were frequent, yet any mention of her powers were met with pages obviously torn out and censored, which was particularly irritating when she found the section on the beginning of the Civil War and Ilune's Living Death.

Nothing.

"Flowra?"

Flowridia looked up at the curious voice, unsurprised to see Ayla emerging from a shadow beside her.

"You were not at dinner," Ayla said, and when she sat upon the arm of the chair, she gracefully let her hands fall upon Flowridia's shoulders, leaning down to place a kiss on her lips.

Flowridia blushed at the charming gesture. "I was feeling quiet. I needed time alone." Ayla began stroking her hair, wreaking havoc on the flowers and pins stuck into the thick locks.

"First, a congratulations is in order—regarding your foresight in anticipating refugees," Ayla said, conspiracy in her tone. "Another group of Theocracy citizens crossed our borders today and have been diverted to Neolan."

Flowridia did smile for that, to know she had done something right.

"I did not see General Irons much today either. What happened?"

Flowridia quickly went through the day's tense events. "After killing the vampire, I inspected a dead man's body— presumably the vampire's victim, unless it was you." When Ayla shook her head, Flowridia said, "Tomorrow I'll be interviewing his wife." She set the book aside, contemplative. "Will they turn?"

"The husband—perhaps. I would have to see the body. But the woman will not, since she survived."

A chill coursed through her, exacerbated by Ayla suddenly planting sensuous kisses around her ear. "Darling, I have a gift."

"Do you?"

"In your chamber. Won't you come?"

Flowridia nodded, allowing Ayla to help her rise. The cold of Sha'Demoni engulfed them, and they held hands among the shifting shadows. She wondered, not for the first time, where this secret place truly hid. But a part of her enjoyed the mystery of it, and when Ayla whisked them back into Flowridia's home realm, the torches were already lit, the piles of corpses as she'd left them.

The only thing out of place was a living man chained against a wall. Exquisitely dressed, though perhaps a bit dusty from travel, he immediately perked up at their entrance, struggling against his bonds, foreign words rapidly leaving lips. "Yes, yes—scream all you like," Ayla said, and then she spat out a few foreign words of her own, much to the distress of the prisoner. "Flowra, I stole this man from the border of Solvira and Moratham. I do not know his name, but he was leading a caravan of slaves to the nearest market, so I made a few assumptions about his character." Ayla sauntered over to the man, her grin as wicked as her deeds, and laughed at whatever panicked words he cried. "I thought he might be a grand vessel for your first attempt to enact old Solviran justice. What do you say?"

It was easy to speak the words, but another entirely to act, to violate this man in so visceral a way, evil or not. Flowridia's breath caught as she came forward, ambivalent at his obvious fear. "Ask him his name," she said softly, and Ayla spoke what she assumed was the Morathan language.

The man shook his head, pressing against the wall. Ayla's hand whipped out to grab his cheeks, her nails sharp enough to break skin. She asked again, this time he muttered a soft reply. "Helam," Ayla repeated, and Flowridia said it softly to herself.

She would humanize this man, wicked or not. This man who likely had a family, who had children, and who destroyed innocent lives for money. Perhaps he was kind in his private life; perhaps he was cruel. She didn't know, but she forced herself to stare into his dark eyes, determined to know him before she destroyed him. "I don't know how the God of Death did any of it," Flowridia said.

"I am not convinced anyone does. My own research keeps hitting brick walls." Ayla's fangs elongated as she licked the man's blood from her fingers. "As I said—he is an experiment."

"I have influenced living beings before, though," Flowridia mused, recalling the simple creatures she had spoken to, "and it felt the same as controlling the dead. The same words. The same innate knowledge. Perhaps it has been there all along. This is just more."

She reached out and touched Helam's forehead, ignoring his fearful, heaving breaths. When he struggled, Ayla bared her teeth and spoke a foreign threat—he quieted, even as Flowridia felt his life, his body . . . and his mind.

So delicate, this man's brain. So much damage to be done with a mere thought. She felt his pulsing blood, each individual pore on his skin as sweat beaded and fell. No words, but a silent command: *Hello, Helam.*

He gasped, his eyes fully on her.

She had him in her grasp, but what was the next step? The God of Death had granted a living death, but that was not literal. They were alive.

There was something in here. Something to touch, to grasp, to sever . . . Power rose from her fingertips, the barest hints of purple smoke, and she shot the tiniest spark into his head—

The man slumped in his chains.

Flowridia took her hand back, staring at his still figure, then brought it back, tentatively pressing it against his neck.

No pulse. Nothing. Her hand fell to her side, unexpected grief filling her. "He's dead. I failed."

Ayla's arms wrapped around her, her lips brushing Flowridia's cheek. "It will take practice, my love. Do not be so hard on yourself. Miracles take time."

So strange, to think she'd killed a man with hardly a touch. Flowridia stared forlornly at her hands, wondering when every death had become *just one more.* "To what end, though? I perfect this awful skill—and then what?"

"Change never happens without resistance," Ayla replied, and she busied her hands with Helam's shackles, his body sliding to the ground. "The Civil War was fought because the God of Death used her power too liberally. A totalitarian regime settled in too quickly. But we? We use it sparingly. As necessary. Less quantity and more quality. I have already started planting seeds of inspiration into the council's minds—speaking of Old Solvira with fondness, reminding them that while we are unquestionably a great country, we were once *the* greatest. Nox'Kartha rises, and we are stagnant. But you, my darling, are the key to its success. Casvir wields death and has undead to toil in the fields, but you balance light with your death—we do not need undead in the fields if you can grow entire fields of crops in minutes. Our people shall never know famine, and our economy shall flourish when we sell our wealth to neighboring countries. It's incredible, darling—*you are incredible.*"

Despite her anguish, Flowridia managed a small smile. "I see the merit," she said, and in her hand, she summoned a gaseous substance, corporeal death. "What if the ability was linked with the Silver Fire? What if it isn't true necromancy?"

"Necromancy was born with the God of Death," Ayla replied, silver flame bursting from her own hand. "Two sides of the same coin—pure creation and hunger incarnate. The Goddess of Stars was a healer, yes, and the Moon was creation, yet their daughter was neither—she was Death. The most dangerous of magics was born from true love." She dared to take Flowridia's hand, the one seeping potent necrotic power.

Flowridia nearly flinched at its heat, though it did not burn. Instead it vibrated, as though pulsing pure energy through her skin. She gripped Ayla's hand tight, drawn like a moth to flame, invigorated by its might. Discomfort came in tandem with alarming pleasure—this chaotic energy could kill, yes, but it could create life, or so they said.

"They are still different magics, however," Ayla said, mesmerized at the connection between them. "I understand your concern."

They lingered, the powers joining in a swirling amalgamation of silver and deep purple. One had birthed the other in a nearly literal way, and their union was potent but peaceful, culminating in a gorgeous lavender smoke. Flowridia could have watched it for hours. "It's so beautiful."

Ayla pulled her close and kissed her fondly, lingering at her lips. "I don't know that I would dare use this to fuck you, but, oh . . . it is tempting." Flowridia laughed, and when Ayla released her, their magics faded in tandem. "Perhaps once you have joined me in death," Ayla cooed, and Flowridia suddenly had to fight to keep her smile, her blood immediately pumping cold at the reminder.

"Perhaps," she said, hoping her shyness was taken as demure.

"Wait here," Ayla said, stepping back. "Helam was a failure, but we need not give up. I shall return soon with more subjects."

With Flowridia's affirming nod, she left.

Alone in the chamber, Flowridia knelt before the fresh corpse, bidding it to rise with a mere flick of her finger. It obeyed, eerie and lifelike, the grey pallor of death yet to settle.

She told it to sit and placed her hands upon its skull, feeling the stagnant heart, the cooling blood, but most importantly, the intricate patterns of his brain.

Silently cursing the God of Death for not sharing her spells, Flowridia's magic seeped inside the corpse's head, seeking simply to learn.

The Temple of Sol Kareena held high walls and a different sort of architecture than its once prestigious counterpart in the Theocracy. Humbler, the walls were built from dark brick, bearing massive windows to let in the sunlight. "Why are they keeping her here?" Flowridia asked, stopping in the shadow of the holy building.

"I wasn't told," Irons replied, wearing his breastplate and tabard. "Most likely goodwill—to ease her emotional recovery after her husband's death. Potentially to watch her to make certain she doesn't become a monster like the creature who attacked her. Superstitions are commonplace among priests, unfortunately."

"You are uncommonly well-versed in vampire legends," Flowridia said, and Irons scoffed at the remark.

"I trained under General Khastra. She wouldn't allow misinformation of any sort." They lingered before the large, double doors, his smile unexpected. "Years ago, a group of us were jesting over a drink about how to slay Nox'Karthan lieutenants—she overheard and told us that hearsay had killed far greater men than us and to spend time studying instead of drinking. Needless to say, I listened."

Flowridia grinned. "That seems in character."

"She said it far less politely," Irons replied, but his face returned to stoicism as he pushed open the doors.

The inside of the cathedral held an open skylight, though it shimmered slightly, the magic apparent—a barrier to protect the building from the elements. There were no statues, but paintings. Flowridia kept her eyes to the ground, unable to face the goddess she had placed herself at odds with.

A priest approached, and Irons explained their quest. The young man escorted them away from the chapel to a comfortable hallway, bearing dark paneling and candles enchanted to float above their heads. He paused at a shut door, knocking quietly before twisting the knob.

Within, a well-dressed woman spoke somberly to two priestesses, visibly surprised when Irons and Flowridia entered. Her neck was bandaged, and Flowridia saw evidence of bruising peeking out from beneath her long sleeves. Her face bore large, purple blotches on her cheek and forehead, and beneath her dress, her stomach was large and swollen—she held it protectively, and Flowridia understood, recognizing the gesture from Mother's pregnancy long ago.

Irons shut the door. "I am General Irons of the Solviran Royal Guard," he said, then gestured to Flowridia. "I come with Lady Flowridia of Staelash, future Empress Consort of Solvira. We would like to ask you a few questions about your husband's murderer."

The woman stiffened, and Flowridia's heart sank when tears filled her eyes. "I'll tell you whatever you want to know."

"First, you should know that the prime suspect is dead." Both the woman and the priestesses perked up at that, eyes wide in shock. "You have nothing more to fear."

"Did you kill him yourself, General?" When Irons nodded, the woman added, "Then you know I have everything to fear."

Her opposite arm joined in protecting her womb, and understanding settled upon his countenance. "That's why you're here."

The woman's face paled. "I'm due in a month's time. They're watching over me, prepared to, um . . ." She swallowed her words, visibly despondent as she looked to the ground. "Take care of it, if needs be."

"I don't understand," Flowridia said, looking to Irons for clarification.

Irons cleared his throat and said, "When a pregnant woman is bitten by a vampire, there runs the risk of her child being infected. Not a true vampire—vampire spawn, as it's colloquially known. Children of Vampires. A dhampir. I'm surprised you don't know."

Flowridia shook her head.

"Dhampirs are not inherently evil like their vampire progenitors, but most succumb to their desire for blood, even if they don't need it to survive."

"It's also a dangerous labor," one of the priestesses said, "because legends say they're born with teeth. They'll try to bite their way out. So, she'll stay here with us until we know for certain."

Flowridia matched eyes with the woman and saw fear. Something was not right. "May I heal you?" she said, a plan formulating in her head.

"Would it hurt the baby?" the woman asked, and Flowridia shook her head even as the second priestess stepped forward.

"Could it kill it? If it is vampire spawn?"

Flowridia's skin crawled at the implications. "Whether it is or not, I won't allow the magic to touch it. I can also try and sense if there is any undeath in your womb. I have power enough for that too."

The woman agreed. Irons watched, visibly intrigued. With a permissive glance, Flowridia removed the bandage from the woman's neck and saw the brutal bite mark—the man had certainly fed. She touched her hand to the woman's skin, felt her whole body, and read it like a book. She coaxed the bruising to clear, the skin to seal, but focused most of all upon the foreign entity in her womb, keeping her magic well away from its vulnerable form.

She was surprised to feel something different. Not dead, but not alive. Something in between.

Flowridia feigned a gracious, earnest smile. "The child is normal. A perfect, living person."

The woman suddenly sobbed, relief in her heaving breaths. The priestesses smiled with happiness.

"You're safe, and you're healed," Flowridia said, taking her hand. "Will you let us escort you home?"

The woman nodded. "My name is Erial Redwin. Thank you so much. My late husband's estate isn't far, but I wouldn't say no to an escort."

Flowridia helped her to rise and steadied her, her pregnant stomach surely a burden. "Thank you for your service," she said to the priestesses. "We will take it from here."

Flowridia offered an arm to the woman, and the woman, visibly charmed, accepted.

Once out of the church, Flowridia glanced back toward the now-ominous building. "Wait," she said softly, for only Irons and Erial to hear. "Lady Redwin, I couldn't say it in front of the priestesses, but I lied. The child in your womb is a dhampir."

She glanced at Irons for a reaction, but she saw only surprise. Erial placed a hand on her mouth, her tears having never staunched. "You're certain?"

"Yes, but those women were going to kill it, weren't they? That's why you were afraid."

Erial nodded, fresh sobs shaking her figure.

Flowridia looked to Irons. "You won't tell, will you?"

"I'm not in the business of killing infants," Irons said, scowling at the words.

"Do you have anywhere you could go outside Neolan?" Flowridia asked. "Your child deserves the best, dhampir or not, and I fear it will only suffer here."

"With my husband's death," Erial said, "it wouldn't be suspicious for me to move to my parents' estate, in the country."

"Arrange for that. You're due in a month's time, you said; are there midwives trained for this?"

The woman shrugged through her tears. Irons shook his head. "Vampire spawn are rare, and there are very few accounts of women surviving the birth."

Flowridia swallowed her own rising emotions, a dangerous plot forming in her head. "I may know someone. An . . . elven doctor. She won't care if your child is a dhampir. Would you agree to meet her?"

"Yes, I would," Erial said, barely composed. "I can't stand the thought of leaving the baby alone in the world."

"Go to your country estate," Flowridia implored. "As soon as you can. Then send word immediately to the castle that you're safe. Address it to me—I will be looking for it."

"I will," Erial said. "Unless the baby decides to come early, all should be well."

"If it does . . ." Flowridia swallowed, her hope barely a flicker in the darkness. ". . . send word anyway. Send a rider. Where is your estate located?"

"Lorimar," Erial replied, and Flowridia knew it to be only a day's ride from Neolan.

Flowridia offered her arm once more. "Let's take you home. Time is of the essence."

Erial lived in the upper district of the city, not far from the Glass Palace. Flowridia left her at a gated estate, and Irons, reserved for the entire walk, finally said, "You know an elven doctor?"

"Lara does."

"I see," Irons said, his posture perfect, hands behind his back. Hesitation hindered his next words. "Not many people would dare lie to a priestess, no matter what their loyalties were."

"Sol Kareena has a child," Flowridia said. "I can't fathom that she would ever approve of murdering one."

"I'm inclined to agree, though she has been quiet lately."

"The archbishop said something similar. They fear for her."

Irons nodded and said no more. They walked in silence to the castle.

"Absolutely not—I cannot condone this!"

In the council chamber, Jules' face had turned an unflattering shade of red.

"Empress Alauriel," the high priestess continued, "to enforce a curfew with soldiers would only drive our citizens to panic! This is unprecedented."

"They have every reason to panic," Lara said, serene as she lounged on her throne, "given what Irons and my Flowra have said. There is a monster vile enough to attack an innocent woman. It killed her husband."

"A monster they killed just yesterday." Jules had become as stiff as stone, liable to crack at a moment's notice.

"And who else did the monster attack that we haven't discovered yet? And who created it? Vampires populate quickly."

As Jules argued, Flowridia accidentally met General Irons' gaze, and was surprised to see solidarity. He had said nothing except to deliver the account of their morning, but he was not one to silently disagree.

She had asked him to say nothing of the pregnancy or child, and he hadn't argued.

They came to no consensus; instead, once Jules finally raised her voice, Reginal called for a recess.

"Bear in mind, Jules," Lara said, her icy tone reminiscent of Ayla and Ayla alone, "I don't need your approval. It would simply make things smoother. But I *will* push this along without your permission."

Jules stopped in her tracks, the thin line of her lips twitching. "This isn't like you, Lara. I worry about the recent influences in your life."

She didn't look at Flowridia. She didn't have to.

Irons said nothing of it as he left, only stopped to say, "I will keep you informed of any developments. Let me know of any on your end."

Reginal had taken Lara's hand, his aging countenance impossible to stray from. "I do worry you may be taking this too far."

"Reginal, I am willing to do whatever it takes to ensure my citizens' safety, especially in light of so many refugees fleeing to our great country." Lara patted his hand, her smile kind and false—though perhaps only Flowridia could see it. "If it means I am villainized by some, so be it."

"I have great faith in your wisdom," Reginal replied, though his grimace was unmistakable, "but don't forget to consider all sides."

When he left, Lara slumped in her chair, her annoyance palpable. "Gods, they'll be the death of me."

"It's like you said—we don't need Jules' approval."

"No, but it would put the people at ease to hear the Speaker for Sol Kareena in this country endorse our tightening leash."

When she stood, Flowridia followed, grabbing her hand to stop her. "Ayla, there's something else. Irons and I agreed to tell you first."

Hidden in the council chambers, Lara's visage melted away, leaving only Ayla Darkleaf. "Do tell."

Flowridia's smile faded. "I hate to ask this, but I need *your* help. Ayla Darkleaf's help."

Ayla's touch left her hand; instead, the woman sat upon the crescent moon table, scrutiny on her severe features. "You know I would never deny you anything."

"It's not for me," Flowridia replied, hating her own desperate tone. "There is no one in the world who understands biology like you do. You spent centuries cutting people apart and piecing them together for your art, but you knew how to save my life when Mereen punctured my lung. You . . . You could deliver a baby, couldn't you?"

Ayla flinched as though Flowridia had spat in her face. "Of course, I could. Whose baby?"

"The woman. Her name is Erial; she's the woman who was attacked last night. She's pregnant, and the vampire bit her in the same attack that killed her husband . . ."

Her words trailed away when understanding settled onto Ayla's face. She nodded knowingly, her tone pleasant despite her vicious words. "Honestly, that baby would be better off dead."

Flowridia's jaw fell. "How could you say that?"

"Do you think this little half-dead child will be embraced by the world? No, Flowra. It will be a pariah. Hated. Spat upon wherever it goes. Dhampirs live on the fringes of society, assuming they live long enough to make their way there. Vampires at least have the luxury of blending in when we must, whereas vampire spawn keep their fangs all the time. They cannot heal on their own. They do not drink blood for sustenance—they drink it to recover from scrapes and bruises because their bodies do not have the capacity for it on their own. Weaker in the sun, but merely normal at night. Luckily, they're overall stronger than their human half—they need it to survive when they're inevitably captured and burned at the stake."

Flowridia swallowed her grief at the cruel words. "But its mother will love it. Isn't that enough?"

"No." Ayla's cool touch skimmed across Flowridia's jaw, beckoning her to meet her gaze. "You're the type to romanticize a mother's love. Believe me when I say it's . . . *overrated.*"

Shocked at the admission, Flowridia managed to swallow her discomfort at Ayla's nasty sentiment "Ayla, please, just tell me if you'll help."

To her surprise, her intended slipped from the table and held her close. With care, Ayla slid an arm beneath her thighs and behind her back, scooping her up with the same ease Flowridia had once lifted an infant Demitri. She cradled Flowridia a moment, then sat in the once occupied chair, leaving them pressed together. "Yes, Flowra. For you."

Relief filled Flowridia at the assertion, and she finally breathed in peace. Whatever the danger, Ayla could work miracles.

"I have always been sensitive to watching other mothers and how they care for their children," Flowridia said. "When I was a little girl, I dreamt there was a mother out there, searching for me. You can imagine my heartbreak when I discovered I was right, and that she was a monster who murdered her children with no regard." Ayla soothed lines into her hair, letting Flowridia sink into her touch. "I found my first true family in Staelash. Thalmus became a father to me. Later, so did Casvir, in his own way. Etolié is the drunk older sister I never knew how dearly I needed. Even Khastra became something to me, once I was in Nox'Kartha. Never a mother, though." Her smile softened. "Connecting with Lunestra has been rewarding in ways I never could have foreseen. She's made me feel whole.

"When I realized my affection for women," Flowridia continued, her words flowing like an aimless stream, "I gave up any thought of ever having children of my own. I know you've touched men for pleasure, but I don't know that I could even for a child."

"Allow me to put a stop to that line of thinking," Ayla said, a quiet threat to her words. "You're mine alone, my sweet summer blossom." Her glower suddenly faded, leaving stark discomposure. "Do you want children?"

Flowridia's mind played a memory of long ago, of a sweet newborn boy nestled in her arms. How she had loved him, in those short precious moments of his life—her brother by blood. Her stomach clenched at the memory of Mother's knife, and in her nightmares she still heard his cut-off wail when she'd been forced to twist the knife and end it.

"I do," she admitted, forcing monotone lest she succumb to tears. "But it isn't something I would ask of you. I have Demitri. He brings me joy."

"I could very easily find you a baby if that would make you happy. Whatever sort of baby you want. A little human swine? Easily done—the orphanages are piled with them. Or perhaps you are a romantic and would prefer a little elf? I shall steal you twins."

Flowridia stiffened, irked at her love's dismissive tone. "Ayla, you do realize a child is a commitment, right?"

"Not necessarily. You are the empress consort. You can love the little sunspot, cherish its giggles, and when you have tired yourself, I will dispose of it."

Ayla's teasing smile suggested she jested, but Flowridia was still offended on behalf of the elven orphans. "Ayla, that's not at all how parenting works."

"I shall drop them off at the Temple of Staella, and you won't have to worry yourself."

"Ayla!"

Ayla laughed uproariously, despite Flowridia's glower. When she finally tired of amusing herself, she kissed Flowridia's cheek. "Forgive me. I suppose I've gotten carried away."

"A little," Flowridia said, refusing to melt into her sweet gestures. "As human swine raised in an orphanage, I do take this seriously."

"I apologize, then."

Those cool lips kept their gentle peppering of affection. Flowridia shied away from the touch, however, heart heavy at the evoked memories. "If I were ever blessed to be a mother, I wouldn't care where the child came from. But I would like to know what your thoughts were. You don't want children, do you."

Ayla, perhaps sensing the shift in mood, sat back in their shared chair, her hand finding Flowridia's and intertwining their fingers. "No, I do not," she said, no teasing in her tone. "I have no interest in children, nor do I have the temperament to raise one."

Flowridia couldn't disagree.

"That said," Ayla continued, "I would never deny you anything. My teasing aside, I am entirely serious in supporting you adopting a little orphan or twelve, though they would be yours; not mine." Ayla brought Flowridia's hand to her lips, leaving a lingering kiss. "However, given the timeline of your immortality, I would recommend waiting until the bloodlust fades, even if I do have faith in your fortitude."

The thought chilled her blood. "With due respect, Ayla," she said, her good mood failing, "whatever my wish for children, without your support, it wouldn't be worth it to me."

"I just said I would support—"

"No, no." She pressed gently forward, not wishing to hurt her beloved's feelings. "I only mean that as a vampire, I will have enough to worry about besides children, and without you there to run around with them in the sunlight, I don't know that I could do it. Of course, it's possible to parent alone, but whatever your altruism, I don't think you can fathom just how much of my time it would take away from you. And I wouldn't wish to hurt you." When Ayla's face fell into contemplation, Flowridia kissed the worry from her mouth. "I made my peace long ago with never having a child."

The faintest of smiles appeared on Ayla's lip.

"Might I ask," Flowridia said, preferring a change in subject, "of your mother? She must have died a thousand years ago."

"I do not actually know," Ayla said, and when she leaned in for a kiss, Flowridia shrunk back.

"What do you know?" Flowridia asked. Ayla continued to pursue her mouth, and Flowridia slid down and pressed her face into her chest, in that bony space between her breasts. "As your intended," she continued, voice muffled by pale skin, "I'm very curious about my in-laws."

"You will be disappointed by what I can tell you."

She kept her face planted in Ayla's chest, acutely aware of her breasts as Ayla pressed them to either side of her face, slight as they were. "You don't remember them?"

"I truly do not."

"Were you raised in an orphanage?"

Ayla stared expectantly upon her, a single eyebrow raised. "Something like it."

"Then how can you know a mother's love is 'overrated?'"

Ayla's expression remained severe. "I sincerely do not remember the woman who birthed me."

"Do you not want to tell me?"

"No, I do not. My history is my own."

Flowridia would respect that, though her curiosity burned to know more. Ayla seemed unoffended, thankfully, and kissed the top of her head.

"My life before undeath is shattered glass, Flowra. My memories have cracked with time. And in a thousand years, your mortal life will be nothing but a tarnished stain on brilliant bronze." Ayla smiled, conspiracy in her twisted lip. "But I will do what I can to make our wedding spectacular, worth keeping as a mortal memory."

Flowridia recalled a song Ayla hummed in her quiet moments, a memory of her mortal life. But she humored her and returned the offered kiss, though Ayla's words caused her blood to run cold.

A wedding for Flowridia, but a night for Ayla. A spectacular day, for it would be the last time Flowridia would ever see the sun.

Chapter 15

The true hazard of flying was the monotony of the journey. At night, the whole world looked the same.

Etolié stared down at an endless expanse of dark forest, exhaustion from days of denying herself sleep finally assaulting her. Her blinks became heavy; her head bobbed involuntarily. After deciding there was no danger in resting her eyes, she wondered if the horse could steer without her, her grip releasing—

And she plummeted into the sky.

Thankfully, she had her own set of wings, so this wasn't a death sentence. Adrenaline pulsed though her blood as her wings spread wide, slowing her descent.

The horse, obedient little thing, no willpower at all, headed toward the ground. Etolié flew after her, more falling than flying. "Slow down, you shit!"

The horse landed gracefully; Etolié stumbled and fell, skidding across the ground and managing to find herself with a mouth filled with pine needles. She coughed and spat, desperate to purge the horrible sensation from her tongue, before collapsing onto the ground. "Why," she groaned, content to lie there and die.

Hooved footprints approached. Her winged monster suddenly stared down from above, its nose far too close for comfort. "I'm not afraid to throw up on you," Etolié said, and the horse *neighed* in her face.

Soon enough, another set of hooves trotted forward. Etolié shut her eyes at Khastra's approach. "I'm not dead. Don't worry."

"You fell asleep," Khastra said, and with her came the rush of wind that meant the hammer had joined them.

"Did not," Etolié replied, like a liar. "I just rested my eyes. They were watery from the wind." From the air, she summoned her flask, then brought the blessed booze to her lips.

A thunderous *thud* shook her. The literally blessed alcohol splashed out, and Etolié choked as she breathed in the noxious liquid. Fuck, it *stung;* she rolled over and heaved. As usual, Khastra had used her hammer to smash through the base of a nearby tree, which fell with an earth-shaking 'boom.' "There," Etolié heard the half-demon say. "A seat for me, and then my lap can be your bed. You need sleep."

Burning liquid spewed from Etolié's nose as she coughed. Tears welled in her eyes. Khastra's weight fell beside her, and then a giant hand patted her back, theoretically helping though Etolié thought it would be worth it to cough out a lung to get rid of the damn burning in her throat. "Don't. Wanna sleep," she managed amidst her hacking fit.

"Etolié, you fell off the horse."

Etolié's derisive thoughts were lost as she expelled the final flecks of liquid from her throat. Gods, it hurt, but it wasn't the first time. Wouldn't be the last.

She finally sat up, scowling through her unintentional tears, and groaned. "You sure you won't get bored?"

"I have better things to do than be bored."

Etolié might've argued, but then suddenly those lovely forearms and biceps were around her, carrying her, and she did rather like that. When Khastra sat, her head rested on the half-demon's armored thighs. Unconsciousness stole her immediately . . .

The world shook.

Panicked braying filled the air. Trees crashed to the ground. Etolié shoved herself from Khastra's arms, wings wide as she floated above the shifting earth. As she tried to make sense of the tremors, she caught a hint of sparkling wings as the horses escaped into the sky. When Khastra stumbled, Etolié tried to grab her hand like a dumbass—only to be dragged down with her.

It stopped.

The world fell silent. No creatures sang. No breeze. Nothing.

"Khastra, what the actual fuck was that?"

"An earthquake," Khastra muttered, her glowing eyes narrowing in scrutiny.

They rose, and Etolié brushed dirt and pine needles off her illusionary dress. She floated in the air, wings spread wide, not trusting her feet. "So that's what an earthquake feels like? Thirty-four years on this damn realm and I've never felt one."

"No, you haven't—because they do not happen in Solvira."

Khastra's tone sparked a jolt of realization through Etolié's blood. "Soliel."

Khastra's glare remained ever-present. "Soliel."

When Etolié's feet touched the ground, she half expected it to split and consume her—not an impossibility, given this new realization. "That fucking earth orb." The air smelled moist, but the subtle prelude of thunder rolled across the sky. "Sounds like a storm—"

"Hush," Khastra whispered.

Tension radiated from Khastra's physique. Etolié quieted, hearing nothing of note save for the brewing storm. In the stark silence, Etolié lifted the pouch at her hip and withdrew the jeweled box. Holding a breath, she opened it and plucked out the orb.

With the sharp headache came sensation.

Across the sea, the dark orb sang—

And close, so close—

Etolié quickly stuffed the orb back into the box. "Confirmed. He's close."

Etolié spread her wings and flew above the trees. The acrid stench of smoke whispered like a breath on the wind, and an unmistakable orange glow flickered in the distance.

Fire.

She descended. "Khastra, there's fire far up ahead. That must be him."

"Something has provoked him," Khastra replied, the hammer flying back into her grip. "We must keep our guards up."

Just before her feet touched the ground, Khastra took her hand, steadying her when she landed. Etolié didn't need the extra help, but the gesture warmed her heart, nevertheless. "What's the plan, Beefcake?"

"You are certain it is him?"

". . . No, but I'm confident."

Khastra nodded. "Then I will not call the Bringer of War yet. Hold on to my back."

When Khastra crouched, Etolié stepped behind her and wrapped her arms around her demon's neck. With care, Khastra slipped one arm beneath Etolié's thigh and stood, easily supporting her with her massive physique. She took the great hammer in the other. "Ready?"

Etolié replied by kissing the back of her neck. "Always."

She stole a deep breath. Just in time.

Despite her size, Khastra bolted through the trees like a racehorse—perhaps because of her hooves, but Khastra had scoffed at that remark in the past. Etolié ducked her head, protecting herself from the wind and branches, though realistically Khastra more than easily dodged them.

The first hints of violence prickled against her senses. Clanging metal echoed through the night. Thunder rolled; magic brewed, rising in tandem with Etolié's sudden headache.

Static lifted the hair on her arms. Realization spiked. She barely had time to scream, *"Stop—!"*

Lightning struck the ground, not twenty feet away. The trees burst into flame—those that weren't incinerated. Khastra skidded to a stop, holding her arm up to protect her face from flinging debris.

When Etolié looked up, a shadow burst through the flame.

But it was not Soliel.

A feminine figure raced toward them, her pale skin glowing in the firelight. All Etolié saw was worn black leather and braided hair of blonde so white it nearly glowed—before the woman ran past them at inhuman speed.

Then came Soliel.

Like an angel of death, he stepped from the flames, the radiant glow of his halo nearly blinding. Fire coated his body as a second skin, churning as though molten with sculpted pieces of ice floating within. His sword was pure flame, the pine needles beneath him igniting from the sheer heat. Behind his handsome visage was hatred, for he wore no helmet, nothing to mask his golden hair and soft eyes. He gave them no mind, perhaps did not see them—merely kept his stare to the woman in his path.

Again, static rose. Before Etolié could cry out, lightning struck the ground in the distance. A woman's cry echoed through the night, cutting through the deafening blast.

Wings of pure flame burst from Soliel's back. But before he could fly toward what Etolié hoped was not a dead woman, Khastra shucked her off her back. Etolié barely had time to duck before—

A horrid *squelching* noise sounded as Khastra's hammer met Soliel's chest. Ice cracked; fire splattered; Soliel flew back, crashing against a collection of burning trees.

In the distance, Soliel's silhouette shone amidst the burning forest, struggling to stand. Khastra grinned as she brought her forearm to her mouth, slicing the skin with a sharp incisor.

Etolié's racing heart thumped in her throat as Khastra twisted and transformed. Limbs elongated, her stature grew and stretched, the skin threatening to tear as her massive physique became something more. Her armor shifted to accommodate this new, gargantuan form, well over twice Etolié's height and with the mass to match. Her tattoos glowed; fangs grew from her mouth; a bestial roar escaped her lips.

The Bringer of War had come. A shiver shot down Etolié's spine.

In hindsight, Khastra's transformation into her more monstrous self had always gotten her blood racing, but now Etolié freely thought that perhaps her tendency to turn into a giant monster was both neat *and* sexy as fuck.

Khastra lifted her hammer with the ease of a child's toy, swinging wildly as she burst recklessly through the burning trees. Horrid, mocking words left her lips, spoken in her mother tongue—the Bringer of War only spoke Demoni, with the notable exception of Etolié's own name. Fire coated Soliel, but fire wouldn't stop a hammer created by a demon goddess.

Meanwhile, Etolié illusioned armor of pure light, pulling a quarterstaff from the air. Safe from the flame—at least in her mind, given that was how illusionary armor worked—she flew into the fray. Chaos ensued as Etolié attempted to navigate the fiery scene, narrowly avoiding bursts of flame and a hammer made of gems. The Bringer of War swung her massive weapon, all but shattering Soliel against the ground, and when Etolié felt static rise again, her demon pummeled him with her fists, destroying his focus.

That was the pesky thing about magic. All the power in the world meant nothing if a mosquito bit you at the exact wrong moment—or if you were punched in the face by a twelve-foot tall half-demon.

Ice expanded from Soliel's body, reaching across the forest floor, quenching the flames. It rose to consume the Bringer of War, but she cackled. Shadows rose with her malevolent glee. Ice coated her, yet she broke free—over and over she smashed shards of ice with her bare fists, giving no shits if it broke skin.

Meanwhile, Etolié burst into fifteen of herself and swarmed the bastard like wasps. Each doppelganger wielded weapons of different styles, and she thanked her seven-year-old self for illusioning entire orchestras and learning to play all of them at once—her multi-tasking was pretty legendary, if she said so herself.

She stayed back, invisible, content to not be squished by Beefcake's fists or hammer. Soliel swung through the Etolié clones like a knife through cake, but they simply reformed. She knew he didn't believe they were real—but he believed *one* was real, and he didn't know which one.

The Bringer of War, despite appearances, was uncannily intelligent, and bludgeoned her way through the Etolié doppelgangers with no hesitation, taking great glee in grabbing Soliel by the ankle and slamming him into the ground.

A shadow passed across them, faster than the wind, as silent as a still night. Etolié spared only a glance for the figure, lest she lose control of her illusions, as the woman broke into the fray, twin swords wielded in her lithe arms. She leapt with inhuman grace, dodging the growing flames with ease as she twirled and cut her swords into Soliel's cheeks—who had much better things to focus on, like the demon who had retrieved her hammer and attempted to bring it down onto his head.

Soliel, for all his might, had no armor, and for all his power, for all his capacity to heal himself, faced an opponent with no fear of pain or injury, whose strength dominated his own. Etolié's doppelgangers stole his limited focus, taking swipes as they could, diving down to stab the exposed bits of his flesh. And this mysterious woman could not be touched— not by the clones, nor Soliel's flaming sword, or even the Bringer of War's hammer—and her swords slashed deep lines across his face—

Until, in a burst of flame, Soliel vanished.

Amidst the inferno, Etolié shrieked, *"Coward!"* Her doppelgangers vanished as she reappeared, landing beside the heaving Bringer of War. "Nice work there, Beefcake."

The Bringer of War continued pounding the ground where Soliel had disappeared, content to throw her tantrum.

Meanwhile, the mysterious woman stepped lightly across the smoldering underbrush, her face greyed from ash. Ethereal beauty shone in her smile and figure, but the sharpness of her gaze spoke of something clever and coy. Pointed ears stuck out from her disheveled hair. She slipped her swords into the straps upon her back with ease as she approached, tall enough to match Etolié in height. Hands together, she mimed a gesture of gratitude.

"I have questions, lady, but those can wait," Etolié said. "Let me help big, blue, and brawny over here."

She ran toward her favorite demon. "Khastra! Over here, ya big lug. He's gone."

Covered in ash and soot and blood, the Bringer of War looked to her, fangs bared, those glowing eyes impossible to decipher. Her growl bespoke bestial fury. But though permanently hunched, she stood and lifted her hammer.

Countless times, Etolié had decimated slave camps with Khastra during the golden years of Staelash. Normally she would fall into a sleepy heap post-transformation, but undeath had given her boundless stamina—which was terrible, because it seemed she wasn't ready to change back. "Look at me, Beefcake," Etolié said, but Khastra did not—she stared at the mysterious woman behind them.

She roared and leapt over Etolié, hammer swinging. The woman dodged, breathtaking speed in every motion, her reflexes rivaling the most adept of felines.

"Khastra, stop!" Etolié cried, daring to fly into the fray. "What the fucking hell is your problem?" She landed on the Bringer of War's shoulders, grabbed one pointed ear, and tugged. "Stop that right now!"

Quest forgotten, the monster dropped the hammer and attempted to swat Etolié like a fly—but with a restraint that suggested her friend was still in there somewhere, just a little agitated and covered in blood. When she finally managed to grip Etolié's wings, she held them with the gentleness of a butterfly as she set her on the ground.

Still, Etolié glowered. "Don't look at her. Look at me." She snapped her fingers; the monstrous half-demon's attention left the mysterious woman. "Time to calm down now, all right?"

Etolié didn't understand Demoni, but she did understand tone—and the Bringer of War's words were dark and hateful.

"If you would like to turn back into my favorite goat, you can tell me all about your grudge against this nice lady, but until you use your polite words, I'll hear none of it."

Khastra grumbled something, and Etolié clapped to steal her attention back. "Was that sass? You look at me, General. This forest is actively burning down, so let's discuss this somewhere else, hmm?"

To punctuate Etolié's point, one of the burning trees collapsed, sending sparks into the air. Wordlessly, the Bringer of War scooped Etolié into her arms, infinitely gentle as she held her to her armor, coated in ash.

The Bringer of War was rarely around long enough to cradle her, but when she was, Etolié considered it the grandest delight. Always had. She dared lean up to plant a kiss on her chin, but the half-demon suddenly roared—once again, at the woman as she tried to follow. "You listen right now!" Etolié cried. "We can discuss this like civil people once we're out of this inferno, all right?"

The Bringer of War growled but did not bite when the woman followed this time. Etolié didn't see fear, but amusement on her elven features.

She admired that.

The forest was not dense enough for the fire to burn quickly. Etolié prayed it burned itself out but knew there was nothing she could do. Fire couldn't believe in illusions.

When the smell of smoke and ash faded to tolerable degrees, Etolié tapped the Bringer of War's cheek. "Blood still racing, huh?"

A fanged visage faced her, that mouth bigger than Etolié's entire head. She said something hateful, practically spitting when she looked at the pale woman—who easily kept pace with the half-demon's monstrous strides.

"Look at me," Etolié said, softer this time as she coaxed Khastra to face her. When the Bringer of War held her up, she placed her hands on her cheeks to keep her focus. "Just think about me, all right? I'm cute, aren't I?"

In response, one of the Bringer of War's monstrous, clawed hands came up to gently graze Etolié's wing. The gesture shot shivers down her spine; squirming, she batted the claw away. "A little forward there."

Whatever the Bringer of War said, it came with a wicked laugh and a smile to match, eerie with those teeth and giant maw.

"Something tells me," Etolié said, mildly concerned by the sudden warmth pulsing through her own blood, "that this is a conversation to continue in private, hmm?"

She pointed at the elven woman—rather, where the elven woman had been. Nothing but shadows remained.

"Fucking hell, Khastra," Etolié said, but her companion, dirtied from ash and hints of dried blood, merely laughed and brought her free hand to caress Etolié's figure, lingering at her breast and not exactly subtle as she brushed past it.

Etolié pushed her aside, ignoring both the pitiful whine the Bringer of War released and the flood of want pooling between her own legs. "If you actually think I'd let those nasty claws anywhere near my naughty bits, you're insane."

"Etolié . . ." The Bringer of War spoke her name and then smooth words, menacing and dark—Etolié suspected this wasn't her standard Demoni vitriol.

"You know, it would be pretty stupid to let our guard down," Etolié said, actively letting her guard down and certainly not biting her lip as her breathing steadily shallowed. Again, Khastra's massive hand came to touch her. "Soliel could come back any moment now." Whispered words spoke dangerous promises in a foreign tongue; she sighed when lips touched her ear and hair. "That lady could still be watching—"

Again, the Bringer of War's finger brushed across her breast, careful as she lingered, lurid as she grinned. Etolié leaned forward and placed a kiss on her demon's cheek. "I'll likely regret this," she said, and then she placed a few more, not daring to kiss lips wider than her head, but electrified to touch every exposed piece.

There wasn't much. Her cursed armor covered most of her magnificent physique, but the Bringer of War didn't seem to care. Instead, she fell back, the ground shaking from her bottom hitting the ground, and placed her lips upon Etolié's body, who was little more than a large ragdoll in her hands.

Etolié's clothes vanished, embracing the sensation of Khastra's fanged mouth on her entire breast, gasping for her tongue. "I'm still quite serious about those claws on my naughty bits—!"

The Bringer of War's hands were all that supported her, placed beneath Etolié when she suddenly laid flat. Etolié stared into a ravenous gaze, a mouth half agape, and realized what the main course actually was. Excitement coursed through her, the heat between her legs painful and pulsing. "That is a pretty spectacular tongue you got there."

The Bringer of War's vicious laugh echoed through the trees. A large thumb caressed Etolié's wing, the sensitive appendage radiating overwhelming heat through her body.

"You gonna just sit there and look?" Etolié asked, her own hands coming to up to grope her breasts. "If you let me sit on you, you can stare all you like."

The half-demon smoothly fell back, and somewhere in Etolié's rational mind she wondered if this would actually speed along the Bringer of War's de-transformation, but then came the first caress of an extremely large and long tongue across her cunt and her mind flickered out like a match.

She fell forward, legs splayed around Khastra's head as she caught those wonderful horns in her hands and gripped for her life. Hands held and stroked her wings. That tongue motioned across her wanting self, then pushed inside—

Etolié cried loud into the night. Within her, she thought she might burst from sensation, that impossibly large tongue moving slowly within her, tasting her, likely enjoying it for every fucked-up reason imaginable. Etolié simply laughed.

She didn't last long, her body alight with pleasure and excitement as the Bringer of War brought her to climax. Shuddering, she clung to her horns, meeting her gaze in the final throes of passion—surprised to see contentment.

At her final moment of pleasure, she stood up on shaking legs and stumbled forward, clinging to a tree lest she fall. She grinned, depthless delight coursing through her blood as she looked back and watched the Bringer of War steadily shrink.

She was used to the gruesome display, watching her favorite demon's bones shift back into place, her massive physique became familiar once more. Her armor moved to match, sliding and shifting to become smaller. When Khastra looked up once more, it was a face Etolié adored—though it was admittedly widened with horror.

Etolié laughed and knelt to greet her, clothing appearing with a swipe of her hands. "Before you fall into a pit of self-loathing, I just want you to know that I *thoroughly* enjoyed that and greatly look forward to seeing your lovely other half naked." Grinning, she cupped Khastra's face in her hands. "But we'll save that for next time."

Resignation colored Khastra's half-hearted smile. "You should not listen to her. She might hurt you."

"Oh, she was quite clear in her intentions to eat me."

The Bringer of War was not a separate entity, but Khastra spoke of her as such to better seize control of the monster residing within her. The manifestation of her basest urges, bestial and wild—so, of course she'd want to ravage Etolié, who definitely wasn't complaining.

Khastra sighed, then pulled Etolié to lay on top of her. "Very stupid."

"Her idea, not mine." Etolié kissed Khastra, savoring the bitterness on her lips, proof of their amorous affair. "Next time I'll make her beg more."

Footsteps interrupted them then, and that's when Etolié remembered that they were in the middle of the woods on a dark night with a mysterious woman approaching from beyond the trees and a God somewhere in the vicinity licking his wounds. "Oh, um, sorry about whatever you . . . witnessed."

The woman waved away her words, which meant she either plugged her ears until it was over or watched like a pervert. Etolié chose to not ask.

Blushing like a purple fool, Khastra sat up, bringing Etolié with her, who stumbled into standing. "Let's start over," Etolié said, offering a hand. "I'm Etolié, Magister of Staelash, Savior of Slaves, and Chosen of Eionei. Someday I'll streamline that title, but not today."

The woman shook her hand and merely smiled.

Something growled behind her. Khastra, apparently feeling no better about this interloper even in a less crazed state, held a guarded stance, her glare piercing enough to shatter glass. "That is Mereen Fireborn," Khastra said, contempt twisting her lip. "Known as 'Dark Slayer' across the sea."

"Oh!" Recognition flooded Etolié, her studies all coming back. "I read about you! You worked alongside The Coming Dawn; you're a vampire slayer! You're . . ." She took a small step back. ". . . a vampire."

The vampire now known as Mereen grinned broadly, revealing white teeth—teeth that could turn into fangs in an instant, given a reason.

"If you're a Fireborn, do you know a Sora?"

Mereen's expression remained the same, though something in her stance held resignation.

Etolié didn't know what that meant. Instead, she looked to Khastra. "How do you know her?"

"I do not personally," Khastra replied, placing a protective hand on Etolié's shoulder, "but my sister does."

Right. The Coming Dawn—though a select few knew her to be Khastra's youngest sister, Kah'Sheen. "Yes, they worked together," Etolié said. "That was established."

"Kah'Sheen hates her."

Mereen's smile faded.

Etolié frowned. "Not really talkative, are you."

At that, Mereen grimaced and pointed at her throat—then slid her finger across it.

"You . . . can't talk?"

She smiled once more, though it lacked any sincerity.

"Did someone cut out your tongue?"

"She would grow it back," Khastra said. "She is either cursed or lying."

Mereen perked up—not the normal reaction to being cursed, but Etolié was starting to understand her strange mannerisms.

"I just want to know why Soliel was after you," Etolié said, concerned when Mereen's smile turned vicious. "We're here to kill him, you see. But it looks like our goals aren't unaligned."

The vampire looked between them, then opened a pouch at her hip. Upon her shoulder, Khastra's hand tightened, but Mereen pulled out a map?

She unrolled the scroll-like parchment, revealing a thorough map of the continent. She tapped enthusiastically at the little mark called 'Staelash.'

"Yes, I'm from Staelash," Etolié affirmed. "Beefcake here was there for a while too."

A crazed glint shown in Mereen's visage. She tucked the scroll beneath her arm, then pointed at her eye.

All right, so they were playing this game. "I?" Etolié said.

Then, she pointed to both her eyes and scanned her fingers across the horizon.

"Seeing? Looking? Looking," Etolié repeated, at Mereen's grin. "I'm looking . . ?"

Mereen opened her pouch once more and pulled out . . .

An orb.

The green and purple fucking earth orb.

"I *am* looking for an orb," Etolié said, breathless. "Well, that explains why he's looking for you."

Khastra leaned over to steal it, but Mereen dropped it back into her pouch, moving as smoothly as a snake to avoid her touch. "We need that," the half-demon said, but Mereen held out a hand.

The elven vampire tapped her chin, appearing thoughtful. Her smile chilled Etolié's blood as she withdrew the map once more.

She pointed at her eye.

"I?"

She brought two fingers to her opposite palm, then moved them in disjointed sync.

". . . walking?"

She unrolled the map, then 'walked' her fingers from Staelash to . . . the south? Mereen tapped erratically at a spot on the map, and Etolié had to squint to read the small writing. "Abyssal Swamp? You want me to go to a swamp?"

Mereen withdrew the orb once more with a satisfied smirk, then tapped one last time on the little drawing of a swamp.

"If I come with you to the swamp, you'll give me the orb."

Spreading her arms wide, Mereen beamed as she bowed. As she dropped the orb back into her bag, Khastra said, "Or, I kill her, and we take it."

Mereen shrugged as she rolled up her map, looking extremely unworried at the prospect.

"Khastra, there may be bad blood between her and your sister, but right now, the enemy of our enemy is our friend. I don't see any reason to not trust her."

"Vampires cannot be trusted. This is clearly a trap."

Etolié looked to the vampire, sighing as she said, "This *is* more than a little suspicious."

Mereen's apologetic smile suggested that she well and already knew that.

"Could you give us more information? I'll play charades until morning if we gotta—"

Sickness suddenly struck Etolié's stomach. She stumbled into Khastra's side, who appeared unaffected, but even Mereen had frowned, staring into the distance.

When Etolié followed her gaze, her heart stopped to see a familiar sizzling in the air. It pulled into a line, a literal cut through the planes.

Her soul silently pled for it to be Lara, but she knew—fucking hell, she knew.

The line parted into a portal.

Out stepped Imperator Casvir.

The demonic man surveyed the scene like a battlefield, his red eyes relentless as they studied her grip on Khastra's hand, and then Khastra herself—ever stoic, despite the quiet hitch in her breath. His blackened armor shone like new, repaired and polished, perhaps remade. He bore no crown, but sweeping, curved horns, adding nearly a head to his not insignificant height. The corpse-blue shade of his skin blended well with the night. "General Khastra," he said, his voice as deep as the core of the earth, "you are expected back in Nox'Kartha."

Khastra tried to release her hand, but Etolié would be damned before she simply let her go. Her hold tightened as she stood in front of Khastra, as though her small body could stop the onslaught of the imperator. "Why?" she asked cheerily, though she didn't doubt her manic eyes.

Casvir looked at her like a wasp—more annoying than dangerous, but certainly worth swatting. "There is a war to fight."

"And then what?" Etolié said, pushing back when Khastra tried to step past her. The half-demon could have toppled her with a single finger, which meant she hadn't tried at all.

"I do not see why that is pertinent to you."

Fear expanded in Etolié's chest—of abandonment, of loss, of the arrival of this impending doom. She turned around to face Khastra, heart aching at the steel in her glowing eyes. "Khastra, you can't."

"I have to."

"No," she pled, tears welling in her eyes. Not now. Not yet. "Please, I'm begging you. You can't just go. He'll . . ."

The thought was too horrendous to imagine—another vast unknown.

Khastra's hands caressed her hair, her face—anything they could touch as she held Etolié against her armor. "Whatever my fate, I do not regret it. It was worth it, to love you."

Etolié fought as Khastra pushed her away. She flew up to kiss her, to hold her, to force her to stay, to fight—*something* other than to simply walk away.

Khastra grabbed her and held her at arm's length, anguish twisting her features. "Etolié, please, do not do this."

Behind her, Casvir watched, impassive and merciless. Even if they escaped today, he would never stop.

If they escaped, he might shatter Khastra's mind with merely a command.

Khastra set her on the ground. Every instinct within Etolié screamed to fight, but the half-demon's final plea resonated through her head. As she stepped back, Khastra whispered, "I love you."

"I love you," Etolié said, her tears falling fast.

Khastra stepped across the great divide between them, toward a fate unknown but surely hellish.

High above, thunder rumbled. The clouds had never dissipated. Static raised the hair on Etolié's arms. "Khastra—!"

Too late. Lightning shot from the sky—directly into Khastra.

The force of the blast knocked Etolié to the ground. Blinding light radiated across the scene, and when she looked up, Mereen had vanished, and Casvir had also fallen, static dancing across his metal armor.

Khastra knelt on the ground, gritting her teeth and growling as she forced herself to her feet. Smoke fizzled from her body; a raw fractal pattern stretched from her neck down to her armor. She held out a hand, facing the woods, but right as the gigantic hammer returned to her grip, Soliel burst from the woods, his flaming sword prepared to remove her head.

The battle resumed. This time, Soliel held the gift of surprise.

Khastra dodged the risky blow, the momentum of the hammer spinning her around, though her movements were noticeably slowed—Etolié feared what the blast had done, and quickly summoned her doppelgangers, willing them to swarm Soliel.

Casvir merely stood by the line of trees, watching.

As the Etolié clones swarmed, she flew into the air, floating near enough to cry, "Are you going to just stand there?"

Pure indifference laced a single word: "Yes."

Bitch.

Etolié flew back toward the fight, realizing the clones were being ignored—apparently he had simply accepted the risk of decapitation by Etolié's sword and disbelieved them all. Meanwhile, Khastra swung and missed. Shards of ice shot from Soliel's elemental armor, piercing her skin. Pain twisted her visage, but when she tried to bring her arm to her mouth, Soliel's sword sliced across her face.

Etolié screamed as Khastra fell onto her back, the skin visibly smoldering, cauterized immediately but the cut was deep. The half-demon tried to kick him, but missed—

Soliel brought his sword down through Khastra's mechanical heart.

Etolié screamed; Soliel twisted the blade, and with it came an explosion of flame; a horrid shriek as fire consumed Khastra's dead flesh. The inferno raged, as blinding as the sun as it swirled to consume the God of Order and the ancient half-demon—whose scream cut off, though the flame did not relent.

The heat was unnatural, enough to bristle and burn against Etolié's flesh even from a distance. Her shock settled; she dove down, quarterstaff drawn as she bashed it across Soliel's head. The God of Order stumbled, sword swooping toward her as the fire ceased, but the Etolié doppelgangers flew once more, effective now that he knew with certainty one was real.

But as they batted him back, real Etolié fell at Khastra's side. Flame still licked her skin, but the damage lay revealed—

shattered armor, a melted heart sparking as it ticked in its death throes. But that paled to the horrendous burns on her exposed skin—and presumably beneath, if her burning gambeson were any sign. Barely any hints of blue—just red, ghastly red, and black, charred flesh. Her face could not be called that, patches of muscle and tendons exposed beside seared layers of skin.

"Khastra, look at me!" Etolié screamed, but the half-demon did not—there was no glow to her eyes at all, merely charred flesh. "Khastra!"

The half-demon released a pained gasp. Perhaps she couldn't speak at all; Etolié couldn't begin to fathom the damage within.

The doppelgangers warded off the God of Order, but Etolié barely noticed them. She turned to Casvir, who had the audacity to look moderately perturbed by the scene. "You're a necromancer—do something!"

"You care much more than I do."

"Take her to Nox'Kartha!"

He raised a single eyebrow. "Now you will let me?"

"I don't have time for your bullshit," she cried, the fact that he was a foreign monarch at the absolute bottom of her priority list. "You have to fix her."

"I do not know if I can fix that," he said simply. "How badly do you want her saved?"

Etolié simply stared, horrible dread welling in her stomach.

"What will you give me in exchange for her continued life?"

Khastra trembled, that nightmarish visage holding nothing of the woman she loved. A pained and gravelly, *"Do not—"* fell from her lips, and exposed tendons and bones moved with her mouth. Khastra groaned, the noise she made utterly inhuman.

The world slowed as Etolié looked to Soliel, his sword swiping through the clones, the forest steadily burning around them. She thought of Eionei, a god who could not save them, who could help her fight Casvir, but at what cost? Was it worth bargaining to save her? Should she plead for Khastra's final death instead?

With her body destroyed, what pain would await her if Casvir decided he wasn't done?

Etolié silently prayed: *"Sol Kareena—"*

. . . could not save her, even if she were willing. Khastra was not alive or dead, but something else, something no one could heal, not light or dark, perhaps brutal forms of science, but Etolié knew nothing of mechanical hearts nor of the man who had saved her before—much less if that would fix her now.

"No," Etolié sobbed, and Khastra's raspy breath nearly made her retch. She looked to the sky, nothing to respond to her desperate cry for help except the shadows of trees and glittering stars.

It came like a blow to the face—that there was someone who might save Khastra yet.

Etolié threw off her satchel—its contents could not come, and fuck them, fuck the whole world—and dove into the recesses of a power she had not touched in thirty-four years, screaming as she clung to Khastra's ravaged body with her own.

The world vanished.

E tolié's very soul was ripped from her body, then her bones, her sinew and muscles and skin—yes, in that fucking order—as she cut a tear into the world and pulled them through. A blink was a thousand years of agony, every piece of her burning as she stripped herself raw, the power she wielded tearing her apart. She screamed; she *burned*—

Cool dirt cushioned their descent. Eternal night blanketed the sky. Etolié vomited her weight in bile upon tufts of grass and a few unfortunate wildflowers. Sputtering and coughing, spit and tears covering her face, pain pulsed through her body as she stumbled into standing.

But whatever Etolié's misery, Khastra's was far worse. The half-demon lay still—so still—mutilated beyond recognition.

Upon a small hill waited a humble cottage. Etolié sprinted toward it, stumbling over rich, bronze rocks, nearly tumbling into the door. She banged upon it frantically, screaming all the while. "Help! I need help!"

She heard movement within.

"Momma, *please*—!"

The door opened.

Etolié faced a mirror once shattered, a thousand memories of a lifetime past. The woman appeared Celestial, from her full lips and round cheeks, to her up-turned nose and eyes, soft and wide and filled with shock and welling tears. But light burst from every pore, the strands of her hair, even the gentle tendrils of her wings. Not blinding, no, but soothing and beautiful, the sort of gentle light that inspired poetic pieces of hope, the sort that filled a lost soul with warmth and love.

The sort of light the stars were made of.

"Down the hill," Etolié said, barely blubbering the phrase. "Khastra needs help! Please!"

Staella wasted no time as she gathered her skirt, her magnificent wings gliding her down. Etolié wept against the doorframe, forcing herself to collect her strength and join her, wings shaking as she flew down the rocky hill.

Staella knelt beside Khastra, her hand stroking a line down the half-demon's face—not quite touching, merely a hair's breadth away. "Oh, my friend," Staella whispered, her voice never louder than a night breeze, "your spirit is kept here through dark magic. I cannot fix that."

Etolié fell beside them, her tears having never staunched. The sight of her demon made her sick anew, to know this was the woman she so desperately loved. "Momma, she's in pain. There has to be something you can do."

Their eyes met, and time ceased to be. Etolié stared upon a woman whose life she had ruined, who rightfully hated her for all she was, who never wanted to see her again, yet here Etolié pled at her feet, begging for more, begging for the life of the woman who made her own worth living . . .

And she saw no hatred; merely depthless sorrow.

Staella said nothing as she broke their gaze apart. Her hand skimmed lightly upon the ravaged, melted armor and broken heart, along the gruesome burns upon Khastra's skin and finally to her face and softly began to sing.

Soothing words, melodious and light, of a language well before Etolié's time—the ancient tongue of Celestière from before the Convergence, words of depthless power. The pain in Khastra's countenance faded away. Sleep took her; Etolié knew this song well, sung to her when her young mind had been too restless to slow down. It brought the haunting memories of nights she feared, of when her momma was too weak and battered to hold her and instead sang her to sleep, nights when Camdral had finally left them alone and Momma lived in a distant land gifted by the magic he offered.

Even then, she would sing. *The Witch of Celestière*, they called her. Some deemed it blasphemy, but Momma had never minded.

Staella's voice faded, but her focus remained. She took Khastra's hand—charred and ruined, some of the remaining skin unnaturally webbed—and held it to her own cheek.

Glittering light emanated from Staella's body, engulfing Khastra's sleeping form. Twin stars, each radiating throughout the eternal night, and Etolié's heart seized at the reality of what madness she was brewing.

Healing, neither dark nor light . . . but empathic.

The glowing figure that was Staella curled against the ground, the light slowly fading first from Khastra, whose destroyed armor revealed not a mechanical heart in the shattered hole, no—but a smooth, tattooed chest, no ticking beneath her skin and sternum. Her skin was blessedly blue, her tattoos apparent, though all of her was covered in blood and ash. Pristine eyelids protected what Etolié knew would be perfect, glowing eyes. Her sleeping form was flawless, utterly void of pain or injury, save one important detail—her grand locks of hair were gone. Her eyebrows too—incinerated in the flame. Something Momma couldn't fix, it seemed.

Khastra would be indignant, but Etolié desperately hoped she awoke so that could even come to pass. But before she could sob for that sudden hope, her own momma's light faded to a mere glimmer.

All of her momma was pain.

Those same gory burns ravaged the Goddess of Stars. The gentle golden color had gone, save for her wings, instead revealing melted flesh and raw, charred skin. Her light had muted; she gasped and sobbed, then bit it back, trembling as a gaping hole appeared in her chest, the bloodied space beneath her body of light as meaty as any mortal.

Staella trembled, softly weeping. Pain was the price of life—and she was a goddess who accepted the pain and fear from her worshippers, burning it through her godly blood instead, but it could not simply disappear. That was not what matter did. Not without a cost.

She took it upon herself, the pain tenfold, they said. And Etolié simply watched, knowing it would be a small moment, yet unable to move for fear and for guilt.

She ached to see her momma's pain, the sound of those quiet sobs welling anguish from a lifetime ago. "M-Momma?" she said, but Staella did not stir. She merely cried.

She would not die. Gods did not die, except when they exploded across the sky in silver light. Etolié wrapped her arms around herself, her thoughts far away from Khastra, who slept peacefully beside them.

"Can I help?" she asked, as lost as the little girl who pled at her brutalized momma's side all those years ago.

"Will you sing for me?" said a whisper in her head. Not her imagination. Staella was a still small voice.

Etolié obeyed, a simple tune trilling from her lips—one of Eionei's songs, written thousands of years ago as a homage to her momma's glory. A distraction for Staella's mind to grasp:

> *All across the painted skies*
> *Celestial bodies, pink and bright*
> *Glitter across the peaceful night*
> *To the delight of mortal eyes*

Etolié sang, and soon the horrid wounds upon Staella's body slowly sealed. She did not react at all, merely remained tense, silently weeping as the burns disappeared, leaving not even scars—just pure, glowing light.

> *Solvira sings its pledge to thee*
> *Mother Staella, Goddess of Peace*
> *The radiance of your boundless love*
> *Matched only by your stars above—*

A shuddering breath left Staella's lips. Instead of collapsing, she rose, her tendril wings rising to help steady her when she stumbled. Etolié watched helplessly as her momma shivered, her breathing heavy but consistent. Miraculous, what her godly momma could do. Extraordinary, but at what cost?

When she faced Etolié once more, they stared without the pressing onslaught of death, no constraints for time. Yet what words were there to say? Eionei had said them, thirty-four years ago.

"Your mother needs to heal on her own for a time."

The words had broken her fourteen-year-old heart.

"She swears she'll speak to you when she's ready."

And she'd heard absolutely nothing since.

Staella's pose was small, slightly hunched, hands clutched together at her chest. "I do not know how long she'll sleep." Her voice bore soothing femininity, soprano and bright. When Staella smiled, Etolié managed to match it, though discomfort welled in her stomach. "I will return in just a moment."

Staella left, a serene sight among the endless night of the clearing. Celestière was a shattered world, but Momma lived in a small desert oasis all alone, populated with wildflowers in sunrise hues and cacti taller than even the Bringer of War. Etolié looked out beyond the cottage at the thick, white fog surrounding the outskirts of this peaceful place. Like the edges of a children's story book, it signified the end of the scene—beyond, a boundless void awaited.

Some could navigate it, but one wrong turn meant to be lost for eternity.

Etolié scooted closer to her favorite demon and placed her horned head in her lap. Relief weighed upon Etolié's soul, the pain of it overwhelming, even if her half-demon's perfect stillness was disconcerting. She had no beating heart, no need for breath. Etolié's fingers traced the sharp lines of Khastra's cheekbones and jaw, touched her horns and scalp, but she slept like the dead—which she literally was, and Etolié alone was there to appreciate the pun.

Light lit up in her peripheral. Staella approached, a large pile of blankets in her arms. "Her body has been through an awful ordeal. She may sleep for some time. I cannot speak for you, but I haven't a hope to try and move her."

Etolié smiled, though she struggled to maintain it as Staella unfurled the first blanket. "I can take off her armor," Etolié said, and when Staella nodded, she did so, though an awkward silence brewed between them. She began at the half-demon's limbs, removing her vambraces and greaves, but struggled at her cuirasses until Staella helped to lift Khastra's leg—those slammin' thighs did come with a few drawbacks, but Etolié elected not to joke about that right now.

Only once did their fingers brush—and they both flinched, nearly dropping Khastra's thigh.

Alone, Etolié pulled at the straps on Khastra's shoulders, which she had years ago discovered counted as locks for the purposes of her magic. Thus, she had little trouble.

In the end, they had a pile of what used to be armor and a naked half-demon covered in blood and ash. Staella draped a blanket across Khastra's body, then carefully placed a folded-up one beneath her head. "She looks much more comfortable."

Etolié agreed. "Thank you," she whispered, and Staella's smile filled with light.

A tentative light, like a fragile, flickering candle, as told by those desperate eyes, and Etolié hated that she didn't understand. "I-It's no trouble," Staella said, which was a fucking lie because empathically burning yourself down to the bone was realistically the very definition of the word. "Can I get you anything? If you'd like to come inside, I-I could put a kettle on."

Etolié studied her, a strange and horrible sickness welling in her to see how . . . *healthy* her momma looked. "No. But thank you. I don't want to impose."

"Oh, no. No, it's not . . ." Staella's words trailed off, boundless hesitation in her enormous eyes. "Well, if you need anything at all, I'll be up there."

Etolié's mind reeled, but she managed a nod. "I'll stay here until Khastra wakes up. Then we'll be on our way."

Sorrow marred Staella's smile, but Etolié didn't understand it at all. "It might be a while," her momma said. "I . . . I'll be there."

She turned toward her house, slow as she traversed the hill. Etolié watched her, the longing in her heart threatening to spill out and bleed all over the rocks. She didn't understand, only realized a horrible truth.

Momma seemed to be doing perfectly well, and that stabbed her heart like a fucking dagger.

She warded away tears, failing miserably until a new figure emerged from the fog. "Staella!" he cried, and though Etolié longed to greet him too, she instead clutched Khastra's sleepy hand and willed them out of sight.

She hadn't seen Eionei in the flesh for nearly as long as she hadn't seen her mother. Lean and handsome, even by mortal standards, Eionei's face bore the sharpness of his wit, and his wings were a fractal design, vanishing and reassembling with every flicker. He was a topaz in shade, a brighter yellow than her mother's gentle gold. But instead of the mischief Etolié knew and loved, his face bore evidence of tears, shining in streaks down his countenance of light.

Staella stopped at the cry of her name, waiting as Eionei ran to her. "What's happened?"

"It's Etolié—she's gone. She's missing. Last I know, she was fighting the God of Order, then called for Sol Kareena's help but now—" His breath bore evidence of a sob. "She's gone."

Staella spared the faintest glance for Etolié's spot, the scuffled dirt surely revealing their precise location. "Oh, goodness," Staella said, placing a hand upon her heart. "That's just awful."

"Awful!? She might be dead!"

Eionei couldn't sense her presence when she was in Celestière, Etolié recalled, watching her chosen deity fall into tears.

"Oh, I doubt that," Staella said as Eionei fell into her arms, and had Etolié not known better, she would have thought her momma was perfectly sincere in this charade. "Didn't you say she had that nice demon girl with her?"

"You aren't taking this seriously," Eionei said, somewhere between anger and anguish, and Etolié struggled to stay quiet. "Starshine might be dead!"

Staella's gaze held depthless kindness and light. "I am. Do you think Khastra would let anything happen to her?"

"No, but—"

"Then I'm not worried. Not until they find a body. Have you thought of sending a search party? Where were they when they disappeared?"

"In a forest in Solvira. I . . . I could contact a nearby temple."

"You could." Staella smiled, revealing nothing as she patted his shoulder. "You always worry, and then it's nothing. Remember the attack on the City of Light?"

"I feel like that one was justified."

"It was. And this one is too, but I truly believe in my heart that all will be well."

Etolié could only see the interaction to a small extent, but Staella had him eating out of her hand. "If you're sure."

"Send that search party, and let me know."

They hugged, then Eionei disappeared into the fog. Etolié and Khastra flickered back into view. "Thank you," Etolié said, and she dared to leave the half-demon behind and approach her glowing momma. "I don't want to worry him, but he doesn't really like Khastra, and I don't have the emotional capacity to handle that argument."

"He's mentioned it once or twice." As they stood before the other, Etolié realized she towered above her progenitor, who scarcely reached her chin. She hadn't remembered her momma being so small. "If you don't mind me saying," Staella continued, "I was overjoyed when I heard you had met her. More, when I heard you became friends."

That . . . was not what Etolié had expected. "Eionei doesn't quite agree with that."

"No, he does not," Staella replied, and Etolié wondered how often they spoke of her, surprised they spoke of her at all. "I told him to leave you alone about it, but I'm not surprised he didn't listen. Etolié, I have great respect for Khastra, and I knew if she were with you, you'd be safe."

Etolié nodded, remiss to admit she'd recently taken up the habit of naked cuddling with the aforementioned friend. "I love her," she said, and there was no lie to suspect. "Didn't realize you knew her that well."

"Goodness, I met her a long time ago. She was there on the day I first met Ku'Shya to try and make a bid for peace between us—and that was over nine thousand years ago."

An unfathomable amount of time, to Etolié. "I suppose she was in Solvira, too, when you were in charge."

"She was, and you'll be amused to know Eionei hated her then too." Staella smiled, but when Etolié could think of nothing to say, an uncomfortable silence welled between them once more. Her momma's hand clutched her opposite arm as she gazed up at her, a full head shorter. When Etolié had left, her momma had matched her in height.

Staella opened her mouth, but then Demoni words grumbled behind them. Startled, Etolié turned to see General Beefcake muttering in her sleep in her mother tongue. An idea bubbled in her head. "Do you have a place we could put her inside?"

"I do. Is she waking up?"

"No. But she's highly susceptible to suggestion when she's sleep-talking." Etolié ran over and knelt beside Khastra, gently tugging on her horns. "Good morning, sleepy."

Khastra muttered something most likely non-inflammatory in her native tongue, followed up by Etolié's own name.

"You fell asleep outside, ya lug. Will you come with me? I'll walk you inside."

With the obedience of the undead slave she was, Khastra rolled over, Staella's sleep song far too strong to allow her mind to awaken. But when she stumbled into standing, all eight and something feet of her, she groaned and muttered more, and Etolié cursed herself for never learning more words in Demoni.

If seducing the Bringer of War was part of her incentive, it was a rather good one. But for now, she took Khastra'a callused hand and coaxed her along with soothing words toward the cottage. Her momma held the door open. "Bend over, Beefcake," Etolié said, the way she might talk to an unwilling puppy, amused when her demon obeyed.

The cottage was of Celestière design—rounded and hollow within the inner rooms, for the sake of absorbing light. Staella rarely ate; she merely basked in the starlight for sustenance, her wispy wings absorbing the blessed light.

Staella followed them inside, and Etolié was thrust backward in time.

Messy and cluttered, a nest of scarves lay in the center of the front room, one path leading to a food preparation area, dusty from disuse, and another disappearing into a hall, where Etolié's childhood bedroom waited.

But there were frightening things hidden among the quaint sight, humble for a goddess, former or not. The slight dent in the wall, invisible to anyone not seeking it, perfectly shaped for her momma's head, or the scratches at the arm of the couch, where Momma's nails had gripped while Camdral—

"Follow me," Staella said, earnest as she escorted them down the hall.

But Etolié slowed when she passed her old bedroom, the door slightly ajar. Loneliness filled her, to see her childhood so clearly displayed. A bed, perfectly sized for a Celestial adolescent, sat centered among shelves of toys, a wardrobe in the corner, and, by appearances, a quaint and happy little spot, even if Etolié's memory reeled.

Perfectly maintained. Not a speck of dust upon the shelves. Ready for a guest at a moment's notice, and Etolié . . . wondered.

She passed on, saying nothing on her way to Momma's room.

And a very different room it was, all evidence of a male interloper absolutely gone, along with any signs of living—if the nest of scarves in the front hall were any indicator, Momma slept out there. This bed, rounded in the usual angelic style—they slept on their stomachs, lest they squish their wings—hadn't been used in years, Etolié suspected, and when she entered and brushed her hand across it, there was dust.

This room was never touched, if the stagnant air were any indicator.

Perhaps it was too much for Momma.

"This should be large enough for her," Staella said, lingering in the doorway. "If you wouldn't mind getting her settled, I will go clean up outside. Will you want to take a bath?"

Etolié glanced down at her illusionary dress, noting the ash and blood and flakes of Khastra's crispy skin. "Yes."

"I can—"

"I remember how to do it," Etolié said, because Staella had already done too much.

"Will you need new clothes?"

"No. But thank you."

Etolié tugged Khastra into bed as Momma shut the door. "Come on," she said, her disoriented friend falling onto the dusty sheets. The bed creaked but did not break, though Khastra's legs hung off the bottom of the round blankets. Etolié gave a good attempt at pulling the covers out from beneath her favorite demon but was met with failure.

Whatever. She wouldn't be cold here.

Instead, Etolié dared to spare a moment to curl up beside her, intrigued at the smooth skin of her brow. "Go back to sleep," she whispered, and in her sleepy haze, Khastra nodded. When Etolié kissed her, the half-demon kissed back, the sweetest of smiles pulling on her full lips.

Etolié's heart soared for that.

She ran her fingers down Khastra's bare chest, seeking to rewrite the memory of burnt flesh. So strange, to lay in perfect silence, no gentle ticking to punctuate the scene. Her true heart was restored. Even the scarring had gone, from both her sternum and her face. Khastra was perfect, more perfect than before.

She was still dead. Her momma could not restore the dead to life. But her body was repaired, and her spirit remained trapped within it.

As Etolié stepped from the bed, she paused a moment to study the half-demon—*her* half-demon, and oh, it was a remarkable thing for Khastra to be. Without the burden of war and politics, Etolié's heart swelled simply to look at her. Nothing had changed, yet everything was new, her dearest friend more hers than ever before.

Khastra's face held peace, and Etolié wondered if it was the first she'd felt it since before her death.

After washing away the dirt and gore, Etolié illusioned the same dress, hoping it would detour any questions about where she had gotten a new one.

She stepped down the familiar hallway, appearing in the entry room where a pile of ruined metal, the remains of a once-grand set of armor, sat neatly arranged. Staella stood by the door. Her eyes lit at Etolié's entrance, and somehow it hurt to witness. "I was about to leave for Vanir Sol," she whispered. "I don't keep much food in the house, but . . ." She smiled sweetly, everything about her demure, and Etolié hated feeling so much larger than her momma.

Even if Momma had always been small.

"Would you like to join me?"

Countless complicated emotions were tethered to the layered question, all of which Etolié immediately swallowed. "You know I can't do that."

"Letter of the law says no," Staella replied, her wispy words bearing mischief, "but the spirit of it says you and I both have illusion powers and what they don't know won't hurt them."

Amusement twisted Etolié's lip. Most childhood memories of Vanir Sol held joy. "All right. Why not."

"We can leave a note if you like," Staella said, rummaging through a drawer as she spoke. When she withdrew an old quill, Etolié found the blending of worlds too strange for words. "In case Khastra wakes up."

When Staella offered a strip of parchment with it, Etolié quickly scribbled the words: *Be back soon!* With the addition of a few artistically scattered hearts, there would be no question who it was from, unless Momma was the sort to scribble hearts around otherwise benign notes, but she was fine to rely on context to hopefully convey that it was her flirting and not her momma—which was a thought process she promptly shut down because *ew*—at which point she remembered the aforementioned momma was watching and likely wanted an explanation, so Etolié said simply, "We're just really good friends."

And Staella, who had previously held an agreeable smile, kept it, but Etolié had to commend her commitment to not showing the stark confusion in her widening eyes. "I don't doubt that."

"We always put, uh, hearts on notes to each other," Etolié said, casually blowing on the ink, aware of the hole of lies she was digging. "It's what best friends in Staelash do. It's, uh, cultural. Totally normal."

Staella nodded, her interest palpable, visibly hanging onto every word, but Etolié got the strangest feeling that it had less to do with the words and more to do with, well, that they were her words. "I think that's sweet."

"I'll just . . ." Feeling awkward, Etolié pointed at the direction of the bedroom, then left without another word to deliver the parchment scrap.

She placed it idly on the bedside table, sparing a moment to watch her favorite Beefcake. Khastra laid as still as the dead. Coldness permeated the half-demon's skin, slowly overtaking the familiar warmth. Without a ticking heart, Khastra's blood no longer pulsed.

Something akin to dread filled Etolié's stomach, but she pushed that aside. For now, Khastra would sleep until Momma's spell faded away.

When she returned, Staella offered a pleasant smile. "Through the mist, then? I'll lead the way."

Etolié followed her momma out into the endless night, the glittering, peaceful stars a gateway into a perilous journey. Staella lingered at the edge of the mist, the swirling border of white opaque and all-consuming, then tentatively offered a hand. "I must insist. If you're lost, you'll never be found."

Etolié accepted her hand, the warmth of it pulling an unwilling blush to her cheek. She barely held Momma's fingers, the space between them insurmountable even when touching, it seemed. "Lead on."

They stepped into a void of white.

Unlike Sha'Demoni, which stretched but never shattered, Celestière held islands of organized matter among a fragmented world, the broken bits filled with nothing at all. With every step into the white, cloud-like world, Etolié's feet sunk into the ground, and though she knew if she stopped it wouldn't consume her, it certainly felt like it. Her grip tightened; she held her momma's hand properly now. There were those, like her momma, who could navigate the mists, pure instinct and age leading them on, but most residents of the world could not, either staying put on their little islands— some bigger than others—or relying on others for safe passage.

They walked, nothing before them except white fog, but Staella made deliberate turns, and Etolié wondered if she counted steps.

"I hope Khastra recovers well," Staella said, her voice echoing within the broken space. "A body is not meant to go through so much trauma."

"It's still strange to think you know her," Etolié admitted. "Is she older than you?"

Momma's smile was so full of light, shy as it was, and Etolié burned beneath it. "No, though only by a few years. Khastra came to Celestière many times, serving as an envoy between Solvira and Neoma, though Neoma wasn't particularly fond of her. But Khastra had a good heart, and I trusted her honor. I tried my best to make her feel welcome in my home." Her light faded by small degrees. "I do not know if we're friends or ever could be, but did you know she saved my life once?"

Etolié shook her head.

"I'm not surprised. I know she harbors guilt for what she did during the Civil War. Khastra and . . . and Ilune, they . . ." Momma hesitated, and Etolié found it so surreal, to speak of Khastra like she didn't know her at all. "They were allies. When I came to visit Ilune near the end to speak peace, she tried to have me killed. Khastra betrayed her to save me."

Khastra had never said a word of that before, and Etolié's heart stung. Thankfully, the parting mist stole any bitter words she might have conjured about that little fact.

The brilliant world of Vanir Sol awaited.

The white mist had integrated itself into the world, yet light shone from cracks surrounding it—resulting in an endless, cheery day. Stone paved the path before them, taken from the mortal realm thousands of years ago to build it, along with other emblems of mortality—homes built of wood, familiar plants upon windowsills, and clothing bearing silks and wool from the world Etolié called home.

Like her momma's home, mist surrounded the outskirts, but Vanir Sol was enormous, the epicenter of angelic life. Bustling citizens filled the path the farther they stepped from the mist. Grass grew in the space beyond, likely sown generations ago, and shopkeepers sold Solviran delicacies, trinkets—things familiar and not. In the far distance, impossible to miss for it rose high into the sky, placed upon what appeared to be a cloud, was a great castle, created of pillars of stone, largely open and filled, Etolié knew, with gifted art and beauty from mortals to their grandest goddess.

Sol Kareena lived there. Etolié's heart sank to know she was unwell.

Celestière was a broken world, though very few were old enough to remember what it had been before the Convergence. Sol Kareena used to tell bedtime stories of the unique ethereal beauty, of plants and creatures as luminous as angelic wings. Eionei made silly songs of it, and there were others, yes, but so few. With the extinguishing of Celestiere's Triple Suns had come the death of nearly all matter. Anything reminiscent of plant or animal had come from the mortal realm or from Sha'Demoni.

Small signs remained—stone that did not shine in any way that was mortal, dirt bearing small flecks of sparkling matter. Momma's stars back at home were something like unto the old world as well—luminous and bright.

Those who saw and recognized Staella immediately parted for her passing, her wings setting her as different than most. A few bowed, but she paid them no mind. They paid no mind to Etolié at all, and she wondered if it were a spell.

Knowing her momma, yes.

"No one will see you unless they know to look," Staella whispered, in response to her unspoken question.

There were no children among the array of people— but children were rare and valuable. Staella smiled to a few who spoke her name, even greeted some when they stopped her, and to see her momma so timidly vibrant punched Etolié in her stomach.

Staella was well, if reclusive and shy.

Still, fond memories floated through Etolié's head, of times spent with Eionei admiring wares, of playing in fountains and elegant parks. Countless times, she had slept in Auntie Kareena's castle, who was strict but ultimately kind, and who knew something was wrong in Etolié's home but not what. Her gaze lingered upon the distant castle as Staella led her on, then realized their hands still touched. Etolié resisted the impulse to flinch, instead debating the appropriate course of action. Her mother began chatting enthusiastically with a seller of some strange, tentacled meat, but Etolié said nothing, not wishing to overstep more than she already had, but also uncertain of how to break this physical contact between them without drawing further attention to it.

In the end, Etolié's decision was made when Staella withdrew her hand herself, idly poking through the offered food.

She missed it already. Sparing a glance to the mists far behind, Etolié quietly hoped they would return soon, if only to hold her momma's hand again.

"What do you think?" Staella said, startling her jittery self. "Traded from Sha'Demoni—do you think Khastra would like it?"

"Khastra likes everything," Etolié replied, then quickly added, "b-but she'd probably find it thoughtful."

From the air, Staella pulled a glittering handful of dust and offered it to the Celestial merchant, whose eyes lit up with delight. He told her to take whatever she liked, even offered her a basket, and realization struck Etolié like lightning through her core—a sensation she was unfortunately very familiar with.

Stardust.

There was no money in Celestière—only trade. As Staella filled her basket with tentacles and what could only be Demoni plants, Etolié's attention shifted to everything and nothing, mesmerized by the home she had been banished from. Something swelled in her heart to look upon what she'd been forced to leave behind.

"Etolié?"

Startled, Etolié glanced back to her momma, holding a basket with a few ingredients.

"This may take some time," Staella continued, her soft voice somehow cutting through the crowd. "If you wish to wander without me, I won't be offended."

Truthfully, Etolié wanted to spend every second at Staella's side; to equal degrees, she wanted to hide and never see her again. She forced a smile and said, "All right."

"I will be able to find you, don't worry," Staella said, and Etolié believed her.

And so Etolié left, passing homes with open roofs, designed so their inhabitants could feel the light. Though they could eat as mortals did, angels needed light to live, absorbing it through their wings and bodies like a plant, and many Celestials were the same, though with the passing generations, most required food in varying levels to supplement. Once, there had been three suns, and the angels had thrived beneath their light, condemned now to the inferior light of the mists, but there were outliers like her momma who prospered beneath the stars—and Etolié was grateful for that, given it had been her inheritance.

Despite living among them, most Celestials worshipped the angelic gods, though it was more a station of royalty than godhood. All were loyal to Sol Kareena here in Vanir Sol, but Eionei was a popular figure. Celestials and angels loved their booze, and as Etolié passed a temple to Eionei, she knew it held that in plenty. For a moment, Etolié was tempted to join what she knew was a riotous party, revel in the music surely playing behind the walls, but if she were to be recognized anywhere, it was her grandfather's domain.

There were many minor deities, and Etolié couldn't name them all anymore. It was rare that anyone new rose to godhood anymore; Etolié was the nearest thing to a 'Newer' God anyone had, and she was hardly a demi-god yet. Smaller temples passed, many bearing symbols Etolié once knew but had forgotten. She held fond memories of coming here with Eionei, of being taught the various rulers and their domains, but she had been a child then. Now she had to fill her brain with politics instead of stories.

Eionei had sung and taught many tales of the gods of Celestière—even of Neoma, the late Moon Goddess, who though gone was far from forgotten. Her temple remained as a reminder of what was lost, decorated in emblems of the celestial body but also the stars, for her love of the Stars was of legend. Though a thousand years had passed in the mortal realm, time moved slower in the world of angels. Many still mourned. There were so many stories of the Moon Goddess' legacy, but Etolié had resented her for years to see what her death had done to her sweet momma.

Though now that Etolié had someone to love, she supposed she understood how a person could completely fall apart after losing a wife.

Etolié lingered before Neoma's temple—sealed with stone so none could enter, but a statue, newer than the great building, had been erected outside it. A being of power and relentless might, the great statue depicted a woman in a warrior's attire, wielding a sword of fire. It held eyes that followed wherever you went. Neoma was a presence who lingered, even well after death.

The unconventional but perhaps greatest impact she'd had upon Celestière floated through Etolié's head as she came upon a different temple she knew but had actually never entered—Alystra was not a goddess of debauchery, but there were certain aspects of Love and Beauty Etolié hadn't been allowed to learn as a little girl. Neoma's legacy had been to defy the once more conservative views of Celestière, for any way of life that stood in the way of producing the preciously rare angelic children had once been frowned upon. But Neoma loved women, setting a precedent that had never been disputed in Celestière—there were advantages to being the head bitch, after all—and even forged the way for mortals to love who they would as well.

Many years later came Alystra, who walked a different though not entirely dissimilar path—born into a body most might consider a man's, she had proclaimed herself anything but. Etolié knew her intention had never been to become a goddess, but it seemed that was the price for catching the eye of the Drinking God. Eionei flirted by writing songs of her beauty and grace, some elegant and some crass, and soon the mortals repeated them.

The many ostentatious statues of the Goddess of Love weren't surprising, given her entire purpose was to be displayed and adored. Some were old and showing signs of age, but many still bore the perfection only marble could bring. Alystra stood in luxurious poses and in various states of undress, sometimes with only her wings to cover her, her curves and feminine shape a testament of magic and herbology Etolié didn't know the details of.

What was strange, however, was the sound interrupting Etolié's musing. Crying sounded faintly ahead, but not just any sort of cry—a baby.

In a world of immortals, babies were a rare and blessed thing. Even with the rising Celestial populace, conception was a celebration, and birth was reason enough for the small, shattered world to set aside the day for revelry. Miscarriage was a tragedy; abortion was unheard of.

This baby could be only one.

Swaddled and fitful, the infant lay in the arms of the last person she would have expected, who finally got the poor thing to take to the cloth of his feeding bottle.

Alystra wore revealing robes and looked terribly bored until she stared at and studied Etolié. Her aura bore hints of pink and red, subtle glitter in her wings, which held more structure than Etolié's own. Metallic, almost. Alystra was a ruby, even in Etolié's earliest memories. "Etolié?"

"Nice to see you too, Grandma," Etolié replied—even if Alystra looked notably unimpressed at the pet name. But she was Eionei's lover—sometimes—so what else could she be? "Didn't know you could see through illusions now."

"What are you doing here?" Despite Alystra's frown, Etolié sensed no condemnation—merely confusion.

"Just accompanying my mommy to the market," Etolié replied.

"Brave of Khastra, to show her face in Celestière."

"She—" Etolié's remark withered and died in her mouth, her jaw dropping from appall. "I meant my mother. Staella. The woman who birthed me."

Alystra's face remained perfectly impassive. "That's somehow more surprising," she said, and Etolié wanted to die. "Last I heard, you were dead."

Etolié couldn't be taken aback, given how many times that rumor had likely floated around lately—she just hadn't expected this from Alystra. "How recently?"

"An hour ago."

"Clearly I'm fine. Who said otherwise?"

"Eionei."

Right. He had come to Staella's house crying. Etolié supposed it explained why she'd been spotted—it seemed she was on more than a few people's minds.

Uncomfortable silence settled between them. Feeling like a lost child, Etolié frantically thought through a hundred different excuses to leave, when Alystra said, "I don't suppose you want to meet your cousin, do you?"

Etolié looked from Alystra to the restless boy—to Soliel, who she knew grew up to be a monster—who unlatched from his feeding bottle, his eyes large and fixated upon her. Wordlessly, sat beside Alystra, accepting the infant when offered. She released his pudgy hand from the swaddle, impressed by his strength as he angrily waved it about.

There rose the innate urge to protect the tiny Celestial, yet for a brief and damning moment, she wondered again what would happen if she snapped his neck, whether it would destroy the monster back home and stop his onslaught, perhaps even erase his memory and all that had fallen into place because of it.

Meira. Malakh. The dragon, Valeuron. Even Khastra, in a way—so much blood in this little boy's future—only eight months old in mortal time, and even less in Celestière. Time moved slowly here, though it was difficult to measure, given there was only day in Vanir. But he bore the appearance of a month-old Alauriel, perhaps a week or two more—helpless and sweet.

Would all be made right again, if she ended it now?

Khastra had said it wasn't worth slitting his throat on only a hunch.

When Soliel grabbed her hair, Alystra helped to free it from around his chubby fingers, and Etolié kept her horrible thoughts to herself. "Cute kid," she finally said. "Why are you watching him?"

Alystra pursed her lips, her glower conveying very well how she felt about watching the little sunspot. "Eionei was supposed to. Kareena is still recovering and has needed extra support—which Eionei is happy to give. He loves babies and children. But then you had to go and get yourself killed, so he dumped Soliel and a bag of his things on me as I was leaving my temple so he could go find your carcass." She placed her fingers on her temple, as though a headache were brewing. "But Kareena is my friend. This is fine."

Were Alystra trying to convince herself, she was doing a terrible job.

"Um, if you don't mind me asking," Etolié said, grimacing when Soliel's face scrunched in endearing, infant anger; apparently stealing back her hair had been an insult, "what *is* wrong with Auntie Kareena? People in my realm have been saying she's quiet. Eionei says she's ill."

Baby cries filled the otherwise peaceful temple grounds. Etolié tried in vain to shush him, bounce him, but he seemed content to raise a ruckus instead.

"We are not entirely certain, though this has happened before," Alystra said, concern marring her beautiful face. "We gods gain our power through worshippers, pledges, but if those worshippers are suddenly silenced in large numbers, it leaves us weak, deflated too quickly. Kareena is mourning, but she lacks the strength to help at all. Not all her power is stolen, but the largest bastion of her worship was slaughtered in a night—and that has left her crippled."

Etolié brought the baby to her shoulder to burp him, but he only screamed louder. "She'll be fine, right?"

"We believe so. Tortalga remained lost for years after the leviathan ate the merfolk of Stelune, and your mother suffered quite a blow after the civil war in Solvira. They both recovered, though they were distant for some time."

"Is it possible for her to die?"

Alystra's ensuing shrug was unnerving. "No one has died from this before, but we do not have a particularly large sample of dead gods to choose from for comparison."

There was only one, and Etolié habitually didn't bring her up.

Again came that awkward silence. Thankfully, Staella appeared then—out of pure air, Etolié reckoned—sparing her from further awkward engagement.

Well, in theory. Etolié had a talent for sensing vibes, and Alystra and Staella had always had tension.

Except . . . Momma seemed genuinely at ease. "Lovely to see you, Alystra." She went straight for the baby; Etolié passed the shrieking infant off to her momma, relieved to rid herself of his baby aura.

"Likewise," the Goddess of Beauty replied, her perturb to be expected. "You have a lot of nerve, bringing Etolié here."

To no one's surprise, Staella's mere presence was the necessary remedy. Soliel's cries lessened, especially when Staella made a *puff* motion with her fingers, and down came a rain of illusionary glitter. "I see no harm in it, assuming you don't tell anyone."

"Considering I was an outspoken opponent of her banishment? I'm offended. Not even Eionei will know."

Etolié hadn't known that. Astonished, she opened her mouth to speak, but Momma beat her too it. "For the best, though he's very worried. He wouldn't do anything to her, but she's not the only illicit guest in my home."

"You really do have a lot of nerve."

Instead of commenting on the matter, Staella smiled at Soliel, who released a delighted gurgle. She gently redirected his little hands from her own silver locks. "Oh, he's so handsome, isn't he?".

Alystra's bored glower—her default expression, in Etolié's memory—reemerged. "You don't want to take him, do you?"

"I would if I could," Staella said, conjuring another *puff* of glitter, watching as Soliel sought to grasp the mesmerizing cloud, "but I'm busy harboring fugitives."

"Fair enough."

Etolié's mind still dwelled on the *Alystra defended me* part of the conversation, even as her mother handed Soliel back to his unwilling keeper. "Speaking of," Staella said, "I didn't anticipate having guests, so I'm a bit behind on synthesizing any teas for you. Will you be all right waiting a day?"

Alystra waved her off, clearly unbothered. "I have a massive stockpile. Don't worry about me until your fugitives have gone home."

With care, Staella returned the infant boy and shared a polite farewell, but all Etolié could summon, despite thirty-four years apart, was a small wave.

Something akin to bitterness rose, to see momma's residual joy as she walked away from the baby. But she wouldn't speak of that. Once away, she asked, "What did Alystra mean, when she opposed my banishment?"

"Exactly as she said," Staella replied, her basket held in the crux of her arm, filled with a plethora of strange meats and what she presumed were plants. "And she wasn't the only one, but none of that came about until after you had left Celestière."

"Oh." As they walked through the streets, Etolié soaked it all in, the atmosphere and radiant energy cities brought, surprised at her own melancholy.

"Alystra was particularly angry about the whole situation," Staella continued, "and blamed Eionei."

"Eionei?"

"Because if he hadn't told, we suspect the entire, um . . . *incident* would have been swept under the rug. She . . . She isn't the only one who shares a similar opinion."

Etolié didn't miss her mother's sudden tension.

She hadn't come here to discuss Camdral.

"Why are you giving Alystra tea?" she asked instead, assuming this to be a far less traumatic line of questioning.

"Well, as I believe you know, Alystra's body needs a bit of help staying as it ought to be, and since I can help, I'm more than happy to. There's a lot of magic in what I do."

When Etolié said nothing more, neither did Staella, mutually silent until they reached the mist. Staella offered a hand, and Etolié held the tips of her fingers, unable to encroach on her any more than that.

Together, they stepped through the mist. Staella finally said, "Soliel is the sweetest thing. I haven't had a baby to dote on in so long." She remained apprehensive; Etolié hated to recognize her emotions so well, to read every twitch of her momma's eye, every minute change in her lips. "He has been good for Kareena and I, too. We hadn't spoken in a while, before his birth. And now she's so sick. I've been helping to watch the sweet thing."

Etolié could not bear to poke the tension in that. "What about his father?"

Staella gave an idle shrug. "I don't know who he is. No one does. She won't tell."

Strange.

"Sweet Soliel has no shortage of people wanting to love him. He'll grow up to be a fine heir to his mother's throne, assuming that's his path."

"I don't know if—" Etolié quickly bit her tongue.

Staella frowned, her eyes wide and demure. "Pardon?"

Etolié wanted to shake her head, to deny she had an opinion at all, but recently a dragon had said some ominous shit, and not two hours ago, a time-travelling god had incinerated her favorite demon. With wavering resolve, she said, "Can I say something insane? You have to keep it secret."

Staella fervently nodded, even stopping in the endless mist to face her properly. "Anything, and of course."

Etolié heaved a great sigh, then told the story as she knew it—that the God of Order had returned, that he was keen to separate the worlds and kill the residents of Celestière and Sha'Demoni, and that he had been, somehow, a little blonde infant cooing as his aunt illusioned puffs of glitter. "He confirmed it himself," she finished, no longer holding her momma's fingers, "to my friend."

Staella listened without interruption, finally nodding. "Eionei had mentioned something of the Old God returning, but he hadn't said it was Soliel."

"I didn't tell him. I didn't want Sol Kareena to know."

To Etolié's surprise, Staella appeared thoughtful. "He's truly her son. But grown? How strange." She offered her hand once more, and Etolié, feeling slightly more in her mother's good graces, managed to grasp her fingers.

As they walked through the mists, Staella said, "I was young when the first accounts of angels falling into the mortal realm emerged, but I remember them well. Eionei was the first, promptly worshipped by the humans who found him. Angels could appear in your world back then—the barriers hadn't solidified yet. But he returned with the news and brought Kareena with him. They were friends, even all those years ago. But news spread immediately of how the mortals fell to their knees in her presence, and we learned it was because of her resemblance to their Old God of Order—both in appearance, and in spirit. Neoma followed her sister at her behest and was worshipped the same—as the Old Goddess, Chaos, who ruled many realms, including the moon. It was how they became the greatest among us.

"And so I find it curious," Staella continued, "that Soliel's mother took his place. Curious and intriguing."

"You don't think . . ." Etolié braced herself to speak the forbidden name, but she had to know. "You don't think Chaos is Ilune, do you? Daughter of Neoma?"

Staella's breath caught. But she continued walking, kept her pace through the mists. "I suppose I wouldn't put it past her, but she was born a long time ago. If the God of Order returned upon Soliel's birth, I doubt a Goddess of Chaos would be so subtle as to remain hidden for a few thousand years after her own. But it does spark a thought—that if Soliel bore the likeness of Kareena, that Chaos, whoever she is, will pose a likeness to Neoma—in body, in spirit, or both."

Staella kept freely saying the once-forbidden name— *Neoma*—and Etolié's gut twisted with each repetition. When Etolié was a child, it had been a name she'd muttered only in sorrow or when soothed by the noxious drugs Camdral brought.

And more than once, in that same dream-like state, she had called Etolié by her first daughter's name, too far out of her mind to know.

"It could be one of your descendants," Etolié said. "I wouldn't put it past a single one of those Solviraes to reach godhood."

"Nor would I. Let me think on this. It's an interesting conundrum."

"You can't tell Sol Kareena, though," Etolié implored, and Momma quickly nodded, to her credit. "I don't want her to think about her baby that way."

"The child she birthed is innocent." Staella took a step through what appeared to be a particularly thick patch of cloud, and there came her hidden desert clearing. "Whatever the God of Order's crimes, Soliel's future is not set in stone. Fate is a word we use to discuss the past, biased by our own sentiments. Anyone can change."

She released Etolié's fingers.

At the cusp of the mist, Etolié lingered, the words weighted even if her momma hadn't meant them to be.

Anyone can change.

She gulped back the rising something in her throat. As Staella walked across the desert soil, toward her cottage bathed in night, Etolié's longing only grew—though for what, it was difficult to say. She quickly followed, though, lest Staella know her aching heart and rebuke it.

Anyone can change. Yet Etolié, for all her growth and all her accomplishments in her short, immortal life, would have given all that away just to know her momma loved her still.

Chapter 16

Back in momma's home, Etolié sat at Khastra's side, unnerved at the increasing coolness of her skin. She held her callused hand, stroking lines along her palm, knowing in her mind Khastra was fine, but she held the chill of death, and Etolié feared what that would mean.

She stayed by Khastra for some time, feeling too awkward to step out and face her momma again. If good intentions had a time limit, she had surely hit it. It would be less uncomfortable for everyone if she stayed in here.

Even if, deep down, the idea of leaving made her want to weep.

A light knock sounded. When no one entered, Etolié shyly said, "Come in."

Staella peeked inside. "Is everything all right in here?"

Unwilling to voice her ineffable fears, Etolié forced a smile and nodded.

"Can I make you anything? Some tea, perhaps?"

"I don't want to impose—"

"You're not." Staella's resolute words immediately withered, followed by her stance. "Y-You're not imposing."

Tea sounded grounding, but Etolié couldn't summon the confidence to admit that. She shook her head instead.

What light remained in Staella's eyes faded. She disappeared, shutting the door behind her, the ensuing silence as loud as Etolié's memories.

So little had changed. Etolié still expected Camdral to walk through the door, alcohol and a sweet, smoky smell on his breath. Her stomach clenched, but that was silly—he was gone, his body burned over thirty years ago. Her momma was well, and Khastra was here which meant in the case of some kind of time warp, she'd turn him into a meat pulp if Etolié asked nicely.

Staella suddenly reentered, startling Etolié from her thoughts. "I'd like to show you something. Will you come with me?"

Etolié nodded and followed, her mind spinning as she left her favorite demon behind. All was familiar. All was as it had been. As they entered the front room, the nest of blankets still lay in the center, and Etolié recalled hiding in them as a little girl, popping out to surprise Momma—who always laughed and pretended to be scared.

Not Camdral. But at least he'd only ignored her.

The night sky glittered with millions of stars, the very same visible from the mortal realm. No night creatures sang, for they were alone, but the crimson stone was cool and smooth as Etolié stepped off Staella's doorstep. Neither spoke, giving Etolié far too much time to wonder what the fuck her momma was thinking as she led her out into the beautiful outdoors. A natural path had been pressed by countless steps around the cottage home, leading to a gentle source of ambient light.

It stole Etolié's breath, the beauty she witnessed.

A garden of sorts, with thorned vines climbing a gigantic trellis—some twenty feet high, at least—but instead of flower buds, she saw tiny, glowing lights, radiating the faintest hue of pink. There had to be hundreds, each of them in different sizes, from her pinky nail to larger than she could hold in her arms. Drawn to their beauty, Etolié held her hand above one, finding it warm. "These are stars," she whispered.

"Yes," Staella said, and she sounded so unbearably earnest, yet nervous, and Etolié didn't understand it at all. "Some can take a hundred years to grow to full size—the eldest here aren't even thirty."

Staella beamed at the ones high above. Her translucent wings lifted her, allowing her to touch it with the joy of a mother to an infant. Etolié stayed on the ground, her wings tucked to her back, watching her momma fawn over the celestial rocks. "They're lovely," Etolié said, frustration welling in her stomach, though to name it made her sick.

"It will be a while longer before any are ready to become constellations," Staella continued, gently descending to the ground. When she landed, she resumed her demure stance. "But I have been thinking on it. In all sincerity, I was thinking of commemorating you. I have loved hearing the good you've done in the mortal realm. I'm told they sing praises to the Savior of Slaves. You have saved so many lives, my Starshine. I think it'd make a beautiful story to place in the sky. I've even drawn a few ideas, to prepare. I'd love to show you."

Etolié studied her mother's warm countenance, searched for the lie, for some jest, any spark of insincerity she could cling to—nothing.

Staella was here. And Staella seemed to be doing pretty damn well for herself. She fought to keep her fury down, but Momma said, "Are you all right?"

"What the *fuck* is this?!" With the explosion came the threat of tears, but Etolié battered them down, purposefully ignoring the shock on Staella face. "This constellation bullshit—what the hell are you saying?!"

Staella visibly withered; matchless guilt rose to drown Etolié. "If you don't want it—"

"M-My room was clean. And it wasn't just clean—it was dusted and maintained. I don't understand."

All the glimmering hope in Staella's countenance had gone. "I-I wanted it ready, in case you ever came home."

"But you didn't want me!" Curse her tears; Etolié wiped them on her illusionary sleeve, unable to face her. It hurt Momma, to see her cry. "You told Eionei I couldn't come back, that you couldn't get better if I was around! I was just a fucking reminder of all the shit you'd gone through!"

Etolié sobbed, and it ached, soul-wracking cries tearing from her body. Oh, it hurt, it *hurt,* to face her. To speak her guilt made her feel no lighter.

"Momma, I'm sorry," she managed between cries. "I shouldn't have said that; you weren't supposed to know I knew. I'll leave. I don't want to—I-I don't . . ."

The light before her grew brighter. When Etolié looked past her hands, she saw her momma's tear-streaked face, yet subtle fury steeled her jaw. "I love you," Staella said softly. "You're half my heart, Etolié. And I've thought of you every day you were gone. I've cherished every story they told me of you—you were always destined for brilliance, and hearing that you had saved lives, that you're beloved among mortals, has kept me moving. Because I was told . . ." Staella swallowed what Etolié assumed was a sob, but then anger rose in her countenance. "I was told to stay away from you. I was told you wanted nothing to do with me. I was told you would come to me when you were ready—"

Staella's voice caught. Cold dread washed over Etolié.

"Of course, I believed it," Staella continued, and Etolié clung to every word, shock stilling her tongue. "I failed you as a mother countless times. I've carried that for so long. It was never on you to accept an apology, but I've selfishly dreamed of giving it because sometimes . . ." Her eyes squeezed shut, and Etolié was surprised at the impulse to hug her. "Sometimes, the dream of your forgiveness is what keeps me going, when my mind is dark."

Etolié's mind reeled at the words, still struggling to comprehend them. "What?"

"Eionei has watched over you because he loves you dearly, Etolié. But I think you and I have both been robbed by his self-righteous conviction that he knows what's best for the people around him."

The idea couldn't be true, because Eionei was her grandfather, her friend, and realistically the closest thing she had to an actual father and with whom she held a thousand treasured memories because he'd supported her through every adventure, every endeavor, helped when she called, loved and supported and harped on very specific aspects of her life that he didn't agree with, passive aggressive and straight up aggressive when it came to her proclaimed non-attraction to anyone, or a certain half-demon, or the few times she'd expressed interest in her mother's well-being—

"That. Bitch." Etolié met her momma's gaze, and twenty years of political bullshit had given her the keen ability to know when people were sincere or if they were full of it.

Momma was heartbroken. But behind her sorrow was hope. Etolié fell into her arms.

She was warmer than starlight, heat radiating from her core, and Etolié clung to her with all the desperation of those thirty-four years. Momma was so small, reaching Etolié's chin, yet Etolié felt smaller, especially when her momma's wings hid them behind translucent light. "I love you, Etolié," she whispered, and Etolié continued sobbing. "I want so desperately to know you."

When Staella pulled away, Etolié missed her, craving her affection far more than she disliked touch. But Staella just as soon put her hands on Etolié's face, touching her as she memorized what she saw. "You're so beautiful. I see myself in you, and . . ." Her smile faltered, and Etolié swallowed her own discomfort.

"You can say it," Etolié said, because she knew whose face she held, hated the glimpses of him she saw in the mirror.

"Not Camdral," Staella said, peace settling where there had once been pain. Momma read her well, it seemed. "I was going to say Ilune. Not so much in looks, but I'd thought it once or twice when you were a child; I'd never seen a more mischievous smile, until I saw you."

Somehow, Etolié was happier to remind momma of her evil necromancer half-sister than her asshole progenitor. "You look exactly the same," she said, and Staella laughed, even when Etolié realized it was a lie. "Except, you're lighter, somehow. You look less sick."

"With you back in my life, I can fully heal."

Etolié grabbed her again, clinging to her as though she might disappear once more. Oh, how surreal it felt, to be back here but feel joy.

"I think it will take time," Staella said into Etolié's chest. "You and I have some barriers to cross, but I'm willing to try, if you are."

"I'd like that, Momma."

Staella parted enough to take her hands and led her though the ethereal garden, filled with the legacy she'd once been known for. Etolié hadn't realized she'd returned to gardening, but Etolié knew very little about her mother.

Her bitter heart yearned to know it all.

"Why did you apologize?"

Gripping her momma's hand, Etolié found she couldn't speak. She merely stared, her confusion unspoken.

"When you cried," Staella said. "You said you were sorry. If I'm going to poison Eionei's tea, I need to know what he told you."

The statement might've been funny, given it was said by her tiny momma, but Etolié was the one who spoke fluent hyperbole—not her. As it was, Staella looked quite serious, fury etched into her gentle countenance.

"I'm only here because your life was destroyed," Etolié said, speaking words she'd harbored all those years. Oh, they hurt; they lacerated her heart on their way out. "What am I, if not the culmination of all the bullshit you went through?"

Staella shook her head. "You were my second chance."

Etolié blinked away fresh tears. "What do you mean?"

"After Neoma's death, my world was so dark, Etolié. I'd lost my wife, I'd lost my daughter, and so many times, I wished I was dead, but ..." Hope shone in her eyes, despite her sorrow. "But the day I discovered I was carrying you, something changed. Yes, the circumstances were awful. Yes, I was still controlled by that horrible man, but none of that mattered—there was a little child who needed me, and so I had to live. I wish every day that I had left him for good, but I managed to leave him long enough to not hurt you while you grew inside me. If I did nothing else right, I am proud of myself for that."

"You did a lot of things right," Etolié said, but Staella shook her head.

"You're kind to think well of me, but ..." Staella blinked a moment too long, her tears finally falling as shame filled her countenance. "I don't know your life or what sort of healing you've done or haven't done, but for me, accepting my failings was a necessary and awful piece of it. I failed you. Your childhood was stolen far too young because I kept you in a horrible place. I was supposed to protect you, but just because he didn't touch you doesn't mean he didn't hurt you. You witnessed terrible things. I weep to think about the times you tried to protect me because those were the moments when I saw myself with clarity—that I was slowly tearing you apart."

Etolié rapidly shook her head, panic rising with her momma's tears. "No, that's not—"

"I could have given you to Sol Kareena," Staella said, adamant and pleading. "I could have given you to Eionei. I kept you because I needed you. I loved you so much, but I clung too tight and shattered you. I know this now. I could have told someone the truth about what Camdral did to me, but my mind was so warped that I couldn't bear to part with him, even though I hated him. I've worked to fix myself and become a person again, but my penance was to lose you. And perhaps that's what I deserved, but you were just a little girl. You needed a mother. The cruel irony is that what you did saved my life—but at the cost of your own."

Every fiber of Etolié's being screamed to reject those words. She released her momma and turned away, instinctively rubbing her hands together, desperately trying to wipe off the blood—

"Breathe ... Just breathe ..."

She caught herself and brought her fists up to her eyes. She had cried enough, but now instead of relief and joy, the pain tore her apart anew.

Amidst her rise of cognitive dissonance, a quiet voice said, "It was not your fault."

Unwilling tears spilled from Etolié's eyes, the layers of protection around her heart stripping away, leaving her vulnerable.

"You did what I didn't have the strength to do, and that wasn't right."

She couldn't even feel her limbs—she was a raw and bleeding heart, and nothing more.

Even softer, the voice said, "I'm sorry."

Etolié dared to stare into her life's mirror and look back upon years and years of triumph and pain. She was forty-eight years old. Her body looked no older than twenty. But in her heart, she was fourteen and covered in blood, screaming and sobbing for all eternity.

"I never questioned why you would not ever want to see me again," Staella said, her fresh tears adding a glittery sheen to her already shining countenance, "but it selfishly breaks my heart to know you thought I didn't want you. I have missed you every day."

For the first time in Etolié's young life, she let herself wonder if perhaps she hadn't failed her momma after all. Forgotten memories bombarded her—the countless times she had been hungry, but her momma had been missing, or the lonely moments she'd cried herself to sleep. The fear she'd felt whenever Camdral came still awoke her in tears, and the relief whenever Eionei had stolen her away didn't match her hurt when she'd hear him yell at her momma behind closed doors—always about her. For how much better Etolié deserved.

"You are not expected to accept my apology," her momma's soft voice said. "I've broken free from my addictions, but the consequences linger. I hurt you in irreparable ways. Once Khastra awakens, you can leave and never return, if you want. I would understand."

Something cold and foreign pulsed through Etolié's limbs. Her heart raced. Her blood spiked. For the first time, she felt resentment toward the woman she had made every excuse for, all her life.

When Etolié turned around, something must have shown in her face; Momma looked so small, staring at her from below a cliff face. They had both done better apart, and perhaps it was too soon. Perhaps it was a mistake to even try. What else would it lead to but heartbreak?

Anger escaped her in her tears. For a brief and fleeting moment, Etolié let herself hate her momma.

. . . but that felt wrong as well.

The coldness faded away. Time ticked by, and her momma waited, her watery eyes begging for castigation.

But Etolié had none to give. Instead she pulled Staella into an embrace and wept in her arms. "I love you, Momma," she whispered, and despite what pain and anguish still lingered in her heart, that simple truth brought boundless hope.

Chapter 17

The city beyond the carriage window bustled, forging onward like the creaking wheels beneath her. Watching people without the expectation of interacting was an enjoyable pastime, to speculate about the lives passing before her and wonder of their stories.

"How did last night's investigation go?" Lara asked, and Flowridia turned her gaze from the window. Along with her intended was Reginal and Irons, the latter of whom stole a breath to speak.

"More evidence of vampires, but we have not found more since the man in the tomb," Irons replied, the bags beneath his eyes revealing his exhaustion. "We interviewed a man who survived being bitten by who we speculate is the source of our troubles, given he wasn't torn apart. He described a small woman who apparently toyed with him, asking if he were afraid of death."

"The perpetrator likely has a god complex of sorts," Flowridia said idly, her face entirely impassive—though she gave a light squeeze to her love's hand.

"Sounds like an absolute diva," Lara replied, feigning proper concern. "Certainly someone to worry about. She wants attention."

"That is what we were thinking," Irons replied, but then the carriage slowed and stopped.

Crowds of people were gathered beyond the window, bustling around tents and hastily assembled houses of wood. When the driver opened her door, Flowridia graciously accepted his assistance down the stairs, her rich clothing attracting attention. Ayla had insisted she dress the part.

Lara gazed upon the refugee camp and smiled at an approaching noble. "Lord Xylan, wonderful to meet you."

"The honor is ours, Empress Alauriel," the man said, offering a deep bow. "My people are exhausted, but we are here. Your accommodations are more than generous."

"There is more to come," Lara said, her words gracious and kind. "Proper homes are still under construction, but these will protect you from the elements in the meantime. Did you receive the shipment of food?"

"Yes, your majesty. And thank you for it."

"Any gratitude must go to my intended, Lady Flowridia of Staelash, the future empress consort. She had the foresight to anticipate refugees at our borders and has graciously used her power to provide sustenance for any who come to Neolan."

Lord Xylan bowed to Flowridia, the gesture foreign and strange. "On behalf of the Theocracy of Sol Kareena, our gratitude knows no bounds, my lady. Thank you."

Flowridia's blush burned her cheeks. "It's an honor to help."

"Might I speak?" Lara said. When Lord Xylan agreed, she entreated him to call the masses over.

Flowridia waited in fervent anticipation as the large crowd gathered—dirty, tired faces of children and their parents, who had left everything behind in search of safety. Curiosity colored their features as they studied the Solviran royalty, and Flowridia recalled that these people were hers.

Lara stood atop the carriage, her makeshift platform perfectly suited for her small statue. "Citizens of the Theocracy of Sol Kareena," she said, her voice amplified by Reginal's spell, "I am Empress Alauriel Solviraes of the Solviran Crown, and I welcome you to our grand country. Accommodations are still being built, but we promise to keep you safe and sheltered in the meantime."

Cheers erupted from the crowd, but Lara held up her hands to hush them. "I thank you for your gratitude, but it is not for me. Before I turn the time over to your true savior, I must make one stipulation to our aid—you must pledge loyalty to Solvira and to its royal family. Maintain your loyalties to Sol Kareena and her country. Our mother goddesses were sisters in blood, and so are we. You shall be ours, should you accept us. I simply ask for your allegiance, so we might unite if the threat crosses into our borders as well."

The words went over well, as suggested by the ensuing applause. Ayla had a way of spinning words to make even the strictest of demands a honey-coated pleasure. "But I am not the hero here, as I said. My intended, Lady Flowridia of Staelash, soon to be Empress Consort, anticipated your coming and helmed efforts to provide for you. It is because of her we have the supplies to accommodate you and any others who come. Her brilliant mind and unique magical abilities are why we can be here today."

When Lara beckoned for Flowridia to join her atop the carriage, the crowd gave encouraging applause. With help from the footman, Flowridia joined her beloved on the roof, anxiety crushing her chest. The noise died. They waited for her, for her words. She opened her mouth, but nothing came, her windpipe crushed from fear.

"Speak, my love," Lara whispered in her ear, the words reassuring and kind. She squeezed Flowridia's hand. "They want to hear it."

Flowridia swallowed, holding Lara's cold hand for support. "I—" Her lungs seized but she forced a steadying breath. "I am the future Empress Consort, Flowridia of Staelash," she said, trepidation in every word, "and . . ."

Again, her anxiety threatened to overwhelm her, but Lara whispered once again: "Speak from the heart. Your sincerity is your finest trait."

"A-And I'm so grateful you're here," she said, every eye upon her. "I'm grateful you lived. I'm grateful you've come, trusting Solvira to protect you. That takes courage, to trust." Each breath shook her body, her stuttering lip never stilling, but she forged onward. "I look upon you, and I see brave faces, willing to risk death to protect what you believe in. Your devotion to Goddess Sol Kareena is truly inspirational. Solvira shall honor that. You will find friendship and loyalty here."

At her pause, the crowd applauded. Lara came forward to relieve her of her podium, but Flowridia held her back. "If any of you are injured or sick, please notify me before I leave. Let me help you. Thank you."

Flowridia was assisted off the carriage roof as Lara gave her concluding speech, but she heard none of it. Reginal sat her down on the little bench meant for coachmen and smiled. "You were wonderful," he said, and Flowridia knew he truly meant it.

People came, bidding her to heal broken limbs and gashes, injuries from the road. A few were sick, and Flowridia did not have magic to heal them but knew the herbs to help and instructed a servant to keep a list. She would send supplies. Children crowded her, admiring the flowers in her hair, and she thought of the orphans, wondered how many among the refugees had lost their parents too, and stayed to hold their hands and hug their tiny bodies.

These were her people, and for the first time, she felt that connection like her own blood.

In the evening, Flowridia sat with Lunestra in her room, the fireplace adding warmth to their conversation. "I'm not surprised at all," Lunestra said, seated comfortably in her rocking chair. Flowridia swore she grew older by the day, the idea troubling. "You're a natural charmer; you simply needed practice. Offering your services is the fastest way to win their hearts, and you certainly succeeded."

Flowridia sat on the bed, blushing at the words. "Growing up, my soft heart was often berated. I'm still learning how to let it lead, so thank you. I needed to hear that."

"That's a cruel thing to tell a child," Lunestra replied, lips thin. "But that's often how it is, to be an orphan."

"I don't know yet if I'll reveal myself as the heir, but I'll admit, I felt the weight today. The weight of knowing they're my responsibility."

"It's your birthright, to lead them," Lunestra said. "Were Sol Kareena keen to speak, I am certain she would thank you. She is a strict goddess, but just and good to those who serve her."

Flowridia's smile faltered at that, to wonder what the goddess thought of her. "Given the nature of my magic, I don't know that she would ever fully approve of me, but I shall do my best."

"Have you considered pledging to her?"

Flowridia recalled long ago when Sora had pushed the topic on her 'for her protection.' She also remembered staring into Sol Kareena's visage as she'd held her dead lover and those words of warning: *"Be careful, lest you become no better than the monsters you seek to tame."*

"Yes," she said, though it was barely a drop of the truth. "I will admit that my relationship with her is complicated. You may recall . . ." She swallowed the words, hating the shame filling her to speak of Ayla in front of Lunestra. ". . . at the cathedral, when she came and killed The Endless Night. I'm still clinging to my bitterness."

Lunestra released a tense breath, and Flowridia stiffened at the change of mood. "I see. I suppose I cannot say anything to fix that. But consider the power she could grant you. Your father was renowned for healing and for protecting his people in her name."

Flowridia looked at her hands, knowing they had saved lives yet were stained in blood.

"It would only help in leading your people," Lunestra continued. "Consider, too, the patron of your powers. Yes, you wield powers of death, but only because he granted them."

Not quite, but Lunestra was not entirely wrong. Casvir had not predicted what her powers might be, only that they would be mighty.

"Sol Kareena would surely accept you, if you severed your ties to him. She would grant you a familiar and make you a priestess in her name."

Flowridia clenched her fists. "No," she said, sharper than she'd meant to, but panic pulsed through her veins. Lunestra blinked, taken aback, but Flowridia quickly added, "Whatever Casvir's atrocities, he gave me my familiar. To leave him would mean to lose Demitri, and forgive me for saying it, but he's as dear to me as my intended. It's a different love, but he . . ."

Flowridia swallowed her sudden rise in emotion, refusing to choke and cry despite the memory of a screaming baby boy in her mother's home, bleeding from the knife wound in his stomach—

She drove her nails into her palm, not caring if they bled. "He's little more than a child. He's as dear to me as one. Just because he's grown doesn't mean he isn't my sweet boy. I still remember when Casvir gave him to me. I didn't know who Casvir was; he was just a demon in the woods. But I was handed a bundled little wolf pup, and my whole heart became his. I'd be lost without him."

Lunestra held up a hand to stop her rambling. "I apologize," she said, her words slow and careful. "I forget that familiars granted to witches speak and form a stronger bond."

"He's half my soul," she said, the words oft repeated in literature—that to have a familiar means to find your soul's literal counterpart.

"Bear in mind then," Lunestra said, her words just as mindful, "that Casvir forever holds that over your head. He could take away your power and your Demitri in an instant, should he choose it."

"He isn't the type to do that," she said, praying the words were true.

"I sincerely hope you are correct." With care, Lunestra took Flowridia's hand, her countenance shifting into something mild. "There is news. While you were gone, High Priestess Jules informed me that a letter arrived from Executor Sunblessed of the Sun Elves. She has respectfully declined to accept any refugees, including myself. I will be sent to Staelash once we have explicit permission from their council."

The news felt like a plunge into cold water.

"I know it's for the best," Flowridia said, staring at the decorated carpet, "but for what it's worth, I'll miss you."

"It's a blessing in disguise," the archbishop said, seated on her bed. "In Staelash, you can visit."

Tears filled Flowridia's eyes. "You won't be at my wedding."

"You and I both know that would have been impossible." Lunestra patted the space beside her. "For my grandniece to have captured the heart of a Solviran Empress— I cannot imagine a higher calling upon this earth. I know your father would have been so proud. I certainly am."

The compliment came with the horrible pang of deceit—for Flowridia had captured an empress' heart, yes, but that was not who she married. Lara lay beneath the ground, and Flowridia wed a monster. But she smiled nevertheless, though it wounded her to see the full fruits of her lies.

"In light of all this, I hope you would not mind if I gave you your wedding gift early."

"Not at all," Flowridia replied, shoving away all her bitter feelings.

Lunestra turned away and opened the drawer of the bedside table. She withdrew a crown, one Flowridia had seen before—delicate gold, and often plaited into the archbishop's hair. Lunestra offered it forward, and for the first time Flowridia saw the remarkable detail. Golden prongs created a grand display, meant to sit above her hair, with metal work at the base. Six tiny gemstones were wrapped among the lush design, each in their own unique rainbow hue. "You'll want assistance putting it in your hair," Lunestra continued, "but that is my wedding gift to you."

Flowridia clutched it to her heart, too touched to even speak.

"It was a gift from my mother to me," Lunestra said, a reverent hush to her voice. "She wore it on her wedding day, as it was a gift from hers. I never married, instead devoting myself to my calling as High Priestess. Xoran only had one son, and I would have given it to his wife, had he married. I think it is fitting for you to have it."

"This is priceless," Flowridia whispered. "Thank you so much."

"You're welcome." Her aged hand came to grip Flowridia's shoulder, squeezing affectionately. "Once the wedding has concluded and all the foreign guests have gone, you will hear from me again. I wish to know all about your beautiful day, Flowridia."

Once the wedding had concluded, Flowridia would be a monster.

The words released a flood; she burst into tears, weeping into her hands. Thankfully, Lunestra misunderstood, mistook them for bittersweet joy and simply held her. "I'm so grateful to have met you," the archbishop said, and those were words Flowridia would have never thought she'd hear from the former high priestess.

As Flowridia sought a reply, there came knocking on the door. "Enter," Lunestra said, and a servant peeked inside.

"Lady Flowridia, General Irons has asked for you. He says there is important news."

Flowridia wiped her eyes and tried to leave, but Lunestra held her as tightly as her frail form could. "Whatever happens, you and I are family. I love you, and I'm so proud."

Flowridia remained in the embrace, clinging to this final bastion of holiness in her life.

Flowridia was led to the council chamber, where Irons sat before a large stack of documents. He bid the servant to leave, then said, "I need you to sit down."

No anger in his words, yet Flowridia feared, nevertheless. She obeyed, wary as she sat. "What's going on?"

"Reports came in today of an attack on the road outside of Neolan. This is unfortunately common, often because of bandits, or even slavers if it's in the south, but the victims have been identified, and the details are . . ." He sighed, somber as he stared at the wall. ". . . harrowing."

Flowridia looked to the documents, but he slid them away. "The woman from the cathedral is dead," Irons said, and immediately Flowridia buckled over as though struck. "Erial Redwin. Her carriage was attacked, and the guard and coachman were slain as well."

Shock pulsed cold through her blood. "W-What?" she managed to ask, every part of her chilled.

"It is thought that she was killed quickly," he said, his words cautious, "but the baby was torn from her womb and branded with holy symbols. It was found decapitated and burned, but the markings were clearly visible."

A noise left her throat—more than a sob, nearly a scream—and she covered her mouth, tears spilling from her eyes. *"No, no, no . . ."* she muttered, idly aware of Irons' presence beside her, crying even as his hand pressed gently against her back. She shook, her breaths shallow and quick.

Whatever words he said, she didn't hear—instead, her mind replayed the gruesome tale with vibrant pictures, a mother murdered, her baby tortured and burned. It had been old enough to live without a womb. It might have survived a birth. But no—no matter how difficult its life might've been, it never had a chance at all.

The touch left her back; she faintly heard the door open and Irons call for a servant or guard—*someone*—but Flowridia continued weeping. She had tried to do good, but to what end? Would Erial have died, were she not on the road?

Flowridia sobbed, even when her love's familiar presence settled beside her. "Thank you for calling me, General. You may leave."

When the door shut, it was Ayla beside her, crawling upon the arm of the seat and holding her tight. "Darling, darling . . ."

Flowridia clung to her, her sobs muffled by her dress.

"Irons told me the woman was killed."

Flowridia managed to nod against her dress.

"Flowra, I am so sorry. I know you wanted to help—"

"It's *not about that!*" Flowridia screamed, and Ayla clutched her tight, even as anger surged in tandem with her anguish. "They killed her because they wanted the baby. It's dead! They *murdered* it!"

Ayla's grip became stronger than a cage. "Fear will make monsters out of good people."

"Sol Kareena is a Goddess of Justice—so how could they *possibly think—!*" A tormented sob left her throat, the crushing weight of failure threatened to suffocate her. "How could they?" she whispered, her entire body slumping as gentler sobs shook her.

Ayla held her, stroked her hair, even hummed a haunting tune—perhaps for comfort, yes, but it merely evoked more sorrow. The baby had known no love, no comfort—it had been ripped unwillingly into the world, only to meet a horrific end. Erial had died for no crime except to survive a monster's attack.

"Sol Kareena would not condone it, no, yet she turns away from atrocities beneath her very nose," Ayla said, when Flowridia's cries had finally stilled. "Some call it 'free will,' yet I do not know. This baby is only one among many who have suffered for her lack of action."

"Ayla, we have to do something. This cannot disappear. There has to be justice."

"The crime is done," Ayla replied. "Erial and her child are dead. The news is public, but if we make a grand announcement, what will it do? At best a stir of sympathy but if the masses hear that it was a dhampir child, I fear your heart will only shatter to know . . ." Ayla's words faded; so rare, for her love to hesitate. ". . . most people would agree it was best for it to die."

"Do you agree?" Flowridia asked, and Ayla gently hushed her, her tender strokes against her hair soothing.

"Asking for my empathy in times of tragedy will never end well, my love. But I care that this is wounding *you,* and if there is anything I can do, please tell me."

Flowridia's breathing remained shaky, pained gasps leaving her lungs as tears streamed down her cheeks. "Find out who did this. I wish to meet them."

"I can certainly try. The shadows are drawn to violence in the mortal realm."

When Ayla tried to pull away, Flowridia clung to her, shaking her head. "Stay please. For a minute." Fresh sobs shook her figure, and Ayla acquiesced, holding her tenderly as she cried.

"My dearest Flowra and her gentle heart . . ." Ayla's lips pressed against her brow, lingering to whisper, "It is a powerful thing, to *feel.* I do not understand, but I admire it."

Flowridia shook in her arms, cursing the weight of the cold, dark world. "I wish I didn't care."

"Do not say that."

"I wish I were strong, Ayla." She finally pulled away, revealing her swollen face. "I wish I didn't fall to pieces over death. I don't feel powerful. Casvir said kindness was not a weakness, but I still struggle to understand how. I wish I could be cold and powerful like you, like him, but instead I cry and I feel and I *hurt*—" A sob overtook her words, self-loathing caging her heart.

Softness settled onto Ayla's oft severe features, her touch against Flowridia's cheek as gentle as summer rain. "I would not love you if you were anyone but you," Ayla whispered, the vulnerable words a treasure. "Loving you has forced me to wonder when my own heart became stone, and I am amazed, my darling, that your own remains so open despite the pain and abuse of your past. I admire you. I will never be like you, and that makes you all the more precious to have in my life."

Ayla's hands stole hers, tenderly stroking the skin. "You see the good in the hardest of hearts, and that is a rare and beautiful thing, to love unlovable people. Not always wise, perhaps, but I know I have grown because of your radiant light. I shall never be good, but perhaps I shall be better. You make me want to be better, for you."

Flowridia brought Ayla's hand to her lips and kissed her palm. *"Thank you,"* she mouthed, for it was all she could manage.

"You gave the woman hope in her final days," Ayla continued. "What happened is a tragedy and a crime, and there is nothing salvageable in that. But you did what was right when the world would have judged you. Let me find Demitri; he shall keep you company while I search for your perpetrator."

Flowridia let her go when she pulled away. She stayed in her chair, still feeling like a thousand little pieces, each its own effort to lift.

When Demitri came, he nuzzled her with his cold nose. *Lady Ayla told me what happened.*

Flowridia rested her head against his, her tears still wet upon her swollen face.

Let's go for a walk. You always perk up in the sun.

With his help, she managed to rise, and he helped her find her way.

When Ayla did not return, Flowridia cuddled with Demitri, unaccustomed to sleeping alone. All her life—during her days in the orphanage, in the cottage with Mother, even in Staelash with Demitri's sweet baby breaths—Flowridia had been lulled to sleep by either soft breathing or a presence somewhere near.

Tumultuous thoughts swam in her head, preventing sleep—Lunestra's words, vile, if accidentally so. Would Casvir truly hurt Demitri if they ever were at odds? Would he spite her so viciously? Her heart said no, but her heart was often foolish. She recalled the letter he wrote, the one Ayla had nearly destroyed, and knew he would never say kind words idly—he said nothing idly.

That same foolish heart ached to remember Erial and her unborn child. Her head hurt from crying, her whole body exhausted, yet she did not sleep.

An ineffable presence filled the room late in the night. Flowridia swore her love made every place colder, and when Ayla carefully laid behind her, she grabbed her hand and squeezed.

"You should be asleep," Ayla whispered.

"Were you successful?"

"Yes."

Flowridia sat up, mindful of Demitri, though he could sleep through a hurricane. "Where are they?"

"I did not know what you wanted done with them, so currently they are chained up in your secret chamber. I cannot say it will be easy to implicate them in the crime when there were no witnesses except the demons of Sha'Demoni, but as the empress, I would happily toss them into the dungeons anyway."

Flowridia stood up, aware of Ayla's glowing eyes upon her. "Take me there," she said, teeth grit at the words. "I want to look them in the eye and ask why."

"You will be exposing yourself," Ayla replied, still lounging on Demitri's side. "If they don't know you now, they will recognize you when you oversee their trial."

"I never said they were going to trial."

Ayla raised an eyebrow, visibly intrigued. "Fair enough."

Flowridia left to grab a shawl, and upon her return, Ayla leaned sensuously against the bedpost, an easy smile spreading across her lips at her return. "You are as pretty as a picture, even in nightclothes."

As kind as the words were, Flowridia's mind was too loud to be flattered. She offered a hand, which Ayla quickly accepted. "Let's go."

Ayla led her through the shadows, the familiar dark almost soothing. Despite the inherent dangers of Sha'Demoni, Flowridia saw subtle beauty in the broken world, even if the distant eyes remained eerie.

She thought of the task at hand, unsure of what the next few minutes would bring. Still, the mere thought welled fresh anger within her; she was far too exhausted to cry.

Soon, they appeared in the dark chamber, the clinking of metal cutting through the black ambience. Flowridia waited as Ayla lit the torches on the wall. Among the corpses, three living men struggled against their chains, stopping when they noticed her stare.

One spoke her name. "L-Lady Flowridia?"

There was nothing special about them. They were human, or perhaps Celestial—difficult to tell when the blood was so diluted. Flowridia stepped forward, ignoring Ayla who danced around her, lighting torches for her benefit. "Yes, I am Lady Flowridia of Staelash, and you three . . ." Her breath caught, lip suddenly trembling. ". . . you killed someone in my charge. Erial Redwin's blood stains your hands. You murdered her baby. Do you deny this?"

One of the men spoke—the same who had said her name. "S-She was carrying a monster, my lady. We had no choice."

"No choice?" Flowridia's rage surged at that. "Given the choice to kill an innocent baby or not, you had *no choice?*" She laughed, too furious to even speak, and so she cackled, doubling over as it overtook her. "You made the decision," she said between heaving spurts of laughter, "to track down a woman travelling by carriage, out of the city, to kill her party, to slit her throat, and then *rip* her unborn child out of her womb. And *torture it!*" She wiped tears from her eyes, hysterical laughter wracking her entire body—only then did she see the thick fog of purple seeping from her skin. "And you had no choice at all? None?"

Past her misted vision, the three men watched with wide, wary eyes. Beside her, Ayla was a rapt audience, curiosity in her gleeful gaze. "Tell me," Flowridia continued, "are you worshippers of Sol Kareena? What would she say, as a mother, to hear you slaughtered an infant?"

Cowering, one of the men managed to say, "M-My lady, it was—"

"A dhampir?" Her laugher finally quelled, her smile remaining as she gazed upon their frightened visages. "Feel free to ask her yourself—perhaps I'll rip back your souls to tell me the answer."

Between her outstretched hand and the first of the men, a crackling stream of virulent purple energy connected them, pulsing his life into her. He screamed, and she groaned, the sensation a unique and potent pleasure. When he withered, she willed the stream to slow, reveling in his screams, his suffering. It would only be a fraction of what he had delivered upon his victims, and she would watch him die in agony.

All things had to end; when the stream of power bled dry, the man collapsed as a shriveled husk. Flowridia inhaled, the coursing energy burning hot through her blood. "Don't worry," she said to the remaining two men, both cowering in their chains. "You won't share his fate."

From the power she stole, she offered a sliver back, bidding the freshly dead man to rise. "Eat them," she commanded, and the ghoul dove upon the helpless men, ripping into one with its teeth and claws. Tearing flesh and screams filled her ears, and she watched every moment of it, refusing to hide from her begotten horror.

"You always surprise me," came the sensuous call in her ear. Before them, the ghoul tore into one man's stomach, making a mess of his entrails, but Ayla's whisper remained an enticing treat. "I still stand by everything I said about your kind, gentle self."

Flowridia stared upon the gory scene—the ghoul left the eviscerated man to scream and clutch his falling organs, instead gnawing on the face of the second.

"But let the whole world fear for the unfortunate soul who breaks that tender heart of yours."

Ayla's cold embrace wrapped around her, joining her in witnessing the brutal deaths—the ghoul chewed on the second man's throat, his body finally stilling in the throes of death. A far quicker demise than the first, who screamed. Flowridia met his eye; he pled before her: *"Lady Flowridia, please!"*

Idly, she shook her head, jaw grit when the ghoul returned to unraveling his insides.

Only when the final chorus of his screams faded did she bid the ghoul to still. It fell as a lifeless corpse, and Flowridia felt peace.

And vindication.

"These were likely good men in their daily lives," Flowridia whispered, staring upon their remains. "They surely had families, went to church, yet they were capable of an unspeakable evil. It boggles my mind."

"And you're the future empress consort," Ayla cooed. "Hero to the refugees, secret heir to the Theocracy's throne, beloved of all you meet . . ." Ayla chuckled, dark and alluring. "Yet you live a masquerade, engaged to a phantom after the true empress' death. You are a necromancer, condemning men to die a gruesome death. Monstrosity lives in us all. Whether or not we act upon it defines who we are."

Discomfort brewed in Flowridia's stomach, the words poignant and everything she had been avoiding. "I . . ." She steeled her jaw, fists clenching. "This can never happen again."

Ayla pouted. "No more 'death by undead evisceration?'"

"No, I mean these crimes cannot happen." Resolve straightened her stance. "We haven't done enough. I will keep trying to unravel the God of Death's mysteries. We will protect those who cannot protect themselves from the monsters of the world. Solvira's greatest threat is itself, if this is any indication."

"Well, and Nox'Kartha," Ayla added. "Perhaps Moratham, though that particular feud has been quieter in recent years."

Lunestra's haunting words replayed themselves inside her head, the reminder of the power Casvir wielded over her, but Flowridia refused to entertain this unfounded fear. He cared for her, she reminded herself. Perhaps at the wedding, they could reaffirm that. "Either way," Flowridia said, "we need to be doing more." Her fist clenched. "Whispers of vampires in the night are one thing, but if we want to speed change along, they need a true monster to fear."

Ayla straightened her stance, taken aback at the aggressive words. Excitement twisted her grin. "The Endless Night?"

"Not in name, but certainly in spirit."

"And what say you about me disposing of the Solviran prisoners?" Ayla pawed at her bodice, nearly cute. "Jules is a nuisance, opposing me at every turn, but what if they were simply dead in their cells?"

Flowridia shook her head, but when Ayla pouted, she said, "Bring the worst of them here. Why kidnap slavers from Moratham when our own citizens are capable of . . ." She gestured to the brutalized corpses, tempted to spit on their remains. "To slay the innocent in our quest would run contrary to our goals; we have to protect them, but bureaucracy gets in the way."

"It runs contrary to *your* goals, my love," Ayla cooed, her wink salacious and cruel. "I could not care less. But I will happily play by your rules."

For a brief and jarring moment, Flowridia contemplated where the path might lead. But was damning herself for the greater good actually damning? Intention mattered. "We need a plan. Let's talk."

Ayla grinned, eerie and wide. "Indeed. Let us talk."

Time passed differently in Celestière than on the mortal plane.

Khastra slept, but Etolié forgot to worry. There was peace despite her heartbreak, her talks with her momma exhausting but more treasured than gold. They spoke of Etolié's years in Staelash, of the friends she had made, the triumphs she'd earned. Staella knew quite a lot, her stories coming directly from Eionei, but there were a lifetime of questions between them, and Etolié's soul felt whole, to answer a few and hear some answered in return.

Only one secret remained with her—the truth about her and Khastra's relationship. It was precious and new, and Etolié was afraid to know what her momma thought, to think her Starshine loved a demon woman nearly as old as her.

After that first long night of conversation, she fell asleep on the couch by her momma's side and awoke in her lap with glowing fingers in her hair and Staella's own deep breathing to soothe her.

She lingered a little longer that morning.

Staella grew more in her garden than stars—*"They don't call me a witch for nothing, Starshine."* Etolié was reminded of Flowers and told her as much, which made her sweet momma laugh. *"I used to have a massive garden,"* Momma had mused, her reminiscence peaceful. *"I grew all my own ingredients for tea. I'm trying to do so again. I finally have a substantial collection of herbs, though not all of them do pleasant things."*

Etolié was oddly gratified to think her mother dubiously grew poison.

Nigh inseparable, the two of them, except when Staella slipped away to find food or when Etolié escaped to bathe.

They cooked and drank tea; they laughed and cried, a lifetime of memories passing between them. So many years had been lost, but Etolié found both a momma and a friend.

"I just don't understand why Eionei would lie to us."

Staella became quiet at that, contemplative for a few long moments. Setting aside her tea, she beckoned for Etolié to come closer, then withdrew a handkerchief from the air and dabbed at Etolié's watery eyes. "Eionei loves you sincerely, Etolié. When you were a baby, he was your hero. As much as I loved you, I didn't always understand you, but he had a way of connecting with you that truly, deeply warmed my heart. When you would sit in the corner and illusion your glitter, he would bring his own and toss it with you for hours, just to hear you laugh. He could help you through your meltdowns in ways I simply couldn't—both from lack of understanding, and because I was unwell.

"And I want to think," Staella continued, the handkerchief disappearing when she finally tossed it away, "that he did it for you. He loves you. Truly. But..." She collected her words with the same care as she did all things—meticulously gathering herbs, cooking, even simply listening to Etolié's many words. "I don't wish to stain your view of your grandfather."

"He's done a wonderful job of it himself," Etolié said, still unsettled over it all.

A melancholic smile came to Staella's face. "When Neoma was alive, he was a friend kept at arm's length, but a friend, nevertheless. Then she died, and he stepped in to care for me when I fell apart. I took no joy in breaking his heart when he confessed what I already knew, but even if I did have feelings for him, he has not ever, not in over nine thousand years of knowing him, shown that he would be a good partner. His treatment of Alystra is appalling—and his actions very nearly wrecked the friendship she and I have. She resented me for a long time because of how he doted on me after Neoma's death—and I don't begrudge her that. His intentions weren't innocent, even if his actions were. It wasn't until you were gone that we were finally able to speak of it and set it aside; it was a part of my healing. She thankfully became a support, once you were gone. I think she was one of the only friends I didn't push away—Eionei had an agenda, and Kareena..."

Mist rose to cover Staella's lavender eyes, a mirror to her daughter's. "...Well, I am a Goddess of Forgiveness, but I have been failing in that. Now she has a son, so perhaps she understands how deeply she wounded me, when she sent you away." The statement lingered, bitterness clenching Staella's jaw; Etolié's gut twisted. "The tragic truth is, I cut her out of my life after she sent you away. We only began speaking again because of Soliel, and I will not deny her the help she needs right now—I know what it's like, to be too sick to help your own child."

Etolié's mind reeled from the words, because Momma spoke so earnestly, so *angrily*, but everything within Etolié fought it. Auntie Kareena had saved her.

. . . right?

"I fear, Starshine," Staella said, idly taking Etolié's hand, "that this was all a part of Eionei's need to be my hero as well—to be yours and to be mine, because if I had you during my healing, I wouldn't have needed him. Suddenly Camdral was gone, and so he had a chance. It didn't work, but now I know how insidious his plan truly was. Misguided, yes. Villainously cruel. I may even hate him now, and that is not something I say lightly. I don't even hate Morathma anymore; I feel nothing for him." Though she remained calm, Etolié sensed something simmering beneath her speech. "But those are my thoughts. I will not tell you to hate him as well, because he has done so much for you—"

Her words cut off when Etolié hugged her. She wept into her momma's shoulder, her heart torn in so many ways.

But for as much distress as discussing Eionei brought, there was a worse pain. Only once did they speak of Etolié's father. Of his death.

While staring at her cleaned bedroom, unrecognizable from that final, bloodstained night, Etolié dared to whisper as Momma passed: "Were you really going to just throw him into the mist and be done with it?"

"Yes."

Etolié clutched the doorframe, unable to face her. "Do you think I'm awful, for what I did?"

Etolié had healed. Etolié had processed that despicable truth—that her drunk father had raped her, no matter what part she had played to encourage it. Staella had found her naked and covered in blood, standing over a corpse.

But did she know the truth?

"No, Starshine. I don't. Not in the slightest."

Etolié shut her eyes, and all she saw was a corpse on the floor, still warm. Her body had been far colder. "Even though I . . . Even though he and I—"

The words caught in her throat when small, glowing arms wrapped around her from behind. Staella held her in absolute silence.

Somehow, that was more powerful than any words she could have summoned.

Time passed slowly in Celestière, and so when Etolié and Staella fell asleep a second time, she knew far longer had passed in her mortal world.

She awoke to a silent house.

As she stepped softly through the hallway, she paused a moment to check on Khastra. In her momma's room, the half-demon remained still, and Etolié might've feared she'd truly died had she not rolled over. She had no breath—not anymore.

Her skin was ice. Etolié idly touched her sternum, still unaccustomed to her silent heart.

She soon moved on to a room she didn't know well, and when she peeked in, she saw Staella seated on a bench, surrounded by old crates. The room itself was scarce, save for a bed meant for guests and piles of fabric stacked along the walls. Staella studied something, but she perked up at Etolié's entrance. "Good morning."

"Good morning," Etolié said, curious as she came closer. "What are you doing?"

Staella beckoned her forward. Etolié sat beside her, realizing a small box waited on the opposite side. In her momma's hands was a moonstone, attached to a chain, sparkling in the minimal light. Etolié's headache panged like a warning at the proximity.

This necklace bore power.

"When we were married," Staella said, her soft voice a delight, "Neoma gave me this in lieu of a ring. She wanted to recreate as many mortal traditions for the ceremony as she could but knew I wouldn't be able to wear a ring in my garden." Her smile faltered slightly, the light in her countenance fading. "Your father hated it. He ruined so many treasures of my former life when he was drunk, and so I hid it, and a few others." She held the stone to Etolié's hair. "It would look lovely on you. Perhaps if you ever marry, you would accept it as a gift."

Etolié shook her head. "I couldn't take it from you."

"It would bring me joy to see it worn," Staella said, but she didn't push the matter further. Instead, she placed it gently in a small box, which she shut and positioned inside the larger one beside her. "Part of my healing was learning to look fondly upon the past. For so long, I could not even think of Neoma without sobbing. And what kind of an existence is that? I should be able to think about the woman I loved without tears."

"Can you now?" Etolié asked, discomfort welling in her stomach. As a child, they never spoke of this. Not unless Momma was well out of her mind.

"Most times. I still have moments of sadness. I always shall. But Neoma brought me thousands of years of joy. No matter how much I may hurt now, I would do nothing to erase that."

Once, Staella had not held that sentiment, content to forget her sorrows with all the vile gifts Camdral gave her. Etolié remembered. She feared she would never forget.

When Staella sifted through the box, Etolié said, "I'm happy you're doing all right."

"With you here, I can finally be whole," Staella replied, and the words soothed something inside her. Her momma withdrew a small portrait, easily held in her two hands, painted and ancient yet still vivid. A baby gazed up, glowing like the angel she was, her wings far larger than her body. Swirling silver and gold made up her figure, as well as a tuft of black hair. "I created this," Staella continued, and Etolié realized her momma's aura had faded even more, "days after Ilune was born. She was the greatest gift Neoma ever gave me."

Etolié accepted the portrait when offered, feeling surreal to gaze upon the countenance of her half-sister. She had seen artwork in Solvira, yes, the few pieces not destroyed. But this was so innocent, so intimate—her momma's view of a baby just born, created from Silver Fire. So different than the paintings of the God of Death in the Glass Palace. So different than the imprisoned goddess somewhere underground. "It's lovely," Etolié said simply, unwilling to unearth the heavy words in her soul.

Staella's gaze lingered on the painting, her jaw trembling. "Ilune broke my heart. But not a day goes by where I don't miss her. She'll always be my precious girl. I've come to peace with that."

Forgiveness was something Etolié struggled with as a rule—but if Momma could forgive Ilune, perhaps she could forgive Momma fully someday. The idea gave her hope.

"I didn't know if my body could carry a baby," Staella continued, reminiscence in her words. "I don't know if Eionei told you I had been pregnant when I was with Morathma but lost them. Twins—two perfect little children born far too soon."

Staella's gaze became distant as she stared upon the portrait in Etolié's hands. Etolié knew enough of her momma's time as a deity in Moratham, thousands of years ago—The Stars that Glitter Above the Desert Sands.

"I think about them sometimes," Staella continued. "I had them named. They were so dearly wanted. The pain of their loss has never fully subsided, yet if they had lived, I might have never left Morathma. As an immortal, I cannot look back and dwell upon 'what if.'" She rested her head on Etolié's shoulder, affectionate and light. "If Neoma had lived, I wouldn't have you."

Years of insecurity prevented Etolié from finding anything positive in that sentiment, but she forced a smile all the same.

"Neoma was at my side, day and night, for the latter months of my pregnancy with Ilune," Staella continued. "We had discussed having a child for years, so she knew what it meant to me. She had never been as enthused toward children as I was but knew how dearly I wanted one and admitted that the idea of raising one with me filled her with quiet joy. I presumed at first we would adopt a little child in need, but silly me for underestimating the Goddess of Fertility and Creation." Her smile softened; her glow increased. "It's incredible, what the Silver Fire can do."

"Create life," Etolié said, just in case this were a sex thing and she needed to derail it.

But Staella's smile broadened as she nodded. "Neoma thought it was dangerous knowledge, to create life from nothing, and so chose to keep it hidden. To tell one would mean to tell them all. I didn't agree, but it was her secret to keep; not mine." With care, she took the portrait of Ilune from Etolié's grasp and placed it back inside its box. "Perhaps I should display these again. How would you feel about that?"

"I don't see why that's my choice to make."

"Because . . ." Staella set her hands on her lap, visage thoughtful. The wing on Etolié's side came to wrap around her; Etolié was embraced by pure light. "Because you and I are new and fragile. We have this wonderful second chance, and I don't wish for you to feel overshadowed by the dead."

Etolié leaned into her momma's side, comforted beyond measure by her presence. "They're your family. Which means, in a way, they're mine too." Etolié looked at the box, to the portrait of the infant half-sister she had never known. "Even if it's just as a memory, I should know them."

In a gesture both foreign and unbearably sweet, Staella kissed Etolié's hair. "Ilune always begged for a sibling as a little girl; you and she would have been absolute menaces together." Her smile faded by degrees, but not her glow. "In that same fictional world where you grew up with Ilune, Neoma would have been everything you deserved in a mother."

It was as Staella had said—that an immortal should never dwell in the world of 'what ifs,' and every word cut like a knife through Etolié's heart. But she saw such hope in her sweet momma's eyes, and so she smiled, though she didn't mean it at all. "Doesn't matter what I deserved. You're the only mother I ever wanted."

Perhaps someday, she would feel worthy to receive that motherly love, from the woman whose life was destroyed by her eldest daughter, who was raped by an evil man, who had lost everything only to be given Etolié as a piss poor consolation prize.

"And I want you, Etolié. I never regretted you. Not for a moment."

When Staella embraced her, Etolié was grateful to have that love, nonetheless.

Chapter 19

"**I**f there's one thing I have learned in my years serving Solvira," General Irons said, "it's that anonymous tips only lead to trouble."

The sun dipped low in the sky as they traversed the town square. The streets had mostly cleared, and those remaining were ushered away by General Iron's small battalion of paladins following behind them. Clad in plate armor and bearing tabards depicting a sun and spear, they moved as a unified force, and Flowridia didn't question their worth on the battlefield.

"That's a funny way of saying 'a message written in the blood of a disemboweled prisoner left by the castle gate,'" Flowridia replied, grateful when he returned her wry grin. "It will lead to trouble assuredly, but the perpetrator has promised to reveal itself."

Sunset. Town square. Those simple words had been written in blood, as beautifully as though painted—as was Flowridia's suggestion. Ayla had wanted to write some poetic diatribe; Flowridia had insisted on something simple and bestial.

The compromise had been the handwriting.

"I would like to reiterate that I think you're a fool for coming along," Irons said, standing at attention as those in his service told the townsfolk to go home. "Though if you die, I may sleep better."

"Your honesty is refreshing. I promise to not tell Lara you said that."

Technically it wasn't a lie. She would be telling Ayla. Still, Irons chuckled, even as the final flickers of sunset disappeared behind the horizon.

Even with the evening chill, the whole world became colder.

The darkness settled by unnatural measures, and Flowridia braced herself for the inevitable shadow before them. Pure blackness rose, like an unnatural fog.

"Take formation!" Irons cried, and he drew his sword, his face twisted in concentration. "Lady Flowridia, stand behind me."

She obeyed. From the darkness emerged a shadowy figure, bearing Ayla's physique but all the characteristics of the Sha'Demoni denizens—wispy and dark, consuming all light, with eyes that glowed like vibrant stars. Flowridia suspected she illusioned herself, but perhaps Ayla truly was in the Shadow Realm—there was so much she simply did not know.

"Seems you received my invitation," Ayla said, her voice sultry and cool, as pervasive as the night breeze. *"Delightful to make your acquaintance, General Irons."*

Irons kept his sword readied. "Are you going to talk or are we going to fight, fiend?"

Ayla's laughter permeated the scene, sensual and musical both. *"I would revel in a fight with you, but first . . . empress consort? What an honor, to stand in the presence of so angelic a beauty."*

That . . . was not on script. Not that Flowridia had been given anything to say, but she did draw her lips into a line.

"I had intended on slaughtering you all," Ayla crooned, her voice permeating the air like fog, *"but I could be convinced to let a few of you walk away, if her majesty-to-be would grace me with a kiss."*

Flowridia looked to General Irons, whose bafflement threatened to overshadow his murderous intentions, and said, "Can we cut off her head now?"

"Gladly."

Irons and his brigade of paladins rushed at his command; Ayla laughed and disappeared into the shadows.

They were left alone, searching for a villain that would not show. Irons beckoned them all to cover each other's backs, and in the same move implored Flowridia to stand beside him. "If she's taken an interest in you, we can't risk her trying to kidnap you."

"I don't disagree," she replied, though Ayla likely wouldn't—there was only so much attention to draw.

Then came a vision from Flowridia's nightmares.

From the darkness emerged a gruesome figure, spindly and monstrous, standing above the buildings, even on four limbs. It remained a shadow, not appearing in full flesh. Despite knowing the ruse, Flowridia's blood chilled; she had not seen The Endless Night since its death, and those glowing pits of eyes still evoked dread, the outline of its slack jaw grotesque.

Beside her, Irons kept his sword readied. "What is that?"

Flowridia said nothing, merely prepared her spell of holy light.

The Endless Night slashed a shadowed claw down upon their small battalion, scattering them with the ease of a child to a pile of toys. Flowridia remained standing, however, even as men and woman in armor toppled to the ground. General Irons rushed to the monster, only to be met with its claws, flung several feet away. Flowridia feared a moment, until he stirred, then clenched her fists and walked boldly forward.

"Kiss me, then!" she cried, and the monster turned its eyes onto her. "Kiss me, and leave Solvira."

The shadow monster came closer, and when a collection of paladins came with their swords, Flowridia bid them to wait. She stepped forward, beckoning to the monster. It did, bending its head down to face her, its mouth alone large enough to swallow her whole.

It appeared as little more than dark fog with glowing eyes, yet when it opened its mouth, ever so slightly, she swore she caught a flash of fangs. Determination filled her as her hand touched corporeal shadow—far colder than her love, so perhaps they truly were a world apart.

No matter; she leaned in to kiss the beast, but instead evoked a great burst of holy light. She became a blinding sun in the square; the monster screeched and reeled back, retreating with an intensity that she presumed was false, yet the smallest twinge of worry twisted her gut. It screamed and flailed, vanishing like an extinguished fire.

As quickly as it came, The Endless Night's shadow vanished.

Flowridia's light faded, and she joined with the rest in surveying the damage. A few broken bones, but no deaths this night.

"You're conniving, but tonight I approve," Irons said. "I shall write up a report for the council tomorrow."

This would need to be reported, she supposed. After all, the monster had finally been revealed.

That night, when Flowridia returned to her room, that same shadow greeted her.

"Are you all right?" Flowridia asked, but Ayla simply laughed and kissed her soundly.

"Gods, you give me a rush."

Ayla's joy welled her own, and Flowridia happily let her love lead her to bed.

Chapter 20

The monster had come.

Rumors spread rapidly throughout the city, some claiming to have seen the dark shadow from their windows. Flowridia and Irons spent the next day hearing their accounts, reassuring all they passed that they were doing what they could. She suspected there would not be much pushback on curfew, this night.

Exhausted from a day's worth of walking and inquiry, Flowridia returned in the evening and decided to explore something uplifting. With only Demitri, she traversed to a place of legend.

Empress Alauriel had first taken her to the Solviran Library, a memory far more bitter than sweet. Flowridia entered a magnificent room with a ceiling a hundred feet high at least, with shelves lining every wall and thin windows spanning the vertical length of floor to ceiling. Ladders and lifts stretched high into the sky, but at the center of the hexagonal room, a deep pit circled down. Flowridia approached and peered over the railing, realizing several floors stretched downward, though she couldn't say how deep. Lara had said the Skalmites were down there, along with their crystal of maldectine.

Flowridia found the staircase leading down, curious to see it for herself. Had she not met Etolié's bookkeeper, she might not have had the courage, but the Skalmite had been friendly and kind.

Guilt filled her, to remember their fate, but though it had been her doing, it had not been her fault. The parallels of their fate to the Theocracy's were not lost on her, but with the realization came anger.

What kind of cruel fate was that, to be handed the survival of an entire people without being told the stakes? Was it fair for her to feel guilt for something she could have stopped but hadn't known? She worked to rectify the wrong of the Theocracy, but could she do anything for the Skalmites? Did she owe them anything?

No. It was not duty that led her down those many flights of stairs—but her bleeding heart.

They hiked downward for what felt like miles, the underground shelves lit by ambient, glowing orbs floating in the air. Obscure subjects passed her by—historical accounts of dead civilizations, ancient legends of monsters and magic, tax records a thousand years old, and so much more. Boundless knowledge, some of it useless to most, yet there was not a single floor where she did not pass a sleepless scholar digging through shelves.

She stopped at the Solviran History section, procuring a few more texts on the God of Death's powers. So far, not a single book had shed light on the intricacies of her powers, well beyond coincidence. Surely not all the accounts were censored—or perhaps the Great Necromancer was just that hated here, in the kingdom she had nearly destroyed.

It didn't give Flowridia much peace of mind.

Deep underground, the halls and staircases finally stopped—and the architecture looked newer. As she walked, she came across a set of iron doors guarded by two men playing cards, their weapons set aside.

They glanced up at her entrance. "You lost, your majesty?" one said.

"Is that where the Skalmites are?" she asked, pointing to the metal blockade.

"Yes."

"Might I see them?"

The guard shook his head. "With all due respect, they aren't zoo animals to be gawked at."

"Let me explain," she said, gesturing to her own self. "I was present during the genocide of the Skalmites by The Endless Night." The men paid attention now, intrigue in their gazes. "I have no wish to gawk. Merely to see for myself that they are safe. Perhaps meet with them."

The men looked to the other; one nodded. "Don't spread word around that we did this," one said as they stood. "Knock when you wish to leave."

They pulled the doors open. Ambient green light filled Flowridia's eyes—maldectine lined the doors. Already, a pulse of muted energy filled her. "We won't be able to communicate in there," she said to Demitri.

I'll survive. Let's say hello.

Flowridia set her books by the door and stepped inside, the muted wash of the crystalline environment enveloping her. Demitri's presence in her mind faded as her familiar became merely a being beside her, instead of part of her.

Rough stone touched her feet. When the door shut, blindness engulfed her. Skittering footsteps, like branches against stone, echoed across the walls. Damp earth filled her senses. As she stepped forward, her eyes slowly adjusted to the strange lighting, able to decipher a faintly glowing rock of green, suspended high above. "Hello?"

Figures appeared in her peripheral as her eyesight fully settled in the dim light. Shadows of insect-like creatures tentatively approached, their bodies reflecting the faint green of the crystal. Gigantic eyes watched her, their spindly bodies not unlike a mantis.

"My name is Flowridia. I don't know if you remember me, but I was part of the party of Staelash. I was there when the monster came."

One Skalmite stepped forward, as tall as she as it scrutinized her with crystalline eyes. It mimed a line down her chest, then spat on the ground.

"Yes, that was me. I was cut open, and your people saved me."

The Skalmite pointed to her dress, then mimed ripping it in twain.

Flowridia smiled. "Yes. I helped to bandage your wounded—"

She gasped when something tugged her skirt—hard enough to rip. When she turned around, a small Skalmite cowered, a few strands of beading in its fingers. Flowridia knelt beside what she presumed was a child. "You have my attention."

When the child didn't smove, Flowridia lightly gestured for its hand. Tentatively, the child offered it, and she gently grasped it, then led it to her beaded skirt. Spindly fingers stroked the elaborate designs. Though she could decipher no emotion from the insect face, it clicked in rapid succession— Flowridia assumed that to be good.

More approached, all tentative and shy. Flowridia greeted them as they came, allowing their curious hands to touch her clothing and skin, amused at their curiosity. Demitri, too, was a subject of fascination, his thick fur of notable delight.

It was a strange and charming encounter, for they could not speak. Yet they interacted as friends, and Flowridia's heart filled to the brim. They offered some gelatinous substance which she politely declined, assuming it to be food, and when they rummaged through her pockets, she showed them a few jingling coins—which one tried to steal, but was reprimanded by a larger one.

An hour passed at least before she bid them farewell, wishing all the while she had Etolié to interpret for her—and wondered how in the world the Celestial had managed to learn the language. When she knocked on the door, it opened, the blast of light bombarding her sensitive eyes.

But she emerged and heard an amused guard say, "Have fun?"

"They're delightful company. I only wish I could speak to them properly."

Demitri's voice startled her. *That was nice. I like them more than people.*

"They are people, Demitri," Flowridia chided, gathering the books she had left behind. "They just look different than us."

Not people. Much better than people.

She rolled her eyes but said no more of it. "I don't know about you, but I'm exhausted."

I think spending months in the Nox'Karthan Palace made you soft. You never would have whined when we were in the woods.

Flowridia stuck out her tongue. "Well, this will be a much longer journey back. You'll hear me whine a few more times."

Demitri blocked her path and pressed his stomach to the floor. *I'll carry you, I guess. Since you're royalty.*

"Can't do a good deed simply because you like me?"

My incentive is to not hear you whine.

"When do I ever—" She shut her mouth. Like all wolves, Demitri was only capable of a small range of facial expressions, but there was no mistaking that wry glint in his eyes. "I don't care how big you are—you're a naughty child."

Next you're going to tell me you're not my real mom—assuming you plan on stating the obvious again.

Despite his petulance, Demitri carried her—up the round staircase in the center of the floors and floors of shelves. The soothing smell of dust and ancient pages reminded her of Staelash, of months listening to Etolié prattle on about whatever her interest of the day was while cleaning up and organizing after a midnight reading binge. "Can you even imagine having time to read all these?"

I can't read, so no.

Flowridia chuckled. "Do you want to learn?"

What would I possibly do with that knowledge?

"Become the very first wolf to ever learn how?"

That's not bad incentive, actually.

She scratched the base of his skull, his thick fur engulfing her hands.

It was a happened glance to the side that stole her attention. A book read *A History of Sol Kareena Worship*, and Flowridia said, "Stop a minute."

Demitri did; Flowridia slid down, curiosity piqued as she perused the vast array of books before her. *I thought you were tired.*

Flowridia didn't reply; she had found her quarry. She withdrew *Evandalin's Fire: The Tragedy that Defined a Nation*—written by Archbishop Lunestra—and sat with her back against the shelf. She opened the cover, the copied script old but not ancient by any means. It might've been the youngest book on the shelf. "This is one of the books Lunestra wrote."

That's very neat.

Demitri sat beside her, peering over her shoulder as though he could understand the Solviran characters. Flowridia thumbed through the old pages, wondering what the policy was for borrowing books, then came across a small drawing of a monument—a statue of Sol Kareena embracing a child. She stopped, perusing the words, but her heart sank to see a list of names.

The names upon the monument. Children whose fates were met with horror unbound.

There were names with no surname, a few with unique ones, but most with the surname 'Light' which she presumed was a bastard name. A few foreign names, or perhaps simply antiquated. Twenty-four in all—

Ayla Darkleaf.

Cold washed over Flowridia. She blinked, but there it remained. Not her imagination. Written in deliberate script: *Ayla Darkleaf.*

It was the only name of its syntax. The only name with that surname. The only Sun Elf in the cathedral—not an orphanage, but *something like it.*

"Demitri . . ." She struggled to summon a breath. It must have been a mistake. A coincidence. Ayla Darkleaf was a grown woman, cursed by a demon god, sung to as she was buried by a woman named Sarai Fireborn, whom she had loved. Flowridia knew so little, but Ayla hadn't died in a cathedral fire—

Scrawled upon the altar in blood—the elven word for *burn.*

She slammed the book shut, a puff of dust swirling in her face. In her ensuing coughing fit, her head swam; her chest clenched, and not from dust coating her lungs.

What is it?

She swallowed, struggling to breathe. Demitri couldn't spread secrets, and so she said, "Ayla's name. Ayla Darkleaf. It's on the monument."

That doesn't make sense.

"I don't think she died, Demitri," she whispered, her next words spoken by trembling lips. "I think she burned it down. She escaped."

Well, that doesn't explain why she makes art out of people, but it's a start.

"I need you to not make jokes right now." Flowridia dared to open the book once more, studying the table of contents until she saw the brutal truth she sought: *Chapter 9— the symbols in the fire.*

Flowridia skimmed the first paragraph, voice trembling as she softly said, "Demoni symbols were written on the altar in blood, just like Lunestra said." The symbol depicted looked nothing like the one for The Endless Night, yet it did not answer the awful question of *why.*

Flowridia returned to the table of contents and selected a different chapter: *Chapter 2—the treatment of orphans:*

"Speculative writings suggest that orphans in that era were subjected to all manner of neglect and abuse," Flowridia read aloud. *"Under High Priest Renald's tutelage, corruption remained rampant beneath the cathedral's roof, the evidence of inhumane punishments, such as kneeling in buckwheat for hours during prayer or being locked*

in the dark basement, well-documented among ex-priests and priestesses, stripped of their vestments for perpetuating the abuse." She skimmed further down the page, silently reading of beatings and abuse, even deaths, documented and not, as her heart beat in her throat. *"It wasn't until High Priestess Evandalin took control that the cathedral became a haven once more. Hailed for her efforts to rehome the younger children and educate the rest, she was beloved among the people for both her devotion to Sol Kareena and her warm demeanor."*

Demitri's large paws paced around her. *So why would Ayla kill her? She made things better.*

Flowridia recalled her beloved's own words: *"My life before undeath is shattered glass, Flowra. My memories have cracked with time."*

Did she even remember? Or was Ayla merely a tangle of hatred with no origin? "I don't know. We don't even know if it was her. This might mean nothing."

Tears filled her eyes—she remembered her own childhood, her friends and her habit of sneaking away to practice magic with Aura. As an orphan, she had longed for a family, always felt a piece of her heart was missing, but it had been a charmed life. She had been fed and clothed, tended to strictly but never cruelly. Her life had fallen to hell under Mother's tutelage, but she had been fifteen when she'd knocked on her cottage door.

She hugged the book to her chest, fearful of its contents. Surely the answers were somewhere here, this mystery she had stumbled upon. Anxiety welled in her stomach, though she could not fathom the source.

For a brief, debilitating moment, the image of a tiny elven girl cowering in the dark became the backdrop of her mind: *"The Shadow Realm adopted me when I had no one—"*

"Demitri, I don't understand it at all," she said, cursing her sudden rise in tears. "It makes sense . . . but it *doesn't.*"

Ask Lady Ayla. She promised to be honest with you.

Her gut had known it all along. Clutching the book, she stood and smoothed her skirt. "Let's go back."

When she and Demitri finally crossed the threshold into her bedroom, she knew not what time of night it was—only that she was bombarded at the entrance by an irate Ayla. "I try to respect your privacy, but forgive me for worrying when you're gone *all day* with no explanation . . ."

The door shut behind them. Flowridia hardly heard her rant, merely stepped forward in a daze, her breathing shallow and pained.

". . . five minutes away from tearing apart this castle to find you— Are you even listening?!"

Flowridia merely stared, making no effort to hide her sorrow.

Ayla's voice came gently this time. "Flowra?"

Trembling, she showed Ayla the book, the title faced up. Mist obscured her vision as Ayla stared warily at it. "I found something."

Flowridia opened it to the page with the monument. She presented it again, her finger tapping the damning name: *Ayla Darkleaf.* "Do you remember anything at all?"

Ayla's worry froze, as though painted, her expressions suddenly unnatural. "The name 'Ayla' was quite common back in that era. *Darkleaf* was a bastard name. This means nothing."

"Ayla Darkleaf died in the cathedral fire, then?"

"Apparently."

Behind her, Demitri's voice filled her head, a welcome bit of warmth amidst Ayla's ice. *Ask her about the high priestess.*

"Ayla, the book talks about the high priestess— Evandalin. Did you know her?"

"I might have." Ayla's forced nonchalance was increasingly terse. "Depends on what it said." Apparently, Flowridia hesitated too long. In only the span of her taking a breath, Ayla swiped the book from her hand. "What did it say?"

"Only that she reformed the orphanage and made it safe again," Flowridia stammered, and Ayla seethed before her as she gripped the book—

And *ripped* the thick tome with her bare hands. Flowridia's heart seized—Lunestra had written it, each line handwritten and precious—but Ayla carelessly dropped the pieces, the paper scattering across the floor.

"You do know something of it," Flowridia said, her shocked gaze shifting from the book to Ayla's severe face—her glare withering. But Flowridia stood her ground, unafraid of the monster before her, a monster who was once a child, like everyone else—a bony elven child with rich black hair and vibrant eyes, whose fate might have been very different with a mother to hold her at night. "Do you remember anything?"

She swore Ayla growled, but she held her tongue. Instead, Ayla remained still as her nails pierced her forearm, steadily digging in and puncturing skin. "No, I do not. And if I did, it would not be your business anyway."

Flowridia swallowed her fear. "Ayla, did you start the fire?"

"If I say yes, will you drop it?" came Ayla's tense whisper.

Flowridia's stomach churned; panic filled her, but she didn't dare come forward. "There were demonic symbols on the altar. Was that you?"

Ayla's fist tensed, ripping the pierced skin with it.

"I read what they did to the orphans. Did they hurt you?"

"Flowra, shut up," Ayla said, louder by thin degrees.

But Flowridia came forward, pleading as she said, "Ayla, I know the shame that comes from abuse. I know you feel like you can't talk about it, that it makes you weak, that you're to blame." She waited for reprimand, but Ayla merely met her eye, pure ice in her vacant stare. Gathering her courage, she peered into the battered recesses of her heart, and softly said, "Once, while living with my mother, I managed to burn the bottom of our dinner. She slapped me hard enough to bruise and told me if I healed it, she'd hit me with the burning pan next."

Ayla didn't speak—instead she tore her gaze away and stepped back, deliberate as she stomped toward the window.

"She always threatened to cut off my hair in my sleep. When she was angry, she'd grab it and rip chunks of it out." Flowridia blinked as fresh tears fell down her face. "I was afraid any time she passed. I didn't know when she would do it again."

Ayla gazed into the dark night, her hands coming up to cover her face.

"Ayla, I . . ." Flowridia dared to come forward, longing to touch Ayla and comfort her. "Please know that I will never think less of you for what someone else did—"

When Ayla turned around, her nails tore her flesh as they left her face, leaving gashes thick enough to show her teeth, her skull. Ayla's lips parted for a smile, thinly veiled mania in her tone, every word deliberate and enunciated. "You sweet, innocent thing. Be grateful your mother was merely cruel."

Flowridia stared into a monstrous void, Ayla's fangs dominating her face, her smile twisted with hatred. Her face healed, yet the nightmarish memory lingered.

"I never knew my mother, but I knew Evandalin," Ayla spat, and when she marched forward, Flowridia stumbled back, startled by her love's predatory features, "and may she burn in whatever hell Sol Kareena tosses her into. We children *adored* Eva. She was warm and kind—the very picture of motherly love—but I was her favorite; she told me so in whispers and private places, lavished me with kisses, hugged me and held me, let me sleep in her bed. I called her 'Eva' at her behest; I was her 'little dove.'" Ayla smiled, but it was vicious, a thin barrier between Flowridia and her seeping rage. One of her hands remained at her cheek, methodically scratching it open, over and over. "On my ninth birthday, she bought me a cake and a new dress, told me I was the prettiest thing she'd ever seen. That night was the first time we fucked."

Flowridia didn't recognize the word—not at first, not for a few tense seconds following Ayla's casual reveal. She tried to speak; instead her jaw fell slack. "A-Ayla—"

"Oh, my apologies—was that not what you expected?" Ayla's mutilated visage twisted in mockery, nothing mortal in that gaze. Her face was in tatters, and Flowridia's heart broke and bled. "You precious thing—you wanted to hear how she broke my arm over spilled porridge or whipped me when I was late to my prayers. Perhaps hear that she starved me when I was sick and hoped aloud that I would die. You want a nice, clean crime with a villain you can spit on and hate. But no, that was not Eva. She drove those people away, protected me from the cruelty of the world. I'd probably be dead if not for her."

Flowridia dared to come forward, shaken from Ayla's words—the latter began to yell.

"Of course, I am no stranger to shame, but *you don't understand.* You don't want to know the lies I told to protect her. You don't want to know how desperately I thought I loved her. You don't want to know that she raped me for five years and convinced me it was love, *so don't you dare preach to me about something you know nothing about!*"

Ayla's face remained ravaged, assaulted by her nails over and over, clear markings of flesh and skull behind her torn skin. Flowridia heard every damning word, yet she dared to touch Ayla and try to heal her brutalized visage, offer tenderness in the face of cruelty, but Ayla was faster.

Her hand gripped Flowridia's wrist. Demitri snarled; Flowridia merely swallowed, facing the monster and her colorless eyes. "Ayla—"

Ayla's own cry came when Demitri's massive jaw closed around her arm. Bone snapped as he tore her away from Flowridia, knocking her down. From the floor, Flowridia cried, "Demitri, no!"

Demitri had Ayla's entire arm in his mouth as he dragged her away, throwing her down before snarling in her face. Ayla's arm hung unnaturally, clearly shattered, but she hissed at him like a cat, her fangs long and strong enough to tear out his throat.

When Ayla stood, she favored her broken arm even as the bones inside it shifted to heal. She kept a fighter's stance, pupils black and void of any focus except the massive wolf before her. Demitri planted himself between she and Flowridia, his growl low and threatening. Claws readied, Ayla rushed him—

And stopped just as quickly, as though pulled back by strings.

Flowridia stumbled into standing, blocked from coming forward by Demitri's massive self. But as she looked to Ayla, gazed upon the black pits of her eyes, Ayla looked more vulnerable than ever before.

Ayla stepped back, her footwork graceful even in retreat, and before Flowridia could cry out and stop her, she stepped into the shadow of the bookshelf and vanished.

Demitri kept his ruffled fur and defensive stance, but his growling ceased. Wherever Flowridia touched him, his fur settled down, his body steadily relaxing as she stroked across his coat. Finally, he looked to her, his body no longer poised to attack, and licked her cheek. *Are you hurt?*

"No," she said, and she hugged him, hiding her face in his fur as her panic settled—replaced by fear.

I'm sorry I hurt Lady Ayla.

"Don't say that." Flowridia held him, her mind rapidly replaying the wrenching scene—Ayla poised to fight, to kill . . . only to run away instead.

I was just trying to protect you.

The words broke a shelf holding damning truths, and Flowridia cried as she drowned in the bitter flood.

She could hardly breathe, and so she clung to her familiar for stability. "You're the most important thing to me," she whispered, and the words were true, in that different sort of way. Demitri curled around her, and she sobbed well into the night, vulnerable and afraid.

Not afraid of Ayla. Afraid she might never return.

"I'm not surprised they had it."

In the late morning, Flowridia walked in the castle garden with Lunestra. The old woman was spry for her age, needing no cane nor support.

Flowridia would never be old. Her wedding day loomed. Two weeks.

"But I am flattered. Did you read it?"

"Pieces of it," Flowridia replied. "I couldn't read it all in one sitting."

And now she never would, because Ayla had torn it apart. When she had awoken, all the pieces had disappeared.

"It's a heavy subject. Not for tender hearts." Lunestra smiled, the sun illuminating her kind visage. "You can't fool me—what's wrong?"

"My soul is heavy," Flowridia admitted. Behind them, Demitri sniffed at every new thing, birds scattering well before he could reach them. "My heart aches from reading—anyone's would." The wind sang through the trees, the path paved in stone and clicking beneath Demitri's nails. A sigh escaped her lips. "And Lara and I had a disagreement last night."

Ayla hadn't been there when she'd awoken. It was afternoon, and she had still seen no sign.

"I'm told it's good to fight before you've committed to someone," Lunestra replied, her good nature startling. "It lets you see their true character."

Flowridia couldn't shake her own part in this—she had pushed for something Ayla wasn't ready to give, but give she had . . .

And Flowridia still wept to think of it.

"Productive fights lead to solutions."

"She stormed out," Flowridia admitted. "I haven't seen her since."

Lunestra stopped before her, a slight frown etching deeper lines into her aged skin. "I won't ask why. It is not my business. But has time apart given you a clearer head?"

Flowridia nodded, though it was a lie.

"Do you feel like you can discuss it calmly now?"

Again, she nodded, unsure if it were true or not. Perhaps she could. But she wasn't certain Ayla could speak of it at all. Ayla had reacted like a cornered animal and lashed out. And then Demitri stepped in . . .

"I love her," Flowridia whispered, her voice no louder than the breeze. "I love her dearly, but she's difficult sometimes."

Lunestra offered an embrace, which Flowridia graciously received. The archbishop smelled faintly of peppermint and spice, and Flowridia found it soothing. "I don't know how Empress Alauriel is behind closed doors," Lunestra said. "My meetings with her over the years have shown her to be a reasonable and kind woman. But if she isn't what we think, if she is more difficult than she is loveable, you do not owe anyone in this kingdom your presence."

"I don't want to leave," Flowridia replied, and that was true, yet her soul remained heavy. "May I ask something?"

"Always."

"You wrote the book and drew the monument. You wrote down the name of each child who died in that fire and wept for them, prayed for them . . ." Flowridia gathered her courage, suppressing the innate shame at the mention of that infamous name to her progenitor—shame she struggled to label. "Ayla Darkleaf. That name was among the deaths. You must have known."

"I recall," Lunestra said, resignation in her tone. "To this day, I don't know what to make of it. When she came to work for Nox'Kartha years ago, I did what research I could— and while I found out plenty about The Endless Night, there was little about the name 'Darkleaf.' Some texts indicated it was a bastard name in that era, so perhaps it means nothing at all. There's no reason to think she's the same, but I agree that it's odd. I didn't think you would seek it out, and so I didn't mention it—lest I reopen old wounds."

Flowridia nodded, her stomach unsettled.

"Is that what you and Empress Alauriel fought over?"

Too tired to lie, Flowridia said, "Among other things."

The sunlight filtered like glitter through the trees, the first hints of leaves finally beginning to sprout. Spring would soon come, and Flowridia would die before she could bask in it. Lunestra, High Priestess to the Sun Goddess, lingered in sunny patches; Flowridia felt condemned to the shadows.

She loved the shadows, but could she truly live among them?

"She haunts you, doesn't she," Lunestra said, and Flowridia couldn't deny it. "You gave a compelling speech regarding her character in the woods, when my party and I followed you and the imperator. I haven't forgotten it."

"Well, you did ask me again about the body at Marielle's wedding," Flowridia replied, a scoffing smile at her lip.

"Yes, and you were devoted enough to not trade it for the orb, which was foolish but admirable." Lunestra's smile conveyed compassion, and Flowridia recalled that dark time, when she had plotted a murder she hadn't performed, yet reaped the consequences, nevertheless. "I presume disposing of the body on your own didn't bring you the closure you wanted?"

A dangerous question, though Flowridia suspected it wasn't meant to be. She offered a shrug.

"Do you still love her?"

The question, posed with no animosity, brought a plethora of complicated sorrows—because of course she did, she always would have. Even if her life weren't a lie and she were truly engaged to Alauriel Solviraes, her heart would be torn to shreds.

As it was, Ayla was hers, and her heart was bruised over a death that shouldn't have been.

"If you want me to say I don't love Ayla, I can't," Flowridia whispered, the words stolen by the breeze. She wondered if Ayla listened or if she were sulking far away. "With time, I see her more clearly. I know what she is."

"You said she was a monster," Lunestra offered, when Flowridia's own words faltered. "I never doubted you at least knew some of the truth."

"Yes," Flowridia affirmed, but her mind dwelled on the violence of the previous night, of Ayla's broken arm and her crazed antics. "But before that, she was a child who may have survived the cathedral fire, and I hope you can understand why that haunts me."

"Perhaps she didn't survive," Lunestra said, but Flowridia shook her head.

"It isn't how she died. I don't know how she did, but what little I do know tells me it couldn't have been that."

"My point still stands," Lunestra replied, and Flowridia looked to her curiously, asking for more. "Perhaps the little girl who was once Ayla Darkleaf lived through the fire yet died in the cathedral, nevertheless."

Flowridia's gut churned at that, and a lump in her throat rose and threatened to choke her.

Footsteps rapidly approached. A young man ran to them, through the garden path. "Archbishop Lunestra," he said, bowing deep. "Lady Flowridia, your presence has been requested."

"By Lara?"

"No, my lady. By General Irons."

She looked to Lunestra, who waved her away. "Go on. I'm having a wonderful time in the sun."

Flowridia managed a smile and followed the servant out, Demitri in tow.

General Irons waited in the council room. "There's news," he said, sliding paperwork across the table. "Perhaps you heard already, but there was a fire last night."

"I hadn't heard," she said, studying the top sheet of paper.

"At the Temple of Sol Kareena."

The words stuck like a knife in her stomach.

"Thankfully it was contained, but the temple is unusable for the time being. The spire was set ablaze, and repairs must be done before the roof caves in. There's evidence of arson, though that in and of itself doesn't pertain to us. But look at the symbol on page two."

With numb hands, Flowridia obeyed, breath catching at the familiar Demoni character.

"That was found written in blood on the door," Irons said. "An ancient legend—the symbol of The Endless Night."

Flowridia knew it. It had been written in her blood a lifetime ago, used to summon a monster and slay the Skalmites and dwarves.

Oh Ayla . . . What had she done?

At her silence, Irons continued. "Apparently this was some sort of vampiric monster a thousand years ago. Likely not the real thing, but we should investigate. It almost certainly relates to the sudden surge in vampire activity in Neolan."

She managed to nod. "Let me put on something warmer."

Flowridia stumbled out, lightheaded and appalled, hot pulses of anger bringing life back to her cold limbs.

There was little to be found that day.

Irons had underplayed the damage done—the steeple had been set ablaze, most of the roof charred and damaged, and the smoke staining the walls and priceless art wounded her greatly. Worshippers stood on the outskirts, sending prayers to the goddess, but Flowridia stared in silence at the covered-up symbol, written in blood, and feared what it meant.

Yet not so much as she feared what could have been. What might still come.

If she had any damn inclination to where Ayla was, she would feel far more at peace. She questioned what game Ayla played, if any at all, wondering if this were a punishment or her merely coping.

"I think it may be time to conduct an investigation at night," Flowridia said, as she and Irons returned to the castle. The sun had barely set, the last vestiges of daylight reflecting from the Glass Palace.

"Are you sure you wish to join us?"

"I have dealt with far worse."

"As much as I hate to say it," Irons said, "it would be useful to have you."

Shocked at the admittance, Flowridia stopped in her tracks. "I'm flattered."

"Don't think too much of it," he said, but Flowridia swore she saw a smile pull at his beard.

Perhaps they might have spoken more of it, but a cry suddenly interrupted the quiet evening. Wordlessly, Irons drew his sword and ran for the palace, where the scream had originated. Flowridia followed, though even weighed down by his armor, he outpaced her.

Flowridia followed the distant, metallic footsteps as she entered the castle, for Irons had vanished from sight. Servants bustled, some coming to investigate, but Flowridia ran straight to the council room, hearing Irons' cry of, "Die, fiend!"

The scream she heard was inhuman, yet something familiar chilled her blood. Flowridia burst into the room. A woman lay prone on the floor, blood seeping from her neck. Irons swung his sword, glowing with holy light. But the vampire he sought to slay grabbed the divine blade in her hands, glowing with silver light as the weapon grew muted, and then shattered.

Ayla Darkleaf's face was coated in blood, her fangs long and monstrous, her black dress something light and tight and with a skirt that flared when she leapt at Flowridia.

Flowridia screamed, shoved to the ground by the bloodstained villain, though a hand cushioned her head from the floor. With their faces only inches away, Ayla said, "Oh, you're *gorgeous*." She licked a line from Flowridia's jaw to her ear, who flinched at the contact. "You smell simply decadent."

Fangs pierced Flowridia's throat.

Instinct took over. Flowridia placed a hand on Ayla's face, releasing a spell of healing magic, terrified at the image of black pupils and elongated fangs.

Ayla screamed and ripped herself away, clutching at her seared face. Irons rushed her, a dagger in his hand, but Ayla, screeching, disappeared into a shadow.

Flowridia sat up, trembling, surprised when a gloved hand offered her assistance. "Are you all right?" Irons asked, and Flowridia managed to nod, despite feeling a faint trickle of blood trailing down her throat.

Once she had steadied, Irons ran to the crumpled figure on the floor. The religious vestments meant she knew the woman, High Priestess Jules' attire unmistakable, but blood had turned the once holy vestments into a vision of horror. Her throat seeped life, and Flowridia placed her hands on Jules as Irons steadied her, searching for a pulse.

She still lived. Flowridia's senses expanded, commanding the brutalized skin to mend, and the deeper wounds to come together. Jules' heart slowed, but Flowridia refused to give it the luxury. "Live, please," she whispered, tears welling in her eyes as she focused on repairing each damaged cell.

Blood would drown Jules if she stayed lying down, the thick liquid having dripped down her throat and possibly into her lungs. The skin repaired; Flowridia heard her cough. "She will need a healer, but she's stabilized."

General Irons glanced from Jules' brutalized neck to hers. "What about you?"

"It's nothing," Flowridia said truthfully. "I'll heal it on my own." She helped Jules sit up as she violently wheezed, blood coming up with each labored cough. "Jules, can you tell us what happened?"

"Came from—" Jules continued to cough, gagging as she spat out blood and fluid. ". . . t-the shadow."

Flowridia trembled—from fear or rage or shock she did not know.

Then, a scream echoed from the doorway as Lara ran inside, making a show of genuine terror. "Flowra— Flowra—!" Lara gasped, her dramatics truly gag-worthy, to any who knew her. "You're covered in blood!"

"I'm fine," Flowridia replied, forcing her voice to calm. "Lara, just breathe."

"What happened to Jules?"

"Shh . . . Lara, breathe," Flowridia said, her patience wearing thin from Ayla's theatrics. "Jules was attacked by a vampire."

"She could freely enter the castle," Irons said, still kneeling beside Jules. He looked to the nearest of his guards. "Set the castle on lockdown. High alert. We have an intruder."

"Agreed," Flowridia said.

"We shall spend the night in my room," Lara said. "Send guards to the door."

They left Irons with Jules, entering the hall and then the lift.

Once truly alone, Lara cracked a brilliant smile. "You played your part well."

"You nearly killed Jules," Flowridia said, realizing she still shook. "Ayla, how could you?"

"What is one more casualty? A wonderful bit of drama—"

"Ayla, this isn't funny!" Flowridia stepped angrily from the lift when it stopped, high atop the castle. She stormed toward Lara's bedroom.

"Oh, darling, are you angry?" Lara blocked her path with her small body, hands pawing at Flowridia's dress. "I thought it was a grand addition to our plan. Was the flirting too much?"

"Ayla, you scared me." Emotion choked Flowridia's throat, but she shoved it down. When she breathed, it hitched, and she cursed the tears welling in her eyes. "You *bit* me."

"Nothing I haven't done before." Lara's visage vanished, leaving only Ayla Darkleaf, her face covered in blood. She placed her hands upon Flowridia's waist. "I thought you liked it when I stole a bit of your blood."

"Under the right circumstances, it's intimate, yes," Flowridia said, realizing she hurt, oh she *hurt*. "I let you drink from me because I trust you. But when you shove me down and steal it—" Her breath caught again; her threatened tears fell. "You scared me, Ayla."

Ayla's frown held ignorance, held innocence, and when she opened her mouth to speak, her wide eyes sought reprimand. "I . . . Flowra . . ." So strange, to see Ayla subdued, but her entire posture shrunk to match. Despite her bloodstained features, her pointed fangs, she looked helpless and small. "I am sorry."

As Flowridia gazed upon her, a modicum of empathy pierced her bruised heart—for the woman who was so lost, who truly didn't understand at all. "Don't do it again," she whispered, swallowing her tears. "I can forgive you for this once, but please . . ."

She couldn't finish. The words were too heavy, too much. When Ayla pulled her into an embrace, Flowridia, despite all her anger and hurt, felt relief. "I was scared you wouldn't come back," Flowridia admitted, and Ayla merely clung to her, hands grasping Flowridia's dress.

"I am sorry. For last night. I did not mean—"

"Ayla, no," Flowridia said, uncaring of the blood staining her dress. Another one for the furnace, and let it burn; Ayla was more important. "I pushed you. You didn't want to answer, but I wouldn't let it go, and—"

"I nearly . . ." The first of Ayla's sobs sounded against Flowridia's shoulder. Flowridia offered a gentle *shh* . . . "I nearly hurt him."

"But you didn't, and that means so much more."

When Ayla pulled back, just enough to face her, her vibrant eyes held tears. "I do not know what came over me."

"It was you who tried to burn down the cathedral, wasn't it? The one here, in Solvira."

"Like I said, I do not know what came over me. It . . . It seemed like the best way to purge those awful feelings."

Awful feelings Flowridia had dumped on her, and despite Ayla's crimes, Flowridia's guilt rose. Yet Ayla still awaited castigation; Flowridia smoothed her hair, prayed her gentle touch could be enough. "Last night . . . You were right; I don't understand. I don't, and I can't, and if I disregarded your pain . . . Ayla, I'm sorry. I pushed you, and I'm sorry."

"It's all right," Ayla whispered, and she touched Flowridia's face, her hair, desperation in the gesture. "It's not something I often think of, nor something I have ever told a lover. I . . ." She nearly crumbled, visibly fighting to stay composed. "Gods, it was like you punched the air out of me, and I do not even breathe."

Flowridia struggled to find a reply, then gasped when Ayla suddenly kissed her. She savored her intended's lips, uncaring of the blood, conveying her apology and forgiveness both.

Ayla finally parted their mouths, then tensed. Flowridia feared she would crumble, but instead she looked over Flowridia's shoulder, claws suddenly digging into her dress. Her voice held a warning: "Flowra . . ."

Flowridia looked back, following her gaze.

And there stood Lunestra, watching the exchange.

Ayla tried to pull away, but Flowridia held fast, instead turning to stand between Ayla and the archbishop, whose wide eyes held horror. "Lunestra, it's not—"

"What is the meaning of this?" Lunestra said, condemnation in the words, and Flowridia felt her perfect world begin to crumble.

Flowridia sought an answer, dug inside her soul for words, but Ayla spoke up instead. "I am charmed to see you again, High Priestess," Ayla said, her grin salacious and starved, "though I heard a rumor you exchanged that title for a higher one. Pity about your brother." She returned her attention to Flowridia, ever the actress with that predatory gaze. "Where were we? Right, I was *kidnapping you.*"

The emphasis seemed to be for Flowridia's own benefit, who remained rooted to the spot, managing only a tense, "Ayla—"

"That is why I have come to the castle," Ayla continued, through grit teeth, but Lunestra's reproving stare suggested the lie meant nothing. "Shall I laugh manically for emphasis?"

"Ayla, please," Flowridia said, daring to release her and come forward, a supplicant before Lunestra, before her progenitor who loved her. "It's not what you think."

"I had heard a rumor that The Endless Night's symbol was written on the cathedral door," Lunestra said, standing her ground, her withering stare falling to Ayla. "I disregarded it. There are always rumors." She looked back to Flowridia, tension in her jaw. "What is this?"

"I . . ." Flowridia's throat choked with unspoken words, panic steadily rising in her blood.

"What would your intended say?" Lunestra said, her gaze darting between them, still aghast with horror, "to see you fraternizing with this woman? To see you weeping in her arms?"

"It's not what you think," Flowridia repeated—foolishly, aimlessly, willing the world to simply stop so she could think.

Lunestra shook her head, cautiously stepping back. "Flowridia . . ."

She disappeared around the corner, her steps echoing across the walls.

Flowridia's panicked heart pulsed with life. She ran after Lunestra, the woman's cry of, *"Guards! Come quickly!"* a betrayal.

Ayla ran faster, disappearing into a shadow, and when Flowridia rounded the corner, she saw Ayla emerge at Lunestra's side and effortlessly drag her into the nearest room.

Metallic footsteps sounded. Flowridia ran to escape the approaching guards, knowing the castle was on high alert, and joined Ayla in the small parlor room, heart breaking to see her love's arm around Lunestra's neck, and the other covering her mouth.

"Your decision, Flowra," Ayla said, and Lunestra didn't struggle, merely looked to Flowridia with anguish in her aged gaze. "I can break her neck; she will be dead before she can feel it. Or I can drop her in the Morathan Desert until you think of something better. Your decision."

Flowridia wanted none of this. Her tears fell fast as she met Lunestra's eye, vicious repercussions in every action, every choice, and she cursed the unfairness of it, this twist of fate.

Yet a quiet voice inside her whispered wicked words— that she had earned this. Happy endings were not for creatures like her.

Flowridia knelt before her, a final, impossible hope shining through the bleak future ahead. The God of Death could condemn you to a living death, yes, but Ayla had also spoken of feats of a smaller scale, to pluck out memories, to toss them away, and when Flowridia put her hands on Lunestra's skull, she placed all her focus forward. The magic was the same; she had not succeeded yet, but . . .

"Forget this," spoke the spell, and familiar nothingness came to numb her heart. *"The last ten minutes . . . Let them go—"*

Something shifted beneath her fingertips, the delicate nature of the brain too complex to know precisely what, but something changed, the barest hints of necromancy seeping through—

Lunestra slumped in Ayla's arms.

Flowridia pulled back, tension rising as she stared at the limp body in Ayla's arms. "Did it . . . Did it work?"

When Ayla's hold relaxed, the archbishop fell as though sleeping, helpless in her grasp. Ayla placed two fingers to her neck, face inscrutable as she waited.

Something had changed in Lunestra's head, and Flowridia looked to her hands, still trying to make sense of what she had felt. Her blood pounded, adrenaline surging.

"Flowra."

Flowridia looked up, pulled from her musing.

Ayla's face remained impassive, forcibly neutral as she whispered, "There's no pulse."

All that hope, all her grand ambitions, the family she finally found . . . crumbled.

The first of Flowridia's sobs broke silently, guilt and shame rising to follow. She fell forward, weeping into the carpet, and soon Ayla's cold embrace surrounded her. Her mind thought nothing, feeling only agony and guilt, disregarding whatever gentle tidings Ayla whispered in her ear.

She wept in Ayla's arms.

Chapter 21

The next morning, news came that Lunestra had died in the night—from old age, presumably, but Irons was convinced vampiric activity was the cause. Her familiar had flown off through the window, for without the magical connection, its mind had become that of a normal bird.

Flowridia remained impassive at the news, instead excusing herself to sit alone in the garden.

Ayla became a shadow by her side, tossing away her empress duties to console her. *"Why don't we go to your secret chamber? Perhaps you might distract yourself with work?"*

Seated in the speckled daylight, the thought of returning to somewhere so dark and cold chilled her blood, yet not so much as the thought of her own power. The garden might have been a welcome comfort, but she felt empty. "Ayla . . ." She shut her eyes, unable to summon the will for even tears. "I'm sorry, but I can't. I can't do it anymore. I'm not the God of Death, and I never shall be."

To her surprise and relief, Ayla gently took her hands. "All right. We let it lie, my sweet summer blossom. There are mysteries that can simply remain as such. You are useful for far more than necromancy."

"I feel like I finally understand what everyone warned me about, regarding necromancy," Flowridia said, the morning breeze lifting the natural curls in her hair. "A dangerous path, but I never saw it. I couldn't fathom it, yet for all the good I claim to be able to do, it's all lies. Yes, I can raise little dead creatures for my amusement, and that's harmless enough, but death is death. They're still dead, and there's nothing I can do about it."

She pulled one hand away from Ayla's, then willed a vibrant spark of light into her palm. "Yet the more I grow in darkness, the same can be said for my healing. I can coax pure life into plants or take what they already have and make it more. Perhaps someday I could raise the dead without necromancy."

She thought of Lara, slain for Flowridia's cause. She thought of Lunestra, her blood link to a family she had never known.

"It would be a cruel fate," Ayla replied, "to those who do not want it."

"What do you mean?"

Ayla looked warily to the bright light in Flowridia's hand, all the while stroking soft lines into her other. "As someone cursed to never die, I wonder sometimes if I might appreciate life if I were ever in danger of losing it. I wonder about the Beyond and if I might have ever found peace had I been allowed to move on after my natural death. Doubtful, I suppose—Izthuni had already sunk his claws deep in my head. I'm self-aware enough for that."

"How did . . ." Flowridia swallowed her words at Ayla's sudden frown. "There must be some way for you to move forward," she said instead, her sorrow muted as she contemplated this great mystery. "Do you want to?"

"I have not given it much thought, to be honest. I suspect my soul is so damaged, I would simply cease to be. But given that my vampirism is because of a curse, it could feasibly be broken—at which point I would crumble into dust. I truly do not know the answer, however. Izthuni has never spoken of it, nor have I asked."

Flowridia's hand closed around her beloved's. "For what it's worth, I'm grateful you're here now."

"Me too," Ayla said, her smile soft and rare.

Flowridia thought of the path ahead, of the woman she had killed—and of the stark rejection in her eye, though rightfully earned. "Lunestra said once that her nephew—my father—had a woman he loved. He made mention of a family to Casvir. I have to wonder if perhaps . . ." Tears finally did well in her eyes. The divine light in her hand extinguished as she wiped them on her sleeve. "It doesn't matter. I'm not worthy of that name."

"Perhaps not," Ayla said, and Flowridia was grateful to not be coddled. "Lunestra was your blood, but there's more to a family than that. Odessa was your blood, but I'd sooner see her be consumed by Onias' Hell than hear her call you 'daughter' again. You spoke a time or two about Staelash adopting you when you had nothing, did you not? They can be your family instead."

Flowridia said nothing, too dazed to even move.

"And what of Demitri and me? You'll never be alone, my Sweet Flowra." Ayla's dark chuckle felt cold amidst the sunlight—but Ayla had never been suited to dwell in the light. "Surely that counts for something. Flowridia Solviraes to the world . . ." The gentleness in her smile twisted into something vicious. ". . . but Flowridia Darkleaf in my bed. Is this acceptable?"

Flowridia nodded, unable to staunch her tears.

"Oh, Flowra . . ." Ayla came to her side and held her in her arms. "Darling, cry all you need to. And I am sorry if I am callused—I never understood your affection for her, but I do understand the sting of failure, and I know you must mourn. I have already spoken to Reginal about a small funeral—but what do you think, my love? As her next of kin, do you think it would be wise to reveal her to her people?"

Flowridia held her, accepting that the comfort was sincere, even if held an edge of coldness. "I . . ." Though her tears still fell, she pushed her sorrow and guilt aside—this was a political matter. "It would be to Solvira's detriment, for Casvir to discover we held her here. It should be a small funeral. Let rumors circulate that she lives among the refugees. Hope is all they have, false or not."

"I shall handle the details, my Flowra," Ayla said, her nails writing soothing lines across Flowridia's back.

Flowridia wiped her eyes, soothed by the sun and by Ayla's presence. "I still wonder if she's still alive. The woman my father loved. She must be Solviran, or perhaps even Morathan, given how far south he was travelling."

"While I would do everything in my power to help," Ayla said, still grazing her nails across Flowridia's back, "I do not have much to go on—Solvira and Moratham are large countries."

Flowridia looked at her hands, the blood running through them bearing a noble lineage—a lineage she spat upon for who she loved. "I suppose you're right."

Mariam, she thought to herself, but the name meant nothing. Nearly twenty years had passed. She might be dead.

When Ayla hummed—that familiar tune of long ago, sung to her by a lover of ages past—Flowridia simply wondered, her mind grappling with a great many things.

A gloomy aura permeated the day, though perhaps it was all in Flowridia's head. Ayla sensed it, tried to offer comfort through sex and flowers and food—any and all possible romantic gestures, but while Flowridia forced a few smiles, she politely turned it all down, save for the flowers.

Moonlilies. She hadn't seen them since the Valley of Neoma, and before that in her garden in Staelash. She spent the evening replanting them in Solvira's Royal Gardens, busying herself instead of succumbing to more tears.

She ached, but she managed to sleep that night at Ayla's behest, who coaxed her into bed with honeyed words and tender kisses.

Ayla was gone when she awoke, replaced instead with Demitri who, having learned his lesson, placed only his head on the bed. His golden eyes met hers. "Good morning, Demitri," she said, idly placing a hand on his soft head.

Lady Ayla said she has a present for you, for the funeral. But she felt sad about leaving you alone.

A scoffing bit of laughter escaped her throat before she could stop it. "Sweet of her."

She doesn't know how to help you, but she wants to.

"I know," Flowridia said, and her heart did warm for that.

She dressed, her characteristic colors forgotten for an ensemble of black. As she stared at her reflection in the mirror, the lush, dark fabrics highlighting the auburn tones in her hair, the richness of her russet skin, she wondered when her image had so starkly, ineffably changed—once a little girl, abused but not broken, and now . . .

She touched her cheekbones, which she swore must have developed overnight, or so slowly that she hadn't noticed. Her once gangly form had gained symmetry, the curves of her breasts and hips lithe yet suited for an adult figure. She would no longer be mistaken for twelve, as Etolié had once jested, nor for fifteen. She remained youthful, the final vestiges of childhood content to cling, but despite her sorrow, she carried herself as a woman.

From the dresser drawer, tucked safely away, she withdrew Lunestra's gifted crown.

It was a piece meant for royalty, for a role Flowridia had rejected and now betrayed. With care, she caressed the gemstones embedded in the gold, and when she held it up to the top of her head, she saw an empress consort.

She thought idly of her father, who had an entire kingdom as his inheritance, who had people who adored him, accolades unparalleled, yet loved someone forbidden and supposed she had inherited one small thing.

Are you going to wear it?

She looked at Demitri through the mirror. "I don't know that I should."

But it was a present.

With some apprehension, she nestled it back into the drawer. "I'm not worthy," she said simply, and proceeded to pin back her thick locks of hair with the provided finery on the vanity.

Soon, a knock sounded from the door. Lara entered, already dressed in black, a decorative veil over half her face— far more dramatic than when Flowridia had seen the true Lara at Khastra's funeral. "Flowra," she said, shifting to become Ayla as she quickly shut the door behind her, "they would like to begin soon."

Flowridia placed a final pin, deeming it good enough. A sad smile tugged at her lips when Ayla offered her a black violet, the dark center bleeding out into shades of purple. She tucked it behind her ear, finding it completed the outfit well. "Thank you."

Soft lips brushed across her own. "Darling, you are perfection, even in mourning," Ayla said. "Come with me. And I hope you will forgive me, but I took a . . . a leap of faith."

Confused, Flowridia accepted her offered hand, her expression remaining the same even as she shifted back into Lara's form. "Demitri did say you had a present for me."

"I do," the false empress said, leading her to the door. "I know when I am out of my depth, Flowra, and I am not too proud to admit that I have absolutely no idea how to console you, aside from simply holding your hand and listening to your tears."

"That's generally all I need," Flowridia replied, but Ayla shook her head.

"Darling, I know when to delegate," she said, and when she twisted the doorknob, Flowridia gasped and nearly sobbed for who waited outside.

Dressed in black, Thalmus stood nearly too tall for the hallways—hallways designed for even Khastra to walk—meek as he smiled down at Flowridia. "Hello, Flower Girl."

When she fell into his side, he caught her, held her, his familiar smell of earth and fire grounding and beloved.

"I took the liberty of quietly informing him of Lunestra's worth to you," Lara said, appearing at their side, "and brought him here this morning. I hope you do not mind."

But Flowridia wept, content to fall apart in his arms, this man—this father—who loved her in every pure way.

They buried Lunestra in an unmarked plot, in the graveyard beside the castle designated for royals and their kin. The gravestone simply bore the sigil of Sol Kareena—a spear and the sun—and Flowridia thought it fitting.

Thalmus kept a hand on her shoulder all the while, even as Lara gave a touching speech to the small crowd—only the inner council was present. Jules had come, shaky but standing, having recovered at least physically from the attack.

Dirt fell to cover the body; Flowridia's tears fell to match, her guilt only rising.

She had done this.

She couldn't stand watching the rest and quietly slipped away—from Thalmus' touch and from the crowd. He followed, and when they had left the small group of mourners, Thalmus softly spoke. "There is still no news of Etolié or Khastra. I would not begin to know how to reach them."

"They'll be told of Lunestra's passing upon their return," Flowridia muttered, but her jaded heart added, "assuming they do." Her gaze drifted to the sun, still low on the horizon. "Kedira," she softly whispered, the name a sacred thing, but Thalmus shook his head.

"Today, I named it for you," he said, and Flowridia managed a smile even in the somber atmosphere. "Flowridia Makosa—that is your name, isn't it?"

She nodded, shame filling her at the surname.

"The family name of the Theocracy's monarchs is well known, even if they shed it upon taking their mantle." Thalmus stood behind her, joining her in absorbing the sunlight. "I'm so sorry for your loss, Flowra. I know what it means to lose a mother—and she was near enough. There is no pain quite like it."

Flowridia wiped quiet tears from her eyes as she leaned against his side, content to be a child again and hide in Thalmus' shadow. His greying hair betrayed his age, revealing a life of work and strife, for he was young enough to be her father, despite appearing older. "Thank you."

"I hope it isn't inappropriate to congratulate you," he continued. "Every ending brings a new beginning. Lunestra has passed, but her legacy continues with your impending marriage. I know it's not a comfort now, but she died knowing you were continuing the cycle of life, and there is something to be said for that."

Except . . . she hadn't. Flowridia clenched her fists, for Lunestra's final moments had been confusion, rejection—knowing without question that Flowridia loved a monster.

"Before she died, we . . ." She swallowed her threatened sob, trying to gather her scattered words. "We had a disagreement. And I wish so dearly that it was different."

"It doesn't mean she didn't love you at the end," Thalmus said, "but I understand why that would hurt."

She could only hope. When she said nothing, Thalmus said more. "When the mourners have left, tell her what you wish your final words could have been. I believe she will hear them. The dead know our words."

Flowridia nodded, eyes still seeping quiet tears. "How long will you be staying?"

"A few days. Zorlaeus has agreed to oversee my duties. Whatever my initial reservations about his character, he has proven himself to be a good man." Thalmus' smile flickered and faded. "Marielle often visits Nox'Kartha, usually without him."

Flowridia frowned, unsettled by his tone. "Why?"

"She claims she is meeting with the viceroy for political purposes, but between you and me . . ." A glower overtook his oft stoic features. "Something isn't right."

"Murishani is manipulative," Flowridia affirmed, his mere memory enough to bring her blood to boiling. "But she can agree to nothing without Etolié or Sora—and Etolié might be gone, but Sora isn't a fool."

"No, she isn't. But while I do care for Marielle, she's impulsive. I worry."

"Have you ever asked to accompany her?"

Thalmus shook his head. "I don't know what good it would do."

They settled into silence, the news of Marielle's antics disconcerting at best, but Flowridia's still dwelled upon the sorrowful day. As she contemplated this new world, her name and all it meant, she realized something she had forgotten in the madness. "Thalmus, may I ask something?"

He merely looked at her, kindness in his expectant gaze.

"This may be inappropriate timing, but I need to ask, in the absence of any blood family, not that Lunestra could have done it, but . . ." Flowridia swallowed her sorrow, for this was supposed to be a happy thing. "In Solvira, it's customary for the bride and groom to be escorted by a parent—usually of their same gender—but I don't have anyone. Lara, I think, shall be taking Etolié. But would you walk with me?"

Thalmus' smile was marred by tears, but of a joyful sort. He agreed.

When they headed back to the gravesite, Lara waited alone and immediately embraced her. "The mourners have gone to lunch. Will you join us?"

"I would like to be alone for a moment, actually," she said, smiling fondly at Thalmus. Lara kissed her cheek as they parted, leaving with the half-giant.

Flowridia knelt beside the mound of dirt. "Lunestra . . ." She shut her eyes, a choking sob immediately tearing from her throat. "I'm sorry. By every god—I'm so sorry."

She could manage nothing more. She simply wept upon the grave, every blubbering word an apology.

"**M**y *darling, I had a dangerous thought. Won't you let me show you something?*"

That was the cryptic warning Ayla cooed in her ear that night. Flowridia followed, unsurprised when their destination became Sha'Demoni. "I told you—I'm done trying to emulate the God of Death."

"Oh, this entirely different. I thought we could have some fun."

The word 'fun' hardly soothed her.

Ayla escorted her to her secret chamber. The familiar cold and putrid smell seeped into her skin, chilling her to the bone. All was as she had left it—shambling dead making slow laps around the perimeter, piles of corpses in the corners— save for a large table in the center, a corpse neatly arranged upon it. Releasing Ayla's hand, Flowridia approached, cringing at the ghastly display. "Ayla . . . what is this?"

A single head lay attached to a naked torso, but its arms were severed, instead surrounded by three different arms on each side, artfully displayed like an insect. The normal legs were attached, but Flowridia suspected a nasty plot. "In my own experimentation," Ayla mused, "I had wavering luck through the years in assembling unique creations. The only ones that ever survived for long were already dead, given life by Casvir in Nox'Kartha. But their bodies were always so fragile, no matter how minute my stitches. Useless for combat, or even lifting. But you . . ." Ayla grinned; it sent a shiver down Flowridia's spine. "You could seal them properly. Make them strong."

"I can seal what can be attached, yes," Flowridia replied, biting at her lip at the task ahead, "but I don't know that I could create new nerves or bones or muscles—it would be useless, simply hanging there."

"No, because it is dead. You control the dead and the dead hand moves—that is necromancy. Right?"

Ayla had a point. Still, she hesitated, grimacing at the macabre sight. "You truly want this?"

"I do." Ayla's cool hands suddenly pawed cutely at the collar of her dress. "He will be a spider. It's funny."

"I don't know that 'funny' is the word I would choose."

Ayla placed a lingering kiss on the side of her lip. "Do it for me, darling. What does it hurt?"

Though she groaned internally, Flowridia agreed, mildly amused by Ayla's delighted claps. She refused to look too closely at the corpse's face, lest she humanize this monstrosity, and ran her fingers along its bare shoulder, studying the severed appendage. The cuts were done with medical precision—this was not rot. "Did you do this?"

"His original arms were too damaged. I did not wish to waste your time."

Flowridia blew out a breath, the air fluffing the hair by her face. "Thank you, I think."

She placed the first arm by the gaping hole, finding it simple enough to attach. Time consuming, yes. This was not the corpse's actual arm, so while it did not resist like a living being would have it seemed . . . confused. But she coaxed them together, sealing them as one, then repeated on the other side.

A normal corpse lay before her. "Do you have a knife?"

Predictably, Ayla did. Flowridia cut slits into the corpse's side, then lined the next arm against the gruesome wound. At her will, the skin sealed, though her stomach revolted at the sensation, the flesh closing unnaturally. Layers and layers of skin attached, muscles knitted together where they were never intended to. Flowridia soon stared upon a gristly sight, then swallowed her revulsion and repeated it, again and again.

All the while, Ayla hovered like a hummingbird, but not near enough to disturb her. Her keen eyes studied every movement, every motion, and when Flowridia finally finished, a broad grin spread across her face. "Give him life. Let us see if it works."

Therein lay the easier part. Flowridia bid him to rise, and the monster did. The unnatural limbs moved on their own accord, bumping against the others, but seated before them was a six-armed man, as Ayla had requested.

Ayla's laughter echoed across the stone walls. Her thin arms wrapped around Flowridia's torso. "Oh, he's fantastic!"

So strange, the things that delighted her love. "I'm happy you like him," Flowridia said, honest in that. Happy that Ayla was happy.

At her silent command, the monster rose, unsteady from the added weight up top, but he did not topple. Ayla stepped around him, inspecting the gruesome work. "This opens up so many possibilities."

"With your artistic mind, I'm sure the ideas will never stop," Flowridia said, concerned her words were prophetic.

"You don't seem so thrilled," Ayla said, peering out from behind the monster's torso. "Is this too much?"

Flowridia looked upon the creature she had crafted, knowing it was abominable, though it technically hurt no one. "It's not my personal taste," she replied, careful in her word choices, "but it's not offensive." A sigh left her lips, long and heavy. "It is also very good for me, for practice."

"Wonderful," Ayla said, almost cute as she poked the undead creature. "Do you think they have a place as soldiers? Like Casvir?"

"Against anyone but Casvir, yes. They would fall to his will. He's stronger than I am."

"Pity." Ayla came to stand beside her. "Might we make another? I have so many ideas."

When imagining a future with Ayla, Flowridia could not say she had anticipated nights creating nightmarish monsters, but Ayla's joy was radiant, and, admittedly, it was good to have a hobby they could do together. Ayla followed her around like a duckling when she gardened; why not appreciate Ayla's hobbies as well?

She agreed, and Ayla immediately dove into working, prattling on about balance and art, all while Flowridia simply rolled her eyes, amused above all at her love's antics.

For hours they entertained themselves, and Flowridia lost herself in the oddly pleasant horror of their activities.

"I was always told necromancy came from peace," Ayla said amidst their work. "From an absence of feeling. Yet you're often angry when you cast your spells."

"I was told that too," Flowridia replied, watching Ayla assemble the monster upon the slab. It had to be past midnight, but her creativity knew no end—this creature was enormous, mapped out with limbs and excess skin and organs to accommodate its size. "But I can't say it's been true for me."

"Do tell," Ayla said, clearly listening though her eyes remained on her project. "I find your anger invigorating."

Flowridia bid one undead servant to fall upon its hands and knees, another to stand beside it. She sat upon the makeshift chair, long ago desensitized to corpses, their cold touch and smell familiar. "My first outburst," she said, recalling months ago, "was in the woods. I was mourning your death but felt betrayed. Betrayed by you."

Ayla glanced to her, curiosity in her slight frown.

"I was heartbroken when I discovered your history. I told you that. Back then, I had tried to let you go, but my mind wouldn't allow it. I dreamt of you. I missed you. And one morning I ran away from my camp with Casvir and let it all out." She shut her eyes, recalling the desecrated forest scene. "It was the first time I'd felt invigorated at the concept of power, but I destroyed so much. It scared me."

"Does it scare you now?" Ayla asked, her focus returning to her work.

"A little," she admitted. "I think it always will. But it's strange, to actually feel angry. I hadn't felt angry in years; I'd repressed it. I'm slowly accepting that anger is neither right nor wrong—merely a tool to wield. Hammers can build houses, or they can kill."

"My hammers generally kill," Ayla said, which was not a revelation, but Flowridia would not deny her the chance to speak her heart. Ayla was so rarely introspective. "But I would argue that I was the opposite. Looking back on my life, it is difficult to recall a time I was not angry."

"Are you angry now?"

"No, and that was why meeting you was so aggravating. I kept instigating, and you merely offered kindness. You did not feed my rage—instead, you soothed it." Ayla turned to her, flecks of ichor upon her cheek. "Would it be different now? Had I met you as you are instead of as you were? A little girl delivering breakfast for my poor, hungover self?"

Ayla grinned, but Flowridia studied her, forced herself to look back upon the monster her love had been, the cruel games she had played. "I can't say. I might have still made you breakfast, but I would have had the courage to be more upfront about my intentions for you."

"Oh, really?"

"Yes." Flowridia smiled, humming slightly to watch her love, content in her admittedly abhorrent element. But there was no harm in it here. "I'm still a little shy, but I can at least speak my mind. I would have told you I thought you were beautiful, that I thought your dance was the most wonderful thing I had ever seen, and that I'd like to know you better."

Ayla laughed uproariously at that. "I would have eaten you alive, but not until after I'd had my way with you. As cruel as it sounds, I would not have given you a chance. Pardon my upbringing, but I would have never *allowed* myself to fall in love with a human—instead, I had to be tricked."

"I know half-elves aren't looked kindly upon," Flowridia said, purposefully putting it lightly. "I suppose their parents wouldn't be either."

Ayla shook her head. "Forgive me, but I do not know that you can fathom the scandal of it. Imagine a man came to you and claimed he had fallen deeply in love with his cow and that they were expecting a child. A little revolting, is it not?"

It stung, but Flowridia buried that. "Am I your prized cow, then?"

"Do not even jest," Ayla replied, her frown almost amusing. "You are my Flowra, and you are perfection—from your little round ears to your vastly denser bone structure."

Flowridia laughed, for it was so unbearably Ayla. "My denser bones?"

"Elven bones are more hollow, similar to birds." Ayla sat up tall, studying the macabre arrangement of corpses. "Start sealing it together, would you? It needs something more, but I do not wish to risk ruining anything."

Flowridia agreed, settling into sealing the arrangement of flesh into a single entity. At Ayla's behest, she began at the bottom as her vampiric love sifted through the piles of bodies. The creature, when complete, looked to be around ten feet tall, a macabre monster on normal legs but supporting a massive, bloated torso. Two heads waited at the top, half-rotted and twisted in their eternal scream, but Flowridia was desensitized to death and found sealing the unnatural blending of flesh increasingly simple to do. "These aren't all from the same cemetery, right?"

"Oh, no," Ayla replied, knee-deep in corpses. "I gathered them from all over Solvira. I would not dare poach from Nox'Karthan cemeteries, given they are legally property of Casvir. But if you ever want me to find more exotic corpses, I think it would lead to some incredible artistry."

"I won't stop you."

"Regarding what you said," Ayla mused, idly gazing upon their collection of corpses, "it is strange to think upon how many lovers I have kept, how many people I've had. I never liked them. I kept them for convenience, fucked them to gain what I needed. Would it . . ." Ayla visibly wrestled with her words; Flowridia paused in her work and waited. "Would it be strange to admit how rarely I found them actually desirable? I would go through cycles of having an insatiable itching for lust, but even then I found them boring to look at, no matter how skilled they were in bed."

"Did you ever find any of them desirable?"

"Well, most notably—you. I find you truly breathtaking, my darling. And I am not saying that to appease you. I found you objectively pretty when we met, but annoyingly beautiful the longer I spent trying to break your heart. You were like a puppy—the more you kept sniffing around, the more I became attached."

Flowridia chuckled, despite the errant reminder of their difficult past.

Yet . . . things *were* different now. Truly. For all the pain their history had brought, she was happy to be here now, elbows-deep in corpses, listening to that same love prattle on about her plans for them.

It was a lovely thought. Ayla had grown.

"I would lie constantly to stroke egos," Ayla continued, her musing truly contemplative, her voice distant and lost, "but besides you, I suppose there was one, but that was during my mortal life, so it is far swept away."

Flowridia instinctively knew it—surely the minstrel. Sarai Fireborn.

"It needs more heads," Ayla muttered. "A De'Sindai head would look brilliant with those horns, but I shall have to make do for the night."

Flowridia kept her focus on the task at hand, until Ayla approached, holding something small. "What about this head? I think it's a delicious bit of horror."

She looked up to face whatever gruesome madness Ayla had concocted—and froze.

For a brief and blinding moment, Flowridia stood not in a stone chamber but a moist, warm cottage, smelling of rot and mildew, facing a woman who screamed abuse, but not so loudly as the screeching baby boy, not so vividly as the visceral wrenching in her stomach when she had twisted the knife—

"Flowra?"

Ayla stood before her, worry etched into her face. She idly held an infant's corpse; it dangled by an arm.

Flowridia breathed but drew no breath. Her legs lost strength. Grasping the table with trembling hands, she slowly dropped to the ground. Oh, the world had turned so cold, and all her mind could do was replay his scream, over and over and over . . .

"Flowra, what's wrong?"

She felt a touch on her shoulder, but Flowridia merely held herself, kneeling on the ground, bent over toward the floor. Pins and needles lacerated her hands and feet; she could feel nothing else. She saw nothing else, save blood behind her eyelids.

"Flowra, look at me."

She couldn't. She saw only his precious baby body, alive in her arms for mere minutes. How she loved him. How she adored him in those fleeting moments—

A hand touched her forehead. Flowridia gasped and fell backwards, breathing shallow and quick, but it was not Mother here to berate her. She faced Ayla Darkleaf, her betrothed and beloved, whose eyes spelled fright. "My darling, are you sick? You are cold as ice. Gods, your pupils are pinpricks."

From behind the shade of her hair, she saw the body idly laying on the floor, carelessly dropped. On hands and knees, shaking upon her numb limbs, she crawled to it, the first of her tears falling.

The baby was cold but bore no horrible gashes in his stomach. Rot had eaten his soft flesh, but that could be repaired, and she wasted no time in sealing his skin, repairing the tender bits of flesh. Oh, he was small, a newborn perhaps born dead, as small as the boy she wished had been, to save him a painful end. Cradled in her arms, he looked merely sleeping, his tiny fingers curled into fists, his tuft of hair as flawless as sunrise.

She stroked his cheeks, fingers brushing his long eyelashes. He was perfect, save for the teardrops marring his peaceful, eternal sleep.

Only then did she notice Ayla seated across from her. "Flowra, you are worrying me."

Flowridia took a breath, feeling air for the first time in minutes. She looked back to the baby, knowing she appeared as a madwoman, but she held him to her shoulder, embracing his small body in her arms. "I don't remember precisely what I told you of my mother," she whispered.

"Very few specifics," Ayla replied, concern in her wary gaze, "but enough to paint a picture of her abuse."

"She was pregnant for the final months of my stay." Flowridia shut her eyes, the body cold yet a healing balm as she stroked a soft line down his back. "And she was nearly kind. To watch her change as her body held this new child, and to hear her speak of it . . . It's difficult, because they're memories I cherish. I helped her as she labored. I was the very first to hold him. I cleaned him and soothed him when he wouldn't stop crying—" Her breath caught. Tears fell freely down her face, yet she felt calm. "I loved him so much."

Flowridia curled around the infant boy, her words foreign and peaceful. Never had she spoken them. Here, they flowed like a gentle stream. "But my mother couldn't stand to have birthed a boy child. She told me to get rid of him." In her hands, the baby was a comforting weight. When she opened her eyes, Ayla watched, hesitation in her gaze. "I had to kill him. I had to, because when I refused, she . . ." Her hands shook; she heard his wailing, and so she clung tight to the fragile baby in her arms, protective and firm. "She stabbed him. He was in pain. And I ended it."

Freed of the words, her limbs loosened. She brought the baby down from her shoulder, cradled once more against her breast. "I don't know what came over me. I'm sorry."

Ayla shook her head. "Strange things can well up awful memories, my love. I do not mind."

"His death was what pushed me to finally try and run away. That was when I coaxed Aura in and she . . ." Flowridia held the words in her mouth, then swallowed them back. She had said them once before to Ayla, and that was enough. "You know the story from there."

With the grace of all her thousand years, Ayla slid beside Flowridia and set her arms around her, holding her close. "Well, I know now to stop jesting of disposing children."

Flowridia laughed, though it was choking and pained. "I would appreciate it."

Ayla kissed her cheek, then lingered at her hair, stroking the thick locks. "You blame yourself, but the blood is on her hands. It's a cold and merciless world, but you gave him comfort during his short life, then provided the only kindness you could."

Flowridia curled into her embrace, still cradling the infant. "Thank you," she whispered, for there was little else to say.

"I think we should be done for the night," Ayla said. "You should bathe and sleep. Would you like to join me in placing the infant back in his tomb?"

Flowridia nodded. Ayla helped her to her feet, then led her to the shadows.

A somber mood lingered when Ayla brought her back to their room. Flowridia bathed alone, washing the residue of dirt and corpses from her body, careful to keep her hair tied up atop her head.

Despite the weighted admittance, she felt lighter.

When she emerged from the washroom, dressed in a nightgown, Ayla sat with her back to her upon the bed, facing an open window. Distant stars illuminated her silhouette, the faintest outline of silver around her. When Flowridia came to sit next to her, she kept her face to the window, contemplation on her sharp features. "I despise introspection," Ayla said softly, the quiet night whispering outside, "yet I would be blind to not see the sacrifice it is, for you to be with me."

Flowridia brought her arm around Ayla's shoulder, silent as she waited for more.

"Watching you with the baby reminded me of the life you'll never have." Her gaze fell to her hands, clasped in the other, their tension revealing her own. "You should have had it. You chose it. You deserve it. But fate intervened, and Empress Alauriel fell."

"I don't want—"

"But you could have." The words held finality. Ayla's jaw clenched, her gaze severe. Flowridia feared her nails would puncture her skin, but when she reached to softly touch her hands, their tension didn't change. "I hold no sorrow for her death, yet . . ." Her words trailed off as she stood up; Flowridia withdrew her embrace. Ayla reached into the shadow of the bedside table and withdrew a book.

Evandalin's Fire: The Tragedy that Defined a Nation lay embossed on the fine leather, and Flowridia gasped as she accepted it. When she opened the first page, there was Lunestra's writing, neat and unmistakable.

"After I ruined the copy you found, I went hunting for another," Ayla admitted. "I stole this from the Nox'Karthan Library. You deserve a piece of your progenitor, and truthfully . . ." Where a mortal might have sighed, Ayla remained perfectly still, resignation in her visage. ". . . none of it matters. I skimmed through it. It does not say my story, except the little pieces you found."

Flowridia hugged the book to her chest, a thousand questions brewing her in mind. She voiced only one. "Thank you. Though I fail to see what this has to do with Empress Alauriel."

"She wouldn't have destroyed a family memento, for one thing," Ayla said, bitterness staining the words. "And, well . . ." Acrimony marred her features, yet her posture slumped in defeat. ". . . watching you with that baby reminded me of the beautiful mortal life you will never have."

Oh, Ayla.

Flowridia set the book aside, sadness filling her for the guilt in her lover's heart, but Ayla continued. "More than that, Lunestra would not have died were you betrothed to her. You would be in proper standing with your family in Staelash with no need for lies and consider yourself worthy of your family name."

"Flowridia Darkleaf was the name I dreamt of for all of your death," Flowridia said, standing to embrace her. Ayla reciprocated, the softness of her demeanor startling. "It's the one I want."

When they parted, they kissed, but when Flowridia sought to escalate their touch, to show Ayla with her body that her love was sincere, Ayla pulled away, lingering a moment before approaching the window.

Beyond, the silver moon waxed, their wedding day looming. Ayla remained tense, her words said in bitterness. "I sincerely don't know who my mother and father were. Likely, I was a bastard born to a servant raped by her master, given to the temple for the hope of a better life. It was a far too common story in that era. Yes, I was abused in the cathedral. I learned to set broken bones at a young age, learned to clean cuts and wrap them so they would not bleed—you'd be beaten more if you stained your clothing or bedsheets. We were told it was a penance to the goddess for our sins, even if that sin were as benign as spilling oatmeal. A few of the children were violently preyed upon, but thankfully I was too ugly for that. I kept to myself, kept in the shadows, but even that was not enough. I was beaten half to death more than once, but though I could not seem to die, I saw others who did. No one cared for orphans. We were a list of names and nothing more."

In silence, Flowridia wrapped her arms around Ayla. The woman fit so well in her embrace, tiny in every dimension. Weaponized, her body, a dexterous knife capable of beauty in her macabre art. But here she felt so small. As a child, Ayla would have been so much smaller. Flowridia shed a tear for that, for the precious elven girl who became a weapon, too sharp to touch.

"That is everything the book will tell you about me," Ayla said, leaning back into the touch, gently clutching her arms, "yet it is only the prologue of my story. Even those hateful bits about Eva ... It means nothing. She twisted my mind, but I think I have mostly cast her out—even if I still cringe to think of that damned pet name. *Little dove.*"

When she said nothing more, Flowridia kissed her hair. "You owe me nothing, my love. You don't have to tell me."

"I trust you, Flowra," Ayla said. "But it's hard. The first person I might have trusted enough to speak plainly too ..." Her grip on Flowridia tightened; were she wearing shorter sleeves, Ayla's nails would have punctured her skin. "Well, I did not marry Sarai Fireborn, as much as I desperately wanted to, so it is a foregone conclusion that it did not end well."

Tragedy laced her tone. Flowridia wondered, but she did not press.

"But you are not her," Ayla said idly, her hold finally relaxing, "and I am not Empress Alauriel. They were both our hopes for righteous lives, but fate intervened—" Ayla's voice caught. Silence settled as she looked out into the beyond.

When she spoke again, she was calm. "Though for my part, I have never known why. And I think it is why I am gutted to this day. I reflected, for a time, on why I was so defensive when you pressed me for my history, why I panicked and nearly hurt Demitri. Because it does not matter. I am not ashamed. But I am terrified to bear my whole heart to another person—even to you. I love you so much and have told you things no other lover has known, but still I hoard my secrets behind iron walls."

Flowridia kissed her hair, her pointed ear, reveling in the coolness of her skin. "Like I said," Flowridia whispered, "you don't have to tell me anything. My love isn't predicated upon knowing every detail of your life."

"You have shown time and time again in your own vulnerability that you trust me." Ayla twisted in her arms, facing her. Exhaustion shone in her eyes, the silver overtaking the cerulean color. "You have given your power to me with no strings, offered every piece of your heart. Yet for all my insistence that I love you, I have never offered that same power in return. Let me, please." She blinked heavier this time, the barest hints of mist clouding the brilliant colors. "I'm trying hard to love, and I do. I am learning what it means to be in love. It hurts because it's new, like . . . like working a new muscle, or learning a dance. I am left sore but elated, and I know you are the cause. For centuries I have guarded my heart, but I want to be open to you. I want to be your equal— and isn't that so strange? It is to me." Her smile held joy, even as a tear fell from her eye. "I am afraid but excited to think it will only make me love you more, to tell. As I said, I am learning. My history is a knife—and you'll have the power to stab me, if you choose." The joy in her smile faded, her eyes shutting as more tears fell.

Flowridia gently tilted her chin up to face her, their eyes meeting, though Ayla's expelled quiet tears. "I will cherish anything you give me and keep it secret and safe."

Ayla fell forward into the crook of her neck, content to hide, until she finally whispered, "Yes, I burned the cathedral down. I was fourteen. I killed Eva at Izthuni's behest and drew his sigils in her blood. I sought only to burn the body, but instead the entire cathedral erupted in flame. I think it was his doing. I merely facilitated the act. Which is not to say I regret it; I do not know that I've ever experienced a more brilliant catharsis than watching it burn."

"So Izthuni spoke to you, even then?" Flowridia asked, and when Ayla pulled back, she feared she had misspoken.

Instead, Ayla sat on the open window frame, perched like a bird. Her thumbnail idly scratched at her opposite wrist, the repetitive motions sure to break the skin. "Burning the cathedral is the end of the chapter. It begins when I was very young. Despite my proclivity to hide, or perhaps because of it, I was often thrown into the basement as a punishment. You spend enough time in darkness, and it becomes a part of you. It was salvation in a way; when it was dark, I was safe. The priestesses were afraid of what lurked in shadow. I must have been only five when I began seeing eyes staring back. Time was elusive. But I screamed at them, then begged. I asked them to take me."

As Flowridia had feared, Ayla's thumbnail slowly scratched a deep hole into her wrist—first revealing raw skin, then veins and finally bone. Her stomach churned, but she forced herself to listen, knowing the moment was fleeting and rare. "That was my first time in Sha'Demoni. I savored my freedom from the totalitarian temple. The demons played with me, let me chase them, chased me back. Unfortunately, we drew attention. The presence of a mortal caused a stir. That was when Izthuni came—"

"Wait," Flowridia said, holding up a hand as she went to the nearby bookshelf. In the dark, she perused the books as well as she could, until she found *A Dictionary of Magical Terminology*. Boring and innocuous, the book wouldn't be missed. She returned to Ayla's side and carefully sat herself on the ledge, then opened the book and tore out a page from the middle. She ripped the page in twain and stuck her hand out beyond the window, letting the papers flutter out into the darkness. Then she offered the book forward. "Tear at this instead. Please don't hurt yourself."

Contrite, Ayla accepted, the wound on her wrist already sealing shut. She tore the paper as demonstrated, ripping it into tiny bits, letting them fall as rain. "Izthuni is an evil god," she whispered, "no doubt about that. But even he would not kill an innocent child in cold blood. He told me to go home and never return, saying Sha'Demoni was a dangerous place for a child. Of course, I begged for him to let me stay. I barely knew how to speak, but he bade me to and granted me the speech of Demoni. He asked why.

"I told him they hurt me. That they beat me, burned me. I told him I prayed for Sol Kareena to bring me my family, my mother, but that she did not listen. He laughed and dropped me back into the darkness of my home. From then on, though, I was never alone. He was always whispering—told me to paint Sol Kareena's symbols in blood upon her altar, to sacrifice birds in her honor." Ayla paused in tearing apart the book, a small pile of paper disappearing into the dark like snowfall. "I would find the prettiest ones I could. Sol Kareena loves birds. I would cut out their hearts, select the loveliest of the lot, and leave it on her altar. The rest I kept for me, though it always wounded me when they would rot away. She never answered, though, and the clergy only beat me more. I was labelled as difficult, considered a freak."

With care to not interrupt her, Flowridia reached to rip out a piece of paper as well, joining her in tearing it apart. Ayla's smile spoke of solidarity, and Flowridia knew she had done right. At the pause, Flowridia said, "When I was young, I would tear petals off flowers to show to Aura. Not quite the same, but she reprimanded me for it, saying they were lovelier alive than dead."

"We had very different mentors, you and I," Ayla said, the gravity of it never truer. Her hands paused in their idle tearing, falling instead upon the open book. "When I was eight, the public became aware of the treatment of us orphans when one of the younger priests quietly gathered evidence of abuse to present to the archbishop. The high priest of the cathedral was stripped of his vestments, along with several of his lessers. High Priestess Evandalin was sent to us." She resumed tearing the paper, her tone increasingly monotone, void of attachment. "You know where the story goes. I loved her; we all did. When I tried placing bird hearts on the altar, she did not reprimand me; she simply listened and taught me to pray and keep the voice in my head away. She let me sleep in her bed when he spoke during the dark nights. Soon enough, Izthuni vanished. I was free . . ."

Ayla suddenly tore the book down the middle, through the leather seam, her nails puncturing the thick stacks of paper. "She saved my life in a literal way yet left me to flounder all the same."

Half the book fell from her lap, collapsing onto the floor. Flowridia tentatively stood up and came close, then knelt beside the agitated woman, who very purposefully didn't face her. "She made the choice," Flowridia whispered, reaching up to steal her hand. She clasped Ayla's forearm; Ayla did the same to hers, though she would not face her. Her gaze remained fixated upon the stars and the sky. "She could save you because she had power over you; she made the choice to corrupt it."

Ayla's thumb tenderly caressed her skin, and from below, Flowridia watched the subtle trembling of her jaw. Still, when she spoke, it was smooth. "She told me it was love, even though it made me sick inside. But I loved her; I would have done anything to please her, and knowing I was her favorite filled me with pride." When Ayla withdrew her hand, Flowridia reluctantly released her, standing instead as Ayla said, "Gods, my mind was warped. But I was her little dove; she carved me open and plucked out my heart."

Ayla resumed tearing the paper; Flowridia stood beside her and caressed her hair, offering comfort through the dark locks. "I outgrew Eva in time," Ayla said, utterly monotone, her vibrant eyes misted though they shed no tears. "At fourteen, I finally left the tenuous bounds of childhood—bled my monthlies, grew tits, all those garish female things—and she grew bored of me. Tried to send me off to an apprenticeship—shattering my heart, of course—and found a new little girl to groom and charm." Ayla smiled, vindictive and cruel. "I cried under the altar. It had been my favorite hiding spot as a child. But in the darkness, I heard that familiar voice. He mocked my tears, laughed at my pain, reprimanded me for leaving him. Sol Kareena abandoned me, but he had never left. He offered to help, then said words I shall never forget: *'Become the greater monster.'*"

Ayla stared, calm and cold in her fury, save the barest trembling in her hands. She twitched incessantly, and Flowridia forced herself to merely listen. "When she came back, I attacked her. Choked her with my bare hands. It was gratifying, watching the veins in her eyes pop."

"And then you burned the body," Flowridia said, understanding now, the dramatic ending to the first chapter of Ayla's life.

"I burned it. The cathedral was collateral damage. It seems they thought I died." She made a show of tearing a page down the center, then crumpling it with her hand. Once she had thrown it outside, she watched it fall, her keen eyes surely able to see much better than Flowridia's. "I set sail across the sea, for Zauleen. I stowed away on a ship, nearly starved to death but was never discovered. I was used to darkness. Meanwhile, I practiced returning to the Shadow Realm. I saw the cracks between worlds as clear as the lines on my palm, came to know them instinctively. Izthuni followed, whispering wherever I went—even to Ku'Shya's dreaded kingdom, though he sent only a shadow of himself.

"But in Falar'Sol, the Sun Elven Homeland, I moved on from birds to larger creatures at his behest, and finally to travelers in the woods, sometimes lost children. He taught me every secret of the world—how to pick them apart, how to skin them, make them into something new and beautiful. You likely find that abhorrent, and I suppose it was, but I did not feel for them. I did not feel anything at all. I simply ... *was*. Which meant I travelled often, lest I was caught. I was something of a legend, a monster in the woods, a warning to children to say in their beds. And all was well, until one of my victims was Mereen Fireborn's husband."

A strange thing happened, then. Ayla's posture relaxed as she reclined against the side of the window frame. She released the book. And she ... smiled. Softly yes, barely perceptive, but it was genuine and sweet. "I lived in the woods outside Sune. Sarai came to live with Mereen, to help care for her son. But she would often walk through the woods—just walk. And sing. I heard her one day, and I had never, and still never have, heard anything more beautiful. It was pure silk, pure light, an absolute joy. I thought I might cut out her throat and try to make it play at my whim. But then I saw her." Ayla looked down at her hands, settled into her lap. Her smile remained, and Flowridia felt discomfort. "She was as beautiful as her voice, and when I introduced myself, she was just as charming."

Flowridia struggled to explain the sudden lump in her throat. Her discomfort at seeing Ayla's enamor to speak of Sarai stung, and her jealous self wished to know everything about her—did she look like Mereen, with her perfect body and smile? Why did she write her song at all? What were the words?

If Sarai stepped out of the woods right now, would Ayla go with her instead?

She released Ayla's hair when the woman silenced. Instead, she sat across from her again, watching Ayla's smile turn from joy to cynicism. "No one had ever loved me as purely as she," Ayla said, and Flowridia's bitter heart softened when she saw fresh tears in her eyes. Ayla's words struggled to escape her lips. Flowridia sensed the dam threatening to burst, but she knew it had to, even as tears seeped through the façade holding back an ocean. "She saw me immediately as a broken person and sought only to build me up. She sang little songs to make me smile, bid me to eat, to sleep, even taught me to dance. I loved her. I would have left my whole life behind for her and become someone new—"

Ayla's voice cut off. She blinked, her tears falling faster as she turned away. Her fists clenched when she tried in vain to stop them. A quiet sob escaped her throat.

Flowridia ran to her, held her when Ayla clung to her, still seated, her face pressed to her stomach. With care, fearing she'd fall, Flowridia coaxed her off the window and to the floor, where Ayla wept, sobs tearing from her throat. Flowridia had seen such anguish on her betrothed only once before— when she had revealed her horrible crimes all those months ago and conveyed her apology.

Amidst her cries, Ayla's gasping words were simply, *"I'm sorry,"* and Flowridia gently shushed her, heart aching. Somewhere between her love for Sarai and her slaughter of hundreds of thousands was soul-wrenching pain. Flowridia did not know what it meant, much less what to say, and so she merely held her, even as her cries finally stilled.

"I'm sorry," Ayla whispered again, and Flowridia clung tighter, shaking her head.

"Gods know I've cried enough to you. It's all right."

Ayla had grown quiet. Defeated. "It was my birthday," she said, the unleashed flood now run barren and dry, "and I had asked her to write me a song. Instead, she told me she loved me. She held me, she kissed me, and she asked me if I trusted her. She told me to close my eyes."

Dread filled Flowridia's stomach.

"She stabbed a knife through my chest—" Ayla bit back something, perhaps what might have been a sob had she anything left inside her. "And I don't know why."

Coldness filled the room, the lingering silence as heavy a burden as Flowridia had ever felt. The defining moment of Ayla's existence, the stubborn hate that had caused her to fiercely cling to life and twist into a monster—not hate at all.

Love. Brutalized, twisted love, an abused girl who clung to kindness like a starved prisoner to food. Flowridia understood. This was what broke her. This was what fueled her. And this was what she spent nearly seventeen hundred years chasing and destroying.

And this was what Flowridia, unknowing and innocent, had tried to heal.

When Ayla spoke again, her voice raspy and worn, it took all Flowridia's focus to decipher that nigh inaudible whisper. "And as my soul lay suspended between life and death, I heard her singing. The words spoke of heartbreak, of regret, but it was what I had craved—a song for my legacy. In the darkness, another voice broke through the duet of soprano and harp—my one constant for decades."

Ayla's paled face glistened with tears, shined droplets of rain upon a marble statue. "Izthuni, God of Shadows, whispered in my ear. *Become the greater monster.*

"My body twisted, transformed by his power and by my own stubborn will. I clawed my way out of my coffin, and out of my grave, Sarai's song echoing through my head all the way."

Flowridia kissed her hair, heart heavy from grief, as Ayla said, "I decimated the entire village she had come from, turned them into vampires, and burned them alive. Mereen was among those that escaped, unfortunately . . ." Ayla's eyes fluttered shut, serene despite her awful words. "Sarai wasn't there. I never found her, never saw her again."

Ayla's hand came to rest on Flowridia's chest, at the neckline of her dress where she gripped for comfort. Flowridia's hand came to rest upon it, coaxing a sad, slight smile to Ayla's lips. "The books will have told you the rest. There are no secrets there. I look upon so many of my accomplishments with pride, yet I cannot deny how empty I was, and so the victories feel hollow, even now. When mindless murder no longer appeased me, I became calculated and creative, and when loneliness overwhelmed me, I returned to the world, climbing the social and political ladders of the time. Always seeking feeling, because I would so quickly become desensitized to anything I grasped. And that is so . . . sad. So abysmally sad. And then, of course, Mereen finally locked me in that damned box."

Ayla fell silent a moment, yet a small smile slowly spread and became something beautiful. "There is a quiet sort of joy that comes from sitting in your embrace. For all the grandeur of my former life, this peace was what I wanted all along."

Flowridia kissed her scalp again, lingering as Ayla turned to meet her lips. Tears stained her tongue, tasting of salt and sorrow.

A rare spark of light shone in Ayla's glistening eyes. The smile at her lip twisted, conveying unequivocal joy. "Understand the weight of my words when I say it was worth it, if only to have you by my side." Ayla's hand came up to cup her cheek, cold hands stroking soft lines along Flowridia's jaw. "To be your wife is a fate I would not trade for anything. Flowra, I love you. And I'm so happy."

When Ayla touched her, Flowridia succumbed, her heart raw and craving comfort—and Ayla's did as well, it seemed. She removed her dress, helped Ayla throw aside her own, and they clung to the other, their bodies intertwining, content to house the other.

They made love in the purest sense, each glowing kiss a tender affirmation. As one, they moved within each other before the celestial lights beyond, their touch as deep as soul.

They could clash as violently as a hurricane, fight as fiercely as wolves. But by every god—Flowridia loved her so and knew, from that beautiful, tender glint in Ayla's eye, she was loved in return.

Their hearts beat as one that night. Flowridia felt peace amidst the storm.

Chapter 23

In a realm of endless nighttime, Etolié couldn't say how long Khastra slept—only that Etolié slept three different times. She didn't know how long that translated upon the realm she called home. She didn't care.

She and Staella sat on the couch one day, giggling over something Clarence Vors had said twenty years ago—the most boring man in the world left more than a few zingers to his legacy—when footsteps from the hallway interrupted their happiness. Etolié perked up, heart soaring when Khastra stumbled out and leaned against the wall, visibly disoriented. "Good morning, Beefcake."

Khastra rubbed her eyes, visibly processing the scene before her. At least she'd had the good sense to wrap her naked self in the blanket. "Goddess Staella?"

"Hello, Khastra," Staella replied, standing from her perch on the arm of the couch. "Etolié brought you here, and it was a good thing she did."

Khastra looked as groggy as the morning after a late-night drinking marathon and spoke about as coherently. "How are you doing that?"

"Listen," Etolié replied, "given the volume of nasty I puked up, my limited capacity for teleportation isn't something I *tell* people about. I've also only done it twice in my life, and a few days ago was one of them."

The other had been thirty-four years ago. Consequentially, she only knew how to teleport to and from one place—Momma's house.

"How are you feeling?" Staella asked, but when she came close, Khastra held out an arm.

"Well enough to know I smell very bad."

"You're covered in some nasty stuff," Etolié helpfully added. "I'll get you into a bath if you would like."

Khastra grimaced. "I do not mean to be rude."

"You are not rude in the slightest," Staella said, her smile endlessly kind. "While you bathe, I will go to Vanir Sol and see if I might find something for you to wear. You're a rather unique size."

"I would prefer to not be naked and will not argue, but know that I appreciate you."

Staella smiled. Etolié grabbed Khastra's hand—unprepared for her cold and clammy touch—and escorted her out. "You've never mentioned you were so friendly with my momma," she muttered, once they were out of earshot.

"I met with your mother many times during my years in Solvira."

When Etolié looked back, Khastra had the frown of *'I'm being needlessly attacked and you know it, Etolié'*—which was greatly exacerbated by the fact that she had no eyebrows. "For over twenty years, I refrained from bringing up your mother because any mention of her has only wounded you," Khastra whispered, sparing a glance to where Staella had vanished. "Please do not be angry with for me for this. I did what I thought was right."

Etolié stole a breath, then released it, defeated. "You're right. I'm sorry."

Khastra squeezed her hand. "But you two have reconciled?"

Etolié looked at their intertwined fingers, a smile spreading across her face. "I think we have," she said, unprepared for the joy that came with those words.

"I will hear whatever you will tell me."

"I don't even know where to start, Beefcake."

Within the hollow center of the home, illuminated by lamps and the stars high above, were several separate alcoves, each with their own purpose—a place to sleep, to read, and more.

One room was to bathe, though it looked more like a pond. Etolié told her story while Khastra let her blanket drop, speaking of what Staella had done to save her life as Khastra inspected her blood-covered, naked self—until the half-demon's hands suddenly flew to her head. Etolié's voice faded as Khastra glossed her fingers across her smooth scalp.

Anger darkened Khastra's visage—enough that Etolié nervously grinned and said, "My mom couldn't, uh, fix that. Good thing there're plenty of hairdressing sorcerers in Solvira!"

Her good humor faded as Khastra glared into the pond's reflection. "Soliel has done a great dishonor to me," the half-demon seethed.

"We could probably draw on your eyebrows in the meantime."

"Etolié, please stop trying to make this better."

Khastra very rarely snapped at anyone, much less Etolié. She shut her lips and quietly watched her beefcake run her fingers across the juncture of her horns and smooth skin. Call it panic or ingenuity—or perhaps a mix—but Etolié willed a silent spell, and the illusion of braided lavender hair flowed down to her digitigrade knees once more.

Khastra frowned at her, but it lacked any true anger— merely minor annoyance. "Thank you, but until I scalp him on the battlefield, it will have to stay as is."

"Why? Is this a Sha'Demoni thing?"

"It is cultural to the elves, actually. Though not in the last . . ." Khastra's lips became a line, a certain wonder in her furrowed brow. ". . . several thousand years."

"I think that means you're off the hook."

Khastra entered the tub, uncharacteristically petulant as she scrubbed grime from her arms. "I will consider it."

The half-demon paused in her washing, her hand lingering where her heart now was. Disbelief widened her eyes, and then her breath caught.

The half-demon revealed nothing in her face, yet Etolié sensed her agitation. "Do you still feel Imperator First and Last inside your head?"

"I do," Khastra said, and Etolié's vain hope dissipated. "But we are so far away, it is like trying to hear a single raindrop in a storm."

Resisting the urge to tease her over that fancy-ass metaphor, Etolié instead resumed the tale of her time with Staella, perching herself at the side of the pond-like tub as Khastra washed herself.

When they emerged, Etolié gathered up her towels, then conjured illusionary clothing for Khastra.

Holding Khastra's hand was a wonderful sensation, even with this new, almost clammy cold radiating from it.

Always had been, innocent and endearing and probably a manifestation of her mommy issues, but Etolié wasn't going to ruin something lovely by overthinking.

Still, it was a short-lived joy—as soon as she heard her mother's voice, she released Khastra's hand and beckoned instead, praying she understood.

Momma was singing, and when Etolié peered into the front room, she saw her glowing figure in the kitchen, standing before a large pot, alternating between leisurely chopping the creepy tentacle meat and stirring. There was magic in the words, but Etolié suspected it was less *'poison whoever consumes this draught'* and more *'may this bring joy and also not be over-spiced.'*

In her happier moments, Staella had always been practical.

Staella turned from her chopping, visibly amused as she surveyed Khastra up and down. "There are some garments your size on the bed, but I won't be offended if you don't need them after all."

"Oh, those aren't real," Etolié said. "Illusion magic."

Staella, to her credit, accepted that with no question.

"I will return shortly," Khastra said, and when she had gone a few steps down the hallway, Etolié took a tiny swipe of her hands.

Khastra's clothing vanished. The half-demon promptly turned and frowned, but Etolié merely winked and mouthed the word, *"Nice."*

Khastra chuckled as she disappeared behind the door.

As Etolié stepped into the small kitchen, she realized how vastly dominated with food the space had become. Angels didn't need to eat much, their diet consisting predominantly of light, but the Celestial populace significantly outweighed the pure-blooded angels and so space for food was commonplace. Staella actively chopped what Etolié assumed was a Demoni plant, all while a large cauldron simmered with some sort of soup.

"As far as I recall," Staella said softly, her attention on her chopping block, "Khastra eats a little more than the average person."

"Yes, to put it lightly."

Etolié recalled that Khastra hadn't eaten since she'd un-Bringer of War-ed and understood why Momma had brought home a small mountain of food.

But a terrible thought came with it. "Momma, with Khastra being fully undead, I don't know that she can eat."

"Oh," Staella said, though not with any ire. "Well, at least she can smell it, right? I think it smells lovely. Relaxing, even."

Etolié agreed, appreciating the savory aroma as sat at the small table, having been chastised before for offering to help in the kitchen. Khastra returned, wearing a dress woven from a thick fabric, decorated in embroidered designs, with two decently high slits up the sides to accommodate her digitigrade knees. "This is lovely, Staella. Thank you."

Staella beamed from her place before the stew. "Etolié brought up the understandable issue of your undead appetite, or lack thereof as the case may be. So, while you're more than invited to eat, please don't worry about offending me if it will hurt you."

With a scowl, Khastra placed a hand on what Etolié knew was a chiseled abdomen. "It seems the changes to my physique have affected my appetite. Strange, to not be hungry. I think I will only eat a little. Thank you. For everything." Khastra, polite and classy, picked at her food, genuinely smiling at the strange tentacle meat as the conversation commenced.

"You're too cute, demon-spawn," Etolié said. Khastra struggled to swallow, and Etolié wondered how a rubbery tentacle actually *felt* going down your throat and resisted the urge to grimace.

As she lifted her spoon, the hint of a suckered tentacle peeked from the broth. With a glance to Staella, whose attention remained on the cauldron, she placed it back, careful to only get broth.

A knock sounded at the door. They all turned to stare.

The voice was as familiar as Etolié's own. *"Staella?"*

Tenor and masculine and unquestionably despondent, Eionei stood on the other side. Etolié looked to Staella, who already carefully set her tools aside. "I'll take care of it," she said pleasantly, but Etolié watched the faint twitch of her smile.

A miracle occurred; Staella managed to open the front door just enough to whisk herself out, then shut it before the figure beyond could peer inside.

Clever. Etolié opted to follow, quiet as she placed her ear against the door.

"... no sign of her, Staella." Eionei sounded heartbroken, and Etolié realized who he was referring to. *"They found a burned satchel, and gems, and that giant, bloody hammer in the middle of a charred forest."*

Oh shit. The bag. The bag once holding an orb. Etolié winced, for this confirmed her worst fears, and shoved that dilemma in a box for her future self to handle.

Momma spoke. *"Don't lose hope, Eionei. Etolié is too clever to have gotten herself killed. Perhaps she's hidden herself."*

"I just don't know what I'd do if ... if ..." Etolié swore she heard stifled tears, and she might've pitied him were she not still contemplating his murder.

Momma, it seemed, was a better actress. *"Fear not. I haven't given up hope, and you shouldn't either."*

There was silence for a time; Etolié suspected they were hugging. But the next words prickled the hair on her neck. *"Why ... Why does it smell like soup?"*

"Stress eating. I made soup."

"You don't ..." His voice trailed off, and Etolié was mightily concerned with whatever his rather sharp mind was contemplating. *"I-Is she here?"*

"Eionei—"

Etolié managed to stumble back just in time to not be slammed by the door.

There he was, his glowing form clearly distraught. He said nothing—merely bombarded Etolié with his body, stealing her into a hug. Her skin prickled, but it was grandpa; she hugged him tight. "Hi, Grandpa."

"Etolié, all of Celestière has been ..." His grip tightened, and it was sweet—protective, maybe, but that was just the polite way of saying 'possessive.'

Etolié tried to pull away, but Eionei kept his hold even as she turned enough to follow his gaze, unsurprised to see him staring daggers at Khastra, who politely smiled. "Eionei. Good to see you."

Staella suddenly stood between Eionei and the half-demon he'd happily leave for dead between worlds. "Eionei, don't. She's here as my guest."

Eionei shook his head, his stare fixed on Khastra. In his grasp, Etolié bristled, anger steeling her jaw. "You know she can't be here, Staella."

"For what crime? For following the orders of the man who owns her mind? She means no harm here. In fact, she saved Etolié's life." Momma didn't actually know that—they'd spoken little of the City of Light—but it seemed she thought better on her feet than Etolié would have given her credit for.

The words managed to steer his hateful gaze away from Etolié's demon. "One saved life doesn't justify the slaughter of thousands. She destroyed the City of Light. Sol Kareena is bedridden because of her actions."

"I suppose you're right," Staella replied pleasantly. "Sometimes cruel men force us to do things against our will, but it's still our fault, and the consequences are ours."

As Eionei sputtered something about how, *'It's not the same, Staella,'* Etolié realized she'd never considered it that way, that Khastra had been violated mentally and bodily—by every god, she thought of Khastra's new heart and her silence, her pain and her secrets, and suddenly her tears before Sol Kareena's statue bore a new and impossible weight.

"Celestière is in crisis, Staella, but you would cast them aside for her?"

"Someone has to stand up for her—"

"You'll be demonized if they know she's here—"

"Listen, *grandpa!*" Etolié said, and with a furious shove she escaped his embrace. "This is Momma's house, and she can make her own *fucking decisions!* Maybe if you pulled that self-righteous stick out of your ass, you'd see you don't fucking know what's best for everyone!"

Eionei looked kinda startled, to his gods-damned credit. "Starshine—"

"I was there, you self-righteous bastard scum! I saw people *die!* A child was nearly torn from my arms and *murdered* because a monster decreed it so, but listen mother*fucker,* because Khastra risked her life to try and save us! She recognized me when we were holed up in the tunnels, and she tore the fucking walls down to protect us from the undead, so don't you fucking spout any bullshit about her lack of sincerity! If Casvir knew that, he'd fucking disassemble her and break her brain—and then, guess what? *She'd still work for him!*"

Furious tears streamed down Etolié's face, but she'd be damned before she stopped, because the resident asshole called Eionei had the audacity to give a reply. "If she truly cared, she'd have had her brain broken before she led the undead to destroy the City of Light! Defend her all you want, but she chose the selfish route—"

"Are you *kidding me!* Listen, you homewrecker, she's a fucking *hero,* and if you could look past your old-fashioned, racist bullshit, you'd see it. What if it were me? Would you disown me because I was an undead slave to the imperator?"

"It's different—"

"It's not different, you gods damned, cunt-licking bastard! So the fuck what if her mother is a demon goddess? My friend Khastra has more honor in her dainty-ass goat hooves than you've ever had in your entire *life* you deep-throating cock-sheath—"

"Friend?!" Eionei yelled, a challenge in his furious word. "Funny, that's an awfully loose term to give someone you've been fucking."

The words stole Etolié's retort, so shocking they were. "I—"

"Clever of her—"

Oh, shit. The hickey.

"—to twist your misguided affection for her right before she murdered—"

There really couldn't have been anyone else who gave her that, damn.

"—an entire city's worth of people. Starshine, you have a clever brain but a tender heart when it comes to monsters—"

"Fuck you!" she cried, because *oh, that was a fucking word, that bastard—* "Call her whatever the fuck you want, because that's what fucked your precious Starshine. And I keep coming back for more, so take your gods-damned bigotry somewhere else. Your little angel is a demon-fucker, and you can't fucking stop her, you meddling asshole. Why? Because she has a life. She has a life! She has a life she'd like to fill with demon fucking and *visiting her mother every once in a while!"*

Ah, so she was gonna have this chat. Eionei only blinked.

"How fucking *dare* you lie to my momma and me! Who in Onias' Hell do you think you are, keeping us away from each other?! She's my mother, and I thought for *thirty-four fucking years* that she *hated me* only to find that she's been waiting for me to come home, and what kind of *sick fuck* would have the audacity to keep a momma from her baby, hmm? *Tell me!"*

The bastard was apparently stunned into silence; again, he just sorta blinked.

Fresh rage filled her. *"Listen—!"*

"Etolié," came a gentle voice, and though her fury wasn't tempered, Staella's careful touch on her arm did interrupt her tirade. Etolié remembered there was world outside her small bubble of rage, and she saw Staella looking kind, then glanced back and saw Khastra, whose glowing eyes had widened in horror.

Staella kept her touch, defensive as she placed herself between her and Eionei. "Eionei, you should go."

This forced Eionei's slippery tongue. "S-Staella, you—"

"I'm standing by my daughter and her beloved, Eionei. Leave."

Eionei stumbled back, betrayal in his features as he spared Etolié a final look.

Something severed between them, a nasty little word called *trust*. "I'll talk to you when I'm ready," Etolié spat, hoping the poetic justice wounded him as much as thirty-four years without a mom.

Eionei said nothing; he simply nodded and left.

Beside her, Staella gave a slight squeeze to her hand before leaving.

And to her surprise, Staella stopped beside Khastra, upon whom she gazed with tenderness. Stark shame shadowed the half-demon's countenance—shame Etolié didn't understand, because Khastra was stoic and proud. "For over twenty years," Staella began gently, "I've been hearing Eionei rant and rage about your friendship with my daughter, and I want you to know that I simply laughed through it all. I thank you, from the bottom of my heart, for caring for her."

Relief was painful as it washed over Etolié, leaving her limbs tingling and her head light. Khastra's smile held warmth as she faced Staella. "Thank you."

"No, I should be thanking you. I know you'll treat her well, and there's no greater relief than that for a mother."

Etolié wiped her angry tears from her face, her momma's words healing Eionei's scars. When Staella smiled at her, Etolié said, "I'm sorry I didn't tell you."

"From the sound of it, you hadn't told anyone," Staella replied, returning to Etolié's side. "I'll talk to Eionei. Your grandfather is set in his ways, but he loves you, and he may never love Khastra, but he will accept it as truth, in time."

"I thought you were gonna poison his tea."

Staella laughed, and Etolié loved it so, though she had so few memories of the comforting sound—now, however, she could make new ones. "I will do nothing to stop you from receiving the vindication of an apology."

Etolié's regular, non-angry tears fell now. "Thanks." When Momma grabbed her hand, Etolié pulled her into a hug. "I wanted to tell you, but it's so new, and you and I are also new, and I didn't know if you'd accept us."

Staella held her tight, conveying the comfort Etolié had craved for all those lonely years. "Etolié, Khastra is a good woman. All that matters to me is that you're treated with kindness and love."

"I know, but she's half-demon, and I'm a Celestial."

"That's not forbidden."

"Yes, but it's not exactly normal. And her momma's an elf-eating demonic god, and you would never."

"No, I would never eat an elf," Staella replied, and Etolié nearly laughed at how nonchalantly she said it, "but she considers us friends, so I consider us friends too."

Etolié groaned. "And let us not forget the uncomfortable fact that Khastra's, you know . . . your age."

"Khastra's a few years younger," Staella said, mischief twisting her smile—probably because 'a few' was literal. "But Ilune always loved much older women too. I'm very used to the idea."

Staella laughed and pulled away, something downright conspiratorial in the wink she offered Khastra—who had clearly overheard, judging by the flat line of her lips.

But despite Etolié's awkward inner world, Staella kissed her cheek and prattled on about benign and lovely things.

Chapter 24

The gentle sunrise filtered through the window, stirring Flowridia from her rest. Beside her, Ayla looked asleep for how serenely she lay, her body even warm from the bed. In the quiet peace, Flowridia admired the porcelain perfection of her skin, each individual eyelash, lush and dark. Vampirism warped one's appearance, perfecting what already was, but Flowridia wondered at the shortness of her natural hair, the severity of her cheekbones. Her ribs showed sharply above and below her breasts, highlighting years of starvation and stunted growth. Ayla was so small, far littler than any grown elf Flowridia had met, as few as they were. How lonely and fragile had she been, when Sarai plunged the knife?

Now she held slight curves, ineffable allure from her unholy existence. She was not beautiful, but her poise and grace were perfection, her confidence utterly enthralling, and Flowridia found her unbearably attractive. Still, Flowridia wondered if she could have loved the strange woman in the woods the way Sarai had.

Would she have killed Ayla as coldly? What did Ayla not see, to have loved someone who would so cruelly murder her? Ayla claimed Sarai was kind and good, had uplifted and loved her, but Flowridia hated her—her apparent charm and beauty, her voice, her betrayal. All of it. It broke Flowridia's heart anew to consider it, to consider everything, and she curled around her still lover, knowing she did not truly sleep.

Ayla responded by clinging tight and slowly batting her eyes, heaviness lingering behind them. "Good morning, Flowra."

"How are you?"

Ayla slid her hand up into Flowridia's hair, caressing her scalp as she tangled her fingers within the thick locks. "I feel tender," she whispered. "Very raw."

Flowridia kissed her hair, content to hold her a little longer. "I'm so proud of you, Ayla."

"Proud?"

"Growth always hurts, my love. You were scared, but you trusted me. It's an honor to hold your secrets, and I swear to keep them safe."

"I have always felt safe with you." Ayla's tender smile was precious beyond compare, and Flowridia realized she would burn the world to preserve it. How strange, to see Ayla as someone to protect. "Does the world await? Or can I keep you here a moment longer?"

"I'll hold you as long as you need it. Today can simply be for us."

Ayla's ensuing groan held her usual dramatics. "No, it cannot. We have refugees to discuss. We have monsters to invent. I think a vacation would take more planning than a wedding."

"Then may I simply offer my company? Aftercare for something like this won't end overnight, and that's all right. I don't want to leave you alone."

Ayla truly did have a lovely smile, in her soft moments. Her small lips remained shy in her quiet joy. "Even now my pride wants me to reject you and call you a fool." Instead, she melted further into the touch, their bare skin sealing them as one. "But my heart is so full, Flowra."

At those vulnerable words, Flowridia simply kissed her hair and let her linger.

"If I may make an observation," Ayla whispered, innocently held to Flowridia naked chest, "you've ceased talking in your sleep. Are you having fewer nightmares?"

Flowridia pondered that, wondering when it had last been. "I suppose I am."

Surprising, considering the guilt she carried. But perhaps she had grown and healed in other ways.

When they did finally part, the sun had shifted, and they helped the other to dress, cherishing each passing touch between them. Morning meetings awaited, a looming threat to tear apart their blissful peace, but Flowridia's heart overflowed with love.

To hold Ayla's secrets, her hurts and shattered dreams, to protect them and ease her love's burden . . . Something new and beautiful had come to bind them, their standing with the other finally leveled.

Ayla owed her nothing, but Ayla trusted her with no reserve, and that was worth more than the world.

Still, the world did not seem content to mirror their sanctuary of peace. In the council chamber, High Priestess Jules had infuriating words.

"More refugees are the last thing this kingdom needs."

Flowridia bristled at the statement, her anger spiking enough to actually speak. "How can you say that? We have more than enough resources to feed and house them, and when they're back on their feet, they will pledge and become citizens. This is an investment as much as a good deed."

"But at what cost to our current populace? This rise of monsters and vampires and vigilantes cannot be dismissed, and the coincidence of their timing doesn't require much wisdom to see. The cathedral fire makes me worry that some may even be bitter toward their goddess. She has become quiet in her grief, and even I have become concerned. However, that doesn't change the reality we're facing."

Her logic was sound, even if Flowridia knew for a fact there was no correlation. "And we should punish an entire country of innocent people because a few vampires decided to take advantage of a situation?"

"I'm saying we care for the ones already here and redirect any new ones. Solvira has done more than enough."

"Where? Where will we send them? To Moratham? To Tholheim? Neither would accept them."

"Lady Flowridia, I know it sounds callused, but sometimes it takes a callused heart to see the greater good. There is a monster hiding somewhere in this kingdom—can we even protect them? We cannot protect ourselves."

"Now, now, Jules," Lara chided, her smile disarmingly pleasant, "my intended's wisdom is not to be idly disregarded."

"I am in no way disregarding her," Jules replied, her simmering offence palpable. "But I worry she's affected by the archbishop's death. We all watched the two bond and become close, and while her death is a tragedy, unquestionably, it doesn't mean it's an insult to her memory to think of Solvira first." She looked severely to Flowridia, but with a weighted sigh her expression softened. "I understand you're mourning, but this cannot impair your judgement. If you are going to assist in ruling this country, you must be loyal to Solvira above all."

Flowridia grit her jaw, angry to know Jules was likely correct. But she had come here for one purpose, one reason—to protect the people she'd failed to save. Her people. Her blood.

"I cannot stand idly by and allow it any longer," Jules continued, "and if you continue down this path, Lara, I will have no choice but to speak out against it. My people deserve to know where I stand."

Lara stood; Flowridia's stomach knotted. "Really?" Lara said, her quiet fury utterly unlike the late empress. "This is the hill you would die on?"

"It is," Jules said, her glower returning. "And while I'm at it, I must say how deeply disappointed I have been with your behavior surrounding your intended."

The mood shifted, and even General Irons watched with minor appall. Reginal tugged nervously at his beard. "Jules, Lady Flowridia may be inexperienced, but I find her outside viewpoint refreshing."

"That is entirely beside my point," Jules replied, and then her attention returned to Lara. Flowridia bristled in her chair; Jules acted as though she wasn't even there, couldn't hear every toxic word. "Lara, since your engagement, you have become unreasonable, combative even, when it comes to matters pertaining to your intended. Love often blinds people, but you are the ruler of one of the largest kingdoms on this realm. Your actions have consequences that dictate whether people live or die—but lately I feel as though Lady Flowridia is the empress and you are the parrot who echoes her naïve words."

Silence settled a moment, the atmosphere choking, so heavy it had become. Flowridia bit her tongue, offended but waiting to see what course her beloved took. Lara forced a smile, though obviously fake, and coolly said, "Meeting adjourned. No decisions will be made today."

No one objected. Lara helped Flowridia to rise, then swept her out of the room.

She said nothing at all, until they reached a private room. Lara locked the door and dropped her illusion, revealing Ayla instead. "Oh, that she had died when I tore out her throat."

Flowridia took her hand and stroked tender lines across it. "She is becoming a problem."

"I have not ruled out crushing her skull, but that would be suspicious after her performance." A guttural growl echoed deep within Ayla's throat, her predatory instincts manifest. "I know you swore to stay by my side all day, but I need a quest. I need to get out of this castle and breathe. Metaphorically."

"I won't be offended. I'm just worried for you."

"Do not be. Or do. But I have been thinking on something and wish to test my theory. I swear to return before tonight. If the castle panics, so be it."

Flowridia kissed her soundly, feeling her tension and curtailed rage. "Go. I'll take care of things."

"You are incredibly understanding."

"I also don't want Jules to die without considering the fallout first."

Ayla's wicked chuckle stirred excitement in Flowridia's heart and body both. "Be safe. There's a monster afoot."

After a wink, she disappeared into a shadow.

Flowridia stood still a moment, contemplating what to do with her free day.

She didn't often think of the wedding details—ruling a kingdom took up far more time. But it would come in less than two weeks.

Ayla would surely have a wedding present.

Flowridia thought a moment who to ask, who might know the town well enough to help her in procuring the gift she had in mind, then went off to find General Irons.

Surely he knew something of specialty knives.

"Good evening, my love."

Well after sunset, Flowridia sat in their room with tea and a book, content to spend her time in silence. But at Ayla's appearance and her entrancing gaze, relief filled her. "Hello, Ayla."

Ayla held a large book, and her saunter, though alluring, was curtailed by her thoughtful expression. "I would like to propose something."

"Go on."

"I know you said you were done trying to emulate the God of Death—and I fully respect that, I do—but I may have actually found the answer to why it did not work." Ayla held out a large book, written in a language Flowridia did not know. "Would it bring you closure to know?"

In her quiet moments, Flowridia still felt the moment of death, the disconnect in Lunestra's brain and her body slumping. Still, the truth was said to set you free. "I think it would."

"I found it strange," Ayla said, perching on the arm of the chair, "that every single book on Solviran history had removed any mention of Goddess Ilune. I even snuck into Nox'Kartha's library while you were sleeping one night to look for it—again, nothing. But my most recent adventure was actually to Moratham; if someone were censoring Solviran literature, they would not have access to the libraries in Moratham, at least in theory. I was right. I stole a book, and it has potentially paid off." She placed the open book into Flowridia's waiting arms, revealing lines and lines of unfamiliar characters. "I am not quite so fluent in Morathan as I am in Solviran or most other languages, but I am passable. This book speaks of the ancient rivalry between Moratham and Solvira—and while that feud has quelled since the Moon Goddess' death, the history remains." Her sharp nail skimmed the lines, until she stopped at one. *"We speak in whispers of the Living Death, bestowed by the melding of Necros and Flame*—from here it elaborates, essentially saying it is not necromancy nor pure Silver Fire, but both. The God of Death wielded both and so could blend them together."

"All along, it was futile," Flowridia said, despondent at the words. "Lunestra died for nothing."

"Lunestra's death is unquestionably a tragedy, but do not hate yourself for this. You did not know. No one did." Ayla kissed the top of her head, but Flowridia stared at the unfamiliar words, finding clarity within her tumultuous inner world.

Tears welled in her eyes to think of Lunestra, her sole link to her family, the condemnation in her final gaze. But she swallowed that, something new rising to fill the void her anguish left. "I don't wield Silver Fire, and you don't wield necromancy. But it isn't unheard of for witches to work together in spellcasting. I wonder..." She met Ayla's stare, unashamed of her watery eyes. "I wonder if this is something we could do together and find the same results."

Contemplation stole Ayla's attention. Her sharp features softened as her gaze became distant. "We could try. Are you willing?"

Perhaps Lunestra's death did not have to be in vain, but a tragic stepping stone. Perhaps their quest for Solvira's future did not have to be thrown away. "Yes," she said, resolve brewing. "I think it would be a better use of my grief."

"I will find you a whole volley of wicked men and women to practice on," Ayla said, her words tender despite their evil intent. "Set tomorrow night aside for practice."

Their lips met, the innocence soothing after the sorrow of the past few days. When Ayla slipped into a shadow, Flowridia was left alone to consider it all and wondered how guilty she should feel.

Wicked actions could be done for good intentions. Solvira would flourish. The refugees would be safer.

All would be well.

The next night, Flowridia stood within a dungeon of depravity and death.

The people chained to the wall came from every species—mostly human, but a few De'Sindai and one half-giant, men and women both. Most were gagged, though a few cried freely; some merely stared.

"I perused records," Ayla cooed beside her, her sensuous grin reminiscent of a snake, "and found debauchery among the wealthy, absolved of crimes because of money and influence. The murderers, the rapists, the pedophiles—those who spit upon those they deem lesser. Trivial, to kidnap them from their beds."

They were all dressed well, sure signs of finery on their persons despite their nightclothes. "These people haven't gone quietly in the night," Flowridia whispered. "News of kidnappings are spreading. The commonfolk are starting to be scared."

"They will stop, once they realize the monster's pattern. Those with no crimes—or even petty crimes—need not fear. We've already seen a significant decrease in thefts since distributing food."

Flowridia approached one man, gagged and chained to the wall. The rich fabric of his nightgown bespoke wealth. Recognition shone in his eyes—the whole world knew her, it seemed.

Rather, they thought they did. As she met the man's gaze, he knew her better than any who walked the realm, save Ayla herself. "Who is this man?"

"His name is Silas," Ayla replied, because of course she would remember every detail; Flowridia counted on it, "and while he presents the very picture of civility in public, a hefty sum of money was donated by his estate to the family of a peasant girl in exchange for her silence—and the forfeiture of rights to the child she carried, conceived in a drunken rape."

Any guilt Flowridia might've felt for what she intended to do faded away. Perhaps what she would do was not even enough. "Hold my hand," she muttered, and Ayla obeyed.

She recalled the union of their powers, the magnetic pull between them, and felt it anew as Ayla's fire rose in her hands, melding with the cloud of purple from hers. Necromancy had been born with Ilune, the magics two sides of a coin—one created, held the capacity to touch souls and pull them from bodies; the other with the capacity to kill, to pull souls from the void and place them back into their corpses.

It was nearly bliss, yet verged into the realm of too much, too stimulating. When she met Ayla's gaze, she saw the feeling reflected, the idyllic adoration only intimacy wrought. "What does necromancy feel like, to you?" Flowridia asked, forgetting the man and his crimes, forgetting their macabre bearings—there was only Ayla and the fire cast across her visage.

"Soothing. But somehow invigorating."

She longed to kiss Ayla, to steal the intrigue from her lips, but elsewhere the man groaned, plunging her back into the present. "All right. As discussed."

"As discussed," Ayla affirmed, and they placed their hands—the ones not clasped together—upon the man's head.

Flowridia could not speak for Ayla, but she was immediately flooded by the inner workings of the man's physiology, felt the intricate pieces of his musculature, the pulse of his blood, but most importantly his mind, separated by a thin veil of bone and flesh. Necromancy consumed life; Silver Fire consumed magic. The delicacy of his brain was familiar. Every victim had held the same fragility, the gentle line between life and death requiring only the faintest breeze to push one over the edge.

Yet, with the melding of magic came further awareness, and Flowridia grasped not flesh nor spirit, but the invisible space in between.

The victim slumped against the wall. Flowridia gasped and pulled back, releasing Ayla as her magic dissipated. "Did . . . Did it work?"

He appeared among the dead, but Ayla held a hand to his neck. "I do not know, but he has a pulse."

When the man stirred, Ayla gracefully took her hand away. He did not struggle, merely stared vacantly, a strange emptiness in his eyes.

Ayla stared curiously upon him. "What is your name?"

The man spoke frankly. "Silas."

"You will refer to me as 'my lady,'" Ayla replied curtly. "Answer again—what is your name?"

"Silas, my lady."

Speechless, Flowridia studied the pleasant twist in his lazy smile, even as Ayla whispered in her ear. "I want to know what more we can do. This man can never return, though I shall be certain to question him further and see what personality he still retains. But I would say we succeeded."

Flowridia managed to nod, breathless as she faced her great work. "This is incredible." Unquestionably so, though whether the apprehension within her would cause her to cheer or collapse and hyperventilate had yet to be decided.

"I have a few ideas for how to preserve a bit more personality," Ayla cooed, "if you would like to . . . *play* around with me. Honestly, Flowra, in a perfect world, we would take the time to perfect this skill, remove all risk of failure, but we do not live in that world, and I would like to know—what of High Priestess Jules?"

Flowridia frowned, though not because of Ayla. "You wish to test this on her?"

"Considering she's threatened to speak out against us if we don't change course? Yes, absolutely. And soon."

Flowridia thought of Jules, of her service to her kingdom—she was a good person, righteous by every definition. Deep down, Flowridia's soul sickened at the thought.

But at the cost of countless refugees? Jules stood so starkly in the way of helping worshippers of her own goddess. She valued Solvira above all, which was understandable, but the monster was Flowridia's creation—Jules did not understand.

"The greater good demands it," Flowridia muttered, "even if I find it distasteful."

Excitement glinted in Ayla's eye, even as Silver Flame engulfed her arm.

Flowridia's power rose and seeped from her pores. But instead of grasp her hand, she cupped Ayla's cheek and kissed her soundly. Their magics melded, the Silver Fire licking harmlessly against her skin, even as it caused the hair to rise from her arms. Wherever Flowridia touched, Ayla responded with quiet moans, the dark magic apparently quite appealing. "We should practice," Flowridia whispered, though her body yearned for something a little more intimate.

Ayla lightly bit her lip, evoking a gasp from Flowridia. "We should, yes. But after . . ." Her grin bore wicked intent, her pupils expanding to fill her vibrant eyes. ". . . I want to feel that power *deep* inside me. Understood?"

Flowridia's blush surely dominated her face. "Understood."

"I have never romanced a necromancer before you," Ayla said, her hands wandering to Flowridia's bodice, shameless as she skimmed across her clothed breasts. "Such an oversight."

"I'd never romanced anyone before you," Flowridia offered in return, and Ayla laughed and held her hand instead.

And despite the macabre atmosphere, the rank smell and palpable fear, laughter and joy remained between them.

Flowridia slept late, awoken by a sun already risen. Demitri lay on the floor beside her, which meant Ayla had gone—and to punctuate that was a note written in elegant script—a script that was unnervingly *not* Ayla's, even if they were her words. Ayla's artistry extended to penmanship, and thus her ability to perfectly mimic the late empress:

Darling, I have meetings to attend, but you looked so peaceful and calm. I could not bear to wake you.
Find me. I miss you all the time.
-Lara

Simply 'Lara,' free of titles and damning surnames. Flowridia's gut clenched as she tucked the note away.

Little reminders of her crime remained, perhaps forever so—journals written by Lara, tucked into the bookshelves, trinkets that were her taste and style, instead of Ayla's. That damned bouquet—too suspicious to move—remained a stain. Perhaps Flowridia was a masochist, determined to punish herself.

But as she dressed and made sense of her auburn locks, a knock sounded, causing Demitri to lift his head. *Smells like smoke. It means it's Thalmus.*

Flowridia said, *"Just a moment!"* and finished putting on her gown, adjusting the bodice just so. Apparently Solviran fashion had finally stolen her heart; she was actually content to show her collar bones lately, even give the mildest suggestion that she had breasts, and wondered if it were another sign of adulthood—to love her changing body, instead of hide it.

Perhaps it came from having someone to cherish it. Ayla always made her feel beautiful.

When she opened the door, Thalmus smiled kindly; she couldn't help but match it. "Good morning. I hope I didn't wake you."

"You didn't."

"Empress Alauriel said you hadn't come out. Emotions have been running high, and I wished to make certain you were well."

Touched, Flowridia took his hand and led him along, the childish gesture familiar and beloved. He had to duck through doorways, but otherwise fit perfectly well in the expansive castle. "We had a late night," Flowridia said, "and Lara was kind enough to let me sleep. I'm well; I promise."

"I'm glad, truly. I would rather err on the side of caution and be wrong." He squeezed her hand as they approached the lift, but neither moved to release the other. "I shall worry for you when I leave. I think tomorrow is the day; there is still no sign of Etolié, and Staelash does need maintenance."

"But you'll be back for my wedding, right?" Flowridia asked, and she winked for she knew the answer.

His smile bespoke simpler times, of days spent in silence watching him work—whether it be at his kiln or his office. "I wouldn't miss it, even if I will miss you."

"You'll still see me." Flowridia leaned her head against his arm. "Solvira is a portal away."

"Yes, but while you'll always be my little flower girl, you aren't a girl anymore."

The words were said in kindness, but Flowridia felt their bittersweet weight. "Thalmus, I don't know if I've ever met anyone more sincerely kind and thoughtful than you. I spat at you once that you weren't my father, but the truth is . . ." Her heart swelled to consider it. ". . . you chose to be my father, all the same. And I'm blessed for that."

A tender mood settled as the lift stopped at the first floor. They might've hugged, but an approaching voice said, "Flowra! Good morning!"

Lara approached, accompanied by High Priestess Jules.

Flowridia blushed at the light kiss on her cheek. "Good morning."

"Flowra, I was just speaking to Jules. We have made peace, she and I."

Jules nodded sagely. "Our disagreements still stand, but I think we've at least explained ourselves calmly."

"But, Flowra, darling, you wanted to speak to her as well, didn't you?" Lara batted her lashes cutely, but there was a certain intensity in her eyes. "I think now is as good a time as any to speak in private."

Flowridia nodded, her mind still catching up to what she was agreeing to. "Of course, yes." She released Thalmus, offering a grin before turning her attention to Jules. "I would like to speak."

Lara quickly escorted them to an empty room, and Flowridia finally realized the ploy. Nerves prickled against her skin; cold flooded her limbs.

What would it mean, if they failed?

In a private sitting room, Lara discretely locked the door behind them. The illusion of the empress remained, but her smile twisted cruelly as Jules politely sat upon a chair. "Jules, before we begin, I should warn you—if you scream, I will snap your neck."

Shock widened Jules' eyes. "I beg your—"

Quick as a whip, Lara appeared at her side, immediately wrapping her arm around Jules' neck. The high priestess didn't scream; instead, she struggled to breathe. "Flowra, won't you help?"

Fear flooded Jules' countenance as she struggled, but unholy strength bound her, far greater than any manufactured bonds. Golden light suddenly shone from her skin. Lara gasped and flinched—her skin burned, and Jules scrambled to rise—

Flowridia pushed her, the older woman's frail body falling back into the chair. Purple smoke rose from Flowridia's hand as she held it forward, near enough to Jules' face for it to reflect in her eyes. "Sit down," she commanded, and the words were hers, but the voice was a stranger in her ears. True fear fell upon Jules' visage, and she felt . . . *powerful.*

Lara's burning hand clasped hers, the perfect melding of Necros and Flame. Together they touched Jules' forehead.

It was as simple as rifling through parchment, and only a matter of finding the right one to tear apart.

The spell unleashed. Jules slumped forward.

Flowridia released Lara's hand and stumbled back, the adrenaline rush as uncomfortable as it was invigorating. Lara helped Jules sit up and placed a finger to her neck. How Flowridia loved that grin, filled with brutal triumph.

Jules' eyes opened, a certain vacancy shining through.

"High Priestess, look at me," Lara said, and Jules obeyed. "Tell me who you are?"

"Jules of Kent, High Priestess of Solvira."

She said it as sweet as pie, void of any personality.

"Who am I?" Lara cooed.

"Empress Alauriel Solviraes."

"Call me *Lara.* I have a few documents for you to sign. Won't you lend me your signature."

Jules agreed, that blank smile ever-present. As Lara withdrew the requested papers, Flowridia's stomach churned from the implications, from the thousands of ways this could go wrong.

If it all fell apart . . . well, the monster had attacked the castle before.

Jules' signature remained the same, so surely something remained of her, but Flowridia couldn't begin to fathom the long-term consequences of this spell.

"Sign there, and there . . ." Lara snatched the papers back, nothing of the late empress in that twisted grin. "Now be on your way. Be scarce. Sit in your room until dinner."

"Yes, Lara," Jules said, and as she rose, Flowridia assembled her own objections.

"Ayla, what about when she comes across Reginal, or another of her friends?"

Lara kept her gaze to Jules as she left, her triumphant pose never faltering. "I plan to keep an eye on her from the shadows. See how she acts and figure out how to counter it. Honestly, she may not be here much longer. Once she has served her short-term use, I shall have her announce an early retirement, then slit her throat that night. Or she can live out her days in the temple, if that would suit your sensitivities better. I'm honestly indifferent."

"I'll think on it," Flowridia said idly, her mind still dwelling on Jules' fear and then her glazed countenance. She looked at her hands, recalling the surge of *want* that came to watch Jules cower.

Something of it lingered, though muted behind the crushing waves of horror. "Ayla, could you be you a moment?"

Her love obeyed, and Ayla's form came to replace the empress'. "What is it, darling?"

"I . . ." Her stare remained on her hands, knowing a cloud of death waited at a mere thought, mere desire. "I don't know if we should do this again."

Ayla approached, a frown stealing her triumph as she took those offending hands in her own. "Why?"

"I enjoyed it," Flowridia whispered, the realization making her cold, yet the temptation remained to bask in her ever-increasing power. "I saw her fear and felt . . . *amazing.*"

"Entirely normal, I assure you."

"That's not what I meant. I told you once I was afraid of who I would become if I continued down the path of necromancy, and I fear this is who she is—someone who revels in taking someone's power away." Disappointment fell upon Ayla's features, and Flowridia's panic rose. "Ayla, I just—I don't mean—"

"No, no—Flowra, please don't . . ." She struggled with words, her subtle glower the worst punishment of all. "We have worked so hard. We are victorious, and now you don't want it? I don't understand."

"Am I a hypocrite if I say I'm afraid?"

"A little," Ayla replied, but her tone held no judgement. "Perhaps a lot. I am willing to put a hold on this and reconsider, but I will not lie and say I am not disappointed."

When Ayla tried to release her, Flowridia merely held tighter. "I don't want to disappoint you. I need time to wrap my head around all of this. Life is changing so quickly, and I don't know when I've last had a moment to breathe."

Ayla remained still, eventually withdrawing her touch; this time, Flowridia let her go. "I should go watch Jules," Ayla muttered. "Perhaps I will send a few disposable servants in to see what she does. If she can behave normally with direction, she can stay."

Flowridia watched Ayla go, her heart settling in her throat. Once alone, she sat upon the couch, uncertain of what to call the torrent of feelings within her. Sorrow, yes—to have hurt Ayla. Fear for herself. *Of* herself.

Wasn't this for the greater good though? Jules was a good person, yet she stood in the way of saving the lives Flowridia had committed herself to. Flowridia had only practiced on reprehensible folk. Most had lived.

What she and Ayla could create together was magnificent. She loved feeling so connected to her love.

A knock sounded. "Come in," she muttered softly, though it was apparently loud enough.

The knob twisted. "I saw Empress Alauriel leave," said Thalmus' voice. "Are you all right?"

"Ruling a kingdom is complicated." When she turned, he was familiar and warm, the legacy of a simpler time—when she was a child, when her world made sense, and when the strings of morality hadn't become so twisted. "But I think I'm done making decisions for today. Would you come to the garden with me? I'd like to enjoy your company while I can."

He agreed, of course. She stood by his side, and when the blissful sun embraced them outside, the crippling reality of the future fell upon her—that her wedding night would mean the end of these quiet times with Thalmus.

Once upon a time, he had said words doomed to haunt her future self: *When all is right in the natural world, the dead remain dead."*

When she turned, would he seek her death to right that world?

Instead of dwell, she swallowed her pain and grabbed his hand, speaking of simple things instead.

At dinner, Flowridia saw no sign of Lara or Jules.

Reginal and Irons rarely ate at the castle, except for lunch, understandably preferring to spend their morning and evening meals with their families—the exception being when Irons worked late, investigating with Flowridia. Jules was a wild card for attendance. She had no family but was often at the temple or in her room in the castle.

Instead, she ate with Thalmus—a guest and thus invited to join the royal family. A royal family of two today, and it made Flowridia miss the chaotic days in Staelash, where most of its royal employees lived in the manor and so were forced to mingle closer than they'd often prefer. But it had resulted in hilarity more often than contention—Marielle waxing poetic on Zorlaeus' latest visit while Etolié rolled her eyes, Meira speaking teachings of Sol Kareena with Sora echoing like a parrot, Thalmus sitting stoically beside her, also quiet, even Khastra who had only joined them sporadically—her time split between the council and her soldiers.

There was comfort in chaos. Flowridia sometimes missed it.

She bid Thalmus goodnight, unsure of what she would find when she returned to her room.

To her surprise, Lara found her in the hallway—accompanied with Jules.

"Lady Flowridia, what a pleasure to see you," the high priestess said, unnervingly friendly but perhaps only because Flowridia knew to be suspicious.

"Delightful to see you as well," Flowridia replied, though she looked warily at Lara—who simply smiled, the barest hints of victory twisting her lip. "What have you two been up to?"

"We have spent a wonderful day talking, haven't we, Jules," Lara said, impish and cruel. "Versing you in the ways of the world."

Flowridia didn't know what that meant, even more confused when Lara bid Jules to go off the bed. "What's going on?"

"I watched her a while, then decided her transformed mind simply needed some guidance. She'll be quieter, but she'll at least know she's supposed to laugh at Reginal's jokes and pleasantly agree to everything you and I say."

Flowridia glanced back to where Jules had disappeared, catching the final glimpse of her fluttering robes. "I don't know that I fully understand, but I trust you."

"I have taken care of everything, Flowra. I promise there is nothing to fear." Lara wrapped her arms around her, her countenance softening at the touch. "Darling, are you feeling better?"

"I don't know what I'm feeling," Flowridia admitted, "except that I'm worried we are fighting, and that's the last thing I want."

"We are not fighting. We are . . . *discussing*. There is an impasse between us. I figure, for my part, that if I am to convince you it's all right to move forward, I have to prove that I can care for what we have already done—hence, the reeducation of High Priestess Jules."

"It's more complicated than that, but I appreciate you taking responsibility. Can we be alone?"

Wordlessly, Lara led them to their shared room, their little haven of privacy in this political world. Lara shed her façade, leaving only Ayla Darkleaf. Again, she held them together, but there came a small bit urgency with it, a passion she never exhibited with her empress disguise. "What is wrong?"

"Nothing more than what I said before. I don't have anything to add to it. I simply fear."

"Fear what, my darling?"

Flowridia sighed, silent a moment before she chose instead to press their lips together.

Words were a difficult thing, but bodies spoke their own beautiful tongue—a language of impassioned moans and silent affirmations, of a thousand complicated feelings and a few simple truths. As Flowridia led her beloved to bed, she cherished the loving gaze she met, savored the lust in Ayla's eye as she shed her dress and underclothes. Whether they made love or fucked or something in between, Ayla looked at her as a goddess, touched her in every perfect way, and Flowridia quickly succumbed to her radiant presence.

Lost in their lovemaking, Flowridia forgot the world for a time, more entranced by the mouth on her breast, the touch deep inside. For a moment, Ayla was the universe.

To the world, her climax was a small moment, but here in their private domain, in this bed where they alone ruled, it shook the very foundations.

Once upon a time, she had stood at a crossroads. Flowridia didn't know when precisely she'd crossed it, when she'd chosen, what deed set her on her path or if it were the compilation of many.

But as she held Ayla, luxuriated in the aftermath of ecstasy, the truth settled as gently as a dove.

Once, she had feared becoming like her mother.

Now, she feared becoming herself.

In Celestière, Etolié remained in a pocket of peace—a peace now punctured by Khastra's awakening.

Etolié lingered, knowing she was wasting precious time. Soliel had four orbs now. It was only a matter of time before he found Mereen. Kitty really was their greatest hope.

This should bother her. The reality of it would hit the moment she touched back down in Solvira. But her momma was here, and there were thirty-four years to bridge, thirty-four years of loneliness and pain, of thinking she wasn't wanted.

All along, she had been loved. Her momma loved her.

It was unnerving, however, how easily Khastra and Staella fell into a rapport, if only because Etolié had been anticipating anything but. Intellectually, of course they'd known each other, but to see them laughing about jokes two millennia old was . . . weird.

Etolié fell into another nap, signifying that time still passed, even in this world of limitless night.

When she awoke, groggy and disoriented, she had been carried to bed—the bed once occupied by the half-demon corpse she adored, though cleaned of blood and ash. As she stumbled out, she quickly swiped through a number of dresses, trying to imagine one she hadn't worn here before.

Staella hadn't questioned where she got her extra clothes yet. Perhaps that was another conversation to breach soon.

Etolié shuffled down the hall and overheard the end of whatever Khastra and momma were discussing.

". . . generally live my life as though Ilune were dead, with all possible respect. It is easier that way."

"I understand," came Staella's mild retort. "Be all that as it may, I never stopped seeing you as a daughter, just as she'll also always be mine. It is strange to me, I will not lie, but I don't question your honor. I will become used to the idea, in time."

Etolié stopped at the word 'daughter' and illusioned her steps away, though she didn't dare peek in. Momma couldn't see through illusions, despite being able to cast them—that was a Silver Fire ability—but Khastra often saw through her, simply because she knew to look.

"I have never told Etolié about Ilune and I, but it would be best to now. Better she hears it from me, than stumbles upon it in a history book."

Frowning, Etolié crept closer, because everything about that statement was mildly alarming.

"If you'd like, I can try and gently breach it."

"No, it is best from me. If she is angry, I would rather it be at me than you. She will forgive me, in time, though if she decides it is too strange to be with me, I would understand."

Per usual, Etolié decided that thinking was overrated— and opted to open her mouth instead. "The fuck?"

Both Staella and Khastra looked properly shocked at her entrance. Momma recovered first, her smile characteristically sweet. "Starshine—"

"Are you insinuating that you *dated* my *half-sister?*"

Khastra didn't blush because she currently wasn't biologically capable of it, but the widening of her glowing eyes suggested she was mightily embarrassed. "Yes, Etolié. For many years."

Etolié frowned, uncertain of what to name this volatile blend of feelings inside her. "Is this a 'Daughters of Staella' fetish?"

"No, Etolié."

"Am I a consolation prize?"

"No."

"Do you ever think of her when we do the fuck thing?"

"Never."

"Do you still secretly love her?"

"I do not. That love has been dead for a long time."

Etolié looked at Staella, her frown remaining. "Ilune liked older women too, huh?"

Staella cringed, which she damn well deserved. "This is a strange situation, and I apologize if I made it worse."

"Joke's on you," Etolié replied, leaning back on her hip. "It's only strange if we make it strange."

Internally, she grinned at their ensuing surprise. This time, Khastra recovered first. "You are not angry?"

Etolié opened her mouth, but shut it just as quickly, accepting that this did deserve a thoughtful answer. She quickly ruminated, then said, "In twenty-four years of friendship, you never once brought her up." She held up a hand before Khastra could find an excuse for that. "Which tells me that you really, truly, don't equate us or compare us at all."

"I truly do not."

"Well, there you go." Etolié's frown faded, any lingering perturb vastly overshadowed by the gratification of their shock and discomfort. Joke truly was on them. "Look, it's weird. I'd prefer to continue not talking about it. But this would be a stupid reason to leave you, when you've done nothing but show that . . ." Even that bit of perturb finally left, replaced by something she couldn't name, but left her feeling misty-eyed. ". . . that you care about me, whether we're fucking or not."

Sure, she'd said 'fuck' twice in front of her mother, in context of it being a verb with Khastra, but Khastra's smile made that all right. Etolié stood behind the arm of the couch and hugged her.

"What's actually got me fucked up," Etolié continued, "is that duty calls, and we've already overstayed. Soliel might've burned the world down by now; I just don't know."

"Well, if the God of Order had succeeded, we would all be dead," Staella replied, oddly nonchalant for someone discussing the destruction of her world, but she did have a point. Her posture fell, however, and Etolié's heart bled at the sadness in her visage. "The world needs you more than I do."

A lump formed in Etolié's throat, tears rising to choke her. "Yes, but I need you more than I need the world."

When Staella stood, Etolié released Khastra and fell into her momma's arms. It wasn't goodbye—not forever—but after finally reuniting, she would have been happy to stay and replace the childhood she'd lost.

"You can always pray to reach me," Staella whispered, the gentle glow from her skin as soothing as a candle in the dark, "and when you want to come back, I'll bring you here. And I do mean *when,* Etolié. I know we have barriers to overcome. I know the damage I caused can't be undone overnight. But if you'll give me a chance, I want you here. I want to know the beautiful, grown woman I'm blessed to call my daughter."

Etolié's tears fell fast as she clung to her dearest momma, unprepared for the wash of pain. Within her, nasty voices still said she couldn't do this, that she wasn't worthy to be in Staella's arms.

The past could not be erased, nor could thirty-four years of longing, of thinking she wasn't loved. But that chapter was closed. Perhaps this one could be better. All Momma asked for was a chance to try.

"I'll miss you."

"Like I said, I'm only a prayer away."

When they parted, Staella cried as well.

A loud knock roused Flowridia from sleep. Claws pierced her arms as Ayla's protective hold tightened, the only sign her beloved predator had heard. Her head swam, her grip on Ayla mutually defensive, well worth the slight stinging across her skin.

But the knock pulled her groggy mind from sleep. Ayla's form shifted, but nothing changed in her touch, the illusion only surface deep. "You may enter," Lara's voice said, and an apologetic servant stood in the door.

"My apologies for the early hour," he said, "but Magister Etolié has returned. General Khastra of Nox'Kartha is with her."

Flowridia sat up at that, holding the blanket to her bare chest. "Where are they?"

"In the council chamber. Magister Etolié has insisted upon a meeting this instant. She claims to have news of the God of Order, among other things."

Though clearly annoyed, Lara did not radiate murder. "We will be there," the false empress said, and the servant left with a bow.

Ayla's form returned, and to Flowridia's surprise, she wrapped her arms around her naked body, sealing them together, skin on skin. "I am coming to despise the outside world," Ayla seethed. "Always interfering in our lives."

Flowridia kissed her, tried to leave, but the undead woman held her in a frozen embrace. "Ayla, love, we should go."

"I know, I know," Ayla replied, her unwillingness shown in her molasses pace. "Etolié awaits."

They dressed quickly, the time for finery after sunrise. Flowridia elected to let Demitri stay asleep, and so they went down to the council chambers alone, hand in hand.

Within, Jules wore what Flowridia suspected was a nightgown, whereas Reginal was dressed in his usual finery, though he appeared half asleep. But General Irons was wide awake, as was Etolié, who sat on the reflective table, looking not completely miserable for the first time in all Flowridia's days knowing her.

Flowridia's breath caught at Khastra's appearance, and she struggled to determine whether this was the sort of scenario in which to ignore her bald head and lack of eyebrows or mention it. Politics were complicated, but the half-demon stood against the wall, arms crossed, expression wary as she studied Jules. Then, her gaze shifted to Flowridia and Lara, narrowing onto Lara herself, a slight frown twisting her lip.

Which, given her lack of eyebrows, was excruciatingly frightening, even for the half-demon. Dread welled in Flowridia's stomach.

Whatever Khastra had noticed, Lara didn't, because her own stare settled onto Etolié. She glanced to Flowridia, then to Khastra and the council members, failing to hide her bafflement. But she smiled. "Hello, Etolié."

"Moonbeam, it's been one helluva time," Etolié said, apparently content to stay seated on the table. "I have a story, and I'm only telling it once, so sit down."

Flowridia sat beside Lara, joining in the awkward throng of people around the Celestial, still half bouncing on the table. "We found Soliel. Kicked his ass, actually. The coward disappeared with his undefined teleportation powers. But the interesting bit is that he has one fewer orb than we thought. Turns out, he's been preoccupied chasing down a woman who *stole* the green one."

A horrible trepidation filled Flowridia. Suspicions raised, she carefully asked, "Who?"

"A vampire named Mereen Fireborn," Etolié said, affirming Flowridia's worst fears. "Bitch couldn't talk for some reason, but she was keeping an orb away from Soliel. Helped us fight him. We were trying to strike a deal with her for the orb when, uh . . ." She looked to Khastra, her good mood falling slightly. "Imperator Casvir showed up."

The room fell into a hush at the name. Flowridia couldn't say if she felt relieved or not, but Lara's grip tightened by slow degrees.

"He came to collect his general," Etolié continued, gesturing to Khastra standing stoically by the wall, "and would have succeeded if Soliel hadn't come *back*. We didn't do as well in that fight. Khastra's hair is the most notable casualty, but she might've been gone for good if I hadn't done something stupid even for me . . ." Etolié shrugged, and Flowridia braced herself for news she wouldn't like. "I, uh, took us to Celestière to find professional help for Beefcake over there. The help ended up being none other than one of the founding goddesses of Solvira herself—Staella, Goddess of Stars. My momma."

Visible intrigue showed on everyone's faces, but especially Lara's—who had thankfully been informed that she worshipped this particular deity. "Really?"

"Really, really. She wants to be more involved with her kingdom. We'll discuss that at length some other time, Moonbeam."

"What about the vampire woman?" Flowridia asked.

Etolié shook her head. "We came straight here, unfortunately—" Her mouth shut abruptly, and she looked at Flowridia's hand, idly sitting on the table. "What the fuck is that?"

When Flowridia followed Etolié's stare, her eyes landed on the ring on her left hand. "Oh, you don't know."

Perturb flattened Etolié's mouth into a line as she looked at Lara. "The fuck is that?"

Lara's shy smile and blush said enough. She lifted her own left hand, revealing a rather gaudy piece. "It has been a whirlwind affair, but I have never felt more certain of anything in my life."

Flowridia genuinely couldn't say if Etolié were going to puke or burst into laughter. She glanced at Khastra and realized the half-demon still frowned.

"Well, that's wonderful!" Etolié said, a little too happy as she slid down from the table. She stood between their chairs and embraced them as well as she could. "When is the big day?"

"Eight more days," Lara said, practically sighing the phrase.

There was no mistaking this time that it was puke Etolié was holding in. She looked at Khastra. "How long were we gone?"

"Not very long, Etolié."

"Guess I need to get on finding a gift," she said, her ensuing giggle only a little forced. It abruptly stopped, however, as she returned to her spot on the table. "I presume Solvira is hosting."

"Of course," Lara replied.

Etolié stared at Lara, then Flowridia, then finally at Jules. "Well, we need to get the archbishop out of here." In the ensuing silence, Etolié's forced goodwill faded entirely. "What happened to Lunestra?"

"There was an attack on the castle, three nights ago," Reginal said, looking to Jules, her gaze vacant and pleasant. "Our own lovely high priestess was attacked. We don't have proof that it's what killed Archbishop Lunestra, but the correlation is suspicious."

Etolié grunted like she'd been punched in the stomach. She looked at Khastra, who met the startled gaze with sympathy, then managed a shaky breath, increasingly pale. "What?"

Irons quickly explained the situation—rumors of vampiric attacks, he and Flowridia's investigation, the fire, and finally the night of the attack. "What we saw," Irons said, "was unlike any vampire we'd ever seen. Lady Flowridia and I investigated the fire, but when we returned, we found Jules nearly dead and a woman who matched the description of one of the monsters we had been searching for. She attacked Lady Flowridia but was warded off by her magic."

Etolié peered over to Flowridia, who shied at the attention. "You burned it, didn't you."

Flowridia nodded.

"Poetic justice at its finest." To General Irons, Etolié said, "Please, go on."

"The vampire woman disappeared into a shadow. That was when we went to help Jules—"

"Hold on," Etolié said, staring at Irons as though he'd suddenly removed his clothing. "You said she disappeared into a shadow?"

Flowridia gripped the arm of her chair, internally crying, *no, no, no!*

Irons offered a nod. "I had never seen anything like it."

"We have," Etolié said curtly, gesturing to Khastra. "And so has Flowers."

Flowridia shook her head. "Etolié, it wasn't— It couldn't have been—"

"What did she look like? Did she say anything?"

Flowridia said nothing, but Irons had an answer. "Her face was stained with blood, but she was unnaturally strong for someone so small. Dark hair. Bone thin." He stopped and looked at Flowridia. "She did speak to you, didn't she?"

Flowridia stammered, "I-I barely remember, to be quite honest—"

"She said you were 'gorgeous,' I believe was the word. And didn't she ask for a kiss the night the beast came to the town square?"

Etolié's face lost all amusement. What else could Flowridia do but play stupid? "Etolié, it can't be. We watched her die."

Etolié pointed to Khastra.

"Etolié—"

"I watched Casvir get flattened like a pancake, but he seems to be doing fine."

Reginal interrupted, curiosity in his words. "What are you insinuating?"

Khastra spoke, darker than usual. "The tiny one has a dead lover who matches that description."

Lara's words were tentative, broken. "You mean Ayla Darkleaf?"

"I absolutely mean Ayla Darkleaf," Etolié replied, her knuckles white from clutching her dress. "And if it is, she's taunting you." She looked to Irons. "Tell me about this 'beast.'"

"There was a gigantic shadow monster. It seemed to be some sort of demon. Lady Flowridia warded it off with holy light." Etolié looked like she would scream, but he looked to Flowridia, who felt she might suffocate; the walls steadily closed in. "Who is Ayla Darkleaf?"

Flowridia answered, her voice barely a squeak. "As Khastra said, she was someone I used to love. She was a vampire, or something like it. And she had the ability to step into Sha'Demoni at will. But she's dead. Sol Kareena came and personally ended her. There's no way that—"

"Flowers," Etolié said, her voice deathly serious, "I know this is difficult to swallow, but we can't discount what this looks like."

"Does this correlate at all with the symbol written on the church?" Irons asked. "The Endless Night?"

Etolié threw up her arms. "By Eionei's Asshole, Flowers—you're a real piece of work!"

"It can't be," Flowridia said, praying her denial could sway their minds. If they knew Ayla lived, all would be suspect. Their carefully constructed castle of glass would be cracked, certain to shatter.

"Flowra—"

Flowridia looked up, surprised to see Lara standing beside her, expression as soft as her silver eyes.

"Flowra, my love," Lara said gently, and she stood and knelt beside her. "Etolié is right. We cannot simply dismiss this out of hand. The investigation will continue, but perhaps it would be best if you stepped back from it."

"But Lara—"

"And I *swear* to you, Flowra," Lara implored, her words laced with sincerity, "you will be kept safe. Our wedding will be filled with people willing to give their lives for you. There is nothing Ayla can do to hurt you."

Flowridia's breath caught. In tandem with anguish came simmering anger. "You are very naïve if you think this can't hurt me."

Lara took no bait, instead lifting Flowridia's tense hand from her chair and holding it with her own. "All will be well, Flowra."

But Flowridia stole it back, then scooted her chair away from the crescent moon table. "I need a minute alone, please."

No one stopped her, much to her surprise. Etolié's gaze followed, but she cast it aside. Even if the Celestial suspected, there was no crime to pin her to.

The door shut behind her. Flowridia ran.

Frustrated tears fell before she reached the room upstairs. She quickly found her prize, her beloved wolf who lounged on his room.

Flowridia collapsed into Demitri's side, the enormous wolf rolling over to smother her in affection. *What happened? Why are you crying?*

"They know," she whispered. "General Irons told Etolié of the vampire who could walk through shadow, and she knew. *She knew.*"

How much does she know?

"Only that Ayla is possibly alive and taunting me. But I don't know what to do."

Demitri nuzzled against her cheek. *Talk to Lady Ayla. She always has a plan.*

"Her plans created this mess. I fear what she'll do to fix it."

Coarse fur rubbed against her body as Demitri shifted to engulf her in his warmth. *True. But you also know Lara will do anything to protect you from the monster, including kill Lady Ayla.*

But would she? Ayla's pride seemed to only grow. "We'll see, Demitri."

Restless, she bid him to follow her outside. Gardening always brought comfort.

"I would like to adjourn this meeting," Lara said, and Etolié noticed her tense posture, the way her hands fidgeted behind her back. "We've discussed what we need to, and ... well ..." She smiled, but Etolié saw no joy in the gesture. "I worry for my intended."

Etolié said nothing, instead taking a long sip from her flask as the room cleared out, praying sobriety left her soon. The grating ambience of the mortal realm slowly enclosed her skull, radiating white noise and pain.

First Jules left, then Irons and Reginal, but when Lara tried to leave, Etolié placed a hand on her forearm. "Wait a moment, will you? There's something we should discuss."

Lara lingered in the doorframe. "Etolié, I am concerned for Flowra."

"As am I," Etolié said, "but sit a moment. If Flowers hasn't been stolen already, I don't think Ayla will strike now. Not in broad daylight."

Lara obeyed, frowning as she sat beside Etolié. "What is it?"

"I know you're worried and understandably so." Etolié savored another drink of the noxious liquid in her flask, then offered it to Khastra, who accepted. "If I may be so bold as to say it, Flowers was always weak for Ayla."

Lara's frown remained, twisting into something uglier than Etolié had ever seen on the empress. "What is your point?"

"Between you and me, if confronted by Ayla Darkleaf alone, I genuinely don't know what she would do. And that isn't to say I don't think the world of Flowers, but I don't think she ever fully healed from Ayla's death or her abuse."

"Again, your point?" Lara's expression darkened, opaque in its worry.

"Have a heart to heart. That, or I will. But if she's reacting this strongly to the idea of Ayla still being alive, we need to puncture that boil, so to speak."

"I will speak with her," Lara said, but Etolié grabbed her hand when she tried to leave.

Poor thing was cold, clammy even, and Etolié worried. "Listen, I love you. I don't want you to worry." She slid from the table and embraced her tiny moonbeam, who only barely reached her shoulder. "Take it easy, but try not to be alone too often. That dominatrix bitch doesn't have to care about Flowers to want to keep her as a pet, and I don't doubt she'd flay you alive in front of her just for fun."

"I do not doubt that at all," Lara said, her expression unreadable, and Etolié worried to imagine what she knew. Lara was theoretically Flowers' confidant now; hopefully it had come up.

"Let me take over for her on this investigation bullshit. It isn't safe for her, but I do, in fact, have Auntie Kareena in my arsenal as a final resort." She frowned, all the details of this new world still falling into place. "I wonder if Momma could do anything."

"While you think about that, I have plenty else to think about."

Lara left without a goodbye.

Etolié collapsed into the nearest chair. "Khastra, this is very bad. First small, pale, and sneaky is back and now those idiots are getting married." Etolié withdrew her flask, not drunk enough for this.

Khastra came to kneel beside her. "If it is a mistake, it is theirs to make."

"This isn't some star-crossed couple—this is the *Empress of Solvira* and a necromancer. If they fuck it up, that isn't something a kingdom recovers from." She took several long sips, sneering all the while. "This is exactly what I wanted to happen. But not like this. Not this *fast.*"

"Have you considered the issue of an heir? Lara is the very last of her blood."

"I sometimes forget that mortals have to reproduce, I'll be honest." She tossed her flask aside, letting it fall back into its pocket realm. "That's a problem for future them."

"It is not a small problem." Khastra frowned as she looked to the door, something vicious suddenly settling into her countenance—but perhaps that was just her face now, given the lack of eyebrows made everything a little more menacing.

Etolié groaned, never drunk enough for this. "I need to go." She pulled herself up from her chair. "I have a lot to discuss with 'the tiny one,'" Etolié said, but Khastra placed a hand on her shoulder.

"I would like to speak to her, actually," the half-demon said. "I am concerned, and I think she may respond better to a . . . how do you say . . . *motherly* figure."

"Oh, so I'm not motherly?"

"You are not."

"You're right, but ouch." Etolié sipped from her flask, taking several deep gulps as Khastra lingered at the door.

"Nap, if you can. At least until you can readjust to the mortal realm."

Etolié shook her head, even as she groaned into the open flask. Her growing headache finally ebbed, the promise of relief in sight. "If I slow down, I'll think about Lunestra, and I don't think I have the resolve for that."

"Then go harass Reginal with tales of the crazy vampire bitch."

"Now we're talking," Etolié said, chuckling as Khastra laughed.

Her sobriety slowly faded, and thank the stars for that. Etolié prayed to be wrong, but she never was.

Ayla was a cancerous plague on Flowers' sanity.

The sun had not yet risen, but Flowridia walked through the frosty garden, shivering in her shawl. Beside her, Demitri remained a constant shadow. *You could still leave.*

"I don't think we need to resort to that yet," Flowridia replied, her initial panic finally easing with each chilled breath. She focused on the barren trees, seeking signs of life, but the frost would still kill any tiny growths daring to peek out. Winter kept a bitter grasp upon the world, but she prayed it might relinquish soon—her heart yearned for spring, to see blossoms illuminated by the first light of sunrise a final time before her wedding night.

Her breath caught at the thought.

Do you think Lady Ayla will be able to fix this?

"I don't know . . ."

Her words trailed off at the approaching steps— hooved and unmistakable.

Khastra had a pleasant smile, utterly neutral as she traversed the path to join them. "You are predictable, tiny one. You always go outside when stressed."

"I think I have justifiable cause to be stressed," she said softly.

"You do, because you are either the biggest idiot on this realm or the wickedest woman to walk it."

Fresh panic pulsed in Flowridia's blood. Khastra's glowing eyes narrowed in disdain, scrutinizing her every thought and motion. "I beg your pardon?"

"Lara smells like Silver Fire," Khastra replied, her great height never so imposing as she loomed above her. "It is an unmistakable aroma. The magic is potent, even countless generations later. And the woman in that room smelled of it— but she is not Lara, is she."

Flowridia froze, every instinct inside her screaming to run. "Um—"

"Vampires also have a distinctive aura," Khastra continued, and Flowridia wondered if she imagined the slight growl in the back of her throat. "They smell like the dead, yet sweeter. More refined. Tell me, tiny one—tell me to my face that you are an idiot and do not realize Ayla Darkleaf is masquerading as the Empress of Solvira."

Beside her, Demitri said, *I'm going to go find Lady Ayla.*

But Flowridia shook her head. "Demitri, stay here," she muttered, still maintaining eye contact with the half-demon leering above her. "You seem to already know the answer."

"Thank you for your honesty," Khastra replied, making no effort to hide her contempt. Flowridia suspected she would not leave this conversation alive. "I would like to bargain with you. It is imperative that you listen, lest I proclaim your crime to the entire castle."

Sensing she might not immediately be squished into a pancake like her mentor, Flowridia stood tall and nodded.

"I will not ask what you have done with the real Empress Alauriel. What I know of necromancy and blood magic tells me she is long dead. I am curious to know why Ayla bothered to slay the archbishop, however."

The statement lingered. Khastra held the upper hand in the exchange, and so Flowridia said, "She didn't."

"No?"

"No," Flowridia affirmed, and when Khastra waited, she finally said more. "I did."

It was difficult to decipher those glowing eyes, but Flowridia thought the half-demon might have been surprised. "Did you?"

"Not on purpose," Flowridia said, and despite Khastra's scrutiny, she managed to say more. "She saw Ayla and I together. And I . . .I tried to use necromancy to wipe her mind." The memory remained raw; it took all her will to stay stoic.

Khastra furrowed her brow. "You have been studying the God of Death. You failed on Lunestra and were successful with Jules."

The statement lingered, the implications damning. "It seems you've made up your mind on that too—"

"I was once pledged to Ilune, tiny one. I know the scent of her magic. It is dangerous, and you are on a dangerous path."

Realization expanded in Flowridia's gut, the suspicion dangerous and damning. "You . . . You're the one who tore pages from the history books, aren't you."

"Yes. After the Civil War, when I returned to Solvira, I made it my mission to erase that part of history. If it is not written, it is forgotten. The powers you are seeking brought a nation to its knees and *killed* its patron goddess." Khastra's glowing gaze narrowed. "I enlisted Kah'Sheen to help me track down every book I could. Ilune was an evil woman, and it is better she rots in her cell, forgotten and alone."

Flowridia nodded slowly, questioning once more whether she would be leaving this interaction alive.

"But you found it anyway."

"In a library in Moratham," Flowridia admitted, and Khastra's glower darkened.

"Tiny one, unlike you, I recognize the supreme magnitude of the situation, because while I might be able to slay Ayla Darkleaf in honest combat, she is not known for that—instead, she is known for grudges. This will end in blood. In exchange for my silence, and for your continued life, you will give me your promise that neither you nor Ayla Darkleaf will touch Etolié."

It seemed such a small thing, yet Khastra had damned herself for Etolié's well-being before, and Flowridia didn't doubt that Ayla was only a tantrum away from burning the world anew. "I accept your terms," she said, and she offered a hand.

The half-demon lifted her own, but held it back and said, "Believe me, tiny one, there is nowhere in this realm, Sha'Demoni, or even Celestière that she can hide you. I am a woman with only one thing left to lose—and if she is gone, there is nothing to stop me from eating you alive."

Having seen the Bringer of War, Flowridia suspected that was literal. "I believe you, and I'll make certain Ayla does too."

Khastra's callused grip was firm and predictably painful. "Do not mistake this as me condoning whatever you have done. Ayla Darkleaf was a threat to the world before, but you have made her a match to lesser gods, giving her those powers. I will smile at your wedding. I will give my congratulations. But you tell your lover my terms—that if she touches Etolié, I will not hesitate to rip you in two and tell the whole world of your crimes. Your palace of glass will shatter in time, with or without me. As I said—you are either the biggest idiot or the wickedest woman to walk this realm." Khastra scoffed, the condemnation in her gaze enough to cripple Flowridia's will. "Or perhaps you are both."

And Khastra walked away; Flowridia didn't breathe until she was well out of sight.

"Etolié thinks dangerous things, Flowra."

When Flowridia entered her bedroom, the curtains were drawn, but the hair upon her arms raised—for she was not alone. "Ayla—"

"One more death," Ayla cooed, her breath stroking like a lover across her ear. "I shall even turn her remains into a gift for you."

"Ayla, no," Flowridia said, and cold hands grabbed her dress, pulling into an iron embrace.

"A slip of the knife. She will not even feel it. My gift to you is a quick death for your beloved Etolié—"

"If you kill her," Flowridia said, "you'll be signing our doom. Etolié suspects, but Khastra knows."

Ayla released her, her performative glee vanishing. "What do you mean she knows?"

"She knew what we did to Jules. She knows who you are. But she's sworn to say nothing so long as you don't harm Etolié."

"Or I slay them both. The Bringer of War falls first—then there is nothing to protect that idiotic angel—"

"If you kill Etolié," Flowridia spat, "I won't meet you at the altar. I'll leave."

She stood tall, unafraid to meet Ayla's withering eye. "You love her more than you love me?"

Flowridia refuse to accept those baited words, clenching her jaw as she said, "I love you more than anyone. But if you kill her, you'll show that you love yourself more than you love me."

"She despises Ayla Darkleaf! She had the audacity to accuse me of abusing you. You really wish to keep around someone who *hates* your beloved?"

"Ayla," Flowridia replied, forcibly calm despite the typhoon of her beloved's rage, "when Etolié met you, you were monstrous to me. You admitted it. You apologized for it, and I have watched you be better. But she holds to that image. She was there to hold me after you all but shattered me against the wardrobe."

Ayla said nothing at all, her gaze pure ice.

"I see you trying," Flowridia said, daring to steal one of her hands. "Every day, you try to be a better person for me. To me. You have vowed to be better, and you are. I won't pretend that I understand you all the time, but I don't question your love."

Ayla's gaze fell to the floor. She shut her eyes, fists clenching.

"I love Etolié. I love her as a mentor, and as the drunk sister I never knew I needed," she said with a laugh. "But I don't love her like I love you."

"I would rather keep you to myself," Ayla whispered, spite in her words.

"I love my friends, Ayla, and they love me. I am a better person for that love. But I reserve a special piece of myself for you."

"You gave that to your 'friend' Lara, too."

"I don't mean sex, Ayla. Otherwise, you would have nothing special to give back to me." In tentative motions, she hugged her, pressing Ayla's face to the crux of her neck. Upon the table, she saw the dreaded bouquet, the reminder of Ayla's insecurities and pain, and held her tight. "I don't know how to reassure you except to say that you're not my friend; you are so much more. You needn't be insecure."

Muffled words said, "I would cage you, if I could."

"I would fly away." Flowridia looked up, saw Ayla's glistening, silver eyes, and whispered, "Do you trust me?"

Ayla shut her eyes and nodded.

"Trust that I love you above all else."

Ayla's stance shifted; her legs buckled. Flowridia gently led her down and hugged her when Ayla settled into her lap. "I will never leave you," Flowridia whispered, and she felt her love crack, felt each line etch into Ayla's carefully constructed defenses. "Let's not go back out today. We'll disappear. Just you and me."

"They will think Ayla Darkleaf stole you," Ayla replied, bitterness in her quivering words.

"We'll leave a note, signed by both of us." Flowridia kissed her hair, her scent clean and rich.

"What about Mereen?"

The name pulsed dread through her limbs. Flowridia clung tighter to her love. "What use does she have for an orb?"

"I cannot begin to fathom. She cannot wield it—not without study, and that would take years." Those pale eyes held hatred, more silver by the day. "It has been a mistake, to ignore her. But you must understand, Flowra, that if Mereen wants to stay hidden, she will. She can elude even shadows, despite living among them. Otherwise I would have killed her hundreds of years ago."

"She can steal from a God, and that's no small feat," Flowridia said, "but that gives you a place to start. Ask the shadows of Soliel. Mereen will be near him."

"As always, you are wiser than me." Ayla leaned back, posture small as she whispered. "I am sorry. I do not mean to hurt you."

"I'm not leaving," Flowridia said, but Ayla remained still. "If I have learned anything from our time in Solvira, it's that when we are united, there's no force on earth that can stop us. You have shown me that you trust me—but that sort of love requires work. You can't just trust me in one big moment; you must trust me in little things, every day, just as I must trust you." She placed a tender kiss upon Ayla's lips, lingering as she whispered, "I love you. I want you and only you, my love."

Ayla returned the gesture, no urgency in the kiss—only easy sensuality, the soft ending to their spat.

"Mereen must be our first priority," Flowridia whispered. Yet when Ayla stood to leave, she stopped her, holding her small wrist in her hand. "I don't want you to leave, feeling like this."

With a dancer's grace, Ayla helped her to rise. "You have already told me you love me, and I believe you. I will be fine, Flowra."

Flowridia came forward and held her from behind, appeased when her love relaxed against her. "Yes, you should look for Mereen, but there's been so much stress and sorrow lately. Ayla . . ." Flowridia ran her fingers across Ayla's back, content to convey affection. "Everything has been dark and heavy; I know I could do with a bit of fun." It might have been innocent, but desire bled into her words; Ayla should know she was wanted. "Wholesome or otherwise."

"I am a fan of 'otherwise.'" Ayla stole her lips into something carnal and raw, kissing with her open mouth, leaving Flowridia a melting heap when she suddenly pulled back. Her grin bespoke mischief and lust. "Though we still manage perfectly well to steal time for that."

"Yes, but what about something different? If I must throw a tantrum to get us a full day alone before the wedding, I will."

Intrigue twisted Ayla's grin. "What kind of different did you have in mind?"

"I don't know. Perhaps a luxurious inn, or a romantic picnic in a meadow."

"How do you feel about ropes?"

Startled, Flowridia managed only to blink. "Ropes?"

Ayla chuckled, dark and alluring. "Ropes, yes. Or whatever I have on-hand to tie you up and leave you helpless with."

Judging by the surge of heat between her legs, the idea sounded euphoric. "Yes. Yes, I think I would like that."

"Of course, if you change your mind, you tell me." Her ensuing wink pulled a blush to Flowridia's cheeks. "I shall put some thought into it; depending on how elaborate we want to go, it may have to wait until after the wedding . . ." Flowridia supposed she couldn't fathom quite what Ayla referred to with that little tidbit, but her love continued on. "In the meantime, I will handle Mereen. This gives me something to look forward to."

"Stay a moment longer," Flowridia whispered, and Ayla curled into her embrace. "Ayla . . . you are so loved."

Ayla settled in, a docile monster, and Flowridia savored the beautiful moment of peace.

"Let me get this straight—you knew this Mereen lady. Like, you knew her on sight."

In the hallway, Étolié and Khastra refrained from holding hands. All the world was still in disarray, and Solvira was technically taking a risk even keeping the general here at all.

"She smelled like a vampire and matched my sister's descriptions, yes," the half-demon replied.

"But you also expect me to believe that you *didn't* know who Ayla Darkleaf was the second she stepped into the manor back in Staelash? You know—eight months ago? I mean, she was pretty *up front* about her name."

Khastra shook her head. "I suspected she was a vampire, but it was not pertinent until the tiny one started pursuing her."

"Yes, you told me that, but you didn't say she was *that vampire.* You know, the extremely famous, genocidal one."

"I was in Solvira during that time," Khastra said, nonchalant despite Étolié attempts at interrogation. "She was across the sea. I only gave her any mind because Kah'Sheen decided to care. Besides, Ayla Darkleaf is not an uncommon name."

"What? Don't tell me people name their kids after her."

"No, but there are countless 'Darkleafs'—it was a bastard name, given to orphans. It fell out of favor with The Endless Night's rise to power, but you do still find some."

Étolié frowned, the idea far too strange. "And, what— was 'Ayla' the most popular girl's name of that year?"

"It was a common girl's name for many years. It has come back into favor now, since she is dead."

"Was dead, Beefcake. This is an important distinction."

"My point," Khastra said, utterly unperturbed, which kinda pissed Étolié off, "is that I did not know, and my suspicions were not worth voicing without cause. When she turned into a demon and killed the Skalmites, that was probable cause. Then I knew."

Étolié stopped, blocking Khastra's path with her hands on her hips. "And you still said nothing."

"You are greatly overestimating how much I cared about The Endless Night. I accept that as a failing."

"Last time I saw the bitch, The Endless Night rammed a claw through my best friend's heart, so you should care a little more."

She felt some vindication at Khastra's slumping shoulders. "I had not considered that, and I am sorry."

"It doesn't matter how many times I watch you get stabbed in the heart," Etolié spat. "It doesn't get any easier."

Khastra pulled her into a hug, and the feeling of cold skin beneath her dress chilled Etolié's blood.

"Etolié?"

They both turned, and Etolié blinked for a few seconds before finally spitting out the name, *"Thalmus?"*

The half-giant stood nearly too tall for the ceiling, but thankfully Beefcake's horns required a few extra inches of stonework up above. His reserved gaze drifted between them. "Good to see you back."

It wasn't that he cared—he likely would have been indifferent if she'd died—but there was a clear question in the words. "We got back this morning. Didn't quite kill Soliel, but it's about the journey—not the destination."

"I see."

He looked about to leave, but Etolié stood her ground, given she had a few questions of her own. "Forgive me, but what are you doing here?"

"Empress Alauriel asked me to come for the funeral and to stay a few days to help comfort Flowra. She took the news hard. I had planned to return to Staelash today."

That goddamn mom of a man. "Well, good call. You and Flowers have always had, uh, a special connection."

The conversation quickly fizzled into awkward territory, and with a curt nod, Thalmus left them. But just as he might've escaped, Etolié remembered the most important news of the day. "By the way," she called, figuring it didn't matter who overheard, "we have a threat-level maximum going on—there is solid evidence that a certain small, pale, and stabby has returned from the dead."

He stopped in his tracks, looking at her with more clarity than he ever had before. "Ayla Darkleaf?"

"Correct. So, stay alert."

Thalmus gave a slight nod. "Perhaps I will stay a few more days," he said, and then he left.

When he had finally disappeared, Etolié said, "You were quiet there, Beefcake."

"I do not wish to offend him with my presence more than I have to," Khastra replied, and the words immediately boiled Etolié's blood.

"I respectfully disagree with the sentiment, but you do you." She dared to take Khastra's hand, quietly resolving to find them the alone time she had been craving and led her onward. "How did the talk with Flowers go?"

"As well as it could have," Khastra said.

"Did she say anything?"

"She knows as little as we would expect her to."

"Got it," Etolié said. Flowers, for all her growth, was still the naïve idiot Etolié had found in the woods.

Upon her death, Khastra's room in Solvira had been disassembled, all her belongings transported to Staelash. A pity—Etolié had loved that gigantic bed. Instead, she directed them to Etolié's permanent room in the castle.

Within, the room smelled cleaned and dusted—the maids were efficient above all else. The bed had never been used and remained as perfectly well made as it had been twenty-four years ago, when she'd first been dragged to this castle. "The bed's a little small, but I think you can find a use for me and my tits."

She laughed, but Khastra did not join her. The half-demon locked the door and said, "I need to tell you something."

Etolié withered at her tone. "What's going on?"

Khastra gently led her to the bed and bid her to sit. She joined her, the bed sagging slightly for her weight. "My body is dead. Staella restored me to a perfect form, but it has undone all that Casvir did to me." She took Etolié's hand and traced a line down her palm. "I cannot turn into the Bringer of War in this state."

The statement was so obvious in hindsight, but Etolié hadn't considered it at all. "Your heart isn't beating."

Khastra shook her head. "No, it is not. I would ask that you not speak of it to anyone, however. The world does not need to know that I cannot protect you."

Etolié set her hand on Khastra's bicep, which her hand did not even halfway wrap around. "Clearly you're useless."

A scoffing grin took Khastra's melancholy for a small moment, but then her face fell anew. "And what that means for us is that intimacy will be different."

Etolié frowned, the implications falling into place, but frantically shook her head. "If all this Ayla bullshit has reminded us of nothing else, it's that undead can have all the sexy-times they'd like."

"Vampires are unique," Khastra said. Her callused hand came to stroke Etolié's hair, her glowing eyes infinitely soft. "My love for you has not changed. You are breathtaking, Etolié, and to see you naked would still have its joys. But my body cannot become aroused. I can still pleasure you and would happily do so, but if this is something that would come between us, I understand."

Etolié pulled back her hand and sat up on her knees, a rapid rush of *annoyance* flooding through her. So much so, that she flicked Khastra on her dumbass nose. The half-demon reeled back in shock. Etolié said, "Are you fucking kidding me?"

"Etolié—"

"You've been my favorite person in the cosmos for twenty-four years, and you really think I'd leave because you can't get off?" She sat back on her ass and crossed her arms, kinda steaming if she were being honest. She pursed her lips; she released a huff. "Khastra, I realize that for most people sex and romance come in the same package, but that's never been who I am. Even if we never have sex again, I would love you just the same, and not just because of my unresolved codependency issues. Sex with you is special and wonderful, and I love the feeling of being so close, but cuddling naked with you gets me just about as high. I know it sounds weird, but it's the truth, for me. It's like you said before—exactly the same, but with sex. We can just be 'exactly the same' for a while if we need to, as long as you'll still be only mine."

Khastra smiled, and Etolié stuck out her tongue. "Oh, Etolié—"

"Don't 'Etolié' me. I'm pissed—"

She squeaked when Khastra pulled her against her clothed chest. To illustrate her point, Etolié let her clothing vanish, content to be naked with the woman she loved. "I'm happy to cuddle, but get a blanket first, Beefy. You're freezing."

Khastra removed her clothing and stole Etolié into bed. Peace settled, though Etolié's mind was loud. Khastra held her, but not as the protector, no—like a child to her beloved doll, something to comfort her in the darkness.

Etolié's face settled against the hollow that was Khastra's heart, finding it strange to not feel scars beneath her fingers. "Nox'Kartha isn't here," she whispered, her hand tracing those elaborate tattoos. Khastra's chest illuminated at her touch. "Imperator Casvir can't touch you here. You're safe. There's nothing to be afraid of."

Khastra's grip tightened.

It was a lie, for Casvir loomed like a shadow ahead, The Endless Night had come to torment Flowers' soul, and Archbishop Lunestra was dead—and with her, one of the few beacons of hope left in the world extinguished.

Etolié's next words were shy. "I love you."

The reply reverberated against her entire body; she felt it down to her bones. "I love you, Etolié."

There was so much to cry for, and Etolie softly did— for Lunestra, for Khastra, for missing her momma after only just finding her again . . .

Something dreadful waited ahead, but they had pushed it off for a few more days. Etolié would fight against finality until the day she died.

By evening, Ayla had still not returned. Flowridia chose to not fear, and to the few who asked, she said that Lara was researching somewhere down in the recesses of the library— something to deter them from looking but enough to dissuade any worry.

Ayla Darkleaf was prowling about, after all.

To the outside world, she might've shown no sign of self-preservation, except she acquired a shadow sometime midmorning who lingered all through the day. As she contentedly gardened, Thalmus spoke of Staelash, of home, and Flowridia didn't need to ask why he chaperoned like a protective parent, even if Demitri would likely be a better deterrent of any vampiric threats.

"In light of you moving to Solvira," Thalmus said, in the late evening, "I told the gardeners on staff to care for your garden. They don't possess nearly the talent you did, but it remains a place of peace. You've left a legacy."

Flowridia smiled to think of her little sanctuary. "Thank you."

"That said, with the recent threat of Ayla's return, would you consider returning to Staelash? It might be safer there."

Flowridia shook her head. "Who's to say she won't follow?" With her skirts stained in dirt, Flowridia continued coaxing tiny blossoms to grow, urging spring to come a little faster. "Solvira could offer greater protection, with due respect."

"Yet you sit outside, without any formal protection."

The subtle sternness in his words evoked a frown from her lips. "If she wanted me, she would have taken me already. No amount of guards could stop her."

They truly could not. Thalmus' quiet acrimony suggested he knew she was right. "Be that as it may, someone should be around to sound the alarm if you're taken."

"Currently that someone is you," Flowridia said, annoyed to be placed in this position—vainly defending herself to a man who was, by all accounts, completely correct. "But that's assuming she doesn't kill you to silence you." She looked to Demitri, quiet as he enjoyed the chilly evening. "To be honest, Demitri is the best hope for warning people; for all of Ayla's wicked intentions, she wouldn't hurt him. She always liked him."

"You may be right," Thalmus said, as footsteps approached from the garden path.

As the last vestiges of sunlight disappeared over the distant horizon, there came subtle footsteps. Flowridia swallowed her relief when Empress Alauriel approached, her clothing more revealing than the weather should have been comfortable for.

Thalmus bowed. "Good evening, your majesty."

"Good evening," she said politely, then beamed at Flowridia. "Forgive me, but I must steal Flowra away. There are wedding plans to settle."

"I would be happy to escort you," Thalmus said, and Lara, to her credit, kept her face perfectly calm, "assuming you don't plan to bring guards."

Her polite laughter conveyed no ire. "And why would I do that?"

"Begging your pardon, your majesty, but there was recently a clear threat on Flowra's life."

"Ayla Darkleaf is more than invited to try stabbing me in the back and stealing my intended, but I suspect she'll find me more difficult to kill than the average person, assuming that's her plan."

An unspoken standoff occurred—between Thalmus, immovable and stubborn, and 'Lara,' whose apparent hubris would have been alarming even to Flowridia, were she not acutely aware of the truth.

It was Thalmus who eventually released a stiff sigh. "Find me when you're done," he said to Flowridia, then he bid them both goodnight.

When he disappeared, Ayla's true form shifted, and Flowridia was surprised to see evidence of snow upon her dress. "Protective, that one," Ayla whispered, but though the night was dark, she could perfectly imagine every quirk of her eyebrows, the twist of her lip. "Walk with me?"

Flowridia let her lead, their fingers intertwined as they stepped away from the garden's edge and into the copse of trees surrounding the outside of the castle. In the dark, the shadows flickered, the waxing moon not enough to cut through the thick leaves and castle walls, enchanted glass or not. Yet what fear could she have? The monster in the dark was hers to hold and love.

"What news do you have of Mereen?"

"Nothing." Gods, Ayla was a vision in the night, her alabaster skin practically glowing, reflecting the scattered flecks of silver moonlight. "I stalked Soliel for hours, but he also found nothing. I eventually grew bored and approached him."

Taken aback, Flowridia's breath caught. "You what?"

"What can he do to me, Flowra? He facilitated my return. He clearly wants me around."

A fact that haunted Flowridia to this day, but she managed to merely nod. "What did he say?"

"We had an interesting conversation, he and I," Ayla mused, idly releasing Flowridia's hand as she moved sensuously through the shadows, all but dancing—how graceful and smooth her motions were, as alluring as the day Flowridia first saw her. "He had also lost Mereen, feeling flashes of her occasionally but never for long enough to know where to go. Apparently, she has eluded him for some time, but he holds hope to find her, or so he claimed." She paused in her ruminations; her small lips pursed as her eyelashes fluttered. "We spoke of Casvir. He has healed, as Etolié said.

Apparently Casvir tried to engage him in some kind of bargain, but Soliel would not hear him."

"Strange," Flowridia said, the thought disconcerting, "but Soliel has alluded to bad blood between them before."

Ayla hummed, her hand stroking along the bark of a tree as she passed. Flowridia followed, as she always did. "Stranger still was that we spoke of you. Nothing of great value in the end, tragically. But I asked him the pressing questions of your heart—specifically why he would kill your beloved Lara and aid in bringing about my return. He would not say. He merely chuckled and said it was not for me to know— because I would kill myself anew to run from my fate." Ayla turned to her then, quiet reserve on her severe features. "Not exactly a comforting thought."

No, it was not, yet Flowridia still vowed to hold a knife to his throat and force him to speak the truth someday. "Did he imply to have known you, in his time?"

Ayla's stoicism twitched, a frown threatening to mar her perfect lips. "I suppose he did," she muttered, "or at least enough to allude to know what becomes of my life. However, whatever my thoughts on the concept of fate, I believe in choice above all. And if fate ever leads me down a path I reject, well . . ." She smiled, wide and leering, the shadows revealing her teeth and little else. "I don't know how to kill myself, but you know I'm stubborn enough to try. Certainly stubborn enough to walk away."

Flowridia approached her love, hidden in the shadows of the trees. There was freedom here, outside the castle. The night brought chills and an icy breeze, yet she relished the sensation, for to watch Ayla in her true, most perfect form held greater reward than anything Solvira could offer. When their hands touched, Ayla gripped hers tight and pulled her in for a slow, sensuous kiss.

Flowridia relished the touch, sighing into her lover's mouth when Ayla's hands stroked around her waist. There they remained, the heat between them merely simmering, and when Ayla finally pulled back, her eyes were but a ring about a void. "And that was all," she whispered, her fangs glinting in the scattered pieces of light. "A strange encounter. Can't say I would do it again, except on your word."

A strange encounter, indeed—with a strange and malevolent entity Flowridia felt an unwanted kinship toward. "Could you kill him?"

"Likely," Ayla cooed, and then her grin widened. "That would be a spectacular announcement of my presence to the world, now wouldn't it—The Endless Night slays the God of Order, leaving his remains within a crater of black sand. Would you permit it?"

"He wields holy light as a weapon," Flowridia replied. "I fear it would end the same as your encounter with Sol Kareena."

Ayla's grin faded, but her eyes held the same wicked delight. "After all the trouble he went through to bring me back? Doubtful." To Flowridia's chagrin, she had a point. "Besides, you're implying he is better than Sol Kareena. I cannot stand up to her because I am not a god." She released Flowridia's hand and held hers up, just as the first emblems of flame ignited at her fingertips. It slowly rose to consume it, reflecting off her face, flickering eerie light and shadows. "Not yet."

The statement brought only dread. "Is that what you want?"

"Who am I to deny myself the world? Casvir asks for pledges of godhood in exchange for citizenship—but Solvira is vast, grander than Nox'Kartha, thousands upon thousands of years of history to bolster its strength. He and I were both born to nothing, yet he has built an empire; I destroyed one. Now I wield a godly boon, the greatest power upon this mortal plane. So why would I not?"

"Do you have a plan?"

Ayla hummed, contentment spreading across her countenance with her grin. "Don't I always?" She chuckled, the fire emanating across her bare arms, immune to the chill of night. Her black dress conveyed vanity and pride, but the fire did not burn it when it touched the scant edges. "The Nox'Karthan threat has only spread. Casvir will wreak havoc upon the Theocracy, decimating it entirely. All their citizens shall be ours by the end. He will only grow more powerful, and who can save us? Neolan can withstand his forces for countless generations, but the same can be said for Haven. Nox'Kartha's weakness is that all its power lies at the head—Casvir falls, and his armies fall with him. To defeat him will not take an army, but a hero. Solvira already believes there is a threat and willingly allows me to tighten the rules. They trust me, so I entreat them to pledge, to pray to me as they would have their founding goddess, Neoma. And once the power has been granted to me, I destroy Nox'Kartha." Pure malevolence shone in her countenance. "Then the power is mine to keep."

"Your plan is brilliant," Flowridia said, though she hated it for reasons her heart could not name. She watched Ayla's fiery display, mesmerized and appalled, yet the fear coexisted with boundless love. "But after you destroy Nox'Kartha, what will you do with that power?"

For the first time, Ayla frowned, her flawless features etched in contemplation. "Does it matter?"

"Yes."

Ayla's flame slowly dissipated, smoldering against her pores in effervescent light. "I have not thought that far ahead."

Drenched in darkness, Flowridia's hand instinctively sought her love's, even as her eyes steadily adjusted to the natural light of the moon. "And where I do exist in this narrative?"

"You will be my wife," Ayla replied, the bare beginnings of shock leaving her jaw slack. "Whatever you wanted, I would give you. I would even worship you, pledge my power to your name so you could have a piece of it."

A strange notion, that a god might pledge their power and bestow it upon another, but Flowridia supposed it made some semblance of sense. Despite her fear, she smiled, for Ayla, no matter what terror she wrought, loved with all her heart. "I suppose if the path to stay with you forever leads to godhood, I would do it for you."

Ayla smiled, and it was soft—as soft as the precious few days they spent in the time before, when Flowridia was little more than a child and Ayla had unwittingly fallen in love. "I wonder if I could absorb Soliel's soul."

"Lara thought it was possible," Flowridia said, burying any unwilling emotions that came with the name. "Could you steal his orbs?"

"If Mereen could, why not me? I'm better." With a hum, Ayla brought her hands to Flowridia's hips, where they settled contentedly. "I wonder if I could absorb Casvir's." A sullen frown overtook her features. "He sent a letter today. Not addressed to anyone in particular, so the courier read it. He will be attending with a small entourage. No Murishani."

More and more lately, Flowridia held mixed feelings toward the man she still considered a dear friend.

"Perhaps Etolié will consent to not placing extra guards in his room." She laughed, but at Flowridia's bafflement, she paused and added, "She is adamant about security. I overheard her proclaim that guards would roam the halls all night and perform mandatory check-ins at random hours—lest Ayla Darkleaf make off with any guests. She is quite concerned about a scandal—which I find ironic given she's the one swanning about in illusionary clothing. Did you know that, Flowra? Gods, she was *naked* all along. I will say this solves the scientific impossibility of her clothing, however. You have no idea how much that vexed me during my time as a diplomat."

Flowridia's stomach sank, but not for the non-realization. "I know she's naked. Could you not dissuade her?"

Ayla shook her head. "Jules speaks on my behalf, per my behest, but Etolié has been telling all sorts of lovely stories about me. She has the rest eating out of her hand." Bitterness stained the words. "Forgive me if I snap and rip her spine out."

The threat might have been comical, had Ayla not looked so deathly serious—and had Flowridia not seen that very act performed. "Ayla, we discussed this—"

"I know," she snapped. "I will not touch her, lest the Bringer of War smite us all. I know."

"We have to do something to dissuade her," Flowridia said. "Something to make her think Ayla Darkleaf isn't a threat to our wedding. Perhaps you could talk to her."

"I already said—"

"No." Flowridia studied her undead lover, wondering how amiable she would be to insanity. "I mean that Ayla Darkleaf should talk to her."

Visibly unimpressed, Ayla raised a condemning eyebrow. "What, I should swoop in from the shadows and proclaim my good intentions? I struggle to imagine anything more suspicious. And that is assuming I can speak to her away from her demon-blooded lover—who won't hesitate to tear me into pieces, if she sees me as a threat."

Her choice in words took Flowridia aback. "Etolié and Khastra aren't lovers."

Ayla frowned, though not with any anger. "Yes, they are."

"No. Between you and I, Khastra harbors secret feelings, but Etolié would never return them. They're an odd pair, but they are only friends."

Ayla's expression remained the same. "Strange. My point still stands, however."

"You and I both know you're too clever to be so straightforward." Flowridia crossed her arms, letting the statement linger until the first hints of calculation distanced Ayla's gaze. "This is our wedding. Please don't let Etolié ruin it for paranoia's sake when you hold the power to fix it."

Amidst the dark atmosphere, Ayla Darkleaf grinned. "Perhaps I do have a plan."

Despite Ayla's change in mood, she dwelled upon her words, the ominous whispers of the future. When Flowridia pulled away, she studied her lover's undead visage, nearly glowing in the darkness. "You would become a god to slay Soliel?"

"As I said, if you would permit it."

"Yet you spoke only of Nox'Kartha. You have refrained from explicitly saying you would slay Casvir, but that is your intention."

"I hold no grudge against Soliel," Ayla replied, though quiet acrimony settled within the thin line of her mouth, "aside from the day he threatened you. But Casvir has done far more to hurt me than he has."

"Forgive me when I say I don't comprehend it." Flowridia took her hand. "He is my friend. Though I'm appalled at what he's done to the Theocracy . . . I can only be so angry, given you're the love of my life and have done just as much wickedness, if not more." Ayla's shrug conveyed a forced nonchalance, but Flowridia realized she had misspoken. "Which isn't to say I compare the two of you. I simply . . ."

Her words trailed off at Ayla's finger on her lip. "Well, he did cut off my ear," the elven woman said, and not without some petulance. "If that is not a reason to hate someone, I cannot fathom what would convince you."

"I never questioned that you hated him—"

"Furthermore, while he did perform the blood ritual to resurrect me, he promptly forced me into slavery. 'Until his death or mine' means very little among immortal beings. Sol Kareena did me a grand favor, to be honest. I am not a woman who can bear a cage, gilded or not. He gives all the world to those who please him in their service, but I would rather live in the dirt and be free than chained by diamonds and gold."

Ayla's lips pursed, biting back some further retort. "His punishments are as spectacular as his rewards," she continued, "but pain is not something I fear anymore. You need not have pity for me, given anything I did to piss on his station generally involved murder, or attempted. Yes, I tried countless times to seduce him—how embarrassing, in hindsight. I tried to kill him. I killed others. When I realized I could take no power from him, I did all I could in my limited control to make him regret ever enslaving me—my one joy for years was knowing I was succeeding. He took everything from me, but with that comes a strange sort of power—I had nothing left. I walked the line of usefulness, still his grandest servant so he would not throw me into his dungeons and torture me, but I still dared him a thousand times to destroy my soul and let me go. To say that and mean it is power in and of itself."

Ayla's words brought triumph to her sharp features, but Flowridia's chest felt tight. She recalled her days in Nox'Kartha, remembering the agonized screams of Khastra upon the surgical slab, and wondered if Casvir and Ayla were more similar than either would ever admit.

"To be honest," Ayla continued, her joy fading, "that was what made loving you so fearful to me. Suddenly, there was something to lose, something I cared for more than I feared for myself. I loved you, and that infuriated me, but it also terrified me, to think what he might do to you. It likely startled him too, to know the girl he had put years of investment into was being romanced by his most dangerous monster, but I could not have known that. You spoke wistfully of coming to Nox'Kartha, but I would have never let you under his roof."

Flowridia pulled Ayla into her arms, heart aching for how small her love felt. "I'd never considered that," Flowridia whispered. "I hadn't . . ." Her sigh deflated her entire body. "It's difficult to reconcile the many images of him."

It was difficult to reconcile the different images of many figures in her life.

"You are marrying me," Ayla said, still clinging tight. "Not him. Not that it was ever an option, but you understand my meaning. You are marrying me. You are ruling at my side. You are *mine*, my love." Vehemence shone in her visage when she looked up. "He chose you, but you chose me, and that is enough."

Flowridia's smile came easily this time. "I'll choose you every day, my love."

"Someday, he shall fall for his hubris. I do not doubt it. And I shall not overtly seek his doom, for your sake. But I would like to be prepared to deliver it. I would like to hold some power over him, considering he holds supreme power over you."

The chill of outside seeped into Flowridia's blood. "What do you mean?"

"He is the demi-deity who granted you your magic. He is the reason you have your darling Demitri. It would be trivial for him to take it away if you ever defied him."

"Lunestra said the same thing," Flowridia replied. "That's not something I'm prepared to consider, yet. But I know he would not do it lightly. He's spent too many years watching my powers develop to simply throw me away."

"I genuinely hope that is true." Ayla stole her hand, quiet as she looked up to the grand castle. "If I can be nothing else in this life, I would like to be free. I will never be under his power again."

Freedom meant so many things. Flowridia joined her gaze. "When the castle becomes a cage, we can leave. We can always leave."

Ayla simply kissed her, then in silence escorted her back.

Chapter 26

When the sun hung low in the sky, pregnant with the promise of night, Etolié stepped through a shit-stenched slum, a small assembly of guards following behind. Khastra had stayed behind—at Etolié's insistence. *"I don't wanna waste time illusioning away those goat hoofprints."*

"There was an anonymous tip," General Irons muttered, casting his gaze across the crowd, "concerning bodies found in an abandoned, underground cellar."

"Anonymous means suspicious," Etolié said, her attention only half upon the task at hand.

"I'm inclined to agree."

Her mere presence drew the populace's attention, having decided to not illusion away her identity. Innumerable eyes watched her. Her glowing wings and silver hair revealed her angelic heritage, some staring from curiosity—others from wonder.

"Chosen of Eionei," she heard the crowd whisper. *"Savior of Slaves."* Unquestionably, she had liberated some of these very citizens, saving them from slavery, only to throw them into the slums.

She should be out destroying slave camps. She should be adventuring to slay Soliel. There was work to be done, yet she sat in a palace, sipping wine and sleeping in a warm bed. There were people who needed her, but she could not save them all.

Etolié wouldn't say she was friends with Irons, but she'd known him for years and he was considerate enough to not ask about her sudden silence.

They took a turn down a dark and rather shady alley. As the sun set, Irons knocked on a moldy door, bearing hints of frost. "High General Irons of the Solviran Royal Guard. You are hereby ordered to open this door."

Etolié side-eyed his gruff. "What if no one's there?"

"Then I cannot be reprimanded for kicking in the door."

And he did—in one motion, the door broke from the hinges. One of the guards carefully moved it aside as the rest entered, Irons in the lead. Etolié kept her wings visible, their light helpful in navigating the filthy shack.

Rats sounded from dark corners, skittering when the light touched their nests. Cobwebs hung in tatters, caressing her hair as she ducked beneath them. Ancient farming equipment lay rusted on the floor, some covering a trapdoor. "Is this our cellar?" Etolié whispered.

Irons nodded, then motioned to his men. "There's no telling what we'll find, so stay alert."

Etolié illusioned a sword—an exact replica of the one he wielded—and waited, tense as the guards moved the tools aside as quietly as possible, which admittedly wasn't that quiet.

It took three to upheave the ancient door—which landed with a *thud,* its iron hinge still holding. The scent of blood bombarded them, as did horrid screams.

Etolié cursed herself for losing that damn white orb as she followed Irons down, bracing for whatever horror they were about to walk in on. At the very least, the man's screaming meant they had a chance of not being heard themselves—small victories.

The stairs led to a dirtied, stone hallway. The thought occurred to Etolié that she could make the soldiers behind her invisible, but not only would they undoubtedly fall or attack each other, Ayla Darkleaf would smell them before they landed a single hit.

Assuming they could hit her at all.

Light shone from the seams of a shut door. "Let me," Etolié whispered. She gripped the doorknob. "Keep your men out here. I want to get her talking. I don't know what we're about to see—" The man inside suddenly wailed, and Etolié winced. ". . . but she won't kill me without monologuing first."

Irons held his sword readied. "Just you and me, then."

"With the promise of your self-control, why not."

Etolié twisted the knob.

The smell assaulted her first, seeping into the very pores of her skin—fresh blood and putrid rot. Etolié stared upon a small slaughterhouse of horror, pieces of bodies strewn about, walls stained with gore. Living people stood chained to the walls, most weeping, some stark white from shock. Drawn in blood, an abominable painting of a woman covered one wall, though Etolié spared it little mind. At the center stood Ayla Darkleaf herself before a table, running a knife along an unfortunate man's skin—Etolié couldn't quite see and frankly didn't want to know the details.

Ayla looked up at their entrance, genuine shock on her countenance. That, or she was a brilliant actress, which Etolié would also accept.

It had been six months, and that hadn't been enough time for her to wipe the creepy fucker from her memory. "Hi, bitch," Etolié said, sword aloft. "Thought I'd seen the last of you."

"Delightful to see you too, Starspawn," Ayla said, her crazy eyes fixed on Etolié alone. "Will there be no charade of politeness?"

"Last we spoke, you rammed a claw through my best friend's heart, so no." Etolié watched her movements, though Ayla seemed relaxed for now. She could vanish into a shadow and slit either of their throats in seconds, and Etolié was seriously questioning what the hell she had been thinking, coming here.

Well, she had been thinking they were investigating a creepy cellar. Which, they were. But this was something else. "You also half ripped me and Eionei in two, which wasn't very nice."

"Mm-hmm," Ayla hummed, and then she looked away and resumed whatever torture she was inflicting. His screams echoed through the chamber.

Etolié dared to step forward, avoiding the fearful eyes of the people chained to the walls. "Listen, bloodsucker, I don't know what game you're playing—"

"Game?" Ayla pouted, those crazy eyes wide. She tossed aside her knife, to Etolié's relief, then crawled upon the man she tortured and stroked his bleeding chest like a lover. The man softly cried. "Whatever do you mean?"

"Cut the bullshit—you're toying with Flowers."

As though the nasty fuck could get creepier, she grinned, her expression almost dreamy. "What about my Flowra?"

"She's not your Flowra. She's getting married in a week."

Ayla gave a dramatic sigh. "I know. I stole an invitation." She pointed to a wall. Beside the wall-sized painting was an invitation stuck to the stone with a knife—a painting Etolié realized was Flowers herself, naked and laughing.

Or screaming. Admittedly, Etolié couldn't tell. "Why is it that every time I talk to you, I want to light myself on fire?"

"Sounds like a personal problem," Ayla cooed, but she cooed the words into the man's face, who continued his soft weeping.

"You're playing with her," Etolié continued. "All of these killings—it's to get her attention. You stormed the castle and attacked her just to call her pretty."

Ayla's ensuing laughter was not quite like a girl in love—more like a creepy girl currently lounging on a bleeding, naked man who wasn't having the best time. "Was that her?"

"Stop playing stupid."

"Oh, all right," Ayla said, dramatically rolling off the tortured man, graceful as her bare feet touched the dirty ground. Blood stained her dress and exposed skin, coated her hands, but she brought her hand up to cup her cheek, nevertheless, apparently not caring about the red marring her skin. "I suppose I have gotten a little carried away. It began as harmless fun, but she is a difficult woman to reach. I had to try a little harder."

It took all Etolié's will to remain put when Ayla approached one of the chained prisoners—she hardly reached the man's chin, but she stroked down his clothed chest, leaving a bloodied line with her nail, ignoring his obvious flinch.

"Has it occurred to you that this is exactly the sort of behavior that made her choose Lara over you?"

Again, Ayla pouted, casually licking her finger as she gracefully stepped toward the next—an old woman, not crying but clearly in shock. "Oh, you moronic little firefly," she said, grabbing the woman's cheeks in her hand, forcing their gazes to meet, "do you think I would subject my Flowra to anything so ghastly?" She smiled, and Etolié spared a glance to Irons, who looked entirely revolted. "She is light and joy, the single, pure white daisy among my blood-soaked fields. I would end myself to preserve her innocence."

"Kindly get on that then."

Ayla leered a little too close to the woman's neck for comfort as she released her face, blood streaming down from the marks her nails had left. Her hand caressed the woman's neck instead, her teeth ghosting across the skin. "Flowra can do as she will. Her happiness is paramount, and I would do nothing to ruin her perfect day, even if means losing her to that harlot empress." Instead of biting her neck, Ayla *licked* the blood dripping down the old woman's cheeks, ignoring her struggling, and Etolié stomach sickened—but to move would guarantee they all died. When Ayla turned back, blood dripped from her lips. "I even have a gift prepared."

"You don't have to do that—"

"Oh, but I do. What is a lifetime except for a small moment? She needs to know I shall wait for her."

Somehow, despite those being the words Etolié had needed to hear, she felt absolutely no reassurance. "You'll wait, huh?"

"I am a patient woman. When I take her, it will be forever—so let her have her fun now, hmm?"

Etolié openly looked at Irons this time, who visibly quivered trying to hold himself back from decapitating this woman—or trying to, at least. The Endless Night had murdered the Bringer of War, and even alone, this woman was one of the most prolific murderers to ever walk the realm. "You're a creepy motherfucker, you know."

Ayla cackled. "And you are a demon fucker with palpable mommy issues—sorry, thought we were stating the obvious."

Furious, Etolié blushed and refused to look at Irons, who of all people would know there was only one demon in her life to fuck. "Listen, walking dead—"

"Hush now, lest I change my mind on surrendering."

Etolié sputtered but managed to shut her mouth.

"Seems I have been discovered," Ayla continued, placing a dramatic hand on her forehead. "My secret lair, desecrated. Take your victory and go, Starspawn—and give my love to Flowra, would you? Tell her I shall be weeping on her wedding night but shall forgive her in time—anytime I touch myself, I cannot seem to get her off my mind."

"You yeast-ridden cunt—"

But Ayla, that bitch, disappeared.

When Etolié looked back to General Irons, he had gone sheet white, as pale as their escaped quarry. "So, uh, about that demon fucking—"

"It is best I don't know the details," Irons replied, "but I cannot say I'm surprised."

Etolié grimaced as she surveyed the scene. "We should clean up," she said, and Irons called for his guards to enter, imploring them to brace themselves. "We should also definitely not tell Flowers anything she said." She cringed at the bloody painting. "Or did. We say just enough to reassure her that her wedding will most likely be safe."

"Agreed."

They busied themselves with helping the unfortunate souls in the makeshift dungeon.

Etolié's heart hurt for something it had missed for years.

Alone, she traversed the familiar streets of Neolan, still suspicious of every shadow as evening settled. Ayla Darkleaf was a nasty fucker, but as far as she knew, there had been no new killings.

Anything could happen at weddings. Etolié would be on alert.

She found her quarry in an old district of town, renovated and given funding by her moonbeam—*For Whom the Stars Shine,* a sign said.

The Temple of Staella. A shrine to her momma.

Etolié entered the unlocked door to the small cathedral. Within, it held all the ancient architecture of its original construction, the floorboards creaking, wooden beams supporting the old structure. Staella was a humble goddess, even at the peak of her worship, and so her temple held a subtle beauty, bereft of opulent displays. Instead, rows of wooden pews, a few holding silent worshippers in prayer. A large painting of her momma's figure hung at the front, and she was beautiful, a perfect likeness to her glory as she gazed forever upon her supplicants.

A priestess emerged, followed by a child—one of the children from the City of Light, and Etolié's heart soared to see her. "Lady Etolié!" the little girl said, perhaps seven years of age, and she ran to embrace her, giving no mind to the praying supplicants.

"Hush, now," the priestess said, somehow managing to yell and whisper at the same time. "No running in the cathedral."

But Etolié hugged the little girl—child hugs were far less itchy than adults.

"My apologies . . ." The priestess' words faded, her hand coming to cover her mouth. "You are the Daughter of Staella."

"In the flesh," Etolié replied, releasing the little girl.

The woman stared as though she gazed upon an angel, and Etolié supposed there were perks to letting her wings show. "It is an honor to speak to someone of my goddess' blood."

"If you wouldn't mind, could you find me a private room? I'd like to speak to my mother."

The priestess nodded and beckoned for the child to follow. Etolié was led into a hallway to the side, then to a simple wooden door. The priestess knocked, then bid her to enter.

Within, a small altar had been placed before a freshly pressed mat. A skylight showed the waning sunset, and Etolié sat below it, knowing her momma's light was ever-present, even in the day. The altar bore her momma's sigil—a circle of four-point stars—and Etolié lit the provided incense, resolving to leave a generous donation.

The incense slowly swirled in leisurely wafts. A cloying, sweet smell filled Etolié's nostrils, but she forced herself to breathe deep, knowing this was part of the ritual. Her head spun, but she carried on, for momma communicated with mortals in their sleep.

Thus, the scent provided a waking sleep, which was a polite way of saying 'hallucinations.'

When the world fully spun, Etolié laid on the mat, face toward the skylight, and shut her eyes, letting the sensation overtake her. All was quiet. All was peace.

And then a soft touch came upon her shoulder.

When Etolié opened her eyes, the room had darkened, save for the illuminate light of her momma standing before her. "My sweet Starshine," Staella said, and she helped Etolié to rise and then embraced her.

It remained surreal, to accept her momma's love. She wasn't truly there, but illusions were as real as you believed them to be—and Staella's were the most powerful of all. "Hi, Momma."

When Staella pulled back, her smile held more light than even her glowing form—and her wings were easily twice the span of Etolié's. "Wonderful of you to come see me."

"I wish it was purely a social call," Etolié said, and when Staella beckoned for her to sit, she did. Her momma placed an arm around her shoulder. "I'm scared as shit. Lara's wedding is in three days, and security has theoretically been handled, but fucking hell—I still can't relax."

"Lara's wedding?"

Oh. Etolié frowned and looked to her glowing momma. "Has she not told you? Empress Alauriel is getting married."

"No!" Staella's free hand settled upon her heart. "Oh, that's so wonderful!"

Even in moments of joy, Momma's voice never raised above a whisper. "I think it is," Etolié said, her quiet worries ever-present. "She's happy, even if I think the whole affair is a little rushed."

"She is marrying for love, then? Not treaties?"

Etolié nodded, and upon momma's face came a dreamy sort of joy.

"I adore weddings," Staella continued. "Who is the young man?"

"*Her* name is Flowridia. She's my bookkeeper, turned diplomat, turned empress consort. Quite the social climber, but she's sincere above all else. And she's a witch, which I think is a wonderful bit of irony, considering Solvira's history with witches."

Staella removed her hand from Etolié's shoulder and beamed as she stood up. Contemplation settled peacefully upon her face. "Alauriel is the last legitimate heir, is she not?"

"Khastra voiced similar concerns about babies, don't worry. On one hand, it's technically selfish for Lara to end the Silver Fire by marrying someone she can't bear a child with, but on the other, I also don't endorse having sex with men, so I shouldn't be a hypocrite."

"I never approved the Solviraes' obsession with preserving their bloodline," Staella mused. "All the hate, all the incest, all the murder—it broke my heart, to watch my descendants destroy each other in the name of blood purity. But I was never one who understood the need for power, so perhaps I cannot cast judgement." Her expression fell. "No, I truly cannot. I abandoned them, in the end."

"Momma, it's more complicated than that . . ." She stopped when Staella shook her head.

"Don't try to justify my wrongs, Starshine. I have made mistakes, and it is my duty to rectify them. Might I ask for something?"

"Anything."

"I would like to attend the wedding. Do you think they would mind?"

"Um, no." Etolié laughed at the audacity. "Gods forbid an actual goddess come to support."

Silence settled as Staella's gaze became distant. She smiled, yet it was far away. "I have a gift, though Neoma shall have to forgive me."

Etolié listened closely, curious to know more.

But Staella said nothing of it. "What did you mean by security concerns?"

"Flowers' crazy undead former lover has been causing problems, and I'm worried she'll do something to upset the wedding. I actually spoke to her, and she claims she has nothing planned, but I don't trust the bitch as far as I can throw her."

Staella hummed, and it was melodious. Etolié loved to hear it. "I can offer a ward of peace. Would that suffice? It would not detour any unwanted visitors, but it would dissuade violence within its bounds."

"Dissuade?"

"Heavily dissuade," Staella replied, and Etolié nearly laughed when she winked. "I was a Goddess of Peace and Mercy. I neither enact violence nor condone it, though there are those I shall look away from when they beg for mercy. So that is what I can offer."

"I accept."

"There might be wards you could set. Which have you practiced?"

"Approximately zero," Etolié admitted. "I can't set wards."

"Have you ever tried?"

Etolié shook her head.

"It's possible you cannot, but I suspect you have more of my power than you realize. I know you inherited my powers of illusion—to greater measures than I think any of my lineage before. Perhaps next time you visit, we might try and coax a bit out?"

The question held layers, Etolié realized. "Once the wedding is over, I could use a vacation in Celestière."

Staella's smile softened. "I would love that."

"I'll need something to distract me from Khastra being dragged back to Nox'Kartha, anyway," Etolié said, unable to hide her bitterness.

"Tell me of Khastra. How is she?"

"She's well, I suppose. Imperator Casvir will be coming to the wedding, so that's the new end of our perfect world. I wish she would let me hide her, but she won't listen. She says Casvir will find her one way or another. She won't fight at all. She says it was inevitable from the moment she left with me and the dragon."

Saying it out loud gave it weight. A lump formed in Etolié's throat.

Momma took her hand. "I cannot save her, and that is something I deeply regret. But I can promise two things: One, that I shall watch over her, for there are few places I cannot be. I will comfort her. I shall take what burdens I can. And if she meets her end, I will personally guide her to her final rest."

Mist blurred Etolié's vision, but she refused to cry here and now—not when her momma tried to offer hope.

"The second is not a promise, but an assurance of what will come to pass, which is that if Casvir destroys her forever, he will make an enemy of Ku'Shya, and that is a fearsome foe to have. Some say she is more powerful than Sol Kareena, and I believe it."

The words sent a chill through Etolié's blood.

"But Ku'Shya, as strange as it sounds, is my friend. Should you ever be in dire need, you can always call upon me, but if I am not the one who can save you, she would be your ally."

The statement was too jarring to fully contemplate. "Why?"

But even as she said the words, she remembered a heartbroken demon goddess at Khastra's funeral, all those months ago, who would speak to Etolié alone.

"Ku'Shya is an evil woman," Staella said, her sigh holding the weight of thousands of years. "Many of her actions are appalling, unquestionably. But she is odd. She would love you, because Khastra loves you."

"I'll keep that in mind," Etolié said, though Ku'Shya lived both a world and a continent away. "Thanks."

Momma released her hand. "Tell me more of your fears, my Starshine. Perhaps I can be of some help."

Etolié did, the hours spent bonding with Momma as precious as gold.

Chapter 27

The morning before the wedding, Flowridia awoke with her head on Ayla's thigh, lithe fingers slowly stroking her hair. Ayla perused a book, patient as her mortal beloved slept.

When she joined Ayla among the dead, what would she do with the boundless energy? Perhaps acquaint herself with the moon with the same dedication as she gave the sun; find solace in silver light and be content to forget Sol Kareena's domain.

The thought smothered the joy of the peaceful morning, of laying in her beloved's lap. Flowridia shoved it aside, though the time to confront it steadily approached.

"Flowra?"

Flowridia looked up, smiling when she saw Ayla gazing down from her book. "Good morning, Ayla," she said, and she curled into the blankets, the soft nightgown a comfort to her panicked heart.

Ayla moved her hand from Flowridia's hair to her back, soothing her through the thick blankets. "Stay as long as you like," she cooed. "Duties can wait."

Ayla so desperately craved her attention, clever in how she spun her words, as though to convince Flowridia that it was not so, but the other way around. Flowridia knew better.

She snaked a hand up from the covers and wrapped it around Ayla's waist, her fingers brushing against taut muscles behind the thin fabric of her dress.

Flowridia willed the sunrise to slow, to let her bask in this peaceful moment for a while longer. The day would progress, the guests would come, and before she knew it, tomorrow would arrive—her final day.

Her hand grasped the fabric of Ayla's dress, wishing it could be a tangible way to still the ever-ticking clock of time. In measured breaths, she calmed her heart and smothered her fears with Ayla's scent and presence.

But soon, sunlight filtered through the curtains. Her body grew restless, unaccustomed to lingering in bed. Her stomach growled, and finally she sat up, hair surely tussled and tangled, her breath stale, lips dry, but Ayla's mouth descended to meet hers anyway.

Flowridia's hand settled on the back of Ayla's head, her thumb caressing the sharp line of her cheekbone. Perhaps it was only meant to be a quick peck, a small piece of affection, but Flowridia lingered, desperate to cling to the moment a little while longer.

She rolled away from Ayla's lips and let their foreheads touch, breathing in the presence of her chosen love. "Flowra," Ayla whispered, and when Flowridia opened her eyes, Ayla's were wide with worry, "is something wrong?"

"No," she said quickly, praying her capacity to lie extended to convincing her betrothed. "I'm well."

Simply afraid. So afraid.

Flowridia placed a quick kiss on Ayla's lips, then pulled away, accepting that time stilled for no one, no matter who she prayed to. "There are arrangements to make, surely—"

"Flowra, I'm caring for all of that.

When her feet touched the floor, Flowridia slipped her nightgown from her body, blushing when she felt Ayla's eyes on her slight curves. "I'm anticipating it being a long day."

"Yes, but we get presents," Ayla said brightly, and she stood from the bed and moved to change her dress. Flowridia had once berated her for wearing the same dress twice in a row. Ayla often neglected to wear nightclothes, but why would she if she never slept?

One more day as a masquerading peasant. Tomorrow she would be royalty, but she was still expected to don the cumbersome jewels and complicated gowns of Solviraes monarchs. From her dresser drawer, she withdrew a treasured possession—Lunestra's crown.

"Would you like help plaiting that into your hair?"

Flowridia's thumb stroked the intricate gold, mindful of the subtle shift in texture as it glossed over the small gems. "Ayla, I . . ." Behind her eyelids, memories of vacant eyes followed wherever she went. Tears filled her own. "I shouldn't. I can't."

"Why not?" Ayla plucked the crown from her hand. "Your great-aunt would have wanted it."

"Someone might recognize it," Flowridia said, but that wasn't a reason someone like Ayla would accept. "Ayla, I'm not . . . I'm not worthy of it."

"*Worthy* might be the wickedest word language has ever invented, my love." Ayla sat herself on the vanity, blocking the mirror as she faced Flowridia. "It keeps us in self-imposed cages, constantly questioning our value as people. Don't think, just speak—do you want this crown?"

Flowridia quickly nodded.

"Then take it, darling." Ayla offered it back. "Who gives a damn what anyone thinks? This is your birthright by blood, and no one's opinion can change that—not even yours. It is merely fact."

Flowridia accepted the crown, admittedly not feeling much better.

Perhaps it showed. "At least try it on?"

"I can do that," Flowridia said, managing to smile when Ayla sat her down.

Watching from the mirror, Flowridia witnessed an amusing bit of drama—Ayla's stark confusion as she set about parting the thick locks of her hair. Trying to, rather, given the curls clung to each other, and when Flowridia winced from tugging, Ayla's lips tightened into a line. "This may take time."

"It may take months of practice," Flowridia said, laughter in the words. Sensing Ayla's rising frustration, she stood and kissed her thin lips. "Call for Reginal. He'll know someone who can help."

Ayla's petulant glower remained. "I have braided flowers into your hair before."

"And you do a wonderful job at that." Flowridia lifted the crown, displaying the prongs in the comb on the bottom. "This will take more skill."

"Fine," Ayla spat. "But tell no one of my failure."

"I would never."

Ayla left to find Reginal.

Flowridia looked upon the crown once more and wondered, for the first time, if it might honor Lunestra at least a little for her to wear the crown on her grand, penultimate day.

Many guests would arrive tomorrow, those native to the kingdom and of less esteemed status, but the castle would be housing several foreign royals and their entourages.

Flowridia spent the afternoon in the throne room greeting a line of noble guests, most of whom claimed to know Lara. To her credit, Lara smiled and laughed with each of them, thanking them for their presence. A spectacular actress—Ayla's charm was practiced and perfect.

To Flowridia's surprise, Etolié stood among them, leisurely tapping her foot, staring off into space as she followed the slowly trickling line.

But her heart beat rapidly when her beloved Staelash approached. Thalmus stood among them, his calm smile grounding among the room of mostly strangers, whereas Marielle practically jittered with excitement. Zorlaeus looked rather pale, and Flowridia could not say if she were surprised or not that Sora was not among them.

It was best to not remind Ayla that Sora existed.

At their turn, Flowridia stepped down the stairs leading to the throne and ran to them, greeted first by Thalmus' embrace. "Congratulations, Flowra," his soothing voice said.

"Flowridia, this is the most wonderful day of my life!" Marielle proclaimed, nearly choking her in her cleavage— some things never changed. She smelled of rich soap and new clothes, and Flowridia clung to her familiarity. "Second only to tomorrow, which is sure to be perfect."

"What about your wedding?" Flowridia asked, amused at the hyperbole.

"I am allowed to have more than one favorite day." Marielle squeaked and ran to her supposed cousin—and Lara, to her credit, smiled even when Marielle released her from her crushing hug.

Zorlaeus offered a shy hand, his grip limp and sweaty when Flowridia accepted. "Congratulations, Flowridia. Weddings truly are magical."

"Thank you." She glanced back in the line, though did not spot what she sought. Her voice lowered. "I should warn you that Nox'Kartha will be here."

The man's maroon features paled to nearly baby pink. "And I appreciate the warning."

Lara remained civil, kind even when greeting Staelash's royal couple. Flowridia took the moment to speak to Thalmus, knowing time was short. "I hope my request to have you walk with me isn't too much."

"Not at all," he replied, and she noticed his clothing—cut to his figure, or well enough so, old but perhaps the finest he owned. His hair held a more elaborate braid than she'd ever seen before, falling down to his belt, and she thought he looked wonderfully handsome. "It's the least I can do for my little flower girl."

The name brought joy, and she hugged him once more, saddened when he and the rest of Staelash were escorted away.

Lara's smile was sweet, but in the short lapse of guests, she said, "Gods, that woman is insufferable."

"Marielle means well," Flowridia whispered, "but if it's any consolation, I don't know that Lara thought all that highly of her either."

Lara's grin became wicked at that.

Flowridia greeted countless nobles, all leaving gifts in an ever-increasing pile. Members of the Solviran council with spouses came through as well, and Flowridia was charmed to see Reginal's husband, Erlyn, as well as their adopted daughter once more. Ceile was dressed like a princess with beautiful braids tightly wound in her dark hair.

Flowridia told her such. "I don't think there needs to be a princess here when you come to visit."

General Irons came too, standing beside an attractive woman who matched his middle age. "Lady Flowridia, this is my wife, Margritte," he said, and he nearly smiled.

Margritte's eyes sparkled when she offered a hug. "My husband has said fine things about you."

Flowridia's heart warmed. So strange, to think she had made an unexpected friend.

Eventually, Etolié reached the front, and Flowridia marveled briefly at her gown, though she knew it to be a mere construct—ethereal and pastel, nearly translucent and with an otherworldly feel, the sort mere mortals could never truly emulate with fabric alone.

Lara said, with a laugh, "Etolié, you're not a guest."

"No, but with permission I would channel one. Goddess Staella wanted to give her regards and a gift."

Those within earshot hushed at the words. "Of course," Flowridia replied. "We wouldn't wish to keep Staella waiting."

"Eh, time is different in Celestière." But Etolié stepped back and shut her eyes, the space around her clearing of people. She clasped her hands together, inaudible words on her lips. Before their eyes, a blinding light shone, as brilliant as the sun, and Flowridia had to cover her eyes.

What else were stars, but distant suns?

Etolié's form morphed, growing tall and soft, gently curved in a way her thin physique wasn't. Staella wore the gown Etolié had donned, her features matching the familiar Celestial in so many ways, yet the curve of her lip was wrong, fuller, her cheekbones less defined, though her hair shone a familiar silver, glittering as vibrantly as the night sky.

Most illustrious were her golden wings. Wispy yet magnificent, power radiated from the outstretched appendages. They nearly touched both walls when they stretched to their full length, and Staella smiled with lips even wider. "Alauriel Solviraes," she whispered, her voice feminine and almost childlike, soft and warm, "it is a joy to see you."

Then, her attention settled on Flowridia, and she was reminded of the fallen empress, whose tender gaze had drawn her in the moment they settled upon her in a garden long ago. "And you are Flowridia. Etolié speaks lovingly of you."

Staella came forward, standing demurely as she looked from one to the other. "Your union brings peace, both to this kingdom and to my heart. Alauriel and Flowridia Solviraes, I have a gift."

In Staella's hand appeared a scroll, small for the Goddess, but appropriately sized for a mortal. She offered it forward, the tied string radiating magic, but the scroll itself seemed to be mere paper. "The contents of this scroll are for your eyes alone. My gift to you both."

Lara accepted the offering, gazing at the scroll with curiosity. "Thank you, Goddess Staella. We will not abuse your trust."

Flowridia saw sincerity in Staella's smile, but it laced with heartbreak. She knew the stories, that Staella was a broken goddess. A thousand of years had passed, but once the Stars had ruled the night sky with her beloved, the Moon—until the Moon had fallen. The Stars extinguished. The world had never been the same.

She was curious at the gift, unable to fathom what Etolié's mother would offer her, but she smiled, truly grateful for her presence. "It is kind of you to come here and wish us well. Thank you for your gift."

"You are truly welcome," Staella said. "Fate works in wondrous ways, that the world would align to bring you two together. I will not take up more of your time, but I will return tomorrow for your wedding day. Best of luck, and farewell."

Staella's aura dimmed, her size diminishing, and within seconds it was simply Etolié, swaying slightly. When she stumbled, Flowridia came forward to catch her. "That wasn't as difficult as I anticipated, hosting her."

"Your mother is lovely," Flowridia replied, her heart torn to shreds for all her mixed feelings.

"Isn't she?"

As Etolié walked away, Flowridia swallowed her guilt—to know it was all a ruse, that this so-called fate was only a lie, that she would break the heart of the one goddess she ever sincerely contemplated pledging to.

The guests continued with their well-wishes and their gifts. Flowridia kept glancing at the door, waiting for an announcement from Nox'Kartha, any sign of their coming. Casvir's death was sealed so vibrantly in her memory, and she would feel no peace until she saw him again.

Faces became a blur, and Flowridia tired, going through the motions of greeting her guests, until one voice stood out. "This is awkward. I hope you don't mind."

The man before her was an elf, his white-blonde hair unmistakable, as well as the scarring on his face and ears and exposed skin. He dressed in fine clothes, suited for his handsome figure, bearing no weapons but holding a small, wrapped gift. On his shoulder, there was perched a little bird.

"I didn't actually receive an invitation," Tazel Fireborn said, an apology etched into his countenance, "so I hope it isn't presumptuous that I came."

Flowridia took the gift, passed it to the waiting servant, then embraced her dear friend, the one who had helped her through her most harrowing moments of grief. "Tazel, my friend, you could never be a bother."

As she turned to introduce him to her betrothed, she recalled, like a punch to her stomach, that Ayla knew Tazel perfectly well. But Lara's smile held boundless kindness as she offered a hand and accepted his work-worn one. "It is a delight to meet you. Any friend of Flowra's is a friend of mine."

"I am overjoyed for you both," he said, his smile suddenly forced. "Goodness, you have a firm grip."

"My apologies," Lara replied, her smile showing teeth.

"Flowridia," he said, shaking out his abused hand, "I am so happy. I am . . . relieved. Relieved that you're happy," he quickly added, and Flowridia forced herself to laugh because he had known her intentions all along. "I hope you understand why I can't stay for the wedding itself. One of your guests is an imperator I owe a great deal of time and money to, and I have no intention of paying up."

"The fact that you stopped by is more than enough," she said. "Visit anytime."

They said their farewells, and when he had gone, Lara's visage flickered into ire for just a moment. "Anytime? Really?"

"I like him, and he's my friend," Flowridia replied, and she resumed greeting the next guest.

She fell into a lull of greetings, exhaustion coming in waves. But the guests kept appearing, the line never ending.

The first hint should have been Lara's sudden, subtle sneer, but Flowridia's overstimulated mind struggled to make sense of the unrecognizable figure suddenly before them. Yes, there were his glowing red eyes, his stark white hair pulled into a signature tail, even blue-tinged skin, marking him as more corpse-like than not. And horns—sweeping horns— adding height to his already substantial presence. Yet, while he did not appear small—his skin seemed ready to split for his muscled bulk—he did seem somehow undersized, lacking the imposing menace Flowridia had come to recognize.

He stared expectantly, and Flowridia stared back, the silence punctuated by only the soft gasps and whispers of the guests around them.

Flowridia realized, in that moment, that she had never seen Imperator Casvir dressed without his armor. Instead, covering his substantial figure was a well-tailored and oddly stifling suit, the sort she often saw among military nobility. High fashion should've been laughable on the demon-blooded necromancer, but Flowridia would never tell Casvir he looked out of place.

447

In fact, he looked nearly handsome, at least as much as the menacing De'Sindai could.

She stared too long, it seemed, because Casvir quirked an eyebrow. "Lady Flowridia?"

Flowridia had expected tears. Tears came easily—always had. But something blocked the natural flow of emotion, a strange sort of perturb she had no name for. "I had heard you were back."

"It has been a few weeks, yes," Casvir replied, the familiarity and comfort of his voice only burning her more.

"And you didn't think to tell me?"

Casvir, however, appeared nonplussed by her growing fury. "I have been busy."

Yes, the utter disregard was rude, but it was a statement so unquestionably Casvir, and Flowridia's annoyance faded away. She fell into his arms; he knelt to meet her. "I have missed you, Flowridia."

She clung tightly to him, her small arms wrapping around his neck. Casvir made no move to extract her embrace. Only when she stood and stepped away did he nod in deference to Lara. "Empress Alauriel, I remember you taller."

Surely he knew the ruse, with a greeting like that. Lara smiled, though there was resignation in the gesture. "You would forget your head were it not attached to your disemboweled body."

Casvir's lip twisted upward at the jest. "Your humor is *biting.*"

"Would you prefer I hammered it down a little?"

"*Anyway,*" Flowridia interrupted, the mood between them unquestionably tense. She realized, for all their pomp and bitterness toward the other, she had never actually seen them together. "I'm delighted you could come."

"I was surprised to receive your invitation," Casvir replied, and Flowridia still could not shake the oddness of his outfit, "but not displeased."

"I couldn't not invite you. You're far too dear to me."

Casvir shook his head. "It was not the event itself, but the actors." He looked to Lara now instead, the barest hints of amusement twitching on his lip. "Now I understand. I only hope, with Lady Flowridia as Empress Consort, we might continue our neutrality."

"That's for the future to tell," Lara said, and there was nothing of the empress in her stance and stare—Ayla Darkleaf grinned, and Casvir merely nodded.

"It would be rude of me to steal more time from your other guests," Casvir said. "But I will be here to enjoy the festivities. Seek me out if you wish for company."

Flowridia spared a glance for the line of well-wishers, surprised when Lara spoke up. "Flowra—"

Flowridia turned around, astonished at the soft resignation in her expression.

"Flowra, go with him. Enjoy his company, and that of your friends. I can greet guests on my own."

"That would be so rude. I can't."

Lara made a show of sighing, then beckoned for the nearest guard. She whispered words into his ear.

The guard cried, "The couple will be taking a break for the next half hour. Refreshments will be provided while you wait."

Lara then turned to kiss her, stealing the shock from her mouth. "Tomorrow is our wedding," Lara whispered, "so go spend time with the people who matter to you. You are tiring, so make the time count. I will see you in half an hour."

So much sincerity in her loving gaze, and for a moment, Flowridia saw only Lara, the woman who lay dead in her grave. But they were Ayla's words, Ayla's touch. Flowridia squeezed her hand before she left.

In a vacant hallway, Flowridia's worry welled anew. "Casvir, how are you, truly?"

Casvir's usual stoicism remained. His steps were much quieter without the metallic echoing of his armor. Very flatly, he said, "I have had better months."

She hadn't assisted him, and she felt some guilt in that. Still, her wry comment could not be contained. "I'm glad you managed to pull yourself together."

Casvir opened his mouth, but shut it just as abruptly, a flickering a smile twitching at the corners of his frown. "I regenerated, but you are as clever as always."

"Did you genuinely not realize who I was marrying?"

"Murishani informed me that you had been successful in your quest, but when I received your invitation, I no longer knew what was true."

Flowridia took Casvir down the lift, his relentless stare aimed at the daylight filtering through the glass windows of the lift.

"How can this be, though?" Flowridia asked, for here they were truly alone. "Watching the God of Order cut you in two was horrific enough, but I accept that you survived. How in the world did you live through what Khastra did?"

"Truly proficient necromancers gain a mastery over all death, including their own." The lift stopped, and Casvir gestured for her to lead. "I cannot be killed, because I decreed it so many years ago."

Servants and guests were scattered through the hall, and Flowridia withheld her reply as she stepped through the crowd, politely acknowledging those she passed. Casvir followed, radiating an aura of menace, which Flowridia suspected he had practiced to get him out of social interactions.

The more you knew a person, the less frightening they became.

She led him outside, the cool air invigorating after so much time spent indoors, surrounded by bodies. The winter air chilled her throat when she breathed. Hints of frost clung to the shadows, and Flowridia led Casvir to the expansive garden. "Ayla called you something," she whispered. "A lich."

"That is the name for it," Casvir replied. "When a necromancer wishes to gain mastery over death, he or she will carve out their own heart and seal it inside a specially crafted box. This is called a phylactery. Unless the box and its contents are destroyed, your body will manifest after your passing, no matter what its state. It results in a state of living death—my body is cold because there is no heart in my chest, but I maintain the capacity to do a great many mortal things."

Flowridia lingered beyond the garden's reach, the sunlight infinitely precious, but she refused to contemplate that notion now. "How does one learn this?"

"If you wish, I will teach you when you are ready. But failure to execute the rituals properly will result in death, at best. At worst, you rip your soul from your body, condemned to be a ghost haunting a corpse."

A strange hope filled her, to think there might be another way to live forever.

"You are not ready," Casvir continued, dashing those hopes into pieces. "There is much for you to do with your mortal life, and even more to learn. As I said, the consequences of failure are dire."

Flowridia stepped into the shaded garden space, embracing the chill and letting it distract her. Casvir offered a solution to her dilemma, but it might be years before this could be accomplished, if ever. Would Ayla be willing to wait?

Was it an inquiry she even dared to make?

Her burdened heart longed to tell someone, and Casvir had helped to carry her heavy soul before. But he would think her foolish, at best. Were he so opposed, he may even reveal Ayla's true nature to preserve her life for his own means.

Flowridia simply smiled. "Then it is good I am young and have time to wait."

The garden promised to flourish in the spring, the trees and bushes biding their time in the cold air. Longing seized her heart—would she be here to see it? By night, perhaps. But never again would she feel the first whispers of sunrise upon a new bud; never again would she feel the morning dew nor watch it reflect morning light.

"May I ask something?"

Flowridia glanced up, praying her heartache did not show. "Of course."

Casvir appeared as a stone guardian among the beauty—not marring it, but certainly changing the peaceful aura. "Have you taken any precautions to keep your wife-to-be in line?"

The words shattered her forced peace. Offense rose. "I beg your pardon?"

"I do not ask for my kingdom's sake. I ask for yours. You have taken a risky gamble. If rumors are to be believed, your kingdom has been plagued by a recent onslaught of vampiric activity."

Smile forced, she said, "My betrothed is not a child who needs parenting."

"You are allowing this?"

Strange, to face her sins and feel the full weight of their judgement. Casvir waited for a response, a justification, and Flowridia had none to give. "We have a plan," she said simply, praying he would cease.

"There are rumors that Ayla Darkleaf herself is behind it all."

"That was Etolié's doing," Flowridia replied, the air suddenly difficult to breathe.

"I have heard, too, of the reformations you have helmed to accommodate refugees from the Theocracy." He said it with no ire, merely as fact. "I commend you. Your foresight is admirable, and your use of your magic is generous. It is everything a proper monarch should be."

She waited for a catch, but he did not give it. Instead, she forced a smile, knowing all his compliments were to be cherished as the rarities they were. "Thank you."

He watched her, studied her, his red eyes staring past her many layers. Casvir had always known her too well. "Are you happy?"

"Yes, of course—"

He held up a hand, then repeated his inquiry, slower this time. "Are you happy?"

Flowridia matched his gaze, refusing to wither beneath it. "She is all I have ever wanted."

"But are you happy?"

Was she?

Flowridia faced away from him, taking idle steps down the path. "She and I are very different people," she admitted, "and while I don't know that I ever dreamed of any specific future, this isn't what I imagined. I think I would be happier living a quiet life, but a part of me accepted that someone like Ayla never would, even before she came back. And she's outlandish, yes, but . . ."

Her memory drifted to their quiet moments alone, to Ayla's tears as she spoke of her history, her strange contentment at assembling dead men into 'spiders.'

". . . it's wonderful, seeing her so happy. And I am happy, Casvir. Truly." She shut her eyes. Beneath the shadows of the trees, the sun felt so far away. "She's the one who proposed coming to Solvira. She wanted the power. I agreed to come because I wanted to help the people of the Theocracy. Your actions appalled me. Had you told me the stakes, I would have abandoned my quest and taken my throne. I came here to try and rectify the tragedy I could have prevented."

"Is that why you wear a Theocracy crown?"

She slowed her steps, finally stopping as she contemplated the slight weight on her head. "It was a gift."

"Do you know where the archbishop is?"

"The Beyond," Flowridia said, aware of his presence behind her, "but not before I revealed myself as her grandniece. We became close, her and I."

"My condolences for your loss."

Before she could stop it, a bitter, scoffing laugh escaped her throat. "You can't say that. You wanted her dead."

"I do not regret her death, but I do regret your loss."

"Casvir, if you truly cared for my feelings, you would have told me what I was walking away from. You asked me if I wanted the throne, and I said no. You didn't tell me that the alternative was the destruction of an entire city. Thousands lost their lives. I know that means nothing to you, but it means everything to me. So now I'm here, trying to salvage any hope I can for those left behind, even as your troops march on to slaughter the rest."

Her jaw trembled—from sorrow, from rage, or from the grand betrayal of his character, she couldn't say. Inside, something virulent brewed, but she swallowed it back, refusing to show weakness to her mentor and friend.

"Your ire is hypocritical," he said, the barest hint of a scowl on his features, "considering who you have placed on the throne beside you."

He might as well have struck her; she reeled back all the same. "I beg your pardon?"

"Ayla Darkleaf has killed hundreds of thousands more than I have, yet you turn a blind eye to her crimes and condemn mine?"

She heard his words, yes, yet her mind refused to let them settle, couldn't bear to let their meaning sink in. He waited for an answer.

"I know," she said curtly. Rather than scream, she turned on her heels, studying the trees, the trilling of birds—anything other than that wicked truth.

Casvir remained quiet for a time as the air cleared between them. Then, his large hand gripped her shoulder, gentler than his size would have predicted. "I apologize. Sincerely. I have not meant to offend you."

Stiff beneath his touch, she managed merely a nod.

"This conversation is not going well," he said, and the abrupt honesty broke her tension; she laughed, scoffing and pained, grateful when he gave a small smile.

"You're an ass," she said, for he was the same, always and forever. "But it doesn't mean you aren't my friend."

"You are the only person I have ever allowed to call me that."

The statement warmed her heart, but she managed to grin. "Ass? You can't tell me Murishani doesn't call you that daily."

"I was referring to 'friend,' and you know that." But he smiled, her jest having landed well. "Flowridia, your success in restoring Ayla's life genuinely fills me with pride. The throne you have secured is worthy of your name and talents. I cannot commend you enough."

Though her eyes still watered, she smiled. "Thank you."

"I must ask—did you slay the empress?"

With those words, Flowridia's joy faded. "Her blood was used for the ritual, yes."

She hadn't slain Lara, but she struggled to find the words to say it.

"Not a simple task."

She shook her head, face downcast. Shame filled her, for she had done nothing in the end. Perhaps she didn't deserve his accolades, just as Lara hadn't deserved to die.

And so, she forced herself to speak her guilt; Casvir had always been a listening ear. To the ground, she said, "I didn't slit her throat. Soliel did."

"Why?"

"I don't know why he did it." She clenched her fists, refusing to cry for this. Again. "But he threw her body at my feet and bid me to complete my task. He had overheard me falter and killed her instead."

"Strange." A few moments of silenced passed, but then he added, "When I tried to speak to him in the woods, he said something unnerving."

Ayla had mentioned Soliel saying that, she recalled. Flowridia met his eye, intrigued to know what someone like Casvir would find 'unnerving.'

"I tried to bargain with him and offer him my aid in exchange for his."

"Why did you want his aid?"

"That is irrelevant. But he refused my offer, and instead stated his own terms—that he would do anything I wanted, even abandon his quest for the orbs, in exchange for my phylactery."

Flowridia frowned, taken aback by the words. "The box with your heart?"

"Correct. I said no, and so he left." Casvir joined her in frowning. "It has left me unsettled."

"I suppose the only question now..." Flowridia grinned, cheeky and wide. "...is whether I could give him your phylactery instead, in exchange for not destroying the worlds."

Casvir's frown disappeared, replaced by that familiar, neutral face he gave whenever she said a particularly wry pun. "I encourage you to try finding it. Truly. Good luck."

"But you wouldn't give your life to save the worlds?"

"No."

She rolled her eyes, not surprised in the slightest.

They spoke of lighter things, though Flowridia's mind wandered.

Late in the evening, when the mingling dwindled, Etolié crept toward a guarded room.

Fortunately, the stationed patrol did not question why she would have need to inspect the large room filled with presents and let her pass. There was a particular one she needed to find.

But despite her wish to draw as little attention as possible to her quest—there, seated leisurely upon the gift pile, was Lara.

In the empress' hands was a scroll of unfathomable worth—truly, since no one knew the contents except Staella herself, and now Lara. She glanced up from her reading, eyes wide from an emotion Etolié couldn't quite decipher. "Oh. Good evening."

"Avoiding the party?"

Lara nodded. "I am exhausted from people."

"Understandable. What are you doing?" Etolié said as she approached, trying her best to appear nonchalant as she searched the nametags on the presents. No need to worry her moonbeam needlessly.

Lara rolled up the scroll. "Nothing of importance."

"That's not nothing. That's my momma's scroll."

Lara shrugged, casually retying the string—well, trying to be casual, but the subtle sneering of her lip said otherwise. Etolié frowned as she floated up beside her, trusting herself to be light enough to not crush any of the gifts as she landed beside Lara. "What's wrong?"

Lara smiled, and it was the smile Etolié knew and adored—radiant and warm. "I am perfectly fine."

"You're full of shit is what you are. You can't lie to me."

There was little to read in her expression; Lara was a politician, and she could hide her feelings behind an iron mask when necessary. "Etolié—"

"Don't 'Etolié' me. Between you and me, I've been worried about you." Etolié placed a hand on her moonbeam's arm, frowning at how cold the poor thing was. "I'm not your mom, and I'm a piss-poor stand-in for one, but someone has to ask if everything is all right. One of the biggest days of your life is tomorrow. If . . . If you're having doubts or worries, you can talk to me."

Lara had been moody lately, unpredictable and stressed in the way any sane woman would be in the days leading up to her wedding, but to Etolié's relief, sincere joy overtook her countenance. "I feel like I've been waiting for tomorrow my entire life," she whispered. "When I think of her, I only feel peace."

Etolié might've bought it, so nearly did, but Lara's hands looked ready to wring the scroll like an enemy's neck. "So, it isn't Flowers that's bothering you. Good." Etolié tried to steal the scroll, but Lara's grip only tightened. "But that has you tied up in knots."

Lara brought the scroll to her chest, hugging it tight, her lips a thin line. Etolié had no fucking clue what it meant. "Fine. It does. But I cannot speak of it. Your mother didn't want anyone else to know."

"If you need to talk, I think she'll forgive you for talking it out with me, her daughter." Etolié removed her hand from

Lara's shoulder, wishing she had a pile of blankets to bury her in.

Lara's face hardened, then she slipped the scroll into a shadow, some extra-dimensional space, as she shook her head. "It does not matter. Flowra will understand." Distress settled upon her features, some hesitation Etolié didn't understand. "She has to."

"If this has you this fucked up, you should talk to her."

But Lara simply shook her head, her lips nothing but a thin line.

Etolié, feeling well out of her depth, brought a hand to her moonbeam's back. "In my personal experience, relationship ending secrets never live up to their name. Khastra and I have been through a few wringers, and we're stronger than ever—our friendship, I mean. We're very good friends."

Lara smiled like she knew shit, but Etolié wasn't ready to confirm. "Thank you."

"You're clearly not fine," Etolié said, Lara's weirdness only welling further worry. "But if you don't want to talk, that's fine too."

"No," Lara said softly, and it only added to Etolié's pile of worry. She smiled sweetly though—sweeter than pie. "But I may take some time tonight to pray. Would that appease you?"

"As long as it helps. I love you, you know." Etolié squeezed Lara's hand, then carefully descended the gift pile, sensing the quiet shift in mood. She had come with a task in mind, and it proved to be laughably easy—for there, upon a small pile near the back, was a wrapped gift in black and red bearing a tag with the perpetrator's name: *Ayla Darkleaf.*

It bore a heart as well. With a proper eyeroll, Etolié lifted the gift and went to the door.

"What do you have there?"

Etolié glanced up at Lara, still seated on the pile of gifts. "Nothing important. But trust me. This one needs to go."

And she left without any further explanation. Lara was worried enough.

Gift in hand, Etolié's illusionary heels clicked down the hallway, her commitment to the aesthetic what truly made it shine. Sound effects were second nature. Still, her mind wouldn't quiet about a great many things, the number one of which were the contents of this particular box, so her focus was forced to be deliberate lest it falter—

"Magister Etolié, may we speak?"

The voice from her nightmares had come.

Forcing a smile, she saw Imperator Casvir standing behind her, regal and imposing. Strange, seeing him without his armor, but it did not mean he was any less dangerous. "Imperator Casvir," she said politely, adding a nod for show, "delightful to see you. I can spare a moment, though I am on my way to deliver a stolen package."

Casvir didn't take the conversation bait. "Where is my general?"

Dread welled in Etolié's stomach, but she kept her smile. "Somewhere, I'm sure. Haven't seen her much today."

"Tomorrow, once the couple has left at sunset, I shall be taking my leave," Casvir said, unquestionable menace in his voice. "I do not care what she does in the time in between, but she leaves with me."

Imperator First and Last made his exit, but fury rose in Etolié's blood. "Imperator," she said, barely composed, "may we speak in private?"

She could decipher nothing on his neutral features, but was surprised when he said, "We may."

Etolié opened a door to the small closet—hardly a proper place for two monarchs to speak, but it was large enough for them both, including Casvir's substantial girth, assuming he didn't knock over any brooms. When he entered, she shut the door behind them, letting her wings show and illuminate the small room. There was hardly two feet between them, but she didn't care. "I won't waste your time. Let's talk as friends. You're not a monarch, and I'm not the daughter of a goddess. Level with me, Casvir—is my favorite demon about to be stripped into a thousand tiny pieces? Because I can always slit her throat myself. Toss her head into Celestière. Save her some pain."

Casvir, to his credit, did not look annoyed to be addressed by merely his name. "You are not entitled to that information . . . Etolié."

Her name was an afterthought and clearly a point of pain, but she respected him working through it. "Fine. Then I'll take her to Celestière again until you lose patience and just let her go. Or break her brain."

"Or I command her to slay you."

Etolié's eyes narrowed. "Fair. And she would succeed, assuming my godly momma doesn't cast her into eternal sleep first. I genuinely don't know who would win that one, but good lucking getting her out of Celestière. My point is that unless you give me a fucking reason, I'll do whatever it takes to make certain you never see her again."

Those red eyes sharpened. His lip twitched; he looked nearly pleased. "I would consider that an act of war."

"Bring the horde, then. Wouldn't be the first time Solvira has battled an army of the dead."

Silence settled between them, the tension as thick as the corporeal light of Etolié's wings. "Knowing your persistence," Casvir finally said, "you will see my general again."

"Alive?"

"She is not currently, so no."

Etolié opened her mouth, but just as quickly shut it. "All right, ya little shit, I see how it is. I want that in writing, though. Or at least a fucking handshake."

Casvir shook his head. "I do not owe you that."

"Are you gonna torture her half to death first?"

"She is already—"

"Oh, fuck *off* with your literalism. You know what I mean." Etolié crossed her arms, no longer trying to fake a smile. "You don't understand love, and that's fine. I thought I didn't until about six weeks ago. But if I thought I could take her place, I'd offer it—and if that doesn't tell you how stupid I'm willing to be to protect her, nothing else will. She's the most important person in the world to me, so don't push me to strap explosives to my chest and walk into your castle to protect her."

His raised eyebrow spoke volumes. "You are free with your words."

"This is a talk between friends, remember?" she forced a grin, unable to quite suppress her crazy eyes.

He held eye contact; it took all her willpower to match it. "If I tell you, will you agree to let her go without causing a scene?"

"Assuming I let her go with you at all, yes."

"I have no intention of harming her, assuming she behaves. Her privileges and luxuries in my castle shall be renegotiated. A contract shall be penned between us dictating her precise roles and responsibilities, as well as a list of banned behaviors, among which shall be wielding her hammer against me."

He said nothing more, merely waited for her reply. Etolié knew it didn't matter how hard she glared; the bastard was immune. "All right," she said, though the feeling of dread hadn't waned. "Thank you."

"While we are speaking as friends, I have an inquiry."

"Go for it."

His gaze finally shifted—to the package in her arms. "Why are you holding a gift from Ayla Darkleaf?"

The gift's tag showed. Even in the dark room, the script practically glowed. "Ah well, funny story—rumor is, she's back. And by 'rumor,' I mean that we had the great misfortune to have a conversation while she molested some poor sap with his chest ripped open." Etolié smiled, but it was not a smile at all—just her pulling her lips wide while her eyes remained dead. "If you see her, kindly smash her head in."

"I would not hesitate," he replied, and though his face said nothing, those words said a whole fucking lot.

Etolié offered a slow nod. "Nice to know we agree on one thing." She extended her hand. "Good talk. Let's hope we never have to be friends again."

He did not take her hand. Awkwardly, she drew it back, then let herself out of the closet, taking no care to make sure the door did not shut in the imperator's face.

Though unnerved beyond reason, she could not yet face real life. Instead, she resumed her quest and took the gift to an unconventional place, full of the only people in the castle who would understand. With a polite knock, she entered the large suite set aside for the guests of Staelash.

Within, she saw the predictable assortment—Marielle babbling about her honeymoon, making a few too many mentions of Murishani for Etolié's comfort, and Thalmus, who politely listened, as well as Zorlaeus, who must have been half deaf to be able to listen to her constant chattering. That or he liked it because he truly loved her, but Etolié settled on that first one.

"Good evening, friends," she said, not making eye contact with Thalmus. "I need emotional support."

She came forward with the gift. "What's that?" Marielle asked, gesturing to the seat beside her.

"You all need to know this, because the more eyes on the lookout, the better. Rumor says Ayla Darkleaf is back and swanning around Solvira."

The mood immediately turned cold.

"And by 'rumor,'" Etolié continued, "I mean confirmed by yours truly. We had a delightful talk, and by 'delightful,' I mean I wanted to puke afterward." Etolié placed the gift on the table, the tag clearly visible.

"You spoke to her?" Thalmus asked, his deep tone severe.

"She insists she won't be doing anything to disrupt Flowers' day."

Thalmus' judgement showed in his severe features, and Etolié shifted uncomfortably. "And you believed her?"

"No, so we should all be on alert. She said she would be dropping this off, though, and Flowers doesn't need this sort of negativity in her life."

The red, satin bow was tied to perfection. Etolié gave it a tug. Everyone's eyes remained fixed to the box; Etolié carefully opened the top, revealing a smaller, wooden one. "Moment of truth," she muttered, cringing as she lifted the lid.

Zorlaeus looked faint; Marielle's eyes went wide. Thalmus probably growled, but Etolié groaned. "Of course."

A heart, moist and raw, lay in a bed of silk, and upon the inner lid of the box was carved, *My Heart is Yours Forever.*

"But is that her actual heart?" Marielle said, asking the important question.

"It could be," Zorlaeus said, affirming that he still had a voice. "She doesn't need it, and hers will slowly grow back if removed. And, well, it fits her style of dramatics."

"You would know," Etolié said, forcibly remembering not to use the name 'Lae Lae'—which was a struggle. It was damn catchy. "Oh, she's nasty."

Perturb appeared in the thin line of Marielle's lips. "Why must her packages contain a body part every time?"

Etolié shut the box. "We never tell Flowers."

"Never ever," Marielle affirmed.

All were in agreement.

When she'd bid her friends goodnight, Flowridia stood alone in a dark hallway, finality settling upon her.

The last night.

She ran her fingers across the skin of her forearm, feeling warmth yet imagining cold, and wondered if Ayla would feel warm when she became as dead as she.

A crushing hand gripped her heart, her panic ever rising, but she swallowed it, breathed, and wrapped her arms around herself.

Ayla had said to set her affairs in order. She had spent the day loving those who needed it. Loving those she would never see again, the ones she would lose when she became one with the night.

Would Casvir disown her for stunting her growth? Would Thalmus hate her for the radiating cold of her skin? Etolié might love her still, but she was close to suspecting dangerous things.

Steeling her courage, she marched through the halls, finding her way to her room.

Ayla was nowhere to be seen. Flowridia sat on the bed and waited, her gaze settling on the bouquet upon the table. She still hadn't mentioned it, knowing Ayla's proclivities toward jealousy.

She loved Ayla. By every god—her very soul yearned for Ayla, to hold her, to house her, to love her all her life. Yet, the world was better without her. Each day, more blood stained Flowridia's hands as she willfully turned away.

If she saved as many as she allowed to die, did it all balance in the end?

Whatever the state of her soul, she would lose it tomorrow.

Idly, she stood and stepped toward the bouquet, its eclectic colors as erratic as her scattered heart. She studied the display, heart aching to recall Lara's joy when she had received them. A drunk night of kisses and nothing more, but Lara had been easy prey, already smitten, so effortlessly lured to her doom.

A doom Flowridia hadn't delivered.

Her bleeding heart hardened. Forever discontent she might be, but her choice had been stolen. Fate had been decreed. Whatever her conflicted heart thought of Lara, whether or not they might have found happiness together or grown to resent the other for who Lara was not, the God of Order had interfered.

The thought did not bring sorrow . . . but anger. A final few questions still lingered.

The shadows flickered. Ayla stepped inside, as herself, holding a wrapped box. "I have been searching for you."

"As have I, but I suspected I would find you more quickly if I just stayed put." Flowridia studied her, the woman she would marry when this cold night had ended, and mourned the cost of love. Because by every god, she did—to look at Ayla filled her with joy, yet she could not disregard her fear, the blood in the streets, the monster's legacy surely to be made anew. People would die, yet as Ayla's expression softened, Flowridia did not see The Endless Night, the Scourge of the Sun Elves, nor any of the other ghastly titles bestowed upon her love.

She simply saw Ayla.

"What's that?" Flowridia asked.

"A present. My wedding gift to you," Ayla said, hesitation in her stance. "Are you all right?"

"No. I'm not. I would like your assistance in settling one final affair."

"Anything, my love."

She forcibly ignored the bouquet, wishing to draw no attention to it. "Soliel. You could find him. I want to speak to him."

Ayla's frown held no fury, merely contemplation. "Why?"

"He wouldn't speak to you, but he might to me. His actions burden me, the questions he's left too heavy for me to carry into death. He has spoken freely to me before—so let me try one final time. Will you take me to him?"

Ayla nodded. "Let me find him first; then, I will return. Dress warmly, my love."

Ayla placed the box on the vanity and vanished into a shadow. Silence filled the room.

Flowridia dug through the expansive closet to find a shawl that matched her dress. When she emerged, there was still that damned bouquet.

Truly alone, she trembled as she lifted it. Its colors were luscious. Necromancy fueled it. The beauty would last for eternity.

Tomorrow, she would marry.

And for a final, bruising time, she thought of Lara and her silver eyes; she thought of her laugh and her gentle soul, her fear of spiders and acceptance of skeletal foxes. The world would mourn her once it knew the truth, and rightfully so. Flowridia mourned her now.

She dared to hold a mirror to the dusty corners of her heart and ask . . . if this fate were what she truly wanted.

She might have been happy with Lara. It was an undeniable truth, if only because Flowridia could not see the future.

Tears filled her eyes. She sought answers that simply were not there.

In her hands were flowers destined to last until the end of days, yet Flowridia saw them clearly for the first time. Whatever their beauty, whatever potential they once held, they were dead. Nothing could fix that.

With a breath, she took the false life back, small bits of energy flowing through her as the bouquet wilted, desiccated and grey. She walked to the balcony and stepped outside, facing the grand kingdom she would soon rule. A bitter chill stung her face, yet as she looked to the dried flowers, the resentment inside her faded away.

She crumbled each petal, every dried bud, blowing the papery remains into the wind, one by one. Her tears fell freely, yet for the first time, she felt relief. She stared into the dusty places in her heart and swept them anew, allowing herself to mourn a life she wouldn't live.

Burying Lara hadn't meant to bury her guilt, nor her feelings. As each bud flew away, there came freedom. "Whatever else is true or false, you died to save my life," she whispered into the night. "I am indebted to you for that. Alauriel . . ."

The name lingered on the wind, bearing depthless power.

"Thank you."

The final flower drifted off into the night, cast off by her breath. Finality settled into her soul. She threw the handful of dried stems into the air, their weight causing them to fall far away.

As she returned to the bedroom, she wiped her eyes. Her tears finally ceased.

Ayla stepped from the shadows, hints of frost upon her scalp. Before she could speak, Flowridia pulled her into her arms and held her. Just held.

Ayla settled into the embrace, docile and calm. "Are you all right?"

Flowridia kissed her head, the words as poignant as they'd ever been as she softly said, "I love you."

And I am happy, she did not say, not wishing to reveal the end to her personal tale. Some things could be for her alone.

Ayla took her hand. "I have found the God of Order. Are you ready?"

Flowridia nodded. She followed Ayla into the night.

Flowridia appeared in a brilliant, white wonderland. Moonlight reflected from the snow, even through the thick trees. Every breath was fog, her steps crunching through virgin snow, leaving their mark. Winter was nearer to the end than the beginning, but while Solvira held merely frost now, some of the northern forests remained an ethereal realm of ice.

Yet, light shone from between the trees, and Flowridia held her head high as she approached her quarry. A campfire cast contrasting hues across the landscape, golden fire against the silver reflections of snow. She heard a strange snort from the odd creature he had called a 'camel'—it stared at her with black eyes, and she noticed its legs were wrapped in furs.

Soliel himself sat before the fire, wearing no coat, his nose and cheeks pink from cold. The radiant illusion of a halo forever emanated from around his head, conveying his holy stature, though fallen now. His blonde beard bore flecks of grey, and though he was enormous—without his armor, Flowridia could see the outline of his musculature, easily rivaling Casvir's—his figure was hunched before the controlled flame, making him appear so much smaller. In his hands, he held the fire orb, clutching it for further warmth.

He was not magnificent. He was . . . tired.

It shone in his eyes, this bone-deep exhaustion. "Lady Flowridia. A pleasant surprise."

The polite greeting boiled her blood. She pulled the shawl tight around her, cold quickly settling in. Ayla watched from the flickering shadows and could whisk her away in an instant, but she had many words still to say. "Good evening, Soliel. May I join you?"

He gestured toward a log adjacent to himself. After brushing off what snow she could from the seat, she settled in, the fire pleasant against her hands. The camel seemed perfectly content with its wrapping of furs, oblivious to its shivering master. "Aren't you cold?" she asked.

"Yes, but it will not kill me. It more benefits my resources to warm her instead." He gestured to the camel, who came to meet his hand. Affection showed in the touch between them; there was kindness there.

Flowridia said as much. "Noble of you."

"Her kind is not suited for the snow. I can heal her if it becomes too much, but it's best to keep her comfortable as much as possible."

Flowridia studied him, this monster who had slain Lara in cold blood, her father as well, who had bisected Casvir, who had led to Khastra's demise and thus her undead servitude, beheaded a dragon he had once called a son, whose sole purpose was to separate the mortal realm from Celestière and Sha'Demoni and cause the slaughter of millions . . .

Here, she saw none of it. Not a monster who was one of two Old Gods. Merely a man weary of travel. Somehow, this irked her more.

"I would offer food, but I have none," he said, interrupting her musing. "Why have you come here?"

"I'm getting married tomorrow."

He nodded in deference. "Congratulations."

"Is that what you wanted, when you murdered Empress Alauriel?"

His laughter echoed across the silent night. "You have strange priorities, being so angry with me. I only finished what you started."

She would not take his bait. "Is it what you wanted?"

He shrugged. "It was what *you* wanted."

"Why, though? You threw Empress Alauriel Solviraes at my feet," she spat. Her fury rose, to finally voice her great inquiry. "You bid me to rise and move forward, despite my heartbreak. Why?"

"You could not have done the deed yourself. I heard your confession."

"And you took it upon yourself to finish my quest for me. Stop evading my question; I understand what you did. I cannot fathom why."

Silence settled between them. Snowflakes fell, gathering ever so slowly in her hair. Soliel's jaw grit. "Because our goals," he said slowly, deliberate in every careful word, "were not unaligned."

Discomfort settled in her gut, yet she couldn't comprehend the source. "What does that mean?"

"It means that Ayla Darkleaf is a person of such gravity that her actions dictate the very fate of this world. You need her to fill a vacant hole in your heart; I need her to lay out the path for the future."

The words lingered, swirling in Flowridia's mind as she desperately sought their meaning. She forced her face to reveal none of her confusion, calm despite the storm within her. "You told Ayla she would kill herself to run from her fate."

"I stand by that."

Ayla listened from the shadows, heard every condemning word. Flowridia stared upon his visage, searched him for any hints, any indication of what it meant. But she could not read minds; only take what clues she could. "Every answer you give brings more nonsensical questions, Soliel. Speak plainly."

"Is it not enough to have her back?"

He spoke a poignant truth. Flowridia had all she wanted. Perhaps she should be appeased.

Yet, she was slowly accepting that her fate was to be forever discontent. There was nothing to lose in asking for more. "Have you considered that you being here has already drastically altered the world? Perhaps you've repaired one piece of it, but consider all the lives you've stolen. All the events you've irrevocably changed."

"I wish to tear the worlds apart, Lady Flowridia. Has it occurred to you that to change the course of fate was my plan all along?"

"Yet you bothered to right this one piece? It was not a small thing."

The silence lingered, and as Flowridia stared into his visage, she understood a strange and fundamental truth—a truth she saw reflected in her own heart, a truth he had all but claimed those weeks ago, in the woods.

He took a breath to speak, but she spoke first. "It's her, isn't it. It's Chaos. None of this would matter, but you want her back. You're reconstructing the narrative you nearly rewrote."

"Where there are villains," he said, "so must rise a hero. Balance in all things. Without Ayla Darkleaf, there is no Chaos, for she became a harbinger to her rise to power."

"But what will it mean," she asked, hoping to bait him for more, "for Chaos to return only to see all this horror you've wrought? You wield orbs stolen through bloodshed, but that's hardly a drop in a bucket. The blood of millions will be on your hands, Soliel. You said she isn't evil. You said she rose to fight a monster—yet you killed her son. What will she think, to see you've become a monster too?"

For the first time, Flowridia saw the faintest flicker of doubt on Soliel's features.

"Love is sometimes selfish," she continued joylessly. "So, take the selfish path. Forget the world. Abandon it. Find your love instead and live in peace."

Soliel said nothing, merely scrutinized her as she sat as tall and proud as her nerves would allow. He smiled, and she was surprised to find it sincere. "I am selfish to want her back. Somewhere, her spirit waits, just as mine did for ten thousand years. I am also selfish to hope she is wracked with the guilt of her sins, to know she has damned the worlds we fought for eons to try and save."

"What?" Flowridia asked, for she knew not what it meant, but Soliel continued.

"The blood of millions shall be on my hands, yes—yet even that is merely a drop in the ocean for all the lives that shall be lost if I fail again."

She merely stared. "Again?"

"I cannot speak of it."

"But there's a reason," she said, nearly pleading. "You've claimed all along that you're righting her wrong—"

"I am—"

"But something happens, doesn't it," Flowridia's breath caught, and though she could not begin to fathom it, panic rushed through her. "Something that slays more than the millions due to die at your hand. How would separating the planes save the world?"

Soliel's visage became stone. "Have I answered your questions?"

"Soliel—"

"Have I answered your questions?" he repeated, though it was a finale and nothing more.

Flowridia glared, wondering at his pride and cryptic nonsense, his awful words about her intended, when a fundamental truth struck her like a knife. "You're so high and mighty, but I think you're forgetting what kind of leverage I have in this negotiation. I don't know that I could kill you, but that's not what it would take to stop you. Mereen Fireborn could steal from you; so, what's to stop me from asking Ayla to do the same?"

Something in his countenance shifted, subtle anger settling instead.

"You won't kill Ayla; you went through hell to bring her back," she continued. "And something tells me you won't kill me either, or you would have months ago. Ayla isn't a god, but you aren't quite one either yet, are you. Give me a reason, or I'll take back those orbs, one way or another."

"These are words you'll regret," Soliel replied, as dark as she had ever heard him sound.

"Will you kill me then?"

"There are answers you aren't ready to hear."

"That's my decision."

Soliel suddenly stood up, and Flowridia feared she had misjudged, that perhaps he would strike her dead.

But instead of violence, he offered a hand. "There is more. I will show you. And then you will walk away."

Hesitant, Flowridia spared a glance for the woods, silently pleading for Ayla to interfere if she sensed danger. But Soliel, though a threat to the world and to those around her, had only ever feigned being a threat to her.

She took his hand. The world disappeared, replaced with a backdrop of pure darkness.

All that remained was she and Soliel. "In the future, though not far enough away, a new God will rise. One who will destroy us all."

Flowridia voiced her greatest fear: "Is it Ayla?"

"No."

The sea of darkness remained, yet figures appeared within, gruesome and rotting. An army of mindless undead, some small and others unnatural, abominations created from the same wicked powers Flowridia wielded. They moved as an unstoppable storm, consuming all they passed.

And there at the helm—

"Casvir," she whispered, an omen on the wind.

The army vanished, leaving only the imperator, stalwart and menacing, standing as a statue until two new figures appeared—one of whom Flowridia knew.

Ineffably younger, radiant, righteous, Soliel wielded a sword and holy light, his battle against Casvir an orchestra of divinity and darkness clashing in discordant chords. Flowridia would be a fool to forget his holy heritage—the son of Sol Kareena, the antithesis of Casvir's powers—and to watch him fight in his prime was exhilarating. She wondered if he were yet a god, this vision she saw, but Casvir, it seemed, was.

With him, though the darkness obscured her feminine form, a woman bore her own boundless aura, her movements a perfect amalgamation of finesse and magic, her speed unnatural, her precision suggesting a manipulation of the very fabric of the world. She wielded fire, magic, darkness—Flowridia swore she even saw a familiar cloud of necromancy surrounding her. To seek patterns in Chaos' power was foolish.

Soliel's voice played as a backdrop to the battle at hand. "We fought Casvir for centuries, gaining power in tandem with his. But it was not enough. We called upon allies; we called upon gods. The armies of the world joined together—those not already under his might—to stop his onslaught. But we failed; we all failed."

Flowridia saw visions of gods she knew—Ku'Shya's shadow, Izthuni's might, and a tentacled being she knew as Onias. They joined Soliel and his counterpart—the Old Gods to be—and Casvir's army rose anew.

"The Gods of Sha'Demoni fell first, for they believed us when we said he was a threat and joined in our fight."

One by one, the shadows of the demonic gods faded, replaced by glowing figures of light.

"The next to fall were the Gods of Celestière, for they came too late. He invaded the Angelic Realm and destroyed them all. They would not bend to his will."

They extinguished, but Casvir's army remained.

"From there, he leaves this world, his power great enough to find others to conquer—broken worlds attached to this one, and then even beyond. He accepts those that will bow and destroys who will not. It is his way."

Everything vanished, leaving pure darkness.

Flowridia reeled, for it was everything Casvir had already proclaimed—that he would become a god.

And he succeeded.

"We slayed him countless times, yet he always returned," Soliel said softly. "We never, in a thousand years, found his phylactery, and so his spirit always lingered. And when he gained enough power, he banished us. I suspect he sought to slay us, but instead we became lost in time—and landed thousands of years before the Convergence."

"And you became the Old Gods," Flowridia whispered, and then the world faded back to what she knew—to the dark woods and the snow, yet the bitter chill was nothing to the ice in her limbs.

"And so, I seek to separate the worlds and stop this monster before he can become god," Soliel said, countless years of exhaustion in the words. "Celestière and Sha'Demoni will be destroyed and much of this world too, but that was already fated to occur. Is it not better to sacrifice them before their time to spare the infinite souls in the worlds beyond?"

Flowridia's breath failed her as she stared into the forest, her mind comprehending everything and nothing.

Casvir, her friend . . .

"There is no winning in this game of death, Flowridia. I failed. We failed. This is the one chance left to rectify what we did not do. Perhaps when I succeed in this, I will bow and let Chaos destroy me, as a penance. Or perhaps she will join me when the time comes. I don't know. I never truly knew her mind."

"What of Ayla," Flowridia whispered, for it was all her heart dwelled on, in the end. "You said Chaos rose to fight Ayla Darkleaf, despite the both of you rising to fight Casvir."

"There are truths that would break your heart to know, Flowridia. Please accept it as a mercy."

"Then what is my part is this narrative? Ayla has been a monster all along, but you've called me by a name I've dreamt of since I met you. In your future, I was Flowridia Darkleaf, and I would not stand idly by when—"

She recalled his words, though they felt like a lifetime ago: *"I know your death, Flowridia Darkleaf . . ."*

The truth came like a blow to her stomach. Perhaps it meant tomorrow's dark truth, the wedding night she feared, but she knew in her heart, from his cryptic words and her own intuition, that he meant something far more permanent and dire.

"I'm not there," she whispered, her skin cold from far more than merely the falling snow.

Again, Soliel became quiet, thoughtfulness in his chosen words. "To know your future is to take it away, Lady Flowridia. Perhaps you should go."

"You told Ayla she would kill herself to run from her fate," Flowridia echoed, her breath short. "Is that what you meant? Does she lead to my death? Is she the cause?"

"As I said," Soliel repeated, his tone hard and final, "perhaps you should go."

She could stay. She could fall on her knees and beg to know more, but she struggled to stay composed—both from anger and from anguish.

Could she stand to call Soliel a villain anymore? Despite his crimes? Flowridia's soul felt jarred from her body.

"Thank you for your time," she said brusquely, brushing snow off her shoulders and skirts. "Do let me know if you find Mereen. I have every reason to want her dead, too."

She left; he gave no reply.

Once past the light from the fire, hidden within the thick copse of trees, a pale hand gently tugged her into a dark shadow.

The winter's chill ceased—the Shadow Realm was cold, but consistently so. "You were right," Ayla said, her own quiet fury apparent. "He did speak much more freely to you."

Flowridia's tears fell fast. Idly, she wiped them, then shut her eyes at Ayla's touch on her waist. "What do we do?"

"No need for fear, Flowra. This is grand news."

Flowridia's blood chilled at her love's ensuing chuckle. She opened her eyes, surprised at Ayla's vicious smile. "What do you mean?"

"He has spilled a flurry of threats but forgotten a fundamental truth—that I am spiteful above all and would burn the world to save you." Her grin widened, teeth revealing vicious delight. "But what did he show you, when he took your hand?"

Once upon a time, Flowridia looked upon Ayla's visage and saw a lifetime of love and hope. Yet now, with every step forward, it tore at the seams.

She whispered it, whispered it all, hoping the demons did not overhear.

And all Ayla said was, "Interesting."

"You don't care that Casvir becomes a god and destroys everything?"

"Oh, I care very much. I am simply not surprised. Are you?"

Flowridia sniffed, her tears falling faster. "I suppose not."

"Really, I'm just bitter he succeeds before me." Ayla took her hand and led her forward. "You are half-frozen to death, my love," Ayla said, soothing now instead of cruel. "Perhaps it was a mistake to come here."

"It's what I wanted," Flowridia replied, though it seemed everything she desired was a mistake.

They walked in silence. When they arrived in their palace bedroom, Ayla undressed her, mindful of the goosebumps on her skin as she wrapped her in a warm robe. "My darling, do not fear. I shall protect you from all things. Sleep on this, won't you? There's not much to do with this information yet."

It would be her last night to ever sleep. Tomorrow began an endless night.

"May I give you my present now?"

Upon the vanity sat the forgotten box. "You may. I have one for you too."

Ayla perked up, genuine surprise in the gesture. "Really?"

Flowridia nodded, though she conveyed little enthusiasm as she procured the thin package from her bedside table, wrapped in plain parchment. Her somber mood lingered, but Ayla did not seem to share it.

"Which of us first?"

"Mine leads to an activity," Ayla said, oddly twitchy as she eyed the gift in Flowridia's hands. "I say yours first."

Flowridia offered it with little aplomb, but Ayla's thinly curtailed anticipation did cause her to smile. With ease, she tore the paper, revealing a leather case. She sat on the bed, then carefully undid the silver latch holding it together—and there lay a set of surgeon's tools. Pure silver, Flowridia knew, their handles bearing polished, black stone. The memory of Irons' bafflement as they'd shopped together brought amusement anew, especially when she asked the craftsman for the palest sapphires he could find to decorate the base of the handles.

Ayla said nothing at all, merely stared. Discomfort welled in Flowridia's stomach to watch it, and hesitantly she asked, "Is this not . . . Do you hate it?"

Ayla idly shook her head as her fingers stroked lines across the fine stone of the scalpel, admiring the tweezers with her touch, then lifted a particularly sharp instrument. Tears welled in her eyes, and Flowridia's breath caught. "Ayla, I'm sorry—"

"No, no—I love it so much." Ayla wiped her tears on her sleeve, fighting whatever emotion had struck her so viscerally. She placed the knife back into its spot, then closed the case. With as much tenderness as she had ever seen the woman display, Ayla held it to her chest. "I have never felt worthy of you, Flowra. And I doubt I ever will. But somehow you accept me for all I am, which is the greatest gift of all."

Flowridia embraced her, joy filling her when Ayla melted into her arms. She made no move to rush her, remaining until Ayla herself pulled away, her tears having finally stilled.

When Ayla offered her own gift, Flowridia accepted, then sat on the bed to tug at the ribbon tying it. It fell neatly apart, and so she lifted the box's lid to find . . . a chess set?

Carved from stone, the black held rich flecks of gold, whereas the white glittered from diamond dust, even in the dim light. With care, Flowridia lifted the white queen, the first hint of a smile pulling at her lip. "Oh, Ayla."

Lips brushed her forehead. "Want to play?"

Flowridia looked up to see an impish grin. "I thought you hated chess."

"I cannot promise I will have the stamina for eight hours," Ayla said, already tugging the desk toward her, "but I have come to appreciate the game a little more, upon contemplation."

"Have you?"

Ayla set up chairs around the desk—a makeshift place for them to play. "I have nothing clever to say about it. The simple truth is that I would not have you in my life without those damned games of chess."

When Ayla smiled, Flowridia matched it, heart fluttering as she brought the gifted set toward the table. She quickly set up the pieces, the tapping of stone on stone delightful as she lined them up.

Ayla kissed her cheek. "Hope you've improved. I suppose you shall take white?"

Flowridia shook her head. "Black this time."

They sat and played, the evening filled with warmth. Flowridia found pristine joy in Ayla's laugh and smile.

In the morning, Flowridia was awoken by a kiss on the lips. She opened her eyes, unsurprised to see Ayla's visage blinking prettily. The fading night hinted at an imminent sunrise. "They say it is bad luck to see your beloved before the wedding," Ayla said, and she cupped the back of Flowridia's head, kissing her lips once more. "But if I bid you farewell before sunrise, it hardly counts, yes?"

"I see the logic," Flowridia muttered, sleep still clouding her judgement. She sat up when Ayla pulled back.

"I will be stealing Demitri until the ceremony. Will that be all right with you?"

Flowridia nodded. "Where will you be?"

"Readying myself, of course. Empress Alauriel has an image to uphold." She smiled, her countenance shifting to match that of the late empress. "But all will pale to you, my sweet summer blossom."

Unspeakable softness settled in her vibrant eyes. Flowridia feared she might cry, but Ayla smiled instead. "I will see you at the altar," Ayla said, and then she stepped into a shadow and disappeared.

Alone, quiet dread clenched at Flowridia's stomach. She stood from her bed and grabbed a robe to cover her nightgown, then ran from the room, to the lift, and prayed to reach the outside before the sun did.

One more sunrise, her mind screamed. Oh, she craved it, that warmth and comfort. The windows at the lift bespoke a few minutes more, but she wished for it to hurry, fear gripping her heart.

She ran through the hallway, ignoring any servants or guests who wished her well. Once outside, the cold grass tickled her feet, frost clinging to her skin and hem of her dress.

Between she and the garden, she saw a giant of a man watching the glowing horizon. Flowridia ran forward, nearly ramming into Thalmus.

Thalmus always watched the sunrise.

His enormous hand rested on her back, no words spoken as the brilliant sun burst over the silhouette of distant mountains and trees. Warmth touched Flowridia's face. She shut her eyes, and for a moment—a single, perfect moment—time suspended, the sun's burst stagnant as it warmed her heart and body.

For a moment, she was a child again, back when Thalmus cared for her unconditionally, when the sun brought joy and not dread, and before she had sold her soul for love.

But the light ascended. Thalmus' touch shifted. Flowridia opened her eyes and knew that time ticked forever forward. Her hand came up to clutch his shirt, and she hid her face in the fabric.

Never again would she hold him. Not like this. Thalmus despised all the dead, and he would surely know her for what she was. Wetness prickled at her eyes and stained his shirt, and Flowridia winced at the quiet sob escaping with her breath.

"Flowra?"

Thalmus' voice reverberated against her hidden face. His arms encircled her, or as well as they could with him towering above her.

"Please, talk to me."

Flowridia shook her head, hating her cries, yet still they came. She held him tight, and if she breathed, she could smell his furnace, his melting glass, the days of sitting in silence as he worked.

Yet, like the glass he molded, the tighter she clung, the more broken her heart would be when she broke his.

His thumb caressed patterned strokes across her back. "Empress Alauriel is a good woman, and I am overjoyed that you've found love together. But if you are having doubts . . ." His voice trailed off, his touch slowing. "I will be the first to defend you if you decide to walk away."

Flowridia whispered, "I love her, Thalmus. I love her so much, but I'm afraid."

"What are you afraid of?"

Eternity as an undead monster, to be the type of creature who would slay her loved ones for blood, to lose all her friends, the family she had found . . .

Never again would she feel the sun.

"Nothing tangible," she said, praying her lie sounded more believable spoken aloud. "It's as you said—she is a good woman. And she is good to me."

But wicked to the world; a monster they rightfully feared.

"Flowra—"

"Thalmus—" To berate him only brought her more pain. Her eyes seeped liquid into the cloth of his shirt. "Please, don't tell me reasons to go. I'm looking for reasons to stay."

Thalmus was quiet a moment, and then he whispered, "Etolié told us she met with Ayla Darkleaf."

Flowridia released a breath. Though her tears still flowed, she slowly relaxed. "She and I have spoken of it, too."

"Is she why you're afraid?"

The question he asked was not the one her heart answered, but the pain it brought ricocheted from her ears, to her mind, and finally to where it punctured her tender heart: *Yes, I am afraid. Afraid of the woman I love.*

"If Ayla is alive," she said carefully, "I think a confrontation between she and I is inevitable. But if she has any residual love in her heart for me, she will do nothing to disrupt this day." She released another breath, this one pained. "I would be lying if I said she was not the reason I'm afraid, though."

"I would give my life to stop her, as would Etolié, and as would Lara. And Imperator Casvir is here. Ayla can do nothing when he is near. But you will not be left alone today, Flowra. She will not take you."

Not until tonight, when the festivities ended. Ayla would take her in every possible way.

Flowridia turned away from Thalmus' shirt and looked to the sunrise, watched it rise steadily higher. For a moment, she let it settle on her face and imagined a future where every morning she could savor the dawn.

"Thank you, Thalmus," she whispered, though her sorrow remained, for in that future she lived—and broke Ayla's heart. "I need to get ready. Will you come with me?"

"Of course."

They left together, the sun to their backs. When they stepped inside, she mourned the loss.

Servants pulled and yanked at her auburn locks, all under Marielle's watchful ire. "Flowridia, have you ever cut your hair?"

Staring at her appearance in the mirror, Flowridia saw a young woman steadily blossoming into an empress consort, each strand of hair tucked into place creating a picture fit for noble company. Her golden crown, her family heirloom, sat regally atop her head. Beneath the vanity, her fists clenched. "Not recently, no. My mother did once."

"There's residue matted into your tresses, Flower Child. We can try to soak it out, but it might be easier to simply chop it."

"Well, it's lovely, but there's so much!"

Flowridia's heart thumped in her throat, her apprehension higher than even her annoyance at Marielle's remark. In the corner, Thalmus sat silently, her ever-present guardian—for now. She forced a smile as she glanced at him, though her eyes remained dead. "Someday, it'll be as long as Thalmus'."

Except it wouldn't. She wouldn't be alive for it to grow.

The door to the guest room opened, and Etolié and Khastra slipped inside. "All is well for baby number one. How is Flowers?"

"Flowers is doing well," Flowridia replied, praying she appeared merely breathless and nothing more.

Before Flowridia could react, Etolié stole the ring from her left-hand finger. "You all right?"

"A little nervous," Flowridia said, her false smile clearly forced, "which I think is normal."

"I mean, yes. But you're gonna sweat all over your dress." Etolié helpfully dabbed her forehead with a handkerchief, then lifted her arms by the wrists and dabbed her armpits, which under any other circumstances would have been hilarious—or embarrassing, she truly couldn't say which—but Flowridia felt faint.

"The crown is pretty."

When the servant pushed the final pin into her hair, most of it still fell in thick waves. "It was a gift," Flowridia said absently. "Thank you."

Etolié stole her hands and helped her to stand. "Your dress is in the next room," the Celestial said. "Khastra, tell Thalmus to stay."

Khastra merely looked to Thalmus, who clearly overheard.

With Marielle in tow, the three of them escorted Flowridia out. Hands covered Flowridia's eyes, and she let her friends lead and have their fun. A lock clicked. A door shut. Etolié removed her hands.

The dress waited, displayed on a wooden mannequin, white and cream and embroidered in every shade of pastel. Floral patterns climbed their way up from the expansive, layered skirt, the fabric so thin it was nearly sheer. It would show her arms, but the modest design was to her tastes, the chest embroidered with jewels and thread, each stitch intricate and perfect in its placement.

The skirt and train trailed well beyond the base. It would even cover her feet.

Ayla had made this. Flowridia knew the style, and she resisted the urge to sob—once she started, she wouldn't stop. The dress signified both the beginning and the end—her bridal and funeral gown, both.

"Lara says you've never seen it," Etolié said, and Flowridia nodded, unable to articulate that she had seen it half-completed in a basement of horror.

Gods, Ayla was sweet. She deserved better than a hysterical bride. Flowridia swallowed her rising apprehension, fearing she'd break skin for how tightly her fists clenched.

With Marielle and Etolié's assistance, she removed her nightgown and stepped into the immaculate dress, careful not to disturb her hair. Flowridia stared into the floor-length mirror, admiring how the gown draped and turned with her movements. With tender care, she ran her fingers along the delicate embroidery at the bodice, refusing to let tears mar perfection. Still, her eyes were rimmed in red. She hugged her bodice, the first of her tears finally falling. Truly she was the princess of the castle, royal perfection, and all she wanted was to vomit.

Etolié set her head on her shoulder, not quite hugging, but not quite not. "You look perfect," Etolié said, thankfully misinterpreting her tears, and Flowridia thought it might be the sincerest thing she'd ever heard the Celestial utter. "I'm so happy for you."

Marielle sobbed at the sight, wiping away tears as she said, "Weddings go by in the blink of an eye. Slow down and remember today."

"I hope today never ends," Flowridia said, for it would be her last.

They escorted her to a room outside the ballroom, with Etolié to illusion her away from the guests. Thalmus' face remained puffy and red, hardly proper, but he hadn't stopped tearing up since she'd emerged in her dress. It touched her that he would be so overwhelmed on her happy day.

"You're looking pale, Flowers," the Celestial said, dabbing at her brow with what Flowridia hoped was a different handkerchief. "Remember to breathe."

Flowridia moved to wipe her eyes with her sleeves—but was stopped by Etolié, who offered a new handkerchief from the air. She dabbed at her eyes, desperate to calm herself.

"Marielle, make sure they didn't give away my momma's seat," Etolié said, and the queen agreed, leaving the duo alone. "Are you sure you're all right? You don't normally sweat this much when you're nervous. If you're sick—"

"If I'm sick, I trust that you'll illusion away the vomit," Flowridia said, failing to lighten the mood.

"Well, I'll be hosting my momma, so I won't really be able to . . ." Her words trailed away, and Flowridia feared what her frown meant. "Do you want a blessing or something? I'm not officially pledged to my mom, but I doubt she'd be offended if I acted on her behalf."

Flowridia shook her head. "Thank you, though."

Etolié looked ready to say more, but instead she looked to Thalmus, some silent interaction passing between them. "Take care of yourself. Everyone loves you."

She left, leaving Flowridia with only Thalmus.

"Flowra," came his quiet voice, "you're awfully tense."

When she released her tight hold on her skirts, her hands shook. But she refused to think on it, refused to think what this wedding meant, what would happen tonight—

"I stand by what I said before."

Frantically, she shook her head, unable to articulate her words.

Scratching at the door pulled their focus. Thalmus answered, and Demitri bounded in. Flowridia gasped, laughing at what she saw. "Demitri, are you wearing a bowtie?"

Lady Ayla said I had to. I'm the ring bear.

"You mean, 'ring bearer?'"

No, I mean 'bear.'

Attached to his bowtie were two familiar rings. "Dearest Demitri, you look so handsome," Flowridia said, and she kissed his nose, mindful to not get his fur on her dress.

And you look much better than death. Demitri nuzzled against her face, and she giggled at the contact. *What's wrong?*

"I'm fine," she said, forcing her smile.

I feel your feelings, stupid. Why are you scared?

"Please don't ask me that," she whispered, and she kissed his furry cheek. "I love you, dearest Demitri, but my intended might skin you alive if you don't get into place."

She has the knowledge, too. But he lingered, clearly torn by how he shuffled. *Mom, are you sure?*

She forced a smile and a nod. "Get in line, Demitri."

Demitri left. Flowridia went to Thalmus' side. "Demitri says he's the 'ring bear.'"

"The name bears a nice ring to it."

Flowridia laughed, but it evoked fresh sobs. Thalmus' hand clasped her shoulder, and she gripped it like a lifeline.

Gods, waiting was agony.

Would it hurt? To die?

Music wafted through the hallways and into the room. Thalmus made no move to follow the cue. "This is your decision, Flowra," he said, a calm in the storm. "Whatever you choose, I will support you."

No, he wouldn't. He wouldn't accept her as an undead monster. When all was right in the world, the dead stayed dead.

"Thalmus ..." She squeezed his hand tight, knowing she had to act, she had to move forward—the end was near, this was her promise, her bargain ...

A wedding for her, and a night for Ayla.

One foot, then the next. Thalmus walked beside her, holding the door open for her approach.

Rich music played, a blending of harps and violins. Floral scents met her nose. The entrance to the ballroom was a short walk away, but she couldn't feel her feet, couldn't feel Thalmus' hand, the music slowly waning to the thumping of her heart in her ears.

Her tears fell fast. Her head swam, but not from nerves; the swamp in her chest rose, but she clung to the prospect of immortality, a never-ending future with the love of her life. She breathed a stabilizing breath, willing herself to relax.

How she loved Ayla. How she longed to stand across from her at the altar and pledge her love. Yet her tears fell quickly down her cheeks, and she knew Thalmus noticed.

By every god—they would be wives. So why wasn't that wonderful?

This was what would bind them—not matrimony, but a bargain for eternity, for Flowridia's silly sentiments of love and a family name as well as ... death?

She reeled at the thought, fear surging in her veins. Breathing in, a sob tore at her vocal cords.

"Flowra?"

Flowridia wrenched her hand away from Thalmus' and ran.

Past the ballroom doors, leaving them far behind, instead racing down the hall. Instinct said to flee, to hide, and at the nearest open room, she slammed the door behind her, frantically barricading it with a simple chair.

A sitting room, empty, with a couch and a cold fireplace. Flowridia collapsed into the corner of the room and sobbed.

In her beautiful dress, her crown, with hair done up like royalty, she wept into her hands, gasping cries surely revealing her presence. But she couldn't breathe, much less quiet herself, and shame steadily piled upon her, crushing her to the floor.

She spilled tears upon her immaculate dress, staining it with sorrow, and her thoughts raced in a thousand different directions.

Get up, her mind screamed, but she trembled and shook, screaming into her hands from visceral *fear.*

Move forward, her body urged, but she frantically cried, head swimming as she wept.

And then, cutting through her tears, a gentle knock.

A timid voice: *"Flowra?"*

The door jostled, and the chair beneath the knob did nothing to stop it.

Lara peeked her head inside, turning quickly to someone outside and whispering something.

Then, she stepped inside and shut the door behind her. Her visage disappeared, replaced with Ayla—a vision in white and silver, everything Flowridia knew and loved, save for the alarm starkly etched on her face.

Ayla came forward. "Flowra—"

Flowridia tried to stand, to run; Ayla's fingers snagged her skirt. Sobbing, Flowridia fell at her feet, crumbling into a ball as torrential cries ripped from her throat. "I can't do it, Ayla. I can't." Flowridia gripped the skirt of Ayla's wedding dress, staining it with her tears. Over and over, she repeated that panicked plea: "I'm sorry. I can't, I can't . . ."

A cold voice broke through the reverie of her begging. "But why?"

"I know this was our promise. I know, I know . . ." Her rambling became as erratic as her breathing. "But I can't," came the fearful sob, and then she turned her sight upward.

Tears clouded Flowridia's vision, but she saw the severity of Ayla's stare. Shrinking, Flowridia released her dress and cowered on the ground. Words shriveled. Fear staunched her tears.

Tension rose. Ayla dove down. Flowridia shut her eyes, bracing herself for fangs and castigation.

Cold claws grabbed her. Flowridia gasped.

But in place of pain, a soft embrace.

Cradled against Ayla's chest, Flowridia dared to open her eyes, fear still freezing her heart. Ayla's hand held her face to her breast as lips kissed her hair. Wetness dripped onto Flowridia's face; soon, their tears mingled.

In silence, Ayla held her. A whisper met her ears. "All right. We will not do this."

The affirmation shattered Flowridia's shaking resolve, and her tears burst forth like a flood. She wept, fear and relief and soul-aching *guilt* staining her beloved's dress.

A soothing touch gently caressed her back, soon joined by Ayla's soft singing, her breathy alto a distraction enough for Flowridia's frantic mind to grasp to. She focused on breathing, her vision finally gaining substance around the edges. Still, her tears fell, and when she finally looked up from the shield of her hair, Ayla's eyes were shut, quickly expelling their own tears.

"I'm sorry," Flowridia whispered.

Ayla's eyes opened, their silver hue shined and rimmed in wetness. "It's all right."

"No, Ayla . . ." Flowridia sat up, but kept her hands to herself, knowing she was the cause for her love's own anguish. "You've given me everything. This wedding . . . This dress . . . It's beautiful. It's perfect. And I . . ." Her words faded, but when Ayla reached to touch her face, she shied away; Ayla's hand dropped. "I'm sorry."

"I do not understand," Ayla pled, her watery eyes spelling heartbreak. "I wish you would have said something. This day should have been joyous, not filling you with dread."

"Ayla, no." Flowridia gripped Ayla's arms, daring to touch her silken sleeves. "You were so excited at the thought. I couldn't ruin that. You put so much time and effort into making certain this wedding was perfection, and I'm only sorry that—" Her breath hitched; the truth would finally come. "I coerced you into this with the promise of letting you turn me into a vampire."

"What?" Ayla said, and Flowridia heard heartbreak in the word. "Flowra, did you think I would only marry you for that?"

Flowridia struggled to find a response, a wash of cold seeping through her to realize what she had finally voiced.

"Flowra, I love you." Ayla's voice broke at the last word, quickly devolving into sobs. "It is not rational or conditional. It is selfish, yes, and I often fight with myself to be someone worthy of you. But please know that I would have married you from the moment I first said, 'I love you.' Turning you had nothing to do with it." Ayla broke from Flowridia's grasp and instead clung to her, buried her face in her neck. "Is that what this truly is, then? You're afraid for tonight?"

"Yes," Flowridia replied, limbs aching from her pulsing blood.

Ayla released her, tears falling fast. "Eternity broken-hearted is better than never knowing you at all. For you to choose to live your short, fragile life with me is enough. I am hurt, yes, but I can set that aside if . . . if you will still . . ." Ayla stole her hand, her own trembling as she clutched it. "More than anything else, I want to marry you. I want to be your wife. I want you to be Flowridia Darkleaf—or I shall be Ayla Makosa, if that would suit you better. I do not care. I love you. I want you. Do you still want me?"

"More than anything, yes," Flowridia said, and when they embraced, she swore she finally drew a breath. With her face buried in Ayla's hair, she whispered, "We'll find a way. I've sworn to never leave you, and I won't. There are other ways to achieve immortality." Her lips brushed Ayla's hair, and her eyes shut tight, willing her senses to be filled with Ayla alone. "And if not, then you turn me. Give me a few years to sort out my affairs, but I swear you will never be alone."

Ayla looked up, her face stained with tears, eyes glistening, but the barest hints of happiness shone in her smile. "There are worried interlopers waiting in the hallway. You caused a bit of a stir. Will you . . ." Hesitation stilled her tongue, vulnerability in Ayla's precious gaze. ". . . walk with me? Down the aisle?"

The promise of vampirism and matrimony had been twisted as one, and Flowridia saw now how tainted both had become because of it. But Ayla wanted her, all the same.

For the first time in perhaps all her days, the future felt bright. No looming shadows. "Yes, Ayla. I want to be your wife."

Their lips touched, sealed by relief and love.

They held hands when they left the room, both of their faces stained with tears.

Waiting, though visibly trying not to look *too* anxious, were an array of beloved faces—Thalmus, of course, standing in the front, with Demitri beside him, Marielle behind them looking very concerned, even Casvir standing a ways off, stoic of course, but his presence suggested he cared very much.

Reginal peeked from behind Thalmus' arm, and near him was Irons, looking far more confused than worried.

Strangest, however, was the glowing figure not too far off from Casvir—Goddess Staella herself watched with her hands clasped, though she ineffably bore Etolié's face—who would be concerned for her moonbeam. Far smaller than she had been in the throne room—in fact, she looked Etolié's height.

For a blissful moment, Flowridia didn't care that it was a lie—in the held breath before her decision, her friends loved her.

Lara's doppelganger smiled but looked to Flowridia and squeezed her hand, her cue crystal clear. "Lara and I had some misunderstandings about what this wedding would mean for me, and for us," Flowridia said, knowing they deserved an explanation for her meltdown, or at least a few hints. "And I was afraid, so I didn't speak up. We've spoken now; we're on the same page." She smiled at Lara's visage, but it was Ayla's soft gaze in every perfect way. "Once my face has stopped puffing, we'll be getting married. Give me a few more minutes."

Relief flooded their small audience, especially those in the front. Demitri bounded to her side; Thalmus hugged her; Marielle cried. Reginal shook her hand and embraced Lara— even Irons wished her well.

One by one, they returned to their places, though Thalmus did say he would wait at the ballroom door.

Goddess Staella approached demurely. "Etolié said she doesn't wish to outshine my presence and has asked that I say she's relieved and unbearably happy for you both. As for me, I have a certain weakness for empresses who marry for love instead of money or gain. For you both to have found each other fills me with unparalleled joy."

Then, to Flowridia's surprise, Goddess Staella offered her hand, the invitation clear; Flowridia accepted it, marveling at her gentle warmth. "Always speak your truth, Flowridia, even when you think it is selfish. I so despise the negative connotations of that word. To be selfish means to put yourself first and nothing more. It is neither wicked nor good—it simply is. There must be balance in all things, and that includes how we treat ourselves versus how we treat the world. Etolié has spoken of your kind heart; as you serve my kingdom, don't forget to care for your heart as well."

Staella released her then, and Flowridia wondered at her words.

The Goddess of Stars looked next to Lara. "Care for her always. If you value and cherish the other, nothing can stop you. United, there is no force more powerful than love."

Staella left, but the words lingered.

Casvir was the last, and he approached with arms crossed before his chest, his formalwear different than the previous day's but no less magnificent—or strange to see. "Did she threaten you?" he said simply, and Lara bristled.

Flowridia spoke before she could. "No. I'm thrilled to be getting married. Truly."

"Good." And after a curt nod to Lara, he left them alone.

Lara withdrew a handkerchief from her bodice and used it to dab Flowridia's face. She pressed her chill hands to the space beneath Flowridia's eyes. "I'm aware that my touch is a little colder than most. This will help the swelling."

Flowridia laughed, and it felt so freeing.

Lara smoothed Flowridia's hair and dress, restoring her to impeccable form, and in a few minutes, she deemed her perfection.

Hands held, they went to the ballroom. Thalmus waited at the door, smiling at their intertwined fingers. "I'm honored to have walked you this far," his deep voice rumbled, "but perhaps it would be most appropriate if you escorted each other, given everything."

Flowridia thanked him silently, her eyes filling with fresh tears. Thalmus walked ahead.

The deep green carpet bent like grass beneath her feet. Flowridia marveled at the sea of people, but more so at the vines of flowers wrapped around the pillars surrounding the ballroom, and the sky above bearing a blue and sunny day, perhaps enchanted to reveal what lay outside. She searched for faces, her eyes landing first upon the Goddess Staella, standing to the side of the altar, where Etolié would have stood after escorting Lara down the aisle.

There was a woman Flowridia did not know at the center of the altar—the High Priestess of Staella, as was appropriate. Demitri watched across from them, his bowtie untied and in the priestess' hands. Thalmus stood near him, waiting in his place as her chosen escort.

When she looked upon Lara—Ayla's—face, she saw tears of pure joy.

Flowridia had reminisced once or twice as a child at the prospect of a wedding. Something to wait for, yes; something to find when she was older, perhaps. But Ayla had waited a thousand years and more, and after the betrayal of her first love she would have set aside this dream, if it ever were one.

Yet here Ayla beamed, she wept, and when Flowridia stood across from her, she seemed ready to jump into her arms for how badly she twitched. From her peripheral, Flowridia saw the Tyrant of Nox'Kartha, stoic yet at peace. She briefly saw Zorlaeus and Marielle, and farther back, Khastra loomed.

But she reserved her gaze for Ayla, whose silver eyes glistened.

The priestess gave a grand speech about love, and Flowridia swore she tried to listen, tried to pay attention, but all she saw was Lara, or Ayla, rather, for she swore the illusion grew fainter with each day she observed it.

Rings were exchanged, and Flowridia let it all flutter along, barely listening, only watching. Their wrists were tied with strings woven from threads from the Moon Goddess' dress, or so they claimed, and then Flowridia heard words that reverberated in her head:

"Presenting, Empress Alauriel Solviraes and her wife, Empress Consort Flowridia Solviraes, as they exchange their first kiss as wife and wife."

Ayla nearly jumped forward, crushing their lips together as thunderous applause sounded around them. Flowridia savored the touch, the intimacy, public as it was. When she opened her eyes, it was Ayla's she saw, as vibrant and sincere as the first time she had said, "I love you."

Flowridia pulled her into an embrace, overcome by the love she felt pouring out.

The applause faded, as did the world. For a moment, there was only them, only her wife wrapped in her arms.

When the applause faded, the ballroom was cleared for festivities, food, and dancing. Well-wishers came to give their congratulations.

The first among them was Goddess Staella. Despite her grand appearance and wings, and despite the crowds that parted as she walked, the angel held herself as though small, her hands fidgeting, her posture slightly slouched. Silver tears fell from her glowing eyes, glittering down her perfect face. "The ceremony was beautiful, and I thank you for allowing me to share in your love. I will be taking my leave so Etolié may properly enjoy herself, but I wish you both every happiness."

Flowridia sniffed, still combating her emotions. "Thank you," she said.

"A lifetime of love takes work. Remember to cherish each other," Staella said, and then her form shrunk, her shine dimming.

Standing there instead was Etolié, whose red eyes bespoke her own tears. "Good, uh, good work, kiddos," she said, wiping her eyes on her false sleeve. "I need to sit before I faint."

Then came the crowd, far more than Flowridia could keep track of. So many names and faces, none of whom she could remember, most of whom she would never see again. Amidst the endless sea of guests, she saw the chairs flicker out of existence, revealing a splendid dance floor, and when music played, the crowd dispersed.

She was surprised when Casvir stepped forward and offered a clawed hand. "May I have the first dance?"

Flowridia glanced at Lara, expecting objection, but Lara simply waved her hand, her face stained with dried tears. "Go on. But do save a dance or two for me."

Casvir's talent for dance was stiff yet accurate, his movements on the ballroom floor as precise as they were on the battlefield. Flowridia couldn't comfortably reach his shoulder, so she kept her hand on his forearm instead and let him lead. "I didn't know you could dance," she said, laughter in her words.

"It is what nobles do," he said. "Murishani is a far more accomplished dancer, but not so much as your wife."

He was the first friend to refer to Ayla as Flowridia's wife, and it brought a blush to her cheeks.

At the conclusion of the dance, Casvir let her go, but within seconds, Thalmus stole her hand. "I don't know much of dancing, but—"

"Oh, Thalmus, that's all right," Flowridia said, and she placed his hand on her back, though he had to hunch slightly, leading as they swayed in time.

They spoke of Staelash, her garden, his work, and when the dance concluded, she beckoned for him to kneel. Flowridia planted a kiss on his cheek.

She looked, then, for any sign of her wife, but then Etolié tapped her shoulder. "One bride down, now to dance with the second."

The Celestial did nothing to hide her beautiful, ethereal wings. Flowridia beamed and let Etolié lead. "Your mother is wonderful."

"She was so funny. Worried that you would mind if she came. I told her she was crazy."

"I'm touched she cared so much," Flowridia said sincerely. "I do need to ask, though—do you know what her gift is?"

Etolié shook her head. "No fucking clue."

When the dance ended, Etolié passed her off, straight to Khastra. "Tiny one, did you know I can dance?"

Flowridia shook her head. "I never saw you attend the dances at Staelash."

Khastra, though taller than Casvir, still managed to position Flowridia well, and led her into the next dance. "I am the one who taught Etolié."

Khastra led her through twirls and complicated steps, yet Flowridia found it easy to keep up. "Will you be taking your leave after this?" the general asked, to Flowridia's discomfort. But no one would overhear them here, upon the dance floor.

"We're staying," she said simply, and Khastra dipped her as a gentleman might, suspending her in the half-demon's arms.

Khastra's glower held menace. "Tread lightly, tiny one."

The song ended, but not soon enough.

Reginal came next, gushing about the event, conveying his congratulations. "I always liked you," he said with a wink. "I knew the rest would come around."

When the song ended, a hand tugged on Flowridia's dress, pulling her away from Reginal. Flowridia turned, surprised to see Lara looking petulant. "Will the whole world be dancing with you before I get the chance?"

"I don't think you'll give them the opportunity, now that you have me," Flowridia said, placing a hand at Lara's shoulder. "Will you dance with me?"

Lara's expression softened as she took Flowridia into her arms. "I told Reginal I had taken dancing lessons, in case there were any suspicions regarding my talent."

"Clever of you." Flowridia let Lara lead, her skill and experience surpassing all in attendance, even Khastra.

And for a moment, she was a child again, dancing with Ayla Darkleaf among lights and a small crowd, learning for herself what it meant to fall in love. Though the atmosphere was grander than the embassy of Nox'Kartha, Flowridia felt the same rush of joy, the same breathless exhilaration in her wife's embrace.

Flowridia saw Marielle dancing with her husband and recalled her words, that weddings go by in the blink of an eye, and realized night had almost fallen. She saw Khastra steal Etolié from the table full of ale and drag her out for a lively jig, saw Casvir silently watching the scene with a mug full of noxious liquid, saw Thalmus with his puffy face and red eyes sobbing as he watched the married couple dance.

The sky changed to reflect the outside. Through the walls, the last flickering of sunlight disappeared beyond the horizon.

With night came the rising of the moon. The final dance was announced, for the couple at least. The festivities would go on all night for the guests, but for the late Moon Goddess to bless their union, their marriage must be consummated beneath her light. Even in death, there was tradition.

Flowridia swayed to the final song, Ayla's head falling against her shoulder as they embraced more than danced. No words were spoken.

When the sun had fallen, Reginal beckoned for Lara, enlisting her aid in creating a portal at the far end of the room. The scene through the space was familiar—a meadow dotted by moonlight and flowers—and Flowridia waved a farewell to her friends before stepping through, her fingers intertwined with her wife's.

But not a final farewell. She would see the sun again.

Etolié never did lose consciousness from drunkenness anymore. Though her vision would blur, and the lights might blink, she still maintained awareness. It burned off nearly as quickly as it came, and so she required a near constant stream to stay truly intoxicated.

Once the couple had left, Etolié scanned the ballroom for a familiar face, one who was hated as much as feared.

There Casvir stood by the barrels of ale, casually sipping from a personal stein, and she unfortunately matched those blazing red eyes.

With nothing more than a mental 'fuck you,' she grabbed Khastra's hand and pulled her from the ballroom.

Were there justice in the world, they would have downed their drinks in Lara and Flowers' honor, blessed the union with their own celebratory joy, and had a night of bliss, but with the couple's exit came a reckoning. Casvir would be civil in Solvira's territory, but he would claim what was his.

In the hallway, Etolié kissed Khastra blindly, uncaring of who saw or heard. Khastra was cold, so cold, and the sensation was enough to make her skin crawl. But it was her demon, who was worth it all, and Etolié prayed she could be used to the feeling in time, to find warmth in her cold embrace.

For now, Khastra held her in her arms, supporting her as they kissed, and Etolié focused on her familiar calluses and her horns, her stare, understanding in those glowing eyes.

Time was up.

The door to the ballroom opened, and Casvir appeared. He looked nearly civilized with his coat, but he faced Etolié the way he had stared upon the conquered Theocracy.

Khastra loosened her hold, but Etolié fought the touch, instead clinging to her demon. Her demon, not his, yet entirely his in all the visceral, horror-bound ways.

And were she not his, Etolié would not have her at all. A hellish dichotomy, indeed. "I suppose you'll be going now," she said, struggling to stay composed. He was a monarch; this was neutral territory. Civility was required, even if she wanted to carve his eyes out with a spoon.

"The festivity is over," he said simply, the reminder of his bargain.

Khastra's touch glossed over Etolié's hair. "All shall be well, Etolié."

She released her hold on the woman she loved more than life, and by Alystra's Ass if it weren't the hardest damn thing she had ever done. Khastra leaned down to place a chaste kiss upon her forehead, appropriate enough to display in front of her boss but still lingering, still holding the intimacy Etolié already missed with all her heart.

"Goodbye," Khastra said, and Etolié hated how her gut twisted at that awful word.

"See you again soon," she replied, willing it to be true.

They disappeared down the hallway, likely to gather the rest of their envoy, and Etolié sat on the ground, lest she follow.

Her hands shook. When other guests appeared, she illusioned herself away. Tears fell from her eyes as reality settled into the pit of her stomach.

Khastra was gone.

She couldn't be here. Couldn't stay and face her friends, even the ones she liked. She could shut herself inside her room, yes. Take a walk outside and hope Flowers had placed a few of those wards . . .

Momma had placed wards.

She knew where she needed to be. Shutting her eyes, she reached out to her home, bracing for her soul to rip in twain—

And vomited upon a desert beneath a starry sky.

Chapter 30

Beneath a moonlit sky, her feet caressed by grass and wildflowers, Flowridia embraced the love of her life. The scenery remained bright and bold, just as she remembered, as vibrant as the eyes of the vampire who so gently gazed upon her.

The world was quiet here.

"Which is it, then?"

Ayla's alluring voice cut through the soft ambience. Flowridia smiled and stroked her sharp cheek. "Which is what?"

"Flowridia Darkleaf or Ayla Makosa?"

Flowridia laughed, the golden moment worth every moment of doubt. "I've dreamed of Flowridia Darkleaf for months, but I also now know it's a bastard name. If you need a family name, I'll happily offer mine."

To her surprise, Ayla appeared thoughtful. "The name 'Darkleaf' was a brand more than a name, but I have forged a legacy of spite and embraced it along with everything else. I will happily give it to you, but you did not have a family name when we first met—not one you knew of."

"Be that as it may," Flowridia replied, for there hadn't been much thought put into this frankly humorous dilemma, "I understand you have a weighty grudge against Sol Kareena and the Theocracy—and I would understand if you didn't want to tie yourself to that name."

"A fair rebuttal," Ayla muttered, grimacing at the reminder.

Flowridia kissed her cheek, gratified to see her wife's smile return. "I would be sincerely honored to accept your spiteful name."

"And so it shall forever be," Ayla whispered reverently, depthless joy in her gaze. "Flowridia and Ayla Darkleaf. You are my wife, and that is not something I thought I could ever say to someone."

"Ayla, I'm still so sorry," Flowridia said, but Ayla quickly shook her head. "No matter how you look at it, I broke a promise to you. I've hurt you."

Ayla remained silent a moment, and it was not regret on her features—but a small, sorrowful smile. "I am terrified of losing you. But that is not a problem for tonight. When we have returned from our marriage bed, we can discuss this, but tonight I only want to dwell on joyous things."

Ayla stood on her toes and kissed her slowly, her small lips parting for her tongue. Flowridia savored the sensation, adoring every flush motion, letting it fill her with want—though there remained some uncertainty. Their wedding night plans were wiped away, so what instead?

Enraptured by her love, Flowridia dared to push for more, her hands settling on the bodice of Ayla's gown. Her thumb skimmed Ayla's breast, then her whole hand cupped it lovingly, the gentle curve a temptation through the thick fabric.

She felt Ayla's lips pull into a grin. "I was not certain you would want to make love, after everything."

"Actually," Flowridia teased, "if it's all the same to you, I don't really care to make love tonight."

Ayla's good humor dried up like a barren stream. She frowned, visibly confused. "No?"

"No, Lady Darkleaf." Flowridia batted her eyes prettily, knowing she failed to play the vixen, but perhaps she could be the doe. "I'd like to *fuck*. It's a bit different."

Ayla's jaw fell slack a moment, but soon twisted into a salacious grin. "I think I understand your meaning."

"Ever since you mentioned ropes, I've been so curious," Flowridia replied, giggling at the sudden delight in her love's countenance. "With the wedding planning and running a country, we haven't had time to simply be. But we have tonight. No one will bother us. No one will interrupt. We are finally alone, and I would love nothing more than to fuck until sunrise."

When Flowridia pulled away, she immediately grabbed Ayla's hand and led her to the cottage.

"Darling, I promise to fuck you until you've forgotten your own name," Ayla said, something dangerous in her tone, sparking primal instinct within Flowridia. Gods, she wanted to drown in her.

Instead of comment, she ran, tugging Ayla along, exhilarated and delighted all at once. The cottage awaited, this beautiful and mysterious valley housed them, and when they reached the door, Flowridia winked and pulled Ayla inside, feeling bold as she kissed her perfect lips.

Ayla kept the kiss chaste, a wicked glint in her eyes as she whispered, "The question is—how much pain do you like?"

Admittedly, the question excited her as much as it unnerved her. "The vast majority of my sexual experiences are shared with you, my love."

"Am I allowed to test that then?" Ayla grinned and Flowridia so happily melted in her grasp. "You do have healing powers."

"Just don't break any bones?"

"You have my solemn promise," Ayla cooed, her hands creeping down to grope her ass; Flowridia bit her lip and giggled. "I have a feeling you'll like it. But I promise to start simple. Wait here, won't you? When I return, I want you naked."

Ayla vanished into a shadow, and Flowridia carefully stripped out of her wedding gown. Somewhere deep inside, she still reeled from the fear of the day, yet she grasped this opportunity to end it with bliss, to rebuild the trust she'd inadvertently broken.

She vowed, in the quiet moment, to always speak her truth. The guilt would follow for days to come, but she clung to the sweet aftermath—that Ayla loved her still, even without the promise of vampirism. Ayla would have married her still.

When Ayla returned, she was utterly nude and carried what appeared to be a pile of silken ropes, thick and soft. "Look at you, my darling pet—pretty as a picture already." She set the ropes aside, then caressed Flowridia's face, hunger in her gaze. "Two rules. The first is that you call me 'Lady Darkleaf.' The second is that you tell me what is going on in your head— particularly if you are uncomfortable in any way. You're placing your trust in me, and I shall do my part; swear to do yours."

"I swear, Lady Darkleaf."

Ayla's grin held delight. "If you say the name 'Demitri,' I will cut you loose immediately—not a particularly arousing word. Don't be shy to use it."

She fell into silence after that, placing kiss after gentle kiss upon Flowridia's neck as she grabbed the pile of ropes. As she pulled away, there shone enamor in her gaze. "On your knees."

Flowridia obeyed, kneeling on the bed as Ayla came behind her. She stole her arms, placing them behind her back, carefully brushed her hair aside, then took the ropes and began to weave.

Flowridia gasped when the ropes suddenly tightened around her upper arms, pulling them back, thrusting her bare chest forward. Ayla paused, leaning forward though she kept the ropes taut.

When she caught her wife's eye, Flowridia smiled. "Keep going. Um, Lady Darkleaf," she added as an afterthought, and for a moment, Ayla's serene expression cracked, revealing amusement. A kiss touched her hair, and Ayla resumed.

Flowridia fell into a lull of feeling, as the sensation in her arms dulled and the occasional tugging forced her focus back into the moment. But every touch was so deliberate, so precise as Ayla led her arms through the loops she tied, creating what she could only imagine was an elaborate display. She reveled in the attentiveness, for Ayla's focus to be so drawn, and though she was technically helpless, she felt oddly cherished.

As the time ticked by, her body grew impatient, and she pondered if this truly were the proper definition of 'simple,' as Ayla had promised it would be. But she shut her eyes and relinquished control, basking instead in every glowing touch.

When Ayla came to her wrists, she pulled away and the rope remained taut—was it over then? Flowridia's curious mind compelled her to try and look back, managing to glimpse an array of ropes crossed into lovely knots.

"I'll draw it from memory for you," Ayla whispered in her ear, and her stare was everything. Though she left a decent amount of slack, Ayla tied the two ends of the rope to the bedpost, keeping Flowridia utterly trapped. "You are so beautiful."

Flowridia melted at the words, then sighed when Ayla's arms wrapped around her. She took Flowridia's breasts in her hands, forcibly exposed in their private sanctum, and squeezed. "Are you comfortable?"

"Yes, Lady Darkleaf."

At her affirmation, Ayla sensuously bit her ear, evoking a slight moan from Flowridia's throat. She released one breast—then tugged her hair instead, instantly binding Flowridia's focus. Her entire world became that predatory gaze. "Still keen for pain?"

Flowridia's breath hitched at the question, surprised at her own visceral reaction. "I-I . . . No biting, please. Not tonight."

"Are you all right?" Ayla said, her hold on Flowridia's body releasing. "Tell me the truth."

"Yes, I promise," Flowridia replied, her smile hopefully reassuring. "I feel safe with you. Pain is fine; even some biting is fine. Just don't draw blood. I'm still a little tender at the thought."

Ayla grinned, appeased. Her hands returned to their intended targets—Flowridia's breast and hair—and she forced her head back. Flowridia gasped when Ayla sucked on her neck, apparently content to leave a bruise.

But she just as quickly left her neck, keeping a firm grip on her hair as she came to kneel before her. Ayla directed Flowridia's face to her small breasts—and oh, Flowridia loved to hear her, her gentle pleasure, nearly as much as she adored her lover's easy control. Delight filled her, as well as heat, to romance her wife's breasts, to suck on those precious buds. Ayla held her thrall, yet something in her control relinquished in those darling moans.

When Ayla pulled her away, revealing her blown pupils and rapacious glee, she stood up, never releasing Flowridia's hair. *"You'll have a taste, won't you, pet?"* and she slid down, spread her legs, and held Flowridia's face down against her cunt.

She savored the bitterness coating her tongue, gasping when Ayla began grinding into her mouth. Ayla was not quiet in her pleasure, making a grand show of enjoying her mouth. Flowridia focused on her clit, though still spared some love for the soft folds of her vulva. Ayla might have been in control, but Flowridia still desperately wished to please her.

It took time, and sometimes Flowridia forgot to breathe, but soon Ayla rocked against her, shuddering involuntarily as she came against her mouth. Flowridia didn't relent, the taste of her want exquisite, until Ayla pulled her away. Knowing her face was a mess, she stared up at Ayla, utterly breathless—her own body longed for release, especially to meet the vacant black of Ayla's gaze. "You're so beautiful," Flowridia whispered, and never had it been truer—her beautiful monster wife, and Flowridia longed to be everything for her.

The wickedness in Ayla's gaze faded into amusement, though she visibly fought it. "Gods, you make it difficult to be serious. You are precious."

Flowridia blushed as Ayla sat up and helped her to rise, then came down to kiss her, caught somewhere between desperate lust and unbearable softness, dizzy from need. Whispered words caressed her ear. "Are you still all right?"

"Yes, Lady Darkleaf," Flowridia replied, and Ayla grinned as she kissed her cheek.

Her wife's cold touch traveled to her back, her nails leaving a warning in their wake—though she never drew blood, not once. Flowridia gasped when Ayla suddenly pushed her forward, shock causing her to tense and tug at her bonds. With her face pressed to the blankets, she felt Ayla's tongue lick a leisurely line across her vulva. "Oh, you do want me," Ayla cooed, breathing cool air against her dripping cunt. Flowridia shuddered, the torture of waiting likely to unravel her all on its own, but then Ayla's fingers skimmed across her slick folds. "Say you want me, pet."

"I want you, Lady Darkleaf," Flowridia managed, whining when Ayla set her finger at the crux of her entrance. "Please."

"What do you want?"

"I want you to fuck me."

Ayla's fingers pushed inside her, no softness in the gesture—only lust. The time for gentle touching had passed; Ayla's rough motions pulsed heat through her blood, each thrust dancing the line of pleasure and pain. "Scream loud, my darling," Ayla said, and Flowridia obeyed, cries echoing with each motion inside her.

Claws dug into her hip to steady her, and oh—what a pleasure, to be so exposed. Utterly trapped, all she could do was ride the moment—her ass in the air, her cunt open for Ayla's delight. Climax neared, but then sharp pain suddenly shot through her, her ass pulsing from Ayla's spank.

Oh, she loved that. "Yes!" she cried, and after a few more thrusts, that sharp pain came again, pulsing fresh pleasure through her blood.

Every sensation felt so brilliantly vibrant—each rough movement inside her, the nails gripping her hip, the residual stinging radiating from her ass. "Say my name, pet," Ayla said, menace in the words.

"Fuck, *Ayla—*"

Her bubble of pleasure popped, her wife's name on her tongue; climax writhed through her body. She fought her bonds, her involuntary motions leaving her trapped, yet freer than she'd ever felt, and with a final cry she finished.

Only then did she realize the tears and spit staining the sheets beneath her. Ayla withdrew; she gasped, a new longing settling in with her afterglow—the desperate desire to be held.

"Ayla," she said, and her wife seemed to understand, carefully helping her to rise, only to pull her into her chest. Flowridia remained tied at her arms and wrists, but Ayla placed sweet kisses into her hair.

"I love you, Flowra." Ayla held her close and wiped her tears, her own eyes glistening—how beautiful she was, silver glittering in the moonlight. "You called me the wrong name."

"Oops," Flowridia replied, blushing fiercely.

Like the epilogue to a story, they ended as they began, with Ayla's studious attention as she untied the plethora of knots. Once free, Flowridia admired the red lines carved into her arms, running her fingers across them, wondering if they would last until morning.

"They are impressive," Ayla said, affirming her silent thoughts, but then she winked and added, "but I prefer the handprints on your ass, personally."

Flowridia's blush burned bright. Her entire body hummed in residual pleasure, though some stinging buzzed from her posterior and her hips.

From Ayla's mouth came demure words. "Was that good?"

So strange, for Ayla to be so shy over sex. Flowridia let her amusement show and chuckled. "It was wonderful. And I'd love to do it again."

Ayla's ensuing grin showed teeth. "It has been so long since I have had a partner to tie up and smother with affection—or lust as generally was the case. I have never done this to someone I love. It's gratifying."

Flowridia kissed her, then held Ayla in bed, adoring her nude embrace. "I always trusted you, even when it was stupid to do so." She dared to wink, giggling at Ayla's ensuing eye roll.

"It still is."

But Flowridia shook her head. "Yes, yes—you're a monster, I know. But you're my monster wife, and I think that's reason enough to put my life in your hands."

Shyness showed in Ayla's pose; Flowridia kissed her sweetly—first above and then below.

Chapter 31

"It will take time for your power to grow," Staella said, her voice as soft as night, "but I have no doubt you'll be able to snap a finger and come to me in no time."

Amazing, how what felt like little more than a day could be a week back at home. But the carriage to Staelash had a while yet to travel, and Etolié's kingdom needed her.

Etolié accepted her momma's outstretched hands, their glowing light covered by her own. "Or you could keep volunteering to help me out," she said with a wink. "Save me some nausea."

"Starshine, if you can bring yourself here, you can go anywhere in the world."

Staella squeezed her hand, but Etolié hardly felt it. "What do you mean?"

"It's my blood that allows the Solviraes to travel across and through the planes, but no one has ever been able to come to Celestière." Staella's beaming smile literally glowed. "You hold the potential to be better than anyone before you. Have you ever tried?"

Etolié shook her head. "I've never needed to though, now that I think about it. For the last two decades, I've had the Solviraes at my beck and call."

"You'll try sometime, won't you? For me?"

Momma looked so sincere. Etolié could not shatter that hope. "For you," she said, though the thought made her stomach sick. Given she could not keep her lunch inside for other people's portals, she suspected her own would be just as dreadful.

"I recall you being just a little thing and summoning entire orchestras to entertain yourself." Staella sat across from her, fondness in her reminiscent smile. "By seven, they all played in time, perfect harmonies, and I can't even begin to imagine where you thought of them. If you could do that at such a young age, I can't fathom what you can't do."

She offered her hands; Etolié accepted them.

"Focus with me," Staella said, and Etolié shut her eyes, picturing her little client kingdom. "Feel my power. Remember the sensation. Let that be your guide, next time you try to access this power on your own."

Etolié nodded—

The touch left. The world tilted, but she did not feel sick.

When she opened her eyes, she stood outside the city gates with all her insides properly inside her stomach.

Her feet left shallow tracks in the falling snow—true footprints, if you looked closely, instead of the boots she illusioned. Cold had never bothered her, barely affected her. The familiar streets of Staelash met her, grid-like in their planned perfection. Etolié waved at the few townsfolk they passed. The hour likely neared midnight, the weather frigid, but citizens swept their doorsteps, nevertheless. Work never ceased.

When the gates surrounding the manor approached, Etolié swore her eyesight failed her when it fell upon a familiar figure frantically waving from behind the iron walls. She ran toward the strange sight. "Zoldar?"

Zoldar, that wonderful bug, rarely went outside. Familiar clicking ensued in rapid succession. "Slow down," she said. "Nice to see you too—"

He waved his arm-like appendages, his spindly frame apparently immune to the cold. Etolié's breath left small bursts of fog, but Zoldar's gigantic, crystal eyes seemed terrified as he proceeded to mime.

"The library? What's wrong with the library?" Etolié said, struggling to make sense of his clicking. "Intruder?" Zoldar gave an affirmative but continued his wild motions. "A dead intruder?" Realization struck Etolié like a particularly well-placed stab wound. "Was she small and pale? Black hair? What do you mean you don't see color?!"

Etolié had no time for several things, and the number one thing on that list of several things was vampires. "Well, she didn't kill you, so she probably won't kill me. Take me there."

Zoldar took her hand, his spindly fingers weaving with hers. As they wandered down the hallways and stairs, Etolié mentally documented her options, as well as weaponry she could believably pull out of the air. The fact of the matter was, if Ayla Darkleaf wanted her dead, the only place she was safe was Celestière, which meant she really might be in trouble. Perhaps Ayla was angry Etolié had stolen her wedding present.

Death was one hundred percent worth stealing that nasty piece of work.

In the library, Etolié braced herself for assault, but stopped in her tracks at who waited. The intruder was definitely not hiding—nor who she expected.

Mereen Fireborn beamed at her entrance, casually sitting up from her collected pile of books.

"Looks like you've made you've made yourself at home," Etolié muttered, too shocked to be angry at the mess. "Nice to see you again."

The skylight cast Mereen in eerie shadows. Etolié's wings appeared, giving the room a slightly less disconcerting ambience. Still, vampires practically radiated cold—metaphorical and not. Zoldar released her hand and recoiled at the approaching figure, then rapidly disappeared up into the bookshelves.

Mereen reached into the bag at her hip and offered both a jewel-encrusted box and a set of maldectine knuckles.

Etolié gasped as Mereen offered them forward, heart thumping wildly. When she opened the box, she nearly sobbed from relief—the white orb remained, nestled safely in its velvet coverings. "I take back literally every bad thing I've ever said about vampires." She shut the box, holding it protectively to her chest. "This is beyond even just my own thanks. You might have helped save the world."

Mereen shrugged, then held her bag forward, lifting the covering. A green glow radiated, faint but unmistakable, as Etolié peered in—that blasted green orb—

And . . . a bracelet?

Etolié frowned as Mereen took the bag away, not moving even when the vampire withdrew a scroll from a different pocket. She did not even contemplate just how many goddamn pockets she had sequestered in that leather ensemble. Mereen unraveled the map, but Etolié struggled to breathe. Before Mereen could predictably point at the swamp again, Etolié raised a hand and said, "Where did you get that bracelet?"

Mereen raised a questioning eyebrow, withdrawing the condemning piece of jewelry—and it was, indeed, exactly what Etolié thought. Made of maldectine, it glowed bright green, and Etolié would know that work anywhere. "I may or may not definitely know the goat-hooved manufacturer of that bracelet, as well as who it was gifted to."

Mereen's smile spread wide. She withdrew the orb and held them together.

"No, no. I get that it mutes the orb's power. It is likely not perfect cover because I doubt you know much about magic—no offense— but it's how you've been hiding, and I applaud you. But listen—that was a gift to my former bookkeeper, so how the hell did you get it?"

With gloved hands, Mereen motioned like a wheel—encouraging her to continue.

"You know Flowers?"

Mereen positively beamed. When she placed the condemning objects back into her pouch, she handed the map to Etolié.

"You want me to go to Ilunnes, I know." Etolié glared at the tiny spot on the map—fuck, it was far away. Weeks of travel. "This smells like a trap."

Mereen kept her smile, then tapped the spot once more.

"Listen, you've endeared yourself to me because of that white orb, but this is all sounding very suspicious—" A thought occurred to her, something strange and potentially plausible. "Are you under some kind of curse?"

Mereen held up her hands, sort of weighing them in the air.

"If I could help you to speak again, would you?"

Intrigue crossed the vampire's face.

"You may or may not know that my momma is Staella, Goddess of Stars, known for taking on other people's ailments and shit. I've never tried this, but the worst that can happen is nothing." Etolié offered a hand. "I'll need you to take off your glove."

With a victorious grin, Mereen removed her glove, revealing a lithe hand, perfection embodied. When Etolié touched it, she nearly flinched—exactly like Khastra's, cold as death.

The terrible and petty thought of, *'this is what Flowers lost her flower to?'* popped into her head, but some things were better left unsaid.

She shut her eyes, her focus slowly settling. Given direction, her ability to hyper-focus was realistically quite inspirational. Sensing magic was innate; something did exist here, coating Mereen like an invisible sludge, even beyond the necromancy passively sustaining her.

Careful to peel apart the vampiric magic from this odd curse, Etolié focused exclusively on Mereen, on the sensation of her cold touch, then tried to dig deeper, to touch upon what clung to her. She found this a difficult task, given her general aversion to emotions. Feeling other people's pain was not a thing she considered herself capable of, but Momma had said she held the ability . . .

But Etolié muted it. Constantly. She drank to suppress.

Yet she had been in Celestière for the past few days and had not had a drop.

The world itched. It prickled and burned, but instead of fighting it, for the first time, she embraced it—

Sensation bombarded her. The sludge coating Mereen sloshed away, creeping over to cover her instead. Weightless, yet it felt like mud sloshing over her skin.

Immediately, Etolié released her, lest she invite more. She withdrew her flask from the air, frantically gulping because *oh gods she felt fucking sound.*

"Huh," she heard, surprise in the foreign, sultry tone. "Isn't that interesting."

Etolié held up a hand, not wanting to be rude, but definitely not listening as she slowly swallowed her weight in booze.

Mereen waited patiently, her smile pleasant and false as Etolié finally gasped for breath and tossed her flask away.

She opened her mouth to speak—

And choked on air.

Fuck.

"I'll feel terrible if that's permanent," Mereen said, but something in her tone said she was not sorry one fucking bit.

Damn it all—how had Momma said to get rid of it?

"But let me introduce myself properly." Mereen placed her glove back on her hand, casually stretching her fingers. "Yes, I am Mereen Fireborn. To quell your suspicions, I met Flowridia on the road several weeks ago—I rescued her, actually, from the God of Order. That was when I stole his orb. He's been following me ever since."

Etolié tried to nod, but a sudden kink in her neck froze it solid when she tried to motion. Weird. No words of any kind, it seemed. She tried to illusion letters, and all she could manage were puffs of smoke.

"No words," Mereen affirmed. "'No more words from you,' was her exact phrase—and we vampires are helpless to our creators."

Mereen Fireborn—who fought The Endless Night with Khastra's sister, long ago. Etolié choked once again as she tried to say she understood, but instead released a *hemph* sound and tried instead to mime fangs.

"Yes, a vampire—"

Etolié conjured an image of Ayla Darkleaf. It seemed her illusions were still good for something.

Mereen's eyes flashed with delight. "You do know her, then. Wonderful." She withdrew her map once more. "Go to Ilunnes. I will meet you there, with the orb."

Etolié placed her hands on her hips, glaring at the map as Ayla's image disappeared.

"Of course it's a trap," Mereen said, "but not for you. I want you to see for yourself what has been done, but I will tell you this much—that not two months ago, Empress Alauriel Solviraes entered this swamp with Flowridia, and she emerged as a . . ." Mereen's grin held vicious intent, and Etolié's blood chilled. ". . . a new person, you might say. But I want you to see it. I want you to know, without a shadow of a doubt, the atrocity that was committed. I want you to know the monster who is Flowridia Solviraes, Empress Consort of Solvira."

Despite the fact that her limbs had numbed from sheer terror, Etolié contemplated how to say *fun fact, I can potentially summon us a portal and save us literal weeks of travelling*, but when she finally settled on just illusioning the image of a portal, Mereen had fucking disappeared.

Etolié stared at the space she had stood in, noting the mess and the toppled books, and heaved a heavy sigh. Then, she summoned exploding fireworks—the bitch was hiding *somewhere* in the dark—but no. Lights filled the space, but the fucker had vanished—

Then the earth tremored.

Etolié watched in horror as her shelves swayed, fearful of the walls in her underground library, ducked when books fell into a heap—

But it lasted only seconds.

Etolié trembled from shock, because earthquakes simply did not happen in Solvira, yet she had experienced two in only a few weeks. She took a few tentative steps forward, fully expecting the structure to collapse, but the tremor had been small.

The correlation between Mereen's appearances and ensuing earthquakes could not be dismissed, but that strangely felt like drop of rain in a fucking typhoon after whatever cryptic bullshit Mereen had spouted.

That, and the fact that she was now mute. There were bigger problems at hand.

In her mind, Etolié tried to say magic words: *Goddess Momma*—

Static filled her head, in tandem with a wicked jolt of pain. No. That counted as words.

Exasperated, Etolié bolted from the room.

There was only one person in this house she trusted to go along with insane shenanigans without too many questions. Etolié grabbed a few sticks of incense and ran up the stairs and through the hall, then frantically pounded on a door.

Garbed in a nightgown and with her hair wrapped in silk, Sora opened the door, fully alert, armed with a knife. Upon her shoulder was Leelan, the small bird. The half-elf was one of the few residents of the manor tall enough to face her eye-to-eye, her hazel ones wide and sleepy. When Etolié smiled, she heaved a sigh. "Goddess' Glory, you scared me."

Rather than waste time miming, Etolié offered the incense. Beside her, she summoned a sparkly image of Sora praying, then motioned from real Sora to the illusion.

Thankfully Sora looked more confused than angry to have been awoken at the odd hour. "You want me to pray?" When Etolié smiled, she frowned. "What's going on? Was I dreaming or was there actually an earthquake?"

Etolié pursed her lips, trying to convey the hand motion for *bitch, you don't know the half of it,* but gave up and just beckoned harder, nearly throwing the incense into her hands.

Sora, always down for a bit of insanity, motioned for her to enter. "You're acting strange." She kept the grip on her knife—as she should—but allowed Etolié in, who looked around, curious about the sparseness of the bedroom.

Very utilitarian, void of finery—Sora's bed was unmade but aside from that, the atmosphere was spotless and cold. The only sign of personality was a small statue of Sol Kareena upon a shelf.

Yet, when Etolié narrowed her eyes and peeked closer, little things popped out—the hint of a blade beneath the pillow, another glinting from the closet. Like all things Sora-related, it was more than surface deep.

Sora offered the incense sticks back. "I have no idea what to do with these." When Etolié accepted them, Sora pulled a box of matches from her drawer. "I'm assuming you need these, though?"

It occurred to Etolié that she hadn't seen Sora in weeks, and that the half-elf, one of the rare few to know the nastier truths of Etolié's childhood, was in for a couple of surprises.

Well, too late to make this a smooth awakening.

Using the matches, Etolié lit a stick of incense, then pulled the hidden dagger from Sora's pillow and placed the incense on it, lest it burn down the bed. Handy, that thing. Etolié motioned for Sora to kneel with her and breathe deep.

Sora shook her head. "Why aren't you talking?"

There was not really a good way to mime or illusion the words *vampire curse,* so she huffed a breath and tapped her throat. Then, she shrugged.

"Your voice is gone?"

Etolié smiled, but Sora did not.

"What the hell happened—" Sora cringed as the smoke touched her nostrils. "Oh, that's strong. And I don't say that often."

Sora, connoisseur of hallucinogenic drugs, really would not. Etolié ignored her and breathed deep, relieved when Sora joined her, though she still gripped her dagger—understandably so. "You want me to pray? To whom?"

Etolié illusioned the image of a starry night.

"Your mother?"

Etolié smiled wide.

Sora asked no further questions as she knelt and shut her eyes.

Silence settled. There was not a temple to Staella in Staelash—an oversight, assuredly—and so Etolié hoped she hadn't completely fucked this up, but then a gentle glow filled the candlelit room.

"Etolié?"

Beside her, Sora gasped. Though not quite so corporeal as it had been in the temple, there appeared the image of her momma's wispy, radiant form.

"Oh, and friend!" Staella's gentle voice filled the room with as much metaphorical light as it did literal. "It is wonderful to meet you."

Etolié tapped Sora on the shoulder, then pointed at her own throat. The half-elf looked shocked but managed to gather her words. "Y-You're Goddess Staella."

Very articulate. Etolié rolled her eyes, but Staella gave a small curtsy. "In spirit, yes."

"E-Etolié needs me to tell you," Sora said, stumbling over each word, "that her voice is gone. I don't know why. Honestly, I'm not quite certain this is actually happening."

But Staella frowned as she knelt before Etolié. "My guess is you tried to take away someone else's muteness?" When Etolié grinned nervously, she laughed—and thank Morathma's Whore Mother for that. "Well, let us first be grateful you haven't been left with a gaping wound instead of a few minutes of being mute. You have to let the curse burn through you."

Etolié waved her arms, trying to convey that it was here to stay unless intervention happened.

And Staella . . . understood? "If you can take it, there must be some way to burn it out, but perhaps it is too much too soon. I will help you this time, but be very careful what wounds you take upon yourself. You are not an angel, nor are you a goddess yet." She offered her hand, and Etolié, relieved, anxiously accepted it.

Though drinking had dulled the sensation, she felt the metaphorical gunk coating her skin pull away. "Momma—" She stopped, realizing the word did not immediately choke. Laughter overtook her. "Momma, you're a right piece of work."

Staella smiled, but she said nothing. Now this was her problem, and Etolié did feel a little bad about that.

"It isn't permanent, right?"

Staella's smile held reassurance.

"I hate to ask for more, but I need help getting to a place." Etolié looked to Sora. "Want to join?"

"Oh, why not." Sora stood up and went to her closet. "What am I dressing for?"

"Swamp."

Sora groaned as she disappeared behind the door.

"It's called the Abyssal Swamp, outside Ilunnes," Etolié said to Goddess Momma. "We're going to beat that Mereen lady there by . . . probably weeks, actually. But something big is going on—"

"Who the fuck?"

Etolié had never heard the half-elf say 'fuck.' "Mereen Fireborn," she said, to the wide-eyed half-elf—mostly dressed and staring out of the closet. "Kinda sneaky, definitely a vampire, but also weirdly helpful? I'm assuming this is a relative of yours."

Sora's head fell into her hands and she groaned miserably loud. This was not what Etolié expected. "She's my great-great-great-grandmother, but I always called her grandma. I know her much better than I'd like to."

"Huh. Neat." Etolié chuckled nervously as another piece of important and damning information played through her head. "Speaking of which, guess who's back?"

All the healthy color drained from Sora face, leaving her an ashy shade of amber. "Who, Etolié?" she said, as though she had not immediately known in her gut.

"Some bitch your grandma has a big ol' grudge against."

Sora withdrew back into the closet without further comment.

Etolié looked back to Staella, who waited politely. "Momma, something's wrong with Empress Alauriel. Do you know anything?"

Staella frowned.

"That's what Mereen said. She said Lara was different, I think. Changed? She was cryptic because she needs me to go to Ilunnes, I guess. And Flowers is apparently evil? I do not know. I don't know if Mereen can be trusted, but . . ." Etolié sighed, willing her panic away. "I don't know what to think. I'm just scared. Can you help? Portal? Pretty please?"

Staella laughed, though worry shone in her eyes.

When Sora emerged, the half-elf whispered something to the little bird familiar of hers, then set him on the bed. "It's best that he stays here."

Etolié took Sora's hand, and the world shifted away.

Ilunnes was moist.

Everything—from the cottages, the scent in the air, even the grimy people watching. Etolié's garb and silver hair bespoke her as an outsider, so she let her wings shine, letting there be no question. Mothers pulled their children away from her and Sora as they passed, windows shut, and all around the atmosphere grew cold.

There was a single road leading through town. Etolié found a guard, though he was little more than a peasant with a spear, and said, "Sir?"

The man stared her up and down, the lines of his frown permanent. "You an angel?"

"Mostly. I am Magister Etolié of Staelash, Savior of Slaves, Daughter of Stars, etcetera. I am conducting an investigation. Have there been any strange happenings in that swamp?" She pointed to the collection of trees that formed a barrier beyond the line of houses.

Immediately suspicion stiffed the man's stance. "'Bout two months ago," he said, looking beyond Etolié, "the witch returned."

Etolié frowned. "What witch?"

"Odessa," he said, then he spat on the ground. "The Swamp Witch. Passed through our town and killed a number of us with her witchcraft. Concocted some sort of evil back in her home—twisted the magic in the place, caused an explosion."

"An explosion?"

"You could see it for miles. Looked like a star exploded."

Etolié had the faint memory of a flash of a silver light twisting the magic of the world. "You say the witch caused this?"

The man nodded. "We sent a mob to find her. None of them returned. Anyone who goes in there never comes back."

"Good to know. Thank you for your time."

"You ain't thinking of going in there, are you?"

Etolié said, "Lucky for me, that silver explosion was precisely what I was looking for."

As she walked away, toward the edge of town, Sora leaned in and whispered, "What are you thinking?"

Etolié thought a great many things and realized the puzzle she had hastily assembled no longer fit. "I know that about two months ago, Lara and Flowers were here, and that Lara blew herself up to combat Soliel. I know that Odessa is an urban legend, supposedly a witch who . . ."

Etolié's words trailed away, the name suddenly triggering a memory from months ago.

Sol Kareena had come to save her city, and what was it she had called Flowers? *Your fate is a thousand tangled strings, Child of Odessa—*

"Scratch that, Sora. Odessa might be alive and well." She frowned, glancing back at the town.

They continued onward. It did not take long for the noxious smell to rise.

The muddy ground soon coated Sora's boots, and Etolié wished she had brought real ones for herself. Instead, she spread her wings wide and floated along, already sick of the dank atmosphere. Night hung like an oppressive fog, yet she heard nothing—no creatures, no life.

Unnatural. It made Etolié's skin crawl. She pulled out her flask and drank.

"Etolié . . ."

She looked to Sora, who hesitated as she navigated the murky ground. The half-elf's form, illuminated by Etolié's wings, held reservation.

"I should tell you something." The half-elf braced herself. "If Ayla Darkleaf truly is back, my life is in danger."

"Oh, she's back," Etolié replied, sneering at the memory. "Back and nastier than ever. We're all in danger."

"No, listen." Sora fists clenched—whatever she thought of brought pain, and Etolié shied at her palpable anxiety. "She's the one who murdered me. If she realizes I'm still alive, she'll try to do it again."

"She . . ." Etolié's words caught in her throat—in part because of how obnoxiously rude it felt to forget that someone had been murdered and subsequently resurrected by Sol Kareena herself, but also the many pieces that had suddenly fallen into place. "Ayla Darkleaf is the one who . . ."

"Mutilated me and hung me in the cathedral? Yes."

Etolié felt very cold, despite the disconcertingly warm swamp atmosphere. "Fucking hell—that bitch really has killed all my friends."

First Clarence, then Khastra, and now she knew the truth about Sora.

The fact that Flowers was still alive was a gods-damned miracle.

"Why though?" Etolié asked. "Was it because you were a Fireborn?"

Sora's hesitation bespoke something terrible. "I never spoke up before because I didn't, and still don't, want the person responsible to be held accountable. She did not know better. She was a stupid girl in love—"

"Oh, fuck no." Etolié stopped dead in her tracks, feeling suddenly faint. "Oh, Flowers . . . Flowers, no . . ."

"In her defense," Sora said, "I did threaten Demitri."

With that, Etolié's sympathy ended. She reeled up and stared at Sora, jaw slack. "You threatened a baby boy? Bitch, I don't feel bad for you anymore. He was just a puppy. I would have let Ayla murder you for that too."

"I suppose that's fair."

"Look, what happened to you was awful, but what a way to make everyone hate you." Etolié shook her head, her steps resuming.

"I've felt awful about it ever since."

"Good." The word seemed mean, especially given Sora had probably been tortured a bit before she had had her heart stabbed, but Demitri had been a little puppy.

Subject change, then, before Etolié had to further admit how little compassion she felt for her friend. Still, it remained a gruesome memory—but with it came the undeniable miracle of Sora's resurrection.

Sol Kareena had saved Sora. Not Khastra, though, and Etolié had thought she had made peace with that. Something new had come to replace it.

"Sora, do you remember the conversation we had in the carriage?"

"You mean the entire week we spent dissecting the night you and Khastra—"

"No, no—not that conversation," Etolié said, unable to find humor in the segue; not today. "About Sol Kareena."

Within the dark swamp, Etolié's wings remained the only light, casting Sora's ensuing nod in soothing, golden hues.

"I'm learning that what she did . . . when she basically banished me . . . it wasn't a popular decision. Do you think she could have been wrong?"

Sora slowed her careful steps, the moist suction of her boots in the mud an unpleasant backdrop. "She must have had a reason. She's the greatest of all the Deities of Celestière."

But she had not always been, Etolié was keen to remember. And Momma had said Ku'Shya was even greater. Her stomach twisted, not emotionally prepared for even minor cognitive dissonance. Not today, when her mind already reeled from Mereen's cryptic bullshit. "She was following the laws," Etolié muttered, but there were no laws for children—certainly not for children who murdered their fathers.

Etolié was hardly an adult, but she was grown. She thought of Lara, who at fourteen was simply a child, versed in the ways of politics but still much more focused on prettying her hair and reading her books—and if she had killed a man, Etolié would have happily utilized whatever dark magic it took for the opportunity to kill him again.

That seemed to be how Alystra had seen it. And Momma. Etolié's stomach hollowed, and despite the humid air, she was awash with cold.

"What did you mean by Flowridia being evil?"

Sora's words jarred her from her spiral, though it took her a moment to latch on to her meaning. But once her mind had returned to the present, Etolié explained what Mereen had said—all the cryptic nonsense. "I don't know what any of it means."

"Grandma isn't a liar," Sora said, her eyes fixed to the swampy ground, "but I also know she'll say or do anything to get what she wants if it has to do with Ayla Darkleaf."

"You think this has to do with her?"

"It has to. There would be no other reason for her to care—"

The ground suddenly shook. Violent tremors rattled the earth. Etolié instinctively let her wings carry her up, just a few inches, then helped steady her half-elf companion, lest she fall into a bog. Trees unearthed; water sloshed; the muddy earth shifted—

And just as quickly, the world settled.

Etolié landed, eyes wide as she looked to Sora. "What the actual fuck?"

"That's not natural," the half-elf said, visibly shaken. "Earthquakes don't . . . They don't happen here."

"No, this isn't natural," Etolié muttered. "Question— let's say, hypothetically, if handed an orb, would your grandma know how to use it?"

"I don't think she could. Mereen doesn't understand magic at all." Sora stared as though expecting more; Etolié had nothing more to give.

They fell into silence, aside from the splashing of water as they avoided puddles. Fumes of gas erupted from bubbles. The place would ignite at the drop of a match.

Farther in, Sora said, "Follow my lead, Etolié. Unless you trust yourself to navigate the bogs."

"I'd rather not risk my fake dress," Etolié said, instead floating a few inches off the ground.

Sora did not comment, instead hopping over rocks and ditches.

They navigated for hours, with Etolié directing Sora toward where her headache grew worse. "It amazes me," Sora remarked, "that we haven't found any animals. No crocodiles, not even insects."

Etolié listened a moment, realizing Sora was correct. No chirping of birds or bugs—only the faint wind in the trees. "That's unnerving."

"I agree."

Soon, hints of light peeked through the trees. Day had come. Yet, the darkness remained, omnipresent, the land sickly from lack of sun.

A strange something lay in the water. At first it appeared as a pale rock, then Etolié realized it wore rotted clothing. "Sora—"

Sora stopped, eyes wide when she followed Etolié's gaze. "Goddess' Glory . . ."

Etolié thought her head might split from pain, but there would be time to drink once they had found whatever it was they searched for. "There's one missing townsperson." She kept walking forward, close enough to Sora that the half-elf could grab her if she fell into a bog. "And look there— another."

The body itself had begun the slow process of decomposition, hindered by the lack of animal life. Waterlogged, covered in filth and gore, it lay face down, yet

Etolié wondered if the bite marks torn into its flesh were from before or after death.

They continued onward. Underneath a dense collection of trees, was a cottage. Dilapidated and beginning to mold, it looked to have been abandoned for years, and around it were thick trees serving as supports. One tree appeared burned, the rotting remnants of rope lying at the charred base.

But all this paled to the stench and the horror lying in the bogs. Strewn about the water were bodies. The corpses were in various stages of decomposition, some nearly skeletal, yet they all bore visages of terror—those that still had faces, at least. Etolié cringed as they passed the bodies by, noting how pale Sora had become, and guessed there to be at least fifty. Likely more.

"Bog bodies don't rot," Sora said, the words as ominous as they were confusing. "Not the way buried ones do. But look—that one looks to have been eaten by insects."

She pointed to a particularly nasty corpse, face up and missing its jaw.

"Not all of these died at the same time."

Etolié stepped carefully, not wanted to brush against gore or accidentally trigger some trap. As they approached the cottage, she swore she saw a flicker of light from the window. She stopped, holding out an arm to warn Sora.

Nothing moved. Nothing emerged. Wood creaked when Etolié placed her foot on the porch. Politeness dictated that she knock. The damp wood absorbed the noise. Only a mild echo sounded within.

When nothing collapsed or shrieked, Etolié pushed the door open.

Within, a damp, putrid odor met her nose, a pungent mix of blood and mold. Etolié watched her step, feet carefully navigating the piles of upturned earth and evidence of fungal growth. Her radiant wings revealed a cozy home, though the obvious aura of evil did take away from the comfort.

Beyond the dirt was a moldy sitting room. A barren fireplace had been built into the wall, and there stood the entrance to a kitchen up ahead. To her right, two doors, each slightly ajar.

"If Odessa is truly dead," Etolié muttered, "I would bet an ample amount of Eionei's brew this was her home."

"I'd say it was abandoned for years, but some of those bodies are only a few weeks old, I'd guess," Sora said. "Someone's been here."

Something strange and familiar leaned idly against the wall—a spear?

Flowers' spear.

Etolié took the light wood in her hands, the design unmistakably Thalmus', even if she hadn't observed it up close before. "She was definitely here."

Placing the weapon aside, Etolié pushed open a door, taken aback by the large cauldron, as tall as her waist. Large, metal hooks dangled above it, bearing evidence of blood scrubbed away, and shelves stocked with jars lined the walls.

"Mereen sent us here for a reason," Etolié finally said. "I don't know what puzzle pieces we're seeing, but this isn't nothing."

"I don't recognize most of these ingredients," the half-elf said.

"With due respect to Flowers, there's a reason witches are often so feared." Etolié skimmed the jars, most written in Solviran. Herbs, obscure and not, were sealed inside— wormwood, moonlily, listrous root, and so much more—but also various biological components, the names of which Etolié couldn't even begin to guess, though a pair of eyes stared at them from within one.

Etolié touched the offending jar and turned it around. "Let's keep looking," she said, and when they backed out of the room, she froze when faint light shone from the kitchen. Something blue emanated from around the corridor. Etolié summoned a quarterstaff into her hands. "Sora?"

Sora held a dagger at the ready.

"Whoever it is must know we're here." Then, louder, Etolié said, "Hello?"

They stepped toward the kitchen, as silent as their feet could be. The blue light had a source. Etolié stopped dead in her tracks.

A ghost shone bright, animated as it stared back with intelligent eyes, arms crossed. Her revealing clothing appeared stained, and the ghostly knife jutting from her throat showed the source. But her eyes were familiar, large and innocent, though her frown was callused and cruel, but every bit of her Etolié swore she had seen in a younger, less confident stance.

Jaw agape, Etolié finally said, "You're Odessa."

The ghost woman raised an eyebrow. "In the flesh," she said, a sardonic twist to the grin pulling at her lip, "so to speak."

"You look like your daughter," Etolié said, and Odessa's eye lit up with malevolent glee.

"You know my Flower Child?"

Etolié nodded. When she glanced at Sora, the half-elf kept a fighter's stance, prepared to leap and strike the incorporeal woman—not that it would do much, but Etolié appreciated the dedication.

"She's a delight," Etolié continued, wary of the ghost's reaction. "I went to her wedding, not too long ago."

Odessa's smile lost all sincerity. "A pity she didn't invite her dear mother, after all the work I did to save her beloved."

"You met Lara?"

The ensuing pause in conversation held enough tension for Sora to slash with her dagger, as Odessa looked oddly taken aback. Then, her countenance lit with pure delight. Hilarity stretched Odessa's cheekbones wide as she cackled. The ghost floated on her back, her laughter filling the entire cottage as she floated past Etolié and Sora and into the larger sitting room. "Oh, I certainly met Lara," Odessa said, and she wiped fake tears, so great was the amusement shaking her incorporeal body. "Tell me, sweet interlopers, are you close to my Flower Child?"

"I would like to think so," Etolié replied. "She worked with me, for a time. I'm Magister Etolié of Staelash."

"The Savior of Slaves comes to visit?" Odessa placed a dramatic hand on her chest. "Oh, what an honor." She turned her gaze to Sora. "And you are?"

"Sora Fireborn, High Priestess of Staelash," the half-elf replied, wary as Odessa continued her fit of laughter.

"The Savior of Slaves *and* a priestess of Sol Kareena? To what do I owe the honor, friends of my wayward whore of a daughter?"

Odessa watched with sincerity in her visage, and Etolié felt a few puzzle pieces fall together, at least regarding Flowers' sanity. "I have so many questions for you," Etolié said, "but to answer yours, you don't know a vampire named Mereen, do you?"

The enmity in Odessa's visage seemed so natural. Etolié wondered if Flowers were even capable of mimicking it, despite being this woman's near doppelganger. Odessa held lines in her face, faint but distinct, curves to her figure granted from childbearing, and a lighter hue of skin, but their appearances were near mirrors. "Mereen Fireborn? Yes, she stopped by a few weeks ago. Can't say we hit it off—got herself a little tied up." Odessa's wink meant something; Etolié just wasn't certain what.

"She sent us here," Etolié replied, unsure of what to make of Odessa's wicked smile. "We're supposed to meet her. She said something about Lara leaving here changed and Flowers being several shades of nasty."

The ghost woman floated closer, and Etolié resisted the urge to step back, even as icy cold radiated from the woman's ethereal form. "Tell me about my Flower Child's wedding."

"The wayward whore of a daughter had a beautiful ceremony. Lots of dancing, lots of ale, and two overjoyed brides. But you know Lara?"

"She wasn't particularly talkative."

Odessa kept that evil smirk, one that sent shivers down Etolié's spine. "I didn't realize Flowers had brought her here."

"She was dead-set on it," Odessa cooed. "And I would say that Lara left here *truly* changed."

Dread welled in Etolié's stomach. This woman knew something, hinted at something, and there was clear disdain in how she cooed over her 'Flower Child's' name. "You're playing with us," Etolié said, patience wearing thin. "Why did Flowers bring Lara here?"

"The poor empress blew herself to bits during her fight with the God of Order. Tell me, Daughter of Staella, what do you know of blood rituals?"

Etolié's memory immediately went to the large cauldron and blood-stained hooks, horror steadily rising. "It's old magic," she replied. "Life is the most potent form of power and—"

"And the more powerful the blood," Odessa interrupted, "the more powerful the ritual."

Etolié could no longer feel her hands, so cold the room had become. "That's common enough sense. What's your point?"

"Mereen must bear a weighty grudge to send you to me," Odessa continued, clearly reveling in the words. "All the evidence you could ever need is here, Magister, but if you wish to play the fool, I'll give you a hint."

Etolié could barely draw breath to speak. Instead, Sora spoke for the first time, though Etolié's muddled mind barely heard it. "Tell us."

"I've met other famous vampires, and a particular one *very* recently. Something tells me you know her too."

"No," Etolié said, and all the air in her lungs suddenly left, leaving her lightheaded. "No, Flowers would never—"

"Etolié?" Sora offered an arm to steady her. "What are you thinking?"

Etolié shook her head. "No, no, *no . . .*"

Powerful blood made a powerful ritual. And what blood was more powerful than—

"Flowers would never," Etolié spat, though her heavy breathing caused her heart to race. "You're lying."

Odessa put up defensive hands. "Perhaps you're right. My Flower Child married the empress, and Ayla Darkleaf is—"

"No!" Etolié cried, and inside her head, the betrayal played in a damning loop. Flowers would never— Lara could not be— But Ayla was—

Ayla was alive.

"So, you know the name?" Odessa said coolly. "An interesting match for my dear Flower Child. Not particularly pretty but alluring in her own way. Ayla was kind enough to banish me from my home, at least temporarily. Quite the set of powers she inherited. The Silver Fire in the hands of the Scourge of the Sun Elves? Well, if this world wasn't damned before—"

"You're lying!" Etolié cried, angry tears threatening to burst. "Flowers couldn't have known. She couldn't— She couldn't—" Etolié swayed; Sora caught her as her legs gave out.

Flowers and Ayla . . . But then what of—

"Lara. W-Where's Lara?" Etolié managed to stammer, but then a shadow in the doorframe caused her to choke.

Mereen Fireborn leaned casually against the doorframe. "Fancy seeing you already—"

"What the fuck—*how are you here?!*" Mereen flinched, but Etolié was having potentially the new worst day of her life, so fuck her. She stomped forward, the entire house creaking. "You were in Staelash just a few hours ago!"

"I could ask you the same—"

"I have a godly momma; this isn't a secret! How the fuck did you—"

Realization slammed Etolié like a punch from the Bringer of War.

"You worked with the Coming Dawn," she said, hardly breathing.

Mereen waited expectantly, her smile twitching.

"You . . ." Etolié shook her head. "No, but you have an orb, you can't be travelling through Sha'Demoni—"

The earthquakes.

"You were taking the orb into Sha'Demoni," Etolié said, breathless at the realization.

Mereen shrugged, deftly plucking the green and purple orb from her bag. "I saw no harm in it."

Mereen could walk in shadow. Of course she could. "You do know that slowly unravels the fabric of the world if you take it out of this one, right? They all have to be in balance at all times, or else."

"Truthfully, no. I know little of magic." Mereen's wicked smile turned to Sora. "Sora," she said, showing her white teeth, "by Sol Kareena's Light, how long has it been? Fifteen years, at least."

"Something like that," Sora said, positioning herself equally distanced from Mereen and Odessa. She kept her dagger poised, but Etolié suspected it would do nothing against her progenitor.

"I anticipated it taking you much longer to get here," Mereen said, her gaze drifting to the ghostly woman. "It doesn't matter. The body is gone."

Etolié sunk to her knees, unable to draw breath. "Lara is . . ."

"She was laid to rest in a truly heavenly field beyond the swamp," Mereen said. "Even granted a guardian of sorts. But now the grave is empty."

Etolié saw only static, unable to speak.

"Well, well," came Odessa's voice, sultry and smooth, "seems it all falls to me. I know who took her."

Though she could not feel a gods-damned cell in her body, Etolié forced herself to look at the ghost, to stand on shaking feet. "Tell me."

"We've already fully damned my sweet Flower Child— thus giving me my vindication." Odessa floated upward, dramatic as she cast her gaze to the ceiling. "I might need . . . *incentive.*"

"What kind of fucking incentive?" Etolié spat, and when Odessa laughed, she nearly screamed.

"As you can see," she said, gesturing to herself, "I am a little, uh, *hollow*. I need a vessel—someone near death, preferably a young woman up to my standards of beauty."

As Etolié studied Odessa, silently asking herself to what levels of depravity she would descend to for the sake of her moonbeam, she noticed Mereen casually striding toward Sora. Faster than lightning, she whipped out her sword—

Only for metal to sing as Sora's dagger narrowly stopped it from decapitating her. Her weapon clattered to the ground, the force of the sword too much, and she ducked when Mereen struck again.

"No!" Etolié screamed, but Mereen relentlessly pursued the half-elf, uncaring of collateral damage and she leapt onto the table, clattered dishes to the floor with her swords. Sora ducked and rolled, on the defensive, with skill enough for Etolié to wonder if she had played this game of death with Mereen before.

Fire rose—across the walls, the furniture, and in a line between Mereen and Sora. The vampire stumbled back, visibly agitated by the flame, while Sora, breathless, fell behind Etolié. Heat rose. Smoke threatened to choke them. Odessa howled, anguish in the sound, but Etolié stood tall, knowing perfectly well it was all an illusion. "Put down your weapons, Mereen," she said, "or I'll burn this place to the ground."

Odessa continued wailing, but Mereen glared with firm determination, maintaining eye contact as she placed her swords onto the ground. Instantly, the fire vanished, leaving no trace of heat or smoke.

Sora's heavy breathing became the only sound; Etolié helped her to rise.

Meanwhile, Mereen looked to Odessa, who had ceased her dramatic cries. "I tried," she said, sardonic as she curled her lip. "Trust in my honor that if you tell us, I shall bring you the quarry you seek."

Odessa glared at Etolié, ice in her eyes. Etolié kept Sora behind her, one eye on Mereen all the while—she had proven herself the greatest threat. The ghost floated back to the ground, pouting as she tossed her hair back, petulant and vain. "Mereen Fireborn, I trust in one thing, and it's that you want my daughter dead as much as I do. The body, I would guess, is in Nox'Kartha."

The words came like a punch to the stomach. Etolié reached back to grab Sora's forearm, lest the half-elf do anything stupid.

"Imperator Casvir stopped by a few days ago," Odessa continued, "followed by that simpering puppy he calls 'viceroy.' When he threatened to burn down my home, I told him what I knew—that the body was beyond the swamp because I could not feel it, but surely not far. If you say it's gone, he found it."

Casvir . . .

"You fear fire," Mereen said coolly and Odessa leveled with her stare, fearless before her.

"No. I fear the destruction of my home. It is all that keeps me here. I need a body so my spirit can latch to something else."

"Understood," Mereen said. She withdrew the earth orb once more and rolled it on the floor, toward Etolié. "A bargain is a bargain."

Etolié stumbled down to get it, the power surging immediately through her veins. Her headache spiked. She clutched it to her chest.

"Go on then, Daughter of Stars," Mereen continued, her stance triumphant. "Find the proof you need. Then serve the justice I cannot."

Etolié grabbed Sora's forearm once more and dragged her from the house.

Outside, she said, "I need to see it."

"S-See what?" Sora asked, her breathing still heavy.

"The grave. Come with me."

And they did. Etolié flew up in the air and saw what she swore was a landing of snowfall.

They reached it within the hour, silent all the while.

An odd mass of white appeared at the edge of the tree line, within a large meadow. What was white was not snow, but flowers, thousands of them—a sea of white, beautiful tulips.

Etolié ran forward, uncaring of the flowers she crushed as she came to a great tree, whose branches hung like a protective mother embracing a child—

And there it was—an empty grave.

It lay beside a large, untouched mound, and within the pit, Etolié saw discarded fabric, bloodied and torn—

Embroidered with moons and stars.

Etolié collapsed before the grave, the delayed anguish crashing upon her. A wail tore from her throat. Sora approached, but she didn't care; she screamed and cried, blinded by tears, by sorrow, by *rage*.

"Goddess Momma," she said out loud, *"send Sora home. And set me on Casvir's doorstep."*

All the world shifted.

When Etolié opened her eyes, she faced undead guards.

Before the great palace in Nox'Kartha, two skeletal guards held up their weapons. "State your name," one commanded, its voice emanating without any true source.

"Magister Etolié of Staelash, Daughter of Staella," Etolié replied, uncaring that she was a tear-streaked mess. "I must speak with Imperator Casvir immediately."

"Imperator Casvir is currently detained."

Etolié steeled her jaw, her brilliant, ethereal wings brandished wide and magnificent, though she surely smelled of swamp and filth. She did wield an orb, however, and that certainly meant something. "Let me repeat myself—I am Magister Etolié of Staelash, ally to Nox'Kartha, so perhaps an exception can be made."

"Imperator Casvir is currently detained."

Blood boiling, Etolié smiled and said, "Then allow me to sit in his throne room until he is not."

"Imperator Casvir is currently—"

"Oh, fuck this."

She launched herself into the air, shooting toward the nearest window, straight above.

Etolié dove through the glass window and fell to the floor. From the side, a shadow approached—a pillar of black sand became a swirling vortex. She covered her face, but the sand swarmed her, swirling about, and where it touched it *burned.*

It ate at her skin. Etolié whimpered; where it touched left nothing, not even a scar—just raw skin, like a burn.

The room she entered seemed to be an office, empty, and she ran to the door, despite the sand slowly eating her alive. She cast an illusion—of herself praying the sand could be taken for a fool.

But though the doppelganger Etolié batted at the sand, it was not swayed by the false image.

From her pocket, she withdrew the maldectine knuckles, and concentrated on creating a shield.

Energy expanded from the weapon in her hand. Where it enveloped, the sand fell, harmless and muted. Around her, the sand darted angrily against her shield, only to fall at her feet.

She spared a moment to inspect her wounded arms, flinching at the patches of raw skin exposed by the sand's necrotic powers. But she had succeeded in breaching the walls, and went to the hallway, taking a different approach. "Khastra! Khastra, you useless dead demon, where are you?!"

She called the name until a De'Sindai servant—a young man with horns that curled around pointed ears—approached. "My lady, are you lost?"

"Yes! In fact, I am," Etolié said with a dramatic flourish. The last of the sand still beat upon her shield. "My name is Etolié, Daughter of Staella, and Magister of Staelash. I'm lost and I'm livid, so either take me to your dark and scary leader or to his general. Your choice."

The young man bowed, visibly quivering in her presence. "My apologies, Magister Etolié. I was unaware of any royal guests—"

"Time is of the essence, kid."

He beckoned for her to follow—and to Etolié's surprise, the sand stopped trying to eat through her shield. Instead, it swirled away, docile for reasons Etolié truly didn't know. She wasn't going to question her one stroke of luck for the day, however; she illusioned away the orb in her hand and marched onward.

It took only a few turns before he motioned to a door. "Don't tell anyone I took you here," he whispered, and then he darted away.

Etolié suddenly understood the merit of employing the dead. Loyal to a fault. Living servants could disobey. Without knocking, Etolié pushed open the large door.

A magnificent table stood in the center of the room, supporting a gigantic map and numerous metallic figures placed upon it. Casvir himself loomed over it, but other important looking folk—mostly De'Sindai, but a few humans—sat or stood around it, listening with rapt attention.

Casvir's deep voice dissipated with the open door. He barely turned his head, a slight frown pulling at his lip. "Magister Etolié, it is considered rude, in polite company, to come unannounced—"

"It's also considered *rude,*" Etolié all but spat, "to loot graves, but if sources are correct, you visited a swamp recently."

Casvir's frown deepened, but no one among the small collection of people seemed shocked. "You know."

"Tell me I'm wrong," Etolié seethed, yet furious tears welled in her eyes. "Tell me this is a sick joke."

Casvir's silence spoke volumes. Etolié's breath hitched when she looked again to the map between them. It was a map of the continent, every figurine placed in Solvira.

Around Neolan.

"So, it is true," Etolié whispered, and the first of her tears slipped down her cheek. "Flowers sits on the throne with an imposter. A-And you . . ." She could not even speak—fury stilled her tongue.

"Consort Flowridia sits on the throne with someone who wields the Silver Fire," Casvir said, "but she did not marry Empress Alauriel. How did you find out?"

Etolié fell against the doorframe, fighting the sobs shaking her body. "Flowers knew; she fucking *knew.*" Her pleading eyes settled on Casvir, but Etolié knew not what she pled for. For answers, for justice, for the honor of tearing his head from his body—she did not know. "And you're planning an attack."

Casvir's voice turned her heart to ice. "It has been in the works for some time."

Etolié didn't love Solvira any more than she didn't love any other place on this realm, but to think of it falling to this bastard cut like a knife to her stomach. "Without Khastra?" she said, for Casvir was the only one here she knew.

"She is currently detained."

The words bespoke a nightmare, but Etolié had to swallow that for the moment. "Where's Lara's body?"

"Would you like to see her?"

Etolié's breath hitched as she nodded.

"Then wait outside while I finish."

No room for argument in his tone, and Etolié was too defeated to even try. She stumbled out of the room, hearing it click shut behind her, and pinched herself, willing blood to flow back through her limbs. Before she could work herself into a panic, however, familiar laughter cut through her spiraling, anxious thoughts.

Queen Marielle Vors of Staelash turned the nearby corner, standing far too close to Murishani, their laughter too friendly, the way their hands brushed too familiar. Etolié's breath hitched, too furious to formulate words—merely glared when Marielle finally looked in her direction. "Etolié?"

Etolié clenched her fists, plastering a wide smile onto her face. "What the actual fuck are doing here?"

Marielle flinched at the remark. "You can't talk to me like that. I'm the—"

"Seriously?!" Etolié stomped forward, quest forgotten in her red-hot rage. "You're the queen of a fucking *oligarchy*, Marielle! Your power means *nothing* without Sora or I, so get that through your gods-damned skull! What the hell are you even doing here?! You're supposed to be traveling with Staelash!"

Marielle's posture bristled, her painted lips a flat line. "I'm visiting my friend, Murishani." Beside her, Murishani stood in mimicry of her pose, the pout of his lips infuriating. "We became close during my wedding and have decided to stay in correspondence. He invited me to stay in Nox'Kartha and save myself the traveling time."

"Without your husband? Where is he?"

Murishani spoke up. "Oh, don't worry about Lae Lae—big cities give him anxiety so he—"

"Don't call him 'Lae Lae'; he hates that name!" Etolié forced a furious sigh after that outburst. She cared about Zorlaeus, yes, but a polite reprimand would have sufficed—even if that weren't what this was about at all. "Marielle, get your ass to Staelash. We'll discuss this when I'm done here."

"Well, what are you doing here, *Etolié?* I thought this was an oligarchy."

She had a point, but Etolié wouldn't admit that. Instead, she glowered and said, "One of us isn't in bed with Nox'Kartha, *Marielle.*"

Etolié didn't even have time to appreciate the appall on Marielle's face—confirming Etolié's suspicion—because Murishani's sycophant voice had to ruin her day. "Um..." Murishani made it a point to make his 'um' as dramatically overstated as possible. "Incorrect. My apologies for correcting you, Magister Etolié, but you are explicitly in bed with our general."

Damn it, he was right. Etolié summoned a breath to speak, uncertain of what those words would even be, when the door behind her opened.

A line of important people exited, keeping their distance to Murishani and herself, and Etolié forced a smile when Casvir himself finally appeared. "We'll discuss this later, Marielle," she said, perfectly pleasant, as sweet as she could muster.

At Casvir's beckoning, she followed him instead.

Downstairs, they went, well below the first floor. Casvir led her through a hallway, across a plush carpet, until they reached an expansive set of double doors.

Within, books lined the walls and shelves, organized chaos at its finest. Under other circumstances, the Nox'Karthan Library would have been a treat to explore, but her anxiety pulsed too cold to consider that. Casvir gestured for her to enter.

Etolié went past shelves, to the center of the room, and what she saw caused her breath to fail.

Silver eyes. As large and vibrant as the moon—even more now, for how they had clouded over. The woman who held them sat at a table, surrounded by books.

It was not the Lara she had once known. A horrendous gash marred her throat, stitched shut, nearly severing her head. Much of her flesh had been eaten away, her face revealing bone, though enough of her remained for her to stand and touch the books around her. Her hands were missing nails, her mouth missing teeth, her exposed skin frozen in the first stages of liquification, hanging loosely around her face. Yet her hair was impeccable, braided down her back, recently done.

Lara's shock manifested in a slight cry, one that masked a sob. Her decrepit hands covered her face as she gasped, and when she stood, she toppled over the chair.

Etolié ran to her, uncaring of her putrid form. Lara collapsed, sobbing into her arms, clinging to Etolié's clothing and body. Her smell bore the sanguine sweetness of death, yet with it lingered the barest hints of magic Etolié recognized.

This *was* the Lara she had once known.

"Lara, I'm sorry." Etolié's eyes shut, thick droplets of tears streaming down her face. "I didn't know. I'm sorry."

Lara shook her head. "You couldn't have known," Lara said, though her voice echoed unnaturally, some spell cast to allow her to speak, but when she looked up, Etolié saw only the baby girl she had loved and helped to raise, the woman whose life was cut short by a crime too evil to speak aloud.

Trembling, Etolié held Lara's face to her chest, protective as she turned back to Casvir. "You can't keep her."

"Can I not?" he replied, a challenge in his tone.

"She's the empress of a foreign country—"

"Who in death belongs to me, according to the laws of my land. If her kingdom wishes to dispute this, let them come."

Etolié hated his words, hated the truth he spoke. Lara's kingdom was helpless to act, assuming they even would. "So, you'll march? Do you think Solvira will simply bend?"

"I plan to expose the empress as an imposter first."

"And then destabilize the country, leaving it vulnerable to your . . . *justice?*" She spat that final fucking word, furious at him, at the bitch on the throne and the flowery traitor who had brought this all together. She remembered the horror of the Theocracy, decimated in a night. "This is what you wanted all along."

"Placing a false empress upon the throne was not my plan," Casvir replied, his countenance utterly unreadable. "But this is what I have wanted."

Etolié shook her head. "If you march in, it's another genocide. Solviran citizens are proud. They won't bend to your influence just because you have the biggest dick. You'll rule a graveyard."

"That is their decision."

Etolié's hands brushed across Lara's pristine braid, the reminder of her presence both grounding and a curse.

"Guards, arrest this woman."

Before Etolié could comprehend those ominous words, armored, skeletal guards appeared and grabbed her shoulders. When she resisted, a sharp sting radiating across her arms as they yanked, forcing her to release Lara. "What the hell are you doing?! This is an act of war."

"I am already going to war," Casvir said, and the guards held Etolié's arms behind her back. "You may leave once my troops have marched; otherwise, your character dictates you will warn Solvira. You know too much."

When Casvir said nothing more, the guards shoved her forward.

"Wait," said Lara, and the skeletons and Casvir paused. Even in death, Lara held herself like a monarch, grace in every action and word. "Imperator Casvir, surely some bargain can be struck for her freedom."

"She is welcome to propose something," Casvir said, indifferent to the weighted mood. "In the meantime—"

"Casvir," Etolié said, because titles were for people she respected. With a pained gulp, she swallowed her pride, praying silently for forgiveness for all who would hate her now. "What if I help you."

Casvir crossed his arms—an impressive feat, considering their bulk and the armor he wore. Intrigue furrowed his brow. "How?"

"I'm highly respected in Solvira. I'm the daughter of their mother goddess. If I walk in and proclaim the bitch on the throne an imposter, they'll listen."

His expression remained the same. "What do you want in return?"

"Your promise that it will be a peaceful transfer of power—or as peaceful as it can be." Etolié looked to Lara, wishing her a silent apology for this betrayal. But she was there to see the Theocracy's destruction; she knew the stakes.

And Solvira had already fallen.

Her chest clenched when Casvir shook his head. "While your word would be valuable, I have resources enough to expose Ayla Darkleaf as an imposter without your aid. The ensuing political storm will take years to settle—peace is an impossible dream."

"Then . . . what if I stayed?" Her words lingered, surprising and horrid even to her. "As I said, I hold considerable influence. If I remain to act as a diplomat, bloodshed could be avoided."

She swore his red eyes flashed, pleased at the prospect his next proposal. "Twenty years."

Etolié tensed. "I beg your pardon?"

"Sign away your services to Nox'Kartha. Your mind and talents would be of great value to my kingdom. You would be well-cared-for during your stay. You could even spend time with Alauriel."

Etolié's throat choked. Twenty years. Hardly a blip in her lifespan, but an eternity to Staelash. How would her small country fare without her?

Yet the cost of failure was hundreds of thousands of lives, either to an empress gone mad or to an imperator capable of genocide. "I . . . I accept."

"I will write us a contract. Guards, release her." The guards obeyed. Casvir left, and Etolié ran back to her beloved moonbeam.

Lara said, "What has happened to my kingdom?"

Too sick to speak, Etolié simply shook her head. "We'll talk. I promise, we'll talk. But let me hug you first." She kissed Lara's hair, held the girl she adored in her arms.

Lara cried, though her dead eyes shed no tears.

"I'm sorry," Etolié said. "I'm betraying your kingdom. B-But the Theocracy—"

"You are not the one who betrayed my kingdom, Etolié."

They wept for a time, the injustice of it unbearably cruel. Only when their cries had stilled did Etolié say, "Tell me what happened."

The empress told her story.

Etolié mulled over a thousand different things as she detoured to Staelash, orb in hand. The world was heavy. She'd never felt so lost.

Gods, she hated leaving Lara alone.

But though her world had shattered, the greater plot remained—that a mad God sought the greatest sources of power in the realms, and she had one exposed in the open.

She'd be damned before she left it with Casvir either. Besides, she had a box in her library.

But the moment she landed before the gates of the manor of Staelash, she was swept with the ineffable knowledge of something being terribly wrong. The morning was quiet, in ways mornings in Staelash never were, the crisp snow falling in gentle sheets, a tension in the air the clenched Etolié's stomach.

There was no one by the manor's gates. They hung open, slack.

She clutched the orb to her chest and ran forward. Kneeling before a pillar supporting the entryway, sticking to the dark shadow, was Zoldar—his crystalline eyes looking like they'd seen a bit more shit than normal.

Before him was Sora, laying awkward against the same pillar—with her boots and trousers coated in ice, frozen to the ground as Zoldar tried to chip them free. Scattered throughout the snowy landscape were guards—whose feet appeared to have met the same fate.

Sora waved her down. "Etolié," she said, though it was more of a groan, "he's here. The God of Order. We . . . We couldn't do anything. He used his orb to stop anyone who tried to pursue him—"

The door swung open, and out came Soliel holding a maldectine encrusted box.

The manor had been built with Khastra in mind, as well as half-giants, so the oversized deity fit easily in the doorframe, silhouetted by his own radiant light. They held stark eye contact a moment, then he looked to the orb in her hand. "Convenient."

"You . . ." Rage spiked in Etolié's blood—this man, this *bastard*—had murdered Lara. *"You . . !"*

"Give me that peacefully," Soliel said, indicating the orb in her hands, "or I will burn you little country to the ground."

Three vibrant orbs orbited Soliel behind his back, each capable of their own unique, virulent destruction. The fourth lay hidden in the box he held. Etolié clutched the earth orb, which would assuredly bypass all subtlety and cause an earthquake capable of doing the job of destroying Staelash itself.

The bastard had the upper hand. But he'd also killed Lara.

Zoldar suddenly placed himself between them, reminding her who would perish if she stayed to fight. He clicked something frantic, and Etolié knew it meant *run.*

Etolié chose to fly instead.

Her wings burst into view as she shot into the sky. Zoldar toppled as Soliel shoved him aside—and grabbed her ankle and slammed her into the ground.

The shock stilled her more than pain. As the Old God's shadow covered her, she curled around the orb, clutching it to her chest like a baby. Her wings wrapped around herself like a cocoon, but when rough hands grabbed her hair, Etolié panicked.

Stupid times called for stupid decisions. Etolié screamed and warped out of the realm—

Mereen had taken the orb to Sha'Demoni, hadn't she? Sure, the world had reacted accordingly, but she theoretically had a few minutes before the realm began imploding in on itself without the stability of earth.

Right?

That thought fueled her as she screamed, tearing herself through the veil between worlds, all the way back to the one place she could feasibly go.

She puked onto a patch of wildflowers, dust rising around her. The orb shrieked in her head, pressure building, reacting like a fish out of water. *"Momma!"* she screamed, and thankfully a gentle, glowing light soon covered her.

"Etolié, what's happened—"

When Etolié looked up, shock showed on Staella's beautiful face. The orb seemed to absorb her light, while Momma's golden hue reflected in shades of green and purple. "Oh, that's very bad," the Goddess of Stars continued.

"Soliel took the white orb. He stole it while I was gone. He must've sensed it when Mereen brought it back—"

"The nice vampire girl whose curse you stole?"

"Yes, but I only have a few minutes until the realm starts eating itself—"

Momma touched her, and once again the world tilted. She was pulled through space, her stomach churning—

Only for her to retch once more, her stomach emptying entirely with her second upchuck of mostly booze. Tears stung her eyes, and the taste was nearly as bad as the smell.

The orb had calmed. Yet . . . Momma still stood beside her.

Etolié looked up, trying to make sense of wherever Staella had taken them. Brilliant stars cast their light from above, and a lush meadow surrounded them, dotted with moonlilies. A mountain range kept them enclosed from the world, creating a quiet haven. "Where are we?"

"The Valley of Neoma," Staella whispered, and when she offered a hand, Etolié accepted, though she held on for support a few moments more. The orb lay in the grass, its power bringing a blistering headache. "The veil is thin here. It's one of the rare places the Gods of Celestière can manifest in your world."

"So, we're . . ." Etolié gazed across the peaceful scene, noting the creek and distant cottage. After the wedding, Flowers would have come here with . . .

Her countenance darkened, and though her adrenaline still pulsed, any reminder brought pure rage.

"Explain again what happened," Staella said, and Etolié told her—everything, from her discovery in the cottage, to Nox'Kartha and the false empress, and finally to Soliel.

Who now had four orbs.

"Momma, I can't believe it," she said, words wavering from her falling tears. "Lara's dead. Flowers . . . she . . . and now I've sold my soul, and I . . . I didn't know what else to do."

Staella embraced her then, holding her close as she whispered, "You did what you had to."

"Momma, Solvira's finished. The Solviraes are dead. You have no lineage anymore."

"Lara's death is a tragedy," Staella continued, her voice as soft as the precious breeze, "but she isn't the last of my blood. I have you, remember? And I have Ilune."

"I'm not exactly planning on continuing the line, if it's all the same to you."

Staella simply smiled, her touch against Etolié's hair tender enough to not trigger her instinctive bristling at any physical contact. "That doesn't matter to me. You matter, and that's enough."

Despite the kind words, Etolié shrugged them away, this moment of peace undeserved after what she'd done.

"And you say she has the Silver Fire? This imposter?" Staella asked, and something in her countenance bespoke concern.

"That's what it looks like. The blood ritual to restore her . . . Something happened there."

Staella's silence brewed plenty of worry into Etolié's stomach. "I may have made a terrible mistake," her momma muttered.

"What do you mean?"

"Later, my Starshine. First, we must find a home for this orb."

But Etolié's panic only rose, to speak of what she'd done. "Can you help?" she whispered, breathless and afraid. "In Solvira?"

"It is not my place. War is not my domain. Nor can I betray my people."

"Even if they've already been betrayed?"

The words lingered in the ensuing silence.

Staella became contemplative, something somber overtaking her countenance as she gazed upon the distant mountains. Etolié wondered what this place meant to her— *Valley of Neoma.* Everyone said her momma and the moon goddess had first made love here, which was a strange thing to know about her own mother, but whether that was literal or not, Momma had once lived here. Momma had likely fallen in love here.

Her momma had lived so many lives. This one, with Etolié, was only the latest.

"Etolié, I regret a great many things," Staella said softly, her gaze a thousand years away, "but allowing my people their free-agency is not one of them. Were I to come down and proclaim the false Empress Alauriel an imposter, it would not lead to peace. It would lead to confusion and anarchy, but it would not lead to them accepting Imperator Casvir. At least with a leader, there is someone to wave the white flag—or incite the war, I know. Solvira can only be led by those who hold the blood of Ilune—the worthiest successor is the one who holds the most of it. That is what the law has said since its founding. What the imposter holds is stolen blood, but it is blood nevertheless."

Guilt filled Etolié, a morass within her soul. "Have I done the wrong thing?"

"No, Starshine," Staella replied, her gaze focusing on Etolié alone now, holding only kindness. "There is no greater agent for peace for my people than you. Sol Kareena has been silent since the fall of her people, and I am but a shadow. But you are real, and you are beloved among them. You have picked what alignment you saw as the surest path for peace, and I would be a hypocrite of a goddess to allow my people free will but not you."

Etolié steadied her breath, secluded in this beautiful place. Perhaps she'd simply stay and forget it all. "I hate this."

"There was no right answer, Etolié—except the one that saved my people from decimation in the dead of night, as would have been their fate had you not acted."

Etolié longed for the safety of Celestière, to run away from the war and blood and memories of betrayal. But her world was not meant for peace this day, if the whole world were to see it later. "I'll do whatever I can."

"I will love you no matter how this ends, my Etolié." Staella placed a kiss on her brow before pulling away, the warmth radiating—and perhaps bearing more power than a mere physical gesture. "But regarding the orb—from what little I know, Soliel cannot cross the sea on a whim, so this gives us time."

Etolié picked the damned artifact back up, preparing a reply when a sudden influx of awareness struck her.

An orb was . . . nearer. Much closer than before.

"Kitty," she muttered, then looked to Staella. "There's a dragon. She has the last orb. Do you think I could bring this one to her too?"

"The worst she could say is no. At the very least, she might know where you could hide it. It will take me a moment to try and find her, though."

Etolié placed the orb into her momma's hands. "Use this."

Staella stared curiously, and a sudden radiation of power bombarded Etolié's senses, her headache spiking in response to the surge of energy. Her momma was a god, and she held an artifact of so-called depthless power. "Oh yes. I feel her."

If only she and the other gods could leave this place. The fight with Soliel might've ended. But with mortals hosting them, their power shrank considerably—Etolié knew this. Soliel's fight with her and Eionei hadn't gone particularly well.

Staella offered the orb back, and while the orb's power remained potent, Etolié's headache shrunk considerably. "Send me a prayer when you're done," her goddess momma said, taking Etolié's hand. "Are you ready?"

Etolié nodded.

The world faded anew.

Thankfully, Etolié had already ejected all the contents of her stomach. It would have been embarrassing to puke in front of an ancient dragon.

Still, Etolié collapsed onto her hands and knees, desperate to keep herself together despite teleporting three times within ten minutes and feeling like death.

The energy here was strange.

Though unsteady, Etolié managed to stand, bringing the orb protectively to her chest as she inspected this strange place. Mist rose all around, though not enough to prevent her from seeing the barren landscape. Dead trees hung as a warning, any shrubbery long dead, and she heard nothing at all—no animals or insects.

The sky was as grey as the atmosphere. But what truly struck her as strange was the ineffable sense of anticipation. Like an aroma, it filled her, her body a sponge to this odd sensation. The very air hummed with brewing energy.

Etolié's steps scuffled across the silent atmosphere. The orb had not stilled, yet it seemed docile, yielding to this grander presence around it. Though her headache had not vanished, it became muted.

In the distance, something upset the peaceful scene. Etolié turned, expecting conflict, and instead saw an unmistakable character.

Kitty rose from what Etolié presumed was sleep—assuming skeleton dragons slept—and approached, her claws churning dust into the air. As she neared, there was no orb in her claw, but instead embedded into a frontward facing section of her spine, like a decorative jewel. There was no aggression in her stance, and so Etolié felt no fear. Instead, a wash of something new overcame her—curiosity.

The dragon's words floated through her head. *"Daughter of Stars?"*

"Hi, Kitty. Quite the home you've found. It's quiet. Peaceful."

"This is my Mother's grave. Her spirit waits here, somewhere. I have not found her, but I feel her."

Etolié's mind buzzed at that, the prickling sensation against her skin never quiet settling. "Forgive me if I'm overstepping, but I think I feel her too."

"Assuredly. Her power grows each day, little by little."

The words were ominous, yet the dragon said them with such purity, like a child waiting for her mother to come home. Which . . . wasn't inaccurate at all, Etolié realized, and it was a feeling she knew too well. "So, the Goddess of Chaos will be coming soon?"

"Soon, yes. But only in the reflection of eternity. I cannot say precisely when, but I think it shall be a year or two more."

The sensation of something brewing, something slowly assembling struck her anew. Chaos would come. What it meant for the world had yet to be determined. "You'll note, I have an orb," she said instead, and she offered the earth orb forward. "I didn't know where else to take it."

"You wish for me to protect it?"

"If you can. Is that allowed?"

Kitty held out her claw, and Etolié carefully set the orb into the center of the boney appendage.

"Soliel—your, um, father—has the white orb. He has four. These are the only two left."

"I will care for it. You needn't fear."

Fear simply didn't work that way—banished by a simple refrain—but Etolié supposed the dragon would know best. "That's really all I came for."

Yet she lingered, for this place was . . . something. Something different. Etolié breathed, the sensation burning her lungs as she let the presence fill her, her curious self wishing the world would stop an hour or two and let her study this strange, ancient magic. Her mind still burned from all Kitty had said before, and Etolié was a scholar at heart.

"What did you mean," Etolié whispered, "when you said I would know what to do? That I knew what to do in the time before. It's been haunting me."

Kitty laid down, placing her head on her claws. Nearly level with Etolié, something kind washed over her, for this dragon projected every feeling inside her. *"Do not fret, Daughter of Stars. If your heart is as good as my Mother proclaimed, you will do what is right, no matter what the outcome."*

Etolié wasn't sure if her heart was pure, but the implication that the Goddess of Chaos had ever spoken of her made her feel . . . weird. "Not to be an asshole, but can you say something that isn't cryptic?"

She swore the dragon frowned, but Etolié felt no anger. *"Perhaps this is also cryptic, but I would know your thoughts on something. I fear this is all a cycle."*

"A cycle?"

"I fear that this has happened before. And it shall happen again, and again unless something breaks it."

Etolié stood in silence, wondering at that. "You mean, Soliel always came and did this?"

"Yes. I wonder if he always killed my brother. I wonder if he always had this quest but was doomed for defeat only for he and my Mother to grow up in the aftermath and eventually be sent to the time before the Convergence to become Gods. I wonder if all we have ever done is foreordained, and if it is useless to try and stop."

"It would make sense, in a time travel sort of way," Etolié said. "You're proposing that in order to stop this for good, something has to change."

"Yes. But not just anything. There must be a key. Something that was missing before. Something that must change for the future to have a chance to flourish and the world not fall into darkness—over and over. That is what I have contemplated, since you told me of my Father's deeds."

"What kind of key?"

"I do not know. I do not know enough of your world. I do not think anyone would know what needs to be changed except, perhaps, my Mother and Father. But even then—they might think they're changing the world, only to repeat the cycle anew."

Anxiety coursed through Etolié's nerves at the dragon's words. "I'll think on this. I don't know how useful I'll be, but if I'm unfortunate enough to run into your Father again, I'll, uh, give him the message."

"I wonder if it might be the only thing to make him reconsider his quest."

Sensing finality, Etolié said, "I don't know if I feel better, but I feel like I have something to work with. Thank you, Kitty." Etolié studied the skeletal dragon, everything about her a marvel of magic. "Though I suppose your real name isn't Kitty."

Quiet laughter flittered through her head. *"No, it is not, though I find it immensely charming. My name is Uluron."*

"Uluron," Etolié whispered, the name holding ancient power.

"You are a marvelous work in progress, Daughter of Stars," Kitty—Uluron—said, and Etolié swore she smiled for how her head tilted, how soft her purple eyes became. *"In your darkest hours, remember that."*

Etolié stepped back and said a silent prayer.

Soon, she was ripped back into the world. The war awaited.

Spring had finally come.

Flowridia's hand touched the silken leaves, each one speckled in sunlight. Gentle buds grew upon the tree's branches, and though frost still came in the early morning, the winter waned, yielding to the changing season, to new life. Her fingers shone in the sun, warmed by the flickering light passing between the leaves high above. So much more precious now, when she had nearly lost it.

In the other hand, she held something cold but oh so dear. Ayla was always near, trailing behind like a duckling to her mother when she was free of her courtly duties.

Balanced between them, the sun and her love, Flowridia felt complete.

Something had changed, something ineffable and wonderful, this feeling of security warming her heart. Ayla was hers in every perfect way, their promise gilded in gold. When she caught her eye, there shone adoration; Ayla must have felt it too, this sense of completeness between them.

"I cannot believe how exhausting it is to open wedding gifts," Ayla said, though with no ire, merely honesty.

"And I can't believe Marielle gave us an entire closet's worth of lingerie."

Ayla chuckled, her touch on Flowridia's waist as precious as diamonds. "I would still happily throw her into a vat of boiling oil, but it is my favorite gift so far."

"I'm partial to Tazel's gift, with all due respect." Flowridia winked, and Ayla rolled her eyes.

"Fine, fine—it was clever. Damned elves and their damned mechanical contraptions."

He had gifted a little wind-up toy, cleverly built to look like a canine, and whether it was inspired by Ana or Demitri, she didn't know or care—it was adorable and precious all the same.

"Goddess Staella's gift must be buried in the pile of presents," Flowridia mused, and Ayla's grip on her hand suddenly tightened. "I'd like to look for it; I'm so curious."

"Oh, I am certain it is hiding somewhere—" Ayla's words stopped abruptly; her form swirled back into that of Empress Alauriel's. Flowridia heard the footsteps then, surprised when a servant rapidly approached. "Good evening."

The young man bowed. "Empress Alauriel, Consort Flowridia—Magister Etolié of Staelash is here. She has requested your presence for a council meeting."

"Right now?" Lara said.

"Yes, your majesty. The rest are already assembled in the throne room. Apparently, there is urgent news."

"Tell them we shall come."

The servant bowed and left. Lara's lips on Flowridia's ear pulled a light gasp from her throat. "After the meeting, we shall see if we can't finish our pile of gifts."

Flowridia savored the touch, wife and wife in perfect bliss beneath the sun's light.

They held hands as they approached the castle. Lara whispered idly about plans to reintroduce the monster within the town square, and Flowridia's smile remained ever-present.

This feeling of love and security, this moment of peace . . . It had not come how she'd imagined, yet it was all she had ever wanted.

Onward to the throne room, and though they were all giggles and smiles, an icy mood immediately washed over Flowridia when they crossed the threshold.

Etolié stood in the center, her wings glowing with all the magnificence of her angelic progenitors. Her dress was pure gold, swaying with each swish of her legs, and at her belt was a sheathed dagger. She wore not a smile but a vicious glare. "Have a seat," she said, no other pleasantries on her tongue.

Discomfort brewed in Flowridia's stomach; her grip on Lara's hand tightened as her wife led her to the massive chair. "Delightful to see you," Lara said. "Why the somber mood?"

Etolié stopped before the throne, her pores faintly glowing with holy light. "I was just telling our friends," she said to the room, severity in her sober gaze, "that I bear ill tidings. Imperator Casvir's forces surround this city. Before the sun sets tomorrow, Neolan will be overrun by the dead."

The hot ire of betrayal pulsed through Flowridia. Not a week ago, she had danced with Casvir at her wedding—and he would dare?

Etolié wouldn't lie.

Around the room, all the guards looked nervous. Reginal tugged on his beard, making no eye contact with anyone, while Jules remained impassive as always, perhaps too much so. Only General Irons held what she considered an appropriate reaction—seething rage.

Yet it was directed at Etolié.

"But why?" Flowridia said, the only one to dare and speak. "Why would Casvir do this?"

Etolié's dominating presence showed no emotion, save for rage. "Casvir leads them, but today, I lead Casvir." Etolié's jaw trembled, her eyes rimmed with red as she glanced across the room, then settled upon Lara. "Empress Alauriel is dead."

The hush remained, and all Flowridia's dreams cracked into a thousand damning pieces, certain to shatter at the next provocation.

The first one to react was Lara.

Her laughter echoed across the high walls as she stood up. "Etolié," she said, her voice more a match to the late empress than it had ever been, "this has been quite the jest, but perhaps you've gone a bit far?"

"They've all seen the proof, but if it's so funny to you, you wouldn't have any opposition to holding this piece of maldectine, would you?" Etolié held out her opposite hand, revealing her brass knuckles, fashioned long ago by the former general.

"Evidence? Oh, please, enlighten me."

But Etolié shook her head. "You'd destroy it. I sent it away."

"You do know that conspiring with a foreign tyrant is treason, yes?" Lara held her hands out wide, but Etolié didn't move. "You are either a jester gone too far or a traitor."

"Hold this, please. If you have nothing to hide, it should be no trouble."

Lara released Flowridia's hand as she slowly approached, descending the stairs of the throne with dripping dramatics. Everything about her, from her dress cut too low to the sway of her hips was nothing like the late empress; Flowridia's gut clenched to watch, knowing Ayla would only deliberately slip. "Say you are not conspiring with Imperator Casvir, then I shall."

"Fine," Etolié said, every line of her face a wicked glare. "I'm not conspiring with Imperator Casvir. Now, hold this."

Lara shook her head, then looked to the council surrounding her. "Arrest this woman. Find out the truth."

The few guards present shared glances, visibly wary as they approached. Reginal broke formation. "Your majesty, I think it would be best if you did what she said," he said nervously, the use of the title more telling than anything else.

"Empress Alauriel Solviraes is dead," Etolié repeated, each word a nail in the coffin of Flowridia's hopeful future. "She was murdered by the God of Order nearly two months ago, in the Abyssal Swamp, then used to revive you—Ayla Darkleaf."

The silence in the room could have driven a soul mad. Nothing in the phrase condemned Flowridia, yet when their eyes met, she saw murder in Etolié's. She didn't dare speak; unfortunately, Lara held no such qualms.

"Guards, arrest this woman. She has given in to delusion."

Reginal approached, standing beside Lara. "Just take the maldectine, please."

"You would dare side with her?"

The magister's face held the highest regret. "I do not know what to believe, but please do what's right."

Etolié offered it forward.

With some trepidation, likely to buy herself time, Lara stepped forward. The faintest silver sheen coated her hand as she reached for the maldectine—

Only for her other hand to shoot up and grip Etolié's when she tried to drive a knife into her body. The Celestial dropped the knuckles, and then Flowridia saw the truth—that months ago, she had gifted a dagger of maldectine to Imperator Casvir, and here she wielded it now. The magic inherent in the blade expanded. Lara's hold released, likely from the shock of seeing her pale hand.

The illusion shattered. The dagger drove into Ayla's Darkleaf's neck.

Gasps ensued across the room, even as Ayla casually withdrew it, and stared upon the clean blade, no blood to spill upon it. The wound sealed shut, and fangs emerged from Ayla's venomous grin. "Clever girl," she cooed—and she impaled the dagger into Etolié's throat.

Blood spurted; Flowridia screamed. Guards rushed, but Etolié collapsed, choking on the light-tinged blood.

It happened quickly—Etolié collapsing as she clutched the dagger impaling her neck; the guards grabbing Ayla's arms, who laughed at the Celestial blood upon the floor. Flowridia ran for Etolié, no regard to anything but the brutalized Celestial. "I'm going to remove it—"

The room burst into flame.

Silver fire erupted from Ayla's form, gushing like a fountain. The guards screamed; some burning, some crying out as Ayla spun from their touch, the flame forming a glittering arc around her. Flowridia covered Etolié's body, but fire expanded to avoid them. "It would be petty to shoot the messenger," Ayla said to the prone Celestial. "Once Flowra has healed you, you shall be allowed to leave. Tell Casvir. Tell him I do not yield."

Flowridia acted, forced to quickly toss the dagger aside lest it suppress her magic.

Ayla kept speaking, vitriol in every word. "How unfortunate that your empress should be so changed. More unfortunate, still, that you would be foolish enough to turn to Nox'Kartha for aid. Whatever my treason, I did not kill Empress Alauriel—I merely wield her power. Yet you have sold this kingdom to the highest bidder, and somehow that seems the more traitorous part." Her visage returned to that of Empress Alauriel, though no kindness shone in her face— merely the predator, a monster sprayed in Celestial blood. "I wield the Silver Fire. The Blood of Ilune permeates my being. I hold the right to the throne."

"Don't you understand!" Etolié cried, all but shoving Flowridia off her—her skin was sealed and pristine. "This is the peaceful option! Casvir will send his forces to flood Neolan if you don't surrender."

"And we give in to Casvir?" Flowridia said, the words filling her with fury—at Casvir's betrayal, yes, but also at Etolié's sudden loss of conviction.

How dare she.

Etolié rose into the air, wings spread wide. "Better to hand this kingdom to Casvir than to the monster you took as your wife!"

She cried it all before the council, before the guards, and before Ayla herself, who glared at Etolié like an annoying mosquito buzzing above them.

"You played us all for fools, but I *believed in you!* Flowers, I loved you. But whatever wickedness you've embraced—" Etolié's voice caught, and Flowridia, from the ground, watched her wrestle with her tears, forcing back the emotion choking her throat. "... you didn't kill Lara. You desecrated her body, you allowed this *monster* to serve as her imposter, had the audacity to feign a happy ending, but you didn't kill her. Had you had your way, she would have lived. You're just a sucker for opportunity."

How Etolié had been convinced of the truth by Casvir, Flowridia could not guess, but to deny her crime now would be an insult to their friendship, past or not.

"Come with me," the Celestial pled, and Flowridia's hands clenched into fists. "Redeem yourself. Imperator Casvir does not want you in the line of fire, so come with me."

Flowridia kept her stare to the glowing Celestial she had once called friend, her fury rising at her audacity. "Etolié, whatever I've done, I've made my bed. I will lie in it with my wife."

"Flowers, don't be stupid—"

"This is my choice," Flowridia dared to summon her power, let that void fill her soul as swirling mists of purple smoke seeped from the pores of her skin. Should Etolié choose to strike her down, Flowridia refused to let her win so easily. And should Etolié try to touch her, steal her despite her protests, she would be burned for it.

Instead, the Celestial burst through the skylight high above and escaped.

Amidst the rain of shattered glass, Ayla turned her attention to the silent audience. Fire rose to blockade the exit. "I shall make short work of them," Ayla said, and Flowridia shut her eyes, steeling herself against the ensuing screams. When a splatter of warmth stuck her neck and face, she flinched, yet grit her teeth.

The cost had been inevitable, as had the end of their reign.

"Flowra, a thought for you."

When Flowridia opened her eyes, the throne room had transformed—once a place of magnificence, now a sea of blood. Guards lay strewn across the ground, gore spilling from their throats and severed heads. Ayla stood triumphant among them, blood coating her pale skin, starkly vibrant against her monochrome. Like walking into the cathedral beneath Nox'Kartha's palace, this place, once a thing of beauty, was now sacrilege.

There remained three survivors—Reginal, Jules, and Irons, the latter of which remained in his chair, arms crossed, jaw stiff. Jules sat passively on her seat, her pleasant smile a betrayal to what truly went on in her head now.

But Reginal was on his knees, facing his false empress. "I need not kill him," Ayla cooed, silver flame rising in her hand, "should you ask it. Perhaps he could share Jules' fate."

Flowridia's heart held too many walls to say she loved Reginal, and so to see the fear in his eyes brought no guilt. "I think—"

She was stopped from agreeing, for there was another face whose fear she hadn't seen and couldn't bear to imagine. Sweet little Ceile, who had asked if she were a princess, waited at home, doted upon by a father who had chosen her, who loved her.

Ayla held a knife to her other father's throat, metaphorical or not. "Ayla, let him go."

Startled, Ayla lowered her hand, the fire extinguishing. "What?"

"Let him go. He can't stop Nox'Kartha's onslaught, so he can't change what we have to do. Let him go home."

"This man holds influence. If he speaks out against us, it could bear consequences."

Flowridia looked to Reginal, finding no gratification from the fear in his eyes. "Leave Neolan," she said, resolve in her voice. "You have magic enough for that. Take your husband and your daughter and go."

Reginal said nothing as he stood, his gaze shifting warily between she and Ayla, whose glower remained on herself. "For Erlyn and Ceile," he said, defeat in his stance and voice.

He walked freely out.

Ayla turned on her heels, Irons her new target.

"I won't descend so low as to call you 'empress,'" came Irons biting tone, "but I will ask you to hear out a proposal."

Ayla stopped before his seated form, hip cocked in a luxurious pose. "Are you about to impress me, General?"

"I'm going to help you. You need me."

At those words, Flowridia came to join them, lifting her skirts to avoid staining them in blood—more blood, rather, given what had splattered across her side.

"Tell me more," Ayla said, intrigue slowing her words.

"The soldiers will listen to me and only me," Irons said, subtle rage in his demeanor, "and you don't know the defenses this kingdom has. But General Khastra of Nox'Kartha does. And correct me if I'm wrong, but you don't know how to lead an army, much less maintain a defense against a siege."

"Continue," Ayla said, her smile wicked and pleased.

Irons stood but kept his arms crossed and away from the sword at his hilt. "Lady Etolié's powers are vast, and her loyalties are compromised. Imperator Casvir has a knife to her metaphorical heart, and if my years of knowing her have taught me anything, it is that she would fall on her own sword to protect Khastra. Were you aware they were romantically entangled?"

Flowridia shook her head, appalled when Ayla nodded.

"Whatever her motives," Irons continued, "the facts are this—Etolié has brought Imperator Casvir to our doorstep and asks us to let him in. When this war is over, I won't hesitate to run my weapon through you, but more than I believe in the Solviraes' right to rule, I believe in Solvira. I believe in my country. And the day Nox'Kartha fills the streets with death is the day they crawl over my dead body to get there."

He offered a hand. Ayla chuckled as she accepted. "I believe you, General Irons. Believe *me* when I say I feel the same. When the war is over, I shall happily accept honest combat between the two of us."

"I'll keep your secret for now," he said, and then his gaze settled onto Flowridia. "Funny. I was right about you."

She said absolutely nothing, waiting for whatever cruelty would punctuate his words.

"But you have done right by Sol Kareena and the refugees from her kingdom," he continued, much to her alarm. "You did right by Reginal, despite the risk. I do not trust you. I think you are an evil woman, but I also believe that even the most wicked among us are capable of good." He steeled his jaw. "Just as those of us who consider ourselves good can align with evil, for the greater good."

"I will not betray you, General," Flowridia said, and though apprehension threatened to choke her, though her shame rose, burning down to her bones, above all soared a single, vibrant emotion—

Rage.

For Casvir. For Etolié. For all she would now lose.

So be it.

Etolié coughed, the spittle flecked with blood. Phantom pain still prickled at her throat, the memory of the knife and the sound of her own spraying blood making her head swim.

Painful heaving sent more fluid to the ground. Etolié trembled, acutely aware of the imperator in her midst, and the hands of the fallen empress supporting her as she bent over. Even rotted and cold, Lara's touch was a comfort.

Once she had expelled what she could from her lungs, Lara led her to the ground, the grass warmed by the setting sun and evening air. She pulled a drink from her extra-dimensional space and chugged deep, the liquid burning her raw throat.

A deep baritone asked, "Flowridia will not come?"

Etolié shook her head, affirming the frantic words she'd been able to spit out before falling into a coughing fit.

"I see," Casvir replied. "I have one more tactic at my disposal. Perhaps your words were not the ones she needed."

What surrounded them churned Etolié's stomach. Swarms of dead, those raised only from walking past the small towns bordering the Solviraes kingdom, stood in ordered disarray, prepared to move at their master's command. She had been reassured that there would be more when the time came—ironic, since more dead folk were generally the opposite of reassuring.

Blocking them from the sun was an impossibly large shadow, cast by a gruesome creature. The dragon, Valeuron, had been a nightmare in the Theocracy, but here he was docile, perfectly still. She remembered the patches sewn into his ruined wings, the obvious signs of burning beneath them, and of course his head was attached only by metal bars. His hand had been reattached. But there was something different in his chest, obvious signs of surgical intervention.

Thank Eionei's Asshole there was no spirit in that undead body.

She finally removed the flask from her lips and wiped her mouth, ghostly pain still searing her throat. "I'm glad I warped you out of there, Moonbeam. Who knows what Ayla Darkleaf would have done."

"She killed everyone, though?"

"As far as I saw, yes."

"A-And Flowridia—" Lara's voice caught, and Etolié waited, unsure of where the empress stood on that particular subject. "Never mind."

"Moonbeam—"

But Lara shook her head, stopping Etolié's words. "It does not matter."

Sickness struck Etolié's stomach. She nearly vomited anew when a hole tore between the dimensions, causing Etolié's headache to spike from zero to over the moon. But she managed to keep her stomach together, even in her weakened state, as what appeared to be an enormous carriage rolled through, though nearly a small house in sheer size. It radiated magic, the great wheels made of iron, capable of carrying more than a few half-giants.

Etolié asked, "You don't have the capacity for that degree of inter-dimensional travel, no offense. So, how do you do it?"

"I do not owe you my secrets, Magister," Casvir said, and the skeletal steed he claimed approached. "Perhaps when you have devoted a few years to my cause, you will figure it out."

Etolié bit her tongue, lest she tell him to shove a cactus up his ass, or his own self-righteous dick. But rather than tell her new employer to go fuck himself so early on, she jumped when the carriage suddenly shook. Something banged around violently within.

With the portal still open, Casvir said, "Alauriel, come with me. You shall be returned to Nox'Kartha." Then, he looked at Etolié. "Do not open that. I cannot account for your safety if you do."

"All good. My plan is to go sow discord among the people. Tell them the truth about Empress Imposter."

Lara clung to Etolié's hand as she stood, then squeezed it with a tragic smile before approaching the portal. When she disappeared, Casvir followed.

The portal vanished.

Etolié spread her wings, prepared to return to the Solviran walls and yell like a maniac in the streets. But, again, the carriage shook, as though struck by its own small earthquake. Etolié stopped, wary as she watched. With the warning in mind, she tentatively approached, noting that there appeared to be no windows—except a small viewing latch build into a presumably locked, iron door.

Casvir had said not to touch, so curiosity said she must.

With trepidation, she reached for the latch—

"I wouldn't do that if I were you."

Etolié jumped back, heart skipping when she saw Murishani smiling pleasantly not two feet away. "Where the fuck did you come from?"

"Assume I'm always here and watching," he said sweetly, which was potentially the worst sentence ever uttered in all of history. "But, uh, don't touch that. Or do, but . . ." He shrugged. "Well, it is your choice."

"You clearly want me to open it."

The carriage rattled, yet the sound was oddly muted. Etolié frowned, realizing it must have been some sort of silencing spell—simple enough.

"I do, but Casvir does not, which means it has to be *your* idea and not mine. But you see—I think you should." His smile remained, but his nervous laugh spoke volumes. "Truly. Much better you find out now than on the battlefield."

With that, Etolié knew. Or at least, thought she knew. Heart racing, she opened the latch, though it was barely a slit, the faint light revealing the barest hints of glowing tattoos and chains. "Khastra?"

Silence. Etolié slipped her fingers through the tiny opening and wiggled them to draw her attention. "Hey, Beefcake—"

The full weight of the transformed Bringer of War struck the door, her roar unquestionable, incomparable. Though startled, Etolié pulled open the locked door—her strange magic simply a habit now—and her wings cast light onto the monster before her.

The Bringer of War wore chains and nothing more, revealing the ghastly, raw red on her chest—not a mechanical, exposed heart, but smaller, metallic pegs, as well as a splitting, brutal gash between her chest, bound shut with metal prongs. Etolié didn't know what it meant, but when their gazes met, she saw no humanity in that monstrous visage, her glowing eyes spelling hunger and nothing more. "Khastra—"

Khastra roared and fought to reach her, but when Etolié stepped in and offered a hand, an enormous claw tore open her arm. Etolié screamed, the welling blood pungent and drawing immediate intrigue from the Bringer of War. Etolié sensed no mischief, no jest—no recognition at all.

When the monster tried to grab her, she darted back, out of the cage, and Murishani slammed the door. "Oh, that looks like it stings," he said unhelpfully, but Etolié couldn't summon the words to mock him.

Yes, it stung, but in twenty-four years of friendship, Khastra had never hurt her once. Tears welled in Etolié's eyes, for the betrayal hurt far worse. She summoned the illusion of bandages and slowly wrapped the wounds.

Murishani spoke as she worked. "She has been like this since her surgery, a week ago. We fear attaching probes to the correct heart has made it *too* powerful. She has yet to calm from the bloodlust. All attempts to sedate her and remove it and insert another mechanical one have been met with failure—and death for a few unfortunate guards and doctors. Casvir still wishes to try and use her as a directed weapon against Solvira, but he has accepted that she may be too dangerous to keep long-term."

Etolié's lip trembled as she stared at the door. Hating his words, but not nearly so much as she hated Casvir, Etolié opened the slit anew, resolve in the gesture. The Bringer of War's glowing eyes were all she saw; they met her own—

Again, a fist slammed on the door, and Etolié stumbled back, accepting that she was about to do something extremely stupid. *Goddess Momma,* she silently pled, *help.*

Staella could lay wards of peace; she could calm virulent storms and take on burdens Etolié couldn't fathom trying to bear.

But Etolié had tamed the monster once before, hadn't she? In the catacombs, pleading for her life and those of her wards—she had sung.

Momma sang, and it brought peace.

You already know what to do, said gentle words inside her head, and Etolié understood. *I will protect you.*

Trembling, she returned to the door, ignoring Murishani, who watched with notable intrigue. "Beefcake?" she said, and the first of her tears finally fell.

She hummed. No particular tune. She simply sang from her heart, hand quivering as it gripped the latch to open the door anew.

The Bringer of War bared her teeth but did not strike, stance prepared to fight. Etolié swore she was larger, taller, the taut skin looking ready to tear in places—and already had, in a few, rips on her arms and thighs following the curves of her hulking musculature. Etolié shut the door behind her, the only source of light her wings and the glowing tattoos, and kept her wordless, lilting song. The monster roared, but when she rose a hand to strike her, Etolié beckoned it down, relieved when she obeyed, and held it to her body, for it was half her size, soothing gentle lines across it with her fingers. The touch was warm, much too warm. When Khastra's thumb came near her mouth, she kissed it, then let the Bringer of War lift her, fearless as she was brought to her face.

Amidst the clinking of chains and monstrous rumbling, Etolié's song eased the tense atmosphere. Between Khastra's breasts, the skin revealed raw scars, surely painful. When she was held to the Bringer of War's face, she fearlessly touched her cheeks, her enormous fangs, caressed the skin around those glowing eyes. Etolié's voice stopped only in the moments of gentle kisses, anything to calm her beloved's soul.

Khastra was not a monster. Etolié would not let her die as one.

Soon, her voice faded away, replaced by soothing words. "I know you can say my name, Khastra. Will you? *Etolié.*"

She was met by a blank, grotesque stare. Khastra's eyes wandered down her body, lingering at her breasts, and a shiver shot down her spine—of primal fear. "Look at me," she said, and the Bringer of War obeyed—she understood, thank every god. "Etolié. Can you say it? *Eh-toh-lee-ay.*"

Behind the monster's bared fangs came a growl.

"*Eh-toh-lay,* then! I love that you can't say my name. It was one of the first cute things about you."

When the monster's face came too close for comfort, Etolié failed to resume humming, unable to quite force a tune through her sudden, ramping fear. "Khastra, please," she pled, and with one free wing, she floated it before the Bringer of War's face, nearly sobbing when those glowing eyes followed, like a moth to flame. "Pretty light. Follow the pretty light."

Khastra did, even taking one of her hands from around Etolié to follow it, like a child reaching for a firefly. Etolié braced herself for contact when the Bringer of War grabbed the soft tendrils—the feeling immensely uncomfortable, violating.

Fresh tears filled her eyes. Forcing a breath, she sang anew, this time, a true song:

> *I love you when the sun is gone*
> *I love you when it rises*
> *I love you when the ocean storms*
> *I love you when it's quiet.*

A simple song. A children's ditty. Eionei had sung it to her as a baby; sometimes Momma had too. She had hummed it to Lara a time or two, and now, Khastra's gaze left her crumpled wing, mesmerized anew.

Etolié dared to grab her face, directing it to stare at hers. She sang, and with it came a silent prayer: *Goddess Momma, help.*

Keep singing, said the unquestionable swelling within her.

And Etolié did, running through every song she knew—a damn near endless assortment, but she sang through them twice. Silly ones, religious ones, offensive ones about Morathma, Ku'Shya—anything was fair. But she sang them sweetly, directing all the focus she had toward the woman she loved.

As time went on and Etolié's voice rang, the Bringer of War sat, then later laid down, still holding her, but less like a conquest and more like a doll. Etolié touched her as much as she dared, traced the tattoos she could reach. Between songs, she kissed her hands, then quickly resumed, knowing the magic happened only in singing.

Time passed, and she grew tired. The Bringer of War was docile when Etolié's eyelids drooped . . .

Then blinked open rapidly.

Etolié sat up, breathing heavy, panic filling her to realize she had sung herself to sleep.

Then she saw the much smaller figure nearby, fast asleep.

Relief flooded her, cold and painful. She crawled toward Khastra, her true self, and pulled her limbs out of the far-too-large chains and placed that horned head into her lap. She was naked, dirt and dried blood staining her skin, and upon the ground were those ghastly staples holding her chest together—instead Khastra's flesh remained raw and red. She stirred when Etolié jostled her, her glowing eyes blinking fitfully.

"Shh . . ." Etolié soothed, her fingers tracing lines down her face, lingering at her neck, feeling for a pulse.

It was quite fast, disconcertingly so.

"Etolié?"

The name brought tears. "Yes, it's me. Just focus on deep breaths, all right?"

With her head still in Etolié's lap, Khastra's arms reached up to hold her at her hips. Her body curled in fetal position, vulnerable in her naked, dirtied form.

Something inside Etolié shattered. Fury rose to replace it, but she forced it down, choking as she swallowed.

Casvir would pay someday. But today, Khastra needed her.

Upon Khastra's arms and thighs remained that awful tearing, and her chest was a nightmare. Etolié lowered all defenses as she held her, focusing instead on Khastra and her pain.

The initial flood walloped her like an ocean wave, and Etolié forced it back, shutting her eyes and gripping her love tight. "Not everything," she whispered, though only to herself.

She couldn't risk any repair to her heart, lest the torture begin anew.

Instead, her fingers skimmed lightly along the gashes on Khastra's biceps, her own flesh tearing as the skin beneath her hands sealed. Etolié bit her lip as the pain lacerated her tender flesh, forcing her voice to still, ignoring Khastra's silent plea to stop as she gazed up at her. When Khastra's thighs sealed, Etolié's tears fell rapidly down her cheeks, her teeth drawing blood as they bit her lip to stay quiet. She focused bitterly upon the skin and muscles on her chest, willing it all away from her heart—even as a knife cut across her own. Bone cracked. A small cry escaped her, lip bleeding to hold it back.

When the final gash on Khastra's chest healed, Etolié focused on the pain, knowing it had to hurt in order to fade. *Goddess Momma . . . help.*

It took time, and she swore the pain increased, excruciating as it ripped across her arms. She wept, cursing her tears, knowing Khastra counted each one.

But in time, a faint pulse of magic touched her, and Etolié knew it wasn't her own. She wiped her eyes as her wounds disappeared.

"Etolié, you should not have," Khastra said, and it bore the stain of guilt, her eyes watery and wide.

"You need to breathe easy. If this helps, it's the right thing." Etolié touched the half-demon's familiar tattoos, soothing tender lines across them. They illuminated, revealing the potent magic. "You just breathe, all right? Just breathe."

Etolié sang as she traced the lines, praying it was enough to comfort the most important woman in the world.

"I worry I am foolish to trust General Irons," Ayla said, mulling over her handwritten notes.

Flowridia paced as Demitri idly watched. They prepared in their bedroom, secluded and safe, while the outside world buzzed with anticipation, holding its breath before the war. "I trust him," Flowridia admitted, "but more than that, I trust that he loves Solvira and truly doesn't want it to fall under Nox'Kartha's rule."

"That is a feeling I can relate to," Ayla said, returning to her study. "Well, I shall be speaking to him at length about Nox'Kartha's military after my speech. Casvir will not show his full might in his first onslaught, and so neither should we. In the meantime, my speech shall be grand. Just a few minutes more and the masses shall be assembled. They will pledge to me as their goddess, I join the fight on the morrow, and we crush them. Casvir is a fool. He placed far too much trust in Etolié; he cannot win this war."

Anxiety clenched at Flowridia's chest, her heart thumping rapidly. With the quelling of her anger had come contemplation. "Is this the right plan?"

Ayla looked up from her speech. "What do you mean?"

"If we fight . . ." Her breath shuddered, lip trembling. ". . . we can't anticipate the death toll."

"On our side it will be nothing if we can properly defend against the siege."

Flowridia's heart raced, but not for reasons she could entirely unravel. Her stomach fluttered; she nearly felt ill. "But what if hubris is our downfall? Are we truly more powerful than the Deathless Army?"

Ayla's frown tugged severely on her lips. "You underestimate my power. Casvir may have his army, but I have the Silver Fire and the blessing of a demon god."

"But our people . . ."

"Will die if we do nothing, and who am I to stand aside and let that happen?" By slow degrees, Ayla stood, her spine cracking as it lengthened to its full height, unimposing as it was. Ayla did not need height to be a dominating figure; her presence came from her will and poise and the sneer on her lip. "This is our darkest hour, Flowra. Casvir comes to collect his perceived dues far sooner than anticipated, but it matters not—he will fall all the same to Solvira's might. My people shall pledge to me as a god, and I shall stand between them and that bastard's army."

"If Etolié knows and Casvir comes to support her, then all of Staelash knows as well," Flowridia said—and oh gods, her heart ached to think of them. Shame filled her, reaching every dark corner of her soul. "We could encourage our people to surrender."

Ayla's glower darkened. "Do you truly think I will stand by and allow *Casvir* to walk in and steal what is mine? Whatever my qualms with ruling, I will not bow to that bastard's will ever again. I was a slave; now I rule a kingdom greater than his, and that irks him. It was only a matter of time; I just never thought he would descend so low as to manipulate that Celestial cunt."

"Ayla, you aren't a Solviraes. You don't hold the right to rule. They will not accept you."

"Who will tell them? Casvir? They will not believe him. Etolié? If Irons is not convinced, they'll likely be just as difficult."

Flowridia shook her head, her words increasingly frantic. "No one will die if we simply leave. We send a message to the people to surrender."

"That will not work, Flowra."

"We've done enough damage—"

"We've done ample amounts of good, I would argue."

"Ayla—"

"*Flowra!*"

The sharpness in her pet name caused Flowridia's gaze to dart up. Ayla's eyes had turned cold.

"Is this panic?" Ayla spat, ever graceful as she came to confront her. "Is it regret? Explain this to me, Flowra. Where is your conviction?"

Flowridia's breath failed her as she faced Ayla's severe countenance. "I-I . . ."

Ayla waited, though her habit of forgetting to blink had never been more disconcerting.

Flowridia wallowed in a swamp of shame. "I fear judgement," she said, lightheaded as she sat upon her bed. "I fear losing my friends more than I ever could have anticipated. Etolié, she . . ."

"Yes, she hates you," Ayla said, and her nonchalance lacerated deep. "Swallow it. Accept it. You knew from the moment you set out to slay Alauriel Solviraes that she would—at least you should have. There was a time for regret, but it has long passed."

Words from long ago filled her head: *"Damn yourself. Damn yourself, and have no regrets."*

"We have come upon the cusp of victory, but you're faltering," Ayla continued, her frustration palpable, yet bearing the undercurrent of sorrow. "Just as you did when you came to slay Alauriel Solviraes—you could not stab the knife."

Flowridia opened her mouth to speak, but Ayla continued first. "Once again, you come to the brink but remain too cowardly to accept the consequences. I know you wish to live in bliss and love, to dance in the sunshine and grow your garden, but have you ever, even once, looked at the road you are building? Flowra, I love you more than the moon loves the stars, but it *infuriates* me that you act so horrified every time consequences come to claim you. I have forgiven you for the broken promise of our wedding night, but don't you see it is the same? And what of Jules when we bestowed the living death? Your fear piles high, and then you run."

The words were cruel, yet Flowridia couldn't deny a single one. That same shame grew, threatening to drown her. She grasped at life rafts—any excuses to alleviate it. "Your pride will get your people killed—"

"Then I shall burn the greatest kingdom upon this realm!" Ayla spread her arms wide, her presence as expansive as the walls. "I will not go out as a candle in the dark—I am Ayla Darkleaf, The Endless Night, and the whole world will remember it soon. If I must drown this kingdom in blood, so be it." Furious tears welled in her eyes, but she spoke smoothly, nevertheless. "I will not run. But I will also ask nothing of you. If you wish for me to whisk you away to a garden plot somewhere far away and safe, so be it; I have said my piece and will not hold it against you. You need not face your friends. I will protect you from your crimes."

Flowridia said nothing, stunned into silence.

Ayla stood tall, smoothing her skirts as her face twisted to fight her angry tears. Wordlessly, she snatched her notes and stepped into a shadow.

Flowridia's entire body slumped, the first of her tears finally falling. When Demitri came over, she held his neck, unashamed to stain his fur with her cries. "Demitri, I may be the worst person on this planet."

Well, you did let some bad men be eaten by a ghoul once, but Lady Ayla killed an entire country, so I think she's a little worse.

A pained laugh left Flowridia's throat. "Why do I tell you things?"

Probably because I don't judge you. It sounds like Lady Ayla does, though.

Ayla had said cruel words, but by every god . . . was she right?

"Oh, Ayla . . ." she said amidst her sobs, recalling the memory of her tender-hearted wife. In their quiet moments, everything was perfect.

But the life she'd built was not meant for quiet moments.

A knock sounded, interrupting her cries. "Yes?" she managed, quickly wiping her tears.

"Consort Flowridia, there is a visitor here for you. He wishes to speak to you immediately."

He could only be one man, and Flowridia had a few choice words for him. With a few stabilizing breaths, she approached the door, though surely her face remained swollen and raw. When she opened the door, a servant awaited. "Bring him here. I will wait."

The servant bowed and left.

She waited, petting Demitri, calming her tears, until another knock echoed through the room.

"Flowra?"

That was not Casvir.

"Come in," she said, breathless. When the door opened, there stood a man she adored, who loved her like a daughter.

Thalmus wore simple clothes, the sort he donned in Staelash when he spent time in his workshop. He had to duck to enter, and his face conveyed heartbreak. "Hello, Flowra," he said gently, his voice a haven of peace amidst the turbulent storm brewing outside.

Surely he saw her tears, her swollen face. Shame filled her; if Etolié knew, so did he. "Hello."

The door shut behind him. Silver streaks marred his black braid, stress and age having taken a toll. "Imperator Casvir sent me," he continued, infinite softness to his words. "I will never bow to him, but we share one ideal in life— keeping you safe. Even he fears your death in the conflict ahead. Come with me. Please."

Thalmus was sincere in all he did, deliberate and careful. Every word held weight; Flowridia's resolve bent beneath them. "If you know the whole story, then you must know why I cannot," she said, subdued and calm.

"Is this what you meant, the morning of your wedding?" His face held only love, fatherly love, an affection she craved. "You said you were afraid."

"Part of it." The words lingered. She could not speak of her broken promise, the eternal night she had nearly given her life to.

He remained by the door, nothing threatening in his stance or gaze. "I want you to know," he said, "I mean what I've always said, that there is nothing you could do to destroy my love for you. I am not your father, but I've never seen you as anything except a child to love." He smiled; it held heartbreak. "I'm afraid for you. I fear you've been manipulated. You are on a dark path, and it can only lead to pain."

Flowridia shook her head, defensive at the words. "I chose this. I was not—"

"You did not kill Empress Alauriel." Thalmus kept his gentle words, and Flowridia wished he would simply yell so she could scream. But he would not. It was not who he was. "Perhaps, if the God of Order had not come, you might have still been wed in this palace."

By every god, she hated his words.

"There is goodness inside you. If you come with me, all can be as it was."

Fresh tears welled in her eyes. Flowridia blinked, forcing them away, his offer of love too much. "Whatever Ayla's wickedness, her love is true."

"Perhaps it is," Thalmus replied, the only sign of his inner turmoil the subtle clenching of his fist. "Perhaps it is not."

"To come with you means to give up all I've gained," she said, and she thought of Ana who had been sweet, no malice in her undead nature. Necrotic energy seeped from her hand, a gaseous cloud of opaque purple, and she stared, contemplative of its great cost.

Her destiny was greatness.

She had never wanted to be great.

Only to be loved.

"There is more to life than gaining power," he said, echoing her deepest thoughts. "But if that is the driving force in your life, perhaps this is the path for you. I don't believe that is true, though."

He was right.

The power ceased its flow, the purple gas dissipating into the air.

"My little flower girl, I will not force you," he continued, the tremble of his lip subtle and telling. "I will always love you. But if you continue down this path, I can no longer protect you."

By every god—her heart ached. When she matched his eye, she saw only love. That different sort of charitable love only a parent could convey, the rarest and most enduring of all. The love Flowridia had sought all her life and only so recently found. Unconditional.

"Where is she now?" he asked in the ensuing silence.

"Masquerading as the empress and gathering support for the war," she replied, voice muted as she drowned in a thousand different voices, a thousand different conflicting wants.

She never had quite chosen, had she. She walked the grey line, never committing. As Thalmus had said, she had not killed Lara. Soliel had brought the knife to her throat.

Compliant. She always had been.

Compliant, even in love.

"It was both of our ideas," she continued, "to come here. She wanted the power. I wanted to save the people Casvir was trying to destroy. If I go with you, I sacrifice them to him all the same."

All she had fought for threatened to tear at the seams.

"Between you and me, I tried to get her to run away with me. But she won't. Ayla's chosen to stay and fight."

"Flowra," Thalmus said, his tone holding depth now, a stern foundation, "whatever persona she has presented to you, no matter how sweet her love, it does not mean it's right."

Flowridia thought of Ayla, sweet Ayla and her fragile heart, her tears as she spoke of her shattered childhood and her death, how she had been reborn and sobbed at her feet while coated in blood.

"Please, come with me."

Flowridia thought of The Endless Night, the blood she'd seen drip from Ayla's mouth, the secrets dwelling beneath the castle in Nox'Kartha, the children she'd murdered, the genocides she'd enacted, the Sun Elves, the Skalmites—hundreds of thousands, dead. Casvir had asked how she planned to control Ayla, lest it happen again.

She thought of Etolié and her slit throat, of Khastra, her spine severed by The Endless Night, of Sora's cruel and tortured demise. All of Ayla's recent crimes had been done with only a reprimand for her lack of secrecy, and Flowridia wondered when she had become so compliant in monstrosity.

She wondered when she'd become a monster herself.

"Ayla's love is true," Flowridia said, daring to look up once more, "and she desperately craves it in return. She gives and gives and asks for nothing—the price of her love is merely acceptance. Yes, she is cruel and wicked to the world; she is a monster, and to love her means I am the same. I am a monster. I am as damned as she for following her."

"Is that what you want?" Thalmus said, heartbreak in his countenance.

What did she want?

Behind her swollen eyelids, Flowridia saw a tender scene, of Ayla's gaze—for it had always been Ayla, even behind the empress' façade—across the altar, their hands tied in a sacred ritual, true love proclaimed. A pledge to love the other, sworn before a goddess neither of them worshipped, but what need had they for a goddess when they spent their nights worshipping the other?

Flowridia loved her wife.

"I've pledged my heart to Ayla," Flowridia said, steeling her resolve, "and I will no longer be compliant in loving her. If resurrecting Ayla wasn't the final nail in the coffin of my good intentions, then today I seal and bury it."

Thalmus' eyes held tears, yet her own did not. "If this is truly your choice, I will not stop you."

She dared to approach, taking tentative steps toward the man she loved. With trepidation, she wrapped her arms around him, breaking when he returned the gesture.

So gentle a motion, to sever her heart in two. "Thank you," she whispered, "for everything."

Hesitation stilled his tongue; she felt it in his stiffening stance. But then . . . he softened. His words came like warm, summer rain. "I hope this brings you happiness. It is all I ever wanted for you." So familiar; so grounding, and she clung to the sound a moment more, the final farewell to a childhood she would never see again. "Goodbye, my flower girl."

They lingered.

They pulled away.

Flowridia held his gaze as she left the room, followed by Demitri, refusing to shed her tears.

Off to fight the war.

"*Citizens of Solvira, I regret this horrible turn of events. This is truly our darkest hour . . .*"

Flowridia heard the words from behind the balcony door. The guards did not stop her when she opened it, letting both the night air and her love's words caress her.

"*. . . and so, I must ask you for your trust. To defeat this army, we must slay the man who controls it . . .*"

A massive crowd had gathered, by decree of their empress. Torches decorated the inspiring scene, lighting the shadows cast by the setting sun. Flowridia gazed upon a sea of supplicants, of faces seeking hope. Empress Alauriel stood upon a jutting platform, her voice enhanced to project for miles, it seemed. Behind her was Jules, nothing amiss as she nodded her idle approval. Irons stood at her opposite side, hands clenched behind his back.

"This is an elective request, but know that every pledge means one more boost in power; one more step toward matching the might of the Nox'Karthan Army . . ."

Flowridia's hands were clenched. She did not regret, because she could not regret. General Irons stood beside her, as stiff as she.

"Keep your loyalties to Staella, to Sol Kareena, or to whomever you have pledged your allegiance to. But pledge also to me, to the Empress of Solvira, as your goddess. Trust in me; let me save you."

And a truly magical, foreboding thing occurred: each and every person in the crowd bowed. There was no unison in their chants—a cacophony of prayers surging forth. Lara stood with her hands wide to accept them, but Flowridia saw through the illusion fully, perhaps for the first time—it was Ayla, wicked Ayla, gaining the power she had always sought.

Something stirred in the air, a force Flowridia could feel but not touch—it was not for her, but for her beloved. The barest hints of light glowed at Ayla's feet, the beginnings of silver flame.

Something different coursed through Flowridia's blood. Her apprehension faded away, and in its stead came pride.

Ayla, for all her evil intentions, was unquestionably magnificent. Unbearably so.

Victory did not seem so impossible.

"Send couriers to every city in my kingdom and tell them my request," said Ayla Darkleaf, empress to the greatest kingdom in all the world. "My will shall be made known. We will defeat this army and its master once and for all!"

When the crowd cheered, Ayla basked in its noise, her grin cruel and poised to kill. Flowridia stepped up behind her, placing her hand on Ayla's back. A question shone in Ayla's eyes as she looked to her, her grin faltering. "Flowra?" she whispered, and the crowd did not hear it.

Flowridia did not care for the guards, for the general, nor for the populace of people down below. She kissed her wife upon the platform, a message for all the world to see— but more importantly, for Ayla to know, to feel, to never question again. She savored Ayla's lips, for they melted into one flesh, one heart, one soul, and Flowridia vowed to cherish that love until her dying day.

When she finally pulled away, there lay confusion and wonder in her wife's countenance. Flowridia leaned toward her pointed ear. "I don't know my fate with you," she whispered, courage steadying her tongue, "but my very soul demands it. It might even be to hell, but I'll follow wherever you go, my love."

A subtle bit of softness shone in Ayla's vibrant eyes. Her smile returned, the very same Flowridia had seen facing her at the altar.

Flowridia went down to one knee. Shock showed in Ayla's eyes. "I'm trusting you," Flowridia continued, "my empress . . . my goddess. I pledge my life to you. And not only in love," she added with a wink, but Ayla's jaw had dropped with no indication of rising again.

Apart from Jules and General Irons, all the people upon the platform followed suit, but Ayla's eyes were only for her.

"I trust you," Flowridia said.

Ayla finally smiled, this time with elation. "Foolish of you," she whispered, and Flowridia laughed as she stood.

Something different shone in Ayla's stance; something ineffable and bright. To worship someone gave them power— but to fear them granted it as well, to only speak their name in a whisper. Ayla held power from every angle, from those who feared her across the sea and now from those who adored her in Solvira, though they did not know the truth.

"I suppose the war begins now," Ayla said, and Flowridia nodded as she stepped back in her place.

Ayla resumed her speech to the citizens, thanking them for their support and trust, sounding truly humbled, though it was a lie.

"General Irons," Flowridia muttered, and the man stepped a little closer, "our fatal flaw remains that General Khastra knows every mechanism of Solvira's defenses—the very same flaw that decimated the Theocracy in a night. Let us thank every god that Imperator Casvir lost his orb, but the fact remains that we cannot startle his forces; not with anything Solvira has ever had in its arsenal before. He will have the means to counteract anything."

The crowd cheered for Ayla's words, but something in Flowridia's tone must have piqued Irons' interest—he looked almost pleased. "Speak your mind. You have a plan."

"I do. First, we bring in absolutely everyone beyond the wall. The Theocracy refugees in particular are at risk. We clear the streets. No citizen may leave their home. Protecting the populace must be a priority—second only to defending the wall.

"On the warfront, we must be utterly unpredictable," she continued. "Not unintelligent. Not without a plan. But we cannot utilize any of Solvira's usual arsenal, save basic defense. However, Solvira has never had me."

"Perhaps not," Irons said, wariness seeping into his words, "but Nox'Kartha has a more accomplished necromancer than you, no disrespect intended."

"Entirely true." She raised her hand, studying the familiar lines, and the barest hints of purple smoke rose from the pores. "But necromancy has many facets. He has strength in numbers. His army is literally endless. However, I have a few tricks he doesn't know about, and they aren't the sort he can steal, like undead slaves bowing to the more powerful master." She closed her fist, a quick glance to General Irons revealing his distaste at her display. "Take me with you to the wall. We withhold Empress Alauriel until after the first wave has fallen. We won't want to show our true might upfront— and Casvir will not either."

"It will allow more time for the news to spread of her request for pledges."

Flowridia wondered if she should fear the result of those ominous words, wondered if her sanity truly had slipped so far.

"Imperator Casvir can't send his army or his servants directly into our city," Irons continued. "We have magic enough for that. They will have to breach the walls. Our priority must be to defend them."

"Then let's discuss," Flowridia said, and in that moment, she felt a semblance of hope.

Chapter 35

Flowridia walked along the outside of the great wall surrounding Neolan, gazing upon an abyss.

In the far distance, a storm approached, the undead a swirling sea of black. Was this what the Theocracy had seen in the moments before its demise? She saw no dragon, but with the setting sun came a surge of death—the moon rose to cast its shadow upon Solvira.

Her Solvira.

With a piece of chalk in hand, she continued her task of inscribing runes upon the base of the wall—for protection, and for detouring undead. She had done as much before.

She had no guards. Instead, she had Ayla, who silently watched her work. "You say it might not be enough?"

"There is so much wall, and only one of me," Flowridia replied. "I only wish I had time to grow them. But that would be a lot of effort for only a small space." She drew the next one, regretting that it would offer scant protection compared to what she had created in her garden in Staelash. "I mostly fear for when they come from the sky. The gates will be protected, at the very least."

"Your best is more than good enough, my love," Ayla said. Her attention suddenly turned away from the wall, to the darkness beyond. "They're coming."

It was time.

Ayla whisked her away into the shadows, remaining in Sha'Demoni when she placed Flowridia upon the wall.

General Irons stood at attention.

"The wards are set," Flowridia said, already missing Ayla's presence.

"Consort Flowridia," Irons said, staring into the abyss, "given the recent revelations regarding your . . . *loyalties*, I'm surprised to admit I actually trust you, so I am willfully ignoring all my hundreds of concerns about the coming siege."

Oddly inspired by the double-edged compliment, Flowridia nodded. "Are our defenses readied?"

"Everything is in place. My elite paladins await the command to march."

Along the walls, soldiers armed with crossbows stood attention. Hot oil waited in cauldrons—something Khastra would expect, but an effective tactic nevertheless assuming they got close enough. But most importantly were the stationed sorcerers along the wall, prepared to deflect bigger things than Flowridia's wards could provide—like a trebuchet.

Or a dragon.

The storm approached, a swirling collection of corporeal black, a harbinger of doom. She stepped to the edge of the wall.

Shutting her eyes, she turned her focus to the wilds, to the winds, to the woven rope of dried hemp coiled far below in the grass, its length more than enough to span the wall, where she could grasp its opposite end. She still needed an anchor, hence the organic rope, but the small connection did as she'd hoped—she felt the grass beyond, sensed it reeling at the oncoming army. She could not wield light as a weapon, no, but death could fight death, given proper form.

With one hand on the braided plant-life, she held the other out, summoning all her focus.

Beyond, she felt an ominous *boom*.

Within, her power surged.

All life in the field withered and fell, plants and animals alike, though the latter was a casualty she hated to lose. The burn was euphoric, the pain a glorious pleasure as it melded with her body, filling every errant crack and empty space. Her reserves threatened to burst at the seams, but Flowridia swallowed and forced the power to settle and wait.

One.

Never had the purple mist been tangible, yet she swore she could grasp in in her hands.

Two.

By every god, her gluttonous self craved more, more, *more . . .*

Three—

False life surged into the field beyond. Trees blossomed; grass became a brilliant green and then grew. The approaching undead had no fear, no mind to comprehend it, but shrieked when the very ground beneath churned and consumed them. Roots held the earth together; as they shifted, the ground unsettled.

Grass rose, dragging the bodies down into the earth. The trees all but came to life, their roots strangling those who passed, their branches whipping about to damage what walked beneath. A dust cloud rose to hide the scene, but Flowridia needn't see. She shut her eyes and focused on the feeling, on each individual blade of grass at her beck and call, bidding some to simply act and others to listen to every minute command she expelled.

She waved her hands idly, a composer directing her orchestra. The undead fought to dig themselves out, and the plants beat them down, some rooting them into place, growing in the space between flesh, conjoining and becoming one.

Like swimming beneath the waves, she heard words as though plunged underwater. *"Aim and hold!"*

General Irons commanded his troops. She dared to risk her focus and peeked. Hordes of flying creatures dove to slay them.

"Fire!"

A rain of arrows burst into the sky—the flying creatures, some sort of abominable gargoyles, shrieked as their fragile wings were impaled by a volley of arrows. The few who survived the onslaught dove down upon the wall—only to hit a literal wall in the air. Celestial sorcerers, working in tandem, held their focus, and where the gargoyles hit, the air rippled in shades of gold.

Still, a few screams were heard. Flowridia looked to the sky and saw a few human soldiers carried away and dropped. "Can we not stop them?"

"Smaller creatures can escape their eye," Irons said, but then a faint sizzling of light glinted from the dark void.

Flowridia's gut clenched, though no nausea hit—the magic was too far away. But from a portal the size of a doorway poured a second wave of dead.

"Watch out!" she screamed, and thankfully the others heard. Soldiers assembled awaiting orders, along with sorcerers set upon the task of deflecting the sudden rush of undead.

And these were not the simple corpses of before—these were experiments, larger creatures wielding weapons, their strength not only from their numbers—nightmarish giants, some sewn from numerous corpses, others literal giants and half-giants.

Flowridia recalled Ayla's words from their secret chamber, that she and Casvir had never quite perfected these aberrations. "General!" she cried, and Irons looked to her immediately. "Those monsters are fragile. Their purpose is likely more distraction than function. Don't let them divert us from the flying creatures!"

Irons immediately resumed barking out orders, directing a few sorcerers to *'blast the bastards with flame!'* and the rest to keep their eye to the sky.

Below, chaos reigned. The ground had become the aftermath of an earthquake, though the undead still struggled to approach, climbing over jagged pieces of earth and rocks, slowly dragged down into the depths once more.

Soldiers barraged them with arrows, but the nightmarish dead seemed unphased—until a few struck the wall and were instantly repelled, wailing cries echoing in the night.

Gods, they might have a chance.

But some were not detoured, finding places where the wards were weak, where nothing touched the wall at all. As Flowridia had predicted, the smaller dead were a far greater threat than their cumbersome counterparts. At one vulnerable place, not a hundred feet away, the undead bombarded the wall, the smaller ones simply piling against it. They rushed as an ocean wave, crawling upon each other, and Flowridia suddenly realized—

"They're going to climb the wall!"

"Pour the oil!" came Irons' cry, and the soldiers obeyed. A sickening slosh of molten oil rained upon the dead, melting their skin, melding them into a singular pile of gore.

High above, she watched gargoyles fly away with the occasional poor soul—mostly sorcerers, she realized. There was nothing she could do about them, these beasts in the sky.

Flowridia turned her focus to the wall of burned dead, the life beyond them still lush and unsettled. To act recklessly would bring down more of the wall; Flowridia kept her eyes open this time, directing the grass to grab their ankles and drag them under.

Still, they climbed.

She ran to that section of the wall, bypassing soldiers scrambling to obey orders. The first of the dead breached the wall; Flowridia touched their aimless minds, feeling the compulsion to simply *eat* and *kill.* She latched onto the first few, successfully bidding them to leap from the wall, but when she sought to control the first of the giants, something struck her from within.

Pain wracked her mind, thrusting her influence out. Stumbling back, she caught herself against the stone.

So that was what it felt like, to face a stronger necromancer.

The soldiers battered back the undead forces atop the wall, their numbers ever-increasing. Flowridia summoned holy light, bidding it to gather in her palms when one of the dead approached. Though it burned the creature, the corpse attempted to grab her—and might've, had a soldier not dragged her back.

Behind her came General Irons' elite.

A battalion of paladins, armored and assured, glowed like the sun they worshipped as they tore through the nightmarish dead upon the wall. Irons stood among them, yelling orders. They bashed with their shields and slashed through the dead with their swords of radiant light like paper, leaving severed limbs and piles of heads.

Cheers ensued as they battered back the enemy. Flowridia took the moment to breathe, even joining in the applause.

Soon, the wall had been cleared—and though Nox'Kartha's army never retreated, they remained on the ground.

The work had only just begun, but the tides had changed.

A knock startled Etolié's tentative peace.

Partway into the forty-ninth verse of Eionei's epic of Morathma's crimes, Etolié clutched the half-demon, who still lay in her lap, exhausted despite her undead body.

Another knock sounded. The door opened, revealing the night sky and Imperator Casvir's glowing eyes. Etolié instinctively sneered. "Good evening," she said, curtly.

After assessing that there was no monster, Casvir stepped inside, the room illuminated only by Etolié's glowing wings. Murishani peeked from beyond the doorway. "Oh, good. You didn't die."

Khastra tried to rise in Casvir's presence, but Etolié's hold tightened. Yes, the half-demon could overpower her—without even a thought—but the slight resistance was enough, it seemed. Instead, Etolié gently extracted herself and stood to face him herself.

"Impressive," Casvir said, and he stepped right up to Etolié, likely expecting her to move.

He was mistaken.

His armor brushed against her illusionary dress, but she held her ground, facing the space between his armored pectorals. She spoke directly to them. "Anything you want to say to her goes through me."

"That is not the arrangement," Casvir said, inspirationally monotone in the face of disrespect.

"Listen, Imperator First and Last, in times of nudity, she belongs to me. Get her some clothes, let her scrape up some dignity, and then we can discuss arranging a meeting—"

In a motion that could not be mistaken as a strike—Etolié watched it carefully to see—Casvir pushed her to the side. His sheer size and bulk meant it was as easy as directing a toddler; she stumbled away, but when she spread her wings wide to block his view, he did not touch them. It seemed he knew convention.

Khastra managed to stand, shaking on her hooves as she steadied herself against the wall. Casvir didn't rush her—to Etolié's chagrin. As much as she didn't want Beefcake to transform, she'd pay to see Casvir squished like a nasty spider again.

When Khastra finally approached, naked and dirtied from dried blood and dirt and who knew what else, she stood a full head taller than the imperator, who faced her neck—and whose eyes didn't avert to her bare breasts even once, which Etolié had to applaud him for. Defeated, Etolié lowered her translucent wing and illusioned a robe to cover Khastra, preserving her modesty at least in front of the sycophant Murishani in the doorframe, even if she knew Beefcake didn't give a shit.

"Imperator," Khastra said, with as smooth a bow as she could muster, though all her movements remained pained.

For all his faults, Casvir didn't seem bothered by her pitiful bow, given the circumstances. "The war has begun. The initial onslaught of the wall has been a failure, due to unforeseeable circumstances. I would discuss this with you and seek course correction."

Khastra gave a controlled nod, and behind her back, only Etolié could see her press a finger to her opposite wrist—checking her own pulse. "I have no armor."

"New armor has been made, with your enhanced powers in mind. It shall be delivered immediately. We convene in ten minutes."

Casvir left. It took all Etolié's willpower to not wring his neck.

When the door shut, Khastra, with impeccable grace and control, sat back onto the ground, placing her head between her digitigrade knees. Her breathing remained steady, perhaps forcibly slow.

With care, Etolié knelt beside her, bringing a hand up to rub her scalp. "You all right? You gonna transform again?"

"I am trying to not," Khastra replied, though pain grated her rich tone. "Etolié, you cannot speak to him like that."

"Fuck yes, I can."

"He will not stand for any disrespect of his station."

"Let me play that game. You worry about you, all right?" When Khastra said nothing, Etolié scooted closer, tracing the endless design of tattoos across her skin. "What does it feel like?"

"Like dancing on a knife," Khastra whispered. "I could fall any second. I . . . I feel very sick."

Etolié kept her soothing gestures, tracing the lines along Khastra's back as the silence ticked on. "Are you in pain?"

Khastra nodded, but she said nothing else of it. "I remember . . ." She groaned, fingers rubbing her temples as she held her breath. When she released, it shook her entire core. "I remember little things. I . . . I hurt you."

"No," Etolié said, even as her arm stung from residual pain—Momma couldn't take away wounds that were simply her own, it seemed—not from so far away. Not from a distance. But she quickly illusioned away the already illusioned bandage and wound, praying Khastra hadn't noticed, then placed a kiss on the back of her neck. "Doesn't matter what state you're in, or how far gone—your larger other half has a weakness for me."

A knife's edge. All it would take was a push.

"You are lying," Khastra said, and Etolié did all she could to will peace upon her, upon them both, but the half-demon gasped as though masking a sob.

"*She* hurt me; not you," Etolié pled, desperate to soothe her. "You always say the Bringer of War is someone else, and I need you to believe that for me. You would never. Not in an eternity."

A knock sounded. When the door opened, a few ghostly, hooded figures entered, each carrying pieces of armor.

Etolié helped Khastra to dress, first in a gambeson and then each new, metallic piece. It bore less splendor than the set Soliel had destroyed—no gems, no artistry in its craftsmanship. Stark black, not unlike Casvir's, bereft of decoration. Purely utilitarian, though it definitely had the hidden gears built inside to shift and grow.

Perfect for a slave to the imperator.

The time easily surpassed ten minutes, but Etolié didn't care, briefly admiring her beloved's stance in the armor, elegant even in suffering. When Etolié intertwined their fingers, Khastra managed to smile.

"Do you feel any better?"

"I always feel more stable in armor," the half-demon said, and Etolié supposed that was as good of a response as she could get.

Soon, they met Casvir, who bid them to follow.

Etolié recognized that this should be the path to Neolan, but the upturned field before them was new. Spots of flame shone amidst the darkness, revealing hordes of dead approaching the walls—grabbed, instead, by great vines and dragged underground or sliced apart by blades of grass.

To support Flowers in this betrayal would have been abominable, but Etolié was too damn impressed to be angry.

She spared a glance to Khastra, who simply scowled, and to Casvir who . . . smiled?

It was kinda leering and creepy, but it was a smile, even if she hated it. "You look oddly thrilled for a man watching his soldiers get dragged underground."

"Her potential truly is limitless," Casvir replied, no question to who 'her' could be. "I shall be deeply disappointed if she dies in the attack."

"Ever pragmatic, all right."

Etolié looked to General Beefcake, calculation on her elegant features. "What are you thinking, Beefy?"

Khastra's glare could have melted ice, so hot it seethed. Etolié adored seeing her like this. "We cannot risk any of our heavy weaponry until the tiny one is disposed of." She turned to Casvir, subtle fury in her visage. "Permission to target the empress consort."

Casvir's searing gaze remained upon the distant wall. "She will tire eventually."

"Yes, and your troops will be animated severed limbs eventually."

"Hence why I have only sent the first two waves."

Khastra huffed, visibly twitching as she watched the show. "Take care your sentimental heart does not lose you this siege."

An onslaught of heat attacked Etolié from both sides—from Khastra, who held nothing back in her glare, and from Casvir, who revealed nothing at all save the barest twitch of a frown upon his face.

"Put them at ease," Khastra said, calculation in her glare. "Let them think this is the best we can do. I will think on this." Etolié stood alert when Khastra suddenly turned that steely gaze onto her. "What has your mother said of this?"

"She says that if she interferes, it will make everything infinitely worse," Etolié whispered, the weight of leadership not a burden she would ever be used to. "She's right. She can't speak on my behalf because that means speaking on behalf of Casvir."

"I see," Khastra replied, and she said nothing more, merely placed her hand on Etolié's shoulder.

All would not be well.

By dawn, Flowridia neared collapsed.

She hadn't considered her own stamina, though she held up better than she ever had before. A small battalion of guards delivered food periodically at General Irons' insistence—and thank every god for that, for it was all that kept her going.

But by the third wave of flying gargoyles, Flowridia physically shook, even though she sat in a meditative position.

There was less to do—mostly maintenance of the irrevocably destroyed terrain—a fact pointed out to her by General Irons, who gently shook her shoulder, pulling her from her focus.

"You look like death," he said, his face illuminated by the nearby torches and impending sunrise. "There's light on the horizon, wall is stabilized, and if we want you for the rest of the siege, you need some rest."

"I just wonder why we haven't seen the Bringer of War yet," Flowridia said, hating how her voice trembled.

"And you'll drop dead before she has the opportunity to show up at this rate." He offered a gloved hand; she accepted. "As your commander, I am sending you to your wife. We will call for you if there is an emergency. Otherwise, sleep until you are rested."

She tried to argue, but she stumbled as she straightened her stance, her vision shaky. "Have someone escort me, then. I promise I'll sleep."

A carriage took her to the castle. Within minutes, she collapsed into bed.

She was not alone for long.

Like a whisper along a night breeze, Ayla appeared, quickly falling into bed with her. "You were brilliant, darling. I watched all the while."

"I believe that," she breathed, and Ayla chuckled, stealing her words with a soft kiss.

"I admire your courage and cleverness. I suspect Casvir is shaken—not that he expected an easy victory, but your ingenuity should be commended."

Sincerity shone in Ayla's gaze. Flowridia gently kissed her. "How are you feeling, my wife who would be god?"

"Taller," Ayla replied, her wink punctuating the word. "In truth, I feel . . . brighter. Like there is a burning fire within me waiting to simply combust. It's dizzying—and I have not been dizzy in seventeen hundred years. Sometimes it flares, and it never quite dies down the same. I suspect that is when the news reaches its intended audience, and they pledge." Her hand stroked soft lines along Flowridia's face. "There is little more to say on it. But I think even I may be in for a surprise when I join you on the battlefield."

"I can't wait to see it."

Ayla pressed a kiss to her forehead. "You need to sleep, my love."

"Wait," she said, managing to smile despite her crippling exhaustion. "You should eavesdrop on the Deathless Army."

Ayla's lips skimmed her cheek, her hand tangling into Flowridia's abundant waves of hair. "Forgive me, but I must say no. He will suspect that I would try that and be prepared. My time is better spent protecting you. Casvir will do all he can to steal you away. Let us be grateful he does not have another like me in his arsenal—I am not hindered by the magical protections on this castle. I shall guard your bedside."

Flowridia did not fight this time, adoring the feeling of Ayla's body beside her. She nearly succumbed to darkness, when whispered words caressed her ear. "There is one final loose end, however. A promise to fulfill."

Flowridia managed to open her eyes, heavy with sleep. "What's that?"

"A pledge for you, my love. I promised to do so. Will you accept it?"

The words swirled in her tired mind, not quite settling. "Yes," she said instinctively, though her mind teetered far closer to sleep than not.

Ayla smiled against her ear, then kissed it lightly. "It will not be quite the same as what I have gained, but a fraction is better than none. Izthuni will not mind; not if it's you." Reverence filled her wife's words. "I pledge my life and death to you, Flowridia Darkleaf. As my wife and as my goddess, both."

Understanding finally fell upon her, though with the gentleness of a bird on a bough.

Inside, she felt something warm.

But she could not dwell upon it; Flowridia drifted off into sleep.

Casvir's forces skittered like insects around the city's walls—those that remained.

He did not have them withdraw in the morning light, merely keep their distance—any who came too close took a quick, burning arrow to the face.

Etolié didn't understand the jargon shared between Casvir and Khastra as they debated the next evening's activities. She twitched, feeling hungry eyes upon her. Despite the massive casualties at the wall, Etolié knew it was a drop in the ocean of Casvir's full force. There was no shortage of dead things in the world, and the imperator would throw every last one of them at Solvira's wall if that's what it took.

Countless corpses shambled idly around her, a massive sea of death. The dragon loomed far back in the field, his eyes unseeing, and Etolié spared a thought for Uluron, far across the sea.

This had not gone how she had hoped. Casvir kept his bargains, yes, but what if Solvira simply didn't bend? What then?

She didn't dare find a secluded place to pray. Just because the dead were under Casvir's control didn't mean she trusted a single one of them. Instead, she knelt in plain sight, clinging to Khastra's hand as lack of sleep and stress and sorrow clouded her mind.

"Eionei," she thought, the ineffable feeling of connection suddenly binding her to another world. *"Eionei, I know we're having some disagreements right now, but this is about the greater good."*

A madwoman threatened to run her momma's country into the dust. The Solviraes line had ended, even if the Silver Fire had not. If her godly grandpa could help, she would swallow her anger for a few minutes.

"I understand you might be angry about my decisions, but I'm doing what I think is right to preserve momma's legacy. And Lara's. This kingdom will be—"

Etolié's words were stolen when a *puff* of pink flower petals suddenly burst angrily in the air before her. How flower petals could be so furious, she couldn't say—maybe it was the sudden mood shift. Maybe it was the flower petals swirling to form the image of an angry woman. Etolié couldn't say, but she knew this bitch pretty well. "Alystra?"

Alystra, Goddess of Love and Beauty, formed of flowers petals since she couldn't actually manifest on the plane, placed her hands on her hips as her wings literally blossomed—well, were formed of blossoms, at least. *"I came out of Celestière to tell you to stop."*

Her indifference to Casvir and Khastra was truly inspirational. Casvir summoned his weapon; Khastra looked prepared to pounce, but Alystra was a woman with no fucks.

"I reserve the right to talk my grandfather, excuse you."

"He has a splitting headache and you incessantly contacting him is making it worse. He's very sick, and he won't shut up about it to me."

"What do you mean he's sick? Gods don't get sick."

Alystra crossed her arms, the flower petals forming her lips pursing like she knew shit. *"Well, he managed it. Sol Kareena can't make heads or tails of it. Your mother laughed it off and said we shouldn't worry and offered a few teas to soothe his symptoms. He said yes; I said no. But, like you said, gods don't get sick. So, it is concerning."*

Momma said . . .

"Needless to say, he won't be of much use, given he's been in bed for the past few days, dimmer than nighttime. Won't stop whining."

Etolié forced a smile. "Send my love. Not my forgiveness; I'm still working on that."

"Will do. Though don't bother sending any more messages through me after this—he and I are done."

This wasn't an outlandish statement, but it did still give Etolié pause. *"Done?"*

"It was long overdue. But he told me what happened between you and him. I also chose your side."

"Oh. Well, thanks."

"Try not to die." With that, Alystra's petals fell from formation, collecting in a large heap upon the blighted ground.

Etolié stared where the goddess had left, insanity brewing in her head. "Wait! Alystra!"

Another puff of flower petals, and the Goddess of Beauty returned. *"What do you want?"*

"Can you help?"

It was a gamble, though without much of a downside to failure. But Etolié was surprised when Alystra seemed to consider it. *"Do you have anything in particular in mind?"*

"No. To be honest, I didn't think I'd get this far."

Alystra's flowery form seemed to grin. *"I won't assist in killing anyone. But if you would agree to host me, I may be able to encourage Solvira to surrender."*

"Yes. Absolutely."

"I'll be back."

And she *poofed* away once more, the flower petals floating harmlessly to the ground.

Etolié looked back to Khastra and Casvir, her smile wide. "Looks like Celestière hasn't abandoned us after all."

"Your mother poisoned Eionei," Khastra said, far too matter-of-factly for Etolié's taste.

"I gathered that," Etolié said, shoving her complicated feelings on the matter into a box. "I doubt it's fatal. He would be dead already. This is a warning."

Khastra nodded, as though this were perfectly in character for Staella to do, and Etolié realized there was so much still to learn about her dear Goddess Momma.

"I was not aware a god could be poisoned," Casvir said, his intrigue palpable.

Etolié's gut churned as she contemplated this odd rift in her extended family. "You would need poison as potent as my mother can grow, but as we have all just witnessed, it's possible. If you need someone to conduct negotiations to buy those from her, I'm your girl. For the next twenty years, at least."

"I shall consider it."

Etolié's fucks were few and far between. Sell your soul and sell your morals with it, she supposed.

"But what *can* Alystra do?" she wondered out loud—again, she hadn't thought this through, and she was fighting blind.

"Can she control plants?" Khastra asked, genuine curiosity in her words.

"Just flowers."

But who was Etolié to forget that some flowers carried nasty thorns?

A knock pounded, waking Flowridia from deep sleep.

Her eyes burned as she forced them to open, groggy and pained as she sat up.

Ayla was already at the door, her form disguised as the late empress. "What do you want?"

The hapless soldier at the door looked deeply apologetic. "My apologies, your majesty, but General Irons requests the empress consort back at the gate. There's been an emergency."

"I will inform her and let her make her own decision," Lara said, slamming the door shut.

As Ayla, she returned her attention to Flowridia, who tried in vain to rub sleep from her eyes. "They can wait," Ayla spat, but Flowridia shook her head.

"He wouldn't interrupt my sleep without a very good reason." Flowridia stumbled out of bed, beckoning for Ayla to escort her through the shadows.

What she saw at the wall both inspired and alarmed her.

The ancient gate to Neolan, hundreds of years old, fortified through magic and mechanics and strong metals, lay shattered on the ground.

And intertwined amidst the massive collection of bars and gears were lush roses, their thorns promising a precarious cleanup.

When she peeked outside the gate, the undead shambled in the distance, but climbing up the wall were more of the thorny, luscious flowers—many brushing against and obscuring her wards.

"What happened?" she asked, and Irons shook his head.

"Apparently Nox'Kartha has invoked the aid of angelic gods—my men swore Alystra herself appeared on the battlefield and did this. The roses burst from the earth and grew into the gate before crushing it."

"I would bet that's Etolié's doing," Flowridia muttered, though she knew little of Celestière gods, besides Sol Kareena. "So Nox'Kartha is fighting dirty."

She thought a moment, something dangerous and new sparking in her mind. "Well, if they're invoking gods, perhaps we can too. Defend this gate at all costs—my plan won't work until nightfall."

"Can you do anything about the roses?" Irons asked, and Flowridia immediately stole their life away, leaving shriveled, dried husks.

"Burn them. They'll erupt like tinder. I'll do the same on the wall. Then, we set up any kind of barricade we can."

She spent the next few hours restoring the wall, mulling over her own retaliation.

Shadowed by General Irons, Flowridia marched to the town square at sunset.

"I would like to reiterate," Irons said, his tone as tense as his gait, "my firm objection to this plan."

Flowridia frowned, defensive at his words. "Is this not our darkest hour? Shouldn't we do whatever we must?"

"Do you swear this shall reflect only upon you and not upon Solvira?"

"I do," she replied, contemplative at his question. "You will note I assisted in bringing his hostess back to life. He owes me this."

A ghost town greeted them, the streets utterly desolate by royal decree. "Be that as it may," Irons said, twitching despite his plate armor, "we must hurry. Once the sun sets, I have no doubt the imperator will launch his second phase."

"If this goes well, we won't have to worry about the imperator."

The expanse of brick and stone opened into a large juncture, revealing a grand display of statues, buildings, and a convergence of roads. Before them, she recognized the statues of Neoma and Staella, the destroyed one of Ilune, and approached the spot before it. "Knife, please," she said softly, swallowing her hesitation.

Irons obeyed, handing her a sharp dagger. She held it in her dominant hand, bracing herself before cutting a small line across her finger. Cringing, she dropped the knife and squeezed the wound until a small droplet of blood welled.

She cleared a spot upon the dirty street, brushing aside dust until she saw mostly clean stone. Upon the ground, she wrote a symbol from memory, seared forever in her mind, synonymous with fear.

The Endless Night

The Endless Night was a conglomeration of deities—the symbol would attract its more elusive member.

The sun disappeared fully beyond the horizon, yet the square grew ever darker, unnaturally so, until a wall of black blockaded their sight from anything beyond, rising like a fog. She could not see General Irons. Soon, she could not see her own hand.

Only then, did she hear a voice: *"Child of Odessa. It has been a long time."*

Izthuni's deep laughter reverberated across her body, rattling her bones. Amidst the corporeal darkness, she saw the barest outline of a six-limbed monstrosity. Ayla's benefactor, the God of Shadows, had come. "Good evening," she said politely. "I hope you are well."

"More than well," he replied, and Flowridia saw a flash of his endless rows of teeth within a gaping void. *"Gleeful. Sol Kareena's power has taken a mighty blow, and I celebrate."*

She willed General Irons to say nothing, knowing he was listening. "Happy to hear," she said, forcibly nonchalant. "I would like to ask you for something."

He drew back into the darkness; she could not see him when he said, *"Go on."*

"As you must know, I have married and received a crown."

"All of Sha'Demoni knows your sins, Consort Flowridia."

Oh, that was a damning bit. It took all her will to keep her smile. "My beloved and I are fighting a war to defend that crown. I do not ask your blessing, nor for anything grand. The

Bringer of War fights with our enemies, and I do not wish to stir any conflict in Sha'Demoni. But in deference to the gift I gave you, I would ask you give one to me."

Again, his pervasive laughter filled the space, endless and ominous. *"Demoni Law says that is fair."*

"Time is short. I must speak quickly."

Izthuni listened.

He agreed.

With the coming darkness came a fresh surge of undead.

Even from behind the battle lines, Etolié heard their rattling moans and cries and hated every moment of it. Her wings remained visible for her own comfort, and she wasn't too proud to admit it. They petrified her; in the dark, she feared them more.

"What's the plan, Beefcake?" she asked, and Khastra, who surveyed the scene with glowing eyes, pulled Etolié against her smooth armor.

"The tiny one will surely come again," Khastra replied, a certain cunning in her calculated gaze. Under other circumstances, it might have excited Etolié—not so much tonight, surrounded by hungry dead. "But it is the second night in a row; she will tire more quickly. We maintain the onslaught. When we receive verification that she is gone, we send the ballista—and myself. The walls will be breached before morning."

Casvir approached. In the dark, his glowing eyes bore twice the menace, but Etolié stood proud, nevertheless. "Valeuron is prepared," he said simply. "During the second wave, I shall ride . . ." His voice faded; his vision narrowed. "Magister Etolié," he said smoothly, "please dim your wings."

A strange request, but Etolié obeyed. Her wings vanished, drenching them in darkness—

Yet, though her eyes tried to adjust, the darkness had become thick. Dread filled her soul; something unnatural awaited them. "What the fuck—"

A horrible, bone-rattling laugh shook the world. Khastra immediately grabbed her, hoisting her into her arms; Etolié clung tight to her neck. The great hammer flew to her side as she frantically searched the vast void of darkness. "Show yourself, Izthuni!"

Casvir's materialized weapon glowed, casting faint illumination upon his intrigued smile. Etolié silently told herself that since the god couldn't materialize, he couldn't hurt them.

Right?

From the darkness came corporeal shadow—a massive claw rearing toward them. Khastra brought her wrist to her mouth, prepared to transform, yet the claw did not grasp them—but Casvir.

It pulled him into the shadows.

The darkness slowly dissipated, and Etolié could not stop staring at the spot Casvir had once stood.

Only once the unnatural fog disappeared entirely did Etolié let her wings reappear. "What the hell just happened?"

"Imperator Casvir was taken into Sha'Demoni by Izthuni," Khastra said, palpably stunned.

"Will he kill him?"

"I do not know, but it does not matter. Imperator Casvir is trapped in the demonic realm."

"Grab him and leave him there?" Irons said, disbelief in his tone. "That's so petulant a child would think of it."

"That's why it's so brilliant," Flowridia replied, cold still pulsing through her veins. Ally or not, Izthuni cast a heavy presence. "We can't kill Casvir. Khastra smashed him with her hammer and he came back. But we can drop him into another realm and be done with it. He'll escape eventually; he's too clever to not." A grin pulled instinctively at her lips. "But this will buy us time to win the war."

Irons shook his head. "I don't approve of working with demon gods, but I have to commend you."

"It pays to have friends in strange places." Idly, she pressed her bloody finger to her dark dress, staunching the dripping liquid. "His troops are endless. We take the time to destroy what we can. And then . . ." She heaved a sigh, fearful at the thought. ". . . we send Ayla."

Quiet acrimony on Irons' features. "Will she appear as herself?"

"I don't know," Flowridia said, ignoring his disapproval. "But I'm very curious to see the results of her pledges."

And her own, but she didn't say that.

Etolié sat on her Beefcake's shoulders, her horns a convenient handhold, and watched the ensuing madness.

All was well—the undead would obey any order given until told otherwise—and though Casvir was far away, he still held control.

At least . . . at first.

Disarray came as odd screams sang from far ahead. Etolié could not see in the dark—not as well as Khastra—but clung tight when the half-demon stomped forward and muttered a soft, "Damn."

"What's happening?"

"With Imperator Casvir in Sha'Demoni, his influence is far lower. Tiny one is seizing control of his troops; they are attacking each other." Khastra shook her head, fury palpable. "I have to go in."

"They'll turn on you too." Etolié floated up from her back, wings illuminating the dark field. She grabbed Khastra's face and held it in her hands. "Khastra—"

"Once the undead have breached the walls, Solvira will fall. They will surrender because they have no choice."

"We have to do something, but throwing the Bringer of War like a catapult at the wall without a plan isn't the answer."

"I . . ." For a moment, Khastra dropped the mantle of General of the Deathless Army, a grimace twisting her features. "I could call upon my sister, I suppose. She could find the imperator and bring him back. But that could take a long time—days, even, before I can even get into contact with her, and that is assuming she will agree to help."

"Aren't there other ways to get into Sha'Demoni? I know in Nox'Kartha, the Temple of Izthuni will lead you straight there."

Khastra shook her head. "Those places are rare. Even if you transported yourself to Nox'Kartha, then walked to Sha'Demoni, assuming Izthuni did not kill you on sight, you would have to navigate an entire *world* to find one man."

"I'm less worried about navigating the world and more about that Izthuni bit, I'll be honest." Etolié released her face, the distant cries grating.

Would Staella help? Even if she were willing, could she?

A strange and impossible thought welled in Etolié's head. "Khastra, is it a safe assumption that, because I can teleport myself all the way to Celestière, I could teleport myself to the other adjacent plane?"

Khastra's gaze became dark. "Perhaps, but—"

"Yes, yes—safety. But I wouldn't be passing through the Temple of Izthuni. Izthuni wouldn't take him there—Casvir being in our world means he could just teleport back. It negates the point of stranding him in Sha'Demoni."

"I do not like what you are saying, Etolié."

It was a stupid thing to do. Celestials weren't exactly beloved in the demonic realm. "I have to try. This war is lost without Casvir."

Khastra's breath fogged in the chill night. To Etolié's surprise, she said nothing—merely pulled her against her chest and hugged her tight.

Etolié clung to her. "Will you be all right without me?"

"I will call for the viceroy," Khastra replied, and at that, Etolié was almost glad she was leaving.

"Not what I meant, but solid plan."

Khastra's lips brushed her hair. Etolié's heart soared at the gesture, and she wondered if she'd ever be used to it. "Do not worry for me. You must save that for you. You reek of magic, and that will attract the residents like flies to honey. Use as little as possible. Wield my name as a weapon. None would dare touch what is mine, even in Izthuni's realm."

Staella had said something similar. The thought was certainly intriguing.

When they parted, Etolié blew a kiss. "Wish me luck."

"You have always made your own," Khastra replied, adoration in her features. "I do not care if you return victorious or not—simply swear you shall return."

"You got it, Beefcake," Etolié said with a wink, because winks generated confidence, which she was currently lacking.

She thought of her momma's house, far away, yet merely a barrier apart from her world. She brushed across that barrier, the one leading to Celestière . . . then pushed the other way—

It didn't even hurt.

Etolié blinked and awoke in darkness.

"We may make short work of them," Flowridia said, pride filling her at the thought. She could hardly see in the darkness, yet the sea of death slowly fell beneath her thumb. Hope was a rare thing, yet it fluttered in her heart like a burning ember.

Her influence was small—she was so far away—but it took no effort at all. Casvir was much farther.

"I plan to," came the sultry reply, and Ayla's image shifted between herself and her empress doppelganger—in Flowridia's eyes at least. She wondered what it meant; if she saw through the illusion or if Ayla were slipping. "Though I suppose I do not know what the difference will be, with all this new power. The Bringer of War remains a threat, but at worst I will make an escape."

Flowridia responded by kissing her, uncaring of the guards and sorcerers watching or of General Irons awkwardly looking away. Fear and adrenaline surged; her gentle touch became desperate, mouth parting for her tongue, which Ayla's enthusiastically accepted. With open mouths, they said their goodbye, and when they finally parted, Flowridia's heart palpitated in time with her heavy breathing. "Come back to me."

"We have gone through far too much for you to lose me now," Ayla replied, and she disappeared into a shadow, illusioning a bit of sparkle to make it looked like she had merely stepped into the air.

Flowridia ran to the edge of the wall, quickly joined by General Irons. Far below, the darkness was all encompassing, save for the barest hints of swirling purple wafting from the raised dead. Faint moans rose from the vast field of death, but nothing seemed amiss. Yet the very air held its breath.

And then . . . light.

A radiant beam of silver expanded across the battlefield, catching onto whatever it touched, spreading like the flame it was. In the center, the small figure began a complicated routine, yet with motions as fluid as dew trailing down a leaf. Ayla twirled like a ribbon—like a *weapon*—and the fire moved with her, an extension of herself. A display of grandeur—Ayla moved, and the flame expanded, the Silver Fire a partner more than a weapon. In perfect sync, they danced, bringing death to all they touched, and Flowridia's breath caught for her beauty.

Once, on the fateful night of Marielle's coronation, Flowridia had watched Ayla flicker in and out of her dance like a flame, gracefully stepping through shadow, and felt her very heart and destiny shift. Yet here, Ayla was the flame itself, her control as masterful as Flowridia had ever seen. She was not Alauriel Solviraes, who grasped the tapestry of magic and shot it like a torrent; Ayla pulled the strings of magic in individual, rapid motions, matchless in her control. Despite the power, it remained a work of art, its symmetry an absolute marvel.

This was her love. Her wife. Flowridia had never felt such pride.

The entire battlefield soon illuminated in silver flame, steadily turning to orange. The fire spread as the dead shambled about, highly combustible, it seemed. Flowridia could not hear Ayla's laughter and glee but knew it was there, and well-earned.

"Get down!" Irons suddenly cried, and Flowridia heard distant screams growing ever closer. She froze, seeking the danger, when a hand grabbed her dress and ripped her back—

Narrowly stealing her from the grasp of a horrid, winged gargoyle. With fangs and claws and wings sewn on in messy stitches, the abominable undead looked to have once been a man. It screamed in her face, but Irons slashed his sword, tearing through its wing. The creature left, but another plucked a guard from the wall and disappeared into the sky.

More monsters swooped in, most stopped by the line of sorcerers but some broke through. Flowridia screamed as Irons shoved her to the ground and severed the head from a monster's torso. It fell in pieces. "I think they're targeting you," he said, then swung once more, successfully warding off another attacker.

"Casvir isn't here," Flowridia said, quickly righting herself. "It means someone else is controlling them." There was only one other someone; realization came in tandem with her curse. "Damn, Murishani. We're in danger—"

A great *roar* echoed across the sky.

Flowridia lost her focus, breath seizing to see a great dragon soaring toward them. "It's strong enough to break the wall," she muttered, and Irons nodded knowingly.

"We anticipated that." He looked to his soldiers and barked out orders, and those manning canons on the wall ran to their stations. "Fortunately, you said it can't breathe fire—"

A torrent of flame escaped Valeuron's throat. It attempted to blast the soldiers upon the wall, but the sorcerers' shields held it back with ease. The dragon swooped up, narrowly avoiding hitting the shield himself.

"Fire at will!"

Explosions echoed from the wall, as canons shot toward the great creature. Yet they were crippled from the simple fact that they could not fire inward, toward the city— where the dragon attempted to go. Flame poured from his mouth, spreading across the shield, which undulated like a bubble over the expanse that was Neolan.

"The fire is new," Flowridia said, breathless as the dragon left the city's bounds—only to breathe fire upon the buildings beyond the walls. All were evacuated, but their homes erupted in flame. "Nox'Kartha's ingenuity is endless."

"I've noticed," Irons muttered bitterly, and the canons resumed firing as the dragon destroyed the outer buildings.

One finally hit, tearing a hole into the beast's wing. Valeuron did not roar for that—he could not feel pain—but his flight did falter.

"Aim for the head!"

Below, Ayla held the dead at bay, turning the battlefield into a field of silver and orange death. But up here, panic rose. A volley of arrows shot toward Valeuron, though they had little effect. Only a second blast from a canon caused him to falter. With another hole in the same wing, he teetered, gliding toward the battlefield.

"Correct me if I'm wrong, but they won't want to risk his demise," Irons said.

"They won't, but he can be repaired like a machine. He's completely mindless—"

Her words were stolen when Irons grabbed her arms and dragged her away—the dragon swooped toward them—

And *crashed* into the wall.

Debris flew about, pummeling soldiers, raining down upon the city below. Covered in stone, the dragon tried to shake it off, but the soldiers did not wait for orders—those still standing released a barrel of oil.

Valeuron did not scream, but Flowridia squirmed as the oil burned through the thinner membranes of his wings. When he tried to rise, more of the wall fell.

General Irons held his sword aloft and charged. As the dragon's neck rose above the ramparts of the wall, Irons leapt and brought the sword down—

Nearly severing its head.

Flowridia rushed toward them, realizing that instead of plummeting to his death, he had landed on the partially bisected neck. The dragon rose as a mindless beast, but General Irons hacked his sword against its meaty neck, aiming for the cartilage between the thick bone.

Holy light suddenly radiated from his figure, granted by his goddess. With a final burst of strength, light poured into Valeuron, burning him at the seams, in tandem with a swipe of his sword.

Valeuron's head fell as a separate piece—General Irons with it.

The headless body stumbled back, flailing aimlessly before collapsing onto the battlefield. Despite the cacophony beyond, silence settled. Flowridia stared into the rising dust, as did the soldiers behind her.

Then, from the rubble, a familiar voice cried, *"I'm fine! Light the bastard on fire!"*

Flowridia laughed from relief, joining in the ensuing cheers. Soldiers lit their arrows with torches and shot them toward Valeuron's body—and oh, how lovely it felt to watch him burn.

Somewhere, wherever in the Beyond a dragon might be, Flowridia prayed Valeuron felt true peace.

"Set sorcerers on the wall to defend it! We need to patch this wall!"

A greater battle still waged around them, and Flowridia resumed her post—the goal now to deflect the undead from the hole in the wall.

Screeching filled the air. The gargoyles had returned. Flowridia ducked, knowing she was a target, horrified when one of the guards beside her was plucked from his post.

Something grabbed her hair—

But then a severed, clawed hand fell beside her. "We need to get you a weapon," came General Irons' voice, and the rush of relief made her limbs cold. He had come back.

Short-lived, for another dove at her, only to be beheaded by General Irons.

But the next grabbed him instead.

Flowridia screamed as his sword clattered to the stone floor—

He was already gone. A speck in the night.

Reality settled like a rock, but she had no time to mourn. Amidst the cacophony of so many other people fighting for their lives, what was one?

Claws sunk into her dress. Flowridia's stomach lurched when she was launched into the air.

In the moment of disorientation, she saw the burning fields surrounding Neolan; she saw a dancer in its midst, oblivious to the danger on the wall. A second horde of death rapidly approached the broken wall, and Flowridia feared what would come of it. The majority of their sorcerers were focused on guarding the destroyed gate. She looked behind and saw her captor, its gruesome visage bearing little resemblance to humanity anymore.

One breath . . .

And release.

Light poured through her veins, seeping from her skin; the creature screeched as her holy aura burned its body. It plummeted toward the ground; Flowridia's stomach rose to her throat.

The gargoyle struggled to right itself with its burned wings but managed to vault instead of crash—sending Flowridia tumbling across the charred earth.

On the ground, Flowridia quickly ran her hands across her body, pulse rapid as her mind settled into the present. She surely bore bruises, but no broken bones, and she no longer knew what god to thank for her stroke of luck.

Far away from the walls and their tenuous safety, Flowridia scrambled to her feet, the battlefield illuminated by fire. "Ayla!" she cried, but she did not see her love. Instead, she saw approaching monsters, too mindless to fear fire.

She braced herself, unafraid of the dead, when a new voice chilled her blood: *"How unfortunate."*

From the fire emerged a grandiose shadow, covered in ash yet clean of blood. Flame reflected off the dark metal armor, different than what Flowridia knew. Yet General Khastra's eyes remained cold and impassive as eerie shadows flickered across her face. The hammer strapped to her back flashed like an omen of death. "Imperator Casvir is gone, but I remain. He wants you alive because he is sentimental, but now he is not here; I want you dead because you are a nuisance."

Flowridia took a small step back, wary of the encroaching dead. "And here I thought we were friends."

"We were," Khastra replied, casually removing the weapon from her back. "Then Ayla Darkleaf stabbed Etolié in the throat. Our bargain is done. I will dedicate your death to my mother when I deliver your head on a spike to your wife."

The hammer might be unwieldy, but Khastra could throw it, could crush her in seconds. Khastra was neither alive nor dead—and thus immune to both branches of magic.

Flowridia had one chance.

"I can make this painless—"

The plants withdrew; the earth unsettled. Khastra fell into a sinkhole.

Flowridia ran. "Ayla!" she screamed, and when Khastra hoisted herself out, Flowridia bid the plants to entangle her. She slowed to direct them, wincing each time the general tore herself free of the grass and roots. She was no mere undead slave; she was War Incarnate, a demi-goddess, and when her body suddenly twisted and grew, Flowridia accepted that she was about to die.

Khastra transformed—Flowridia did not stay to watch and instead ran to the wall, dodging fire and undead. "Ayla!" she screamed once more, yet there was no sign of her love.

A horrid laugh echoed across the battlefield, and she swore the very earth trembled. Flowridia kept running, even as Demoni words bid the shadows to rise, even as pounding footsteps rapidly overtook her. Flowridia felt a shift in the wind and tripped—

Narrowly missing a gigantic hammer, hurled through the air to crush her.

The weapon did not stop, and she swore she heard the impact against the castle wall. This was how Casvir would win—his greatest weapon was no weapon at all, but the general he had stolen. She sat up in time to meet the Bringer of War, her monstrous form somehow larger than what Flowridia knew.

Flowridia was quickly running out of ideas, trapped beneath the monster's leering, hungry stare. "Khastra, please," she pled, but the gargantuan half-demon held out an impossibly hulking arm, catching her weapon when it flew back into her grasp.

In the same fluid motion, she directed it down upon Flowridia's head.

Darkness overtook her, but not pain. When Flowridia opened her eyes, the world had become cold and new. "What are you doing here?" Ayla asked, her face dirtied from blood and dirt and ichor.

Here she stood, in Sha'Demoni. Flowridia's heart restarted, fear causing her breaths to shallow. "I was . . . I was dropped."

Though visibly furious, Ayla embraced her, but just as quickly released. "I am taking you back."

Flowridia nodded, unwilling to argue.

Ayla scooped her up, cradling her, when an enormous, clawed hand ripped through the shadows and dragged them into the light—

Flowridia collapsed, Ayla atop her, having fallen back onto the burning battlefield. The Bringer of War leered above them, nothing familiar in those glowing eyes, nothing resembling a soul. She roared in their faces, bestial and deafening, and Ayla scrambled to her feet, wrenching Flowridia up with her.

Again, they phased into Sha'Demoni—but, again, the Bringer of War dragged them back. Ayla kept her footing this time, even as the monster all but threw them. The Bringer of War hoisted her hammer in the air and swung.

Ayla ripped Flowridia aside, narrowly dodging. "Run," she spat, then pushed Flowridia toward the castle—

And leapt toward the Bringer of War, gracefully twirling like the dancer she was, silver flame spewing from her outstretched hand.

Flowridia obeyed, unafraid of the sea of burning death—not when offered the choice between that and the legendary monster. Still, she peeked behind, in time to see Ayla dance and dodge the bulky Bringer of War's attacks.

Perfectly matched, these two champions of their respective gods—the half-demon was no simpleton, her movements far quicker than her size should have allowed. The vast hammer swung, and Ayla flew like an acrobat to counter it, the beauty of her fire never ceasing. All that was accomplished was for Ayla to lure her away, the Bringer of War apparently distracted by bright objects.

The wall remained impossibly far away. From the sky, horrid screeching relayed the gargoyles' return. The sea of death parted at her will, but their flaming bodies still posed a risk, and when the first of the flying monsters swooped to grab her, she barely ducked. Grabbing her hair, she pressed against the dirt, desperately trying to latch onto their minds—only to be cast out, the splitting pain excruciating as it wracked against her skull.

She nearly cried Ayla's name. She nearly pled for help. Yet a quiet voice within her rose, a voice from memory, bearing the faintest echo of victory:

"Become the greater monster."

Her fury rose. Here she was, cowering in the charred earth, but Flowridia was not a worm—she was the child of a legend; she was the heir to a crown she had rejected but a royal nevertheless; she was the wife to a monster the world feared to even whisper of, who had pledged a slice of her power to her.

But who was she to cling to others' legacies? She was Flowridia Darkleaf, and when the next gargoyle swooped down to grab her, she burned with holy light bright enough to challenge the sun. Within a field of burning dead, she cast her spell, prepared for the earth to tremble at her will.

Her light faded, replaced with a gaseous, purple glow seeping from her pores. The earth shook as the bones of the fallen—ancient and otherwise, thousands of years of war made manifest—unearthed and clattered beneath her feet. The bones piled upon themselves, held together by the darkest of magics and her own stubborn will. Flowridia stood at the helm, rising with the towering structure, a tornado of sorts; a typhoon of death with she at the helm, for the storm moved at her whim.

Flowridia looked at the distant wall; she stood nearly as tall. But nearer raged the battle of silver flame and brute strength, where the Bringer of War bashed her love's body against the ground like a ragdoll and nearly snapped her in two.

She gave her silent command: *Bury her.*

Her storm approached, the display of acrobatics and muscle before it inspiring to behold. Flowridia stood atop her gathered hoard of dead, rode it like a hurricane, then commanded it to scatter—

It happened in a blink. Her stomach dropped as the tower fell in a controlled collapse, the bottom pieces swarming the Bringer of War. The Silver Fire extinguished at Ayla's escape into shadow as the half-demon was buried in undead. The monster roared, grabbing at the individual undead with her fists and throwing them away, but the swarm moved forward to consume her, and when Flowridia felt a rising influence try to steal them away, she shoved it like a slammed door.

Her feet touched the ground, the last of her tower of bone and flesh gone to destroy her enemy. When she heaved a sigh, thick gobs of purple smoke escaped her lungs, the magic woven into her very essence.

A cold hand touched her shoulder. She did not even turn, content to stare upon the carnage. The Bringer of War roared, but Flowridia's judgement stated she would not fall. Time was limited. "Are you all right?" she said to the new presence.

Ayla's touched shifted as she stood beside her, her eyes a black void, fangs long and sharp. The injuries she bore healed before Flowridia's eyes. "She nearly snapped me in half. Silly me, thinking *you* needed protection."

"Oh, I do," Flowridia said, amused at the remark. She smiled, her rage fading, and with it the billowing radiance of power. "Still fragile. Still human. You're practically a demi-god."

The bone crunched as a great hammer suddenly tore through them, though more came to fill the void. Yet, she and Ayla merely stared as the Bringer of War fought the hordes of dead, half-buried still. "Don't discount yourself, darling. A candle is delicate, but it can burn a whole city down."

A thunderous cry echoed from the Bringer of War. Yet behind them came . . . clapping?

They turned, revealing a sole figure on the battlefield, slowly bringing his hands together in applause. "Marvelous work," Murishani said, his smile broad and charming. "What is the Bringer of War against the Chosen of Izthuni and Casvir's favorite plaything? Just a delightful show; I'm truly impressed."

Flowridia glared as he came forward. "What do you want—"

Before she could finish, flame burst from Ayla's outstretched hand. Silver Fire engulfed him, surely searing him alive—

Until something far brighter shone from within.

Ayla's fire ceased, revealing a glowing figure, shining as silver as the moon yet with the brightness of the sun. Murishani laughed, his figure godly as he held out a hand. "Thank you. Now here's something back."

Ayla shoved Flowridia aside just as Silver Fire engulfed her. Murishani controlled it with all the finesse of a seasoned sorcerer, and a ghastly realization settled upon Flowridia as she watched from the ground.

He could touch souls. He could travel through the planes. He wielded Silver Fire.

Murishani was . . .

"Surprised? You shouldn't be."

Where Ayla had been, Flowridia saw nothing all. Murishani, his silver flame having dissipated, stood beside her. He brought his hand down, a sizzling line following. "You think Casvir can do this himself? Please."

In the brief moment of Ayla's reappearance, Murishani summoned his flame anew, blinding her before she could strike him in the heart—

He grabbed Flowridia's arm and shoved her through the portal.

She stumbled onto a cold dungeon floor, the portal instantly closing behind her. Scrambling to her feet, she saw only a strange, stone box in the center of the room, but the door called to her. She ran, wrenching it with all her strength. It didn't budge. "Help!" she cried, but then another presence stepped in from pure air.

"Miss me?" Murishani said, and the statement lingered, chilling her blood. "Your intended will burn the world looking for you, and I commend her for that." He lifted the lid of the strange, person-sized stone box, revealing nothing but dust. "A pity she won't find you."

Flowridia stood tall, refusing to bend to this man's will. "She'll strip you into a thousand pieces if you don't let me go."

"Will she though?" His smile looked more like a regretful cringe. "It's not as easy as you'd think, slaying a Solviran necromancer."

"How are you a Solviraes?" she said, the pulsing dread of her own damning past threatening to drown her.

"Emperor Fahrel—your dearest Lara's great-grandfather—loved his whores," Murishani cooed, slowly approaching, "and my mother loved the unborn baby inside her and ran away before they could discover she had conceived a bastard. That's all. A mother's love. There are few forces in this world more powerful and more damning."

He leered far too close. Flowridia stood tall, even as he backed her against the door, their respective skirts brushing at their hems. He stood taller, his experience and power far outweighing her own, but she refused to look him anywhere but in his eye. "If you touch me, I'll be your last."

He had the audacity to laugh. "Oh, you pompous little thing!" he said, amusement in the words. "My bed is always open to you, but you have grossly misunderstood the danger." When he suddenly grabbed her hair, her necrotic magic burst—only to be absorbed by his silver flame. She struggled as he dragged her, his strength against her own, hair tearing out when he yanked her toward the box. Screaming and stomping, she managed to hit his boot with her heel but cursed her bare feet. When she sank her teeth into his arm, he slapped her, his strength enough to make her ears ring.

She fought him; she beat him; she struggled, but when he threw her, she fell—

Into the box.

He slammed the lid shut.

Yet there was no darkness. The smooth stone did not glow, yet ambient light shone upon every surface, each corner, even her hands as she beat on the lid.

She realized then . . . there was no shadow.

No light source. And so, no shadow.

She recalled the story of Tazel Fireborn, who enchanted a coffin to hold no shadow to imprison The Endless Night. And four-hundred years later—

Casvir had found it.

She heard nothing from beyond, nothing to indicate if she were still alone. Her beating heart raced as she pressed against the top, but it wouldn't budge. Frustrated tears fell, and when she finally exhausted herself, her body slumped back, her hair thick around her face, suffocating in the small space.

Ayla would search for her, but there were no shadows here to tell her where to go.

Within her, defeat pulsed hot and heavy.

Chapter 36

Sha'Demoni was cold in ways Etolié had never experienced before. She wasn't affected by literal cold, but something in the atmosphere spoke of dread, and as she gazed upon the shadowy horizon, corporeal spots of light bespoke that she was watched.

Etolié, with her wings and gleaming aura, might as well have screamed her angelic heritage at the top of her lungs, and the fact remained that residents of Sha'Demoni weren't so keen on their Celestière counterparts.

Strangely, she had no headache. Torn on Khastra's warning, she decided to err on the side of caution and use magic only if the need were dire—consequentially, she traversed completely naked through the foreign realm. At least demons didn't care about mortal nudity, but she was left with quite the quandary—either glowing like a lighthouse but potentially finding her quarry faster or using magic and attracting every demon on this side of Sha'Demoni seeking a host. Living demons needed permission, but these shadowy entities were something different. Etolié swore she lit up the entire horizon.

Was Izthuni still nearby? Etolié watched every shifting shadow with suspicion, knowing she was well past Neolan itself by now. The terrain held evidence of the mortal realm, with dark silhouettes of trees, but they were not corporeal— except when they were, and that was confusing, but Etolié didn't have time to question the physics of three overlapping words. No one did.

The grey sky held no moon, no light at all. Etolié wings cast a golden glow, and she remained solid and colorful, an anomaly in the shifting, hazy world. In the distance, she swore the eyes of the watching demons had grown larger and closer.

Time was as elusive as clutching heaps of sand. Etolié walked, and the atmosphere shifted so quickly she could not say where she had landed; perhaps she had reached Nox'Kartha, yet somehow, she doubted it. Staelash? Would she at least recognize the sea?

Khastra had said many times that the continent her mother ruled held color and substance, an alien world of beauty, but the vast majority of Sha'Demoni had been destroyed, leaving large bastions of wasteland, with residents more dead than alive, shadows with no bodies.

At the top of a hill, the world spread out before her. Etolié stared upon the horizon, seeking any sign of the imperator. "Hello!" she cried, yet the sound wavered, as though underwater. "Casvir! Imperator First and Last! I'm here to save your ass!"

Nothing. She heaved a sigh and spread her wings, gliding down the expansive hill. There was no airflow that she could feel, but Etolié's wings weren't reliant on that—though she suspected something like a bird would simply fall.

When she landed, the footsteps she left in the foreign dirt faded as she lifted each foot. The monochromatic landscape spread out perfectly flat before her, leaving no room for any watching demons to hide.

And watch they did.

As she marched forward, the encroaching creatures were ever-present. Great shadowy forms watched her curiously, some as small as she; some as vast as the Bringer of War herself, transformed and monstrous. Most bore extra limbs; all had glowing pits for eyes. The residents neared, not trying to hide their motions or intentions as they watched, no malice in their misty visages. Only intrigue.

It wasn't until the corporeal shadows were a stone's throw away that Etolié spoke up. "Hello, everyone." The shadows gave no recognition of her words, and she cursed her lack of fluency in Demoni. "I'm just passing through. Looking for a friend. He doesn't seem like the type to get himself possessed by any of you lovely folk."

Her words only spurred them into action. A few dared to approach, and Etolié stepped back—yet they came from behind too. Etolié was surrounded. She spread her wings wide. "I'm not afraid to fly away," she said, despite facing a few who reach a good fifteen feet tall—and would have no difficulty ripping her straight out of the air.

"I'm looking for someone," she repeated, "and he's kind of a big deal where he's from, just so you know. Imperator Casvir of Nox'Kartha? Ever heard of him?"

They likely hadn't. They gave no indication of having heard her.

Wispy appendages stroked her wings; she curled them close to her body. Fear gripped her, but with it came the realization that she had dropped the wrong name. "You know who will be pissed if I don't return is Khastra."

The name did give them pause. A few even shrunk back.

"Yes, that Khastra—eldest daughter of Ku'Shya, the Bringer of War."

At Ku'Shya's name, they flinched. A few even hissed.

"Ku'Shya? Don't like that name? Well, the Queen Bitch of Sha'Demoni is practically my mother-in-law, so don't piss me off, all right?"

Though they lived within Izthuni's domain, the name brought palpable terror. A few disappeared back into the shadowy terrain; a few roared, though it delivered no sound.

"Roar to you too, ya wispy bastard!" Etolié said, and when she cast light from her wings once more, they shrunk. "I belong to Khastra, and that's a big fucking deal!"

The thought that Khastra was effectively a princess had never occurred to her in so many words before. But Khastra would inherit Ku'Shya's legacy if the War Goddess ever kicked it, and as Etolié watched the last of the shadowy fuckers vanish into the terrain, she realized it truly was, in fact, a big fucking deal.

"Huh," she said aloud, because shacking up with the heir to the most powerful throne in all the realms hadn't ever been a goal of hers, but someday—whether it be tomorrow or ten thousand years from now—Queen Bitch of Sha'Demoni would be Khastra's future.

Neat.

Consort Etolié of Sha'Demoni had a helluva ring to it, and Etolié skipped along, more than happy to fantasize about that.

Flowridia swore the air had gotten thinner. The coffin hadn't been designed for a creature who needed to breathe.

She had long ago ceased yelling, instead trying to conserve as many breaths as possible. If this had been Murishani's plan to 'accidentally' kill her, it was brilliant.

Consequently, she was left with her thoughts.

One in particular: Murishani had the Silver Fire.

She couldn't have known, yet she berated herself, crying softly in her small confines. She could have slit his throat over Ayla's corpse instead and saved so much heartbreak. Lara could have been spared. Perhaps if she had just told Casvir . . . asked him more of the Silver Fire . . .

But he had given no indication, and she supposed wisely so. One didn't simply advertise that they had a bastard Solviraes as their second-in-command.

Bitterly, she wondered if that had been Murishani's incentive for pushing her along on her journey—to give her a target before she could research a little more.

Curse him. Flowridia sobbed, vowing his death if she ever escaped.

Oh, Ayla, Ayla . . . She willed her thoughts to reach her love, who must've been frantic. Her vision held the barest hints of blurriness around the edges, slow exhaustion settling in. She had time, but not enough. Not enough for the war to end or for Casvir to return and ask of her whereabouts. *Ayla, please—*

Scratching came from outside.

Flowridia gasped, her hope surging. "Hello?!" she cried, and the lid lifted, just for a moment. "Help, please!"

The coffin glowed, the eternal light it emanated growing bright, only to extinguish entirely as the spell dissipated.

The lid lifted. Flowridia immediately sat up, heaving great breaths over the side, blindly wiping her tears as oxygen filled her lungs properly. "Thank—"

Her words failed for who stood before her.

It was the vision from her nightmares, yet she stood so serene. In a demure stance, clutching the folds of her fine gown, was Empress Alauriel Solviraes—rotted, her eyes silver but dull and glazed, throat stitched shut, no doubt the only thing keeping her head on her shoulders. Her hair was impeccably braided, yet she remained a gruesome sight.

And in her eyes, those milky eyes, was anguish.

This was no illusion. This was what Casvir had found. This is what he had shown Etolié. This . . .

Flowridia managed to stumble out, though her words were frozen on ice. The image of Lara staggering to rise from the swampy water, her chest blown open, bombarded her memory, of blood spraying when Soliel had cut her throat—

Upon a second glance, Lara bore little slits at her wrists and fingers, where Flowridia had helped the blood to drain faster. No doubt, they covered her beneath her dress.

Lara glanced at the closed door. "I can send you back to Solvira. Murishani won't notice until it's too late."

Her voice echoed, barest hints of magic in it. Flowridia could say nothing; her mouth opened, yet her tongue remained stale.

"Flowridia, there isn't much time," Lara said, and she offered a hand.

To hear that voice and not Ayla's mockery . . . "Oh, gods," Flowridia whispered, and she sank to her knees, tears falling anew. She could not look away from this pinnacle of horror, from the hell Lara had been granted—instead of the Beyond, like she deserved.

Casvir knew the truth. Of course he came to claim the body. Of course he stole her from an afterlife of peace. Of course he used her as the catalyst for war.

Her heart cracked and bled as guilt unparalleled swamped her.

"Flowridia . . ."

Her words faded when Flowridia grabbed the hem of Lara's skirt, weeping at her feet. "I'm sorry," she managed. "Lara, I'm sorry. I'm so sorry . . ." Her tears stained the fine fabrics. For all her sins, this threatened to upset the pile, enough to topple her already unstable sanity.

Lara, once an empress—now a slave.

Amidst her tears came quiet words. "Perhaps. But you would do it again, for her."

Flowridia looked up with swollen eyes, still hunched before her, a supplicant before a woman too lovely for this world.

Lara's face remained impassive, until the barest hint of a smile twisted her lip, sorrowful as it was. "Congratulations on your wedding. She's everything you deserve."

A monster. Lara didn't have to say it. A monster, just like herself. Shame filled her, to see the rotten fruits of her labor.

Yet Lara's voice remained kind; perhaps that was the grandest insult of all.

"I don't blame you for my fate," Lara continued. "Casvir will do as he will." Her voice caught, though Flowridia suspected Lara lacked the biological function to cry. "I regret many things, but dying in the attempt to save your life isn't one of them."

Flowridia forced herself to stand and face the woman who did not deserve to see her tears. Her guilt was not Lara's burden to bear. "Why are you helping me?"

"My country fights for its soul," Lara said, her subtle anguish apparent. "Yet no matter who stands triumphant among the ruins, Solvira ends. There are no winners, no matter who sits on the throne—whether it be Imperator Casvir or Empress Ayla Darkleaf, Wielder of the Silver Flame. Should the fighting continue, it shall be a kingdom of ash. Etolié sold herself into Casvir's service to try and soothe the transition of power, but her sacrifice will be in vain, for how the pieces have fallen." Lara's vacant eyes looked to the floor, her voice lowering. "And I am a fool shut in a tower, holding a shadow of my former abilities, who can do the least amount of harm by staying here and staying silent. But I would like to do one selfish thing."

Again, she offered her hand.

Flowridia did not understand it at all. As she went to accept, she suddenly paused. "May I heal you?"

Lara frowned. "You cannot."

"I can," she said, for perhaps it would selfishly alleviate her own guilt. "I know it fixes nothing, but . . ." She released a shaky breath, determined to staunch her tears. "If it would bring you even a modicum of peace, let me."

Lara's hand dropped. Her countenance twisted as she fought what Flowridia feared was anguish. "All right," she said, though it was hardly audible at all.

Trembling, Flowridia brought a hand up to touch Lara's cheek, well-used to the dead and their putrid flesh. Yet, to call Lara that bore the stain of disrespect, for she was kind, she was good, and she had deserved none of this.

A victim of Flowridia's wicked legacy.

Stealing a breath, she let her magic flow, radiant purple swirling to cover Lara's skin. Flowridia bid her cold body to heal, to seal the rotted bits, to receive life anew, and watched it obey. Lara's face gained fresh life, no longer sagging, her color restored, and when her throat began to seal, she quickly tugged at the strings stitching it shut, unravelling it in tandem with the miracle repairing it.

Yet the final moment came when her eyes, those beautiful, unmistakable eyes, became bright, their silver sheen restored.

Lara looked nearly alive, and when she gazed upon her hands, touched her face and neck, tears welled in her eyes.

Wetness streamed down her cheeks. Lara shut her eyes, her arms wrapping around herself. She was silent, and Flowridia's heart ached.

This final piece was Casvir's doing, yes. And he would pay. But Flowridia had paved the road for his hellish actions.

"May I ask one thing?" Lara whispered, and Flowridia nodded when she met her eye. "The past is the past, and I can do nothing to change it. But it does not mean I don't wonder. I need to know if I'm lying to myself." Lara's voice caught, yet hope shone in those beautiful, silver eyes. "When you kissed me on the battlefield, did you mean it?"

Flowridia looked back upon feelings she'd buried, upon a past she'd come to peace with and released . . .

The road had once diverged, and she had chosen her path. But once, it had been a choice. The answer was so simple and damning, even if it didn't matter anymore. "Yes."

Amidst Lara's tears came the barest hints of a smile.

"You could come with me," Flowridia said, her conscience unsure of what this meant, where it would go. Lara looked up in shock. "I could try and steal you from Casvir's control, or I could free your soul and let you move on. I'll burn your body so it can't be used . . ."

Her words trailed away at Lara's soft rebuttal. "To what end? If he wants me, he'll take me one way or another. It is what men like him do—they take, and they take, and nothing will ever be enough."

Flowridia thought of Soliel and his prophecy, the vision of the future where Casvir was God. She struggled to accept it, yet in her heart she knew it was true. "There must be something—"

"Flowridia . . ."

Flowridia stared into the visage of the woman she once could have loved, the haunting refrain of rejection sounding before she could even speak it. Their lost future was not a question anymore—not when she wore a ring upon her finger, the symbol of a sacred vow.

". . . time is short," Lara said, the finality clear. "I have to send you to Solvira now."

When Lara offered her hand, Flowridia accepted, clasping it in both of hers. "This is not the end. I will fight for you."

"Flowridia—"

"Twice now you've saved my life, yet I have destroyed yours. But I swear to you, Lara—you will have peace."

Astonishment slacked Lara's jaw, her silver eyes curious, though whatever she sought, Flowridia couldn't guess. "You're different."

"That's a given—"

"No," Lara said, her interruption as gentle as her soul. "When I met you, you were small. Everything about you, from your stance to your confidence. Now . . ." Wariness showed in Lara's countenance, darkness clouding those haunting eyes. ". . . whatever your fate, I doubt the world will ever forget you."

Flowridia felt the final severance, and though it cut, it did not bleed. But although her heart did not belong to Lara, it ached for her, nevertheless. "I promise," Flowridia repeated, though the path to victory was shrouded in fog.

Lara lightly squeezed her hands. "Are you ready?"

Flowridia nodded. There was nothing more to say.

"Prepare your stomach."

Flowridia shut her eyes as the world tilted . . .

And when the weight holding her hands disappeared, she opened her eyes, standing before the gates of the Solviran Castle.

The newfound knowledge that Etolié could just scream, *"Ku'Shya!"* in face of any passing demons made her jaunt through Sha'Demoni infinitely more satisfying and amusing. Etolié was dickish enough to admit that.

It was a power she used liberally, happily singing all the while, trying to draw as much attention to herself as possible and hopefully lure Casvir. Eionei had a plethora of songs dedicated to the Goddess of War, and while they weren't exactly flattering, they were filled with the offending goddess' name. When she forgot any words, she just sang the word, *"Khastra!"* in tune, and so far it had worked wonders. All distant shadows had scattered. She was met with only the eerie, vacant landscape.

As it was, while Etolié couldn't say with any confidence how much time had passed, she had catnapped under a shadow tree at one point—after drawing the offending names into the dirt around her and hoping for the best.

In hindsight, she should have expected attention.

Etolié moved along, carefree as she sang:

Ku'Shya's appetite is great
In summertime, she lays her bait

By autumn, she'll have had her fill
Then load her stomach up with swill

In winter season, she'll collapse
For three long months, she takes her nap

When springtime comes, she's on the hunt
To fill her mouth, as well as her . . .

Her words faded when an enormous shadow suddenly covered her. Etolié stopped, sensing a presence behind her, but when she turned, she had to look more *up* than over.

A demon woman—though perhaps only a girl for how spindly her appendages were—taller than she, perhaps even taller than Khastra, leered over her. Her bottom half was a spider's abdomen, with four skittering legs, but her naked top half bore four arms and four glowing, yellow eyes. Her hair, as long as Etolié was tall, bore elaborate braids, yet while her face held elven features, there was little else mortal about her.

She was not a shadow. She held substance and a daunting aura. Etolié stole a breath to scream a couple of names at the demon's bare stomach, but the girl said, in heavily accented Solviran Common, "What are you doing?"

The high pitch of her voice reminded Etolié somewhat of her momma, but this girl was far from quiet. "Just looking for a friend."

"Goddess Ku'Shya is hearing news of crazed angel woman screaming at demons. I am assuming that is you."

Etolié had quite a few things to be self-conscious about after those words, but thankfully nudity wasn't one of them, given the demon was as naked as she. "A girl's gotta do what she can to get through a foreign world unmolested. Or unpossessed."

"You are not crazy being?"

"That's subjective, but in this instance, no. I have a method here." Etolié looked her up and down, suddenly frowning as realization slammed her like the Bringer of War's fist. "Hold on. I know you. You're The Coming Dawn."

The Coming Dawn—who had once tried to kidnap Flowers, had worked with Mereen to slay Ayla Darkleaf, and was the youngest sister of Etolié's favorite demon. The half-demon girl—though she had to be at least a thousand years old—nodded curiously. "Very few mortals are knowing me."

"My name is Etolié," she said, offering a hand, and even before she could add the clarifying titles, The Coming Dawn—Kah'Sheen, Etolié recalled—perked up in realization.

"You are Magister Etolié?" Although she had mispronounced Etolié's name in the exact same manner as her sister, Kah'Sheen appeared overjoyed, her eerie face adorable as it lit up in a smile. "Khastra is writing about you, yes! I am hearing all about you!"

Several implications fell together—most notably the fact that Khastra wrote home, specifically about *Etolié*, being the most important one. Etolié found the idea rather flattering. "Didn't know she talked about me."

"Oh, yes. For many years, yes. I am especially enjoying stories about you and the ginger man."

Ginger man . . . Clarence Vors? "Huh."

"Etolié, I am wanting to meet you for a long time. But why are you in Sha'Demoni? All alone?"

"I don't know if your mother knows about the war in Solvira—" Etolié cut herself off, because her mother was the literal Goddess of War. "All right, stupid thing to say."

"She is knowing, yes," Kah'Sheen affirmed, her face pleasant and thankfully not judgmental.

"Long story short, Izthuni stole Imperator Casvir of Nox'Kartha and dropped him somewhere here. I'm supposed to find him."

Kah'Sheen frowned, the gaze of her four eyes difficult to decipher and thus kinda spooky. "This is a large world, Etolié."

"Yes, but in theory, he didn't get a big head start."

Kah'Sheen nodded, hopefully not judging what Etolié was now realizing was an insane task. "May I be offering assistance? I am not liking Casvir, but I am liking Endless Night even less."

Etolié hoped she didn't look too eager. "I would be very grateful."

"It is the least I can be doing. You are my sister, yes? I can help."

Etolié's crusty heart warmed at that. "I will happily accept a sister. Thank you."

Kah'Sheen's ensuing giggle sparked endearment in Etolié's heart. "Come with me. I am suspecting you are well off the path."

She followed the charming half-demon across the barren landscape.

Across the indigo sky, the barest hope of daylight shone as a faint line on the horizon. Uncertain of where else to go, Flowridia returned to the wall, greeted by a battalion of sorrowful soldiers. "Consort Flowridia, we feared the worst," one said.

"I am well. What of my wife?"

"She informed us you had been stolen by the viceroy, but she hasn't been seen since—"

A great *boom* shook the wall. Flowridia stumbled into the man's arms. Instinctively, she glanced down the outside of the wall, surprised to see the Bringer of War far below, combating what appeared to be glowing figments.

"The Bringer of War leads the undead," the man said, "but so far our sorcerers have kept her at bay. Their numbers are dwindling, so she can be their focus. I think we may survive the night."

Flowridia cast her gaze to the vast expanse beyond the wall. Flickering embers of flame still illuminated scattered bits, but most had burned themselves out. "Nox'Kartha cannot create more troops until Casvir has returned from Sha'Demoni. Burn all the bodies; might as well make it as difficult as possible for them."

"Your majesty, there is one you should see."

Flowridia's stomach sank as she was led past piles of dead men and women stacked along a section of the wall, ravaged by claws and teeth. These were but a fraction of the casualties, simply the ones not dropped into the battlefield or raised to join the ranks.

But one did stand out, and Flowridia's eyes immediately filled with tears.

In many ways, it was a relief to know General Irons would not join the Deathless Army, that his body would be burned and put to proper rest. But Flowridia's heart shattered to gaze upon her friend, this man she once hated. She knelt beside his mutilated form, his broken neck an awful sight, the gouges in his armor revealing muscle and bone. Despite her betrayal, he had defended her with his life. He had died to save her.

Tears fell down her face as she gently shut the white slits of his eyes, despondent to feel his cold skin. She placed a lingering kiss upon his forehead. "May Sol Kareena bring you peace," she whispered, unsure of what else to say. She rose, unashamed of her tears as she looked to the man who had led her. "Burn his body as well. Inform his wife. Tell her he died to save me. He was a hero."

When the men moved to obey, Flowridia left, unsure of how to reach her beloved wife. Daylight would come soon, yet darkness lingered within the city below. She took idle steps toward it, ignored by the soldiers who cleaned up the dead.

Once on the ground, a dark patch of alleyway sparked the beginnings of an impossible plan. The vacant streets meant she would not be disturbed as she trudged toward it, exhausted from fear, from sorrow—the weight of this night would never be forgotten.

She thought of Lara, remembered her words, and knew something had to change.

In the meantime, she sat in the darkness and stared into the blackest patches, recalling Ayla's words from a confession-filled night—and searched for eyes.

Silence settled. No one moved beyond, confined to their homes for safety. People who would die the moment the walls were breached—when they were breached, her gut knew. Whether it be a day or a year from now, if they did not retaliate, Neolan would be lost.

This was what Lara feared. More than the victor, she feared the deaths of hundreds of thousands.

Flowridia stared into the darkness and saw nothing.

Shutting her eyes, she let her senses expand. The shadow demons were not quite alive, but also not among the dead. She recalled the half-dead baby stolen too soon from life and sought the realm between life and death, pressing against the darkness, seeking any cracks she could.

And though she strained as she pressed, she swore the shadows parted.

Something watched.

Several somethings watched.

Flowridia clung to the sensation, and though she saw nothing move when she opened her eyes, she chose to trust. "I need help," she said to no one, yet she still felt the invisible presences watching. People feared these shadowed demons, yet Ayla had once danced among them as a tiny girl. They hadn't hurt her. They were not innately evil. "I need to find Ayla Darkleaf. Do you know the name? Tell her I'm here. Tell her Flowridia is here. She's home."

The presences all disappeared.

They wouldn't understand the words, but perhaps they understood the names. Flowridia's senses retracted, exhausted from the mental strain. Her posture slumped, her dress surely soiled from the dirty stone.

Lara was still here. Her mind clung to that, refusing to relinquish that damning truth.

Lara was afraid.

Lara had *saved* her.

Flowridia's head fell into her hands, her hair falling around her like a shade. Here she stood upon a legacy thousands of years old, married in on a lie, handed the responsibility of hundreds of thousands—many of whom would rather die than pledge to Imperator Casvir.

Yet, Lara had said . . . Etolié had . . .

Flowridia didn't know what it meant, but she did know Etolié would never attach herself to a cause that would result in the murder of hundreds of thousands.

Yet to walk away would be a betrayal to Ayla. It would be a betrayal to Irons, who would never again return home to a wife that loved him.

All the world had changed, and Flowridia felt dizzy in the aftermath.

As she sat in the dark alleyway, the sun finally cast its light over the horizon, and her love ran out of a shadow.

Ayla's face bore evidence of tears, and she fell onto her knees, immediately bombarding Flowridia with her small body. "Oh, Flowra, Flowra . . ." Ayla sobbed, smoothing her hair, clinging tight enough to bruise, and Flowridia held her, heart swelling beyond her chest to see her again. "When he took you, I thought . . ."

"I know. Ayla, it's all right." Flowridia kissed her hair, her very soul rejoicing to hold her. "Take me to the castle. I'll tell you everything."

Ayla nodded, but she did not move yet. She simply held tight, a shattered soul, trusting Flowridia to gather the pieces again.

Flowridia chose to savor the moment of peace.

When they finally stepped through the threshold of her bedroom, Demitri immediately assaulted her with kisses. *Lady Ayla said he took you! What happened!*

"Exactly as she said, but I escaped," Flowridia said, soothing him with her hands and kisses of her own.

"Flowra, what happened?" Ayla pled, her touch ever-present. "Did he hurt you?"

"No. Well, he dragged me by the hair into a box, but that was the worst of it." Flowridia left Demitri to hold Ayla's face in her hands, the new understanding of her abominable prison filling her with anguish. "He put me somewhere the shadows couldn't find me—your old prison. Your shadow-less coffin."

Ayla's grief twisted into cruelty. "Oh, he'll die."

"Ayla, there's more. He put me in there hoping I would suffocate to death, but . . ." Her words faltered, for here stood Ayla, her wife, the love of her life . . .

Flowridia couldn't begin to imagine how she would take this news.

"I was rescued," she continued, bracing herself for the unknown, "by Alauriel Solviraes."

Ayla's expression became vacant. She said nothing at all; merely remained still.

"Casvir found where we put the body. She . . . She saved my life. She sent me here, back to you."

Ayla's touch fell away, her visage inscrutable, though it barely shifted at all. "And that's all she did?"

"I healed her," Flowridia said, tension rising between them. "She was rotting away, so I restored her. As a thank you. As a penance, paltry as it was."

Any ambiguity in Ayla's countenance shifted, cracks appearing in her thin mask of indifference. "I suppose she would be more fuckable that way," Ayla spat, her smile mocking, utterly infuriating to Flowridia's bruised heart.

Offense bristled within her, cutting like needles through her skin. "I'm to be villainized for granting a small mercy to a condemned woman?"

Ayla didn't speak, instead visibly forcing her mouth shut before turning away. She paced, something inscrutable in the thin line of her lips.

"Ayla, my love, I'm beating myself up enough without your condemnation. Please." Flowridia sat on the bed, pulled apart from every angle. "I don't want to fuck her. I wanted to give her some peace."

Ayla merely seethed before her, and Flowridia wished so much that she could read her enigmatic love's mind.

"I know you can't empathize," Flowridia continued, "but please accept that what I've done to her is unforgivable.

Casvir raised her; he *owns* her, but none of this would have fallen together if it weren't for me."

"Or Soliel." Ayla hands flexed, her tendons skeletal beneath her thin skin. "Only Soliel, *technically*."

The uneasy mood simmered, certain to boil if Flowridia didn't act. She remained static upon the bed, struggling to dig up words. "If she hadn't acted, I would still be in that coffin. I might be dead."

Ayla said nothing, instead pausing before the window. Beyond, the war stood stagnant as the soldiers burned their dead, but the world felt far away.

"Ayla, I don't know what you want me to say."

Ayla's wide eyes held something akin to panic. Instead of replying, she marched forward, past Flowridia, her gaze vacant as her fingers ran fitfully through her hair.

Ayla was spiraling, slowly drowning with Flowridia helpless upon the shore. Feeling useless, Flowridia searched for words, even vain ones, and hated what she found—for there was more to say. "I asked her if she would come with me," Flowridia whispered, and at that Ayla froze. "Not because I want her, but because I want to help her. I can't let her stay in Nox'Kartha as a slave. You would know how awful that . . ."

Her words were stolen by the unequivocable shock upon Ayla's countenance.

"Ayla, whatever else she was or wasn't or could have been, she was my friend."

Ayla said nothing. She may as well have been stone.

Flowridia wondered if it mattered at all, to try and explain herself now. She'd brought the dark clouds; the storm would come. "Ayla, will you please speak?"

"I hate her," Ayla said, bitterness in the words.

Flowridia shut her eyes, sick to see it. "I accept that."

"I hate that she rescued you," Ayla said, her pacing as erratic as her words. "I hate that she means anything to you. And *gods* I hate that she had the audacity to save your life! Twice! I am forced to be indebted to her because without her, I would not have you. How can I accept that?! *How dare she!*"

Ayla's claws tore at her shoulders and arms, ripping skin and fabric both, revealing muscle and bone. Flowridia flinched, lost in the sea of her wife's rage. "Ayla, it's not—"

"Fine! Make her fuckable! Make her beautiful—I don't care! She is perfect and pure—*I get it!*" Anguish matched her fury, and Flowridia watched in horror as fire flickered at her feet, steadily rising to cover her. "You chose her, *so go get her.* I understand, I really do—I am abominable, and she is a gods-damned *saint* who gave her life for you!"

Flowridia stayed small, uncertain of what to say; she only knew her wife was lost. "Ayla, this was never a competition—"

"Is it not though? Did she not step into the arena at my unwilling departure? Did she not comfort you and sweep you off your feet? The undeniable truth is that you walked away from me and into her arms, only torn away because Soliel slit her throat! I had to steal and conspire for everything she could have simply handed you on a silver platter—except from her, it would not all be falling apart as it is now. You could have loved her more than you ever loved me, and if Soliel hadn't slit her throat, *you would have!*"

Despite the rising flame, Ayla's rage quelled, replaced by agony. She sunk to the ground, a burning star, though nothing else caught in her flame. She wept, heaving sobs wracking her figure, a shadow in her own luminous light, curled on the floor with all the grandeur of an insect.

Yet she grew ever brighter, and Flowridia remembered the slave camp, feared she truly would burst. Demitri's fur stood on end, his stance aggressive, but Flowridia coaxed him away. Heart aching, she dared to approach, rising purple smoke surrounding her figure. As she knelt and covered Ayla with her own body, holding her close, she felt that familiar pulsing, radiant energy. Uncomfortable, yes, for it was too much, too stimulating, her body repelled and drawn all at once.

It didn't matter if it were rational. It didn't matter if her wife's words were true or not. Ayla was drowning. "Ayla Darkleaf, listen to me," she whispered near Ayla's pointed ear. "Hold to my voice, and listen."

To her relief, the words were a healing balm; Ayla's flame ceased rising, merely became stagnant.

Flowridia remained in the field of energy, praying her necrotic touch was soothing to her undead lover. "You're right—if Soliel hadn't come, I wouldn't have done it. Everything you said before, about me lacking conviction—it's true, and I'm sincerely sorry for that. I'm trying to be better. But I can't undo the past. I can't deny that I faltered."

Nothing changed. Ayla remained a weeping supplicant beneath her, yet Flowridia was the one praying for absolution.

"You have already forgiven me for something unforgivable," Flowridia continued, recalling their tear-stained wedding. "I suppose if I had joined you as a vampire, that would have shown true commitment. But I hope my vow to love you means something. I hope the name Flowridia Darkleaf means something. I've sworn to never leave you, and I won't. Not now. Not ever."

The flame around Ayla disappeared. She glowed like the moon upon a dark sky, but Flowridia finally saw the strands of her hair, the folds in her dress. The purple fog surrounding them dissipated. When Flowridia leaned down to kiss her hair, Ayla gasped as though awakened, shuddering from restrained sobs. Her words held agony: "Do you wish you were with her?"

"I don't. You're the one I want, Ayla." Flowridia remained on top of her as the glowing ceased. "I would have been happy with Lara, because she's good and kind and would have held my hand down a very different path. You said yourself she was my hope for a righteous life, but I don't want that future."

Ayla remained as still as stone, no need to breathe.

"I have so many regrets," Flowridia whispered, the quiet jarring in the aftermath of the storm. Demitri sat in a corner of the room, his soft breathing the only sound. "I wish Lara could have simply lived and moved on from me, never been tangled up in this madness. I wish I had waited and researched more of the Solviraes' line. I wish I hadn't allowed Murishani to manipulate me into thinking she was the only option. Izthuni said there was one line, but he never said there was only one. I was the fool who made that leap. It's like you said once—sometimes there's no clean villainy. Life isn't meant for that. I've made awful mistakes these past few months, and I regret so many things."

Ayla hadn't moved, not an inch. With her cold skin, she truly did seem among the dead.

"But I don't regret the outcome. I don't regret you."

At those words, her love stirred, peeking out from behind her hair and hands.

Ayla's large eyes were frightening in the dark, but in the light, they held vulnerability, her defensive stance both a weapon and a shield. As Flowridia studied her wife, an indisputable truth fell upon her. "Before you," Flowridia whispered, the words swelling like a breath inside her, "I'd spent my entire life being selfless, being 'good'; I clung to it because I was afraid of any other path—first instilled in me by well-meaning orphan matrons who preached of the evils of witchcraft, as well as Aura, who did all she could to teach me so-called good magic. My mother reaffirmed the commitment because I feared becoming her. But I've seen now that to not be good doesn't mean I'm doomed to be her. To not be good doesn't mean I'm evil—I don't believe I'm either.

"I believe I am selfish," Flowridia continued, and the word felt fitting on her tongue, granted by a goddess and now duly claimed. "I believe when I saw you across the dance floor all those months ago, I felt what it meant to *want,* even if it was wrong. I saw a future I craved, even if I could not have understood the depth of what it meant. I'm a selfish person, Ayla Darkleaf, and it means I will choose you before the world every time. You're my wife, and there is no greater joy than that. Wanting justice for Lara doesn't change that. It makes me feel immutably guilty to know she must suffer. It makes me want to tear Casvir's head from his shoulders to know he's done this. And seeing her broke my heart, but it didn't steal it. Nothing could ever steal it from you. It's yours to do with as you will."

When Ayla stirred, Flowridia finally extracted herself from on top of her, shuffling to the side so her love could sit up. Ayla's face lacked the capacity to puff and swell, but it did shine from tears. "I'm sorry," she whispered, but Flowridia immediately shook her head and pulled her properly into her arms.

"If you didn't know, then that's my failing. I'm sorry you held onto that."

Ayla curled into the touch, as vulnerable as a child. "I thought I had buried it."

"Now you've set it free."

Ayla remained still, the atmosphere finally settling after her vicious words. "Lara is someone I will never care for, but I . . . I want to let this go."

"I think you finally have a chance to now."

Ayla smiled, and that simple gesture meant more than all the realms.

"There's something else we need to talk about," Flowridia said, as Ayla clung to the collar of her dress. "The war. Lara spoke of it and expressed her fear that it will end in blood on every side. There will be no Solvira when this is through."

"I think I established being content with that when I said I would burn it to the ground."

"That's not what I meant. I have been thinking that we could end this without a lengthy siege, and without running away."

"Explain."

"Casvir doesn't want this kingdom destroyed if it doesn't have to be—he wants worshippers, first and foremost. So, we invite him in. We say we want to negotiate."

Ayla frowned, though it held calculation. "Do we want to negotiate?"

"Of course not."

Ayla shook her head. "He will know it is a trap."

"Yes, but he will walk into it willingly, because he wants this over too. We tell him to come alone, or perhaps with a small entourage."

"And you're giving me permission to destroy him?"

Once upon a time, Flowridia had been a child following her mentor in the woods. Somewhere in her heart, she longed for that time again—back when the world was simple, when Casvir was a man she trusted and loved.

She still loved him, but the pristine view she'd once held had shattered somewhere along the journey. "Whatever it takes, Ayla."

Despite Ayla's infantile pose, her visage bore the first flickers of triumph. "I shall send the white flag. Call for a truce until Casvir returns—the more time to prepare, the better. And when the time comes, Demitri shall be sent somewhere secret and safe. I have plan, and it shall be glorious."

Flowridia could not smile, distraught to consider the coming conflict.

"All this because of Lara's words?"

Flowridia feared a trap in the statement. "She asked me for nothing. But her foresight is correct."

When Ayla pulled away, her face still bore evidence of tears, but she smoothed her gown like the monarch she masqueraded as and offered a hand. "You're exhausted, my love. You're covered in ash and blood. Come and rest."

Flowridia nodded, too tired to do anything but follow Ayla to the washroom, her touch tender as she helped remove her clothing. They kissed as the tub filled with water, innocently touched as they slipped into its warmth.

"I was so scared, Flowra," Ayla whispered, settling against her side. "When he took you, I . . ." She held Flowridia tight, protective. "I hate that she had to save you because I could not."

Flowridia kissed her, held her when Ayla curled around her.

"Would you take comfort in making love?" Ayla asked.

Flowridia's hands skimmed across Ayla's hips, her touch tender and kind. "I think I would, nor would I deny you, but . . ." She contemplated her words, knowing they would hold weight. ". . . would you?"

Ayla frowned, visibly perplexed.

"Making love to you is a joy," Flowridia explained, knowing her wife's insecurities, "but it isn't the only way to give comfort. Love can be innocent. You've cried so much today, and if what you need is to be held, please let me."

Ayla stared as though seeing a whole new color, and Flowridia nearly laughed for her befuddlement. "Forgive me," Ayla said. "I . . ." When her eyes misted, Flowridia's heart sank. "I think you may be right."

Some impasse had been bridged; Flowridia sensed it like the moisture in the air. But rather than speak and ruin the idyllic calm, when Ayla settled into the crook of her neck, Flowridia held her there, simply breathing in her scent.

Strange, how even in the midst of hell, there could be peace. Even for the damned.

The journey made some semblance of sense with Etolié's new demonic guide. Kah'Sheen spoke to shadowy entities, bid them for help in a language Etolié recognized but was ashamed she had never learned.

"They are hearing news of a De'Sindai man lost in the realm. Come."

Time passed quickly, the conversations between she and Kah'Sheen seamless and enjoyable, even if their differences in morality were occasionally starkly apparent.

"You're telling me you *knew* Flowers was going to bring back Ayla Darkleaf?"

"Yes, I am knowing the small one's intentions," Kah'Sheen replied, her nonchalance nothing less than inspiring. "But I am not stopping her when it is only intention. Intention is not a crime. That is Demoni way. And I am not knowing how she is planning it. I am only being surprised she is doing it so quickly."

Etolié sickened at the thought. "I can still hardly believe it. I loved her. I trusted her. She was that friend who's too naïve to function and so you'd die to protect her." Scorn twisted her face, and she swallowed back her sudden rise of anguish. Every piece of her felt so raw. "No one expected this."

"Yes, she was seeming very nice. But Endless Night's influence cannot be ignored. I am hoping you are successful."

"Would you want to help us?" Etolié asked, but even as the words left, Kah'Sheen shook her head.

"Mother is forbidding it. She is not trusting Casvir, nor is she having faith in your victory."

Ouch.

"This is as much as I can be doing," Kah'Sheen continued, "though Mother will be happy to know we have met."

Etolié had so many questions, but Kah'Sheen suddenly grabbed her arms and placed a finger to her mouth. "Ahead," she whispered, and as Etolié stepped through the murky terrain—perhaps it was a forest on the other side, for how difficult it was to see—she heard what sounded like a brutal fight.

She wove through hazy trees, the sound growing louder, followed closely by Kah'Sheen and her many limbs.

There he was, appearing in a blink behind a collection of shadowed trees. Imperator Casvir showed no sign of dishevelment save for the white strands of hair seeking to escape their tail, and his red eyes were a shock of color in the monochromatic scene. He bore no weapons—perhaps he feared using magic as well—and instead raised his fists toward a particularly large and nasty-looking shadow.

Her presence stole the demon's attention for a mere moment, at which point Casvir punched it in its fucking face. Kah'Sheen shouted a stream of Demoni curses at the staggered shadow, as well as those lurking, and Etolié would never be tired of watching them scatter like sheep to a wolf.

Casvir kept his battle stance at Kah'Sheen's entrance, but his eyes widened when Etolié joined her. "Magister Etolié," he said, and Etolié applauded his ability to maintain eye contact with her nude self.

"I have never been so happy to see you, Imperator First and Last," Etolié said, entirely honest in that.

Casvir quickly surveyed Kah'Sheen, stance relaxing slightly. "The Coming Dawn."

"Hello," she said, as sweet as a fruit pie, and Etolié couldn't say if she were sincere or not.

"Long story short," Etolié said, "I was sent to find you since it turns out I'm capable of inter-planar teleportation. Ran into Kah'Sheen because I sang a few too many blasphemes about her mother and now we're friends."

"I see," Casvir replied, still visibly wary, but not looking like he'd throw a punch. Kah'Sheen kept her distance, because though she towered above him, he could snap her like a twig, Etolié didn't doubt. "I appreciate you coming."

"I gotta hand it to Flowers—this is the nastiest trick I have ever seen."

Casvir's stoicism was frankly inspirational, given his radiating mood was 'murder.' "I have underestimated her. I will not make that mistake again."

Etolié looked to Kah'Sheen. "We should go. But I can't thank you enough for your help."

"It is what sisters do, Etolié," Kah'Sheen replied, her smile revealing a row of pointed teeth. "If you are needing me, you will call, yes?"

"Yes, absolutely."

Kah'Sheen hugged her then, which itched like a bitch, but Etolié clung back, extremely invested in this apparent sisterhood. "Are you needing an escort back?"

"I think I can do this, but stay until I know for sure, please."

Etolié offered the very armored imperator a hand, and with a frown he gave his back. She held it—oh god, it was *cold;* dead Khastra levels of cold—as she shut her eyes and touched upon the world she knew, knowing she'd only need to lean a little to the left to fall right through, but wished to go farther still, to Khastra—

Cool air touched her, no longer stagnant and stale. On instinct, Etolié illusioned clothing, then opened her eyes to see morning light and a rather sad encampment in the woods. Murishani sat on a throne far too opulent for the environment, glowering at nothing, but upon seeing them immediately stood and clasped his hands together. "Oh, thank the gods. You both look a little worse for wear."

Etolié surveyed the deceptively comical scene, heart clenching to find no sign of Khastra. "How long were we gone?"

"Half a day? A little more."

Etolié frowned. "Time is so fucking warped."

"Before we are distracted," Casvir said, and when Murishani brought a handkerchief to wipe some kind of dust from his armor, the imperator brushed him aside, hints of annoyance in his subtle frown, "what has happened?"

Murishani delivered a bleak tale—that Ayla Darkleaf had decimated their troops with her Silver Fire, that the Bringer of War had been chewed on by 'the tiny one's' undead, and that the assault was temporarily stalled—with the exception of the Bringer of War, who kept throwing herself at the wall without direction.

Casvir remained silent during the speech. Upon its conclusion, he said only, "I see." His gaze turned to Neolan in the distance, the field between them scorched, churned earth and gore strewn about, charred bodies and carnage wherever you looked. "We have underestimated Ayla Darkleaf's might, as well as her wife's cleverness. This mistake will not be repeated." Steel coated the ice in his voice. "Viceroy Murishani, pull from the reserves. Magister Etolié, fetch your . . ."

His words faded when a particularly gruesome creature shambled over, clearly toward them.

It bore no weapons but far too many arms, and subtle scarring sealed the excessive limbs to its torso. Poorly balanced, it teetered with every step; this undead creature would be useless on a battlefield. But most jarring of all was the enormous white flag it wielded—rather, was impaled somewhere in its spinal column.

It stopped harmlessly before them, and around its neck was a scroll tied with string.

Casvir seemed unbothered, perhaps mildly amused as he approached the creature. It did not react when he procured the scroll, merely stood at attention, as though waiting.

Casvir unraveled the scroll, and as he read, a vicious smile pulled at his thin lips. "Change of plans," he said. He looked to the gruesome undead monster. "Inform Ayla Darkleaf that I accept her terms."

Those seemed to be the magic words—the creature lumbered away.

Murishani spoke. "This is clearly a trap."

"Yes, and they know we know it is. General Khastra and Lady Etolié will accompany me. Viceroy Murishani, you shall remain with the troops, in case her trap involves trying to steal them."

"I doubt I would be of any use in a fight like that," Etolié said, her gaze set upon Neolan in the distance, occasionally spotting a dark spot that could only be her semi-mindless Beefcake.

"Perhaps not for combat," Casvir said, "but there is no one else who can tame or heal the Bringer of War."

Etolié stood a little taller at that, happy to have her role in Khastra's life properly acknowledged. "First, we see if I can lure her back here. Wish me luck."

She flew toward the mad half-demon, praying to her momma for luck.

Chapter 38

“Damn it all; they are coming too soon.”

The expansive throne room reflected shades of red and purple, the setting sun still gripping the horizon. Cleaned of blood and bodies, the high windows revealed the night sky behind them, though no stars shone—not yet.

“My part is ready,” Flowridia said. “Sunset will come, my love. I will distract them.”

Ayla adjusted the crown woven into her hair, her countenance torn between conspiracy and worry. “There. Now you are the very picture of royalty. It is all about image, darling, and it would do Casvir well to be reminded what he has stolen from you. Say whatever you must to stall them. Play stupid, slander my name, surrender if you must—I do not care. But waste time.”

Fear chilled Flowridia’s blood, but she nodded regardless. “I love you.”

The words lingered, echoing softly across the high walls. Ayla stopped and seemed to breathe a moment, her spite fading into something sincere. She pressed their lips together, the sensation sweet despite the bitter shadow approaching. “I suppose we could still run,” Ayla whispered, and Flowridia knew the words were not meant as a trap, even though her judgement screamed to agree. “That, or we shall destroy him. Phylactery or not, having your soul ripped out seems like an inconvenient turn of events. Are you prepared?”

“I hope so.”

Ayla kissed her cheek, but when the door creaked open, she darted behind the throne, disappearing into Sha’Demoni.

Flowridia took her seat, uncertain of what she could or should say, then realized Imperator Casvir, First and Last of

630

his Name, Tyrant of Nox'Kartha and Marshal of the Deathless Army had come all alone.

No entourage. No Etolié. Simply Casvir, his metal armor reverberating against the stone floor—they were all alone. "Good evening, Empress Consort," he said, once he had reached the center. "Where is your wife?"

"My who?" Flowridia said, and then she feigned a gasp and placed her hand to her mouth. "Goodness, I knew I had forgotten something."

Casvir merely stared, visibly unimpressed.

"I'm always misplacing her. Silly me."

"Flowridia, come with me."

Relentless, those red eyes, his stare a battering ram. Flowridia, well used to it, was far more surprised by the words themselves. "What?"

"Your wife has no intention of negotiating," Casvir replied, his stance resolute. "It is not her way. We will fight, and you will fall in the collateral damage, and that is not a risk I shall take. You will not be held hostage; merely out of the way. You have my word."

Something in his words spiked her annoyance. "You don't have much faith in me."

"I have utmost faith in you," he replied, and he came forward, his gaze never wavering. "You have impressed me immensely during this siege, even bested me at times, and I commend you. I could not be prouder of your growth and accomplishments."

The words were unbearably kind. Flowridia swallowed the uncomfortable rise of pressure in her throat. Light shone from the horizon, but it steadily shrunk. "Yet you march here to burn each and every one of my efforts down?"

"It would be a waste for you die for something foolhardy," he said, ignoring her subtle rage, "and there is no shame in knowing you are outmatched."

Those words, however, spiked her anger. "You're the fool to think your victory is assumed."

"I assume nothing, save your demise. I do not intend to lose this fight, but once it begins, there is only one throat I can hold a knife to in order to defeat your wife."

Flowridia frowned. "Then why be rid of me? Why give up that advantage?"

"I do not want to see you fall," Casvir replied, and the warmth in his voice reminded her of months ago back in the woods, when their friendship had been simple and her heart hadn't grown so hard. "I would even return this throne to you once Nox'Kartha has secured it, if that is what it takes for you to step aside."

Flowridia shook her head. "At the cost of my beloved's life?"

"She need only surrender. She need not die."

"Casvir, you're a terrible person, did you know? You don't want me dead; in fact, you want me to flourish, but not if it interferes with your plans. Is it personal? I must know—does it enrage you to see Ayla Darkleaf on a bigger throne than yours?"

All perceived kindness in his visage faded, leaving only a glower. "I am not that petty."

"Then why are you here? Why couldn't you have just left us alone?"

The question lingered, echoing across the bounds of the expansive room. Casvir somehow straightened his already perfect stance, his menace radiant—and it invigorated her to think she had actually struck a nerve. "Nox'Kartha's plans have never changed. Alauriel Solviraes' death pushed those plans to the forefront. It was inevitable that I would stand here across from whoever sat upon the throne; I regret that it is you, because I do not wish to see you fall from something so foolish as spite."

Casvir's actions were never personal. But they didn't have to be to lacerate her to her core. Anger burned her cheeks. "I will stand with the woman I love, for better or worse." Her words held finality, yet Casvir did not move. She sensed a change in mood, a shift in the wind of his demeanor but could not place it.

"The question is," he said instead, and Flowridia wished to every hell that the sun would finally disappear, "to whose throat must I hold a knife for you to listen?"

Flowridia grasped the arm of the throne, nervous at his words. "You cannot subdue my wife. Demitri is not here, and to threaten him would undermine your intentions anyway. There is no one left, so you have nothing that . . ."

Casvir ripped his hand across the empty air, a sizzling line drawing open. The portal stood as tall as Casvir himself, yet the undead who emerged were larger still.

They held chains in their unholy grip, and wrapped in those chains was Thalmus.

He wore the same clothes from their last meeting, but he bore dark bruises, beaten and shackled at the wrists and neck and ankles. A gag had been placed in his mouth, but his eyes were free to convey their truth—and that truth was pain and anguish. "This man would die for you," Casvir said, curt and cruel, the depth of his pervasive voice endless. "Will you let him?"

Flowridia trembled as she stood from her chair. "Casvir, this is—"

"If you stay here, his life will be pain until his natural death." Casvir's tone held no place for disagreement; it never had. "Leave this place, and he will be free."

She swore she floated as she stepped down the stairs, so numb her limbs had become. Though she addressed Casvir, her eyes held Thalmus', rich and black. He had been born in chains; it was the cruelest sort of injustice for him to die in them. "Casvir, if you hold any love in your heart for me, you won't do this."

"I would rather lose your love than lose your life," Casvir replied, as fatherly and cruel a phrase as he had ever said. "Choose."

Flowridia blinked; her tears welled. Thalmus could not speak, but he smiled as well as he could when she came a step closer. Not of approval, no—of love unconditional.

She swore the sun lingered merely to taunt her. Casvir would not wait those few minutes more. Daring to come near, her tears fell fast, her decision undecided; her decision unbearable. "Thalmus," she whispered.

He mumbled a line she knew and adored behind his gag: *"Flower Girl."*

His long braid touched the floor, for he was forced to bend, to kneel like a slave. This had been his life, and it would be his death if she did not act.

Yet it would not be the last time. His was a throat Casvir could hold a knife to. This *would* be Thalmus' life, even gilded in gold.

Casvir watched, patient for the moment. Flowridia bent over, her head level to Thalmus' as she embraced him. He could not hold her back for his chains, but his head pressed to hers.

She touched the back of his neck, thumb stroking the base of his braid, and she felt his whole body, his entire musculature, the life pulsing through his veins.

Once upon a time, she had slain a parasite within a small girl, a single organism within a complicated body, the finesse of her magic matchless even then. She had grown so much since.

She hugged Thalmus, a slight sob escaping her throat as she found the clear passage to his heart.

"I love you so much," she whispered, and then she cast her spell.

A single, seeping slip of magic. Pure necromancy. Right into his heart.

His blood ceased pulsing; a painless, gentle end. He slumped in the ghoul guards' arms.

Through her misted vision, she saw genuine surprise on Casvir's face. Swallowing her sorrow, she clenched her fists and walked tall to her throne even as her heart shattered with every step. She wiped her tears; when she looked to Casvir, behind his shock there lay pride.

In that moment, Flowridia understood, in ways she had never so viscerally felt before, how hate and love could perfectly coexist.

The final vestiges of light shone upon her face. Flowridia collapsed onto her throne, steeling her jaw when she felt subtle pressure upon the back of the chair.

In tandem with the fading light, horrible claws, nearly as large as Flowridia herself, gracefully gripped the back of the throne, pale yet shrouded in shadow. A second claw joined the first, and adjacent to her head appeared a monstrous visage—not a shadow this time; no less nightmarish than their previous encounter, when the monster had cradled her to its chest and screamed for the God of Order to *leave*.

Its slack jaw revealed enormous fangs and rows of internal teeth, leading into a void of a maw, as endless as its ghastly title. Holding no pupils, its eyes glowed as vibrantly as twin suns, their silver light a perfect match to her lover's own. It stared upon the imperator, but Flowridia had only eyes for the monster, daring to reach out and touch its cold skin, the back of her hand gently gliding across its smooth head.

The Endless Night emerged from the darkness, rising to its full, gargantuan height. Impossibly thin, skeletal and inhuman, yet still bearing emblems of its hostess' mortal physique, and Flowridia knew it—knew *them*—like she knew her own soul.

Yet, terror rose in tandem with the silver flame upon its skin. The monster *laughed*—a vicious, grating sound; the blending of a god of depthless, underground things and a screeching, ear-splitting siren coursing above—and then it crept forward on all fours, still taller by far than them all, than even the Bringer of War, were she present.

It grinned with all the predatory instinct of its hostess. *"Hello, Imperator."*

In response to that call, the doors to the throne room burst open. An envoy of dead, led by Khastra and Etolié, came marching forward, though notable shock faltered the Celestial's steps. Flowridia saw her fear and didn't care.

From one undead guard, Casvir took a shield and sturdy mace. With the Silver Fire, The Endless Night could not be harmed with summoned weapons, and Casvir had come prepared.

Khastra grinned at her fearsome opponent, and when she cut a line at her wrist, blood dripped into her mouth. Her body shifted, transforming into a monster, but The Endless Night leered, revealing its depthless maw.

It swiped its claw, tossing Imperator Casvir aside in favor of these new opponents. His body clanged against the stone wall, but he immediately righted himself. The dead from his battalion rushed—some elite, some modified, all bearing monstrous scars and ghoulish forms—but The Endless Night stood far larger, all but ignoring them in favor of Khastra's transformed self.

The Bringer of War charged; Etolié swooped into the air. When the half-demon clashed with The Endless Night, Flowridia sought to meld into the background, knowing she was better off out of sight. Casvir joined the fray, his weapon making contact with the godly entity, but The Endless Night hardly reacted.

From her corner, Flowridia kept a wary eye on Etolié, knowing her illusions were crippled in Ayla's eyes but not her own. She crept out of her throne, taking advantage of The Endless Night's sheer magnitude to slip away unseen. Instead, behind the throne, she ran to one of the sweeping windows, kneeling before the one she had cracked a hole into just minutes before. A small bit of undead greenery waited; commanding vines to grow around the outside of the tower had taken time, but it had not been difficult.

At the moment of contact, Flowridia unleashed her spell—

And crashing through the windows, littering the floors with glass, a huge bastion of vines and roots burst into the room.

The Bringer of War managed a horrific blow with her hammer, landing square within The Endless Night's macabre ribs—denting and shattering more than a few. She bashed its head, but The Endless Night merely faltered, its crushed jaw reconstructing before their eyes. From her came a blast of silver light; Flowridia dove against the back of the throne, letting it shield her. What Ayla lacked now in finesse and control she bore in pure strength, and when Flowridia looked back out, Casvir's dead had caught fire—as well as some of her vines.

No matter. At her instruction, the vines grabbed what dead they could. Skulls bashed; bone crunched—and some were simply thrown out the broken windows. She sought Casvir, but he battered them back, some of his dead running to stand between him and the dead plant life.

The Endless Night's lengthy arm suddenly shot out and grabbed Etolié, slamming her into the ground. The Bringer of War *roared,* but The Endless Night laughed and kept a claw on the Celestial's prone form. Immediately, the silver fire flashed, and the monster shot a potent blast of brilliant flame at the Bringer of War, engulfing her utterly.

The Silver Fire could turn Etolié's power into pure energy, she realized.

When the flames subsided, the Bringer of War bore minor burns but did not fall. Behind her, Casvir held his dagger of maldectine, the power dissipating as he brought his mace back out to fight. The Endless Night tossed the limp Celestial aside and met his weapon with glee.

The battle resumed, the clash of demi-deities a calamitous affair. Flowridia's brutalized heart panged with guilt to see Etolié, collapsed and still. Was she dead? Flowridia ran from her hiding space, thankfully ignored by the small army of death as she knelt beside her former friend.

She lay as though dead, but when Flowridia jostled her arm, there came a faint groan. She rolled Etolié over. Bruising marred her face, but there was nothing she could do for whatever the Silver Fire had done. Nevertheless, Flowridia set to work healing the injured Celestial, finding cracked ribs and internal bruising.

She knew all would be well when she heard a weak voice. "What the hell kind of game are you playing, Flowers?"

"I only want Casvir subdued. Not you. Let me heal you," Flowridia replied, and Etolié shut her eyes. Flowridia continued until Etolié's body silently bid that all was well.

Blinding light suddenly overtook them. The Endless Night burst with fire at every side, and Flowridia fully expected to die, but a sudden emptiness filled her, expanding to surround and shield her. All the world became white save for her little bubble—Etolié held her maldectine knuckles, its aura expanding by just enough to save her too.

The light dissipated. Smoldering remains of corpses littered the arena. Her vines were ash. Casvir slashed his claw across the air—from a portal, more emerged. He could not teleport in if he were beyond the shields protecting Neolan, but he could cast all he wanted if he were within.

When the maldectine's aura left, Flowridia offered the injured Etolié a hand. "Saving my ass twice from that monster wife of yours doesn't mean I don't still hate you," Etolié spat, though she stumbled, visibly swaying.

"I fully respect that—"

Another blast of fire approached, and once again Etolié shielded them from silver flame. "There," the Celestial said, her wings stretching wide, "we're even now."

She flew into the air. Flowridia knew she would receive nothing more.

There were more vines in reserve—Flowridia ran to a burning root, commanding what remained to grow and join them.

The vines lashed out like snakes, like tentacles, grasping the unintelligent dead and holding them thrall. The dead battered the thick plant life, but they, too, were necrotic—and thus obedient and capable of tearing the corpses' limbs from their bodies.

A bunch wrapped around the Bringer of War's legs, who roared and had to drop her hammer to rip them apart. In the moment of weakness, The Endless Night's claws swiped and threw her at the window—and missed, to Flowridia's chagrin. She hit a pillar instead.

Vines snaked around Casvir. The dead who were not trapped ran to Flowridia as he fought to free himself. She released them, giving the plants simply the command to *squeeze*—

But The Endless Night grabbed her, gentle as it lifted her to its chest. Still, she gasped, breath failing as she watched the monster wrack its claws across the legion of dead attempting to swarm her. It roared, fire coating its claws as it burned the rest.

They were nothing but ashes when the monster carefully placed her down, but the glow from its skin had not diminished, not a glimmer.

The Endless Night's light grew ever more blinding. In erratic motions, it spewed a smaller array of magical flame, the outpouring from Casvir's portal never ending. Yet there was something off about Ayla and Izthuni's combined motions, and as their light grew ever brighter, Flowridia's stomach clenched.

The memory of Ayla destroying the slave camp, lost in her lust for bloodshed and power—

Except now, she hosted a god.

"Ayla!"

At the call of her name, The Endless Night dared to look at Flowridia, its expression impossible to decipher. "Don't lose yourself!" she cried, but every undead eye suddenly looked to her.

Again, the dead swarmed her, and though Flowridia could try to redirect them, she could not control them all. Holy light poured through her at her command, radiating from her pores—instead of fighting them, she became untouchable.

And she wondered, as she looked to her glowing hands, if she might wield this light as she did with necomancy.

Flowridia gathered her focus, surrounded by hungry dead, and willed her power to expand. Light burst from her figure; the dead howled in pain.

Again, she bid it to expand, but this time grasped it tight, willing it to hold. A shield of light; truly untouchable.

She was being watched, she realized—a vicious laugh escaped The Endless Night before it returned to its onslaught.

The Bringer of War remained the greatest threat; Casvir smartly stayed in his sea of death. Etolié floated out of the way, watching only, which Flowridia found odd— normally she would have summoned some deity to help.

The Endless Night wracked its claws across the battlefield, a burst of fire flowing with it. It glowed like the sun, and Flowridia feared her love hadn't listened. "Ayla—!"

The Endless Night roared its terrible, ear-splitting cry, another burst of fire radiating off its being. Flowridia pushed through the oncoming dead, nearly incinerated by Silver Flame. Oh, she cursed herself for leaving her maldectine; instead she dove toward the throne.

It happened so suddenly—The Endless Night's frozen stare, its scream of pain. The light from its figure remained blinding, despite the lack of fire. "Ayla, breathe it out!"

She heard Etolié scream a warning—*"Ayla's gonna blow!"*

Casvir's dead fell lifeless; he ran to her.

The Bringer of War landed a blow to its head.

Casvir ripped a new portal into the air. In the moment before a clawed hand grabbed her bodice, Flowridia's gaze met that of her monstrous wife. In those luminous, pupil-less eyes, she swore she saw fear.

"Ayla, no!"

Casvir threw her into the portal, and she crumpled on the ground of his familiar office.

She scrambled to her feet, giving no mind to Casvir when he appeared. Static sang in her mind, silent other than the pained echo of her lover's shriek. Uncaring of her fate— merely desperate to see Ayla's—Flowridia ran back toward the portal.

Casvir's muscled arm caught her at the waist. "Release me!" she cried, as she tried in vain to pull herself away.

"Flowridia—"

"No!" Yet her strength steadily failed her. Still, she fought. "I have to—"

From within the void of space came a bright, blinding silver light. It expanded, hurling toward them here, hundreds of miles away, and Flowridia's sob caught in her throat as the portal sealed itself not moments before the light might have consumed them.

Flowridia's legs gave out, but Casvir did not let her fall. Instead, his other arm joined the first, engulfing her. She could not speak. Shock stole every sense. Somewhere in her vacant mind, she knew he lowered her to the ground. She must have cried, because her tears splattered across Casvir's armored chest.

Ayla was . . . gone.

No body to cling to. Nothing to salvage. No tantalizing promise of her return dangled on a string by the same man who held her now.

But it couldn't be. Not forever. She couldn't accept that.

"You made an impressive final stand," Casvir said, and she knew he meant it. His deep voice reverberated against his armor and thus her body, a soothing gesture.

She could summon no reply. She could not bear to look away from where the portal had once been. This was a jest, surely. Ayla would return. It was too soon. Too fast. It couldn't be.

"Had the battle continued, you likely would have won."

A poor consolation. Flowridia gasped a breath yet did not cry.

"It is Nox'Kartha's duty to sentence you for crimes against the Solviran Empre."

Fitting, for Casvir to be the one to throw her to the wolves.

"There will be no trial—only myself as your judge. The verdict will likely be house arrest."

Under other circumstances, Flowridia would have found humor in the punishment. "C-Casvir," she managed, and he waited in the ensuing silence, patient as she gathered her words, "she can't . . . It can't be . . ."

"I truly do not know."

When Casvir shifted, Flowridia stumbled into standing, supported by his arm. Tears fell as she followed him mutely down the halls, legs numb, skin cold. He escorted her down a familiar path—to Ayla's old bedroom, where she had lived a past chapter of her life.

Once upon a time, she had loved Casvir. Once upon a time, she had felt hope.

Now . . .

When Casvir opened the door, all remained as it had been—Ayla's bedroom held all its charm and wonders, the globes of light and pictures on the wall, the couch and scavenged wardrobe. The only piece out of place, though it was no surprise to Flowridia, was Demitri curled up on the floor, who perked up at their entrance.

Flowridia shuffled into the room, grateful when Demitri met her and kissed her. *You're crying! What happened?*

She forced a smile. "Ayla wanted Demitri out of the way for the fight and brought him here," she said to Casvir, who remained in the doorway. "She thought this would be the last place you would look, if you were going to use him against me."

"Wise," he said simply, though Flowridia imagined it was begrudging.

Mom, where's Lady Ayla?

"Food will be brought to you," Casvir said. "Your punishment ends at tomorrow's sunset. Then, we may discuss what future you hold here." Metal shifted as he turned, the sound intrinsically connected to his aura. But he paused, his clawed hand lingering on the doorframe. "I will not give you false hope and say she will return. But she would come here first. In the meantime, life continues. Mourn your loss, and then move forward."

He left them alone.

Stunned into silence, Flowridia remained still, her mind little more than static.

Demitri placed his nose against her leg. *Lady Ayla is gone?*

With clumsy steps, Flowridia stumbled to the luxurious couch. "I don't know," she managed to say, but all she saw behind her eyelids was Lara's destroyed body, blown apart by the Silver Fire.

Yet, that hadn't killed her. She would have lived, had Soliel not slit her throat.

Flowridia sat up, contemplating this new future before her. All she could do, for now, was wait.

She told Demitri the tale.

"Casvir!" Etolié cried from high in the air. "Ayla's gonna blow!"

It all happened so quickly—Flowridia's scream, Casvir's swipe of his claw in the air. He grabbed Flowers by her dress and tossed her through the portal, then followed, leaving it open.

The world became silent and slow.

The Endless Night stared at the portal, at Flowers' captor, then clutched its own body, tearing through skin, releasing fire and burning, white light.

The Bringer of War hurled her hammer beyond the bounds of the castle, the sheer might of the moment blinding even to her.

The monster burst, the explosion of power an inescapable *boom* upon the landscape. Etolié dove, clinging to the Bringer of War's body as the maldectine expanded to protect them.

But there was no Endless Night. No magic. No castle. White mist engulfed them, as painful to stare upon as the sun. Etolié shut her eyes and embraced the love of her life—if death were her next journey, she would meet it at Khastra's side.

Her stomach flipped, and with it came the surreal sensation of falling.

Enormous arms wrapped around her. Etolié opened her eyes and saw nothing, save for the sun and the sky, as they twisted in midair and crashed to the ground, the Bringer of War's body cushioning their fall.

Only then did Etolié let the shield dissolve. She tried to move, but the Bringer of War's strength held her thrall. Instead, she saw only a massive crater of black sand.

The Bringer of War roared as she pounced up, causing Etolié to drop to the sandy ground. Her armor bore evidence of ash and burns, but there was so little skin exposed—Etolié prayed the damage was only what she could see. When the half-demon held out a hand, her gargantuan hammer came soaring back to her, clutched easily in her massive hands. She tried to run up the sandy slope, only to slip back down, over and over.

Around them came a gentle falling of swirling black, as soft as snowflakes and as warm as afternoon sunshine. It landed upon Etolié's face and hair, staining the silver locks. Not ash, but something like it. Etolié stood and saw nothing— no city and no Endless Night.

Only smooth sand.

Etolié's wings spread, and she floated up from the crater, her heart sinking in tandem. Any other time, she would have found hilarity in how the Bringer of War seemed to only sink deeper and deeper into the fine, black dust, but Etolié's jaw trembled, focused instead on all that was lost.

Her wings took her to the sky, and she saw the city—or what remained. The palace was gone. Utterly consumed. And much of the city with it. Etolié heard the screams of those still living, the wails and sobs, saw silver flame licking at the outlying buildings.

Etolié returned to the crater and wept, joining in the wails of the city. On the curtails of victory, they stood, the cost too high to bear.

Finally, the Bringer of War slowed in her vain attempts to climb the slippery slope, her visage ghastly and covered in black dust. Her muscles twitched, prepared to run, but just as quickly she met Etolié's eyes—

Who saw, somewhere within the glowing pits, recognition.

The Bringer of War knelt before her, Demoni words leaving her tongue, words Etolié couldn't pretend to understand. When she offered a hand, Etolié accepted it, though it was more to say she took Khastra's finger, given it was all her hand was big enough to hold. "You're calmer this time," Etolié said through her tears.

"*Etolié.*"

Etolié gasped at the guttural sound of her name. "Lay down, Beefcake. I'll help you breathe."

It took time and plenty of humming, but soon enough Khastra's monstrous self twisted and shrunk. Etolié sat atop her, gently soothing lines across her tattoos, avoiding the superficial burns on her small patches of exposed skin.

Nausea rose within her, and when she thought she might vomit, a portal opened. Casvir emerged, stoic and proud, followed by Murishani, visibly delighted as he clapped his hands. "What a show! A spectacle! Lady Etolié, you have delivered a gift."

Had Khastra not been restraining her, Etolié would have bitten off his tongue. Fury rose, but Khastra said, "Viceroy, if you will be overseeing the accommodations for this city, I will take Etolié back to Nox'Kartha."

"Oh, absolutely! You and she can join the rest."

Khastra moved to stand, but Etolié, still held in her arms, said, "What do you mean, 'the rest?'"

"The rest of your royal council," Murishani said, as though it were as obvious as the north star in the sky. "I summoned them this evening, to discuss the dissolution of your little territory."

Etolié tensed, her heartbeat suddenly pounding in her ears. "The *what?!*"

"The dissolution of Staelash. The Solviran Empire shall be Nox'Kartha's forevermore, and, well—" He laughed good-naturedly, his utter delight the final nail in his betrayal. ". . . you were always their territory. Now, you're ours. After the little stunt you pulled, it's a bit more in shambles than even how you left it, but Marielle and I have been helming the cleanup—"

"What stunt?!" Etolié said, highly tempted to literally tear the smirk from his lip.

"The earthquake. When you took the orb from the realm in the middle of Staelash." Victory and malice entwined upon his countenance. Etolié breathed but felt nothing at all. "It could have been worse, I suppose, though there's not much left of your library—fortunately you don't need it anymore."

"No one told me," she said, barely audible, unable to even articulate her worry for her friends, her populace.

"Marielle and I are discussing the possibility of her serving as duchess," Murishani continued, as though Etolié's world were not falling to pieces. "Once Priestess Sora and Lae Lae arrive, we can divvy out responsibilities accordingly. Of course, you'll have no need to attend that meeting—Casvir has your future laid out for you, eh?"

Too appalled to speak, Etolié wrenched herself from Khastra's grasp, the implications of his words still settling in her head.

"And I shall be taking a new throne," Murishani continued, batting his eyes almost cutely at Casvir, hands clasped to his chest. "No longer shall I hold the paltry title of 'Viceroy.' Instead, I shall accept my father's name and become Emperor Murishani Solviraes, the final true heir of the Solviran Throne."

Etolié simply blinked. "What?"

Murishani snapped his fingers, and a small bit of silver flame lit like a match. "Did you really not figure it out?"

"You . . !" Again, it was a good thing Khastra was here; otherwise she would have gone for his throat and likely died. "You have no right!"

"I have the Silver Fire," Murishani said, pouting as the light extinguished. With a *huff,* he placed his hands on his hips.

"I have Solviraes blood—and per the charter of the land, I reserve the right. The people will accept me once they see—"

"Have you read the fucking charter?!" Red-faced, Etolié released a cry of frustration into Murishani's smug, albeit confused face.

Murishani glanced at Casvir, visibly alarmed at her outburst. "The, uh, Blood of Ilune. Whosoever holds the most blood of Ilune reserves the right to rule. It has been that way since she founded—"

"I know," Etolié snapped, a damn stupid plan filling her head. Freed of Staelash's golden shackles for less than a minute, she offered her wrists anew. "You're not the heir. Technically, Lara wasn't the heir. Malakh treaded *real* lightly whenever I came around, and you wanna know why?" Etolié's wings spread wide for emphasis, her jaw grit, eyes wide. "I have *half* the Blood of Ilune, you bitch."

And for all her anger, for all her hurt and anguish at the destruction of the indomitable city, to see Murishani look genuinely aghast was nearly worth it all. He turned to Casvir like a child denied a favorite toy. "Casvir—"

"Casvir," she said over his pathetic whining, "I hereby offer—nay, *demand*—my services not as Etolié of Staelash, but as Empress Etolié, Daughter of Stars, and the goddamn half-sister to the God of Death."

And Casvir, that absolute asshole, look amused.

In the ensuing silence, Murishani's face became an unflattering shade of mauve. "Casvir, you cannot possibly be considering this."

"I'm working for you for twenty years, Imperator First and Last," Etolié said, casually checking her nails. "Solvira already loves me. It won't take any convincing at all."

"Casvir, I have been your loyal servant for—"

Casvir held up a hand, and Murishani's griping ceased. "Empress Etolié, you do hold the right to rule. And your reputation with Solvira precedes you. Your first order of business, by my decree, shall be to announce yourself to your citizens and offer them hope."

"Anything for you, Cassie," Etolié said with a wink, and when Casvir's claw struck the air, the portal appeared anew.

He stepped through, but Murishani lingered. His smile, however sweet, held murder. "Oh, how I wish your demon lover had eaten you."

Khastra's grip tightened, but Etolié relished his bitterness. "I'll bet you wish you hadn't saved my life."

"Even I make mistakes, Empress Etolié. But I never make them twice." His smile left; he looked nearly menacing.

He stepped through the portal, after which it disappeared.

Etolié leaned back into Khastra's touch. "What have I done?"

"You have done the noblest part, Empress Etolié," Khastra said, but Etolié immediately shook her head.

"And that is the last time you ever call me that, Beefcake."

Khastra leaned down—far down—and kissed Etolié on the top of her head. "What you have done is save their lives."

Etolié looked upon the vast crater around her, listened to the rising, despondent cries beyond. "Anyone who's left, at least."

She wiped the tears from her eyes with her illusionary sleeves. "I have a job to do. Follow me, won't you? Solvira loves us."

Khastra's laughter helped to soothe her rising anguish, despite the half-demon's own welling tears. "We are an iconic duo, yes."

Etolié took her hand, and they climbed out together, ready to face a new world.

Disarray met them, a sea of despondent, panicked people. Yet upon seeing Etolié and her unmistakable wings and Khastra—a traitor yet also the shadow to the Savior of Slaves—they calmed.

Then they came. From the smoldering streets came mobs of people, most expelling tears, all with endless questions.

"What has happened?"

"What of the war?"

"What shall become of us?"

"Magister Etolié—"

"Attention!" Etolié shouted, and she flew above the masses, floating serenely. She willed herself to glow bright, then beckoned her voice to echo throughout Neolan—a spell she had perfected years ago, the capacity to throw it around and amplify its power. "Citizens of Solvira—"

Her voice cut off, for she had their attention, their hope, their lives in her hand. What could she possibly say to explain this awful tragedy?

"Citizens of Solvira and of the Theocracy of Sol Kareena," she began again, unsure of where her words would go, "you know me—I am Etolié, Magister of Staelash, but—" She hesitated, yet she had to tell them, even if to speak it made it real. ". . . but today I accept a new title—Empress Etolié of Solvira, Daughter of Staella and half the Blood of Ilune."

A murmur rumbled across the crowd, but she did not hear displeasure; merely wonder.

"A great tragedy has occurred." Her tongue stilled, her next words crucial, yet the full truth was too terrible to explain, much less justify.

Ayla Darkleaf was a villain, yet she was not the culprit.

Etolié drew a breath, and with the words came pulsing rage. "Empress Consort Flowridia Solviraes has betrayed us."

Flowridia's day of room arrest ended. Her anxiety grew with every passing hour.

Demitri remained at her side, her loyal and dearest friend, and Flowridia distracted herself by studying the wall of beautiful drawings, memories of she and Ayla's time together. The globes of stolen, hoarded possessions became a comfort once again, a spot of hope amidst her worry.

She thought of Thalmus, wept for his death. The sole mercy remained that his body had been destroyed in the blast and was thus safe from Casvir's twisted justice. She cried on her floor at the memory of his heart stopping at her touch and wondered when murder had become so easy, when her soul had gone so far away.

And Lara, how she wept for Lara—who lingered somewhere here, her kingdom destroyed for Flowridia's hubris.

She had tried to save Solvira, yet everything she touched turned to ash in the end. What of the refugees? Who would protect them now? She prayed Etolié's influence would be enough to save them instead—for Flowridia felt the crushing burden of failure.

She did not weep for Ayla. To weep would mean acceptance. Ayla would return; she had to.

On her second day of confinement, she finally left her prison.

With Demitri at her heels, Flowridia wandered aimlessly down the halls, passing servants and guards and pillars of black sand. Perhaps the library would bring comfort, something to distract her agitated mind.

Flowridia descended the final steps to the double doors blocking the library. The groans of ancient architecture met her ears as she pushed them open, the smell of books wafting to greet her. Demitri shadowed her every step, curiously sniffing the air.

Flowridia heard voices—one familiar and one surreal.

Flowridia looked past the final row of shelves and saw a Skalmite, maldectine hanging from his neck. She kept her distance.

If Zoldar were here, that meant . . .

Centered in the library was the radiant beacon of fury that was Etolié, and Lara, quiet and mild.

Flowridia swallowed the lump in her throat. "Lara—"

"I don't care that you'll be living here," Etolié spat, immediately pulling Flowridia's attention. "Don't you *ever* come down here. Never again."

Flowridia couldn't even flinch at the harsh words. Lara's visage held sorrow and pain, her countenance nearly lifelike. "Lara, I—"

"Did you fucking hear me, Flowers?" Etolié stepped between them, blocking the undead, former empress from Flowridia's line of sight. Her sharp features twisted in fury, wings bursting from her back. "If I weren't contractually obligated to never touch you, I'd stuff you in the grave you left her to rot in!"

Though it came at the risk of death, contract or not, Flowridia stepped aside to face Lara. "Lara, I'm sorry—"

"Get out!" Etolié yelled, her wings spread to block Lara from view. "Flowers, you're fucking dead to me, and she sure as hell doesn't want to see you either."

Demitri bristled behind her, but Flowridia knew he would never hurt the Celestial. Flowridia swallowed her grief and coaxed Demitri to follow.

Then came light steps. "Let me speak for myself," Lara said, elegance in her stance—nearly alive, yes, yet irreversibly broken. "The city thinks its empress and empress consort are both gone. They say you, Flowridia Solviraes, drove me to insanity, that I succumbed to the madness of my lineage and destroyed myself and all I love. But they know you live. There're rumors you ran off with The Endless Night."

Flowridia swallowed guilt, though it amassed ever higher. "I tried to end the war."

"You did. And you succeeded." Lara held her hands behind her back, ever the empress with that regal aura. "What do you want?"

"I want to say I'm sorry," Flowridia said, her own fresh tears welling. "I want to give my condolences for what happened to your people. The tragedy is . . ."

When Flowridia's words trailed off, Lara said, "Unfathomable, yes. My home; my loved ones—destroyed. My legacy is gone. Neoma's lineage ends with me, and my empire dies in a blaze." Lara's lip trembled, but Flowridia dared not turn away, though shame threatened to topple what little remained of her pride. This was her penance; she would grant it the respect of looking it in the eye.

"And yet it could have been worse," Lara continued. "The maldectine crystal in the library's basement stopped the explosion when it touched; that's what they found in the rubble. Thousands are dead, yet I'm supposed to be grateful." Lara blinked; tears welled in her eyes, yet they stoically refused to fall. "I remain a fool locked in a tower, and I cannot blame you for my fate. But I can blame you for Solvira's. With all due respect, I don't wish to see you again. It is too much."

Flowridia steeled her countenance as she took a step back. "I understand."

But as she turned to leave, Lara said, "No, you don't. You can't fathom what it means to have your entire life and legacy ruined. But you wouldn't have come this far without lying to yourself."

Flowridia froze, those final words tearing at the walls around her heart, the ones that hid the pieces of her still capable of love toward another person.

Flowridia swallowed tears and left the library, withholding the goodbye at her lip until the door slammed shut.

Demitri's voice wove into her head. *Mom—*

Flowridia ran.

Up the stairs she flew, desperation driving her steps. For the hell she'd wrought upon the world, she knew she'd burn, but there was one casualty she'd never meant to leave. Not like this.

She raced past undead guards and pillars of sand, all of it a blur. Sorrow faded into rage, for this was not a crime she had committed, yet it bore the stain of her responsibility, nonetheless. When she burst into Casvir's office, she cried, "How could you?!"

Casvir turned, intrigue in his raised eyebrow. "Flowridia?"

"You took Lara."

"You are surprised?"

Flowridia flung the door shut as she marched to his desk. "You won the war. You don't need her anymore."

"Her knowledge of magic is unparalleled; she is a valuable servant to keep."

This wasn't Valeuron, who was desecrated but whose soul had remained free. Flowridia slammed her hands onto the hard wood of his desk. "Release her."

Casvir's intrigue faded into something severe, the slight twist of his lip conveying disapproval. "No."

When he looked back down at the papers he read, Flowridia slipped the top one away from his gaze. His glare bespoke her imminent demise, but what did she have to lose now? No titles, no land, and no wife to love—she alone remained to fix this great injustice. "You have no right."

"According to the laws of my land—"

"Then make a deal! You love contracts."

Casvir's stare held absolutely no indication of being impressed. With a quick flick of his claw, he stole the paper back. "Make me an offer."

"You've already stolen everything from me." Though her fury simmered, the sorrow it had drowned threatened to rise and consume her anew.

"You are the one wanting to trade. Time is valuable. Make this worth mine."

Though it tore a piece of herself off with it, she ripped the wedding ring from her finger and placed it on the table. "Take this."

Casvir spared it a glance. "What does it do?"

"Makes the wearer immune to magical compulsion. It was my gift when I agreed—" Flowridia stopped, unwilling to explain to intricacies of her wedding arrangement. "Take this, instead."

Casvir shook his head. "Impressive, but not worth the empress."

Flowridia took her ring back. "Lunestra's crown," she offered, though it wounded her to part with it. "I still have it.

Take it and lord your victory over the Theocracy. Display it as a trophy."

"Tempting, but no."

"Then take my services. I'll work for you. I'll sign your paperwork—"

"In your current predicament, you would perform such tasks either way."

"Casvir, I have *nothing*."

"Then, we have nothing to discuss."

Frustration tore a cry from her throat. She looked to Demitri, who merely stared. "I'll write down every secret my mother ever taught me."

Casvir shook his head.

"Gods *damn it, Casvir!*" she cried, furious at him and at the tears welling in her eyes. "My life, my love, my firstborn child, every flower I've ever grown—"

The pen he held clattered to the desk. "Done."

Flowridia snapped her jaw shut, taken aback, then said, "You think so highly of my gardening?"

"I do think highly of your talents," he said, "but I have no need for your skills in cultivating flowers. I will accept your child."

His intrigue shook her to the core, sudden dread washing over her. "You want my child?"

"Your mother held every bit of potential I could have hoped for, yet you are her superior in every conceivable way. Your child will be even greater and mine to train from birth."

Bumps rose along her arms, in tandem with Demitri's sudden growling. "And who would be the father?"

"Whomever you chose, though I would maintain the power to dismiss unworthy suitors."

Demitri's hackles raised, hatred in those golden eyes.

"I . . ." Flowridia's hands clutched the other, but she hardly felt them. "No. No, I can't."

Casvir gave a deferring nod. "Lara shall remain mine."

He returned to his paperwork. Flowridia said, "Casvir, I can't. You know I could never love a man."

"Love is not necessary for conception."

Beads of sweat welled upon her brow, in tandem with coldness permeating her skin.

"However, I am a patient man," he continued, pragmatic as ever, the betrayal of his character leaving her frozen. "So long as a child is conceived before your child-rearing years end, I will consider the bargain fulfilled. Otherwise, I will rip Lara's soul back from the Beyond."

Long ago, Flowridia had given up dreams of conceiving her own children, instead devoting her heart to any in her charge.

Demitri spoke, always wiser than her. *Your child is worth Lara's soul?*

"I have to make this right," she whispered, but the cost and all that came with it rose ever higher, the more she considered it.

But Lara, who had died to save her . . .

Flowridia shut her eyes, her bitter heart breaking at her next words. "And there's nothing else you'll accept?"

"You would have to state a more agreeable price."

Lara enslaved . . . for all eternity. Casvir never died, per Soliel's words—in fact, he rose to be the greatest villain of all.

And she would hand a child to someone like that? Flowridia's own soul had been sold before her birth to this man; the cycle continued.

Absently, she stroked Demitri's fur, the sweet boy little more than a child despite his size. She did not feel his touch; she felt nothing at all. Not two weeks ago, she had bid a final farewell to Lara and her gifted bouquet, thinking it would be the last time . . .

Was this the true and final end? Was this what it would take to alleviate the crushing guilt in her soul?

What would Ayla say to this?

"I'll do it," Flowridia whispered, though every fiber of her being revolted at the thought. "Take my child, and free Lara's soul."

"As you soon as you sign, she will be released."

Flowridia gripped her arm, her nails driving no feeling into the numb skin. "Deliver the news once it's done. Don't tell her the cost." Emotion rose within her throat, but she swallowed the threatened sob. "But tell her I'm sorry."

Casvir took a blank piece of paper and began writing in perfect, utilitarian script. When her knees shook, Flowridia clung to her familiar for support. Emptiness hollowed her, reaching down to her soul. Too exhausted to be angry, but refusing to cry, all she could do was listen to the scratching pen upon the parchment that would seal her fate.

"Casvir," she whispered, meeting his eye when he had the civility to at least face her, "do I really mean so little to you?"

"Quite the contrary. You continue to surprise me with every step you take. Your talents are unique and boundless in their potential—"

"Yes, and you're so proud, I know." She felt only defeat, and it came out in her bitter words, calm as they were. "I'm counted among your friends, or so you wrote. Always welcome here—me and my progeny. I don't doubt you would love for me to have a seat on your council, though you'd never dismiss Murishani, despite him being the reason I never will. Did you know he plucked me from the battlefield and locked me in a coffin, hoping I'd suffocate?"

"I did not," Casvir replied, a faint glower darkening his features.

"And you'll swat him on the backside like last time, but you won't actually do anything that makes a difference. He's too valuable. You might not like him, but you respect him—" Her voice caught; behind her back, she clenched her fists to staunch her rising tears. ". . . and you may care for me, but you don't respect me at all."

"I have great respect for your talents."

"For my talents, my power, my potential—yes, I know. But not for me. I'm an investment who has paid out well, and now I'll continue paying out for an entirely new generation—congratulations."

He set down his pen, hands clasping on the desk as his red eyes bore into her own. "I am not forcing you to do anything. If you sign, it is of your own free will."

"Yes, after you've backed me into a corner and placed a knife to the throat of someone dear to me." He opened his mouth to speak, but with her rising tears came a burst of anger. "I miss the woods, Casvir. I miss riding by your side. I miss sitting beside the campfire at night as you helped me explore necromancy. I was in mourning, but you comforted me. We found a friendship that was unexpected but brought me so much joy. You believed in me. You supported me. The Casvir in the woods is a vastly different man than the imperator. I know it isn't personal that you've completely destroyed the life I built, but somehow that makes it worse."

"I have not meant—"

"Don't you dare finish that sentence." From his desk, she snatched the document, half-complete, but saw the important words: *For the freedom of Alauriel Solviraes' soul . . .*

. . . before the end of your child-rearing years . . .

. . . who shall be mine to train—

"I have given you everything, Flowridia," he said, the barest hints of menace in his words, "and I can take it away."

It was as she had been warned, yet the threat meant nothing at all to her bitter heart. "Not everything."

She snatched the pen from his desk and signed: *Flowridia Darkleaf, Daughter of Zanoram Makosa and Odessa of the Abyssal Swamp, Beloved of The Endless Night, former Grand Diplomat of Staelash, former Empress Consort of Solvira, and a woman of spite.*

She set the pen down. "I hope your kingdom burns."

As she and Demitri left, she heard, "Flowridia—"

And nothing more, for she slammed the door behind them.

"I don't really understand what it means. All that Uluron said . . ."

In the underground library, Etolié shut her eyes, dwelling on minor existential despair.

"But the idea that this has all happened before is fucking me up," Etolié continued, and beside her, Lara listened, contemplation on her lovely features.

Strange, to see her looking whole. Flowers had been good for one thing. Sorta like lighting a building on fire but spitting on a smoldering ember.

"Did the dragon say what sort of darkness the world falls into?" Lara said, but Etolié shook her head. "Then I agree with what she said—that the only ones who can know the key to changing the future are the Old Gods themselves. But only if they, too, know it is a cycle."

"Uluron suggested Soliel doesn't."

Lara's words held contemplation. "He knows every ripple, but only in hindsight. There would have to be a catalyst to cause him to deviate from the fated course."

"Are you suggesting we stroll up and tell him something has to change? I'd personally rather have the Bringer of War pummel him into paste. That would also solve the crisis."

"Would it though?" Lara said, and Etolié wondered if it might be best to drop this, given they were discussing the man who had brutally murdered her. Yet Lara seemed calm, or at least focused enough on the problem at hand to set it aside. "I'm just as keen to end him as anyone, but killing him may not even be the answer. The dragon is implying that he fails, but the cycle continues nevertheless."

Etolié sat on the table, next to where Lara sat daintily in her chair. "This also means that causing the wrong ripple will mean he succeeds."

"True," Lara whispered. "And that is not a comforting thought either."

At Lara's notable distress, Etolié placed a hand on her shoulder. "We don't have to talk about Soliel."

"I'm trapped here, Etolié. I might as well be of some use." Anguish twisted her features; Lara's eyes shut, and her words came soft and scared. "Am I awful for wishing I were not? This was my quest. Defeating Soliel is the greatest good, but I'm tired, Etolié."

"There was no justice in your death, Moonbeam. But there's just as little in you coming back."

"As bitter as it sounds, I wish I had moved on. There's something else I—"

Familiar clicking stole Etolié's attention. "Zoldar! Bug!"

Her Skalmite friend emerged from the shelves, quite content among the realm of knowledge, or so he'd said.

"There you are. Rumor is you're getting neighbors. They're bringing the rest of the Skalmites to Nox'Kartha."

Zoldar signed, punctuating it with his usual clicks and foreign whirring.

"You don't get a choice, buddy. Imperator's orders."

This time, the bug spat—technically at her feet, but tone was important in this instance. He meant no disrespect

"Nobody's going to try and take you away from me. If anything, you're my first pick to join me in Solvira."

He didn't speak; he just perked up.

"As Empress of Solvira, I have to pick a council, and I'd be charmed to have you as an official representative of the Skalmites, assuming you *don't* want neighbors."

Zoldar gave a few positive clicks, and Etolié grinned.

"You can help me pick the rest. I'll write you a list."

Zoldar clicked an affirmation, then skittered away.

"Can I tell you what fucking sucks?" Etolié said, fresh bitterness rising, to remember Zoldar and Sora's story. "Soliel fucking stayed. He dug Zoldar out of the rubble of the fucking manor, after the fucking earthquake I created. He freed Sora and the rest before they froze to death. And then he walked away. I fucked up, because what other choice did I have to save the world? But he didn't burn Staelash. He's the reason my friends aren't fucking dead."

Furious tears stung her eyes, because the world made no damn sense, that Soliel would murder someone so dear to her heart, would burn the woman she loved beyond recognition—just to turn around and save her friends after Etolié had accidentally condemned them.

He was a monster. He had to be. Etolié clung to that, but . . .

Lara watched, but her eyes were distant. Etolié sat beside her on the table. "You're looking weepy, Moonbeam. This whole Soliel thing . . ."

"It's not that."

Etolié took her hand, prepared for the disconcerting chill of her skin. "Listen, Flowers is a fucking idiot, but if you want me to fetch her and get some closure . . ."

Lara shook her head, her countenance the same. "I'm not thinking about her. It would be better if I never do again."

Harsh, but Etolié was proud of her moonbeam for that attitude.

"There's something far more wrenching to me, actually, that I haven't yet told you." Lara's silver eyes remained as vibrant as they had in life; in moments like this, Etolié nearly forgot the cruel tragedy of her death. "Etolié, I . . . I know what happens to souls destroyed by Silver Fire."

That . . . was not at all the segue Etolié expected. "Go on."

"After my violent end, it was a bittersweet relief, to be in the Beyond. The endless mists were soothing, in their haunting way. But I wasn't alone. When we die . . ." Her breath caught, and Etolié watched her compose herself like the trained monarch she was. ". . . if we were cursed to absorb a soul, they're set free."

The words lingered, the implications leaving Etolié breathless. "You weren't alone. Was it—"

Lara smiled despite the anguish twisting her features. "It was my mom."

Empress Ralaena's death had shaken Solvira, the tragedy unfathomable, her end a noble one, they said, even if Etolié would never understand—or agree. But this . . . "She's not destroyed?"

Lara shook her head, her brilliant eyes shutting tight. Quiet tears slipped down her cheeks. "She was real, Etolié. Her soul spent a lifetime trapped inside me, but she was with me. She was with me all along. And it almost made it worth it, to die but find a piece of my heart I hadn't realized was missing." Lara's happy tears suddenly changed, sorrow twisting her visage. "We traversed the Beyond together, until I was dragged back here again."

The unmistakable, metallic strides of Imperator First and Last sounded behind the arrangement of shelves. Etolié placed a hand on Lara's shoulder as she placed herself between her moonbeam and the approaching tyrant, wishing she could take them both to mom's house, to Sha'Demoni—anywhere but here, where Lara was damned to an eternal servitude. But Etolié's soul would be forfeit, and likely Khastra's too, for there was a knife on her throat forevermore.

Lara stood and bowed, but Etolié merely crossed her arms. "Yes, Tyrant Deathless?"

"Alauriel," he said, giving Etolié no mind, "your soul has been paid for. You will be released from my service. Lady Flowridia asked me to tell you that and to convey her sincere apology."

Damn that Flowers. Etolié hated her with every bit of fire in her veins, but hate was hardly the opposite of love. For all her sickening acts, she still came through for Lara.

Shock showed in Lara's visage. "When?"

"Now—"

"Wait!" Etolié said, arms held up. "Five minutes." The weight of his words became heavier with every passing second, and with it came a rise of desperation. "Please. Let me say goodbye."

Casvir's cool expression never changed. "What is it worth to you?"

"What?"

"A year for each minute—"

"Fine!" Etolié spat. "Five more years. Twenty-five it is. Fuck it and fuck you too. But let me say goodbye."

Casvir looked behind her, presumably to Lara, but Etolié didn't dared follow his stare, lest her tears fall too soon. She would not give him the satisfaction. "Five minutes," he said, and then he turned around.

He marched away, and Etolié stole the girl she adored into her arms. "I love you," she said, her tears already welling.

"Etolié, you shouldn't have—"

"Damn what I should or shouldn't have done!" Etolié pulled back. She took Lara's face into her hands and gazed into those beautiful eyes, ones that hadn't changed since infancy.

Lara had been a baby, once. A tender child who cooed at her touch, who giggled at Etolié's illusionary tales, who smiled at all the lullabies she sang.

"Don't look back," Etolié said. "Leave this world to the living. I swear I will devote my heart and soul to your quest. The orbs will be found. Soliel will be stopped. But, Lara, don't look back."

Lara's face twisted in anguish; her tears had never stopped. "Etolié—"

"I mean it." Etolié wiped a thumb across her sweet face, her tears as cool as her skin. "You'll find no peace here. But maybe there's a paradise for you, yet. Gods know, you deserve it. You were always too good for this world." Etolié dared to smile at the jest, but it shattered as she sobbed. "I'll tell my momma. She'll find you. She'll make sure you find your rest."

She took Lara into her arms, breaking down at the whispered words, "I love you, Etolié."

Etolié held her, stroking the fine strands of her hair in a way that would have garnered a reprimand from a younger Lara—*"You're ruining the braid, Etolié. I spent so much time—"*

She tried to laugh, but it released as a sob. In her arms, Lara shuddered and shook.

Etolié gasped as she struggled to breathe, willing her composure to stay for just a minute more. It would be a gentle end, the final gift to give. Lara deserved a hundred years more, to live a life of love and grace, to grow old and leave a legacy of peace—but fate was not Etolié's to control.

Time was short. Etolié savored the embrace, memorializing the moment. To Etolié, she was worth it all.

"Go on home, Moonbeam," she whispered. "Your family is waiting."

In Lara's words, there was acceptance, and perhaps even relief. "My mom said something I think you should know. She wished she could thank you."

This time, Etolié did laugh. "For what? For fucking you up?"

"For loving me like I was yours."

Etolié saw, again, the vision of the infant girl the emperor long ago placed in her arms, with a dark fluff of hair and precious, grabbing fingers and a cry loud enough to wake the castle—until Etolié sang to calm her down.

Here, Lara cried, and so Etolié sang:

Sleep, little moonchild
The night is not gone.
So be soothed by the stars
And the sound of my song.
Morning will come;
The night turned to day.
But, sleep, little moonchild—

There was no movement. Sleep had truly come.

. . . For my love never fades.

Alone, Etolié wept.

That night, Flowridia tossed and turned but could not sleep.

Thoughts of Ayla drove her mad, her hope fading with every passing hour. She trembled, though she was not cold, yet she felt raw, exposed.

Her bargain haunted her. But her heart, though broken irreparably, felt a semblance of peace. Etolié would hate her until her dying day, but Lara could go; she could rest—Casvir, for all his faults, never lied.

To say goodbye would have been an insult. Instead, Flowridia wept.

When sleep evaded her, Flowridia stood and stumbled toward a bookshelf by the wall, careful to not jostle her sleeping Demitri. Her hand skimmed past her heirloom crown. She let it be, instead stealing a book sequestered at the top, handmade from leather, the binding broken—and bearing the prophetic words *Flowridia Darkleaf.*

Pressed between the cover and the first page, protected from air and the passing of time were words that conveyed joy, even to her brutalized, exhausted heart. Written in love, after a dance long ago, they brought memories of light: *The dance was sublime. I love you, Flowra.*

Her mind conjured thoughts of a perfect night, and if she focused, she could hear the words pristine in her mind, Ayla's voice having not yet faded.

"Flowra?"

Flowridia whirled around; those whispered words were *not from her head.*

There stood Ayla Darkleaf, her demure hands resting upon the side of the bookshelf, her expressive eyes seeking reproach.

Flowridia's strength failed. The book fell to the floor, the binding unraveling and scattering the pages across the floor. She gasped; she sobbed; she fell into those outstretched arms. "Oh, Ayla, my wife, my wife..." The cold embrace warmed her heart.

"I know you must have worried. I am so sorry." Ayla pulled back enough to gaze up into her eyes. In Flowridia's peripheral, Demitri stirred, his golden eyes reflecting the dim, ambient light. "Izthuni dragged me into Sha'Demoni. It took time for me to lick my wounds and walk again. He is still unwell, but he shall live."

"Ayla," Flowridia said, cupping her cheek, stroking her hair, loving every piece of her beloved wife's presence.

Ayla indulged her, her own subtle desperation apparent in how she clutched Flowridia's gown. "I meant to bring you Murishani's head as an apology, but you will never guess what I saw—a public flogging. Well, semi-public. It was in the throne room, performed by Casvir himself, a hundred lashes administered to Murishani before the witnessing crowd of nobles in his castle and any servants who cared to attend."

Flowridia's breath had stopped. "He ..."

"And so, I think I shall let Murishani live another day and carry this shame a little longer."

The idea brought conflict to her battered heart—that Casvir, somewhere in his black soul, still cared.

"Run away with me."

The words were said with such passion, such joy. Taken aback, Flowridia struggled to understand. "Leave Nox'Kartha?"

Ayla cupped her face, radiant light in her countenance. "Can you believe the adventure we have had? My darling, we were monarchs, practically gods—and now we're nothing, but . . ." Her smile remained soft, even as she chuckled. ". . . I think being nothing would be nice, for a little while. Take time for us to simply be. A cottage in the woods—you and me. And Demitri."

Flowridia gave her affirmation, captivated by Ayla's icy blue and silver gaze, for what else mattered more? She beckoned for Demitri, who came to complete their little family.

She thought of Etolié, who sold her soul to save a thousand lives, and of herself, who sold her own to slay them. Lara had said she lied to herself, but nevermore. Here was Ayla, come to steal her away—poetic in a way. When Flowridia took Ayla's hand, she was made anew.

A monster she would be. No turning back.

They kissed, and Ayla tasted of blood and victory, of a thousand cries suddenly silenced. Flowridia took Lunestra's crown as a final bit of spite, then motioned for her familiar to follow.

With hands intertwined and Demitri close behind, Ayla and Flowridia stepped into the shadows.

The sun set upon a peaceful scene, the moon rising in tandem. Etolié's hope exactly—for the moon to rise upon a Solviraes funeral bespoke a good omen, blessings upon their continued progeny.

Though there was no progeny. Not anymore.

Staelash held only one cemetery—unfortunately unsettled after the earthquake. But the damage was minimal, and thank the gods for that. A few of the larger tombstones had fallen, but any with simple markers had survived and still maintained their peace.

Buried among the commoners was the great Empress Alauriel Solviraes, last of her name, wielder of the Silver Fire, benefactor of Staelash, and one of the most brilliant and lovely minds Etolié had ever known. But her tombstone said none of that; instead, to protect her legacy, merely the beloved pet name—*Lara.*

Beside the grave, a second one had been erected. Not a body, but a name, a memorial Etolié had insisted upon. His body had been destroyed in the explosion, but she had failed this man in life. She would give him peace in death.

Thalmus, a father.

Instead of a body, she had buried a spear of unparalleled artistry, gifted to someone he had dearly loved.

Etolié wept, and beside her was Khastra, never more than a touch away lately. "We tell no one," Etolié whispered.

A rough hand rested upon her shoulder and gave a reassuring squeeze. Khastra's voice held utmost comfort. "You have done right by her, Etolié."

Murishani had grossly exaggerated the damage to her small client kingdom—the greatest casualty had been the manor. Most of the walls had collapsed, leaving familiar rubble for her to navigate. The recesses of Etolié's library had suffered the most. The cleanup continued, helmed by Etolié when she could, but she was Empress of Solvira now, and she had more important things to do.

Even if her heart ached to even think of it. This was her fault.

And every time she thought of Soliel, who had not burned it down as he'd threatened . . . She didn't understand.

A few houses had been damaged in the earthquake, which Etolié had insisted be taken care of first—which Marielle, the new Duchess of Staelash, hadn't argued with.

Which was good, lest Etolié have to cut a bitch.

The Temple of Sol Kareena had taken a mighty blow, windows destroyed, most of the walls having fallen. It would be rebuilt, though without its high priestess.

As Etolié looked upon the precious gravestone, she thought of she and Sora's final farewell in Nox'Kartha, not hours before.

"Where will you go?"

"I haven't decided," Sora replied, her stare transfixed upon the great castle in Nox'Kartha. She held Leelan in her hands, clutching him gently to her chest. "I thought, at first, to go to Solvira and give whatever comfort I could to the Theocracy refugees there—but it seems you've done the best anyone can do."

Etolié's bargain meant many things—and with the war over, the lives of the refugees were guaranteed in writing, at least for the next twenty-five years. She had done a few things right.

"There's a temple to Sol Kareena here," Sora continued, "but serving in the shadow of the man my goddess so virulently opposes makes me sick." She crossed her arms, her fingers digging into the sleeves of her tunic. "Viceroy Murishani offered me a position as an official liaison to the elven territories, which is a joke and an insult. I turned him down." She glanced up at Etolié. "I think I'll visit the temple and pray. From there, I don't know."

When she offered a hand, Etolié accepted, her tears falling faster. She squeezed and hoped the gesture conveyed her love. "You're good people, Sora. Don't let this be the last time I see you."

Red rimmed Sora's eyes. *"I'm good at surviving."*

All Etolié's friends, gone away—except Zoldar, but he was contractually obligated to stay. "What's the point of having friends if they just leave?" she muttered, to the only one left beside her.

Khastra stepped up close enough to brush her with her body. "Friends often come for only a season or two, to support you, to teach you, perhaps even become something more."

Etolié's blush overtook her cheeks. "All right, you and your fancy poetry. Still hurts. Especially when they betray you."

Flowers was somewhere out in the world, walking freely with that vampire bitch.

"That will happen too," Khastra said, more subdued this time. "The tiny one has much to answer for."

"That flowery cunt thinks she can just burn the world and get away with it. I'll kill her, Khastra. I'll rip her head off myself."

"And what would Lara think of that?"

Damn her. Etolié looked to the grave, all her fury deflating at the words. "My goddess momma is known for mercy and forgiveness. I'm not her. But I could be the 'Goddess of Biting Her Tongue and Holding a Grudge for All Eternity.'"

"You will be fighting Alystra for that title."

Etolié's scoffing laughter erupted at that, forcing her to smile. "All right, fair. But you don't just forgive someone for blowing up half a kingdom."

"While it was not an insubstantial amount, it was not half of Solvira. It was not even half of Neolan—"

"Oh, fuck off. Let me be angry."

Khastra placed a hand on Etolié's back, scratching soothing lines through the false fabric, mindful of where her wings would be. There was so much to be angry for—for the betrayal of Flowers, the fact that The Endless Night wandered the world once more, that grandpa simply wasn't who she thought, that she couldn't even think about Sol Kareena without the ensuing cognitive dissonance, and Soliel, into whose throat she would still happily drive a knife . . .

The world was complicated.

Her mind considered all that was lost, the people and the knowledge in the once legendary library. Countless years of history—gone. Erased.

But with thoughts of what was lost came thoughts of what wasn't. The Skalmites remained the accidental heroes and victors of the tragedy. Reginal lived. It was a damn miracle. He had told the story of how Flowers had spared him, and Etolié hated her for having a heart, even if it meant someone she cared for had lived.

Khastra interrupted her onerous thoughts. "And you will be staying here for twenty years?"

"Twenty-five, now. Five more minutes with Lara cost me." Etolié smiled up at Khastra, her silver tattoos luminous in the rising moonlight. "Looks like it's you and me again, ya big lug. I always seem to orbit back to you."

Khastra wore no armor today, merely a shirt that showed off the intricate array of body art covering her arms, neck, and chest, and so Etolié felt her skin—warm again, a small consolation for the cost—through the thin fabric and the taut, rippling musculature beneath. "There is nowhere I would rather be than by your side," Khastra said, and Etolié, despite having lost everything—the girl she helped to raise, her protégé, her kingdom, her comrades; thankfully, her dignity had been misplaced long ago—thought that Khastra by her side might be enough.

To the grave, Etolié whispered, "I'll miss you, my little moonbeam," and she prepared for twenty-five years of an unknown abyss.

Save for Khastra, the great planet to her orbiting star.

"Etolié . . ."

Etolié perked up at the words, before realizing she alone could hear them. She squeezed Khastra's hand, then thought very hard. *"Momma?"*

"Etolié, come to Celestière, when you can."

"Is something wrong?"

"Yes."

Etolié released Khastra's hand, all the world fading to what sounded in her head.

"Come to Celestière," Staella echoed. *"We need to talk about the scroll."*

As Sora roamed the streets, she cursed the city's winding paths and baffling placement of monuments. A helpful merchant had pointed her toward the religious district of the city, but somehow the white marbled buildings now all looked the same.

Sora never got lost. She wasn't lost now. She was merely disoriented.

A wrong turn landed her in the district devoted to Demon Gods, and Sora kept a hand on a dagger sheathed within her trousers. In the quiet night, even the distant scuffling of boots caused her heartbeat to rise.

Before her was a familiar sigil placed atop a multi-tiered temple—The Endless Night, Izthuni's Spawn, and Sora knew she had taken a wrong turn.

Screaming from within spoke of agony, yet Nox'Kartha wouldn't allow the residents to freely feed from citizens. Bracing herself for death, Sora ran through the slightly ajar doors, silver knife readied, and saw pure carnage.

Decapitated remains lay strewn across the windowless, stone room, though Sora struggled to see in the dark. Bodies lay in heaps, slaughtered with no remorse.

A blast of light; the room erupted in flame.

Fire caught the rug, and as it slowly burned, Sora saw the final three among the carnage—two of whom were familiar, bearing pointed ears and a shared surname. Tazel Fireborn, wielding a rapier, turned at Sora's stare, green eyes conveying shock, but then his scarred lips turned into a smile. "Sora?"

Beside him was a woman whose features took on the color of the blazing rug, her skin as white as snow. Stark blonde hair—tussled and stained with gore—shifted as Mereen's eyes pierced a hole straight through Sora. Beauty shone in her stance, even the sneer of her lip, revealing her fangs. "Sora," she said, derision in the name, though Sora was well used to it, "fancy seeing you here."

"Fancy seeing you," Sora replied, hand sliding to her dagger, "slaughtering the entire temple."

Mereen's laughter held music as it echoed across the stone walls. She gave no care to the fire on the rug, her booted feet taking slow steps toward Sora. "Haven't you heard? Izthuni is weak and shall remain so, until he heals from his grievous wounds. Who am I to deny myself the opportunity to slay his most loyal?"

Sora hadn't heard, but it made sense. Etolié had said The Endless Night had blown apart, destroying the Solviran Palace.

Beside Mereen, Tazel glanced between the two of them nervously, and Sora wondered, if Mereen pounced, who he would defend.

Near him was a third figure Sora did not know—a young human woman, gorgeous and fair, her fiery hair as lush as autumn leaves. No blood covered her robes; instead, she appeared unarmed, though Sora knew enough of magic to smell it in the air around her. The woman grinned, and though Sora had never seen her face, she knew her smile.

A ghostly woman in a swamp had once held the very same.

"There's a whisper on the winds that Ayla Darkleaf still lives," Mereen said.

"I have reason to believe that whisper is true," Sora replied. Flowridia had disappeared; there could be no other culprit.

Everything about Mereen held power, from her stance to the alluring curl of her lip. "And what have you heard?" she asked, cruelty behind her patronizing tone. "Rumor says you gave up your title, bastard-born—"

"Mereen," Tazel interrupted, sharpness in the phrase. He looked at Sora, an apology in his gaze. "You said you've heard whispers as well?"

Tazel had always been kind; when she'd asked him once, he said it came from travelling the world. *"You learn that everyone has a heart,"* he had told her. *"Not just the people who look like you."*

"Flowridia Darkleaf disappeared from the castle last night," Sora said, the vision of Etolié's furious glower not one to forget. "They say Ayla stole her and her familiar."

Intrigue filled Mereen's gaze. "Ayla Darkleaf is no mere vampire. Her undeath is a literal curse, placed upon her by Izthuni, and to slay her, we must break that curse. But no one, for two thousand years, has known how—except *one*. And now, because of our new companion, we'll have the means to negotiate." She gestured to the human woman, who looked positively gleeful. "Odessa has agreed to assist us."

Odessa winked, and Sora's stomach churned.

Mereen looked to Tazel, her coy stance causing Sora's stomach to grow ill. "The opportunity has been handed to us on a silver platter. We go to the elven lands." Her cruel gaze landed on Sora. "And what about you? Will you join us? Aid in destroying the monster once and for all?"

Sora shifted her stare from Mereen to Odessa, and finally to Tazel, who looked as surprised at the words as she. Unease welled in Sora's stomach, her innate distrust of her vampiric progenitor rising to the surface, yet she spoke of the greater good, the chance to slay a monster.

"Will you try to kill me again?"

"I need all the help I can get, Sora," Mereen said, and though nothing about her held sincerity, the words were true. "And whatever my distaste for your tainted blood, you are a Fireborn. Killing Ayla Darkleaf is our destiny."

Against her better judgement, Sora gave a resolute nod. "I will join you."

Dread lingered in Flowridia's veins, for the bargain she had made.

She waited until they had settled in an inn at the outskirts of Nox'Kartha—her idea, proclaiming they deserved a bit of luxury. After offering extra coin for Demitri's own pampering—his own room with a bath and all the meat he could consume—she stole Ayla away to their private quarters. She lavished Ayla in affection, made love in the bath and later in bed, until both were near collapse from pleasure.

Ayla lay utterly still, curled against her body, while Flowridia slowly caught her breath. She recited words in her head, preparing for the worst, but knowing Ayla to be most amiable in her listless, post-lovemaking state.

"There's something you should know," she whispered in their candlelit confines.

In muted tones, she told her tale, unable to face her love as she revealed her hand—that she had sold something of incomparable worth, and all for someone Ayla hated.

Ayla remained perfectly impassive all the while, even as Flowridia expressed her regret, her dread, yet clung to this as her final good deed, the last shattered piece of her world she had to right . . .

In absolute silence, Ayla sat up, nude as she approached the window and gazed upon the rising sun in the distance. Ice shown in her stare, the silver tones more familiar by the day, though hints of blue remained.

And there she remained, quiet and still, until Flowridia's fearful heart could take it no longer. "Tell me your thoughts," she said. "I don't care if they're hurtful."

"Oh, they are," Ayla muttered, and in a rare release of breath came smoke. "Did you even think for a moment the hellish fate you would be condemning that child to?"

Not the reaction Flowridia expected. She sat up, though did not dare to leave the bed. "I was angry. I was shocked. Casvir's audacity has no end, and whatever love I once had for him . . ." She clenched her jaw, the bitter heat of betrayal pulsing through her anew. ". . . for him to even suggest it, I feel . . ."

The word that came was unexpected. Jarring.

". . . violated."

Ayla finally met her gaze, something new in her calculated visage. "It is what he does, Flowra. He takes and he takes with no consideration to the cost."

"I thought he was my friend," Flowridia whispered, the true tragedy finally settling. "And I think he still is. I truly believe there's a kind man somewhere beneath the mantle of imperator. I met him in the woods; he cared for me when I was in mourning. He's done so much good for me with no thought of reward, and yet . . ."

When her voice trailed off, Ayla spoke instead. "Perhaps you are right. But whatever sentimental attachment you have to him, I think you finally understand my point of view."

Flowridia couldn't speak, but her heart agreed.

To her surprise, Ayla came to stand beside her, gently holding her against her body. "Fear not, Flowra. I swear to you, this will not come to pass."

Flowridia shook her head, gazing up at Ayla from below. "I can't betray my contract. If I do, Lara will be brought back, and I . . . I know you hate her, but I'm begging you to try and understand."

At the mention of Lara's name, contempt twisted Ayla's lip. "I do, and to be honest, it gives me my own selfish peace of mind if she's truly gone. But that is not what I'm proposing. Keep your contract. Leave this to me."

Ayla's nails drew pleasurable lines across her scalp, but Flowridia's stomach felt sick. "Explain."

"There can be no contract if there is no man to come claim his dues. This merely renews my prior conviction." Ayla grinned, ever the predator, and it sent a shiver down Flowridia's spine. "I am going to kill Casvir."

Cold settled as deep as her soul, though Flowridia could not argue against the effective solution. "What of Soliel? What of his words? He tried for hundreds of years to destroy him—do you think you'll do better?"

"I have time to sort that out, Flowra. Per your words, you have . . . goodness, twenty years at least. And that is assuming we don't find your path to immortality. But I digress." Her smile devolved into a truly wicked laugh, and Flowridia felt relief far more than fear. "I care not for cryptic Gods spouting cryptic words, nor shall I be held by the bounds of so-called fate. I will slay Casvir. He is not a god yet, and I will not stop until I gain whatever power it takes to destroy him forever. This is my promise to you, Flowra, and I deem it as sacred as our wedding vows."

Flowridia managed to nod, for above all else, she trusted her wife's conviction.

"First, we rest," Ayla continued. "We find our bearings as a couple, take time to love each other and simply be wives. Then I find his phylactery. It will not be easy, but watch me scour every inch of this world and Sha'Demoni. I will *crush* it in my bare hands, leaving him vulnerable." She released Flowridia's hair, lost in her fantasy, a wistful expression on her sharp features. "From there, I think tearing out and destroying his soul is a tremendously effective way to end someone. What do you say?"

Breathless, Flowridia agreed. "I still feel guilty. Ayla, I'm sorry."

Ayla's good mood flickered a moment, revealing a vulnerable girl. "You should feel guilty," she said simply, "because I am hurt. Yes, there is the cost to you, and I would never downplay it, but consider my feelings. Consider my part in this, to watch you carry some man's child, sit idly by as you're fucked to conceive it. I cannot bear the thought. Or worse, if we—"

She cut herself off, suddenly stepping back like a wounded animal. "What is it?" Flowridia asked, still unwilling to rise.

"Nothing," Ayla said, though far too quickly for it to be true. "Nothing at all, because nothing is worse than that." The anguish in her gaze faded away, however, leaving something soft. Her smile, when it came, was sincere. "But this is not unforgivable. You have given me the respect of at least telling me the truth. All will be well in the end—Lara's soul shall stay in the Beyond and Casvir's head will be a fixture on my mantlepiece."

"What of Soliel's words?" Flowridia said. "Can you defeat Casvir when even the Old Gods could not?"

"Do not forget—he cannot kill me either. Let it be an eternal stalemate at worst, but I will never stop fighting for you, my love."

"You're very forgiving," Flowridia said, still waiting for castigation. "I don't deserve your kindness."

"We deserve nothing," Ayla said idly, but something soft befell her countenance. "I offer kindness because I love you. I ask only for the same in return."

Flowridia's eyes welled with tears for the familiar, treasured words. She came beside Ayla and took her in her arms. In silence, they held the other, sunrise casting light into their bedroom.

In a land across the sea, thousands of miles away, the God of Order stood before the throne of Executor Luc Stormforged.

The executor sat upon a seat of iron, the militant décor of the vast room a testament to the elves' ingenuity; it served as a bunker as well as a meeting hall. No windows, but sconces on the wall, burning torches casting flickering light across the man's features. "Rumors have spread of your return," Executor Stormforged said, his posture perfect, gaze unwavering, "yet I did not believe it. Many have come claiming to be the True Gods of this world, but none have come wielding Convergence Orbs—nor have any so perfectly borne his likeness, even in rags."

Behind the throne, a tapestry hung from the ceiling to the floor, woven from wool and laden with beads, depicting the image of a woman facing a vast void of space, her image shrouded in shadow and flame. Six colorful globes of light, each in their own hue, surrounded her as she gazed upon a palette of pure potential. She was creation. She was inspiration. She was the origin of all things.

Or so they believed.

"We of the Four Kingdoms agree that Nox'Kartha's rapid expansion has labeled them a threat," Executor Stormforged continued. "The writing on the wall is clear; Imperator Casvir will come. The Theocracy of Sol Kareena has been decimated. Solvira has bent at the knee to his regime. Our messengers state he has already marched north to Tholheim—the dwarves would do better to have your aid."

"I have every intention of returning to my most loyal," Soliel stated, "but their weapons of earth and stone will fall to the Deathless Army; I believe your people have the means to engage him in a proper fight."

The executor smiled approvingly.

"Furthermore, I seek a Convergence Orb in your lands. Uluron, the Dragon of Death, has left her mountain home— first enslaved to the imperator, but she has now escaped and come here. I believe it is to seek the Tomb of the Mother."

All hushed at the words—the guards, the council, and Executor Stormforged.

"With the Dark Orb, we can steal the forces Casvir controls. Without the Deathless Army, the necromancer is merely a man. I shall find it; I ask for you to halt the imperator's onslaught. There is no one more capable of holding his forces at bay."

Executor Stormforged whispered something to the woman at his left, who grinned, apparently pleased. *"I shall send a message straightaway,"* she replied, her whisper loud enough for Soliel's keen ears to decipher.

"Great Father," the executor said, standing from his throne, "though you are not our deity, our loyalty to the Old Gods has never wavered. We would be honored to assist in your quest. Allow us to bequeath gifts—armor suited for your great figure. A weapon worthy of your might. Is this acceptable?"

Soliel nodded.

"I must selfishly ask one final query—tell us of our Mother. Does she join you in this quest?"

Haunting, the memories the tapestry on the wall evoked from Soliel—eons of time beside a woman with a soul as black as night and a heart as fragile as gold. Countless nights of passion, yet so many more of pain. To love Chaos meant to embrace the very essence of her title.

He opened his mouth to speak, yet words from an infuriating and fascinating woman played through his head: *But what will it mean, for Chaos to return only to see all this horror you've wrought?*

Damn Flowridia. Her death was an omen of the end of the world.

"She will. The time draws ever closer."

End

Coming Soon

Fallen Gods 5: Eve of Endless Night

"Goodnight, little girl. Now the nightmare begins."

War erupts between Nox'Kartha and the Elven Territories, but the world feels far away for Flowridia and Ayla Darkleaf, living a life of bliss--until a summons from the Elven Council upturns their world. Respect among the elves must be earned, and Flowridia steps into a political regime more dangerous than any she has experienced before. But though their allies are unpredictable, they are powerful, and Flowridia thinks she might've found a place for her small family to belong . . .

. . . until the whole world ends with a click and a *boom.*

Darkness falls, enemies become allies, and family is forged and shattered in the fifth installment of FALLEN GODS.

To learn more about Fallen Gods 5: Eve of Endless Night, go to S D Simper's website—sdsimper.com

Keep turning pages for an excerpt from my Patreon exclusive story *The Moon, the Stars, and the Desert Below!*

Thank you so much for reading!

Tear the World Apart is easily my biggest project yet. It's twice the length of *Blood of the Moon*, longer than the entirety of *Sea and Stars*, and definitely felt like it at times. But I have a deep affection for it and all its twists and turns, and I sincerely hope you have enjoyed the ride.

If you enjoyed what you read, please consider leaving a review! It's the best thanks you can give an author if you've enjoyed a book. It helps with both publicity and with ranking and so many more things – so if you wouldn't mind leaving a line or two on Amazon and Goodreads (and BookBub, if you're feeling ambitious), that would mean a whole lot!

If you want to hear more from me, consider joining my newsletter! Currently I'm offering two FREE prequel novellas to new subscribers—one about Flowridia and her time with Aura, as well as another about everyone's favorite drunk angel and that one time she was blackmailed into running a kingdom (and unknowingly ended up on a date with a certain half-demon)!

You can also follow me on social media for all the hilarious news and cat pictures. I'm @sdsimper on Twitter, Instagram, and Facebook.

Thank you for all your love and support <3 See you next time for *Eve of Endless Night!*

-SD Simper

THE MOON, THE STARS,

AND THE DESERT BELOW

*There are many accounts of the story—how
the Moon stole the Stars from the Desert Sands . . .*

a serial novel by
SD Simper

Updated Bi-Monthly | only on Patreon

Prologue ✦✦

In the moments before the end of the world, an angel crept from her family home.

With a blanket wrapped around her form to hide her golden wings, Neoma slipped undetected through the halls. One room held an open skylight, where she and the rest of her family could absorb the blessed light from the suns. It would provide an easy escape. Night meant she would glow like a beacon, but her parents slept, and hopefully she had waited long enough as she slinked through the marbled halls—

"Where are you going?"

Neoma jumped, frozen in the doorframe before her destination—but there was Kareena, peeking from her room, her wings emanating soft light.

"Couldn't sleep," Neoma said, cursing her own suspicious tongue. She stared upon a mirror, both of them cast in hues of gold; they shared many features, she and her twin sister. "Thought I would, um, go for a walk."

Thank her sweet, naïve heart—Kareena was earnest enough to believe it. "Would you like company?"

"No need. Go back to sleep, Kareena."

Her sister retreated into her room, and Neoma tiptoed into the living space, where the gentle light of stars shone above all. The room bore rounded chairs, split in their centers to accommodate angel wings, and a table, for them to eat and supplement the Suns' light on clouded days.

Neoma loved the night sky and its endless stars, the swirling mists of galaxies spreading subtle, cool hues across the universe. But instead of admire the celestial lights, she folded and discarded her blanket, then spread her wings and floated up and out through the open roof.

The rich city of Vanir spread before her.

Countless rows of marbled buildings, interspersed with richly-hued plants and statues, made up the grand city she called home. Neoma adored her bustling Vanir, the epicenter of angelic life on this side of Celestière, though even the great city slept when night fell and the Triple Suns set. Neoma drifted high in the air on glowing wings, the wispy appendages not meant for proper flight, but still capable of simple levitation. She gently floated down, the sensation twisting her stomach. When her feet touched the dirt road, she ran.

Her brother, Romanth, and his wife lived next door, along with her nephew, Morathma. Neoma did not catch any glimpses of familiar amber light, so perhaps they were out; perhaps they were asleep. Still, an idle glance out the window from any of her relatives would destroy her hopes for secrecy, so she rushed past, not stopping until she reached the end of the long row of homes. Kareena had nearly foiled her; Neoma would take no more chances.

She slowed only when she reached the park beyond the rows of homes. Thick trees hung with their boughs nearly covering the path, their branches thick enough to shelter the path, while the rich blue and purple hues of sprites illuminated her steps, even when she deviated from the cobblestones beneath her and wandered into the lush expanse of green. Neoma loved the night creatures, loved the magnificent jewel tones before her, even reached out to touch one wispy puff, its pale purple shade something to cherish.

As children, she and Kareena often ran in the great fields beyond Vanir at night and caught as many sprites as they could carry, to show their mother how stealthy they were. Now, at sixteen, Neoma knew the sprites were really more like plants in intellect, and that giggling children were hardly sneaky. But Neoma was no longer a child, and what waited before her upon a stone bench confirmed that.

Secluded in a small grove was a secret spot of sorts, and Neoma couldn't fathom its use except for clandestine lovers meeting in the dark. There Astrea sat, startling at the soft crunching of rocks beneath Neoma's feet—only to immediately breathe in relief as Neoma peeked through the thick curtain of vines. Flowering bushes glowed behind her in a rainbow of hues, casting light not unlike their wings—though the gentle amethyst glow of Astrea's wings and skin was more beautiful than any flower.

"Hello, Neoma," the girl said, one of the rare angels to match her in age. Something faltered in her smile today, her full lips struggling to convey any semblance of joy.

Worry hurried Neoma's steps. She sat beside Astrea, near enough for the fabric of their clothing to touch. "Is something wrong?"

Astrea's breath caught at the words, and Neoma feared her fluttering lashes were merely blinking away tears. Instead of speak, Astrea pressed their lips together, silencing her with a kiss.

It was not the first time, yet the fluttering sensation in her stomach never waned. Neoma so dearly loved their gentle kisses, both shy, wishing for more but neither daring to press. Neoma habitually pulled away, but Astrea followed, parting her mouth for her tongue. As their mouths melded into passion, Neoma's moan came from somewhere different, somewhere dormant and deep, roused by the intimate gesture. Something had changed, but Neoma could not speak of it, lest she scare it away. She only knew she wanted more; she wanted Astrea.

Astrea suddenly pulled away, anguish twisting her features. "Neoma, I-I am sorry."

Though breathless, Neoma managed to speak her panicked words. "Astrea—"

"We cannot continue this." When Neoma tried to touch her, Astrea flinched, grief apparent in her welling tears. "We are not meant for this. It is not right."

The small paradise Neoma had built, this precious haven, cracked, certain to shatter. "But, Astrea, when I am with you, I feel—"

"It does not matter what we feel," Astrea said, her tears reflecting the ambient light. By the Suns, she was beautiful, even in sorrow, and Neoma's heart broke for her next words. "We would have the whole world against us, and that is not a battle I can fight."

"I would fight it for you," Neoma pled, but Astrea shook her head. "I would protect you. We do not need them. It does not matter what—"

"You would abandon your family for me?" Astrea wiped her tears on the long sleeve of her nightgown, trembling as she fought to keep her composure. "My father laughed when they banished the two women from Nébleus. He said it was what they deserved, after turning so far from their purpose. Neoma, that would be us. The world would mock us before throwing us into the shadowlands to die."

When Neoma took her hand, Astrea let it stay. She intertwined their fingers, but this time there was no joy in the gesture; merely defeat. "Then we run. We find our own path, our own home . . ."

Her words trailed off when Astrea stood up, though their hands remained together. "Neoma, what I feel for you is dangerous. You are a temptation, and I . . . I cannot keep walking this path. Love is not meant for women like us."

"It could be," Neoma whispered, but it came so small. Astrea's radiance outshone the Suns, but she was more than beauty. Her voice warmed Neoma's heart; her laughter was the purest song. The safety in her arms could calm even the fiercest storms within, and Neoma could sit and listen to her speak for hours—her mere presence was joy. "I have never loved a man. I do not think I ever could. I have only ever loved you."

The confession lingered in the air, a knife to the fragile serenity of the grove. Astrea's blessed face met hers, grief in those lovely eyes.

And in a gesture so simple and final, she shook her head.

Their hands released. "Astrea—"

Astrea froze at the name, her face twisting in anguish. A sob cut off at her bidding, and she ran—disappearing through the grove, down the path Neoma had tread, back toward Vanir.

Neoma remained in suspended heartbreak, the poisoned words swirling about in her head, but she refused to let them settle, refused to accept the haunting message they wrought.

"Love is not meant for women like us."

Damn propriety and fate—Neoma would have fought until the end, if only she'd said yes.

The first of her tears welled, but she cursed them and wiped them away. Her very soul seemed to split, spewing an emotion her young heart didn't know—only that it was toxic, hotter than any could touch. Astrea's ghost lingered on the bench beside her, and so Neoma ran.

The only sound became her rapid footsteps and the sleek shifting fabric of her trousers. Neoma ran through the park's greenery, batting away sprites and the lush vines—she cared not for beauty.

Her world would never be beautiful, if Astrea's words were any prophecy.

Neoma rejoined the city of stone and art, her feet the only sound as they clicked against the stone, and ran until Vanir was a memory, until the final few buildings were but a spot of light. The great expanse beyond the city opened before her, a magnificent field of glowing lights, of plants as keen to absorb the Suns' light as she, though she stayed upon the stone path.

When she finally stopped, her breaths heaving and pained, she stood beneath a clear and brilliant sky, illuminated with the constellations she had always loved, about which she and Kareena would invent tale after tale, to pass the time as children.

Neoma was no longer a child.

An icy breeze cut across her face, stinging her eyes and cheeks, sticky from tears. Alone in the wild, Neoma gazed upon the welcoming stars, the oppressive darkness soothed by their light. The path ahead was illuminated by her wings, their golden light familiar but cold.

Vanir lay far behind, the great city a reminder of all her bitter heart despised. Neoma's lips trembled at the memory of warmth pressing upon them.

The night was hardly silent, the ambience of creatures within the field surrounding her not quite so loud as the city far behind, but inescapable, nevertheless. Yet she remained alone, no travelers on the road, no light from distant, glowing wings.

All her life, loneliness had followed Neoma like a shadow. Yes, she had a family. But while Kareena was vivacious, never in want of friends, the errant, ineffable knowledge of being different had alienated Neoma from the start.

And just as she had finally begun to understand, when she'd finally found someone who understood the unnatural feelings in her heart, even shared them, returned them, had graced her with a kiss that had stopped the whole world . . .

Love was not meant for someone like her.

As she wiped her eyes upon her long sleeves, contemplating the merit of dying alone, a great blast of light split the sky.

A literal hole in the air, rapidly expanding, spreading wider and wider. Neoma stopped in her tracks, awestruck at the glorious sight, until more bursts of light appeared, and from those holes came . . . fire? But silver—blasts of silver light ravaged the sky.

In the far distance, Neoma watched a great falling ball of flame hit the ground. The impact rippled across the terrain, rocks upheaved—Neoma shot up into the air, her wings carrying her as the land shattered beneath her. All around, silver light ripped through the sky, spewing fire and debris upon her world of Celestière.

Neoma looked to Vanir, her bitter heart suddenly afraid. "Astrea," she whispered, struck dumb as fire rained upon the massive city.

Her wings were meant for floating, not flying, and so Neoma returned to the ground and ran, occasionally spreading her wings wide and catching air to avoid jutting chunks of earth. The world erupted into flame, the delicate fauna burning bright. Smoke rose; Neoma choked. Flickers of ember flew about. The heat surged, but she ran, for the girl she loved was in danger.

Yet in the great splits in the sky were awesome sights, enough to slow even her panicked steps—visions of space, of planets she did not know, great explosions of true, vibrant, orange flame. Some imploding; others crashing leaving nothing but chunks of rocks. Images of creatures she did not know—

And strangest of all—the vision of a woman engulfed in silver flame within one of the splits in the sky, glowing with the vibrancy of a Sun, her pose one of peace—

Until she exploded like the rest.

The ground suddenly gutted before Neoma, a great split tearing across the path. She leapt; she soared; silver flame burst as she passed, but she had not fallen yet.

When Neoma reached the great gates, she saw only death.

The city burned, silver light and fire pouring from the sky—and not always the sky, sometimes in the air beside them. From the abyss the tearing evoked came . . . nothing. White mist. Brilliant, blinding light to outshine the Triple Suns. Some angels fell in, disappearing into the cloying mass. Neoma ran, deftly avoiding falling pillars and panicked crowds of people, trying to make sense of the ruined roads and wreckage.

"Neoma!" she heard a young voice cry, and Neoma knew it, adored it, and she fought her way past masses of screaming citizens until she caught of flash of amber wings.

Morathma was thirteen, only three years her junior yet young—so young—and Neoma immediately pulled him into her arms. Smoke diluted his natural glow, but he appeared unharmed.

Amidst the cacophony of screams, she cried, "Where is your father?"

Her nephew clung to her. Panicked breaths panted against her neck. Explosions shook the ground; the boy cried out, then raised a shaking arm and pointed to the wreckage of a fallen, stone building.

Gone.

Though her stomach hollowed from shock, another blast caused her to stumble, wrenching her back into the moment. "I will find us shelter!" she cried amidst the destruction. She tried to release him, but his thin arms clung tight; he wept into her shoulder. "Fine, then hold my hand!"

Adrenaline pulsed through her blood, igniting her veins, giving her the strength to drag the boy as she ran through the city. They risked being trampled in the open, as well as blasted by silver flame, but as the earth shook anew, the stone structure beside them collapsed. Neoma soared up with her fragile wings, narrowly avoiding the toppling building, her own heart stopping to hear the cut-off screams of angels not quite so lucky.

As she floated gently down, she pressed Morathma's face to her neck, praying he did not see the blood and carnage. Fire burst from a tear in the world—close, too close—and Neoma froze to watch two angels caught in the silver blast.

When it relented, they were not burned, but they were perfectly still upon the ground, their wings extinguished.

Neoma's mind fixated upon Romanth, but he was gone. Where was Kareena? Her mother and father? But if Morathma was to live, they had to escape. Clutching the boy's hand tight, she coaxed him to soar up, content to let her wings gently glide them away, then faced a blinding flash of light—

The void opened; Neoma stared upon pure space. All slowed as a blast of silver light tore the world in twain. Neoma shoved Morathma down to the earth, watched his wings catch him before he could fully plummet. Fire burst; heat engulfed her.

It consumed her whole.

It was not heat, yet it burned. Neoma's skin tingled from the radiant light, the pulsing energy unlike any sensation she had ever experienced before. Not pain, not pleasure—simply pure magic, pure energy, electrifying every cell in her angelic body—

She did not fight it; instead, she breathed as it flowed through her and faded.

Strength failed her; Neoma's wings went limp. She fell, her body weightless and serene despite the destruction around her. Rubble caught her fall; pain split across her skull.

She did not rise.

Instead, she blinked in and out of consciousness, uncertain of time but aware of a small body shielding her, watching the terrain change with each moment of clarity—fire burning; smoke rising, brilliant bursts of light . . .

She awoke, and the world had calmed.

Neoma's entire body throbbed, her head most of all. Morathma gasped as she blinked into wakefulness. "N-Neoma?"

She realized she lay in his lap, his small body protecting her. "I am all right."

"Your wings—they're different."

Neoma's gaze spun, but she kept her eyes to her listless wings, splayed upon the rocks on either side. Realization struck—they were no longer gold.

Silver shades of light, reminiscent of the flame that had ravaged her home, shone from the translucent tendrils. With her limited strength, she lifted a hand and saw it was the same—through the pores of her skin glowed light. Not gold—silver.

There would be a time to wonder, but there were other pressing matters at hand.

Her glowing wings revealed her location with their light. Sifting among the desolate terrain were survivors like herself. Eerie peace had settled, punctuated by the occasional scream and the ambient cries of broken angels. As she sat up, assisted by her nephew, she swallowed to see the state of Vanir—for it was a graveyard of stone; bloodied, dull bodies scattered about, their wings extinguished. She looked to the sky yet saw no Suns—light poured from the voids around them. If she stared far enough, she saw an endless wall of mist surrounding the horizon; what it meant, she did not know.

Fear struck her. Morathma lived, but Romanth was gone. What of her parents? What of Kareena?

Invigorated by panic, Neoma said, "Follow me," and burst into the sky, willing her wings to carry her. Her head spun at the sudden motion, but pure adrenaline spurred her onward.

The landscape had forever changed, but little landmarks remained—a crumbled statue bespoke the city's main sector, and there at the edge of expanding mist were the remains of homes, burned and smashed to bits.

She had been consumed by silver flame, so why did she still live?

She saw a spot of golden light and descended, heart seizing. When her feet touched the rubble, she ran to the sole figure kneeling among the wreckage, covered in ash and blood and weeping into her hands. "Kareena!"

Her sister looked up, shock stilling the tears spilling from her eyes. She said nothing at all, merely sobbed into Neoma's shoulder when she held her. "Momma and Papa, they're . . . they're . . ."

Kareena's voice disappeared among her blubbering cries, but Neoma understood. Sorrow swept across her, yet no tears rose to soothe her; merely rage. All around her, people aimlessly wept. Bodies littered the ground; so many were dead. No grand castles or sweeping peaks—all had vanished or been destroyed. Anguish would be their true end, but Neoma's blood boiled for this injustice, for this calamity that had shattered her beloved home.

"What happened?" Kareena asked. Her eyes, swollen from grief, stared in horror at the silver appendages. "Your wings . . ."

"I was blasted by the fire. But I'm all right."

She did not know what it meant. What mattered was that they had lived.

"Neoma, what do we do?" Morathma's small voice asked, his arms around himself for comfort.

Kareena wept, but Neoma pulled away, shock sharpening her mind, though it took all her will to not cry. "I . . ."

Amidst the wreckage, peeking from beneath a fallen building, was a familiar tangle of amethyst hair.

Neoma did not recognize the cry tearing from her throat—it was not hers. It sounded more like an animal. She ran across the rubble, stumbling, sliding amongst the rocks, and collapsed upon her knees before the prone body, halfway crushed beneath the building.

Astrea's wings had extinguished. Blood pooled beneath her, staining those precious locks of hair. Neoma wailed as she fell upon her, uncaring of the gore staining her clothing. She looked nearly sleeping, her eyes shut and serene, and Neoma wished, oh, she wished she could love her enough to save her. Instead, the punctured pressure within her fully burst, and she wept over Astrea's corpse.

Golden light descended upon her. Neoma continued sobbing as Kareena knelt beside her, her hand holding Morathma's. Her sister said nothing, merely put her arm around Neoma, holding her when Neoma turned to weep into her arms. Kareena did not know who Astrea was to her, did not know her worth—

And she never could.

Amidst Neoma's sobs, something new simmered inside, something potent and hot. Here lay her heartbreak, bloodied and broken upon the stone, but had the world not torn them apart, would Astrea have lived? Or would Neoma have died at her side—died defending her, saving her? Neoma would have fought until the end.

The end lay before her.

Her sorrow remained, yet ice rose to coat her bleeding heart, numbing it from pain. Neoma pulled from her sister's embrace, and though she stung from bruises and small, harmless cuts, she rose, her gaze still upon the girl she had loved.

Rage rose to shadow her anguish—anger was the more powerful force. "We need to rally all who remain," she muttered, the voice a stranger in her ears, for this was a person of conviction, who felt nothing, needed no one. "Alone, we're doomed. But there must be more survivors. The world is bigger than Vanir. Together, we have a chance at living, but we must gather . . ."

Her words were stolen by a small, pitiful cry. Neoma and Kareena shared a glance, then both spread their wings, for instinct said to disturb the rubble might destroy this rare and tiny thing. Amidst the carnage of death and desolation, they followed the source, passing bodies and blood and smoldering flames.

Their quarry lay beneath a half-collapsed pillar of stone, the triangular alcove saving it from death—but not the mother who held it, bloodied and still, her wings extinguished. But in her arms, a baby cried, and Neoma knelt beside them.

The infant girl had not even been cut free—her mother must have labored through the end of the world, and oh, what an awful fate. Covered in ash and her mother's blood, the infant girl bore no sign of injury, though her golden wings and skin were rapidly dimming. Neoma gathered the baby into her arms, willing the poor thing to warm.

Kareena ripped a wide strip from her dress, ruined from the smoke and ash and rubble. "Let me," she said, quickly assembling her makeshift swaddle.

Relieved, Neoma offered the infant, her talents having never been in gentleness. Instead, she stole a jagged piece of rock and cut the cord at the infant's stomach, leaving slack enough to tie it off. The baby cried, and beside her Morathma kept his own quiet tears, trying so hard to be strong, and Kareena was not shy at all in her flowing tears, her grief unmitigated by the bundle of hope in her arms. Neoma shut the mother's vacant eyes, a twinge of sorrow striking her—to think that despite the hope of new life, she hadn't lived to see it come to pass.

Yet despite the tragedy of the scene, despite Kareena's flowing tears, Neoma found a rallying cry.

Angels lived to be centuries old, and so children were the rarest commodity in all the world. For the baby to live was the very picture of hope, and Neoma gently stole it back from Kareena's arms, the baby's birthing fluids staining her sleeves. As Neoma rose into the air, she willed it to cry and send her message to every corner of Celestière. The people needed hope, and just as much, they needed a leader.

Something new swelled within her, a beckoning stronger than she'd ever experienced in her young years. The calling pulsed through her blood, hot and invigorating. There were others more qualified. Surely there were elders far more equipped to the task. But Neoma stared upon a sea of weeping supplicants, her tears having dried. Her heart lay shattered along with the rubble crushing the girl she loved—and there it could stay.

She did not need it. Vanir needed her. She was meant for greater things than love.

After years of staying angrily in the shadows, Neoma hardly recognized her own voice. "People of Vanir!" she cried, and all around, scattered, glowing wings shifted to face her. Silence met her; her voice had been heard. "First, we gather the living. Leave no stone unturned!"

And they moved, they acted at her behest—a river, once empty, flowing anew.

The angels were strong.

As Neoma descended to the ground, she stared only at the sky, the lingering question of *why* an oppressive cloud upon the scene. Footsteps signified Kareena's approach, the infant having finally calmed, but Neoma's calculating mind bitterly sought for answers unknown.

"She needs a home," Kareena said, and absently Neoma nodded. Morathma stood by Kareena, close enough to touch, young enough to crave comfort but old enough to have the pride to think he did not. Still a child—not meant to be left alone in the world.

"We shall find her one," Neoma said. "There will be other orphans. Helping the helpless should be our first order of business—the injured and the young."

"Our what?" Kareena waved her hand before Neoma's view, stealing her attention. "What are you talking about?"

Neoma gazed upon the sea of carnage and death, the flash of Astrea's corpse causing her stomach to twist. A lump rose in her throat, but she swallowed. Many more were dead than alive, wingless bodies strewn carelessly about, discarded like children's toys.

Yet despite the gloom, she saw spots of hope among it—shuffling angels digging through debris, the joyous sounds of reunions, not unlike she and Kareena's. She was sixteen years old, yet the weight of something grander than she fell upon her. Destiny was hers, and she clutched it tight. "We are going to live, Kareena," Neoma said, vigor filling her soul, "even if I must drag all of Celestière along myself."

Neoma stepped into the ruins of Vanir, joining the throng of survivors, aiding in clearing rubble, bodies, barking orders and watching them listen.

When Astrea was dug up from the debris, Neoma joined the small band of angels, nails digging into her fists to keep her tears at bay. All her commands had come sharply, vehemently, but in this single moment, humility melded with her words. "I will take her."

Alone, Neoma carried Astrea, this girl of unfathomable worth, beyond the bounds of Vanir, joining in the line of corpses awaiting a mass grave.

Only then did she succumb, for even a frozen heart could crack and bleed. Neoma wept into Astrea's bloody hair, holding her near, for it would be the last time.

Love was not meant for someone like her.

To read more of *The Moon, the Stars, and the Desert Below,* check out my Patreon! You can find that at www.patreon.com/sdsimper.

About the author:

S D Simper has lived in both the hottest place on earth and the coldest, spans the employment spectrum from theatre teacher to professional editor, and plays more instruments than can be counted on one hand. She and her beloved wife share a home with their three cats and innumerable bookshelves.

Visit her website at sdsimper.com to see her other works, including *The Fate of Stars,* the story of a mermaid, a human princess, and a love that will shape the future of the world.